THE DRAGON KINGS OF FIRE AND ICE

SPECIAL EDITION OMNIBUS

BOOKS 6-10

AMELIA SHAW

THE DRAGON KINGS OF FIRE AND ICE: BOOKS 1-5

First edition. January 23, 2024.

Contact: harleyromancepublishing@gmail.com
Website: www.harleyromancepublishing.com

Written by Amelia Shaw.

CONTENTS

THE HUMAN MATE FOR THE DRAGON PRINCE

Chapter 1 — 3
Chapter 2 — 10
Chapter 3 — 18
Chapter 4 — 25
Chapter 5 — 32
Chapter 6 — 39
Chapter 7 — 46
Chapter 8 — 53
Chapter 9 — 60
Chapter 10 — 67
Chapter 11 — 73
Chapter 12 — 82
Chapter 13 — 90
Chapter 14 — 98
Chapter 15 — 105
Chapter 16 — 112
Epilogue — 118

THE PRINCE OF DRAGON MAGIC

Chapter 1 — 131
Chapter 2 — 137
Chapter 3 — 143
Chapter 4 — 149
Chapter 5 — 154
Chapter 6 — 160
Chapter 7 — 166
Chapter 8 — 172
Chapter 9 — 180
Chapter 10 — 188
Chapter 11 — 198
Chapter 12 — 210

Chapter 13   220
Chapter 14   230
Epilogue   235

HIS DRAGON PRINCESS

Prologue   247
Chapter 1   255
Chapter 2   261
Chapter 3   268
Chapter 4   276
Chapter 5   282
Chapter 6   288
Chapter 7   295
Chapter 8   300
Chapter 9   307
Chapter 10   313
Chapter 11   319
Chapter 12   326
Chapter 13   333
Chapter 14   340
Chapter 15   346
Chapter 16   352
Epilogue   359

THE FUTURE KING'S QUEEN

Chapter 1   367
Chapter 2   374
Chapter 3   380
Chapter 4   386
Chapter 5   394
Chapter 6   401
Chapter 7   410
Chapter 8   416
Chapter 9   423
Chapter 10   429
Chapter 11   436
Chapter 12   443
Chapter 13   449
Chapter 14   455

Chapter 15 462

Chapter 16 468

Epilogue 474

THE DRAGON OF HER DREAMS

Chapter 1 485

Chapter 2 491

Chapter 3 499

Chapter 4 505

Chapter 5 512

Chapter 6 519

Chapter 7 526

Chapter 8 534

Chapter 9 542

Chapter 10 550

Chapter 11 557

Chapter 12 563

Chapter 13 569

Chapter 14 577

Chapter 15 585

Chapter 16 592

Chapter 17 598

Chapter 18 606

Chapter 19 613

Epilogue 621

THE HUMAN MATE FOR THE DRAGON PRINCE

USA TODAY BESTSELLING AUTHOR

AMELIA SHAW

CHAPTER

ONE

Anselm

Even after nearly thirty years of marriage, my parents were still sickeningly in love.

My sister Vanya rolled her eyes at me from across the dining table, then spoke to our parents. "Mom. Seriously. You're gonna make me lose my breakfast over here."

I wasn't sure why Vanya was only blaming our mother, but she had to choose someone to lay the blame on. About ten minutes ago, Dad had pulled Mom into his lap where he sat at the head of the table. Mom had her arms wrapped around his neck and they were kissing and caressing each other like a couple of teenagers on heat.

Mom sighed loudly and managed to climb out of her husband's arms and stand up. Then she straightened her long sleeved, royal purple dress and glared at my sister. "When you find your mate one day, young lady, you'll know what it's like... then hopefully you'll stop pestering us."

Dad laughed. "Then it'll be our turn to gripe at you."

"Yeah... promises, promises," my unmarried sister grumped.

Speaking of mates... "Hey Dad. Can I have a chat with you after breakfast about something?"

My father, King Stavrok, was still a strong, large man. He'd kept the people in our kingdom fed and safe for the entirety of his reign. But to me he was 'Dad'. The most loyal family man I'd ever known.

Dad looked up at me, his eyebrows slightly raised. He knew what I was asking for. A conversation away from the females in our family.

"Yes, of course, son." He agreed with a regal nod, then his characteristic grin.

We finished breakfast and my sister Vanya left the dining room alongside our mother. They were chatting about going to visit our other sister, Jessa. She lived at Uncle Erik and Aunt Marienne's castle in the Black Mountains. Jessa had married their oldest son and the couple stayed there most of the time.

Jessa enjoyed the company of her mother-in-law, Marienne, and the queen's penchant to predict the future and cast spells.

It also made sense to learn the way of their kingdom, as Jessa would one day be their queen, as I would one day be the leader of our kingdom. A daunting prospect and a hard act to follow. For both of us.

"Come, Anselm. Sit." Dad gestured to the chair opposite his. He'd moved away from the dining room table and closer to the fireplace, the castle warm considering it was snowing outside.

I sat where my father dictated and waited for him to begin the conversation.

He chuckled, the sound rough yet joyous. My childhood had been filled with that sound and to this day, it still made me smile. "You wanted to chat, son. What's on your mind? Hit me."

I opened my mouth to begin the speech I'd rehearsed a hundred times, then words failed me. I slammed my mouth shut again, self-annoyance making my jaw clench.

Dad laughed again. "Would you like me to guess?"

"No, it's just… I haven't said this out loud before and I'm afraid how it's going to sound." The idea of appearing weak or cowardly in front of my father was one of my greatest fears.

King Stavrok was a legend. A warrior. A man who'd saved the North and defended the South. A king who loved his people, and whose people loved him back.

He wasn't just a hard act to follow. He was impossible.

Dad sighed and settled deeper into the cushions of his armchair. "I don't want you to ever be worried about speaking to me. I love you no matter what."

My parents' ability to embarrass me out of nowhere always surprised me. Not that I was ungrateful for their unconditional support and love. My siblings and I were lucky and we knew it. But Dad always managed to hit me with a comment like that out of the blue. Always. I was almost thirty years old and yet I felt as small as I did when I was five years old, still seeking my father's approval.

"Thanks Dad," I managed to get out. "I love you too. It's just that…"

"What?"

I was lonely, on a level I couldn't even express. Even though I was always surrounded, the gnawing feeling never went away.

Even with thousands of people in the village, and hundreds of servants within the castle.

Even with parents who were overly affectionate and often stifling in their love for me.

Even with sisters that I was closer to than anyone else on the planet… I was lonely.

"I… need my mate." There. I'd said it.

Dad's eyebrows flicked up as though my answer had surprised him, then he nodded. "Yes, I remember that feeling too well. Sucked balls. And not in the good way."

I practically choked on my tongue hearing the expression exit my father's mouth, then coughed to try and clear my throat again. Once again, my dad had shocked me.

"Ah yeah, it does."

Dad nodded, turning his head to stare off into the fireplace. "I was thirty-five when I met your mother. I was going insane with my need for a mate. It didn't matter who crawled into my bed, or how much I ignored the feeling, the anger... the unrest... it grew and grew until there was nothing else that mattered."

I wasn't sure I'd gotten that bad yet, but my future wasn't looking pretty. The depression was beginning to win and I wasn't sure I had the strength to push it away any longer.

I sat up a little straighter, getting to the point of this chat faster than I'd expected to. "I know you credit Aunt Marienne with you finding Mom in the human realm, but do you think it's possible for me to just cross the veil and find her?"

The human world was a thousand times bigger than our hidden realm. My father, a dragon king, had been given a mental map to find his fated mate, Lucy, a human and my mother.

I wasn't sure I was going to be as lucky.

"You know your mom and Vanya are flying over to visit Jessa this afternoon. Why don't we all go?"

If we were going to visit Jessa, then we were going to the Black Mountains. To Marienne and Erik's kingdom. They should all be there, and I'd have the chance to ask the sorceress myself.

I slid forward on my seat. "You think Aunt Marienne would help me?"

Dad shrugged his massive shoulders. "It can't hurt to ask."

I sighed, feeling the weight of disappointment already, pressing down on me. "You don't think she'll be able to see anything. Do you?"

Dad stood up and I followed suit, jumping to my feet. He clapped me on the shoulder the way he did when he was trying to encourage me to go forward with something. "Marienne isn't a crystal ball, son. She doesn't have a lot of control over her visions, or so she says. You can't just rub her head and get an answer. But you can certainly ask and hope that she sees something that will help you."

Hope soared in my heart for the first time in too long. "Thank you, Father."

Dad walked toward the door. I stepped in alongside him. "I'll let your mother know that we'll all go for the visit today. So go and pack, and I'll send a message to Erik as well. His castle is about to become considerably fuller."

I chuckled and ran off to pack for a few days away. If Dad had his way, we'd all fly in our dragon form and he'd carry Mother to the Black Mountains. Our luggage would go via horse and carriage and arrive this evening.

Within the hour we were all packed, the carriage was on its way and we were all standing on the balcony atop the north tower.

"You know this is where your father landed when he brought me home that first time," Mom said, sighing with remembrance.

Vanya rolled her eyes. "He kidnapped you, Mom. No point sugar coating it."

Mom laughed, her body shaking with the motion. "Oh, don't worry. I've never forgotten that part of the story. I know it's not modern, or very feminist, but damn I loved the fact that your father couldn't control his dragon around me, and he had no choice but to take me away."

Vanya put her hand on her hip and glared at her. "What did I say about sugar coating things?"

Mom grinned, her blue eyes lighting up with joy. "Okay... I was pretty pissed off to begin with. But there's nothing like being the sole focus of a man like your father. You'll see. One day."

Vanya groaned and stepped up to the ledge. "I'm out. See you all there."

My sister threw off her fur robe, revealing her naked form. Then she jumped, launching herself into the air and shifting as she went. Her wings extended out as she swooped low over the kingdom, then flew high in the direction of the Black Mountains.

My father chuckled and stepped closer to my mother. "I'll shift then you climb on my back."

She nodded and walked over to me, giving my father room to shift into his dragon so he could carry her for the trip.

Our mother was human, so I was grateful, as were all my siblings, that we had inherited our father's shifting abilities. We could all shift and fly, just as strongly as any full-blooded dragon we knew.

Despite my mixed blood, our people loved our mother and had accepted me as the heir to the throne.

I stared at her for a moment, taking in the look of love on her face as she watched my father ready to shift. It was impossible to miss the devotion in either of them.

"Mom?"

"Yes, sweetheart?" Her eyes were firmly glued to my father, who was now stripping his robe off to shift for flight.

"Is that true?"

She turned toward me now, her eyebrows narrowed in confusion. "Is what true, Anselm?"

I swallowed hard, forcing myself past the natural resistance to asking these sorts of questions. "That you were glad Father stole you from everything you've ever known? That you were... flattered, in a way."

Mom gripped my hand hard. "Son. At first I was fucking furious. There's no sugar coating that. But as I fell madly, deeply in love with him... and met some of his past lovers..." she growled as she shuddered, "I realized that his dragon grabbing me in such a way was the one thing I could hold onto. That no-one else had. He wanted me, and literally fought to the death to save me."

My shock was very real when I gaped at her. "He... what?"

She smiled softly. "I think it's time that we tell you the full story, and there's no better place than the room where it happened. See you at Erik's castle?"

I nodded and watched in awe as my mother pulled up her fur hood and tugged on her gloves. It was freezing for a human to travel in our weather, something I needed to remember if I ever had to transport my own woman.

Mom climbed onto my father's back and clung tight as he gently stretched out his wings and flew up into the air above the castle.

No tricks, or swoops like my sister. My mother wouldn't have enjoyed that.

I stood on the balcony watching their figures get smaller as they moved off into the distance. There was one thing that niggled at me, like a voice in the back of your mind that just wouldn't shut up.

My mate wasn't living in our realm as a dragon shifter. She was human. I knew it as a truth. I didn't know how, but I felt it. I was half human after all, so it made sense in some strange way.

I stepped up onto the ledge and looked down upon my father's kingdom. The township, lands and wealth would be mine one day.

The mantle of responsibility sat heavily on my shoulders, though my father carried most of the weight. He was great and mighty, but one day, he wouldn't be here, and I needed a strong queen at my side to move into the future proudly.

My grandparents were fated mates. My parents' love was an epic story of devotion.

I would not fail to live up to the same expectations of my life. In all aspects.

I threw off my fur coat and let the cold wind chill my skin. I took a large breath in through my nose, enjoying the discomfort. My dragon surged inside me, wanting out. Needing to fly.

I let go of my humanity and my shifter soared through me. My bones extended and my skin changed to the hardened protective scales of my dragon.

My wings unfurled from my back and our connection strengthened. They were each an extra limb, an important one.

I jumped from the balcony, not flying straight away. Instead I fell, letting the adrenaline pump through my blood as I hurtled toward the stones at the base of the castle.

My wings wrapped around my body while I plummeted, then at the last moment I threw my wings open and soared up, across the rooftops of the village and over the homes of the people. My father's people. My people.

A few of them waved, while others shook their heads at my well-known antics.

When I reached the edge of our town I flapped my wings harder to gain height, taking to the skies where the air was thin and the clouds were thick.

It was time to talk to the sorceress and see if she could help me find the future I hoped was waiting for me.

TWO

Anselm

The flight to the Black Mountains was beautiful. It was spring, so despite the cold and scattered snow on the ground below me, many flowers were already in bloom and the lands were unusually green.

I landed on the highest balcony of the castle, noting a servant standing by with a dark cloak. I let go of my dragon, shrinking back to my human form and shivering the moment my skin was touched by a dusting of falling snow.

"Your Highness." The servant called out, scurrying over to offer me the cloak. "I am Thomas and am here to serve you."

I smiled and took the wrapping from him, grateful for its warmth when I threw it over my shoulders. "Thank you, Thomas. Have the rest of my family arrived?"

Thomas nodded and walked beside me over to the large glass door. "Yes, they're all dressing in their quarters. Allow me to show you to your rooms."

We walked inside and closed the thick door behind us.

I shivered at the extreme temperature difference. It was warm in the halls as we moved along hallway and my body began to thaw.

"Your room, sire," Thomas said as we stopped outside a bedroom in the guest quarters.

The servant was an older man and would stand on tradition, I was sure. Even so, I couldn't help but tease him a little. "Thomas, are you sure this is a guest suite? Knowing my sister, she probably told you to throw me in some sort of closet."

As I expected, Thomas's face turned to horror. "Oh no, sire. This room is..."

I laughed and clapped the man on the shoulder. "It's all good, Thomas. I was only joking. My twin sister may wish to stick me in the dungeon, but I'm sure the queen wouldn't allow it."

Vanya, Jessa and I were un-identical triplets. But it was easier to say twin sister, because 'triplet sister' just didn't roll off the tongue in the same way.

Thomas's lips quirked for the first time. "The princess is a lively one."

I burst out laughing. "Yes, she is. She must keep your prince on his toes." Though Marienne and Erik's first-born son, Carlak, was quite the task master himself. I'd grown up spending a lot of time with him; we all had.

It wasn't until Jessa turned twenty-one, did Carlak make his move on our sister. Two years younger than her, Carlak fought off several suitors to win my sister's hand. They were a great match.

Thomas inclined his head, snapping back into a serious tone. "Our prince is very happy."

I chuckled again. "I can imagine he is. Now... where do I find some clothes to wear, and which meeting area are we all meant to be at?"

Thomas showed me where some of Prince Carlak's clothes had been laid out for me inside the bedroom I'd been assigned, then he instructed me to meet the rest of the families in the larger of the dining halls.

"The larger one?" I asked, surprised. There were less than ten of us, unless my information wasn't correct.

Thomas simply nodded and excused himself.

"Doesn't matter, I guess." I said, still puzzling over why we'd need so much space. That dining table could easily seat fifty people.

I dressed quickly and headed down to the dining hall. I'd be the last one there, I was sure. Whenever I flew here, I took my time, enjoying the freedom of flying in my dragon form. When I stepped up to the entry way and a servant opened the door for me, my assumption proved correct.

"Late as always," Jessa declared, waddling toward me.

I hadn't seen my sister in a month and I was surprised to see how big her belly had grown in that time.

"You look ready to pop, sister dearest." I said, reaching out to rub her belly before putting my arm around her for a hug.

She laughed and shoved at me. "I wish I was! Unfortunately, our doctor thinks there's more than one of these monsters inside of me."

I grinned at her. "I'm not surprised. You always were the most like Mother."

Mom had given birth to us triplets, then our younger brother Iain. Surely a multiple birth for Jessa and Vanya was in the cards?

Jessa heaved a huge sigh. "Yeah, yeah."

Jessa and Carlak had been married over seven years, it had shocked everyone that they'd waited so long to birth the next generation, but I had the feeling she'd felt guilty leaving Vanya and I so far behind.

I dropped a kiss on her cheek. "I'm really happy for you, sis. You deserve the world."

She met my gaze and for the first time in a long time, I saw the glimmer of unshed tears in her blue eyes.

She launched at me with her arms open wide, almost knocking me over in her fervor.

"Whoa." I laughed, gripping her so we both didn't topple over.

"I want the same happiness for you." She whispered the words in my ear, holding me tight.

I sighed and hugged her tighter, my heart aching at the love I felt for her. "One day."

We pulled apart and that's when I realized the party was larger than just the two royal families. "Auntie Cass! I didn't realize you were here."

I walked forward to greet the large party standing next to the huge dining table, laden with morning tea. Fruits and cheeses, drinks and breads.

I hugged my father's cousin and our hosts. "Hello Aunt Marienne," I said, giving her a squeeze before moving on to shake hands with Uncle Erik, and Cass's two sons Theo and Bernie.

"Where's Uncle Damon?" I asked, looking toward Cass.

Cass rolled her eyes. "You know Damon. He doesn't like to leave the castle, and I felt like a break from the freezing temperatures."

Theo laughed. "Dad's dealing with a failed crop and more building. Our population has boomed the last few years and we don't have enough housing for everyone."

"If you need help, I'm available," I offered, feeling the need to get my hands dirty again. I'd spent many months at the Winter Kingdom through the years, and the work there was hard, but very satisfying.

Theo turned to me with a grin. "We could use more hands, Anselm. You're always welcome. You know that."

I smiled at the boy who'd become a man since last we met. Theo was at least five years my junior but had grown a lot these past years. He was the heir to his father's kingdom, and we'd grown up together.

"And Veronica?" I asked, speaking of Theo's younger sister. They all called her 'the dragon daughter.'

"She stayed with her father." Cass said with a sigh. "That girl will be the death of me, I'm sure."

Mother, Marienne and Cass all got along famously, as did our fathers, so we were as close as blood cousins. We'd spent many long winters and short summers together. We'd seen each other through childhood and adolescence, and now as young adults, we were ready to see what the future held for each of us. Vanya, Jessa and I were the oldest of the lot but age seemed irrelevant when we all got on so well.

We sat down to a morning tea, laughing and chatting and telling stories. It was great being around the people that I considered my family, both blood and bonded. The darkness in my heart, that aching loneliness, receded at times like this.

When there was a lull in the conversation, I looked toward my mother. "Weren't you going to tell us a story of something that happened here?

Mom's eyes widened, then she nodded. "Yes." She turned to my father, who was seated beside her. "I told Anselm that you once fought to the death to save me. Would you like to tell the story?"

My father's surprise was a palpable thing. His eyes widened, then he stared at my mother, speechless.

She turned back to me to explain his reaction. "The three of us—Stavrok, Marienne and I—agreed we'd never tell you all this story, but I think it's time."

Now I was more confused than ever. I stared at my father, who was still as silent as I'd ever seen him, and was staring at Mom with a quizzical frown bending his brows.

Finally, he spoke. "Lucy, I trust you with my life, so if you think it's a good idea to tell the children..."

"As long as it's okay with you also, Marienne?" Mom asked, casting her question across the table toward my aunt.

Marienne and Erik stared at each other for a long moment, then they nodded in unison.

"What on earth is going on?" Jessa demanded, crossing her arms over her large belly.

I laughed out loud at her obvious annoyance. "If Jessa doesn't know, this must be one huge secret."

"Oh, it was never meant to be a deliberate secret that we kept from you all," my father said. "We just put that part of our life behind us after you were born."

"Shall we leave?" Theo asked, standing up next to his mother, Cass. "Perhaps we shouldn't—"

"Oh, sit down." Cass pulled her son back to his seat. "I was there for all of this. I know the story. And it's a good one. So... go on, Stavrok. Tell it."

My father, now in his mid-sixties, sighed heavily as he sat back in his chair and began to tell us all his story. "It feels like yesterday, but thirty-one years ago, I was unmated..."

Cass slid forward and interjected. "Other than Damon, he was the only unmarried king, and the elders wanted him to hurry up and find his queen."

I smiled at my dad's cousin. Cass had often looked after us when we were little and I had great affection for her.

"Yes... anyway. I held a dinner at the castle, and all the kings came, including Marienne and..." Dad glanced toward Marienne, who finally joined in the conversation.

"My first husband, King Magnik."

"My half-brother," Erik said.

Silence descended and my sisters and I looked at each other, gob smacked. Marienne had been married to King Erik's older brother?

"Seriously?" Barry asked, the youngest of Cass's sons.

Cass flicked her son in the arm. "Yes, seriously."

"What happened?" I asked, a sudden tightness in my chest squeezing a little harder. Mother had pushed for this story to come to light for me, and I wasn't going to miss any of the important details.

The older adults exchanged glances, then Marienne spoke. "Magnik was a power-hungry, evil man. He wanted Stavrok's lands as well as his own, and when he found that he couldn't buy the lands from him..."

"Of course not," Vanya exclaimed, sounding horrified at the idea that our father would sell even a small part of our precious home. "Why would Dad sell our land to any of the other kings? How ridiculous."

"Exactly," Marienne said with a small smile. "But Magnik wouldn't be put off. When I told Stavrok about Lucy, and he went and stole her away from the human realm..."

"Thanks again for that, Marienne." Mom interjected with a grin.

We all laughed, lightening the mood, though my stomach remained tight with expectation. I had a feeling I knew where this was headed. "Magnik took Mother, didn't he?" I asked.

I stared at Marienne, who nodded, her cheeks darkening with a blush.

"Yes, and I'm sorry to say I didn't free her when I could have."

"Don't you dare blame yourself!" Mom said, her tone brooking no argument. "He was an abusive husband and you helped me as much as you could. And look how it all worked out."

Mom gestured to the large table, filled with two and a half generations of royal dragon bloodlines.

Marienne rubbed her forehead, just above her right eye, as though she had a headache. "Well, as you can all imagine, Stavrok didn't take it lying down."

Dad groaned. "She was my fated mate, and although we didn't know it yet, pregnant with my heirs. What else was I going to do but get her back?"

I stared at my father, my heart thumping faster now. "What did you do, Dad?"

My father was a fit man who still trained daily. I knew he had once been a strong fighter, but without war, I'd never seen my father truly unleashed.

Dad met my gaze with an unwavering intensity. "I flew here, to Magnik's castle. He had Lucy tied to a pole—as bait—and he wanted to kill me. We fought."

I glanced at Jessa, who sat beside me, both of us putting the ending together. Magnik was gone, and Erik had ascended the throne.

Did that mean...

"And you won, Dad?" Vanya asked, her voice breathy and hopeful.

Dad's grin split his face. "Of course, I did."

I stared at my father. "And by win you mean..." I needed to hear him say it. Had my father—the calm and gentle king I'd always known—killed another dragon?

But it was Cass who spoke. "Your father killed him, of course." She tsked loudly. "He took out those foolish humans who dared to kidnap and torture my sister-in-law, too."

"He what?" It was Barry again, so Cass launched into another story featuring Marienne's foretelling, fated mates and my father's protective nature.

By the time that story was finished, Dad was actually looking embarrassed.

"Okay, okay. You can start telling stories about something else now."

Cass grinned at her cousin. "Okay. Well, how about how you and Erik battled the wolves to save the Winter Kingdom..."

"The *wolves*?" I asked, staring at Cass for more information before turning back to study my father. Suddenly, I was seeing him in a whole new light. He had rescued my mother from what sounded like an abusive tyrant, fought off wolves...

"Oh, for pity's sake." Dad groaned then picked up his glass of wine and lifted it high. "I'd like to make a toast."

I made a mental note to ask my father more about his war stories, but didn't try and do so now. Instead, everyone at the table grabbed for their glass or filled it to the brim.

Dad stood up and raised his wine glass high. "To us. Three of the royal families of fire and ice. Long may we find great love and defend our thrones, our lands, and our families, to the very end."

"Hear, hear." We clinked our glasses and drank, just as a bevy of servants entered the room and began to serve lunch.

I glanced across the table at my mother, who was beaming with pride and happiness. It had always been hard to see my mom and dad as anything more than my parents. Even seeing them in their roles as king and queen sometimes felt strange to me.

But now my eyes were open. They'd lived a whole life before we were born, and it had been filled with more danger and greater battles that I'd never known.

I could only hope that Marienne would set me on the same path as she had my father. The road to my mate, and the love I so desperately craved.

THREE

Anselm

It was evening, after dinner and a day filled with laughter and games, that I finally managed to get Marienne alone. We were all relaxing in the small dining room, where the fire blazed and the alcohol flowed.

I walked over to the sorceress, who was watching her son and daughter-in-law cuddle by the fireplace. "Aunt Marienne, may I speak to you for a moment?"

She turned toward me, her eyes shimmering with her magic. "I've been waiting for you to come and speak to me, Anselm."

I chuckled and crossed my arms over my chest to hide my sudden awkwardness. "Has my mother spoken to you, then?"

She shook her head. "No. But I've been feeling a buzz about you all day. You want to speak to me about your future, don't you?"

I nodded, my breath catching in my throat. "I do."

She sighed. "I'm happy to help, Anselm. But you need to know I don't have a lot of control over what happens, or what I see. I can be lucky, and the information is ready and waiting for me, but it's been a long time since I tapped into this sort of power."

I gave her my full attention. "Please. I need to find out who she is, then I can go find her."

Marienne searched my eyes, a smile lifting her lips. "You're so like your father. His need for a mate tore him apart."

I ran a hand through my already-frazzled hair. I had been doing that a lot lately. The frustration was intense. "I haven't gotten that bad yet, I don't think. But... it's getting there," I admitted.

Marienne nodded once. "Give me a moment to tell Erik what we're doing, then we'll retreat to the library for a chat."

I watched her go, then my gaze fell on my mother, who was watching me intently.

I smiled reassuringly, and nodded, hopefully communicating correctly that Marienne had offered to help.

I wasn't reassured, however. I was... worried. Terrified in fact, that she wouldn't be able to help me. Marienne was my last hope and if she couldn't see anything, then that would leave me with nothing but this gnawing depression that ate at my heart and grew larger every day.

When Marienne came back, she took my arm and led me into the hallway, down a little way, then into the library. It was a huge room, the space lined with walls and walls of full bookcases.

I smiled as I looked around the room. "I see why Jessa loves it here so much. She always did love reading. She must spend all day in here."

Marienne smiled. "Yes, she does. Now, come sit by the fire."

The lights in here were dim and the room quiet. I shivered as a premonition stole over me. This was the perfect place for a future reading. I followed her to the chairs by the fireplace and sat where she told me to.

"How do we do this?" I asked, assuming she'd whip out some sort of spell book or crystal ball to help her see the future.

"I just set my intent to help you find your mate, then I hold one of your hands and tune into the magic. If there's an answer there, it will come to me."

If... one of the worst words I knew.

"Okay," I said, ready to give her my hand whenever she asked for it.

Marienne closed her eyes for a long moment. I stared at her and waited, holding my breath and counting the loud thumping of my heart in my chest.

One ker-thump. Two ker-thump. Three...

Then her eyes popped open, the irises swirling with a purple mist I'd never seen before.

Aunt Marienne looked so different to her usual self I couldn't control my sharp intake of breath.

Whoa. That's incredible.

"Give me your hand." She slid to the edge of her chair.

I mirrored her move and shifted forward, then reached out for her outstretched hand.

The moment our palms connected, electricity shot through me and I was blinded. I closed my eyes and inside my mind I saw images. Visions of the past. A drunken moment in time. A night I wished to forget. A night I hadn't been able to forget, no matter how hard I tried.

I wanted to wish the vision away, and yet I couldn't. There she was... the woman I'd tried so hard to forget. *Kayla.*

Marienne hissed, almost like she was in pain, then she let go of my hand and everything snapped away.

I opened my eyes, not even realizing that I'd closed them. "Did you see what I saw?" I asked. My voice sounded hoarse, as if I'd been shouting.

"You know your fated mate. You've already been with her... Oh my. You have to go." She cried out, jumping to her feet. "Now!"

"I have to go?" I repeated, rising like she had.

She gave me a shove in the center of my chest, then turned me toward the door. "Your mate needs you. Desperately. It's a matter of life and death, Anselm. She isn't going to survive the..." Marienne shook her head as though she didn't want to say anymore.

Automatically I raced for the door before I stopped and twisted around. "What are you saying, Marienne?" She couldn't mean that Kayla was my fated mate. That was impossible. And, was she in danger? Was she...dying?

I felt ragged from the emotions that rushed through me, but I didn't even understand them, let alone be able to process the news.

How can I not have known my own mate?

"The human woman from the bar..." she said, her voice sounding a little strange. "She *is* your mate, but you didn't recognize her when you should have. She blames you for leaving... oh my. Anselm. You really screwed that up. You need to go to her. Now. Before it's too late."

She didn't need to tell me again.

With the shock of her revelation echoing in my mind, I started running, back to the room where our families were.

My parents were on their feet the moment I entered.

I called out to them from the doorway. "I have to go."

"Where to?" Mom asked.

"The human realm. I have to..." I ran a hand through my hair, feeling despair claw at me. Of all the women to have wronged...

Marienne burst into the room. "Anselm! You need to go. Tonight. Now."

I turned to the sorceress, finally seeing the full might of her power that everyone talked about. It rippled around her, a palpable thing in this moment. "Where is she? Where can I find her?"

"She's at home," Marienne said. "I'll... here." She grabbed for my forearm and co-ordinates exploded into my mind.

The same town I'd visited last time. Which street though? Marigold Road. Red brick. Small house.

Marienne moaned and let go of my arm. "I haven't got anything more."

I lunged forward and hugged her tight, holding her up to prevent her from staggering sideways. "Thank you. Thank you. Thank you."

Then I let her go and started running, up to the balcony I'd landed on when I first arrived. I reached the large glass doors and began undressing faster than I ever had before.

My dad was hard on my heels. "I'll come with you."

I turned around as I unbuttoned my shirt and tossed it to the carpet in my haste. "No. I know the way. I've been there before."

Dad frowned. "When? I don't..."

He'd never given us permission. It was true. Didn't change the fact that we'd gone.

"I flew across the veil with Iain. We never told you."

My father's glare was mighty, as I'd expected.

"When?" He demanded.

"Last summer. Seven... eight months ago."

My father was nodding, breathing hard. His eyes were flashing yellow, his shifter flying up to the surface.

He was trying to control his temper, but I just didn't have time for this.

"Dad, when I get back you can sit me down and lecture me. Punish me. I don't care. But I have to go. Now."

I dropped the rest of my clothes to the ground and pushed open the door to the balcony. The cold air whipped around me and my dragon surged to the surface.

Dad ran onto the balcony after me. "There's a cabin just beyond the veil where you can get clothes. They'll help you."

I nodded, speech impossible now that I was a dragon. We'd managed to carry clothes with us last time, between Iain and I. We'd gone with a clear head, decided first what we'd do and with a plan to execute.

Pity that plan had gone to shit.

Dad backed toward the door and lifted his hand in a wave of farewell. "Good luck, son. Hopefully we'll see you very soon."

I turned to face the ledge and dove straight over the side of the castle wall. I didn't spin and play the air currents this time. Instead, I flapped my wings hard, and headed straight for the veil that separated our two worlds.

My fated mate was human, which I'd always assumed. But it was Kayla. *Kayla!* With her gorgeous smile and warm, luscious body.

I'd met my mate, and then I'd left her behind. Abandoned her.

I growled into the breeze, remembering her face, the way her body had squeezed me tight.

She'd given my soul solace that night, but I'd been too drunk to find out where she lived. Too wasted to even get her last name. My brother had dragged me home and I'd added Kayla to my long list of one-night stands and tried to forget her.

The veil shimmered in front of me. The sky was dark, being nighttime, but my dragon vision was ten times better than my human eyes and I saw the portal clearly.

I flew straight through the portal to the human world, the heat of a spring in the human realm hitting me hard. I began to drop, soaring into the fields of the farms outside the closest town. I landed on the warm dirt and let go of my dragon body, shifting back to human.

"Kayla," I whispered. "I can't believe it." But part of me could. That one night with her had haunted my dreams. Her tender care, the way her eyes had shone when she smiled at me.

But I'd assumed that I'd know my fated mate on sight. Everyone I spoke to said that when you met your fated mate, your dragon was uncontrollable. I hadn't had that issue with Kayla, so it had never come up in my mind.

Even if the sex had been phenomenal and part of me had desperately wanted to throw Kayla over my shoulder and take her home with me, I hadn't. Because all the signs for my fated mate weren't there, and that's what I'd wanted.

My mate. My love.

I marched toward the nearest farmhouse which had a solitary light above the old door. I was a naked male in the middle of nowhere and I desperately hoped my father was right and I wasn't about to be arrested. Or worse. Shot.

I lifted my hand to knock on the door when my eyes caught a sign attached to a large box by the front door.

It read: *Dragons. Please take whatever clothes you need. And God speed.*

I chuckled as I lifted the lid on the large wooden chest by the door. Inside were neatly folded shirts, pants, jeans and jackets.

I grabbed what I needed. A pair of jeans that were a little tight and a light blue shirt, which was too big. They weren't perfect, but they were clothes. Those and a pair of boots were all I needed.

I set off walking toward the nearby town, glad to have the time to think. To call it a town was probably too generous. It was more of a village, but even so, it had officially produced more fated mates for dragon royalty, than anywhere else in the human realm.

The list was growing. I began to tick them off as I walked. "Mom. Sarah. Katerina, and now Kayla."

Was there something special in the water around here? Or had fate decided it was time to mix more human blood into our dragon shifter lineage, and allowed our mates to flourish in a place that was easy to access from our realm?

I didn't have the answers, but I had a hell of a lot of questions. I continued walking, down the road and into the town proper. The small, semi-identical houses lined the streets and due to the lateness of the hour, most of the homes didn't have any lights flickering in the windows.

I followed some strange sense of knowing that lay within me, walking past the center of the town and then turning off the main road and down a side street. I was looking for a sign, quite literally, that would take me to Kayla's house.

I walked past a food-market that was currently dark and silent, then stepped past a butcher's shop and a bakery. I was about to cross the street and continue past the remaining shops on the other side, but there it was, right above my head.

Marigold Road.

My heart began to pound as I turned into Kayla's street and hurried on toward her home address.

I didn't know the number, but I knew what the house looked like thanks to Marienne's vision. I walked until I found it. A small, single-story red brick house. And there was a light in the window.

She was home. And she was awake.

FOUR

Kayla

My back was killing me. I couldn't sleep. Not for love nor money. Because of the baby, I couldn't take anything for the pain, so I didn't bother trying to sleep. I just bounced on the gym ball the doctor had suggested and rolled my hips around, and around.

This bloody baby needed to come out. Like... now.

There was a knock on the door and I glanced up at the clock on the wall: 10:11 p.m.

Who on earth would be coming to see me at this time of night? I checked my cell phone for any missed calls or messages. Nothing.

The knocking sounded again.

I used the ball to bounce myself to my weary feet, then waddled over to the front door.

The security peephole made it easy to look through but it was dark on the doorstep. I needed light to see who it was.

I set up my cell phone to dial for help if I needed it, and flicked on the light.

"No!" I gasped out, my voice denying the truth of what my eyes were seeing.

Anselm, the drunken worm, was on my doorstep.

My heart began to pound. I gripped my belly hard, the baby Anselm put inside me kicking out, stronger than I'd ever felt before. Was the baby responding to my emotions? The upshot in blood pressure? Or was it something else? Surely to God my baby couldn't sense his or her father nearby?

"I know you're in there, Kayla. Please open the door."

I shivered and turned around, pressing my back against the solid wood of the front door. "Shit."

"I just want to talk to you. To apologize. Please let me in."

I rubbed my belly harder, round and round in circles while I tried to think of a way out of this.

I hadn't told him about the baby that had been conceived from our one-night stand. Whether or not I would have told him, was moot. I didn't have his cell number, or his last name.

Not to mention the fact that he'd simply vanished seemingly into thin air after that night.

There had been no way to find out who he was or where he lived. No way to let him know about the consequences of our night together.

I stood up straighter, taking short, sharp breaths while I tried to calm down. "Go away, Anselm. I don't want to talk to you."

Such an unusual name for a man, but then, the name matched the man. He was so beautiful it hurt to look at him. I wasn't usually one to go for pure looks, especially not pretty boys like him. But the night we'd met I hadn't been able to control myself, and now look where I was.

Pregnant and alone.

"Kayla. Please." He called again, knocking three times.

I sighed. *Okay... not so alone anymore. At least, right this minute.*

He wasn't going away, that was for certain. He'd found me, and I was going to have to deal with this. Now.

I reached for the dead bolt and clicked it open.

Then I removed the chain, sliding it along and unclipping it.

I'd imagined this moment so many times—when I would finally confront him about his disappearing act. Those thoughts used to keep me up at night. Now it was my bladder waking me at all hours of the morning.

I took a deep breath, though my stomach twisted and my heart pounded with sickening lurches against my ribs. "Here goes."

I pulled open the door, a glare firmly entrenched on my face.

He was standing on the stoop in clothes that didn't fit him, nor did they suit him. "Have you been raiding the goodwill bins or something?"

His blue eyes struck my face, leaving me breathless. He'd had the same effect the first time I met him. And despite all the anger and resentment I'd built up over the last eight months, seeing him again felt so good.

Too good.

I hauled up the walls around my heart, reaching for the feelings of anger and betrayal that I'd kept burning for so long.

"What are you doing here?" I asked.

But he wasn't looking at my face anymore. His gaze had dropped to my swollen belly, where his child shifted and kicked as though it were on display at the local fair.

"You're pregnant." His mouth gaped open and his eyes were wide in complete astonishment.

I crossed my arms over my chest, not the easiest feat when my boobs literally sat on my belly now. "No shit, Sherlock."

So he wasn't here because someone had told him about my pregnancy.

Interesting.

"It's mine." He sounded as sure as a man had ever been.

"No. It's *mine*," I said. "You left. You didn't give a shit about me, or this baby, so I.... oh..."

Pain hit me low down, hard. A large cramp was the best way to describe it, but it took my breath away.

"You... You need to come home with me. My mother will know what to do."

I tried to laugh but had to breathe through the pain instead. When the cramp finally subsided, I managed to say, "Your mother... are you serious? What's she going to do?"

I'd been having some cramps all day, but nothing like this.

Anselm was breathing strangely.

I narrowed my eyes at him as I finally straightened to my full height once more. "Are you okay?"

Was he having some sort of panic attack or something? I wouldn't be surprised. I'd almost had a conniption the day I found out I was pregnant.

He shook his head, his hands tightening into fists. "We have to go. Do you have a snow jacket? Something warm to wear?"

I rolled my eyes at him. It was spring and the weather was fine. What was he talking about?

"Anselm, I think you need to go home and come back another time." Another tightening in my belly told me that the next time I saw him there might be two of us.

He shook his head rapidly, then pinned me with his gaze.

"What's wrong with your eyes?" They weren't blue anymore. How was that possible?

Anselm took a step closer, and I took one back. Not because I was actually afraid of him, but because he was acting so intensely.

"Listen to me Kayla. I am a dragon shifter from another realm. You're my mate and I am inches away from losing control. I need you to rug up as warm as you can, lock the house, and come with me."

I laughed, because honestly, what other reaction could I have?

"A dragon... what?"

"Shifter." He gasped out.

"I don't believe you."

When he looked at me this time, his eyes were pure silver. "I'll prove it to you. Get dressed in your warmest clothes and... is there something you can sit in that I can carry?"

He began glancing around, then pointed at my car. "That's perfect. Get dressed, buckle yourself in. Then we have to go."

Why do I always fall for the crazy ones?

There was only one thing for it. And that was to call his bluff.

I threw my hands up in the air. "Fine. But when you don't turn into some fire breathing dragon, you go away."

He nodded strangely, his breathing rapid and fast. He was shaking like someone off their meds, and I slammed the door shut, just to make a point. I was not happy that he had just turned up out the blue like this, and started spouting nonsense at me.

"Why, baby? Why?" I asked, then groaned as the baby kicked out at me.

"Fine," I muttered. "But you know he's crazy."

I waddled to my bedroom and pulled out my warmest jacket. I managed to just do it up around my huge belly, then slid my feet into my only pair of fur lined boots.

I was almost out the door when my gaze caught on my packed hospital bag. I didn't need it, of course. He wasn't carrying me anywhere. But something, a cosmic nudge from the universe, told me I shouldn't leave the house without it.

I rubbed my belly again. Almost forty weeks pregnant, I probably should keep this bag in the car anyway. Now that I had a good and logical reason to take the bag, I picked it up and opened the door.

Anselm had stripped off his baggy shirt and was now standing on my front lawn in nothing but those too-tight jeans.

I groaned and tried to look exasperated, but the truth was I could barely drag my eyes from his amazing form. What man looked like that outside of a magazine? He was freaking huge. His shoulders were even bigger than the last time I saw him.

I lifted my chin, despite the fact I felt as fat as a hippopotamus, and waddled over to my tiny car. It was four doors, barely, and had next to no trunk space. I desperately needed an upgrade, but hadn't been able to afford all the baby expenses and a new car.

So I'd invested in a great pram and intended to lose some of the excess weight I'd put on, walking around town and doing my shopping that way.

"You're gonna feel really stupid soon," I said, throwing my bag in the back seat, then squeezing into the driver's side. My spare keys were in the baby bag, so if he went any more nuts on me, I'd just drive away. Not easy with my belly almost touching the steering wheel, but I'd do it if I had to. The local police were only a few blocks away.

I lifted the lever to slide the chair back, to give myself more room, then rubbed my belly slowly as I forced myself to take deep breaths. Even that small amount of exercise made me pant.

Anselm dropped his face next to the window. "Buckle yourself in. And don't be afraid. I'll never let anything happen to you, or our child."

He was serious, and the tone he was using was beginning to worry me. "Okay," I managed.

He was delusional after all. He had to be.

And the best way to prove to him that he was delusional, was to ask him to show me the dragon, and watch him fail. Right? I was sure that's what I'd seen on a TV show. Or something like it.

Anselm stepped back and I watched him through the side window. And what I saw, wasn't possible. He began to change and transform. He grew so tall I couldn't see his head through the car's window, not that I wanted to see his head anyway.

His belly was scaled and gray in color, and his wings... "Oh my God. No way." *He has fucking wings*!

My heart pounded and my baby rolled and kicked in seeming excitement. I hoped the kick of adrenaline wasn't hurting my baby at all.

I reached for the door handle to try and get out, but Anselm took a step toward me and I froze. Was it even him anymore? Would he recognize me? Or would he hurt me if I tried to run away?

The dragon—because honestly, there was no other word to describe the creature that was standing right in front of me—flapped his wings and flew up into the air.

I gulped down the scream that rose and closed my eyes. "It's gone, it's okay. It's gone." I rubbed my belly in calming circles though my heart hammered loudly in my chest. "Calm down. Calm down."

A loud bang, like something had landed on the roof made me scream out, terror shooting through my veins.

I reached for the door handle and tried to push it open, but now a long talon held it closed, stretching over the top of the door and across the window.

"No. No. No."

I pushed again and let out another yelp as the car lifted into the air. My arms flung out, pushing against the door, and the seat beside me. I closed my eyes and began to chant. "This isn't happening. This isn't happening."

I was shaking with fear, and knew I had to be in a dream. But God, did it feel real.

I opened my eyes again and my jaw dropped. We were high, like really high in the air. My stomach swooped and I retched, trying not to be sick.

There was a bottle of water beside me. I reached for it, my hands shaking as I popped the top and took a sip. Then another sip. Trying to calm down.

I put my seat belt on, right?

I checked and I'd done that one strange thing he'd asked me to do. Thank God. Not that a seat belt was going to save me if he dropped us from this height, but at least I wasn't going to accidently fall out the door.

How the hell was I going to wake up from this dream? By having a heart attack probably... but that certainly wasn't the best way. I had to just force myself to wake up.

"Wake up. Wake up." I slapped my cheeks and blinked rapidly. "Come on."

I slid my fingers down to the steering wheel, then moved my hands slowly around the car, grounding myself and trying not to think about the distance to the ground. If he dropped me, I was dead. There was no other possible ending for me, or my baby.

Anselm's words echoed in my head. *I'll never let any harm come to you or our baby.*

I tried to let that reassure me and dropped into my meditative breathing. I closed my eyes and focused on my body, my hands, my feet, my legs, my belly.

I slowed everything down, trying to stay calm. I was sweating from stress and began to unfasten my jacket.

The moment I opened the jacket, I shivered. That was strange. It wasn't cold out tonight.

I opened my eyes and peered out. Snow was falling onto the windscreen. "What the hell?"

I reached out to touch the glass and found it cold. "Where the hell are we?" Because I was almost certain we weren't anywhere near my home town anymore.

Anselm

I beat my wings as hard as they would go. The combined weight of the car and my mate was by far the heaviest I'd ever carried. But I pushed on, through the veil and beyond, soaring on the cold air and using the gusts of wind to help us toward home.

I wasn't sure if my parents would be back from the Black Mountains yet, or if taking Kayla to Marienne was smarter than going back to my family castle. But as pain ripped through my leg muscles and my wings strained against the downward weight, I realized I had no choice.

My home was closer, and the only option. I wouldn't make it to the Black Mountains.

Despite the turmoil of emotion inside my head, I tried to focus on only one thing. Getting my mate and our child to safety. I couldn't slip, nor could I land wrong. The normal place for the royals was the top balcony on the highest level of the castle.

I wasn't sure the car would fit safely on the balcony, and even if it could fit into that tight space by some miracle, I wasn't sure I could land there safely. I scanned the horizon for a safe place to put my mate. The land around the castle was heavily populated with streets and homes, but further out were fields of crops and snow.

My gaze fixed on a field near the entrance to the castle, where freshly fallen snow was covering the ground. That was where I would have to land.

I soared lower, hearing Kayla's muffled shrieks rising up from the car beneath me. I had no idea how she was going to react when I actually landed, but my dragon didn't care. All he cared about was the fact that my mate was now safe, with us, and about to birth the next generation of dragon kings.

We got lower and lower, the snow falling hard and fast. I fluttered my wings at high speed, hovering just above the ground so that I could set the car down as gently as possible. As soon as the wheels touched the ground, I let go of the weight of the car and it sunk down on to the tires.

I launched myself forward so I didn't land on top of the car, and collapsed in the snow in front of the hood. My breath was heaving. Thank God she drove a mini automobile. I would never have been able to carry her inside of one of those larger cars that look like an armored tank.

Kayla flicked a switch and started the engine. *Oh crap.* She was trying to run from me, but her car wouldn't make it far in this snow. I had to stop her before she hurt herself.

She flicked on the car's headlights, effectively blinding me.

I turned my head away, still breathing hard. My dragon was exhausted, but extremely satisfied with the results. We had our mate in the Land of Fire and Ice—that's what my father called our realm.

I let go of my shifter, transforming back to my human body, the freezing cold night air hitting my naked skin like a thousand needle pricks.

Kayla's car was still on, the engine humming and the lights focused on me. But she wasn't driving anywhere. Not yet anyway.

I lifted my hand to shield my eyes and called out, "I'm going to walk over before I freeze to death, Kayla."

She could be hyperventilating, or so mad she'd punch me as soon as I opened the passenger door. Either way, I was getting in that car. I was ready and willing to handle anything she threw at me.

I hurried over the icy ground to the passenger side of the car. The door was initially stuck, but with a bit of tugging and swearing I managed to yank it open and jump inside, shivering as the warmth of the car's heater vents passed over my almost-frozen skin.

"Damn, it's cold out there."

Kayla had her hands wrapped around the steering wheel, her knuckles white in a death grip. "Anselm." She ground out between gritted teeth. "Where the hell are we?"

I turned to her, trying to keep my tone calm. "We crossed the veil into my realm. It's usually hidden and not many humans know it exists."

"Humans." She repeated the word with a strange note in her voice, as though I said something wrong.

"Yes... we're not human. We're dragon shifters. As you just... saw." She'd asked me to prove I really was a fire-breathing dragon, though I hadn't really shown her the fiery part yet.

She was nodding, and gulping, her throat making a weird noise.

I reached out to touch her arm, but she practically shoved my hand away.

"Hey, are you okay?"

She twisted to face me, her dark eyes flashing. "Am I okay? Did you just really ask me that? No! I am not okay. I am... *freaking out*! I cannot be here. This has to be a dream."

I was warm enough now, thanks to the heater in Kayla's car doing an admirable job, but we couldn't stay here forever.

"It's not a dream," I told her as softly as I could. "But we're going to leave the car and go inside the castle gates. This car won't keep us warm very long in this climate."

Not to mention the fact that I was naked, and there weren't any clothes for me to change into in her car.

Kayla glanced down at my body as though she could hear my thoughts, then groaned loudly. "You're going to get arrested for public indecency."

I couldn't help but laugh, which earned me a glare and a punch in the arm from my feisty human mate.

"I'm sorry," I said, unable to remove the grin from my face. "But there's no such thing here. All of our people, well most of them anyway, can shift into dragons at whim. Nudity is not a big deal in our community. It is natural and normal, though not advisable in this weather."

Kayla turned toward the windscreen which was now covered in snow. "What is with the winter landscape? Are you guys behind us in seasons or something?"

I shook my head. "No, we are in spring here also, but there is snow and ice almost all year round. My father calls our country, the Land of Fire and Ice. For the dragons, and the snow."

Kayla was nodding again in that weird way she had, with her wild eyes and gulping in her throat. "So you're saying that I really am in some strange land with dragons and castles? Oh my God. I feel like I traveled back in time, or something."

I laughed softly. "You'll feel like that inside the castle. We don't have a lot of technology, choosing a simpler life for our people, and ourselves."

Kayla wiped at her eyes, where tears fell on to her cheeks.

I reached for her and this time she didn't push me away. "It's going to be okay, Kayla."

"No it's not." She sobbed and my whole heart broke for her obvious confusion and fear.

But what she didn't understand yet was that she was the mate to the future king, and her every whim and desire would be granted, for the rest of her life.

"Let's get you inside," I said, squeezing her arm. "You're probably exhausted and need a hot shower and a warm bed."

"I'm not sleeping with you. *Ow!*" She grimaced then rubbed her big belly. "Bloody baby is so ready to come out."

I made a quick calculation in my head and came up with a scary number. "You'd be almost nine months now, wouldn't you?"

She lifted her head and looked into my eyes, and there I saw all the shadows and doubts that I would need to chase away. "Yes. I'm thirty-nine weeks."

I wasn't sure what that was in human terms, but it was very obvious that both my mate and her babe would be much happier when the pregnancy was over.

"Well, neither of us wants you to have the baby in this tiny car, so how about you button your coat and we walk to the castle?"

She wiped at her face, then reached for a tissue from the console to blow her nose. "What about you? Won't you freeze?"

I shook my head. "My temperature runs hotter than a human. I'll be fine as long as I can get inside relatively soon."

Dragon shifters in their human form could survive naked several hours in temperatures like this. Longer if we had to.

She shook herself and took some deep breaths like she was pumping herself up to conquer a huge task. "Okay. Can you get the baby bag from the back seat, and let's go see this castle. God... I never thought I'd say that in real life."

I grabbed the large duffel bag that she pointed to in the back seat and opened the car door to get out.

She wasn't moving though.

"Are you coming with me?"

Kayla looked over at me. "Can't you just fly me home? Put me back into my warm bed. I promise, I'll never come after you for maintenance, and you can forget about us completely."

I so wanted to lean over and kiss her lips. I'd reassure her that I was never leaving her again. But that wasn't what she wanted to hear, so I kept those thoughts to myself.

"Even if I wanted to, which I don't," I said, "I'm exhausted. I could never carry that car back through the veil, you'd have to ride on my back... which in your condition is probably not the best idea."

Her eyes widened and then she shrieked, "Are you telling me I'm stuck here?"

Oops. "No... no. I just think that consulting my mother might be the best thing here. She's human and has more knowledge than I do about your anatomy."

I'd never understood before how Lucian, King Damon's half-brother, had been able to live in the human world with his mate for a time. But now that I knew first-hand about the strength of the mate bond, I knew I'd do anything to keep Kayla by my side.

Anything.

"Your mother's human?" Kayla squeaked, and I nodded.

"Did your father carry her through the veil against her will as well?"

I presumed she was half-joking, at least about me taking her against her will, since Kayla had actually asked me to shift and prove I was a dragon.

She didn't ask you to carry her here. Shut up.

I answered her honestly. "Well... yes actually. He tracked her down, since she is his fated mate, and when he shifted, she fainted."

"And he kidnapped her?" Kayla asked, her mouth dropping open.

I laughed and turned toward the car door once more. "They tell the story much better than I can."

Kayla huffed. "I bet."

"Come on. Let's get out of here before everyone's in bed and there's no one to open the doors for us."

I jumped out of the car, Kayla's bag in hand, and hurried around to her side.

She'd already managed to open the door and was hauling herself up and out of the car. "Brr... it's freezing."

"Literally," I said, grabbing her hand. "Stay close. We've lost people in blizzards like this before."

She pressed into my side, and I led her in the direction of the castle gates.

The guard standing at the top stared down at us with a surprised frown. I called up to him. "It's me, Thomas. Can you open the castle gates for us?"

"Oh! Yes, sire." The guard ran off to do my bidding.

"What did he call you?" Kayla asked.

I didn't get to answer her because she was too busy gaping at the entry to the castle as the huge gates opened slowly. They pushed the snow into massive piles each side of the entrance and revealed our small village within, containing quaint homes and cobblestone streets.

"Wow. It's like a medieval fairytale," Kayla whispered.

I chuckled. "Yes, but with electricity and good plumbing. We don't have a lot of technology, but we do have both of those things!" All provided by my father for the whole kingdom. No one in our land was without a roof over their head, clean water or heating.

We hurried inside the gates, which closed behind us. We didn't have a lot of enemies anymore, but my father still chose to keep everything secure and we had guards on the walls all the time.

"Sire!" A guard called from the wall, then he threw down a long fur-lined cloak.

"Thank you!" I called back, grabbing the thick robe and pulling it around my naked body.

"Well, you were certainly right about them not arresting you for being naked." She spoke with a raised eyebrow.

"Let's get up to the castle," I said, trying not to laugh.

"Okay... but go slow." She grabbed onto the hand I offered her. "I'm not built to hustle at present."

"Oh... of course." I put my arm around her and directed her through the streets of our town and up toward the castle.

By the time we got to the top of the steps, she was huffing and puffing. "I hope it was worth all that trouble."

"What?" I asked.

"Getting me up here." She seemed to be gasping for air.

I nodded. "It will be. The accommodations in the castle, and the food alone, are well worth the trip."

She bent forward for a moment, rubbing her belly and breathing deep. "You okay?"

She nodded, then stood straighter. "Yeah. I've been getting cramps for weeks now but it never progresses into full labor."

"Maybe our baby was waiting for me to arrive," I suggested, which earned me a glare of the filthiest kind.

"Well, if you'd bothered to call me, or contact me, or follow up even once after our night together, you could have been part of this from the start." Then her face calmed and she shrugged with seeming nonchalance. She stared at the doors in front of us as if she couldn't bear to face me a second longer. "Now it's too late."

I shook my head, my heart squeezing tight in my chest. Hoping I spoke the truth. "No, Kayla. It's never too late."

CHAPTER
SIX

Kayla

I could barely breathe and was wheezing like a pug. I was so unfit, and this baby made things so much harder. He, or she, was squishing my lungs and my stomach, and the extra weight made my legs and lower back ache.

But I'd made it up all those bloody steep streets and now I was standing in front of huge stone doors at the top of a staircase that had almost killed me to walk up. Anselm had better be correct, and our destination worth all this physical exertion.

I was avoiding thinking about the emotional stress at this point. I had a lot to process but I didn't want rising anxiety to adversely affect the baby.

Anselm walked over to the doors and knocked loudly using the large ornate knocker.

I quirked an eyebrow at him, aiming for humor even though I still couldn't breathe properly. "You don't have a key?"

He laughed. "This door can only be opened from the inside."

Hmm... why would they do that? Security maybe?

The doors opened and a man dressed in black robes stepped out into the snow. He looked like a servant. Especially when he bowed low before he spoke. "Prince Anselm. We were not expecting you tonight, sire."

Sire... prince? Oh my God. No. "Tell me you're not who they're saying you are."

Anselm, the cheeky bugger, didn't answer the question. Instead, he grinned at me before putting an arm around my waist and drawing me inside. "Come on. It's much warmer in here."

I forced my aching legs to keep moving and waddled into the foyer. Then I stopped and stared around the entrance area, shocked at how beautiful everything was. The floors were marble, and plush red carpets ran up an enormous staircase.

Where the hell are we?

"You actually live here?" I asked, but he wasn't listening; he was talking to the man who'd let us in the front door.

I turned away from him and took my time absorbing my surroundings. The lights were dimmed, probably due to the late hour, and there was mostly silence in the background, but God it was all so beautiful.

Suddenly I yawned loudly, unable to help myself, and covered my mouth with my hand. The adrenaline from earlier was beginning to leach out of my system and the fact that it was past midnight and I was practically nine months pregnant began to weigh on me.

When Anselm finished his conversation and walked over once more, I spoke up. "I'm sorry, but I think I need to lie down pretty soon."

He nodded. "Of course. And please don't apologize. I imagine this has all been a lot to take in. The servants are getting my sister's room ready for you. It's next to mine so if you need me during the night, I won't be far."

He indicated with his hand that I should follow, so I did. I didn't need a fancy room. All I needed was one of the couches we passed, and a blanket. I was practically falling asleep on my feet.

Somehow, my back wasn't sore anymore and my body was relaxed, more than it had been in months. I had no idea how that was possible, since I'd done nothing but fight and scream while I was carried here, but it was true.

Was it the cold air and unfamiliar environment that had shocked my system out of its aches and pains? Or was it something more complex? Something to do with the man... dragon... shifter... or *whatever* he was, who had brought me here and seemed determined to look after me and our baby?

We walked down a long hallway, then Anselm stopped in front of a wooden door. "This is my sister Jessa's old room. Mine is there." He pointed at a door about fifteen feet further down the hallway.

I crossed my arms over my chest, suspicious as hell. "There's no adjoining door... right?"

Not that a man like him would likely want to force himself on a woman who probably weighed more than he did... but still. I had to ask.

He tilted his head and frowned at me. "Between siblings? That would be weird."

I didn't have the brain power to explain so I just asked, "Your sister won't mind if I sleep here?"

He shook his head. "No, not at all. My parents and both of my sisters are visiting family friends and will be gone for the next few days."

"Okay." I didn't have anything else left in me to fight him. There was a bed inside this room, and it was calling my name.

I pushed open the door to the most opulent bedroom I'd ever seen. It rivaled every magazine cover, ever.

In the middle of the room was a huge four poster bed, with white draping curtains and golden blankets thrown over the coverlet.

"Wow... I..."

I was literally speechless.

"Let me tuck you in." Anselm took my hand and tugged me inside.

There was only a single light illuminating the room. A gold lamp on the bedside table.

Tuck me in? "You don't need to do that," I grumbled, shoving off my large, warm coat and sitting down on the plush bed. "I've been putting myself to bed alone for a long time." I kicked my feet out of my fur boots, or tried to, but my right foot got stuck.

"Shit." I reached down to shove at it—or at least, I tried to—but had issues bending because of my belly. Anselm knelt at my feet.

"Allow me." He gently pulled at both boots and they easily slipped from my feet. Then he set them to the side, stood up and rolled back the bedcovers for me.

I was too exhausted to be angry or fight him. I crawled beneath the blankets—so soft and warm—and put my head on the pillow.

The whole bed felt like a giant cloud, folding around me. "Oh... this is heaven." I rolled onto my side, grabbed one of the many pillows and tucked it between my knees, and closed my eyes.

Anselm kissed my forehead lightly, a mere brushing of his lips against my skin. The sensation sent a frisson of something delightful through my body, but I was so tired and confused, that I couldn't quite grasp what it was.

"I've missed so much, my beautiful mate," he whispered. "I won't miss anything more. I promise."

I didn't know what to say, and didn't bother trying to answer him. There was too much water under the bridge now. Surely he understood that?

He clicked the lamp next to the bed and the whole room fell into darkness. I stayed awake just long enough to hear the door shut, then I slid into a deep sleep.

❦

WAKING up wrapped in a cloud couldn't feel better than the place I woke up in the next morning.

For the first time in far too long, I'd had hours of uninterrupted sleep. Although my bladder was now screaming at me to get up and go to the bathroom, the rest of me was rested and relaxed.

The baby shifted and kicked out, obviously frustrated about being trapped inside me. He or she really seemed determined to want to come out.

"Okay, okay." I groaned, throwing back the covers and rolling up to a standing position.

The plush carpet beneath my toes was exquisite and made the plantar fasciitis I suffered from in the mornings, so much easier to bear.

I pushed open one of the doors off the bedroom and found the most amazing walk-in closet. It was huge. The size of my kitchen at home.

I closed it because, unfortunately, not a single thing would fit me at present, even if I was the sort of girl to borrow and wear another woman's clothes.

Behind the next door I found what I was looking for. A huge white and gold bathroom extended out the length of the closet. It had a huge bath, a walk-in shower and a large vanity with mirror.

I waddled over to the toilet and quickly sat. Peeing all the time was one of the many things I didn't like about pregnancy. I finished up, washed my hands and contemplated a shower. But with no fresh clothes to put on, there really wasn't any point.

As though someone had heard my thoughts, there was a knock at the bedroom door, then a woman called out. "Hello? Kayla?"

I turned toward the friendly voice and walked back into the huge bedroom which showed itself to be even bigger in the daylight.

Seriously. Who are these people?

There was a woman laying long dresses on the bed. Rich fabrics with long sleeves and hoods, that I assumed would assist to keep out the cold.

"Ah... hello?" I answered.

She turned and looked at me, her intelligent gaze taking in my size in a measured heartbeat. "I can definitely alter something of the queens to accommodate that belly. We need you to be comfortable, don't we?"

Perhaps she was a dressmaker, or a housekeeper? She looked about fifty with graying temples and her hair upswept into a bun on top of her head.

"Do we?" I asked, walking back to the bed and sitting down once more, my feet still aching. I stretched my legs, rolling my ankles around and wishing for the pain to subside.

"You must take a bath," she said. "It will help with your aches and pains. I will just take a few measurements, then I'll bring you back some clothes to wear."

I reached out to touch the dresses she'd already brought me. "These are just beautiful."

The woman, whose name I still didn't know, hummed with approval. "Yes, the queen does have nice taste."

"The queen?" I repeated. Was she serious?

"Yes. Anselm's mother, Lucy." The woman finally introduced herself. "I'm Sadie. My mother has been the housekeeper here since King Stavrok was a child."

"Nice to meet you, Sadie," I said. "You probably already know, but I'm Kayla."

She nodded then reached out her hand. "Stand up. I need a measurement, then I'll be on my way."

She whipped out a measuring tape, made a quick measure of my hip, belly and bust, then thrust the tape back into her pocket.

A true professional.

I couldn't help grouching. "I'm sure you won't have anything that fits me. My original body was hard enough to dress. But my belly has just made everything twice as hard."

I was a size eighteen to twenty anyway, and once I'd gotten pregnant my boobs had gone up three cup sizes.

Sadie *tsked* with disapproval. "You humans... always worried about being too big. Your weight is a good thing. It gives you strength, and sexuality, not to mention the ability to birth your babies well."

I glanced down at my hands. I'd always been uncomfortable with my weight. No matter what I tried, it never changed.

I didn't know what to say to her, so I just kept quiet.

"I won't be long," Sadie said. "I'll draw you a bath and you can have a good soak. Then you can dress and go to breakfast with the prince."

I coughed out a laugh, "The prince. I can't believe..." I covered my face with my hands. "He's a prince. A dragon prince, but still..."

When I dropped my arms once more, Sadie was off in the bathroom, running me a bath. I had the feeling that she mothered the prince and his sisters, something I wouldn't mind being a part of. My own mother had died when I was a teenager, and I missed her. A lot.

My dad hadn't been part of my life much, so I had little family. One of the many drawbacks about being single and pregnant, I hadn't had any family to lean on.

Sadie bustled back into the room and picked up one of the dresses from the bed. The one that I'd been most drawn to. The ruby red.

"The queen is buxom, much like yourself," Sadie said with a nod at my breasts. "Don't underestimate the power of a beautiful body in keeping a dragon mate happy."

I managed to smile at the well-meaning housekeeper and ran my hands over my baby bump. I didn't feel beautiful. I felt like a whale.

"Won't be long." She swept out of the room.

The bathroom was beginning to steam up and the running water called to me.

I looked around the beautiful bathroom and sighed. "What have I gotten myself into?"

A man who I'd slept with eight months ago had turned up out of nowhere and swept me up, then carried me to his castle in another realm.

It was like a movie, and I couldn't wrap my head around the idea that this could possibly be happening to me.

Little old, fat... me!

I shook my head and stood up, undressing for the bath.

There was a long mirror on the wall and I took a few steps toward it, grimacing at the picture that flashed back at me.

My breasts were huge and grotesque now, the areola dark and stretched. My belly was gigantic, not a cute little bump like all the magazine women had. And my cellulite... I turned to the side to see my dimpled ass and thighs flash in the morning light. Damn, they were ugly.

But there was no-one here to see me, so I tried not to focus on how crap my appearance made me feel. Instead, I turned away from the mirror and carefully climbed into the huge bath.

The warm water was like a huge hug and I sighed as I swam across to the far side and turned over, letting myself relax into the warmth. My body was buoyed in the tub and I floated in the bubbles, a huge feeling of relief washing over me.

I lay there and enjoyed the luxury, because goodness knows when this dream was going to come to a crashing end.

CHAPTER
SEVEN

Anselm

I slept like crap, all night. I tossed and turned and ached and angered. My mate was in the castle. My mate! The woman I'd scoured the earth for was literally a few steps away... in the room next to mine. The fact that she was so close had actually given me some comfort, but regret ate at me like a disease.

I could have gone back for her at any time. I could have tried to contact her after I'd left her that night. But no... I'd been too ashamed in relation to my behavior, falling into bed with a human and not telling her who I really was. Too angry at my brother for dragging me away when I'd wanted to stay.

So instead, I'd missed out on loving my mate for all these months that she needed me. I hadn't seen her grow large with my child. I'd been alone, and so had she.

Today I would propose marriage and we would alert my parents immediately. We could have a small ceremony in the castle straight away, which would hopefully make Kayla feel wanted and desired, even after I'd ignored her for so long.

My child would be the next heir to our kingdom, and he or she deserved every possibility of happiness and security.

I'd been told by Sadie this morning that she would take care of Kayla, and make sure she was comfortable and dressed warmly. I hadn't even thought about her clothes, or anything like that. *Idiot.* But I was grateful to have Sadie to think of such things in my mother's absence.

You'd think after growing up with twin sisters I'd know something of a woman's needs.

Obviously not.

A knock on my bedroom door was followed by the entrance of my personal servant, Manny. If he played his role correctly, Manny would run the household once I ascended the throne, something Manny was ever so nonchalant about.

He walked in with his characteristic grin, as informal as my father's butler was formal. "So," he began. "The acorn doesn't fall far from the tree, does it, Your Highness?"

I stood up and tugged on my vest. I'd dressed well today, knowing I would be proposing marriage. I didn't want to look like some sort of street urchin.

"How do you mean?"

Manny chuckled. "From what I've heard, King Stavrok stole Queen Lucy from the human realm when he found her. Now you've taken your own human. I never thought you'd follow in your father's footsteps quite so closely."

I groaned. "It wasn't intentional, and besides, isn't it obvious that I've seen her before?"

Manny laughed. "Oh, you mean the pregnant belly? I did wonder on that one, sire. Perhaps that happened when you and your brother went gallivanting off to the human realm for a little sneaky peek?"

I glared at my best friend, the man who would one day be my greatest asset. "You know too much, Manny."

Once again the blue-eyed young man cackled with laughter. "Not much gets past me, sire. Now, I'm here with a message from Sadie."

The woman who truly ran everything around here. I walked toward the door, waiting for the message.

"And?" I finally enquired. "What did she say?"

"She said to tell you to meet your mate for breakfast in the small dining room. Now. Kayla will be ready in a few minutes."

I pushed my hair out of my eyes and nodded. It was time.

Manny put his hand out and touched my shoulder, his usually joker-like face serious for once. "Prince Anselm, I want to tell you how happy I am for you. Truly."

I clapped my hand on Manny's shoulder. "Thank you, my friend."

Then we both straightened, shrugging off the camaraderie we both felt at a base level.

I headed out the door of my bedroom and looked both ways. The hallway was empty, so I hurried along to the dining room, wanting to be there to greet my future wife.

The dining room had been set for guests, with the good white table cloth and the best silver. I couldn't help but smile at the obvious approval from the servants, already treating Kayla like the queen she was destined to be.

I walked over to the fire where heat burst from the logs. I was still slightly chilled from last night's excursions. Carrying that car all the way from the human realm had drained my energy in a way I'd never experienced before.

I was glad I'd done it, for my mate's sake. But I wasn't sure I could again, if I had to.

When the door finally opened, I turned toward my mate with my heart open and my expectations sky high.

She was even more beautiful than I remembered.

Her long dark hair cascaded over her shoulders and her skin shone with good health. The dress they'd chosen for her suited her to perfection, hugging her large belly and accentuating her huge breasts in a way that made me want to rush over and bury my face between them.

But I stayed where I was by the fire, because despite the beauty that was Kayla, she seemed unsure. Her eyes darted this way and that, as though she was expecting something, or someone, to jump out and scare her.

"Good morning," I called as I meandered toward the dining table. "The servants weren't sure what you liked, so they appear to have made everything on the menu."

I'd never seen so much food on a breakfast table before. There were pies, and fresh breads, pastries and whipped cream. Then of course there was toast, and bacon and eggs. Everything and anything a person could wish for.

Kayla glanced over at the abundance, her eyes wide with surprise. "Oh, they shouldn't have gone to so much trouble. I rarely eat much for breakfast."

That could hardly be good for her, or the babe, but I kept my opinions to myself.

"Well, sit and have a cup of tea, or some fresh juice, if you like. No one will be offended if you don't eat anything."

I pulled out the large dining room chair and Kayla stared at me for a moment, then shook her head and sat down.

I pushed the chair in, and walked around to my spot, opposite her. "Is there something wrong?"

A soft smile played at the edges of her lips. "No... it's just that, you talk like you're from a medieval movie, or something. And your manners are... well, they're great, but very unusual in men nowadays."

I shrugged and reached for the stack of pancakes piled up next to the fresh blueberries. "It may be, in human men. I was taught differently."

"Hmmm," Kayla nodded, then reached for a slice of buttered toast, "You were taught to have one night stands with human women, then abandon them. Got it."

My cheeks flushed with the heat of shame. "You have no idea how ashamed I am of my behavior on that night and since then."

She shrugged, causing her breasts to bounce and draw my eye. "It doesn't matter now. What's done is done."

"No, it's not," I urged her. "We can't go into the future with that hanging over our heads. I have to explain to you why I behaved that way."

Kayla reached for the bottle of freshly squeezed juice. "Go for it."

I clenched my jaw tight, then slowly released it. I should have been practicing this speech. Instead I'd spent the night angry and alone.

Now was not the time for regrets. I had to explain. I took a deep breath and said, "I mentioned last night about fated mates, did I not?"

She shook her head. "No... you said I was your mate. Or something. I was a little distracted by the whole dragon thing."

I tried to smile at her but my face was tight. "Yes. You are my mate... my fated mate. You are meant to be my life partner, and I am meant to be yours."

She frowned at me. "You can't be serious."

"I most definitely am." I reached for some of the berries and pulled them onto my plate. "The fated mate bond means that when I saw you, my dragon lost control and I had to shift. I had to bring you home with me."

"Are you telling me you don't have a choice on this thing?" Her eyebrows were high and questioning. "That fate just... points to me and goes, hey, even if you don't love her and you're not attracted to her... go marry her."

A growl rolled up and out of my chest. "I was attracted to you from the first moment I saw you, or I would never have put that baby in your belly."

It was Kayla's turn to seem embarrassed, or that was what I assumed she was feeling since her cheeks turned the same color as her ruby red dress.

She reached for some fresh fruit and placed three pieces on her plate. "You were saying... go back to the night we met at the club."

I ran a frazzled hand through my hair, quickly realizing that unless something dramatically changed, I would not be proposing marriage to my mate this morning.

I honestly thought this was going to be so much easier.

"I've been waiting for my fated mate to appear for... forever. I've felt incomplete, lonely, missing you."

Kayla looked up from her plate, meeting my gaze. I could feel the intensity of that look right down to the soles of my feet, and the fact that she was at least hearing my words gave me some comfort.

She wasn't speaking, so I continued. "I'd been told that when I met my mate, I'd know. My dragon would take over and I'd shift uncontrollably."

Kayla sucked on a strawberry, making my cock ache. Then she said, "Sort of like last night? All that shaking and carrying on?"

"Exactly," I said, trying not to take offence at the way she pictured me.

"Then why didn't that happen when I met you eight months ago?"

I sighed, opening my arms, palm up to show my confusion. "I'm not a hundred percent sure, but I think it was because I was so intoxicated. My dragon was asleep. He couldn't sense you."

Kayla gasped, then rubbed her belly. "Well, something was awake, because I got pregnant straight away."

I nodded, a strange sort of pride blossoming in my chest. "Well, you're my fated mate. It makes sense that we are compatible in every way."

The memories of the sex we'd shared that night had kept me company on many nights since then.

I took a sip of my fruity wine, then the thought hit me. Humans knew more about their babies than we did. "Do you know what you're having? Is there more than one?"

"More than one?" She gaped at me. "I bloody hope not!" Then she went quiet. "I know I'm huge, but that doesn't mean it's twins."

She looked crushed, and that was the last thing I'd meant to do.

"Oh, I didn't mean to imply anything negative! I am a triplet, with my sisters Vanya and Jessa. I was only wondering in case the multiple birth thing is genetic."

Kayla's hands rubbed over her huge belly, over and over. "No... I'm pretty sure there's only one. I've had several scans, and they all showed just one baby."

I nodded. That was a good thing, for a first birth especially. Mother didn't like to talk about it, but I was certain our birth hadn't been easy for her.

"And do you know if it's a boy or a girl?" I asked, not even sure what answer I would prefer.

She shook her head, vehemently. "I wanted a surprise."

I smiled. "That was a great choice." Made the wait even more worthwhile.

She was still rubbing her belly, almost like one would a magical lamp. "Are you going to continue with your story, or is that it? You met me and were so drunk you didn't realize I was your special mate person, then just disappeared forever in the morning?"

She was still angry, that was for sure. I had to try and explain better, make her believe how sorry I was.

"My younger brother, Iain, came for me during the night. He woke me up and practically dragged me home."

She narrowed her eyes at me. "Why would he do that?"

"Because crossing the veil is forbidden, especially for a crown prince. We hadn't told our parents that we were going, and all hell would break loose if they found out."

Kayla stood up slowly, her lips pulled tight. "I'm not feeling great, so if you don't mind, I think I'll go and lie down again."

"Of course," I said, rushing to stand. "I'll walk you back to your room."

"No." She pushed her hand out into the air, her voice forceful. "I need a bit of time to think."

I could tell that nothing I'd said had made her feel any better. If anything, it seemed I may have made things worse.

"Kayla. I wish I'd stayed until the morning and seen you in the early light. I wish I'd known you were my fated mate, and whisked you home with me that night."

She lifted her chin and stared at me with eyes as cold as the landscape outside. "And if wishes were horses, beggars would ride."

Then she turned and walked away, crushing my hopes of a marriage acceptance in a single breath.

CHAPTER

EIGHT

Kayla

Breakfast didn't sit well with me. Whether it was the food itself, or the conversation, I wasn't sure. But I wasn't feeling great. My stomach rolled and clenched like I was on a ship. I knew that I really should lie down and rest, but I couldn't. Not with my mind and my mood on a downward spiral.

I decided to keep moving and set off exploring the castle. I walked past my bedroom door and kept going, needing to stretch my legs. Before long, what had begun as gentle exercise, turned into wonder. I found myself staring out the windows at the most incredible view I'd ever seen.

The village beneath Anselm's castle was small and picturesque, with thatched rooves topped with freshly fallen snow. And beyond the huge gates were fields and mountains.

That's where my poor car still was, in one of those fields, probably frozen beyond repair.

As I pressed my palm flat against the windowpane, the glass was cold to the touch. I'd never survive if I went out there alone. Even if I could escape Anselm and this strange dream I was in, where would I go?

The baby rolled and kicked out beneath my ribs and I rubbed him or her through the thick winter dress. "It's okay sweetheart. We'll find a way home, and soon. I can't give birth to you here. It's not safe."

A large dark shape in the sky caught my attention and I looked up. "Wow." Flying toward us was a rather fierce-looking but breathtaking dragon. He was absolutely huge. Bigger than Anselm had been, I was sure.

I took a step back, not sure where he was going to land, because it didn't look like he was headed for the village.

The dragon began flapping his wings in big, slow moves as he hovered above the castle. On his back, shockingly was a woman. She had her hood pulled over her head and was riding the dragon without fear or worry. In fact, her hand stroked the scales as though she were petting the beast between her legs.

The woman turned her head suddenly and looked straight at me. Anselm's sapphire blue eyes stared back at me. My breath caught in my throat.

Who is that? His mother maybe? One of his sisters?

Then the woman smiled and waved. It was truly the strangest sight I'd ever witnessed.

I wriggled my fingers at her and waved back, because really, what else was I going to do? There was a woman, riding a dragon, waving at me.

They disappeared from my sight as the dragon flew somewhere I couldn't see through the window.

"Kayla."

I whirled around to find Sadie behind me.

"Oh hi. I was just walking around the castle, stretching my legs, and I saw... um..."

Sadie nodded as though she knew exactly what I was talking about. "Yes. The king and queen are home, and they'll want to meet you. Would you like to change into another outfit? Or can I help prepare you in any way?"

I thought about the single change of clothes I had with me, packed into my hospital bag as my going home outfit. They fit me, just, but I would be freezing in no time at all.

I glanced down at the dress that I was wearing. "Will the queen be upset that you altered this for me?"

Sadie smiled for one of the first times. "The queen doesn't get upset about such things."

"Oh, okay." I almost asked what would make the queen upset but didn't have the guts.

"Come," Sadie said, gesturing for me to follow her.

I did, waddling as fast as I could behind the housekeeper.

When we reached the door to the dining room from this morning, Anselm was waiting for us. "Oh, you found her. Thank you, Sadie."

I glanced toward the housekeeper and found her looking down her nose at the prince. "I didn't get her for you. The king and queen are home."

Anselm sighed, as though being told off by the housekeeper was a normal event. "Well, thank you, anyway."

Sadie nodded, and walked off.

Anselm turned to me, his demeanor sad. "I need to apologize to you, once again. I should never have taken you from your home and brought you here. I wish I'd been able to control my dragon and leave you in your own realm."

His words knifed my heart in a way I didn't expect, and I gasped at the unexpected pain. "Well, you can take me home right now if you don't want me here. That's damn fine by me."

He stepped closer and cupped my face with his hands, moving faster than I'd thought he could. "No." He breathed against my lips. "I should have stayed with you. Explained everything. Given you the support and love you deserve. I want you here. I never want you to go. Please stay with me."

"But the baby." I gulped. "The birth..."

"Our baby is part dragon," he whispered, kissing the tip of my nose, "Perhaps speak to my mother about the birth before you decide you need to go home?"

I nodded, because his words made sense, and his closeness was sending my whole body into shivers of delight. "Okay."

He stepped back and straightened his shirt with a tug on the sleeve. "I'm sorry to have to introduce you to my parents like this. I would have preferred another way."

"What way?" I asked even as he took my elbow and turned me toward the double door entry.

"As my fiancée." He proceeded to pull me forward.

I pulled him back as hard as I could. "You can't just drop a bombshell on me like that, then waltz me in to meet royalty!"

One side of Anselm's sexy mouth curled up. "Ah... I'm royalty too."

Not in my book you're not. You're just... mine.

I whacked him in the chest. "You know what I mean, so explain. What are you talking about?"

Anselm tilted his head as though I should know the answer to the question.

I crossed my arms over my chest and glared at him. "Explain it to me. Slowly. So I can check that I understand because I'm almost certain I didn't hear you right."

I couldn't have.... Surely?

"You're my fated mate," he said, as though it were a fact. "I want to marry you and have our children grow up here, in the castle, and..."

"Hang on a minute." I said, uncrossing my arms and putting a hand out in front of me as though that would actually stop him from saying all these things. "You expect me to... stay here? Not just for today, but forever?"

I couldn't believe he thought I should just leave my whole life behind and stay here in this frozen palace. Who was I? Elsa?

I had friends, I had a job! What about my house?

He reached into his pocket and pulled out a navy-blue ring box. My heart leapt in my chest and anxiety shot through my veins. *No...*

When he opened the box to display the most beautiful diamond and emerald ring I'd ever seen, I couldn't help but gawk at it.

"If you married me," Anselm said, "There is nothing I wouldn't give you."

What about your heart? Is that mine too, or have you given it to someone else already?

Before I could even think of an answer, Anselm tilted his head to the side, snapped the box shut and slid it back into his pocket. "Someone's coming."

The double doors in front of us flew open with a loud bang and the biggest man I'd ever seen in real life stood before us. "What's taking you two so long?"

He was handsome for a man who had to be in his sixties. Even with graying hair and wrinkles, I could see the resemblance to Anselm.

"Your Highness," I said, dropping into a pathetic curtsey. I'd never met royalty before, so I hadn't exactly practiced such an awkward move. Not to mention the fact that I was almost nine months pregnant and as graceful as an elephant.

The king had obviously just noticed my belly because he began to stutter. "You're... a... how? Anselm?"

I glanced up at the man at my side. I wasn't answering that one.

"Could we go in, Dad? I'm sure Mom would like to hear the story, too."

The king practically cackled with laughter. "Hell yes, she will. Come on in."

I wasn't sure I wanted to go into the dining room again. Intimidation was setting in, hard and fast. These men were royals, and they were bloody huge! How was I meant to keep my cool and not embarrass myself?

"Come on Kayla," Anselm said, taking my hand and drawing me with him into the room. "It's going to be all right."

The woman waiting for us had a huge beaming smile on her face, and I was surprised to find her to be short and plump, like me.

She walked over and extended her hand. "Hi Kayla. I'm Lucy."

I bobbed a little curtsey as I shook her hand. "I'm sorry. I'm not sure what I'm meant to say or do."

Lucy smiled and twisted her fingers around so that she was now holding my hand. Then she tugged me over to the couch closest to the fire. "You're meant to relax and put your feet up. How far along are you?"

"Thirty-nine weeks," I answered, my hand going protectively to my belly.

The queen stopped and stared at me, "And you flew through the veil?"

"Well... not the way you did," I said. "Not on Anselm's back or anything like that."

The queen turned to her son. Her smile was gone. "Explain. Now."

We all sat down, Lucy and I on one couch, and Anselm and his father on the other. By the time he was done explaining how we'd gotten to this exact moment in time, there was a heavy silence on the room.

The moment the queen turned toward me, the silence ended. "Kayla, you poor thing! You must be beside yourself. Is there anyone we should contact, or call? Parents? Friends? Will anyone be missing you?"

Hot tears blurred my vision before I swiped them away. It had been so long since anyone had mothered me. I'd forgotten how good it felt. "No... I'm on leave from my job, and my mom's gone. There's no-one that will miss me. Not for a few days, anyway."

Not for a lot longer than that.

Lucy squeezed my hand. "We need to get you an appointment with our doctor."

"Oh... I can't give birth here." I said, shaking my head. "I'm booked into the hospital. I have a birth plan..."

Lucy patted my hand and smiled softly. "Sweetheart, even if I wanted you to go, which I don't, I can't let you go to the human world to give birth to a dragon baby."

My nose burned with tears again. "What do you mean? Is it going to come out with scales and wings, or something?"

There was so much I didn't know. So much I hadn't planned for.

Lucy grinned at me this time. "No, not at all. They come out like normal human babies, but they're big, and can be difficult births. The doctors here are well versed in birthing dragon-human babies, and without them... I'm not sure I would have made it through the triplets' birth."

"I could have a caesarean section," I said, my voice turning shrill with worry.

Lucy grimaced. "That's where there is a complication, and one of the few differences with dragon births. The sack the babies, or baby, grows in, is much harder and more resilient that a human amniotic sac. A c-section may not work at all, and God knows what the doctors would do to you, or your bubs, if they found some miraculously tough membrane inside of you."

The tears were beginning to well in my eyes once more. "So you're saying I can't go home, and if I do, I could die? Or my baby could die?"

Lucy moved even closer, reaching out both hands to me and holding tight. "This is one hundred per cent your choice, and if my stupid son has done something that you won't forgive him for, then I will stay by your side until your child is born, and then Stavrok will fly you both home safely. All right? You are not a prisoner here."

A high-pitched sound of pain came from the other side of the room and the queen glared at whoever made it.

I didn't look away from Lucy's face. I was barely keeping it together as it was.

Lucy snapped at whoever she was glaring at. "You're the only one that can fix this. Not me. My job is to keep this girl and my grandchild safe."

I hiccupped then covered my mouth with my hand. "Your... grandchild. I... you would be the only ones. My mom's gone and my father has been out of my life for over twenty years."

"Well, we are in." Lucy grinned. "One hundred percent. Aren't we, Stavrok?"

The huge dragon king walked over and sat behind his smaller wife, his face solemn. "Definitely. I don't know what's happened between you and Anselm, and I pray to the gods that you sort it out and stay here as part of our family. But if you don't, I hope you would allow us to be a part of your child's life."

The amount of emotion and support being shown in this moment brought a sob to my throat. I wanted to tell them yes. That of course I'd have them in my baby's life. To have such doting, wonderful grandparents would be amazing.

But the words stuck in my throat and when I tried to speak, tears coursed down my face. So instead, I nodded and tried to smile through the tears. I couldn't do their kindness justice at the moment, but once I could talk again. I would.

Anselm suddenly stood up and I glanced over to his couch only to watch him walk out of the room, the doors shutting loudly behind him.

I stared after him, the baby kicking out and rolling about in response to the sound of my heart breaking once more.

Anselm

My parents were giving Kayla every excuse to leave our realm and cut me completely out of my child's life. Here I was wanting my mate to stand by side as my queen, to marry me and reign with me through all the years of our lives, and my mother was offering to take her home any time she wanted to.

I could scream with the fury of it all.

I marched down the hall, heading to the closest balcony so I could fly off some of the anger rolling through me.

When I reached the door, I began to strip off the clothes I'd only donned an hour ago.

A servant ran up to grab the garments from me. "Thank you, Cecile," I managed to grunt out, the manners that had been instilled in me since birth forcing me to speak through my anger.

By the time I was done undressing, my father had caught up with me. "Where the hell do you think you're going?"

I opened the door, ignoring my father and walking out onto the snow-covered balcony.

The king, of course, followed me. He wasn't one to be ignored. Never had been.

"Anselm. I love you, but mark my words, if you don't talk to me, you'll regret it."

My shifter was already leaping into my skin. But I gave it one more attempt to appease my father. I turned and garbled out the only words I could say through my teeth that were rapidly becoming those of my dragon. "Dad. I can't. I need... to fly. We talk. When. Back."

My father nodded, an understanding settling into his eyes. He stepped back as my dragon took full control of my body. I didn't waste any more time; I dove off the side of the castle and flew toward the town, twisting my body at the last minute to soar up over the front gates.

Kayla's car lay beneath me in the field, exactly where we'd left it.

Memories assailed my mind. Ones I'd blocked out eight months ago. The night I'd met Kayla had been a sad one. I'd convinced myself that my mate was just over the veil, like so many kings before me.

Iain and I had gotten a few whiskies into us one night and decided to go and check out the human world. It had been against the law, but we'd decided to actively defy our father and just go. What was the worst thing that could happen?

I'd been at the tiny town over the border for only a few hours when my senses had been so overwhelmed by the people and the noise, I'd wanted to go home. Instead, I'd begun to drink their strange alcohol, and drink heavily. I walked the streets looking for my mate, certain that fate would let me fall over her.

By the time I'd found the human bar, packed full of women, I was lost. Kayla had found me and begun a conversation.

She'd been lovely from the very start. Friendly, worried about me being so far from home and not knowing anyone. Her affection had soothed my soul and her beautiful face gave my desire wings.

I hadn't known she was my fated mate. My dragon had not been awake, nor paying any attention to where I was. Or who I was with. Looking back over that night, there were signs, of course. Ones I'd ignored. The irrefutable attraction, when I hadn't wanted any other woman in the whole place. The tingle in my skin when she'd touched me, then later when we'd been in bed together, how right the whole night had all felt.

Feelings that I'd ignored and tossed aside ever since.

Throughout the night Kayla and I had shared far too many wines and when she'd asked me if I wanted to come back to her place, I'd jumped at the chance to push away the loneliness for a few hours.

What I'd assumed would be a relatively quick, cold encounter, had been anything but. Kayla had kissed me like she'd been searching for me all of her life. Long, endless kisses filled with passion and longing.

The lovemaking itself had been slow, but full of desire. Each gasp and touch had been better than the last. My lack of forethought with protection could be put down to my drunken state, but really, I'd wanted to be as close to her as possible. With no barrier between us.

When my brother had come for me during the night, I hadn't wanted to leave. Kayla's big, luscious body had been so warm and beautiful, part of me had wanted to stay with her forever.

But Iain had talked me into going home, telling me that my fated mate wasn't here and that we had to go back to the castle empty handed. I could still hear his words in my ear.

'Dad's gonna eat us for breakfast if we don't get out of here now.'

My God, did I regret that choice now.

How different would this year have gone if I'd brought Kayla home with me that night? Or even gone back to see her a couple of days later and explained all?

I kept flying and was so lost inside my own head that I managed to fly all the way to the Black Mountains without meaning to.

Erik and Marienne's castle loomed beneath me.

I had a choice. I could turn around and fly home, deal with my parents and whatever Kayla had decided. Or I could fly down and speak to the sorceress once more.

I would have to deal with my family once I turned around anyway, but since I was here, why wouldn't I ask for Marienne's help once more?

Can't hurt.

I began to descend, following the same pattern I had only yesterday when we'd all come to visit Jessa at her husband's castle.

A servant, different to the one from yesterday, ran out onto the balcony with a white robe. I landed and let go of my dragon as quickly as possible. My head was downward spiraling into a depression I had fought hard to stay above.

"Thank you." I took the robe and slipped it on over my rapidly cooling body.

"You're welcome, Your Highness. Your sisters are in the family room, talking, if you would like me to take you to them?"

I followed the servant out of the cold and into the warm castle. "I was hoping to actually speak to Queen Marienne."

"Oh, I'd have to ask...."

Marienne marched down the hallway toward us. "You're back already."

I thanked the servant and fastened the robe tie around my waist. "Yes. You were expecting me. Weren't you?"

The smile on the older woman's face reflected what I assumed. "I was... though not quite so soon."

"Slipping, Queen Marienne?" I teased. "I don't think so."

She took my arm and began walking me in the direction of the family quarters. "Erik and I were talking in our suite. Come. Join us."

"Oh, I don't want to interrupt any private time you had planned."

Marienne laughed. "Anselm. We've been married for thirty years. I'm sure we can cope with the occasional interruption to our schedule."

I nodded my head though I had no idea what it would be like to be in a marriage for thirty years, let alone be someone who was comfortable inviting family friends into my bedroom.

We walked up to a large door and Marienne unhooked her hand from my elbow, and pushed open the door.

King Erik was inside and appeared to be trying on clothes. He was holding up shirts and jackets against his naked chest while wearing a pair of simple gray pants.

"Sweetheart, I..." Erik turned and saw us standing in the doorway, then chuckled as he turned back to the mirror. "I still have no idea what looks any good."

Marienne walked over and said, "This one, and... this one." Then she went up on her toes and kissed her husband. "You look good in everything."

Erik's smug smile was that of a man who knew he was loved. He turned away from the mirror and strode over to the wardrobe, grabbing a simple thin white shirt.

"Hello again, Anselm," Erik said with a warm smile. "I hope you'll excuse the informal garb. I didn't grow up in the palace. I prefer comfortable clothes like these when I'm able to wear them."

I nodded, accepting his apology, then laughed when I realized how absurd the conversation was. "I'm pretty much naked, and you're apologizing for preferring well made cotton clothes? That seems a little odd, Uncle Erik."

I often forgot that Erik had grown up poor, the son of his father's mistress who'd been tossed out into the cold when she'd been pregnant. He hadn't expected to ascend the throne, though he wore the kingship well.

"Speaking of..." Erik said, turning his gaze on his wife. "Are you trying to tell me something, my queen?"

Marienne raised an eyebrow. "I don't understand the question."

"You've brought into our bedroom, an almost naked young man. I hope you're not pitching for a new lover. I'd hoped that even after all these years you were satisfied with your choice."

Marienne rolled her eyes and I tried not to swallow my tongue. Was he serious?

I tried to explain, "Oh no... ah..."

"Could you even imagine what Stavrok would say?" Marienne muttered, shook her head, then walked over to her king.

Then, instead of admonishing him for his question, she grabbed his face and kissed him hard. "You are all I've ever wanted, or needed. Now, get serious. Anselm needs our help."

They both turned to face me and I immediately felt lost. I pulled the robe tighter around myself. "What do you mean?"

"How's your mate?" Marienne asked, taking her husband's hand and walking him over to a love seat situated at the end of the grand bed.

I swallowed hard, forcing my feelings of inadequacy down. I'd come here for Marienne's help in finding my mate, and so far she hadn't steered me wrong.

"She's... pregnant. Due to give birth any day." Any moment I realized, taking a step toward the door. I'd made the wrong choice. I needed to go home. Home.

Marienne waved her hand at my movements. "You have a few more days, so save your panic and talk to us."

I took a breath, attempting to calm myself. "Thank you."

When I didn't speak fast enough, Marienne jumped in to ask, "Has Lucy convinced her to stay here to give birth? She must."

I nodded. "Yes. She has."

"Good." Marienne mused, chewing on her bottom lip. "I'm not sure she would survive a birth in the human world. Your child is strong, and large."

It was my turn to bite my tongue. I desperately wanted to know more about my son or daughter, whichever it was. But it would be wrong to ask Marienne, then know more than Kayla.

And after all, it wouldn't be long before I held the baby in my arms. I could wait.

Get back to the task at hand.

"Kayla is angry at me for not finding her sooner, and she doesn't believe in the fated mate link. When I told her about the bond she interpreted it to mean that I had to marry her, even if I didn't want to."

Marienne turned to her husband and raised an eyebrow. "You want to take this one?"

I turned to the king in surprise. Did he have experience in this?

Erik twisted his body, so he was now completely facing me. "That's not completely unusual. I had similar feelings when I met Marienne, however everything stemmed from feeling... unworthy. You must find out what is making your mate feel that way, and appease her worries."

That made sense, however... "She seems to have some insecurities about her body shape, though I don't understand why. Especially considering I jumped into bed with her practically the moment we met."

My face heated with embarrassment, but the king and queen didn't seem to worry about my words.

"You need to reassure her that she is desired and loved," Marienne said.

Loved?

Marienne smiled knowingly. "Oh, you haven't spoken of love yet. I know it is early; you haven't spent a lot of time together yet so you may need to wait until the love has grown between you. When enough time has passed. But she will need to know that you are with her because you chose it, not because you are being forced."

"I'm not being forced," I said, the words sounding repetitive and yet I couldn't stop myself from uttering them.

Marienne chuckled. "Oh, I know that. I've been dreaming of Kayla for months and wasn't sure who she was set to marry, but I knew she was meant for this world. I was grateful to you when you came here yesterday and asked for the reading. I slept like a baby last night knowing you had found her."

"I'm not sure what to do, exactly." I told them. "My parents have offered to take her home after the baby is born. To separate her from me."

Erik's face was serious now, his forehead creased with lines. "Then you must convince her to stay, Anselm. Your future happiness and that of your kingdom, lies in your ability to convince Kayla that you love her. Because I can tell you, without her, you will be lost."

TEN

Anselm

After my illuminating conversation with the king and queen of the Black Mountains, I took to the sky once more. They were right, I had no choice but to fight for the woman who was the key to my future happiness.

When I landed on the rooftop of my parents' castle, a servant rushed out with a cloak, closely followed by my father. His face was ashen.

"What's happened?" I asked, pulling the cloak on and running for the door.

Please, please, let Kayla and the baby be okay.

"It's your mother," Dad said, swallowing hard. "She had an accident. Slipped on the stairs..."

"Oh God no." I pulled the door shut behind us then started hurrying towards their bedroom.

"She isn't there." Dad stopped in the middle of the hallway. "The doctor. He said... She's..."

He didn't seem to be able to speak, and panic skittled through me. How bad was it?

I grabbed my father by the arms and shook him. "Dad. Concentrate. Where have they got Mom?"

"Downstairs," he said. "In the guest suite."

I wasn't sure why they'd put her there, but I started running. Along the hall, around the balustrade and down the spiral staircase to the main foyer.

When I ran for the guest suite, I threw open the door to the hallway that led down to those bedrooms, to find Kayla pacing the carpet, holding her huge belly.

"Are you okay?" I asked, gripping her face, turning her chin left and right. There wasn't a scratch on her, yet my heart pounded and my dragon screamed inside my head. "I would never have forgiven myself if you'd been hurt while I was gone. I am so sorry. I should never have left you."

Kayla's eyes filled with tears. "Where did you go?"

"To Marienne," I answered honestly.

She gulped audibly, the tears spilling down her cheeks. "Do you love her?"

"Love her?" I repeated, then groaned. "Aunt Marienne is my sister's mother-in-law. She's a sorceress. She helped me find you, and is happily married to King Erik, who's even tougher than my dad if you can believe it."

Kayla sobbed and threw herself against me, crying hard.

I wrapped my arms around her and hugged her tight, despite the tragedy of my mother's injury, my dragon began to purr with happiness having his mate close by.

"Let's sit down." I told her, pulling her to the leather couch pressed against the closest wall. "Tell me what has you so upset."

Kayla pulled back to wipe at her eyes. "It was just so horrible. The accident. I was walking behind your mom, because I'm so slow. She was chatting and laughing, then she just slipped. I... I've never seen anyone hurt like that before."

I pressed her head to my chest and stroked her long, soft hair. "It wasn't your fault."

She pushed against my chest, her gaze turning to a glare. "Of course, it wasn't my fault. Did someone say I pushed her? I was standing behind her, but I'd never..."

"Oh, I didn't mean it like that." I tried to reassure her. "No-one said that, but you were just so upset."

Kayla got to her feet, her tears dried and her red eyes flashing with anger. "I'm upset because I'm very pregnant and my hormones are sky-high. Not that you would know that, because you haven't been there for even a minute of these nine months when I needed you."

I got to my feet and reached for her, the tender moment we'd shared minutes ago disappearing into the abyss "Oh, I..."

Kayla pulled back, well out of reach now. "I'm crying because your mother, the person who offered me a choice in staying here or not, is hurt. I'm crying because you left me, again. I'm crying because you flew off to see another woman, just as I suspected. Do you love her? Maybe not. But is there another woman you do? I don't even know. I know next to nothing about you, Anselm. Nothing! I'm having your baby and we've never even slept a whole night in the same bed!"

This was spiraling out of control. "Kayla, I..."

She didn't want to hear my excuses, that was for sure. She turned on her heel and rushed down the hall and away from me once more.

I watched her go, knowing I should stop her and explain everything, give her the answers to every question she had. But her anger was like a shield, and I wasn't penetrating that.

Not today. Maybe not ever.

The door to the guest suite opened and the doctor I'd known my whole life, stepped out. He had blood on his white apron and looked almost as ashen as my father.

"Doctor Tony. What's happening?" I asked, rushing to meet him.

"Anselm, I'm glad you're back."

"Can I help?" I asked. "Does she need blood? A kidney? What can I do?" My mother could have my very soul if there was a way to give it to her.

"There's nothing you can do now." The doctor sighed.

"What happened?" I demanded. "What does she need?"

"She fell on the stairs and has managed to break her leg, fracture several ribs and hit her head. She had massive internal bleeding as well as concussion. She needs a blood transfusion. I've done all that I can."

I began unbuttoning my shirt. "Take all that you need."

The doctor put out his hand to stop me. "She needs human blood, Anselm."

"Kayla," I breathed. "Is that why she was so upset?"

The doctor nodded. "Yes, but not in the way you think. She was happy to donate, but I can't in good conscience allow it. Giving blood while pregnant is very dangerous, especially so close to term."

So, she couldn't give my mother the blood she needed. "Then what do we do?"

"The king has sent a message to the Winter Kingdom, hoping one of King Damon's sisters-in-law can help. Otherwise, we need to cross the veil and find a donor."

"Okay." I nodded, digesting all the information, staying calm despite the desperation of the situation. "I need to find Kayla. Will you call for me if I can do anything?"

"Of course, Your Highness." The doctor bowed his head.

I clapped the doctor on the shoulder and headed back to my mate. She'd locked herself in my sister's room, and wouldn't come out.

"Kayla, please let me in so I can talk to you."

"No. Anselm. Go away."

I turned my back on the door and pressed my spine against it. We needed to talk, but if she wouldn't listen... or perhaps she would.

I slid down the door until I was sitting on the plush carpet at my feet. I smiled as I ran my hand over the surface. "I'd forgotten how soft the carpet is out here. We used to roll around and play on the floor so often as children. But it's been forever since I just sat here on it. Life got serious, and busy."

Kayla didn't respond, but she was quiet, and I wondered if she could hear me even though she didn't want to.

I kept talking, hoping she was listening and that I would say something that might break through the wall.

"I'm just gonna talk, okay? Feel free to throw out a question if you have any."

Silence echoed back, though I could hear her breathing as though she was closer.

I imagined her sitting on the carpet, on the other side of the door, stroking her belly in that way she had while she was agitated.

I closed my eyes and started to talk. "I had a good childhood, especially considering my blood lines. I'm my father's heir after all. Born first. Oldest son. And all that. Most other princes get their asses kicked by their dads. Gotta stay in line and all that. Not my parents. My mother is human, as you know, so super affectionate, over the top actually. She softens my father, makes him more human if that's possible. Like... he's still hard. And tough. And relentless, but he's fair. He's my father first, then the king. His family comes first, and that's rare in a ruler. And I... I'm grateful. I want to be that way. With my kids. With our son or daughter. If you'll allow me."

I let that sink in, and when no questions came, I continued.

"You asked me if I loved someone else," I said, softly, slowly. Hopefully she was listening. "There is no-one else, Kayla. There has never been anyone else."

I chuckled. "Well, of course, I've been with women. It would be a lie to say anything else. But have I loved another? No. Does another hold my heart and is waiting for me to come to them while I'm in the castle with you? Hell no. I've been waiting for my fated mate my whole life."

A second later I fell backward, landing flat on my back on the carpet inside Kayla's room, staring up at her big pregnant belly.

"Ah... hi?"

She walked over to the bed. "You can come in. Keep talking."

I rolled to my feet and shut the door. "Thank you."

Jessa's room had a few large chairs so I chose the one closest to Kayla, and sat down. "Did you hear everything I said? Or do I need to repeat anything?"

Kayla crossed her arms over her chest. "You were saying that you don't have a... girlfriend. Or lover."

"I was saying that I've waited my whole life for you, Kayla."

She wasn't looking at me; instead she stared at her hands in her lap.

I took a leap of faith and stood up, then walked over to the bed.

I sat down beside her and slid my hand into hers. "I mean it."

She held my hand but didn't look up. Then she whispered, "You're just saying that."

I reached for her face, cupping her cheek and drawing her face up to mine. "Look at me Kayla."

She turned her face up to mine and the vulnerability I saw in her eyes took my breath away.

I wished I could say I already loved her, but Marienne was right, I needed to take the time to show her first.

"I want you," I said, my throat thick with emotion. "I want you to stay here with me so we can get to know one another properly. Be my partner, my lover, my wife. Be whatever you want in this world. But please don't leave me."

Kayla nodded softly, but I could tell that sadness still ran through her.

"You still don't believe I want you, do you?"

She shook her head. "No. You're here because Marienne told you that I was your mate. Not because you felt anything for me that night, or even feel anything now."

I hadn't told her about Marienne, which meant my mother probably had.

There was only one way to show her how much I wanted her.

"You don't believe me?" I asked with a smile. "Then allow me to prove it."

I pulled her toward me and dropped my head, pressing my mouth against her lips and losing myself in the process.

Kayla

I so desperately wanted to believe what Anselm was saying, but everything in my past told me that he was lying. He had to be. There was no way that a prince like him, that had already left me once, wouldn't do it again.

But when his lips touched mine, I couldn't pull back. In fact, I grabbed onto his shirt and hauled him closer.

His arms went around my body and held me against him. His lips parted mine and his tongue swept in to taste me. I met his tongue with my own, giving back whatever he gave and losing myself in the moment.

But when his hands began to free-roam my body, I pulled back. That was enough. "Anselm, I'm not sure this is a good idea."

And if we went any further, I wasn't sure I'd be able to stop when I should.

The prince got to his feet in front of me and began to undress. His eyes were almost silver and his smile was contagious. "I think it's a great idea."

He unbuttoned his shirt then dropped it to the ground, revealing his incredible abs and beautiful chest.

"I think the only way to convince you that I love every inch of that strong, gorgeous, luscious body, is to love on you until you beg me to stop."

He unbuttoned his pants and slid the zipper down.

I couldn't stop watching him and my mouth literally watered as he released his cock from the confines of his trousers and shoved them to the floor, too.

When he stood back up, the effect of our kissing was obvious. His cock was already thick and hard and reaching out to me.

"This doesn't lie." He gestured down to his erection. "You can think whatever you want, believe whatever you want, but you are never allowed to think that I don't want you in my bed."

I dragged my gaze up to his face, where I could see his determination. He wasn't lying.

I stood up and began to undress, needing to feel his skin against mine one more time.

Anselm rushed forward, cupping my face and kissing me hard.

I twisted out of his grasp and turned my back to him. "Please. Help me out of this."

The dresses here were beautiful, but almost impossible to get in and out of without someone else to help you.

Anselm drew the zipper down my back, then pressed his lips to my skin. I sighed, my eyes closing in the moment, trying to savor the sensation.

The dress slid down my arms and whispered over my belly to the floor.

I was naked except for a tiny pair of panties that I'd brought with me to wear in the hospital. I turned back around slowly, lifting my arms to cover my huge breasts.

Anselm took my hands and pulled them gently down, exposing my body to his gaze.

Never had I felt so exposed, nor more desired. His erection tapped against my belly, hard and insistent while his eyes raked over my body, desire flaring to life in the depths of those baby blues.

I stood still, shivering with desire as his hands swept up my arms and across to my breasts. He cupped their fullness and used his thumbs to caress the sensitive nipples.

"Hm.... God, you're beautiful," he said, before dropping his head and taking one nipple into his mouth.

I wasn't going to argue with my head dropped back and my hands in his hair, holding him against me.

He transferred his attentions to the other breast, licking the sensitive nub with his tongue before drawing deeply on the nipple.

I moaned, unable to keep the feelings inside.

When he lifted his head, I could see his shifter in his eyes, his once-blue pupils now the color of pure silver.

"Lie on the bed for me. Please." The urgency in his tone made me want to do whatever he asked.

"I need to taste your pussy."

His words made an embarrassed blush heat my face, but didn't stop me from doing exactly what he wanted.

I walked around the bed and arranged the pillows so I could lie down comfortably. Then, as elegantly as one can do at nine months' pregnant, I rolled onto the mattress and lay down on the bed.

I waited, my chest heaving with exertion and excitement.

Anselm's hands grabbed my panties and pulled them down my thighs and off completely.

I was truly naked now.

Anselm slid up to lie next to me, his face near mine. "I've dreamt about doing this to you. It was the only thing I didn't do last time that I wished I'd done."

He kissed me, softly and tenderly, then disappeared from my view once more.

I felt like a beached whale, lying on my back like that.

But then something magical happened. Anselm lay down between my thighs and urged my legs open. As soon as he put his lips to my clit, I was lost. Pleasure shot through me, unlike anything I'd ever known.

His tongue moved against me, flicking my clit from side to side, pushing me toward orgasm at lightning speed. Every move he made was like liquid lightning inside my belly.

I began to gasp and moan and make noises that I'd never heard come from my throat before, so loud I had to cover my mouth with my hands to keep the noises in.

My belly tightened and with a final flick of his tongue, Anselm sent me over the edge and into raptures of bliss. My belly shook and trembled as I gasped out my pleasure.

Anselm kissed my thighs, one on each leg, then slid up beside me to pull me onto his chest and wrap his arms around me.

"That was amazing," I said, still shuddering with the roll-on from my orgasm.

Anselm kissed the top of my head. "You taste amazing. I could do that all day."

I kissed his chest and sighed as I lay heavily on him. "And you?" I asked, letting my hand wander down his body. His cock was still thick and hard. I wrapped my hand around the shaft, running my thumb through the glistening precum at the tip.

"Me?" He chuckled. "Depending on how comfortable you are, I'd love to bury my cock deep in your pussy."

I closed my eyes against the fresh wave of pleasure his words brought with them. "I could roll over?"

I was pretty sure most positions were out of the question at this stage of pregnancy, but there were some still available.

"Oh, yes please." He groaned and I almost giggled as I rolled onto my side, then decided that I'd be more comfortable on my knees.

I kept moving, setting myself up on my hands and knees at the edge of the bed. When I looked up, Anselm was staring at me, passion flaring in his eyes.

Then he was moving fast, off the bed and around the mattress to stand behind me. "Wow," he whispered. "You look fantastic from this vantage point. Your ass is just... hot."

I would have argued, once again, but he pressed his cock to my pussy and the thoughts were lost. The head slid into me, slowly and gently, making me cry out at how much I'd missed him.

"Did I hurt you?" He whispered, freezing in position.

I needed more. I was aching inside. "Oh God no. Please. More."

His hands dug into the flesh over my hips, holding on tight before he thrust forward, spearing me on his cock.

"Anselm!" I cried out, another orgasm clutching my belly tight. "Oh my God."

I shuddered and clamped down on him and the prince groaned out. "Damn, you're so tight. I want to move. Desperately. But I'm afraid I'm going to hurt you."

I'd never said the words before, but I wasn't above begging. "Fuck me, please."

Anselm drove into me deeper, then pulled back, and thrust deep inside me again. With every move, I cried out, getting louder with every moment that passed.

My belly was huge and ungainly, and yet in that moment I felt as beautiful and wanted as the hottest siren on the planet.

Anselm's hands were on me, loving me. His words were around the room, telling me how beautiful I was.

My orgasm hit me out of nowhere, milking Anselm's cock as he continued to drive into me.

I must have triggered him also because he groaned out, "You're making me come. I can't hold on."

I reached for his hand at my hip, gripping his fingers tight. "Please. Come."

Anselm thrust deep and hard, and began to come. The pulsations of heat pulled an echo of an orgasm from my body once more, dragging me into pleasure shakes and shudders.

We stayed like that for long moments, until my legs started to tremble and I fell forward.

Anselm withdrew then climbed on the bed beside me, pulling me up into a cuddle with our heads resting on the pillows.

It was one of the most peaceful moments of my existence. I couldn't keep my eyes open. I was too blissed and drugged out of my head with pleasure.

The sound of our slowing breathing filled the air and Anselm's lips were on my shoulder, against my neck. His hand cupped my breast, then gently moved down to hold my belly.

The baby kicked against his hand and I smiled when he jerked his hand away.

"It's okay," I said. "You'll feel more... here." I dragged his hand to the place I felt the most kicks and the baby shifted and moved for its father.

"Wow." He whispered into my ear. "I thought nothing would make this moment more perfect, and you just managed it."

My heart squeezed tight in my chest. I had to tell him how I was feeling, or we weren't moving forward. He'd been honest with me, so I needed to do the same. "I... convinced myself we didn't need you. Over the last seven or eight months, I was so alone at first, then when I couldn't find you and had no idea if I was ever going to see you again... I decided I'd be the best single mom ever."

Anselm kissed my hair. "Our child has the strongest mother there is. I'm so proud of you for getting through so much on your own."

I nodded. "I was proud of me, too." I never thought I'd end up pregnant and abandoned, but it had happened, and I'd found a way to survive.

"I set up the nursery by myself, I saved money so I could take time off work. I was doing okay."

"Of course you were." Anselm reassured me, though I was pretty sure that a prince from another universe, or whatever this was, had no idea what I was talking about.

"Anselm... I'm trying to say..."

He pulled back and I rolled onto my back to look up at him.

"I know what you're trying to say." He kissed my lips softly. "You went through hell because of me, and you would have been fine without me. Our baby would have had you, and they would grow up strong and independent, just like their mother."

I nodded, a strange feeling in the pit of my stomach. He did get it. Sort of.

"But I wouldn't have been okay," he whispered. "I would have died of loneliness, never knowing my mate or the baby we made together. So, thank you for staying, even if you didn't feel like you had a choice. I thank you, from the bottom of my heart."

I was beginning to feel like I didn't understand this fated mates link very well. The very idea of Anselm never marrying, just didn't sit right with me.

But now wasn't the time to ask. Lethargy had seeped into my limbs and sleep pressed down upon me.

I rolled onto my side and cuddled into his chest. "I can barely keep my eyes open."

Anselm chuckled and wrapped his arms around my back. "Sleep, sweetheart. I'll be here when you wake up."

The words tugged at my heart. He hadn't been there the first time we'd slept together and a large part of me didn't expect him to be there when I woke up this time.

After all, what had really changed?

TWELVE

Kayla

Despite my misgivings, when I awoke and looked up, Anselm was there, sound asleep. I still had my head on his chest, his heart beating beneath my ear. I smiled at the feeling of happiness still present in my heart. Until a sudden wave of nausea rolled through me, and I gasped at the strange feeling. I hadn't been sick in months; what was this? Was it related to the baby?

I sat up, afraid I was about to vomit on my lover.

"You okay?" Anselm asked, reaching out to massage my shoulders.

Another hot wave moved over me and I rushed to slide my legs off the bed. "Feeling a bit sick. Be right back."

I rushed to the bathroom to hang my head over the sink. I waited there for some time, as long as I could, but when I didn't throw up and the nausea began to subside, I splashed some water on my face.

I sat on the toilet out of habit and when I wiped, my bloody show was on display. I gaped down at the red and white mucus, knowing well that meant my labor wasn't far away.

Well, they say sex is the best way to stimulate labor.

I shook my head at my own sense of humor in the face of such a thing, cleaned up and headed out to the bedroom once more. I knew that even with the bloody show, my labor could be hours or days off, so I didn't say anything to Anselm, not wanting to ruin the moment.

At this time, it was just us, and I wanted to treasure the time with him, if not for anything else than because I wanted memories that I could hold onto in the future.

In case this didn't last.

He slid to the edge of the bed and patted the spot next to him. "You feeling any better?"

I swallowed hard, checked my stomach and nodded. "Yeah, I think so. Not sure what that was, actually."

"Is it the baby, do you think? Or maybe hunger?" Anselm looked concerned, as if he wanted me to say it was mere hunger and not anything wrong because of the pregnancy.

I tried to smile reassuringly. "Maybe just hunger. I think we may have missed dinner, or lunch. What's the time anyway?"

He glanced over at the clock on the wall. "Around four. We missed lunch. Definitely."

He could definitely be right about the hunger because, as I moved around the bed and went to sit down beside him again, a fresh wave of sickness rolled over me.

I gulped. "Um… I think you're right. I need to eat something."

Anselm jumped up off the bed and reached for his robe. "Let me grab some clothes from my room real quick, then we can go and get something to eat. The chef will whip up whatever you like."

I nodded, though the nausea had gotten stronger. I just needed a cup of tea or some toast and butter. Something plain to settle my stomach.

Anselm helped me into a pale blue dress that Sadie had altered for me, then kissed my neck. "You look beautiful in these clothes."

I turned to face him, smoothing the soft material around my baby bump. "I must admit I like all the dresses. Very medieval."

"Very royal," Anselm said with a grin, before dropping his head and kissing my lips in a smooth, affectionate, easy move I could definitely get used to.

I smiled because I wasn't sure what else to say. He was a royal; I was not. Speaking of... "How's your mom?"

Anselm's face grew sad, the light in his eyes disappearing. "I got up to check on her earlier while you were sleeping. She's been given a sleeping draught to help with the pain, so she wasn't awake when I visited, but she's still very unwell. The doctor has called for some of our family friends, in the north. Hopefully they'll arrive soon and we can get her the care she needs."

I swallowed hard. "That doctor... They wouldn't let me donate blood." Even though I'd wanted to. Even though I'd practically begged the doctor to let me help her.

I could still hear her piercing scream as she fell. The crack as her skull hit the wall. I'd never been so terrified, or frozen in fear before. One moment she'd been laughing about some story she was telling me, then next, she was hurtling to seeming death.

He smiled softly at me, not knowing the turmoil within my thoughts. "He was right to make that decision. You and the baby need your blood more. King Damon has two half-brothers, both of whom married humans. They're the friends we're waiting on. They'll help by donating blood. I'm sure of it."

I couldn't help but frown up at him. "How come there are so many fated mates that are human? Don't you have enough dragon women here?"

Anselm's smile reappeared. "We don't actually know why the pattern has emerged, but there's definitely more human blood in the royal lines than ever before."

And after this baby is born, there will be even more.

I slid my feet into my shoes and followed Anselm out of my bedroom. We took a few steps then moved over to the room next door. His suite.

"Come in and sit while I change," he said, taking my hand and leading me into his room.

My heart beat a little faster as I took a step into Anselm's bedroom. It seemed familiar, somehow, which was impossible. I'd never been in here before. The bed was huge, with dark ornately carved wood and royal blue sheets and blankets. It was very masculine and suited him, somehow.

Anselm stripped off the robe he'd been wearing, revealing his perfectly sculpted back and ass, then strode into the large walk-in wardrobe.

My pussy ached at the sight of his nakedness in ways it shouldn't, especially after being so well satisfied only a few hours ago. I started talking to distract myself. "Will I need to vacate the room next door soon? When does your sister get back?"

"Jessa?" Anselm asked, his voice coming from deep in the wardrobe. "She doesn't really live here anymore. She married the crown prince of the Black Mountains, and she enjoys living there most of the time."

"A love match?" I asked, shocked I was even asking. Marriages for love were common in the place I was from, though there were parts of the human world that still married for reasons other than love. I had no idea what things were like here. Perhaps arranged marriages were more common than not?

Anselm walked out of the closet, wearing pants, and his arms slid into his shirt sleeves, but his chest was still bare as he hadn't fastened the shirt.

"Oh yeah. Fated mates actually. Jessa wouldn't have married for anything other than forever love. She's like our mother, very... forceful."

I pressed my lips together so I didn't laugh. "I can imagine." Two girls as beautiful and vivacious as their brother? Yes... Jessa would be a force to be reckoned with I was certain.

"What about your younger brother?" I asked. "Where's he?"

"Away working," Anselm answered, moving to the mirror to finish dressing. "There are five kingdoms in this realm and Iain loves the warmer weather, so he tends to work for Vlakid, one of Father's oldest friends. His castle is in the warmest part of our realm, though I wouldn't exactly call it warm. More like... less freezing than here."

Another wave of sickness grabbed at my belly and this time I dry-retched, loudly.

"Are you okay?" He twisted back around super-fast, concern in his gaze as he studied me.

I nodded, swallowing rapidly, unable to talk.

"Let's get you something to eat." He took my hand and gently led me down the hall. The carpets were so soft beneath our feet and the walls so beautifully decorated with art, I took my time gazing around me.

But Anselm wasn't being deterred by my staring and looking around. He got us down to the dining hall quicker than I would have thought possible.

"Did you take a short cut?" I asked, looking around, confused.

He chuckled, but didn't answer, instead directing me over to the large dining table.

I hadn't expected to find anything other than a bowl of fruit on the table, but there was a whole host of things for what appeared to be an afternoon tea.

"Were they expecting people?" I asked, sitting in the seat Anselm pulled out for me at the dining table.

"No." He walked around the table then sat directly opposite me. "The staff always set up grazing tables for us, in case we have visitors."

I marveled at the spread of food. Fresh warm rolls. Pots of butter. Danishes and pastries, jugs of juice and wine.

"Does it all go to waste if no-one eats it?"

Anselm laughed. "Waste? Here? No way. My mother wouldn't have that." His smile quickly became a frown when he mentioned Lucy. I wanted to reach out and touch him, to console him, but the table was too wide for my reach.

Instead, I asked, "What do you mean?" I took a pastry and nibbled on it, enjoying the buttery texture and feeling the lingering nausea recede.

Anselm poured himself a glass of water and grabbed a bread roll. "I mean... my mother would never let anyone starve, or let food go to waste. She was a childcare worker when she lived in the human realm. She struggled for money and came from a poor family. Now that she is queen, she makes sure that no-one in our kingdom goes without. If this food isn't eaten within two hours, the servants would either pack it up to take home with them or offer it to the people in the village. Mother keeps a list of women whose mates have died, or people who are sick. Those in need. And the servants help distribute whatever is left to the needy."

I smiled at the respect I heard in Anselm's voice. "Your mother sounds like an amazing woman."

"She is," he said. Our eyes met, something soft and warm bubbling between us. A growing understanding. Maybe more.

"Kayla, I…"

Voices made a loud kerfuffle in the hallway. I turned toward the sound, then the doors to the dining room burst open and what seemed to be a hoard of people flooded the space.

The men were dressed in nothing but the robes I knew the servants kept for the dragon shifters when they landed. But the ladies were both dressed in thick, warm dresses. I stared at the beautiful women, older than me, but obviously human.

Anselm rounded the table and held out his hand to help me to my feet.

"Sarah," Anselm called, a note of relief in his tone. "And Katerina. You both came."

The two human women bustled over, worry lines creasing their foreheads. "Of course, we came. It's Lucy, after all. How is your mom?"

Anselm went on to describe Lucy's current situation.

The woman named Sarah frowned at Anselm. "Then we'd best get in there fast. It sounds like she needs blood now."

Anselm nodded. "She's stable for now. Doctor Tony has her on some meds that are helping, but I'm sure the doctor—and my father, of course —will be relieved you're here."

I watched the women as their husbands stepped up and wrapped strong arms around their waists. Both of them looked… content. They and their husbands looked right for each other, somehow. They seemed… happy.

They certainly didn't seem beaten down, over-stressed or kept against their will. They moved with confidence, their husbands chatting in the background with no need to take over as their wives spoke with Anselm.

I wanted to know more about these human women and their marriages to their 'fated' dragon princes. But now wasn't the moment for that. Lucy needed them, far more than I needed information about dragon shifter marriages.

Anselm reached for me and drew me closer. "Kayla, this is Katerina and Sarah. They're married to the two dragon shifters you see over there, Dymitri and Lucian."

The two men turned to smile at me when they heard their names, and I couldn't stop the heated blush that stole up into my cheeks. They were both older, much older than me, but still imposing and handsome men.

"Nice to meet all of you," I managed to mumble.

The woman with lighter hair and a big smile, Sarah, nudged Anselm. "You've got a human mate too? And have wasted no time in creating the next heir to the throne, I see. When are you due, Kayla?"

Heir to the throne.... what? Oh my God, that's what he'd been talking about. Anselm was his father's heir, the next king. That would make our child the heir to all that was around me. All that wealth, all that responsibility.

"I need to sit down." I staggered backwards as a fresh wave of nausea hit me.

Sarah grasped my hand, helping me to sit in one of the dining room chairs behind me. "Not long to go by the looks of that. Are you in pain? Cramping at all?"

I shook my head. "Not at the moment." Though I was always in some degree of pain or cramping, it never seemed to progress to anything more.

The two women looked at one another, then back at me.

Katerina patted her husband on the arm. "I'm going to find the doctor and offer my blood up first. Sarah, stay with her. I won't be long, and then we can switch and you can give blood for Lucy and I'll stay with Kayla."

"Me?" I said, not wanting any fuss. I managed to choke through the strange wave of sickness. They were worried about me? "I'm fine. Please, both of you, go find the doctor and help Lucy."

But Katerina wasn't listening to me. She was already sweeping out of the room, taking the two men with her.

Sarah sat down beside me on the chair to my left and reached for some of the cut-up fruit on one of the platters. "You're close to giving birth for the first time, in a castle, far away from home. Kat and I remember that feeling far too well. We're here to help. Not just Lucy, but you too."

For some reason, her words, coming from a complete stranger, hit home hard.

"I... ah... thank you." Lucy was obviously not going to be able to be there for me through this birth any longer. She was hurt and needed the doctors far more than I did.

"Of course," Sarah said. "We're all a little excited, to be honest. To hear there will be two babies in this castle soon. More than two maybe! Stavrok and Lucy must be thrilled to pieces to have grandchildren coming, and so close in age."

"Who else is pregnant?" I asked, my heart squeezing tight. Anselm couldn't have impregnated another woman, surely?

"My sister Jessa is seven months pregnant," Anselm answered quietly. "As I mentioned, she's married to the prince of the Black Mountains."

I nodded; he'd already told me something about them. "Oh yes. Sorry. I really need a family tree, or something, to keep everything straight. Especially with the fog of pregnancy brain in my head."

Sarah laughed and went on to tell me about her half-dragon babies and how much she loved living in the north. It was lovely to see and hear that another human woman had obviously made her home here, but I had more questions for my prince before I committed to staying.

And whether I stayed or not, was completely up to how he answered those questions.

THIRTEEN

Anselm

Sarah and Katerina's blood donations seemed to make all the difference to Mom's condition. I visited her rooms again after the doctor administered the transfusions, and this time she was awake, albeit very sleepy.

There was a tinge of pink in her cheeks too, that had been missing last time I stopped by.

My father, seated by her side at their bed, seemed less agitated than before. That in itself was telling. She had turned the corner, thanks to the transfusions.

"You look so much better, Mom."

"Oh, Anselm." She blinked sleepily at me. "I'm fine. Don't fuss, please." Her eyelids fluttered closed, as if even that was too much energy to expend. I bent and kissed her forehead, being as gentle as I could.

"Take care, Mom. Rest as much as you can."

"I'll make sure she does, son," Dad said gruffly, and in his tone I heard the relief. I think it wasn't until that moment that I realized how ill my mom had been. It was a reminder of how frail humans were, compared to dragon shifters.

Humans like my mom. And Kayla—about to give birth.

My heart skipped a beat as anxiety filled me. I took a deep breath and let it out slowly. Mom was fine. Or at least, she was going to be fine, eventually.

And Kayla was surrounded by those who could support her through the birth. She had me, for what it was worth. I would not leave her again. She would be fine, too, I was certain.

I clasped my dad's shoulder for a moment. "Mom's strong, Dad. She'll make it."

My father nodded, his lips tipping up in a slight smile. "She is the strongest and most amazing woman I've ever met," he said, and I squeezed his shoulder again and left them there, heading straight back to find my beautiful Kayla.

My mate was incredibly strong, too. She had to have been, to have gone through most of her pregnancy alone and unsupported.

Not anymore. She would no longer have to do anything alone.

Sarah and Katerina were invaluable in helping me achieve that aim. Kayla seemed more content with them around, quickly developing somewhat of a friendship with the two human women.

Watching my mate with the royals I grew up with was extremely enjoyable for my dragon. He was happy. She was here. Home. With me. But I could feel her continued reticence. The resistance. Her worry and anxiety that lay beneath the surface layer of her otherwise open smile.

That evening, when we'd all said goodnight, and everyone headed to their bed for the night, I took my mate's hand and walked her to her bedroom door. "I hope you enjoyed dinner tonight. You didn't eat much."

Kayla placed a hand on her swollen belly and chuckled. "I ate heaps, but the baby doesn't let me fill up like I used to."

I nodded, though I wasn't sure exactly what she meant. Perhaps the little one took up so much room her stomach had shrunk? Or perhaps the pregnancy was making her feel nauseous and therefore not as hungry? I didn't know much about pregnancy. "Would you like to sleep alone tonight?" I forced the question out, not wanting to ask it, in case she answered in the affirmative. I wanted Kayla by my side, always.

She stared up at me, not speaking, but her eyes shone with questions.

"I'd much prefer you in my bed," I told her, taking the leap and admitting the truth. "Or I would happily sleep in Jessa's quarters again if you prefer it. Either way, I need to feel you beside me in sleep. But if that isn't what you want..."

I trailed off, holding my breath while she considered my words. Eventually, she squeezed my hand. "I'm very tired..."

"Just sleep," I clarified, with a small laugh. "I wasn't presuming any more than that."

She nodded solemnly. "Then I'd love to sleep with you in your bed."

I couldn't contain the grin that spread across my face. "Wonderful. Come." I pulled her further along the hallway to my door and together, we walked inside. "The royals can be very boisterous. I hope they haven't scared you off staying here."

I walked around to my side of the bed and Kayla wandered over to what would now be her bed forever. Gods willing.

"Oh no," she said with a soft smile on her luscious lips. "I loved them. The loud, happy family vibe. I never had that. It was... really nice, actually. Especially seeing Katerina and Sarah here, so happy and content with their lives and their... um, dragon shifter partners."

"Like you and me?"

"Well, you know..." She blushed so prettily, her cheeks turning a delicate shade of pink that sent a spike of desire through my gut.

I decided to let her off the hook about her and me. "So, you still liked them? Even when my father and his friends decided they would settle that noisy argument with an arm wrestle?"

That had been quite embarrassing in the beginning. My father and his friends, acting like children. I shook my head at the memory.

Kayla laughed. "That was very entertaining, actually," she admitted, beginning to undress. She took her sweater first, then unbuttoned the dress she'd donned for dinner. It had buttons down the front, so my mate didn't need my help getting out of her outfit this time.

"Entertaining? You mean embarrassing!"

She laughed again, giving me a genuine grin. "Oh, I thought that was great," she said with a chuckle. "They're all so fit still. Human men, as a general rule, don't look that good at their ages. What are they, sixty?"

"My father is sixty-five," I told her.

"Wow!"

Unexpectedly, a spark of jealousy kindled in my gut at her reaction. I knew it was ridiculous, but I didn't want her admiring anyone other than me. *Now who's being childish, Anselm?* I gave myself a silent talking to. That is, I did until Kayla pushed the dress from her shoulders and slid it down her arms, revealing her breathtaking body. Then my mind simply turned to mush.

"Wow is right," I said, staring at her lushness, my fingers itching to reach out and caress her beautiful curves. Her breasts were swollen and beautiful, her nipples long and erect. If she wasn't so tired, I would have pulled her beneath me and made love to her all over again.

Kayla turned away, scrambling to cover herself with one of my robes.

"Oh, please don't," I begged. "There's nothing more beautiful to me than your body, especially at the moment. Lush and curved and carrying our child."

Kayla froze, then slowly turned back to me. Her hands moved away from covering her breasts to cup her belly. "Really?"

"Hell yes!" I said, then shot her a wry grin. "Or did this afternoon not prove how desirous you are to me?"

I dropped my pants and straightened once more, showing her my cock that was thickening by the moment and standing to attention. "You're incredible, Kayla. I find you so very sexy. Would you like more proof?"

She shook her head in response to my question, but her gaze landed squarely on my groin, taking in my erection and growing hunger evident on her face. I stood still and let her explore my body with her eyes, only just resisting the urge to give her a little twirl.

When her gaze reached my chest, she stopped there. "I never asked about your tattoo... what is it?"

My hand came up to my left pec. "It's not a tattoo. It's a birthmark. All the first-born male dragon kings have them. My dad. Erik."

"It's beautiful," she mused. "What about Dymitri and Lucian?"

I threw back the covers and climbed into bed. It was obvious we were just going to talk tonight, and that was fine. I loved the idea of getting to know my mate better on every level, not just sexual. "No. They're second and third born, plus they were the sons of their father's mistress. I don't know how the birthmark knows, but... hang on. I'm certain Erik has one and he was second born and to a mistress as well."

Kayla slid under the covers, pulling the blankets up over her belly and to her breasts.

I pushed the blankets down a little, revealing her huge breasts and reaching out to caress her nipples.

Kayla rolled onto her side facing me, giving me full access to her body. "Maybe the mark knows who is going to end up king?"

I ran my fingers over her nipples, then down to her large belly. "That would be even more magical. And in that case, my younger brother won't be king. He doesn't have one."

I guessed she might be on to something, because the pattern fit.

I frowned at her as I pressed against her belly. "Your stomach is rock hard. Is it painful?"

She shook her head. "Not really. A little crampy, but it's fine."

I wasn't sure what to make of that statement, but since I had no plans to leave Kayla's side until she gave birth, I decided to try not to worry about it too much.

"Are you apprehensive about the birth?" I asked her.

She bit her lip and sighed. "I am. But I'm so ready to meet my bubba."

"Our baby," I corrected her, and she frowned as though the words didn't suit her.

"Yes. Our baby."

A wave of pain and sadness passed over me at her pained look. "Why do you say it like that? You sound... disappointed that you have to share our child."

"Oh, it's not that." She rushed to explain. "I'm glad you're back, for the baby's sake. He or she will be a lot happier having you in their life in some way. And your parents, too. They're amazing."

Every word was like a shot to my gut, making me ache and want to be sick. "Kayla, you talk as if you're moving back to the human world tomorrow and we'll be welcome when we visit. I want you to stay here and marry me. Be my queen."

Her gaze dropped open. "Why?" she whispered.

"Why?" I repeated. Hadn't I already answered this question? Didn't she know? "Because you're my fated mate; we're meant to be together. You're about to give birth to my heir, and soon. We should be married. It makes sense, doesn't it?"

She nodded and the shimmering in her eyes immediately turned to liquid as tears spilled over the edges and down her cheeks. "Yes, it does make sense."

She wiped at the tear drops.

"Then why are you crying?" I asked. Surely nothing I'd said was cause for sadness? "I want you, Kayla. I want to marry you. Are you not happy to hear that I want to be with you?"

"You want the baby," she gulped out. "And you only want me because some mythical force has told you that I'm the one."

Did she really think that? "That's not it," I declared, cupping her face. "I went to bed with you all those months ago because I desired you. My dragon shifted uncontrollably because he recognized his mate."

She nodded, but her tears were still falling. I hated that I'd upset her.

"Marienne told you that I was your mate," she said. "As you said before, you didn't recognize me to begin with. You *left* me, the first time. When you didn't know I was your mate."

"No... well, yes. But I wasn't in my right mind or body that night."

She smiled sadly, then leaned forward. "But if I was truly your mate, wouldn't you have known anyway?"

I could barely hear her; she spoke so low. Had she actually said that? Or did I just imagine those words?

I surged toward her, kissing her lips and tasting her sweetness. I hoped she could feel how much I wanted her.

When she pulled back, I grabbed for her, but she was already sliding out of bed. "I think I'll go sleep in Jessa's room."

I sat bolt upright. "Please don't leave. Whatever I said wrong, I'm sorry."

She picked up her dress and held it against her body like a shield. "That's the problem, Anselm, you don't see anything wrong with proposing to a pregnant woman you don't even..." She sighed then turned away, grimacing and grabbing at her belly as though she was in pain.

I tried again. "Please stay here. Or I can follow you and sleep on the floor in your room. I don't care which way you want it."

She stopped and turned towards me. "You want to sleep on the floor?"

Hardly. I wanted to be pressed up against all her warmth and beauty. "No. But I don't want you to be alone. In case you need me. I want to be near you, just in case."

Her lips tilted down and her face pulled tight, but she nodded and climbed back into bed. "You're right. I should stay here. Just in case."

I thought maybe she'd gotten the right message about my intent and desire for her. But after she climbed back beneath the sheets, she rolled away and presented her back to me. Not to spoon or cuddle, I was certain.

Even so, I leaned forward and pressed a kiss to her shoulder. "Good night, my mate."

"Good night," she whispered and shuffled a little further away.

I lay on my back and stared up at the ceiling, listening to the uneven breathing of my mate and hoping she would fall asleep soon. Two things rolled around in my mind as I lay there.

How had I screwed things up so badly?

And how on earth was I ever going to be able to fix it, when I didn't know for sure what I had done wrong?

~

Kayla

I couldn't sleep. I could almost feel Anselm listening for my breathing to even out, so I pretended I was falling asleep, until eventually he drifted off, too. Anselm snored softly, lying on his back, but I couldn't get comfortable. When he rolled over to be closer and he threw an arm over me, hot and heavy, I stiffened.

I hated it for a moment, feeling claustrophobic. Then when I realized he was still fast asleep and he had reached for me without conscious thought, I let myself shuffle back and enjoy the heat of his body, at least for a few minutes.

Despite the stupidity in my heart, I had to admit it to myself at least, that I was totally in love with the dragon prince. I had been, from the moment I'd first seen him.

I'd spied him across the room, sitting at the bar, staring into the depths of a beer as if the depth of life's answers were at the bottom of that glass.

As soon as I'd laid eyes on him my heart had begun to race, my mouth began to salivate and adrenaline shot through my veins. I could have run a marathon at that point, and I wasn't one for the gym.

I'd made my way over to him, well knowing that a man like that would never go for a girl like me. I was the fat chick. The big girl. The friend with a great personality.

But Anselm had turned to me and smiled in a way that made my knees turn to liquid. I'd had to pull out a bar stool just so I didn't end up on the floor beside his feet, collapsed into a puddle. He'd bought me a drink, then another, then another. We'd talked about nothing and everything, and I'd taken the biggest risk of my life by offering him a place in my bed that night.

I'd been terrified he'd turn me down. Say something like 'oh, sorry, but I was just killing time until my super-hot girlfriend gets here.'

But he hadn't said anything of the kind. He'd walked home with me and stripped out of his clothes with seeming eagerness, and then blown my mind with the number of orgasms I'd been gifted that night.

To wake up alone after a night like that had been the hardest blow of all. Sometimes I pretended I'd made him up. My perfect man. But when I'd missed my period and that stick turned blue, I had to be honest with myself. I hadn't dreamed up my perfect night.

I'd simply been abandoned by my dream man.

Somehow, I'd managed to put the pieces of my heart back together, focusing on the baby he'd given me. Something to love. Someone to make my life complete.

The fact that Anselm now wanted to marry me, seemed like the perfect end to our story. But the fact that he didn't love me, and was marrying me purely out of duty, killed me. I couldn't spend the rest of my life married to someone who'd made me his queen out of obligation.

Obligation to fate.

Obligation to the crown.

And most of all, obligation to our baby.

No. I could not let that happen. It would destroy me.

FOURTEEN

Kayla

The cramps across my lower abdomen were getting worse. I couldn't lie here any longer without crying out. Luckily for me, Anselm slept as heavily as I wished I could. I managed to get myself out from under his arm and stand up.

My back hurt and my belly was as hard as a rock. "Ow."

I waddled to the bathroom, peed, then stared longingly at the shower. Would it disturb Anselm if I had a quick wash?

"Oh..." A huge cramp suddenly hit me, low in the belly, lasting way longer than any of the others.

I bent over, breathing hard and trying not to groan.

Then it vanished like it had never been. I rubbed the spot where I'd felt the pain and shook my head. If that was a prelude to what was coming, I wasn't looking forward to the rest.

The shower beckoned. I wandered over and flicked on the shower head, this time not containing the groan as another wave of pain hit me, hard, and in the same spot as the previous one.

Panic descended and I tried to remember the books I'd read. I had to stay calm. This was a marathon. Not a sprint. *Natural pain relief. Hot water. Stretches. Stay on your feet.*

I stepped beneath the hot spray of water and turned to allow the shower spray to beat against my belly. "Oh... yes." That felt truly lovely against my skin.

When another pain hit, I turned to get some relief on my back. The baby wasn't moving too much at the moment and now that I thought about it, he or she hadn't kicked much today at all.

That's normal. They go quiet before the birth.

I shifted around to let the water wash on my belly, then again so it poured down my back.

I stayed that way for a long time, alternating back and front, breathing and counting, envisioning my body opening up to let my child out into the world.

When the pain got too intense, I turned off the water and walked over to the bath. I could feel the panic rising, the fear of the unknown. Of being out of control. I needed to calm down and maybe a warm bath would help.

I flicked on the bath taps and was staring down at the plug hole wondering how I was going to get into the tub, when Anselm walked into the room.

Still naked. Still beautiful.

"Hey, sweetheart, are you okay? When I woke up and you were gone, I got worried."

I nodded. "Yes. But I think I'm in labor."

Anselm's eyes widened, then his face grew tight and serious. "What can I do? How can I help?"

"Can you put in the plug so I can have a bath?"

His intense look dissipated as he let out a laugh. "Seriously?"

I nodded. "Yeah. I'm assuming I've got hours and hours to go. I need to relax a bit."

He rushed over and bent over to put the plug into the bath. Then he held his hand out to me and helped me into the tub.

"Thank you," I said, slowly sitting down and leaning back to rest my head.

"I'll just throw some pants on," Anselm said, and disappeared.

I closed my eyes and ran my hands over my belly. It was so uncomfortable.

"Good idea." The other women would arrive when this labor really took off, and I didn't think Anselm wanted Katerina or Sarah to see him naked. Truth be told, I didn't want them seeing him naked, either!

Another contraction hit and I breathed through it, using more visualization and splashing some warm water onto my belly.

I was calmer now. Whether it was the bath, or Anselm's presence bustling around just out of eye shot, I wasn't sure.

Probably both.

When Anselm rushed back into the bathroom, I opened my eyes just enough to see him. He adjusted the lighting to be dim so we could both see, but it was much more restful.

"Are you hungry? Or thirsty?" he asked. "I'm not really sure what to do to help."

I was grateful for his attentions, but I shook my head. "No, I don't want anything to eat or drink. I'm just going to rest here and breathe for a while. I'll let you know when I need you to go get Sarah or Katerina."

He slid to the floor beside the bath and reached over to clasp my hand in his. The touch of his fingers curved around mine was soothing. I held on tight.

After a few minutes, I lifted my head. "Why don't you try and get some more sleep? No point both of us being awake."

He shook his head violently. "No way. I'm not leaving you. I'm not going anywhere."

And he didn't. He stayed exactly where he was, sitting next to the bath and being quiet and comforting, simply by his presence. For me.

He chatted to me when I needed some distraction through the pains, and then climbed into the bath, trousers and all, and held me in his arms when I wasn't sure I could keep going.

"You *can* do this, Kayla. You're amazing. "You're doing so well." He whispered the words, kissing my forehead which was now sticky with sweat.

Then the pain changed. I rolled onto my side, then onto all fours, feeling a need to bear down. Yet I was terrified to push. I stared up at Anselm, frantic. "I need Sarah. Or Kat. Or your mom. Please Anselm. Please."

He jumped out of the bath as another contraction ripped through me, grabbing hold of my belly and squeezing so hard it robbed the breath from my lungs.

I cried out, "I can't do this. I can't do this."

Anselm ripped off his wet trousers and grabbed a pair of casual pants that were lying in the corner of the room, pulling them up quickly before reaching out to grab my hand. "You can, darling. Squeeze hard. Breathe, beautiful. Please, just breathe."

I sucked in a lungful of air, vocalizing and groaning out my pain. The contraction peaked, then the pain began to subside.

Oh, thank God.

I relaxed into the water and looked up at him. "I'm okay." *For the moment.* "Go. Quickly, please."

Anselm turned and fled. I tried to stay grounded. Stay calm. But with the next contraction soon to hit I found myself tensing up way before I should.

"Argh..." I cried out, thrashing about in the water, trying to find a position—any position—that would be comfortable.

The doors burst open, but I couldn't look up. I was too busy grabbing my belly and crying. "Oh God. Something's wrong. Oh God."

Anselm jumped into the bath beside me, clothes and all, his hand tangling in my hair. "Kayla you're okay. I'm here. I'm back."

Calm descended as I settled against him and I took a breath. I was okay.

I looked up and managed to focus enough to see who was in front of me.

Sarah was there with a huge smile on her face. "You aren't far away, Kayla. When you think you're going to die, you're almost done."

"That's comforting." I let my head drop down once more and took a few careful breaths.

My belly began to tighten again, and I sobbed. *Too soon!* "It's coming back."

Anselm pulled me against his body and held me tightly while I writhed against him.

When that contraction was done, Sarah spoke. "Good girl. You're doing so well. Just remember that every one you get through, you never have to do again."

I nodded. She was right. This was a marathon, and I was at least half way, I was sure of it.

"Do you want a water birth?" she asked. "Or should we get you onto the bed?"

"Ah..." I didn't know. I couldn't answer that.

"Anselm, after the next contraction, see if you can get her to stand up and over to the shower. I found that to be the best place to birth. Helps with the pain and we can see the baby a lot better. I'll get the doctor."

Another contraction snuck up on me, too fast. "Argh... no..."

Anselm was there, whispering in my ear. "Kayla, beautiful woman. You're doing so well. You're going to see your baby soon. So soon. Good girl."

This time, when the peak crescendoed, I let go of the stress as soon as I began to slide down the mountain of pain, relaxing all over.

I could open my eyes this time. "I want to get into the shower," I confirmed. "But the baby. The tiles..."

"I'll get the mattress," Anselm said, standing up and lifting me into his arms without any seeming effort on his part. "Let's get you into the shower first."

"Yes, please." I knew the next contraction would wipe me out. I wouldn't be going anywhere soon. The heavy pressure on my pelvis was so intense, and scary. But once I was in the shower, the pulsing of warm water against my back and belly helped with the pain, making it bearable once more.

Anselm disappeared briefly into our bedroom, then reappeared, dragging the king-sized mattress beside him.

I would have laughed at the sight if I'd been able to. *Thank God the shower is huge,* was all I could think.

"Move just a little, beautiful. I'll put this under you."

"The mattress," I managed to pant. "It'll be ruined."

Anselm put the mattress on the ground and pushed it straight into the huge shower, the water beating down on the sheets that he hadn't taken the time to remove. "I'll buy you another. Whatever you want, Kayla."

I nodded, then fell to my hands and knees on the soft mattress, crawling back over to where the warm water was flooding the sheets.

The next few hours became a bit of a blur as I retreated inside my own mind. Breathing hard, squeezing Anselm's hand and listening to his whispered words of reassurance.

When the doctor arrived, I was starting to panic. "This feels all wrong. The pains are on top of each other. I can't get a breath." I was sweating even with the water now running cool.

"Let me check to see how you're doing," the doctor said. "Can you lie on your back?"

I was on my hands and knees, naked and terrified, but I still managed to glare at the man over my shoulder. "No, I can't fucking roll over. Are you serious?"

Sarah cackled out a laugh. "He needs to check your cervix, sweetie. After the next contraction, see if you can do it, okay?"

I didn't want to, but so far Sarah hadn't steered me wrong, so in between the intense pains, I rolled over and had the man stick his fingers up inside me.

"Ow!"

He stepped away with an apologetic smile. "You're fully dilated, Kayla. When you're ready, you can start pushing."

A song of relief released inside my mind. I was almost there.

"I don't want to be on my back," I declared, hating the feeling, like I was a floundering fish.

"Roll back onto your knees," Sarah said. "It opens up your pelvis. Makes it easier."

I didn't even stop to think. I rolled and pushed up on my hands and knees, my belly instantly feeling better in that position.

I strained back, the need to bear down coming over me. "Anselm," I called out and he was immediately beside me.

"What do you need, Kayla?"

"You." I panted. "Just you. Stay there. Okay?"

He nodded and stayed exactly where I could see him and lean on him as I needed. The pressure between my legs was intense and I listened to the doctor as he told me to gently push. Not strain. *Breathe* the baby out.

I wanted to roll my eyes at him, but instead I listened, slowed everything down. Every time the contraction came, I grabbed that pressure and used it. Pushed down.

It was a relief to finally do something with the pain. Not just sit around and endure.

"I can see the head, Kayla. A few more pushes and you're done."

I was exhausted, my face wet with tears and sweat. But Anselm was there, kissing my forehead and telling me what a great job I was doing.

Even if I didn't believe him.

Even if I thought I sucked.

I was almost there. My baby—our baby—was almost here.

I pushed down and cried out as the baby's head pushed through. I couldn't wait for the next contraction. I bore down and the baby slithered free of my body.

I collapsed forward on the mattress, the pain finally gone.

"Oh sweetheart. You did it. You did it," Anselm said, still with me, lying down next to me on the mattress.

"What is it?" I asked, barely able to lift my head and look up.

"It's a baby." His eyes were still locked on me. "And you are the bravest, strongest woman I've ever known."

I had to turn over. I wanted to see my baby.

"Help me," I said, and Anselm did. He rolled me over and sat up behind me, giving me a wall of strength to lean on as the doctor handed me my infant, wrapped in a white blanket, squirming and angry-looking.

"Your son," he said. "The next in a long line of dragon kings."

I took my baby in my arms and stared down at his perfect face. "If he wants to be, he can be anything he wants."

Anselm kissed my face. "I am so proud of you."

I pushed open the blanket to take a better look at my son. Two perfect little hands. A scrunched-up face and the most beautiful little cry.

When I stared down at his chest I couldn't look away. It was tiny, but it was there. The beginning of the royal birthmark that dictated the next king.

FIFTEEN

Anselm

The doctor cleaned up Kayla and the baby, then we all climbed into Jessa's bed to rest. I couldn't believe the effort it had taken to push him out. Kayla was amazing, and I was in awe of her and our new, perfect son.

"He is the most beautiful thing I've ever seen." Kayla stared down at the baby in her arms. She was sitting up against the head rest, the baby dressed warmly and drinking from her breast.

"You are the most beautiful thing I've ever seen," I told her, staring at her as long as I could, wanting to imprint the image on my mind.

Kayla smiled at me, and for once I couldn't see even a hint of anger or irony. "You're just saying that because I'm holding our baby."

I chuckled. "No. I would have said that before you gave birth, but yes, seeing our son feeding from you like that... wow. I never thought I could love you more, but I was wrong."

"You... what?"

I sat up, wanting to hit myself upside the head for revealing that snippet too soon. "Oh, I'm sorry. I shouldn't have said anything yet."

She turned toward me, cupping the baby's bald head in her hand to hold him in place against her breast. "What do you mean?"

I smiled and shrugged, feeling foolish. "Marienne and Erik said I shouldn't declare my love for you yet. That you would need time to feel it as I do."

Kayla stared at me like I had two heads.

"What?" I asked. "Don't tell me they were right?" *Damn it!*

Kayla shook her head so fast the baby let go of her breast and squawked in protest.

"Oh, I'm sorry darling. Here you go." Kayla crooned to the baby, guiding him back to her breast.

When she looked at me, this time I saw a warmth I hadn't expected to see. "No, they weren't right. Not at all. I... tell me again how you feel. Be honest, please."

I leaned against the back rest and tilted my head toward her. "I love you, Kayla. I have loved you from the first moment we kissed. That first night together was the best night of my life... I dreamt about it for months, and I stupidly thought I was wrong about my feelings for you. So, I fought them. I tried to forget you even though I couldn't. But I wasn't wrong. You *are* the one. And now, seeing you with our baby..."

I gestured and tried not to let tears blur my vision. It wasn't manly to cry. But the depth of emotion I had for her and the tiny baby in her arms was far beyond anything I could ever have imagined.

"Seeing you both here, in my bed, holding you both in my arms, I can tell you the love has grown even when I didn't think it possible to love you more than I already did," I whispered.

Kayla was still staring at me, unspeaking. But she didn't look upset. In fact, her eyes shone with happiness.

"I know you probably don't care for me in the same way." I rushed to reassure her. "Humans don't feel the fated mate bond the way we do, but I promise you I will do everything in my power to show you every day that I love you. And hopefully, one day, you will return the feelings and agree to be my wife."

However long that took.

The baby had fallen asleep now, and Kayla picked him up to put him over her shoulder and rub his back. "Do you want to hold him?"

I nodded. "Oh yes. Please."

With all the commotion, and health checks, feeding and dressing, I hadn't had a moment to hold my son properly yet.

I held out my arms and she carefully transferred the tiny little weight into my hands.

He was warm and snuggled against my chest. My heart broke and was completely remade in that moment. I was a father. This was my son. And I would die to protect him.

There was a knock at the door and Sadie came in, bearing a tray of food. "I've brought a late breakfast, and a guest who won't be turned away. I swear he is about to knock down the door to meet his grandson."

I laughed, imagining my father pacing outside the bed chamber.

Kayla arranged her shirt she'd brought with her from the human world so that her breasts were now tucked away.

I waited for her to be settled then asked, "Is that okay? Or do you want him to come back after you've slept?"

Kayla smiled and reached for a croissant from the brunch tray. "Your dad should meet his grandson."

I turned to Sadie and nodded. The housekeeper didn't even make it back to the door before my father burst into the room.

"Congratulations!" he bellowed, a smile on his face for the first time in days.

He came straight around to Kayla and bent down to kiss her cheek. "Well done, Kayla."

"Thanks." She smiled up at him.

Dad, who looked grey and exhausted, black smudges under his eyes, walked around the bed to stare down at the sleeping baby in my arms.

A strange look of awe crossed over his face. "It feels like only yesterday

I was holding you in the same way. Though being a triplet, you and your sisters were tinier than this little fellow." He held out his hands and cupped them together. "I could hold you here."

"Amazing they all survived so well," Kayla said.

Dad laughed. "Survived and thrived, but they have a strong mother." Dad sobered then, sitting on the bed near my legs but not reaching for the baby.

"How is Lucy?" Kayla asked, shifting the focus to my mom.

"Oh, she's much better," Dad assured us. "The doctor is very happy with how she's healing and I know she'll want to come up and visit you all soon."

Kayla threw back the covers and stood up, arranging her maternity dress to cover her legs. "Do you know if she's awake? Maybe we should all walk down now."

I gaped at her. "Kayla, you just gave birth."

She narrowed her eyes at me. "Yes. And I have no stitches, no damage. I'm not sick. Let's go."

I stared at my father who looked just as surprised as me.

Kayla grabbed one of the gray blankets from her baby bag, took the baby from my arms and wrapped him up like a sausage.

"Here you go, Grandpa." She handed our precious son over to my father. "If it's okay to call you that? Do you have another nickname you'd like to be called?"

My father, the fierce protector of the palace and guardian of our town, turned misty- eyed in the face of his first grandchild. "I... Grandpa sounds... good."

"Are you right to carry him?" I asked my dad, jumping up and out of bed.

It was my father's turn to glare at me. "I held all three of you every day for years, and Iain too, until you were too big to carry any longer. I'll be fine." He adjusted his hold on our baby, tucking him close to his chest and bringing him deep into his embrace.

Kayla walked to the door, her belly seeming smaller already. "Let's go then. I'm sure the queen would like to meet her grandson as well."

"I think she would, too," I managed. The fact that Kayla was going out of her way to bring my mother such joy, made me love her all the more.

Together, we walked down the hall, down the staircase and along to the guest quarters.

"How is she really?" I asked Dad, who had the baby tucked right into his chest.

"She's improving," Dad said. "I've never seen her like this before. It's… confronting."

"Do dragon shifters have a different life span to a human?" Kayla asked, sounding curious.

"No," I answered. "We live on average eighty years; however, we have more healing capabilities so if we're injured we tend to recover quicker."

"Much quicker," Dad added.

We reached Mom's bedroom door and I faltered. I'd seen Mom in bed with a cold, and after she gave birth to Iain. But that was it, until this injury. She'd always been healthy.

"Go on, Anselm," Kayla said softly. "Knock."

I did as Kayla requested though I couldn't remember the last time I'd knocked on a door in my home.

"Come in," came the quiet response.

My mother's strength was gone and my gut ached to hear it.

I pushed open the door and reached out my hand to Kayla, who took it and walked beside me.

"Mom. So good to see you," I said, walking up to one side of the bed to give my mother a hug. She was lying on the left side of the huge bed. She was pale and looked like she'd lost weight, her cheeks more sunken than normal, but even so, she looked better than the last time I saw her.

Kayla walked around the other side of the bed, beside my father. "We'd like to introduce you to someone, Grandma."

Mom struggled to sit up so I took her arm and helped support her. "Oh, my word… Kayla. Anselm!"

"Meet your grandson," I said as Dad handed the baby over to Mom.

"He's beautiful," she said, taking the baby in her arms and tears filling her eyes. "But I'm definitely Nanna. Not a grandma."

Kayla giggled. "I can see that. Nanna it is."

I assumed that was some sort of human name for grandmother, so I just leaned over and kissed my son's forehead, loving the smell of him.

"He is absolutely perfect," Mom said. "What's his name?"

I glanced over at Kayla, who looked back at me with wide eyes. "We haven't talked about names. Kayla? Did you have a name picked out?"

A small smile lifted the edge of her lips. "I did, but it's not exactly a prince's name."

"Tell me," I said.

She blushed, a red-hot flush that covered her face, all the way to the roots of her hair. "I played with the letters of your name... mostly. Hansel. Ainsley. Mason..."

Mother chuckled. "You two truly are meant to be."

I glanced over at Kayla, who wasn't looking at me. Instead, she sat on the edge of my mother's bed, reaching out to our baby and touching him on his beautiful little face.

I wasn't sure what my mother meant, but Kayla seemed to know. And I would obviously have to wait until we were alone to ask her.

Mom asked Kayla lots of questions about the labor and cooed about how perfect our son was. My parents admired him for so long he got hungry again and began to root around and cry.

"If you don't mind," Kayla said, tucking our baby up into her arms. "I'll feed him back in our rooms."

"Of course, Kayla." Mom sighed and settled back into the pillows. "I think I'll have a rest. You should too."

Dad nodded at me. "I'll stay here, and see you both for dinner. Perhaps? If not, then I'll see you tomorrow. Your sisters will be here by breakfast, I'm sure. Good news travels fast."

I groaned. "I think I just lost access to my son for the foreseeable future."

"And your mate." Mom chuckled. "Don't think your sisters are going to let her be."

I put an arm around Kayla and led her from the room. "I think we're going to need to lock the castle doors. Maybe I can bribe Sadie to keep them away."

Kayla giggled as we ascended the stairs once more. "What's wrong with your sisters?"

I groaned. "You're an only child, right?"

She nodded, the light of amusement twinkling in her eyes.

"Then I really can't explain."

We got to the door of her room and I glanced over at my bedroom. "The mattress should be replaced. Shall we return to my room?"

Kayla glanced up at me, then nodded. "Yes, I'd like that."

I put my arm around her waist and led her into the bedroom I'd had since I was a small child. Tonight, we would sort out exactly what was stopping us from having the future we deserved. Come hell or high water, we would uncover the truth.

Because Mom was right. Once my sisters arrived, I'd lose Kayla in the insanity, and we'd never sort out all our issues.

Kayla

Giving birth to my baby boy had been the most amazing experience of my life. One moment I'd truly believed I might die, then the next, I was bringing another living being into the world.

A perfect baby boy, from within my body.

I'd never felt such a high. Such happiness. So much love. Not just for my baby, but for the man who gave me my son.

The servants had changed over the mattress and re-made the bed, purging all physical proof of the birth from the room.

Even so, I could feel the energy in the room. The love. The warmth.

I fed our son, loving the bond I could feel growing, every moment with him.

When he was asleep, passed out and milk- drunk, I wrapped him up and placed him in the small cot the servants had placed by the bed.

Staring down at his small face it was hard to believe that one day he'd be a king. The next ruler of this incredible place. But would it be the right thing to do if we stayed? On the other hand, now that he was born, could we leave? What right did I have to separate him from his birthright?

"What are you thinking, beautiful?"

I glanced over at the father of my child. "Just that... this is the baby's home. He needs to stay here. To learn about his heritage. About... shifting."

Oh God. He won't be safe in the human world.

"That hadn't really occurred to you before, had it?" Anselm asked quietly, correctly reading my face. "Though, I have to tell you that with our son being only a quarter dragon shifter it is possible that he won't inherit the gene."

I almost rolled my eyes at him, but realized quickly enough that it would be rude. "You saw his chest, right? He's got the birthmark."

Anselm's eyes widened. "The dragon king mark?"

I nodded, realizing maybe he hadn't seen it. Anselm had been staring intently at me when I peeked out our baby's chest. The little one had been covered up by the time Anselm held him.

"Yes. So, I don't think he's going to be a non-shifting human type."

Anselm inhaled sharply. "Then that means he'll be the next king of this kingdom, after me."

I nodded again. "So you see, I don't really have a choice." And that was a feeling I didn't like. In fact, it made the independent woman in me downright devastated.

Though, it was hard to feel sorry for the life my son would lead. He would be revered. He would be loved.

"You do have a choice," Anselm whispered, sliding up the mattress to sit next to me. "If you want to go back to the human world, I'll come with you. We can raise our son as human, if you want. I may need to fly back on occasion for my health; it's not good for a dragon shifter to stay in a human body for too long. But I wouldn't be gone long."

"What about your reign?" I asked, horrified he'd even consider such a thing. "You can't leave."

"Of course, I can," he said. "It isn't done very often, but my sister Vanya is very capable of becoming our queen."

My jaw dropped and no words came out. He couldn't be serious and yet, he looked it.

Anselm continued. "I'll do anything to be with you, Kayla. I love you. I never want to be separated from you, or our baby. Ever."

I still wasn't able to get my thoughts into line, let alone speak. He couldn't really be saying he'd give up everything? His whole life, even his throne, just for me?

"Of course, if you don't want me in your life, then that changes things. I... don't know what I'd do then. Die of heart break, probably." He chuckled and threw me a smile to suggest he was joking, though I wasn't sure that was really true. I could feel the tension beneath the words.

"So, I suppose I need to ask you what you want, Kayla. Because you always have a choice. What you do with your life, and our baby's life, is for you to decide."

I didn't think that was fair, either. Anselm hadn't chosen to impregnate me, nor had he had a choice in keeping the pregnancy.

So far it felt like most of the choices had been mine, though I respected the hell out of the fact that he was trying to share those responsibilities with me now.

"I'm not sure what to say, Anselm." I didn't want him giving up the crown. I didn't want him moving to the human world with me. What was I going back for anyway? A lackluster job and no family connections? He was offering to come with me to the human world, but what was there for either of us?

"Tell me if you want me, Kayla. Please. Tell me if you think you could love me, if not now, then one day. That's the only important thing and changes every part of this plan."

I couldn't contain the sob that rose in my throat. "Of course, I love you," I whispered, while covering my mouth with my hand. "I have loved you since the moment I met you. I've loved you... forever. Why do you think I kept the baby? I couldn't..."

The words were impossible to say. My throat closed up when I tried.

When I'd found out I was pregnant, I'd been both devastated and elated. I had a piece of Anselm to love forever. Even though he'd left me after only one night, I'd never been able to forget about the love we'd shared and the things he'd made me feel that night.

I'd wanted to hold onto that memory forever, and I had.

Anselm reached out for me, his hands moving up my arms, to my face. He lifted my chin so I could look up at him. I hadn't even realized that I'd been staring at my hands in my lap.

"You love me?" he asked, his tone soft and incredulous.

I nodded, tears filling my eyes and spilling down my cheeks. "But I never thought you'd love me back."

"Of course, I love you!" he exclaimed. "You're the most beautiful woman I've ever known. Here." He lifted his hand and touched my temple. "Here." He touched my nose. "And here," he said, pressing his hand to my left breast where my heart was.

"I know you didn't grow up thinking you'd be the queen of a dragon realm one day. But I grew up knowing that I would marry a woman just like you, Kayla. With your generosity of spirit. Your tenacity. Your strength. Your heart."

The words were everything I'd ever dreamed of hearing from him, all said with more sincerity than I'd imagined possible.

Then he grinned. "And the fact that you make my cock hard and my heart race because you're so fucking sexy... well that's more than a bonus. That's amazing."

I couldn't help but laugh as I wiped away the tears. "But the fated mate thing..."

"Is a blessing," he said, interrupting me. "It's a gift, Kayla. Not a curse. Fate isn't making me bond with you, forcing me to marry someone I can't love. Quite the opposite. She's an old wise lady, slapping me upside the head saying, 'can't you see what's in front of you?'"

He shrugged. "Sometimes we need it. Us men can be a bit dumb."

That made me giggle until I could barely stop laughing.

"Well, if that's all it is," I responded. "A nudge in the right direction?"

"That's all it is," he agreed. "Trust me. I've waited all my life for the right woman, Kayla. I wouldn't suddenly just marry you because you had my son. That's not the way we do things around here."

"That's not how they do things in the human world either," I admitted. "Especially not in the last few decades."

I had two friends who were single moms because their baby-daddies had just up and left them. No support. No maintenance. Certainly, no offer of marriage.

Just... gone.

He grabbed my hands tight. "Then please believe me when I say I love you. I would die for you. And if you will stay, then please marry me, be my queen. I will spend the rest of my life proving to you how much I love you. I will be loyal, to only you."

That reminded me. I had to ask one more time. "So there really is no-one else? I'm not going to be confronted with five kids and three ex-girl-friends any time soon?"

Anselm sat up straight, then put a hand on his heart. "As far as I am aware, I have never fathered another child other than our son."

I smiled and couldn't help it. He looked so earnest when he said it. I leaned in and kissed his beautiful lips. As a man, and a beautiful, sexual man, declaring that was all I could hope for.

"All right then," I said, nodding my head as a cloud of contentment settled over me.

I could see my life now. If I stayed, our son would be adored. Anselm would love me, and I would love him. We would be happy. I was sure of it now.

"All right?" Anselm asked. "All right, you'll stay? All right, we go?"

I laughed, realizing that I really hadn't been very clear. "I'll stay here. With you."

He dove for me, wrapping his arms around me and drawing me in for a kiss.

I lifted my chin and kissed him back, moaning at the touch of him. God, I'd missed him. For all the time we'd been apart, and all the time before we met.

I'd daydreamed about a love like this for most of my life, and to think it may have come true was too surreal.

When he pulled back it was to say, "Tell me you'll marry me. Today. Tomorrow. Next month. Whenever you want. Just, please marry me."

"Of course, I will." I could already imagine a plan for the when and how, and I knew it would be beautiful, just like our burgeoning relationship.

I pulled him back for another kiss, giving him my whole heart along with it.

EPILOGUE

My plan for the wedding had been simple. Wait until Anselm's whole family was well enough to attend, which meant both Lucy and Jessa were well.

I also wanted time so that my body was healed enough to have a proper wedding night.

That took a little longer than expected. Jessa had given birth six weeks after me, and to twins who were doing very well. Lucy was finally back to her hurricane self, so we'd set the date and it had finally arrived.

Today would be perfect.

Jessa hugged me for the millionth time. "I can't believe you're finally marrying my brother! It feels like I've waited for this day, forever!"

I laughed at Jessa's antics; she really was the whirlwind of the triplets.

"You've waited forever?" I asked, walking over to look in the mirror for the final time. "I'd say that's a slight exaggeration, my friend."

Vanya's head appeared in the mirror, popping up over my shoulder. "We'll officially be your sisters soon, then you'll never be able to get rid of us."

"Who says I'll ever want to?" I answered, poking my tongue out at her. *I really don't want to ever be rid of them.*

Jessa and Vanya had embraced me as their family from the very first moment we'd met.

The fact that I'd given birth to their nephew might have had something to do with their instant support, but I doubted it somehow. These women were loyal to a fault, and their love for their brother shone through every day.

"How's the beautiful bride going?" King Stavrok asked, stepping into the small room.

"I think she's ready," Vanya said with a clap of her hands.

I adjusted the small tiara that sat upon my head and stared at my image in the mirror. My new sisters had done a great job getting my straight brown hair to look nice in an up-do, with ringlets and flowers adorning the strands.

The dress I wore was Lucy's wedding dress, which I'd been honored to be allowed to wear. Lucy, like me, was more on the curvy side, especially as she'd been pregnant when she'd married the king.

Vanya and Jessa were a smaller build and declared that they'd never wear the dress, so I was welcome to it. Sadie had altered it to fit my waist snugly and today I felt as beautiful as a princess.

Which technically, I would be soon.

"Yes. I'm ready." I turned to Anselm's father who would be giving me away soon. "How's Rocky doing?"

After many discussions, we'd chosen to name our son after Anselm's father. Stavrok the Second, who we all affectionately called Rocky.

"He's sleeping like a champ," the king said, and offered me his arm.

I took it, and together, we turned toward the door that would lead me out to the wedding ceremony being held in the small cathedral at the palace.

I took a deep breath and let it out slowly. "Let's do it."

Vanya and Jessa slipped out ahead of us, dressed in burnt orange, my lovely dragon shifter bridesmaids.

When it was our turn, I didn't have a single butterfly in my stomach. Not one worried nerve. I was filled with excitement and happiness to finally be here and be marrying the man of my dreams. Everything felt so right.

On King Stavrok's arm, I walked down the aisle. The cathedral was full to the rafters with people from the town. Family and friends had flown in, quite literally, from the north, and the Black Mountains.

All to see me, little human me... marry the next king.

The queen, Lucy, stood in the front row holding our beautiful baby boy. He was sound asleep, as he should be, despite all the noise around him.

Standing at the altar was my prince, his eyes shining and very clearly only for me. I reached out my hand for him as we got closer and he rushed to grab my fingers, drawing me away from his father and toward the priest who would join us together, forever.

The ceremony was simple, and much faster than I thought it would be.

The feast afterwards was absolutely magnificent and it was there that I finally got to meet the famous Queen Marienne.

She walked toward our table with a soft smile on her lovely face, her long dark hair spilling down over her shoulder. "It is very lovely to finally meet you, Kayla."

I stood up and rushed around the table to embrace her. "Thank you for sending him back to me."

I'd long since stopped blaming Fate for getting it wrong, or Marienne for telling Anselm what to do when he should have known all along.

Marienne chuckled and gently hugged me back. "You are one lucky woman. Finding your fated mate is a blessing few of us can boast."

I glanced across at the nearest table where Stavrok was chatting with a handsome man with short dark hair. "Looks like you found yours, too."

She smiled softly. "Yes, but I had to endure quite a time before Erik came along. But that's a story for another night. Today is your day! You are officially Anselm's wife, and the future queen of this kingdom."

I covered my face with my hands. "That sounds insane."

Marienne tugged my hands down and squeezed tight. "A gift... if I may?"

I glanced down at my hands where she held my fingers. "A gift?"

"Yes. A future vision."

I nodded before I'd really thought about it. Did I want to know the future?

My head was suddenly filled with a dream. Anselm and I sitting on our large bed, graying hair and wrinkled faces.

We were smiling and holding hands. Our children were around us. Four of them. Three sons and a beautiful daughter with dark curly hair.

And before us on the bed was our first grand baby, covered in the same white embroidered blanket that Rocky had worn today.

Tears filled my eyes and I blinked rapidly as the dream in my mind faded away. My vision returned, bringing with it the sights and sounds of our wedding day.

Marienne was still standing before me, smiling brightly. "You have no need to fear, Kayla. Just keep loving your husband as you do, and your future will be beautiful."

I wiped at the tears that slipped from my eyes. "I swore I wouldn't cry today."

She chuckled. "Happy tears are always a good thing." Then she moved back to her table, leaving me with a contentment I hadn't known was possible.

Anselm and I were going to make it. Our love would endure. Our children would thrive.

Children... could I go through all that again? The pregnancy. Then the birth.

I glanced over to where Anselm was talking to other men, similar in age, holding our son proudly.

Yeah, I can do that again.

A gorgeous young man wandered up to me, his blue eyes identical to Anselm's.

"Hey Iain." I greeted my new brother-in-law. "Enjoying the wedding?"

Iain grinned. "It's a great party, sis. You did well getting everyone here."

I glanced around the room at the combination of royals, humans and townspeople. "Yeah, there were a few people to co-ordinate, but it helps that you guys can literally just jump into the air and fly yourselves here."

Iain broke into laughter. "Yeah. You're right."

I glanced around the room, noticing a beautiful blonde girl staring at us from one of the far tables. "Hey Iain, who's the chick casting daggered looks our way?"

Iain stiffened and didn't even turn to see who I was talking about, because it seemed he already knew. "That's Veronica."

"Veronica." I narrowed my eyes, casting my memory back to the guest list. "Isn't she..."

"Yeah, she's Damon and Cass's daughter, so technically she's a cousin."

Well, from what I'd gathered, Cass wasn't a biological cousin of Stavrok's, so there was no blood link there. But still, I understood the connection now. "And she hates you because..."

Iain's lips pulled tight. "Because I... did something stupid a few years ago and she hasn't forgiven me."

There was a story there, and normally I would have loved to dig into it. But I wasn't sure I had the fortitude to deal with anything more today. So instead, I elbowed him in the side and said, "Sounds like you need a chat with Marienne too."

Iain turned to stare at me, his eyes wide with surprise. Then the look of vulnerability disappeared to be replaced by his characteristic smirk. "Welcome to the family, Kayla. Officially."

I reached out to hug him tight. Something about Iain made my heart sad, and I couldn't pinpoint what it was.

"Thanks, bro." I had family now, and I loved it.

Iain disappeared and I was once again swept into the celebrations.

When it was finally time to go to bed, I was aching for some alone time with my new husband. We were finally walking the hall to our marriage suite, and I clung to him like a limpet. "I feel like I haven't seen you all night."

Anselm chuckled as he tucked me even closer into his side and opened the door to his bedroom. "I feel the same way. I've been counting the moments until I could finally get you into our new bed."

Anselm had commissioned a new super king bed frame for our wedding present and we were still in the bedroom he'd grown up in.

Jessa had moved her quarters to another wing so Rocky could be in the room next door, and everything was working out well. We would live in the castle for the time being. Lucy and Stavrok loved having the baby around and I enjoyed helping my mother-in-law every day with her chores and learning the role of queen.

I took a step into the bedroom and my new husband pulled me back to the threshold. "Hang on a moment."

He swung me up into his arms and I grabbed for his neck, squealing like a banshee. "Oh my God. You can't carry me."

Even though I'd gotten most of my original shape and body back from before the pregnancy, I was still no lightweight.

My dragon shifter husband laughed, crossed the threshold with me in his arms, and marched over to the new bed. "I certainly can." Then he tossed me onto the mattress, and I squealed once more.

He walked back to the door and shut it, locking it tight.

The sound reminded me that my baby wouldn't be beside us tonight. "I hope Rocky's okay with your sister."

Jessa had offered to have the baby overnight, breastfeeding him as she would her own daughters.

Anselm chuckled. "They'll all be fine. That husband of hers dotes on her. He'll help."

I nodded. He was right. We had one night alone together, and considering it was way past midnight, it may only be a few hours until I held my son again.

My new husband and I had better take advantage of the time we had together.

I slid off the bed and turned my back to him. "Help? Please?"

Anselm's confident fingers moved to the ties on my dress, releasing me from the confines. Then he turned me to face him. "I love you, Kayla. So much. I can't wait to start our life together, from this moment forward."

I reached up and cupped his face in my hands. "I love you, Anselm. I am so glad we met, and that you came back for me, in the end. And that we have the chance to build a life, together, with our son."

Then I released his face and stepped backward, shimmying out of my loosened wedding gown before shooting him a grin. I was wearing only a lacy pair of knickers, and my smile. "But first and most pressing of all right now, I cannot wait for you to show me how *much* you love me."

I felt bold, basking in his love, and I leaned forward and ran my fingertips over his trousers where they were already beginning to tent. "You did say I had a certain... effect on your body, did you not?"

He chuckled, but there was a hoarse note that indicated my touch had the desired impact. "Indeed you do, beautiful Kayla. And I will be very happy to show you what you do to me, you sexy gorgeous woman."

Quickly he stripped off his clothes, and then stalked toward me until I had no choice but to back up to the bed and fall backwards onto it. He crawled onto the bed with me, leaning over me on his hands and knees. "And now, my sexy wife, I will show you exactly what effect you have on me." He bent and kissed my lips and passion took us instantly to a place that filled my body with joy.

It had been three months since we'd had full sex, and my pussy was practically aching with need for him.

"Oh, God, I've missed you." Anselm groaned, pulling me into his arms.

I moaned, then gasped, my breath catching in my throat.

"What's wrong?" he asked, dropping his head to press feathery kisses to my neck.

I shivered as pure longing coursed through me. I lifted my arms and wrapped them around his neck. "Nothing at all. I'm actually afraid I'm going to come too fast."

My belly was tight and my nipples were erect. At this rate I'd practically orgasm the moment he was inside of me.

Anselm chuckled as he lifted his head. "Now, that is not something to be afraid of. Quite the opposite."

He rolled us so we were lying face to face, and stared at me with so much love in his eyes, I thought my heart would burst.

"How did I get so lucky?" he asked, stroking a random curl back from my face.

I grinned at him. "Well... you know I was designed by Fate, just for you."

He didn't laugh at my joking tone. Instead, he leaned in and kissed me softly, gently.

I pushed on his chest, hard. He rolled onto his back, wearing a shocked expression that turned to a smile as I threw my leg over him and climbed on top of him.

"I love you, my prince," I managed to whisper between the moans coming from my throat. Feeling his hot, hard body between my legs again was a dream. "But I need you to make love to me on our wedding night."

Anselm reached for my breasts, cupping each with a hand and squeezing gently. "Oh, I will."

But he wasn't moving and didn't seem to be in any hurry. Me on the other hand...

I leaned forward to kiss his sweet lips, flicked my legs straight, then slid down his body. I'd missed every inch of him and had been dreaming of doing exactly what I was about to do.

I moved down until I was lying between his thighs, eye to eye with his beautiful cock.

I wrapped my hand around the already swollen staff, smiling to myself as I leaned forward and licked the slit at the tip.

The moan that filled the air wasn't mine, but an answering clench between my thighs made me groan.

I opened my lips and slid my mouth down over Anselm's cock, sucking on the big bulbous head and loving the heat of his flesh against my tongue. I stroked my hand up and down while licking the end, until he grabbed me and hauled me up to straddle him once more.

"Sit on my face," he groaned out. "I'll get you ready."

I shook my head, slid my wet pussy back over his shaft and lined myself up. "Oh, my love, I've been ready for months."

The head of his cock pressed against my entrance, and with one move of my hips, he was inside me once more.

I gasped and moved faster, taking him deeper. He grabbed my hips and thrust up, penetrating me all the way to my soul.

The orgasm hit me out of nowhere, making me cry out as my body went into spasms of pleasure.

Anselm's hands moved up to my breasts, tweaking my nipples and whispering words of love to me while I shuddered.

When I opened my eyes again, my beautiful dragon man was still beneath me, still hard inside of me.

"Told you I'd missed you," I said with a satisfied smile.

Anselm thrust up inside of me and I groaned at the renewed pleasure. I pressed my hands to his hard pecs and began to ride my dragon, sliding up and down his cock.

Moans filled the room as I moved faster, taking him deeper.

I threw my head back, loving the feel of his hands on my breasts, on my hips, his cock deep inside me.

When he groaned, grabbed me and flipped us over, I grabbed onto his arms and held on for the ride. He fucked me into the mattress, over and over and over.

I lifted my legs and he pushed my thighs back, opening me further, hitting those sweet spots until I was seeing stars.

I began to come again, but this time, the mountain pushed me higher, robbed me of my breath, caught me up in a whirlwind of ultimate pleasure where all sights and sounds stopped.

Then I was thrown back into my body, where I was screaming, biting into Anselm's sweaty shoulder while my convulsing pussy squeezed his cock over and over.

My husband, the dragon prince, thrust deep one more time and growled his release, pumping me full of his seed.

I clung to him, his cry of completion ringing in my ears.

When he finally collapsed against me I held him tight, the vision Marienne had gifted me with flashing through my mind.

We weren't just going to make it. Anselm and I would have a love story that would carry on through the ages. I finally felt like the other half of my soul had been found.

Soul mates. A fated bond. It was real, and I knew at last that we would have our happy-ever-after, for all the days of our lives.

THE PRINCE OF DRAGON MAGIC

USA TODAY BESTSELLING AUTHOR
AMELIA SHAW

Anthony

My biggest secret was kept by my mother and father. No one else knew. Not even my older brother Carlak. I had magic and the gift of sight. Just like my mother, Marienne, Queen of the Black Mountains.

Mom always said that her gift created life and gave our kingdom, and those around us, many blessings. After all, it was because of her gift of sight that King Stavrok found Lucy, and years later, their son Anselm found his mate, a human named Kayla.

She was sweet, though not my type. I liked a woman with a little fire under her belt. Anselm, my best friend, had been ready to find his mate and had asked Mom for help. He could have asked me too, since I could see many of the same things my mom could, but no one knew about my magic—not even Anselm—so I was never asked.

Mom was a sorceress, so her magic was an accepted part of her, but I was a dragon shifter like my dad, and everyone knew you couldn't be a dragon *and* have magic. Except, apparently, when it came to me... A magical freak of nature.

Anselm and I had grown up together, more like cousins than friends, and the fact that he still didn't know about my magical abilities was beginning to eat at me. The discomfort of lying to my friend—or at least, omitting part of the truth of who I was—had created a literal pain in my gut that wouldn't go away. I groaned as I reached over the dining table for the pitcher of water, pain tugging low in my belly.

"Your gut still giving you trouble?" Dad asked from the head of the table, where he was carving up his roast lamb pie with potatoes.

My father had spent all of his childhood and teenage years with not enough to eat, so now that he was king, he made sure we all ate well. Including our people who lived within the grounds of the castle.

"Yeah," I said, putting a hand to my stomach as I poured a glass of water.

Mom stared at me from her side of the table, her hands wrapped around her hot cup of tea.

"What?" I asked, glaring back at her.

"You know what I think it is." She took a sip of her tea. "You need to stop lying to everyone, Anthony."

I stared down at my empty plate. "No, it's not that. I'm just hungry." I began piling food onto the porcelain—potatoes, lamb, and baked tomatoes.

"Son," my dad said. "You're my heir, and I'm proud of you, in every way. You're a good man. I don't know why you insist on hiding your magic from everyone other than the two of us."

I wanted to roll my eyes at him but had learned that would only get me a slap to the back of the head at best, and a magical detention in my room at worst. So, I didn't. I may have been twenty-six, but my parents were still my parents. "It's no one else's business." And it wasn't. I didn't want to be judged by everyone and labeled a freak. Or worse, have people I knew want to use me and my magic the way my mother had been used before my father rescued her from her monstrous first husband.

Magic would not be considered a strength in our world for a dragon shifter. My gut clenched and pulled tight. I grabbed my fork and shoved food into my mouth.

I'm just hungry, I told myself. *That is all it is.*

"Well, I'm off to visit Lucy and my granddaughters today," Mom said, standing up. "Would you like to join me, Anthony?"

Carlak and his wife Jessa had twin daughters, born just last year, and had spent the last month at Stavrok and Lucy's castle.

I shook my head, part of me missing my brother, but the other part too jealous to consider visiting them right now. Carlak had been so happy since finding Jessa and becoming a husband and father. And of course I was pleased for him, but I did wonder if I'd ever find that same level of joy. If I'd ever find my mate. I shook off the negative thoughts. I'd enjoyed the peace and quiet since they'd left, so I had to focus on the positives. "No. I have plans with Dad. Work in town."

Dad nodded, backing me up.

Mom sighed. "All right. I'll be home in a few days. But... may I speak to you, Anthony? Alone, please?"

I glanced at my dad who had just finished his last mouthful of food.

He stood up with a smile. "Time for a shower. I'll meet you in the foyer in an hour?"

I nodded.

Mom went up to my dad and kissed him goodbye, their embrace too long for me to tolerate.

I glanced toward the roaring fireplace instead of at them, trying not to flinch. I was an adult now, but still... *ew.*

"I'll see you soon, my love. Travel safe."

Dad nodded and left the room.

Mom turned to me, her eyes rippling with purple smoke, her magic clear for the world to see.

I groaned, this time in annoyance. "What is it, Mom?" She'd lectured me for years about my desire to keep my magic secret, so nothing she was about to say would be new.

"I had a vision last night."

Oh. That *was* new. I sat up straighter, giving her my undivided attention. I might try and deny my own magic's existence, but I wasn't stupid enough to ignore my mother's visions. "What did you see?" It had to be about me, or she would have shared this vision with Dad too.

Mom chewed on her lower lip, worry clear in her eyes and in her aura.

I dusted off my hands, even though they were clean, but it gave me something to focus on. I did not want to get into a weird push-and-pull of a discussion. "Mom, if you don't want to tell me, it's fine." I pushed my chair back and stood up to leave.

"How much of your future have you looked at, Anthony?" she asked.

I stepped away from the table and pushed my chair in. "You know I don't use my magic like you do, Mom." I'd never wanted her to teach me how to use my magic. I wanted to be a dragon shifter, like my father, and I was.

I don't need magic, too.

I was an aberration. The only shifter we knew to have inherited both skills from my parents. No one knew my secret because a sorcerer and a dragon shifter couldn't exist in the same body. Mom couldn't shift because she had magic. My dad had no magic because he was a shifter. That's how it was meant to be. It was wrong that I had both abilities.

"I didn't ask for the vision," Mom assured me. "It came to me in a dream and stayed vivid upon waking. I can't refuse the gift, Anthony. I have to offer it to you." She held out her hand.

I stared at her, long and hard. "I don't want it, Mom." I didn't want to know who my mate was. I didn't want to know the future. Life was complicated enough as it was, and I knew how much my mom had suffered for her gifts. That wasn't the life I wanted for myself.

"I know," she whispered. "But do you trust me?"

The words hit me hard. "Of course, I do." I trusted my mother more than anyone in the world. She'd birthed me, fed me, and kept me safe throughout my childhood and teen years. She would move mountains, literally, for me if I asked her to. There was no one more firmly in my corner than my mother.

"Then take my hand," she whispered again, her arm shaking with the strain of holding it out.

I didn't want to. God, I didn't want to. I could feel my magic rising up within me, reaching out for her and the power she wielded. I fell forward involuntarily and caught the edge of the table. I clutched the wood, not wanting to admit that I was afraid. Afraid of what my mom wanted to show me; afraid of what my magic would do once I opened that door.

I'd never allowed my magic to learn or grow, consciously shoving it down into the black hole I'd created for all the parts of me I didn't want to admit existed. But here, now, I could feel it rising, bigger than ever before.

"Please." Mom gulped out the word.

I was propelled forward by my own powers. I lifted my arm and reached out for her, my fingers straining to meet hers as if of their own volition. When our hands connected, I was thrown into a world I'd long since stopped allowing myself to enter. I threw back my head and my eyes slid closed as I stood up straight and held out both hands for my mother's magic transfer.

There was my future—flashing right before my eyes. A woman with red, curly hair; the flames of desire and passion whirling in her eyes. The image shifted then, and real flames surrounded her. There was a child in her arms. Then the flames were gone. She dropped to her knees, begging me for help. In the vision I stood over her, shaking my head.

Despite the fact I couldn't hear any words, I knew what she wanted. She needed me—my magic—and I was refusing to give in to her pleas. I wouldn't use my magic to help her or anyone. *Not even my own child.*

I gasped and pulled my hands from my mother's grasp, not wanting to see anymore. "No. No. No." I repeated the word over and over, reeling back. "No more." I panted, unable to catch my breath. My magic pulsed inside of me, and I couldn't push it down, no matter how hard I tried. "Mom. What did you do?"

"I didn't do anything." She sounded much calmer than she had any right to be. "I only shared my vision with you."

I staggered further away from her, toward the doors that led out into the hallway. "I... no." I needed to fly, to bring out my dragon shifter. He would push away my magic, burn it all away. He always had before.

"Anthony. Where are you going?" Mom called out behind me.

But I kept going, staggering down the hallway, dragging my left foot that for some reason didn't seem to want to work. Finally, I made it to the balcony doors, and there I stopped to strip off my clothes. I was in my working clothes, so my sweater and shirt, then jeans, soon hit the ground.

"Anthony!" My mother's voice was getting closer now as she rushed after me.

I didn't want to deal with her. Not now. I'd trusted her when she asked me to, and now I was verging on the edge of losing control. I grabbed for the door handle and pushed it open. The cold air of winter hit me square in the face, and I stumbled out into the snow. The Black Mountains were cold, but nothing like the North Kingdom. The Winter Palace.

With thoughts of heading to my friend Stavrok in my mind, I let my dragon shifter take over my quickly freezing body. My wings extended from my back, my skin shifting into scales, and rock-hard muscles. I closed my eyes, enjoying the rush of power and strength that my dragon gave me. I extended my wings and stepped up onto the balustrade, launching up into the wind just as my mother appeared.

She pushed open the door and shouted at me. "You need to act now, Anthony. There's no time!"

But I wasn't listening to her. Not today. I flew high, away from the kingdom of the Black Mountains and toward the North. Toward the Winter Palace. Away from my mother and her magic.

If only I could get away from mine as easily.

TWO

Charity

My name didn't suit me, but no one needed to know that, not until they had to know, of course. "Can I help you, sir?" I asked the bristling hog in front of the reception desk.

"Yes, you can get your manager for me. Now."

Ah yes. You want a white, middle-aged man, don't you?

"I am the manager, sir, and you're upsetting my staff. So, how may I be of assistance?" I ran the largest restaurant in town and my staff were mostly women. Moms who needed extra cash or time off from their families, or high school girls who wanted work after school.

"You can get me a table. Now."

I glanced over at my concierge, Tania, a mom with five sons, who had the patience of a saint. Even she looked harried and annoyed. I made a point of glancing down at our books, even though I knew we didn't have a table to spare. "I'm sorry sir, we're booked out this evening." I didn't offer him a seat at the bar, or an alternative night. Tania would have done so already, and it was obvious that he'd already tried to push his way in.

"No. I want a table *now*. I have clients here from the city and this is the only decent restaurant in town."

I glanced behind the huge lug and there were three other suits, all staring at their phones, ignoring his boorish behavior.

"I understand sir. Would you please excuse me for a moment?" I tilted my head at Tania, and we stepped out of earshot. "Okay, so, we have two choices. I can kick them out, obviously. Or I can offer them the private corporate room."

Tania snorted. "I offered him the private room already, not that he deserves it, but he shut me down. Too expensive."

I grinned at her. "Perfect." I would have loved to have just thrown him out on his ass, and I still might be able to, but I had a much more fun card to play now. "Go check on the staff and kitchen for me. I won't be long."

Tania hurried off and I stepped back to the desk with a grin firmly in place. "Good news, sir," I said, raising my voice for his corporate clients to hear. "Our private room is available for your party. I'm sure you want to spoil your guests with the best of what our little town has to offer." I batted my eyelashes at him and directed my smile at the other men who'd walked up behind him.

"Barry? Have you got a table yet? We're starving."

I put on my brightest smile as Barry huffed and puffed. "Oh yes gentlemen, this way. Barry has booked our corporate room. You'll have privacy and space."

And a five-hundred-dollar bill just for the room.

I stared at Barry, daring him to refuse the only available table.

He nodded. "Yes, chaps. You're in for a treat." Then he stared straight at me. "The manager herself will be serving us in the private room. The cost surely dictates such service."

I had the best staff on tonight, being a busy Saturday night, so unless the kitchen caught on fire, they wouldn't need me too much. "Of course, sir," I said smoothly. "This way." I walked the party of four to our only private room, seated them, and gave them all menus. "I'll be back soon with the specials and to take your orders."

Barry was an ass, but his money was as green as anyone's.

The rest of the night went amazingly fast. Between managing the staff and our temperamental chef, I was busy enough. Add in Barry and his clients, and the bottles and bottles of wine they consumed, and I was run off my feet.

Barry picked up the bill with only a slightly begrudging manner, and the men he dined with left me a nice tip. It was, all in all, a good night.

"Thanks everyone. You did great tonight." I waved off the staff and sat down to look at the reservations we had for the following evening.

"Thanks for taking care of that guy for me, Charity," Tania said as she slung her handbag over her shoulder.

"Oh, you know it's no problem," I answered with a smile. "I'm always there for you." It was the biggest payoff for me with this job. The staff were underpaid, but between good tips and a good working environment, I hoped that I helped to make up for any of the negatives.

The staff went home, then it was time to lock up. Part of me had expected retribution from Barry for tricking him into paying for a very expensive dinner, but he'd been so jolly by the end of the evening, he'd practically rolled out the front door.

I locked up and stepped out into the cold night air. My apartment was only a few doors down, luckily. I hurried along the street, keeping an eye out for anyone and anything that might be a danger. Even in a small town where I knew every second person, it still wasn't totally safe for a woman at night.

I reached my building's front door, opened up, raced inside, and locked it again behind me. My heart was pounding way too fast, again, and I was a little disappointed with myself. Even though I'd taken self-defense classes since I was young, I was all too aware that I didn't have much hope against a man with a knife, or a gun. Feeling truly safe was a luxury I'd never had.

I climbed the stairs to my second story apartment and took several deep breaths to slow my heart rate. It was almost two a.m., and I was exhausted. Even so, I had a quick shower to wash off all my makeup and the staleness of a long day. Once clean, I made myself a cup of peppermint tea, put on my warmest pajamas, and climbed into bed.

I clung to my mug of tea and glanced over at the romance novel I was reading. It lay on the bedside table, tempting me, but the time was fast moving toward three a.m. now. Did I really need to read more tonight? If I was being honest with myself, part of the reason I was putting off going to sleep was because of the disturbing dreams I'd been having lately...

The book I was reading was a paranormal romance featuring dragon shifters and princesses. And ever since I'd started reading, I hadn't been able to stop the erotic dreams that assaulted me. I wasn't even up to a sexy part of the book, yet, but with every page I devoured, it felt like I was drawn into the world, and as soon as I was asleep, I was in that castle. I became the princess in the story book, being ravished by a sexy dragon prince.

After an internal debate about the need for a good quality sleep, I didn't reach for the book. Instead, I drank the rest of my tea, pulled up the warm blanket on the bed, and snuggled down beneath the covers. If I didn't read anything tonight, then surely I wouldn't wake up in a hot sweat, experiencing the hottest orgasm of my life? In the very least, it was sad that my dreams far surpassed anything I'd ever experienced in reality.

I closed my eyes and relaxed on my fluffy pillow. I was as single as a dollar bill and that likely wasn't changing any time soon.

Perhaps I should start looking forward to these dreams? After all, I thought, as I began to drift off. *They are probably the closest thing to romance I am ever going to experience.*

The carpet beneath my naked feet was soft and thick. I wanted to bend down and run my hand across the fibers, but I had to keep moving. We were playing hide and seek, and he was coming for me. I hurried a little faster, through the dark, warm castle. The sconces on the wall were lit with candles that glowed brightly, and there wasn't another soul to be seen.

"I can smell your need for me." The husky voice came from behind me.

I squealed as I ran into a large room. The library. No exit door. Shit.

"I can't wait to make you scream," The voice came again, this time much closer, "while you come all over my cock."

I looked left and right, searching for a way out of the room, but there was none. Only shelves and shelves of books. A large desk and Chesterfield lounges.

"Charity..." He whispered into my ear.

I froze.

His hands gripped my upper arms, then slid down until our fingers intertwined. It was him, my prince. And there was no doubting that he wanted me. Badly.

I twisted in his embrace, my arms going around his neck.

His eyes were blue, almost purple, as they stared down at me. "My love."

I couldn't resist him. He was my love. My man. My everything. I went up on my toes and kissed him, feeling our connection strengthen with every touch.

He growled deep in his throat as his lips opened.

I slid my tongue inside his mouth. I wanted him naked. Now. My hands drifted to his shirt. I tore at his clothing, his skin hot beneath my palms. I undressed him as fast as I could.

Next it was my turn.

He grabbed the straps of my long night dress and pushed them off my shoulders. The silk slithered over my breasts, past my hips, then down to the floor. My prince grabbed me around the waist and lifted me.

I clamped my legs around his hips and wrapped my arms around his shoulders, clinging tightly. I didn't care about my too-big thighs, or my stretch marks. Here, in this castle with him, I was beautiful. Here, I was desired. Here, I was loved. I kissed my prince.

He carried me over to the desk, putting me down only to grab my hip with one hand, then move back to grab his cock with the other hand. "I can't wait." He used the head of his cock to dip into my wetness and paint it over my clit.

I gasped at the perfect sensations. His hot biceps beneath my hands, his hard cock at my entrance, teasing me—promising the world.

"Don't wait." I leaned back and opened my thighs even wider in an unmistakable invitation.

He grinned down at me, dropping his head to focus on my breasts.

I tilted my head back and ran my hands through his thick dark hair, holding him to me.

His lips pressed to the swell of my breasts, first one and then the other, his tongue trailing a path of fire to my nipple, where he sucked strongly.

I gasped as arrows of pleasure shot through me, straight to my core. Oh God... please...

He transferred his attention to my other breast, giving it similar attention to the first.

I groaned and tugged his hair. "Please... Please..." I was aching for him now, a deep hollow feeling between my thighs.

He lifted his head and again a purple swirl flashed at me deep behind his eyes.

"Wow, you're so beautiful." I was unable to hold the words inside.

He smiled, but didn't respond as he grabbed my thighs once more.

I kissed him again, moaning as he lined his cock up with my entrance and teased me with the head once more. I dug my heels into his calves, urging him forward. When he chuckled against my lips, I grabbed his rock-hard ass and tugged him closer.

He slid into me

I gasped.

"Oh damn... you feel divine..." He rocked his hips, the movement taking his cock deeper, one inch at a time.

I leaned forward, sinking my teeth into his shoulder and my eyes slid closed as a wave of pleasure swept over me.

The dragon prince began to move in the sweetest rhythm, slowly at first, teasing both of us. Then faster. His skin was slick with sweat beneath my hands and my lips, but he didn't stop. He fucked me hard and deep, more and more. He filled my body and my soul with every thrust of his body.

My orgasm was building. With every stroke my king stoked the flames of the fire within me. My belly was tightening, the ache inside me peaking.

"Come..." my prince commanded,

And my body obeyed...

I came awake on a strangled gasp, mid-orgasm. "Oh... God..." I rolled onto my back, my pussy still convulsing around the imaginary cock inside me. I covered my face with my hands, my forehead hot to the touch and slick with sweat. "Not again." I squeezed my thighs tightly together, drawing out the aftersensation as a beautiful lethargy stole over my body.

Sleep beckoned, promising deep and satisfying slumber this time. I rolled back onto my side, truly exhausted now. "Please let me sleep..." And I did. I slept through until lunchtime the next day, my dreams still haunted by those beautiful blue eyes with the purple mist circling within their depths.

CHAPTER

THREE

Anthony

Flying to the North Kingdom could be dangerous for a dragon from a warmer climate. Damon and his family were ice dragons and were acclimated to the freezing weather. It was only the beginning of our true winter months, so the weather wasn't as bitterly cold as it would get in a few weeks. Still, I flew low to the ground, staying out of the snowy clouds, and went the most direct route to the castle.

As soon as I landed, I shifted into my human form and stalked toward the balcony doors, the falling snow landing on my heated skin. I opened the door myself, no servants hanging about waiting for visitors. They

143

probably didn't receive many uninvited or unannounced guests. And I hadn't told the family I was coming.

As soon as I was inside, a maid saw me and fluttered her hands in shock. "Oh, sire! I'm sorry there was no one to greet you. Was the king expecting you?"

I shook the snow out of my hair and pulled the door closed. The castle wasn't as warm as my father's castle, but it was clean and well furnished, and warmer than the cold air outside. "No. This was an unplanned trip."

She set aside her broom and nodded. "Let me fetch you a robe and I'll send for someone." She meant someone from the royal family, so I smiled my thanks as she rushed off to find me some clothes.

"Anthony?"

I turned to find Cassandra, the queen, walking toward me with a curious stare.

"What are you doing here?" Cass was still beautiful, her long blonde hair streaked with silver.

"Hi Aunt Cass," I said, greeting her with a kiss to her cheek. "I had a fight with Mom and started flying. I hope I'm not interrupting anything?" I wasn't entirely sure why I'd flown here, specifically, I hadn't even considered going another way.

Is it another sign my magic and intuition are growing?

I pushed that thought out of my head. I simply wanted some company, and Anselm and his siblings would help me take my mind off things.

"Of course not," Cass said, though her characteristic smile wavered. "It's just... we're having a few issues with Veronica."

I grinned and would have laughed except for the fact that Cass clearly wasn't amused. "What?"

She quirked an annoyed eyebrow at me.

"You all call her the Dragon Daughter. She's always been strong willed. How old is she now, anyway? Eighteen?"

She was the youngest of our generation and Anselm was the eldest at thirty.

Cass nodded and brushed the hair back off her face. "Yes, and she thinks she knows everything."

Veronica was young, and fearless. In fact, if she wasn't so much like a sister to me, I would have considered marrying her myself.

"Veronica has a good heart, Aunt Cass. Even as a child she was a fierce protector of everyone weaker than her."

Cass actually smiled this time. "She protects everyone, not just those weaker than her."

I gently touched her on the arm. "She'll be okay."

Cass huffed and shook herself. "How can I help you, Anthony?"

The servant from earlier rushed over with a robe.

I slipped into it. As shifters our nakedness was second nature, but it was still deemed polite to don clothing in our human form. "I don't know, Aunt Cass." And I didn't. I was here. But why?

She smiled softly. "How about some dinner?"

My stomach grumbled as if on cue. "That would be great."

The robe was soft and warm, with thick fur around the collar. "I think I'm taking this home. It's great."

Cass laughed. "Please do. Now, dinner." Cass and I joined her husband, King Damon, at the dining table in their small family eating room.

"Anthony! This is a surprise. How are you?" Damon stood up to extend his arm and shake my hand.

"Thanks for having me on, well... no notice at all." I sat down and slid the chair in, my gaze landing on a beautiful fare of roasted vegetables and steaming hot pies. "This looks amazing."

"Eat, please. I know how flying creates hunger. Then tell us how we can help you... unless I've missed something, and you've already told Cass everything?"

Cass reached for one of the pies and slid it onto her plate. "He had a fight with his mom, which I can imagine would happen on occasion. Marienne is a fiery one."

Damon snorted. "She isn't the only one."

"Oh hush," Cass said, mock-glaring at her husband. "You have to put up with me. We're fated. Remember?"

"Like I could forget," Damon said, reaching for his wife's hand and lifting it to his lips to kiss her knuckles.

It wasn't quite as bad as watching my parents kiss and touch each other, but it was close. I focused on my food, shoveling roasted pumpkin and potato into my mouth. Of the five kingdoms in our realm, my family was friendly with two of them, led by King Erik and King Damon. All three kingdoms had kings and queens who were fated mates. Meant to be, in every way.

"Funny how people used to think that fated mates were rare," I said, breaking the silence and grabbing a pie as well.

Damon chuckled. "Well, I certainly never thought I'd find mine."

"We were both very lucky," Cass said, smiling brightly.

The happy atmosphere was broken by a slamming door behind me and heavy footsteps on the floorboards.

I jumped up and turned, my dragon shifter leaping to the forefront. But it wasn't a threat entering the room, but the Dragon Daughter herself, ablaze with fire. "Hi Veronica." I grinned at the girl I'd always considered akin to a little sister.

Her frown lifted when she saw me. "Anthony! I didn't know you were here." She rushed forward for a hug, whatever tantrum she'd planned fizzling out, at least temporarily.

"It wasn't planned; I just started flying and found myself here."

She pulled back, her hands sliding down my arms to grip my fingers. "You know it's always good to see you."

A vision hit me out of nowhere, like a lightning bolt thrown directly into my brain.

Veronica stood by a window, beautiful in a gown of royal purple. She was heavily pregnant and smiling, obviously happy.

But where was she? I recognized the windows of the castle but couldn't place the location.

Her hand rested on her belly, cradling her babe as she turned toward the sound of footsteps echoing in the room.

I knew instinctively that the man I'd see next was fated for her. I turned to look, unable to resist.

A familiar face stepped out of the shadows, his smile a testament to the love he felt for her.

Veronica pulled away, disconnecting our hands and halting my vision. "What the hell was that?" she yelled at me.

I ran my shaking hand through my hair. "I'm sorry. That's never happened before."

Fuck! How the hell am I going to get out of this one?

"What happened?" Damon demanded.

"Oh, it was nothing," I said, looking at Veronica and hoping she would see that I wanted her to keep my secret.

Apparently not.

"When he grabbed my hand, I saw... I saw..." Veronica gulped, unwilling to share what we'd both seen.

I wouldn't share her secret, but how would we get out of this one?

Veronica turned to her father, her focus shifting in an instant. Clearly, she wanted to avoid that discussion as much as I did. "Dad, why have I been restricted in all my flight paths this month? I tried to organize to go and see Kayla, and I was told I couldn't."

Damon glanced across at his wife, then got into a fight with his daughter about her safety, and her responsibilities, and her age.

I zoned out, unable to focus on anything except the magic still simmering in my veins. Since when had my magic been so unstable? So out of control? Was that what Mom had seen in her vision? My mate amidst flames that were due to my magic? My out-of-control magic? I clenched my jaw hard. I wasn't interested in finding my fated mate yet, but when I did, I would make sure that I kept an iron grip on my power. I would never knowingly allow my magic to harm anyone, especially not someone I cared about.

But what if I lose control and don't have a choice?

The voices around me were getting louder and I backed away from the table. "I think it's time I headed home."

The three fighting dragon shifters turned to face me.

"I'll walk you out." Cass hurried around her husband and daughter to grab my arm. "I won't be long." She glared at Veronica before guiding me toward the door.

Once we were out of earshot and walking along the hallway to the same balcony I'd landed on when I arrived, Cass squeezed my arm. "Why haven't you or your parents ever said anything?"

"About what?" I asked, my stomach twisting with sudden stress.

Cass stopped and held tight to my arm so I was forced to swing around and face her. "You have magic, don't you? Like Marienne."

"Magic? M... Me? No. No. Of course not." I'd never been asked that question directly, so I hadn't planned my reaction properly. I took a breath and willed a smile to my face. "I can shift, you know that. I can't have magic as well."

Cass's gaze was keen, and even though she didn't say anything, I knew she didn't believe me. She nodded. "That's true... so how did you just show my daughter a vision? And although I'm tempted to ask what it contained, I know what you shared with her is personal. So, I'll somehow refrain—for the moment."

I opened my mouth to rebut what was clearly the truth.

Cass raised an eyebrow as though daring me to lie.

I slammed my mouth shut and didn't say anything at all. The last thing I wanted to be was a liar. Though, I was tempted.

The queen lifted her hand in the traditional fashion.

I kissed her knuckles as a show of respect.

"Thank you for visiting us, Anthony. Fly safe." She was dismissing me instead of grilling me further.

I appreciated the reprieve more than I could say. "Thank you, Aunt Cass."

She nodded, turned, and walked away.

I watched her go, too many conflicting thoughts in my head. Should I call out and try to reassure her that she hadn't seen what she thought she had? Or would that just compound my weak attempt at denying the vision? I shook my head and hurried to the balcony door, throwing off the robe as I went. Despite my joking comment about taking it with me, I would never take anything from anyone.

I stepped out into the freezing weather, my magic instantly warming me with a buzz all over my skin.

Damn it.

I hadn't even conjured it that time. Why was my power suddenly stepping out on its own? As uncomfortable as it might be, I had to talk to my mom about it. I closed my eyes and let my dragon shifter take over my body once more. It was time to go home and find out how to turn off this other side of me—this unwanted, flawed side—once and for all.

I just want to be an ordinary dragon shifter! Is that too much to ask?

Anthony

When I arrived home my mother was waiting for me just inside the doors to the balcony landing area in a warm robe and slippers. Our castle was well made, and my father had ensured it was well kept. However, it was mostly stone and freezing to the touch in places, so the slippers were a welcome greeting.

"We have to talk," she said.

I slid my arms into the robe and tied it around my waist. "We certainly do," I agreed. "How do I get rid of my magic forever?"

She gaped at me. "What?"

"I don't want it," I declared. "I never have. And it's getting stronger. I can't control it as I once did."

"You're not meant to control it," Mom said, stepping closer. Her voice was a little short. "You're meant to *embrace* it. Be grateful for it. The way I am, every day."

I rolled my eyes at her.

Grateful?

"You know I'm not meant to have the ability to shift and have magic as well. One or the other, not both. It makes no sense. I'm a dragon shifter!"

"You want to embrace your father's side of your bloodline but not mine?" she accused.

The hurt in her voice stabbed through me. "That's not what I meant. Not at all. It's just... *no one* else has both. It's not right. I'm a freak, Mom!"

"You're not a freak!" Mom corrected in her harshest tone. "You're a miracle. I would have loved to have been able to shift. To soar in the air..."

"Well, you *can* have it," I said. "Obviously it's possible, even though you didn't think so before."

My mother put her hand to her forehead, pressing her fingers into her flesh as though she needed to stop the headache. "No... Anthony, you don't understand. It's your inability to accept your magic that causes... the... *oh...*" She froze, her eyes flashing with purple as her magic took over her body.

Her trembling made me flinch and I couldn't stop myself from gripping her arms. I didn't like sharing my mother's visions, but her magic called to mine, as did my need to help her. "Mom! I..." The vision hit me with the weight of a tree trunk.

My mate was walking along the road... someone was stalking her. She was hit from behind and she fell. He was on her. My mate was screaming. Horrible, bloodcurdling screams of pain. He was hurting her. Making her...

I pulled away, managing to disengage from my mother's magic, my soul recoiling with rage as my dragon rose up within my heart. "Where is she?" I growled, my shifter barely contained.

"She's..." Mom wrapped her arms around her body, shuddering.

My worry rose, almost swamping me with its intensity.

"She's at work. I can show you..." She held out her hand.

This time I grabbed it without a second thought. Flashes came at me.

Main Street. Number 245. A big red brick building. A restaurant. Then a gray two-story smaller building. Blood. So much blood...

I let go of my mom, scales already covering some of my skin. My teeth had shifted in my mouth, and I couldn't talk.

Mom rushed to the balcony door and pulled it open, standing back to give me room. "Go. Go. Before it's too late to save her!"

Too late?

I rushed for the door, barely squeezing through as my dragon body took over my smaller human one. I leaped over the railing, dropping like a stone before completing my shift mid-flight. I spread my wings and flew across the ground, flapping my wings to get up and over the small houses of our township.

The higher I flew the more my gaze narrowed in on the Veil. The air space I'd only flown through once, a long time ago. The gateway to the human world. I hit the portal and tingles coursed all over my skin. Then I was through, into the human world, and immediately warmer.

It was mid-afternoon, and the vision I'd seen had been late at night. Had it happened yet, or was it something that was yet to occur? Should I wait it out, or go to her now? I flew lower, spying a small house in a field. A memory swam into my mind about that house. About the family who lived there and helped the dragons who crossed the Veil.

I made a decision and landed in the field, shifting to human. It wouldn't be good for anyone to see me in my dragon form. The ground was cool and soft beneath my feet as I walked toward the small cabin. The front door had a large sign that read:

Friend, please help yourself from the chest below to whatever clothes will fit you. We are visiting family and will be home as soon as we can.

I smiled at the warm feeling around my heart from such kindness, and wished I'd brought a gem or something for them as a thank you. My magic shimmered inside my hands, and I turned my left palm up and stared as my magic conjured a large ruby from my personal collection at home. I gaped at the stone. "How... why...? Damn it."

My magic really was out of control, obviously even more so here than it had been at home. Nevertheless, I had the gift I'd been hoping for, so I had to focus on the positive in that regard. I opened the chest and grabbed some pants and a warm sweater, leaving the ruby inside the chest while I searched for shoes. The clothes were a little tight in places, but I was grateful for the comfort.

There was no quick way into town, especially unseen. So, I walked, not something I did very often in my realm. We ran or flew. Walking was for short distances, usually between rooms in the castle—not into a town many miles away. By the time I arrived at the edges of town where houses with large yards sported children and pets galore, the sun was setting.

A woman saw me and smiled in greeting, though she was obviously hesitant about me and grabbed her child to her side.

"Hello," I said, not stepping closer but waving instead. "I'm looking for a place to eat dinner. A restaurant perhaps? Could you point me in the right direction?"

She nodded and walked closer to the edge of her fence. "Yes, I can do that. Main Street has all our food places. There's a bakery and a diner, and a fancier restaurant if that's what you're looking for."

"And how do I get there?"

She pointed. "That way, two blocks over. You can't miss it."

I nodded and turned to smile at the small girl clinging to the woman's legs. "Much appreciated." My heart began to pound as I ambled along the street in the direction of Main Street. It was beginning to dawn on me that I was about to meet my fated mate. What would I even do once I met her? Would she recognize me as I did her? Would I be able to leave her once she was safe? So many questions, and none of them with immediate answers.

My older brother had found his mate before he was twenty-one and pursued her with a determination, I'd never seen him display before that time, or since. Would I be the same? Was I ready for the woman who would be my perfect other half? The mother of my children.

I groaned as indecision flooded me. Then a voice in my head whispered, *Trust...* I sighed, yes... trust the process. Trust the universe. Trust fate. If now was my time, who was I to question?

Main Street was not large, but it did indeed have a choice of many shops, including clothing, baby items, and food choices. I walked along the street, forcing myself to stay calm, even though my heart banged in my chest like a bongo drum. Soon, very soon, I would see her. Then what would I do?

Would I be able to control my dragon? Or fail as so many kings and princes had done before me? My hands tightened into fists. The stories of dragon shifter kings turning into uncontrollable beasts at the mere sight of their mate had taunted me since I was a child. Some thought it was romantic, weirdly, but I found it disturbing. I'd never had a problem controlling my dragon, or my magic... though one of those had become quite difficult recently.

A chill stole down my spine and I stopped. Something was familiar here. I lifted my gaze and turned to stare across the road. There it was, the restaurant I'd seen in my vision, with its glowing sign and vibrant warm lights coming from within. My stomach grumbled with hunger, but I had neither money nor the patience to sit with my mate in arm's reach and not say or do anything.

Instead, I found stairs up to a roof terrace opposite the restaurant, and there I rested and kept watch while I waited for Mom's vision to come true.

FIVE

Charity

It had been a ridiculously busy night for a Sunday. The last thing I needed was another run in with Barry from last night, but what was another bully to deal with? I'd been handling them my whole life. I locked up, grateful for the earlier than normal finishing time. Sundays we closed at ten p.m., so I'd be home and in bed before midnight.

Thank goodness.

I was freaking exhausted. Mom kept telling me I needed to slow down, but who was I going to defer to? There was no back up manager. There was just me, and my amazing staff, and the owners who lived hours away in the city and didn't give two hoots if I worked myself into the ground for their bottom line.

I slid my keys into my bag and turned in the direction of my apartment. Mom had dropped off some soup today, so that would be supper when I got home. Something warm and filling on this cold night. I pulled my coat tighter around my body as the wind whipped around me.

"Hey you. I want to talk to you." A male voice slurred the words behind me.

I jumped and whirled around as a heavy hand grabbed my shoulder. When I saw who it was, my heart began to pound. "Barry! What are you doing here?" He looked drunk and mean. His hands were clenched at his sides and his face was slashed with redness. I had pepper spray in my bag... and home was only a hundred feet away. How quickly could I get my keys out of my bag if it came to a fight?

"You!" he growled. "You made me look like a fool, and cost me a fortune."

I opened my mouth to reply, scrabbling desperately in my bag for the pepper spray.

But he swung his arm so fast I didn't even see it coming. His fist collided with the side of my face. and

I fell backwards.

Crack.

My head hit the concrete, and my vision went black as pain swamped my body. I gasped out, blinking, trying to clear my vision. Panic hit. I put my hand up to my head and wetness met my fingers. Was it raining or was I bleeding?

"You fucking bitch," Barry snarled, grabbing my foot and dragging me along the sidewalk.

"Ow... Barry. Stop!" I tried to sit up, but each tug cracked my head back once more. My vision seemed to be returning but I was shaking now, adrenaline zinging along my veins. I kicked out at him but couldn't budge his grip on my leg.

He dragged me into the narrow alley next to the restaurant.

Dirt ground into my back and darkness intensified due to the buildings crowding above my head.

"You owe me." He shook my leg before releasing me, then threw his jacket to the ground.

Holy shit. No.

"I've got cash at my apartment," I gasped out. "I'll pay you back and no one has to know." I had to keep him talking. I had to fight. He already had me at a disadvantage, but maybe I could talk him around?

His foot slammed into my belly.

I screamed as pain swallowed me up, all the air leaving my body is an agonized hiss. I curled up and rolled onto my side, panting for breath. My head was spinning, and I'd long stopped panicking. My thoughts had slowed due to pain and shock, and I couldn't formulate a plan of how to get away.

How am I going to survive this?

Barry's heavy body landed on top of me, and I cried out, pushing at him to try and get him off me.

He pinned my flailing arms down with embarrassing ease and rolled me onto my back, making more pain splinter inside my head.

"Get off me!" I screamed again as his hot breath puffed against my face and his sweaty body gyrated against mine.

"Never." He grunted, grabbing one of my breasts in his rough grasp and squeezing.

A terrifying growl filled the alleyway. I stared up at a dark silhouette as someone entered the space. It was a man, a very large man... maybe. I blinked, trying to bring him into focus, groaning in disgust as Barry squeezed my breast yet again. He was so caught up in attacking me, he hadn't noticed the intruder.

"Help me... please." I whispered the words, unable to call out properly because of the weight of Barry's body on top of me. Hot tears filled my eyes, and I gulped.

The man stalked forward, reached down to pick Barry up, and threw him with sickening accuracy into the brick wall beside us.

Barry dropped like a bag of shit, totally unconscious, judging by the crunching noise when he hit the wall—he had to have broken several bones.

I was whimpering and shaking now.

"I'm here to help you." The man's voice was gentle as he scooped me up into his arms.

I immediately felt protected. I closed my eyes and covered my face with my hands, allowing the unfamiliar sensation to wash over me.

Safe.

Then another deep growl sounded, and I was suddenly being lowered to the ground once more.

What the hell?

I opened my eyes and looked up. And up.

The man above me seemed to have grown and his feet were no longer feet. They were claw-like. They were… talons. How was that possible? Was I dreaming?

Is this a nightmare?

"Do not be afraid." His voice had roughened, and his words were garbled. "I will fly you to safety."

Fly?

His talons reached for me, and I froze as one of them scooped me up and held me tightly against the cool scales on his chest. With a single jump we were soaring up, up and into the air.

I began to hyperventilate, fear striking me hard in the chest as my town got further and further away below us.

What in God's name is happening?

I looked up and that's when I realized what type of creature held me in its talons. A dragon. A real motherfucking dragon! And then the world went dark.

Anthony

I FLAPPED MY WINGS HARDER, aiming for height, reaching for my magic to shroud my mate in the warmth she would need to survive the cold we were flying toward. For the first time, I welcomed the rush of magic, knowing I was helping the beautiful woman in my grip to avoid freezing to death. I wanted her to feel warm and safe and comfortable, and if my magic could bring her a little of that, then for once it was a good thing.

My mate, whose name I still didn't know, was unconscious now, so I tucked both claws around her and held her as close to my body as I could.

God, she's amazing. Gorgeous.

With every beat of my heart, the feeling grew stronger within my chest.

She's the one.

I'd known it the moment I saw her step out of the restaurant. I hadn't known what to do from my vantage point on the roof terrace of the shop opposite. I was frozen in shock at the sight of her. My dragon had surged inside of me, demanding I claim my mate. I'd been so distracted trying to control my shifter that I hadn't noticed the man come up behind her.

When he hit her and dragged her into that alley, I jumped off the roof terrace and reached them as soon as I could.

I hope he's dead, a snarling voice said inside my head.

He'd touched my mate. *Hurt* her. I'd thrown him hard enough. I hoped with every fiber of my being that the one hit against the wall had ended his miserable life. What sort of man hit a woman who couldn't defend herself? What sort of man tried to rape a badly injured woman?

A man who doesn't deserve to live.

I flew higher, reaching the Veil that separated my world from hers. I hesitated for just a moment, worried how my mate would feel about me taking her away from everything she'd ever known. But she was injured, and my mother's magic could heal her.

My dragon fought my humanity back, knowing that we would be able to make her happy. Somehow, we would make it right. Because now that I had her, I would never let her go. I flew through the Veil and the cold hit hard. I pushed more of my magic down through my claws to protect my mate from the snow as I flew, catching the wind currents so that I conserved my energy where I could.

The Black Mountains were in sight. My home. And now, hopefully it would be my mate's home, too. I flew lower, pushing myself to fly to the top level of my parents' castle, where I would be seen by fewer people than if I landed on a lower level. I maneuvered my hold on my mate and managed to land on the icy balcony on one leg. I shifted back quickly, catching my mate in my arms and rushing to the door.

It immediately opened for me, my mom on the other side of the glass. "Come in, come in. I've prepared the bed for her." The top floor of the castle was the wing that Mom once lived in, when she was the widow of King Magnik. When she married my father, she moved into the royal chambers.

I didn't ask questions. My mother always knew everything. So, I simply followed her to the small room where she'd once lived and placed my mate on the clean sheets.

Mom pulled the blankets up and over her. "She's hurt."

I nodded, my teeth tightly clenched together as anger filled my heart.

"But not as badly as in the vision. You saved her?"

I nodded once more and managed to answer. "I think so."

She gestured to the door. "Go have a quick shower and get dressed. I'll stay with her."

"Should I fetch a doctor?" I asked, already moving toward the door.

Mom shook her head and lifted her hands. White magic glowed in her palms. "No. I can heal these injuries. Go get ready. Your mate will be awake soon."

I took one more lingering look at my mate, her eyes still closed, then I ran to my bedroom two flights down and into my shower to wash away the stink of anger and blood. My mate would be awake soon and I wanted to be by her side when she did.

Charity

I jerked awake, then relaxed into a strange sort of lethargy, almost like I'd been drugged and couldn't open my eyes. But I wasn't drugged, and I was *so* comfortable... in a bed with expensive sheets and a soft mattress, and the most luxurious pillows cushioning my head.

But... why am I in a bed that isn't mine?

My eyes popped open, and I glanced around, not moving any other part of my body. Above my head was a bed frame I didn't recognize, with an ornate ceiling and a light fitting that looked like it was from a historical movie set. I tried to sit up, but my stomach hurt, and I moved my hand to cover the pain. "Ow."

"Try not to move," a soft female voice said. "I've done what I can to heal you, but as you're human, you'll need to do a lot of the mending yourself."

I twisted to see a woman sitting calmly beside my bed. She was beautiful, and very regal-looking. With her long velvet dress and her hair pinned up she looked like a medieval princess. "Where am I?" I demanded.

"You're in my home," she answered simply, and smiled at me. "I'm not sure how much you remember, but you were attacked. My son rescued you and brought you here."

"Your son..."

The door to the room opened and a man rushed in, slowing when he saw I was awake.

I managed to lift myself up a little and the woman adjusted the pillows behind me so that I could see the face of my supposed savior.

He rescued me from an attack?

My breath caught in my throat as he walked forward, unspeaking. He was absolutely gorgeous, with bright blue eyes and dark hair with the kind of stare that took my breath away. I bit my lip as I stared at him. He seemed familiar somehow, but he couldn't possibly be.

Where would I have met a man like this?

"How are you feeling?" The sound of his voice caused my whole body to shiver involuntarily. It wasn't unpleasant; more like a frisson of awareness than a shiver because I was cold.

"Ah... I don't know," I managed, pushing myself up to sit higher in the grand bed. "What happened?"

"You don't remember?" He glanced at the woman sitting beside me.

I frowned, searching my memory for something, anything, and came up with a blank. "No. I'm sorry, not at the moment."

"It's okay," the woman said, patting my hand. "Anthony, tell our friend what happened... what's your name, dear?"

"Charity," I answered quickly. At least I knew my own name! I sounded like a dumbass regarding everything else.

The man—Anthony, she'd just called him—moved to the same side of the bed where his mother sat. As he moved closer, I could see the resemblance in the color of their hair and the general aura they both had about them.

They both radiated a sense of honesty and calm. Not feelings I usually attached to strangers.

"Charity," he repeated, a soft smile tugging at his lips.

An answering tug inside my belly surprised me, but I pushed it away and down. That wasn't the appropriate way to respond just because this guy had saved me from some sort of trauma. Gratitude would be normal, but whatever that was... it was something more. Something I couldn't explain.

"I happened to see you leave your restaurant last night. A man hit you and dragged you into the alleyway beside the restaurant. I fought him off and carried you home, here. You were injured, but not badly. We hope."

I covered my mouth with my hand as the memories began to flood back. I gasped loudly. "Barry..." I breathed.

That asshole!

Weird flashes cast images into my mind, of Barry punching me, kicking me... then of a strange shadowy man saving me... There was more there, but my brain hurt to even think right now.

I groaned. "Damn, I have a headache."

"You did hit your head pretty hard," the sexy guy said. "I'm sorry I didn't get there sooner. I..."

"Oh no, don't be. You saved me from a lot worse, I'm sure." Barry wouldn't have settled on just hitting me once or twice. I was pretty sure he'd been trying to rape me and if this man hadn't come along... I swallowed hard and blinked away the tears that swam into my vision. "Thank you."

He inclined his head, spearing me with a strangely intent look. "You're welcome." There was a flash of something behind his eyes—purple on blue. Something that seemed all too familiar. My heart lurched.

It can't be.

"Oh my God." I closed my eyes as my body responded the same way it did in my dreams. With longing and tight nipples and curls of desire flaring to life between my thighs.

"What's wrong?" he asked.

I could sense him step closer. He smelled divine and I wanted to turn my head away so I didn't embarrass myself, but I couldn't move. He was too near, too perfect. "I... um..." I gulped and forced my eyes open.

Be normal. Be normal.

"Nothing. Everything's okay. Sorry about that. It's just the pain and the flashes of memory, that's all," I lied. "It's all a little overwhelming."

This was the man I'd been dreaming about for weeks! He stole my every sleeping moment and turned it into an erotic feast for my senses. My face turned into a red, hot mess, courtesy of the blush that stole across my cheeks. I put my cool hands to my hot face and attempted to look composed, even though I was far from it.

How is this possible? He isn't meant to exist!

"Have you seen my son before?" The woman narrowed her eyes in a knowing manner. "In a dream, perhaps?"

"How did you know that?" I whispered, sitting straight up despite the niggles in my body. The pain in my belly had mostly subsided and, although I could sense some tenderness and stiffness in my back, I was feeling a lot better than before.

The woman smiled. "Let's start with proper introductions first. I am Marienne, and this is my son Anthony."

I tried to nod but found that only increased my headache. "Have you got some Advil or something I could take for a headache?"

Marienne stepped closer. "Would you like me to take your pain away?"

"How would you do that?" I asked, suspicion etched into my tone.

She laughed a little. "Just with my hands. I am a healer, of sorts."

"Oh, like an energy healer?" I knew of some *woo-woo* style practitioners who could lay their hands on people and practically heal them through energy exchanges. Not that I totally bought into that sort of thing, but at this point in time, I was happy to try anything.

"Yes. Just lay back."

I did as she said, though an unease settled into my stomach.

Marienne pressed her fingers to my temples, then stroked my forehead gently.

I tried not to sigh, but her gentle touch was nice and it soothed the pain.

"How's that?" she asked after a minute or so, before taking her hands away. "Any better?"

I opened my eyes, unaware of when I'd closed them. The pain was gone and my head felt clearer than it had in a long time. I sat up once more. "Oh my God, you're amazing!" I grinned up at the woman and her gorgeous son, trying not to let my embarrassment take hold once more.

This couldn't be the man from my dreams, surely? Just because his eyes were blue-and-purple, and his face looked oh-so-familiar...

No. It's impossible.

"Now, about that dream," Marienne said.

"Mom, stop it." Anthony gave his mom a push in the side that didn't move her, so I had to assume it was playful.

Marienne grinned again. "Secrets always find a way of coming out in the end, just so both of you know that." She began walking toward the door. "It's late, so I'm going to head to bed. My husband will be wondering where I am."

Anthony snorted. "Dad will be snoring his head off."

She smiled softly again. "Fine... I'm exhausted. I'm old. Let me get some sleep." She waved at me just before she pulled the door shut. "Nice to have you staying with us, Charity."

"Oh, nice of you to have me," I responded as she shut the door, leaving me alone with Mr. Sexy-Ass-Dream-Guy himself. "Um..." I glanced around the room. "Where exactly am I?"

Why hadn't he taken me to a hospital, or the police, or something? "And what happened to Barry? Did you call the police on him?"

Anthony walked around the bed so he was standing at the foot of my bed, and we could look at each other easier, with a little breathing room. "Um... don't you want to try and get some sleep? It's after one a.m."

I narrowed my eyes at him, suspicious. "Why aren't you answering my questions?" Part of me argued that I should be feeling afraid, but instead I rationalized that if they'd wanted to hurt me, I wouldn't be lying in a plush bed, comfortable and healing up nicely.

He ran a hand through his hair, then looked at me with eyes that shone with heat. "Because I'm afraid to tell you," he said, his tone laced with honesty.

"Tell me what?" I whispered, and even though my pulse quickened, there was no fear in my heart.

He gestured to the bed. "Where you are... What I am..."

"*What* you are..." As though the words conjured the images, more memories flashed through my mind. Memories of a dragon, picking me up and holding me. Carrying me away. Flying through the night... "No..." I whispered almost to myself. "It can't be true. It isn't possible!" He couldn't be some sort of dragon prince in another world like the one I dreamed about every night.

"What can't be true?" he asked, his eyes flashing with the purple mist I'd seen too many times to count in my dreams.

My belly clenched with longing at the sight. I forced myself to pretend calm as I tried again. "Please just tell me the truth. Where am I? Who are you? And... yes. *What* are you?" My heart was beating erratically now, but I wouldn't run. I needed to know the truth, the whole truth, and nothing but the truth.

Anthony sighed heavily. "Mom was right, the truth always comes out, doesn't it?"

He was trying to be lighthearted, but my nerves were already stretched tight and all I could manage was a nod. "Please."

He grabbed the bed end and leaned forward, seeming to brace himself for what he needed to say. "My name is Anthony, and I'm a prince. The second born son of the King and Queen of the Black Mountains. I brought you here to our castle—my home—because I knew my mother could heal you."

Holy shit...

Then Anthony continued and blew my world apart with his declaration. "And I'm a dragon shifter; we all are. Well, my mother isn't. She's... well, she doesn't shift, but pretty much everyone else does around here."

I inhaled sharply, struggling not to laugh out loud hysterically as nerves and the impossibility of my situation swamped me. "Um... say what?"

CHAPTER
SEVEN

Anthony

She didn't believe me, and I didn't blame her. In the human world dragons didn't exist. In fact, they were considered mythological creatures written into ancient fables. Though those stories were most likely written by humans who'd seen one of my ancestors.

"You're kidding... right?" Charity's gorgeous dark eyes flashed with a depth of emotion I hadn't expected. "Tell me the truth."

"I just did." I shrugged. "I saw that man hurt you and I wanted to..." I shook my head. She didn't need to hear about my murderous instincts in relation to protecting her. "I may have thrown him into that brick wall a little too hard, but I didn't hang around to see if he survived. I wanted to get you somewhere safe."

"Safe." Charity repeated the word and paused as if considering it. Then she lifted an eyebrow at me. "Well, I'm sure he got what was coming to him."

I agreed, but didn't say anything more. I could tell she was trying to process everything, which was not an easy feat with a head injury, let alone when what was being said probably sounded fantastical at best and insane at worst. If you'd never known about shifters or magic, it was a pretty big leap of faith to take.

"So, where am I?" she asked, looking around. "In your castle, or something?"

I smirked a little at her incredulous tone. Every eligible woman in my town would have been ecstatic to be in a room alone with me, with a bed in clear sight. But apparently, not my mate. She clearly wasn't impressed by my birthright.

"Well, yes. Though technically, I suppose this is my parents' castle. They still reign, and I'm not the Crown Prince. My older brother, Carlak, will be king one day—not me."

"I don't believe you." She sat up straighter and glared at me with all the fire of a woman who'd been lied to and was getting rather annoyed about that fact.

I gestured to the window. "It's the middle of the night, so you won't be able to see the whole town right now, but feel free to look out. You'll see."

Charity threw back her bed covers and twisted slowly until her feet touched the floor. Her gasp was audible as she looked down at herself. "What am I wearing?"

I tried not to laugh as I walked over to the window and drew the curtains back for her. "One of my sister-in-law's gowns, I believe. Don't worry, that was my mother's doing, not mine."

Charity walked to the window and stared out. We were twenty stories above the town, and in the darkness, it was hard to see any detail, even with my enhanced dragon sight. She huffed out a breath. "I can't see a thing."

Determined not to be thought of as a liar, I marched over to the main door. "Come see the castle then. Or you can wait for morning. Either way, you'll find out I'm telling the truth soon enough."

She narrowed her eyes at me and lifted her head.

I was pretty sure she would have stormed right up to me, all indignation and fire if she'd been able to. I could imagine her poking a firm finger against my breastbone and telling me off, and I had to hold back a laugh at the imagined scene.

She had some fire, this one, which only made her even more desirable in my eyes. Or at least, she *would* have fire, if she were operating at her full capacity. She swayed a little, then moved toward me slowly.

"Are you all right?" I asked, studying her tentative movements. "You took a lot of knocks tonight."

She nodded, but her lips pressed into a thin line.

I opened the door and took her elbow as she reached me. "One short walk, then back to bed. I don't want you passing out again."

"Again? I passed out?" Her voice was slightly breathless.

"Yes, once we got to a higher altitude. I'm not sure if it was fear, or your injuries, but I was worried about you for a good few hours."

We took no more than a few steps before she stopped. "I don't think I can... I'll have to see the rest in the morning." She sagged without warning.

I grabbed for her, sweeping her up into my arms and marching back into her room. "I'm not making a move," I said, trying to be stern. "You just looked like you were going to fall down."

She laid her head on my shoulder and sighed. It felt so right to have her in my arms. "I was, thank you. I wouldn't have made it back on my own."

I placed her back in her bed and tucked her beneath the warm covers. "You're not used to having help, are you?"

She closed her eyes, effectively shutting me out. "I don't usually need help."

I brushed her hair back off her forehead, unable to not touch her when she was this close. "Well, tonight, just accept it. Okay?"

She nodded, though her eyes remained closed. "Okay."

"My room is a few flights of stairs down. Do you think you'll be all right here if I leave you now?"

She opened her eyes and, for the first time since the attack, there were tears shimmering in her eyes. "I'll be fine. I just need to sleep."

The sight of those tears did something to my insides. I felt all squeezed tight, like it was difficult to breathe, and I couldn't stop myself from leaning forward to press a gentle kiss against her hair.

Instead of recoiling as I half expected her to, she lifted her chin and met my lips with her own, surprising me.

Desire burned in my gut and although I desperately wanted to kiss her deeply, the last thing I wanted was to take advantage of her when she was injured. But the imprint of her lips on mine stayed with me, even after I managed to stand straight once more.

My dragon roared inside my head, wanting—*needing*—his mate.

No. I told him. *Now is not the time.*

"Good night, Charity." I managed, then I turned and fled, shutting her door quietly behind me. I leaned against the wall in the hallway outside, my head back and my eyes closed. My heart hammered as aggressively as a dragon's wings in war, and I wasn't sure I'd ever feel the same again.

My mate was strong, beautiful, and fierce. But she was also soft and tender. My dragon was already in love, ready to claim her as ours, forever. But I had a hard job ahead of me. She wasn't of this world, and she certainly wouldn't just fall into my bed, and my heart, without a second thought.

She would need to be wooed, and reassured, and... I didn't even know what she needed, but I was certain our path to happiness would not be straight or easy. I stood up straight and walked down the stairs to my bedroom. My dragon wanted me to sleep on the floor outside of her room and protect her like the treasure she was. But how creepy would that be if she woke up before me, and then practically fell over my sleeping form as she tried to leave her room?

She already thought of me as a liar. I didn't want to make her believe anything else bad about me.

I managed to reach my room, strip off and climb into bed without running back to her. She was safe in my mother's old room. Safer than anywhere else in the world, human or dragon.

My mother's magic filled every room and hallway of this castle. And even though the servants loved her, they also feared her power. No harm would come to my mate while my mother was queen.

And I would destroy anyone who tried to harm a hair on my beautiful mate's head.

~

I MANAGED a few restless hours of sleep before I was up, dressed and heading back up the stairs to see if Charity was well enough to go for a walk. When I reached the door, Mom was walking out.

When she saw me, she held a finger to her lips as though shushing me. "She's still sleeping," Mom said, once she'd shut the door behind her.

"Okay. I'll wait." I stood beside the door like a soldier. I wasn't letting her wake up to an empty room and no help.

Mom nodded. "I understand. The fated mate bond is very strong. You won't want to leave her at all."

I crossed my arms over my chest. "Then why does it sound like you have something unpleasant to say about it?"

She grimaced. "Because my visions of your future haven't changed, Anthony. Until you accept your magic and embrace it... you're both on a hazardous path."

I stared down at the carpet at my feet, anger rising inside my chest. I hated my magic. It made me different from every other shifter. Even worse, it made me dangerous. Which my mother had just admitted seeing in her visions. If I ever lost control, I could hurt those I cared about. Kill them, even. How could she not understand that my magic was a weakness rather than a strength? "Mother, you're a powerful sorceress. You can get rid of my magic, I'm sure of it." I flicked my gaze back up to hers, staying as calm as I could. "I've never asked you for help before, but I'm asking now. Consult your books. See if you can take away my curse."

Mom gaped at me. "It's not a curse! It's a *gift*! And Anthony, you are far more powerful than you know."

I scowled at her. "Yeah, so powerful I'll likely kill my mate someday. No thank you. If this is a gift, I don't want to accept it. I want it gone."

Mom lifted her chin in defiance but conceded. "All right. If that is truly what you want, I'll see what I can do."

"Thank you."

She took a step away from the door then froze. "I think Charity is awake," she said, but in truth, she hadn't needed to tell me.

I could instantly sense my connection with Charity growing stronger as she woke.

"Bring her down for breakfast, would you?" she asked. Then she was gone.

I stared at the door to my mate's bedroom, my gut tight with anticipation. Today was the first day of the rest of my life with her. I just had to convince my human mate that it was also the first day of hers—and that it would be a good thing, not something to fear.

EIGHT

Charity

I was still inside the strange room. It was beautiful, that was for sure, but unlike any bedroom I'd ever seen before. It was so lavish as to be almost fantastical.

Knock, knock, knock.

"Come in," I called out before really thinking about who I was inviting into my personal space.

The door opened and the man of my dreams, quite literally, walked in. "Good morning."

I smiled at Anthony, trying to control my body's irrational response to his presence, and failed miserably. My cheeks burned with the shame of it. "Hi."

He smiled at me. "Mom asked me to invite you downstairs for breakfast. Are you feeling well enough to join us?"

I checked my body and licked my lips as my nerves got the better of me. "I need to go to the bathroom first, but yes. Breakfast would be lovely, thank you."

Anthony indicated a door behind him. "There's an attached bathroom here, with a large tub and shower. Please, take your time. I'll wait out in the hall."

"Thank you."

He nodded once and turned, heading for the door.

My gaze swung down to his ass and the way his slacks clung to him. *Wow.*

As soon as the door was shut, I got up and carefully made my way to the bathroom. I was still sore, but I felt a lot more energetic and revived than I had last night, and less like I was about to topple over at any given moment.

I stared at my reflection in the mirror, a stranger staring back at me. "Holy shit. What the hell happened?" I was pale and wan. I had bruising around my right eye and dried blood still caked in my hair. I looked like I'd been pulled through a hedge backwards... and then thrown in front of a truck. "How am I even alive?"

The answer was clear. Someone had saved me from a fate worse than death, or perhaps death had been Barry's ultimate intention. I didn't know... I still couldn't remember all the details. They remained distant and foggy. I glanced longingly at the shower. I had to wash the blood out of my hair. I couldn't go to breakfast, potentially with members of a strange royal family with blood clinging to my scalp. Injured or not, it would be unseemly and unclean.

I unlaced the bodice on the dress and dropped the heavy garment to the floor. "Whoa. It must be cold here if this is what they wear every day," I remarked to myself.

Had Anthony really carried me to some other town? How had he done that? A brief image of being up high, of air rushing past my face, intruded, but I tamped it down and clung to rationality.

No. Don't go there. Don't think about anything except for what's right in front of you.

I shook my head to clear any lingering worries as I gingerly walked into the massive, tiled shower and turned on the faucet.

One thing at a time.

The water quickly grew hot, and I turned around to let the stream flow over my head and down my body. There didn't seem to be any shampoo or conditioner, but there was a flower-scented soap, so I used that to scrub my whole body, then lathered it into my hair. It felt heavenly to remove the blood and emerge clean and refreshed.

I turned the shower off and found a neat pile of towels near the door. I could already feel my energy fading a little, so I towel-dried my hair and dressed again in the lovely sky-blue gown, but I couldn't manage all the intricate lacing on my own. Eventually I gave up trying and walked back to the door that led to the hallway.

When I opened it, Anthony was there, waiting for me as he'd promised. His smirk told me I looked like a drowned duck. "What?" I said. "It's not like I have this sort of dress in my wardrobe. Where are my regular clothes?" His grimace told me all I needed to know. "Fine." I sighed. "Do you know how to fix this?" I gestured to all the strings and ties.

He nodded, then with expert efficiency, he laced me up, and stepped back. His fingers had been swift and yet he'd lit a path of fire with every fleeting touch.

Does he feel this strange connection, too?

"Do I want to know how you know your way around women's clothing so well?" I asked with a raised eyebrow.

He had the good grace to lightly blush. "You can ask." His smirk lifted one side of his lips, "But do you really want to know the answer?"

I grinned at him, before my gaze found the floor and my cheeks reddened. "Touché."

"Let's go." He offered me his elbow like a gentleman from a historical movie.

I took his arm, because how could I not? Then I remembered our strange conversation last night about where we were. "Weren't you going to show me the view?" I taunted. I was sure we were just inside some beautiful mansion outside the city center, and I would see a familiar landscape when I checked outside. They had bluestone historical homes near where I lived. Not many... but they were around. This was likely one of those.

"Sure," he said with a big smile, leading me to an arched window that looked out over a view that took my breath away.

"Oh... my..." We were high up. Like, *really* high up. This was definitely not a bluestone stately home. I stepped closer, pressing my nose to the window so I could stare down at the village below. It didn't look familiar at all, nor did the mountainous skyline beyond the village. "Where are we?"

"We're in the Black Mountains," Anthony said. "My family rule this kingdom."

Kingdom?

I twisted around to gape at him. "Where's... here, exactly? What country?"

He pressed his lips together and his nostrils flared.

I put my hands on my hips. "Well?"

"You're in a realm not far from the town you live in. We passed through a hidden portal last night. We call it a Veil. It sits between your world and ours."

"We're... in a..." I gulped then swallowed hard. Was he truly saying that he'd taken me to some sort of time travel world, or something? A whole other realm? I felt like I was grasping at straws.

How is any of this possible?

"And what's with all the medieval clothes and stuff?" I said, gesturing to the dress I wore while trying to grasp onto something concrete.

"The clothes are designed mostly for the weather. It gets cold here," he explained. "We like to live a simple life, but we also have modern conveniences if we desire them."

I nodded, registering the fact that I'd used a very modern-looking bathroom only minutes before. "Okay, but..."

Anthony offered his elbow again. "Can I answer any more questions over breakfast? My parents will be waiting."

His parents?

"You mean the king and queen of this place?"

He chuckled. "Yes. Let's go."

I let him lead me down the stairs, along a hallway and down another set of stairs. "How big is your home?" I asked, glancing at everything around me. The furniture, the paintings, the rugs on the stone floors. It really was an actual castle. "This place is amazing."

Anthony chuckled. "It's big. How big? I have no idea." He pushed open a large, carved door and preceded me into a large dining room warmed by a roaring fireplace.

"Wow." I stared up at the stone dragon carvings around the fire and the portrait atop the mantel. It featured a man and a woman, with their two small sons. It was... glorious. There was no other word for it.

Marienne walked toward me, a huge smile on her face. "Nice to see you up and moving, Charity. Are you feeling any better?"

I nodded. "A lot better, thank you."

A man walked toward us, slightly taller than Anthony and with an aura about him that wasn't quite as warm. *Hardened* was the word that came to mind when I stared at him. Anthony's father—which meant he must be the king.

I stepped closer to Anthony, instinctively seeking his protection even though I wasn't in any danger.

The king stopped beside Marienne.

"Charity, this is my father, King Erik," said Anthony, introducing us.

I nodded my head, not sure if I should curtsey, or even if I knew how to curtsey. "It's so nice to meet you."

"And I, you," he answered, his tone more formal than I'd expected.

"Come, eat." Marienne reached for my hand and pulled me toward the massive table. "If there's anything you'd like in particular that isn't here, please let us know."

I gawked at the immense and lavish spread before me. "Ah... is it Christmas Day or something here?"

Anthony snorted out a laugh.

Marienne frowned. "I'm sorry, I don't understand, dear."

Anthony held out a chair for me, stifling his amusement. "No. This is a normal breakfast for us."

"No way." I shook my head as I stared at the plethora of food in front of us. "This is more food than my mom would make on our birthdays and Christmas combined." Not to mention the fact that, for me, breakfast was usually a coffee on the way to work at one p.m. in the afternoon because I always seemed to work nights.

Everyone sat down and began loading up their plates with pancakes and fruit, roast meats and potatoes, pies and stews.

I didn't even know where to begin!

"It's perhaps my fault that we eat so well," King Erik began, his deep tone even more pronounced now. "I didn't grow up in the castle."

"Dad grew up poor and starving," Anthony said, cutting to the chase. "He's always made sure that my brother and I were well fed, and he changed all the laws in the kingdom once he became king so that no one ever goes hungry—not in our town."

I shivered at the emotion behind the words. Anthony was proud of his dad, and I could see why. I simply couldn't imagine the huge man in front of me starving as a child, but it brought a tightness to my chest to even think about it. I swallowed hard. "It sounds like you turned a horrible experience into a blessing for everyone else. That is certainly something to be commended."

The king didn't say anything, but his lips turned up into his first smile since I'd entered the room.

"Please, eat," Marienne prompted again.

I reached for the closest thing, a pot of fruity, red jam and a plate of warm bread rolls. I pulled open the bread and smothered its warm crunchiness in what smelled like fresh raspberries. When I bit into it, I groaned. "Wow. That's amazing."

Marienne smiled. "Our cooks are very talented."

I took another bite and managed to swallow before speaking again. "I've worked in restaurants for ten years and this is top quality."

"Try some of the meat," Anthony suggested, gesturing to the platter not far from me. "It's really tender."

I dug in, eating as much as I would on Christmas Day, enjoying both the flavors of the food, and the simple questions they asked about my work and my family. "So, how far is my apartment from here?" I asked, glancing at Anthony, then Marienne. "I mean... assuming I believe your story about dragons and flying me here, which I can't believe I'm saying out loud, but how far is it to my home?" I laughed to show I was joking.

Marienne looked at her husband with a secretive smile. "She sounds just like Lucy."

"Who's Lucy?" I asked, taking another heavenly bite of roasted sweet potato.

"She's a human who married the king in a neighboring kingdom," Marienne explained. "She was pretty shocked to find out that we existed too."

Um... okay. She sounds serious.

"And did her king save her from a bad guy too?"

Erik snorted.

I looked at him in surprise.

He coughed to clear his throat. "No... sorry. Stavrok stole Lucy from her doorstep."

"He... *stole* her?" I repeated. "Like, kidnapped her?"

Lucy... Lucy... that name sounds familiar somehow.

Marienne giggled. "Yes, exactly like that. She tells the story the best, so we'll have to take you to visit her soon. It's most entertaining."

I glanced at Anthony, then back at his mom. "Well, that would be nice, but aren't you taking me home today?"

King Erik stared at his son.

I glanced over at Anthony, a sudden sense of dread seating itself deep in my gut. "Anthony?" I prompted.

Anthony put down his fork and cleared his throat. "I was hoping you would stay here for a while as my guest."

"Well, I've got to get back to work," I said. Surely, he'd understand that?

"Do you?" He spoke softly, though a little stiffly. "I mean... after the attack, can't you call in sick for a few days, or something? It would seem only reasonable."

I didn't like being told what to do, though he was probably right. If I was home, I probably would have been dealing with hospital bills and the police right now. "Ah..." I glanced at the queen. "Do you really want me to stay?" It seemed so improbable. Why would they want me here? I was no one important.

"We'd love you to be our guest," Marienne gushed. "We have a telephone in the main office, and a computer if you need to give someone notice or let them know you won't be in."

I could call the restaurant and tell them I was hurt. Maybe even find out about Barry... "I suppose I could, but I can't guarantee they'll give me the time off." And I had bills to pay, just like everyone else after all. Not to mention the fact that I still wasn't sure I believed any of the stories I'd been told so far. They were just so far-fetched!

"Please stay," Anthony said, his gaze beseeching and honest. "I'll show you around our town."

I stared at him, the mixture of joy and hope that I always seemed to feel around him rising to smother the dread. I looked away so I could give myself a little breathing space to consider his offer. I hadn't had a vacation in *years*. And even though this wasn't exactly a holiday destination I'd ever heard of, what was a day or two out of my boring and ordinary life?

I lifted my head and caught Anthony's gaze once more. "All right. If I get the okay from work, I'll stay for a few days. Thank you."

Anthony smiled, but there was a strange stiffness to him again that I couldn't place. His parents looked relaxed and happy at my news. But my gut told me that this situation was more complicated than it looked on the face of things. Only, I couldn't figure out why...

CHAPTER
NINE

Anthony

My dragon shifter was angry, huffing and puffing inside my chest. I was struggling, once again, to keep him under control. My mate couldn't leave. She couldn't. The very idea that she expected me to take her 'home' was both shocking and upsetting in the extreme. Against my best judgment, I reached for my magic and asked it silently for help. My dragon immediately calmed down and I could think more clearly once more. "Are you ready for a tour, then?" I stood up and extended my hand.

"Absolutely." She also stood up and shot me a grin. "I've got to walk off that enormous breakfast."

She turned to thank Mom and Dad for the meal, then glanced at me. "Am I appropriately dressed? It's only…" She poked her bare foot out from under the gown.

I turned to my mother for advice on that one. "Mom?"

Mom nodded. "She'll be fine, though make sure you stop and grab a cloak and a set of boots before heading out."

"Thanks. Then let's go." I turned and Charity followed me out of the dining room to the cloak room near the castle's front entrance. "Would you like to see more of the castle? Or should we go straight out into the town?"

"Can you show me how you turn into a dragon?" she asked, her voice as clear as day.

Her request shocked me into an astounded silence.

"Well?" she asked when I was quiet for too long. "You said you were a dragon, right?"

I nodded in response.

"Then show me." Her grin said she didn't think I could do it. It said I was full of it and that there were no such things as dragons.

"I can," I said. "But you have to *promise* not to freak out, especially since you're the one asking me to shift." This was a bad idea; I could already tell. But there was only one way forward and convincing her that I was a dragon was the first step in explaining fated mates, and everything else I had yet to tell her.

She grinned at me, her eyes sparkling with mischief. She was about to get a huge shock.

I dragged in a deep breath, then nodded. "Okay. Let's go out into the courtyard then."

We grabbed her cloak and boots, and then I marched toward a side door and pushed it open.

Charity followed me with a frown on her face. "Aren't we going on a tour?"

"You just asked me to show you my shifter. Which do you want to do first? Shifter display or tour?" A touch of impatience threaded into my tone though I didn't mean for it.

Her eyebrows flicked upward. "I was only teasing," she said.

I groaned. "No, you weren't. You were wanting to prove that I'm a liar. And you're going to keep thinking that until you see the truth with your own eyes. So, you can see the town first, or we can just get this part over and done with now."

She tilted her head, uncertainty clouding her eyes. "I... are you serious?"

I nodded and stormed toward the center of the courtyard. No matter how many times I told her the truth, she wouldn't believe me. I began to strip, pulling off my jacket, my shirt, and my shoes.

"What are you doing?" she exclaimed, still standing with one foot inside the doorway.

"I'm showing you the truth. Dragons are not made-up creatures. They are very real, and you are visiting a country where almost every person you meet is a shifter. When I shift, my clothes get shredded, so I'm removing them for after. I will leave my trousers on, for now—for you."

She crossed her arms over her chest and glared at me as if I was somehow making a mockery of her. "Fine. Show me then."

"Do not be afraid," I declared, letting my dragon rise to the surface of my consciousness. "I am fully aware in my shifter form. I'm not going to hurt you, and you can talk to me just as you are now. I will understand you."

She rolled her eyes like I was the village idiot.

I wanted to roll mine straight back, but instead, I let go of my humanity. My body grew, my scales sprouted, and my chest filled with fire as my senses exploded with shifter acuteness. I smelled fear and heard her terrified shriek a second later. I opened my eyes.

Charity was plastered to the door, her eyes wide and her face pale.

I had to reassure her but shifting back so fast felt wrong. I bent my front legs and laid my head on the stones. My shifter heart ached to see Charity so distressed, but she would need to accept all of me as my fated mate, not just the human side.

Charity dropped to the ground and curled into a ball, her arms around her legs as she rocked back and forth as if she were in an asylum.

I made a purring sound, which probably sounded more like a growl to her, but I was hoping it came across well. If she didn't calm down soon, I would need to shift back.

Her head came up a little at my purr, and her watery eyes stared at me.

I stayed in my submissive pose, wishing she would stand up and touch me.

As though my thoughts had encouraged exactly that, Charity pushed up on unsteady legs and stared at me, her fingers grasping the door behind her. "Anthony? Is that really you?" Despite her fear, her voice was strong.

I nodded my head the best I could without getting up.

She staggered forward, wiping the tears away. "How is this possible?"

I stayed very still, wishing her closer.

Charity took another step toward me, then extended her hand. "May I touch you?"

I nodded my head again and didn't move.

She took another step, her hand trembling as she bit her lip.

I closed my eyes, not wanting to scare her.

Her fingers touched my shoulder lightly.

I was acutely aware of each of her strokes over my scales as she grew bolder and pressed even closer.

"You're... I... can't believe it." She was whispering but my hearing was sharper in dragon form, and I picked up every nuance. Her shock, her fear, and her wonder. Both of her hands touched my side now, moving toward my wings.

I tried not to move, but it was almost impossible. As soon as her fingers touched the delicate webbing I gasped, my wing shivering in a strange blend of ticklish pain and delight.

She jumped back. "Oh, I'm sorry."

It was time to shift to my human form. I let go of my dragon shifter, though he begged to stay and get to know our mate.

Then I was naked and kneeling on the stones in front of her as I looked up.

Charity was staring straight at me, her mouth open in amazement.

I stood up, aware of how her hungry gaze slid over my aroused body. I wouldn't hide my desire for her, which was lucky as, in this state, there was no way I could. "You didn't hurt me," I assured her. "My wings are just sensitive."

She nodded and then her eyes dropped to my erection. She laughed lightly. "Clearly." Then she gulped as if her own forwardness had shocked her, and she glanced behind the door. "Would you like some more clothes?"

I scooped up the pants that I'd torn. "The servants have cloaks. I'll just grab one." I went to move past her.

She grabbed my bare arm. "You can't go into the castle like that."

I couldn't help but laugh at the shock in her tone. "Every staff member here is also a dragon shifter. Nudity doesn't offend anyone. It is normal and natural, and part of being a shifter." My arm tingled where she touched me, but I moved forward and stepped inside the palace once more. "A cloak please."

One of the nearby guards retrieved one for me.

I slipped it on quickly. The door closed behind me, and I turned to see Charity step inside once more. My discarded shirt and shoes were in her hands. I wasn't exactly dressed for a town tour now. "I need to re-dress. Would you like to wait here for me?"

She nodded and shoved the clothes at me.

I took them, then drew her to sit down on one of the chairs in the foyer. "I won't be long. Would you like a cup of tea? Or something stronger perhaps?"

"Um... ah... tea. Yes."

I called over a servant and indicated to Charity. "Get her anything she wants. I'll be back momentarily." I gave her fingers a reassuring squeeze and turned tail. I reached my bedroom in record time, dressed quickly, then rushed back to her side. Half of me expected to find her gone. So, when I found her still sitting on the same chair, a cup of tea in her hand, my hammering pulse began to slow down. "You're still here," I said, unable to hide my relief.

"Where am I going to go?" She took a sip of what I assumed was a fortified cup of tea. "If you were telling the truth about the dragon shifter thing, then you're telling the truth about everything else... about us being in a different realm, and about me being unable to get home without your assistance."

I held out my hand with a gentle smile.

She placed her tea on a side table and took my offered hand.

"Come. See the town. Then you can decide if it's such a terrible thing that you're here with us."

A guard opened the front door for us. As soon as we stepped out of the castle the cold air hit us and she shifted closer, pressing her body against mine.

"It's snowing," she said, holding out her hand to catch a stray snowflake. "I've never seen real snow before."

"It's only a light sprinkle," I replied. "Today, at least. Let's go for a short walk and see how you go. If it gets too cold, then we'll head back."

She nodded.

Together we walked down the main street and around the town, looking at the houses and shops and enjoying the bustle of people as they went about their daily business.

"You said that your father makes sure no one here goes without food," she said when we walked past a small vegetable cart. "How does he do that exactly?"

"Well, one of the first things he did for our kingdom was to lift all the taxes and supply everyone with free electricity, heating, and water. The necessities. Next was food. The new council knows who in the town needs a helping hand, and we provide what they need. Our people work hard, and they rarely need hand-outs, especially with their basic needs being taken care of."

Charity stared up at me, then shook her head, focusing back on the road. "Wow. That's amazing. I feel like I work night and day just to pay the mortgage most weeks. It must be amazing to know that you'll always have a home and be able to keep the lights on."

It was my turn to frown at her. "You don't enjoy your work?" I'd assumed she must, given she wanted to go back to it, but if she didn't, well that would make her transition to living here that much easier.

Her lips twisted as she thought about her answer. "I do... but if I suddenly didn't have to work to pay the bills, would I still do it? *Hell no.*"

That was exactly what I wanted to hear.

She'd mentioned a little of her family over breakfast, but I wasn't sure how close she was with them. Would she miss them if she were to live here? "Do you see your family much?" I asked, assuming of course that she was unmarried. Surely, fate wouldn't have sent me a woman who wasn't available.

"I don't see them a lot," she answered, her voice soft and slightly reflective. "My parents live a few hours away."

"Have you seen enough of the town for now?" I asked, stopping at a fork in the road where we could choose to continue to walk, or head back.

"Yes, I'm a bit tired actually."

"This way," I said, directing her back up the hill toward the castle. "Would you like to rest?"

She was looking paler by the moment, and she nodded

I twisted and picked her up in my arms.

"You've got to stop doing that," she said, but she didn't fight me. Quite the opposite. She laid her head on my shoulder and sighed.

"When you stop looking like you're going to fall down, I'll stop picking you up."

She laughed lightly, but didn't lift her head again.

I got her back to the castle as quickly as I could and walked her up every flight of stairs until we reached her room. The continuing silence was too much for me, so as I lay her on the bed I tried to make conversation. "Did you know these used to be my mother's chambers, before my parents married?"

"But you said your mom wasn't a shifter?" She sounded curious but her eyes were closing. She'd obviously pushed her limits with the long walk.

"No. She's something different again." I pulled the blankets up over Charity, clothes and all. I didn't think now was the time to tell her about my mom being a sorceress. "You can ask more questions later, but first you need to rest."

"I need to call my work," she protested, but didn't move.

"You can when you wake up again." I wanted to reassure her and leaned in to press a kiss to her forehead.

"Why are you being so nice to me?" she whispered, but her eyes were still closed.

I stared at her without the awkwardness of her noticing. She was so beautiful. So delicate. So precious.

Because you're my mate.

"Because you're our guest," I said, chickening out to tell her the whole truth about our situation. "Sleep. I'll come get you when lunch is ready."

She didn't answer.

So, I had to assume she was already asleep. I crept out and shut the door, a wave of relief passing over me at the knowledge that she'd seen and seemed to accept my dragon form. We'd gotten over that first major hurdle, but I was under no illusions. We still had many more to go before I could be confident that Charity would stay with me.

My dragon hasn't sent her running, but my magic might.

And even if she accepted that part of me too, would she quickly change her mind when she found out that my mother had foretold her fiery death—at the hands of my own magic? The reminder of the vision sent a wave of stress and revulsion through me, and I shuddered.

Charity

I woke up slowly, my head amazingly dream-free for once. How embarrassing it would be if Anthony knew what sort of dreams I'd been having about him!

I pushed the bed covers off me. They were too hot and heavy now. Then I stumbled next door to use the bathroom and wash my face and hands. When I was done, the events of the morning suddenly hit me and I began to giggle, sounding strangely intoxicated. "He's a dragon... Like a real, dragon!"

On one level I couldn't really believe it, but everything I'd seen so far was real. His scales, and his wings beneath my bare hands, not to mention his shifting right before my eyes. And the gorgeous little town we'd walked around this morning together was straight out of a fairytale. As was the castle. It was huge, and like nothing from my own life.

A part of me imagined it was possible that I'd been knocked unconscious and was simply in some sort of complicated, long-term coma-dream, but it certainly didn't feel like it. Especially when every time I saw Anthony, a frisson of desire rippled over my skin. That awareness of him —on such a visceral level—felt more real than anything I'd ever experienced before.

By the time I walked back into the bedroom a female servant was laying a beautiful chocolate-brown dress out on the bed for me. "Hello," I said, walking up next to her and reaching for the crushed velvet. "Wow. This is beautiful."

The servant bobbed a little curtsey. "The queen thought you may want to change. Would you like some help getting into the dress?" The girl, who looked to be about sixteen, seemed sweet.

"Thank you," I said. "That would be great. I'm Charity, by the way."

"Elsa, ma'am." Elsa helped me into the dress that somehow fit me perfectly.

"How did you know my size?" I asked, brushing my hands over my waist and hips in wonder.

She smiled. "The queen guessed your measurements, and then I made this for you. If you would like a different color, or fabric, I can make you another."

I grinned at her. "Oh, no. This is perfect. Thank you."

"But what about tomorrow, ma'am?" Elsa asked, blinking at me.

"Tomorrow?"

Was I supposed to be staying tomorrow as well?

"Yes, as Prince Anthony's mate, surely you would like a whole new wardrobe?" The girl stared at me expectantly.

"Mate?" I repeated, my heart sinking in sudden foreboding. "What does that mean?"

Elsa cocked her head and frowned at me, then she gasped. "Oh, I shouldn't have said anything. You're a human and you must have different names for things. I... misspoke. Please forgive me, ma'am." She bobbed again and ran from the room.

I stared after her, feeling slightly numb and a little stupefied at the same time. "Mate?" I repeated it out loud. "She doesn't mean like, a friend, or..." I shook my head to clear my thoughts. The truth was I knew next to nothing about this world and its customs, and I needed to ask Anthony to clarify what Elsa had meant.

Memories of Anthony's beautiful blue-purple eyes within the dreams I'd had before I met him came back to haunt me, sending a shiver of awareness through my body. I needed to find out more about that too. The queen had begun to ask me, but Anthony had interrupted. I had many questions and no answers. Uncertainty ran rampant in my mind.

"Work!" The word spilled from my lips in sudden realization. I couldn't believe I'd forgotten! I had to find a phone. A moment later there was a knock at the door. I walked forward and pulled it open.

There was my dream man, right in front of me.

Oh, the things I've dreamed those lips have done to me...

"Lunch time?" I managed, though my voice caught in my throat.

He inclined his head in a short nod, watching me carefully, but he didn't say anything as I walked out of my room.

"Can you take me straight to your phone?" I asked. "I forgot about work!"

"Of course," he answered, stiffening up again, as he did every time I talked about home.

I made a mental note to ask him about that later, but right now I needed to focus on the phone call. I didn't want to imagine what had been going on at the restraint in my unexpected and unaccounted for absence.

He led me along a warren of hallways to a large and light-filled office.

I was surprised to find a modern computer, desk and multiple cell phones plugged into the power board. "Wow, you guys might live in a castle and wear medieval clothing, but you're really set up in a tech sense."

His grin was brief and disappeared almost as soon as it appeared. He gestured to the bank of cell phones. "Please, use whatever you need."

His arm was vibrating strangely, so I let go of him, picked up one of the phones and called the restaurant.

Tania answered.

"Hi Tania, it's Charity. How's everything going there?"

"Charity! Oh, my God, you're all right! Thank goodness. Where are you? What happened?"

I pulled out the desk chair and sat down, noting the fact that Anthony was hanging around and appeared to be listening intently.

"I'm... away," I hedged carefully. "I was attacked after work the other night, but someone found me and saved me."

There was silence on the phone before Tania whispered. "Was that the night one of our diners was attacked? Barry, I think his name was."

"I'm not sure," I said, my stomach tightening with tension. "I don't remember much. I took a few hits to the head so it's all a bit hazy. Why, what happened to Barry?"

"You were hit in the head!" Tania exclaimed. "By who?"

"I don't know," I lied, my heart racing. "But it could have been the same person. It was just after closing. What happened to Barry?"

"He was attacked too," Tania said. "He's unconscious in hospital at the moment with a cracked skull and broken ribs. They don't know if he's going to come out of the coma or not."

I closed my eyes, a strange wave of feeling washing over me. Was it happiness? Or apprehension? I wasn't sure, but I wasn't sorry that Barry had been so badly injured. Not when I knew what he'd tried to do to me. "That's no good," I managed at last, trying not to sound cold.

"When are you coming back?" Tania asked. "The restaurant's been really struggling without you."

My gut twisted this time, guilt hitting me hard. "Ah... I probably need another day, Tania. I'm still reeling and recovering from the attack."

"Oh shit! I'm *so* sorry, I can't believe I didn't think about that. I'll tell the big bosses that you need a week, and that'll make them send another manager from the city. Or should I say two weeks to give you time? Then they won't say no."

I opened my mouth to say that I didn't need a week, let alone two...

But then Anthony wandered over to the desk, his eyebrows raised high.

I could sense his interest in the discussion, and it made me hesitate. "Yeah, that's a great idea. Tell them I need two weeks, Tania," I said with a gulp as I turned away from Anthony's intent look and focused on the book-lined wall to one side of the desk. "Then at least they'll send you a decent manager to help keep things running. If I'm better sooner than that, I'll just come back in." That was the best solution. It gave me some time to work out what I'd fallen into over here, and my restaurant and the staff would be well handled too.

"Ask for Maree," I added. "She's tough, but fair. Thanks for taking care of things."

"No problem," Tania said. "I will. You just get better, Charity. Don't worry about us."

I huffed out a laugh. "I always worry about you, Tania."

She giggled into the phone. "I'm fine. Oh, I have to go. Delivery truck is here!"

"Okay, go. Talk to you later," I said.

She hung up seconds later.

I sat still for a moment, staring at the phone in my hand. They were fine without me, realistically. They wanted me there, sure. I made things easier for them all, but they'd survive without me with new leadership.

"Two weeks?" Anthony's hopeful voice sounded in the room.

I put the cell phone down, turned in the swivel chair and stood up. "Yes. But that was more for the sake of my staff than anything else. If I have any less than a week off, my bosses won't bother to replace my shifts. They'll just expect the staff to pick up the slack, and they can't. They need a manager there."

"I'm glad you're going to stay a bit longer," Anthony said, his voice soft now. Almost too quiet. "I was worried after this morning that you might wake up from your nap and demand to be taken home."

"Why?" I asked, shaking out my heavy skirt. "Because you turn into a dragon?" I shrugged. I'd dreamed of *a lot* worse things to admit. "It's all good, honestly. Lunch?"

Anthony's eyes widened as if I'd shocked him, but then he nodded and we walked to the dining room, where a table was set for two. "Your parents aren't joining us?" I asked.

He held out a chair for me like a gentleman.

I sat down, admiring the simple yet beautiful fare.

"My parents flew to a neighboring kingdom after breakfast this morning to visit my older brother who's living there with his wife at the moment."

I nodded as though I understood, though I didn't. "So, all the princes and princesses marry each other here? To keep the royal blood lines pure, or something like that?"

Anthony chuckled and reached for the jug of water. "Hardly! We each marry our fated mate, if we're lucky enough to find them. My brother just happened to be fated to a princess, whereas Prince Anselm just married a human woman. Someone from your world." He gulped and stopped talking, as if suspecting that he'd said too much.

I stared at him, my heart pounding a little faster. There was so much to unpack now. From the look on his face, he hadn't meant to blurt all that out, but it was obvious there was no subterfuge in his response.

"Um... what's a fated mate?" I pressed. That was my first, and most important, question. I needed to know.

Anthony began scooping food onto his plate, dropping his gaze so he was no longer looking at me. "It's the word we use for the person you're meant to marry. The one Fate has chosen for you. Together, you're perfect. They're like... a soul mate. Two halves of one whole."

There was so much emotion in his voice, I struggled to hold myself together.

Was that what the maid was talking about?

I took an even breath and carefully asked the next thing I needed to know. "And do you have a fated mate, Anthony?"

His gaze came up and clashed with mine, purple mist swirling in his blue eyes like magical fog.

My breath caught in my throat at the answer in his eyes. "But I'm human," I whispered. "You can't mean..."

"Yes. It's you," he answered, a deep growl behind his words. When he stood up, his chair scraped on the floor and he leaned forward, a soft rumble echoing in the room. It sounded like... a purr. Only, not like any purr I'd ever heard before.

I jumped to my feet and started backing toward the door, the hairs on my neck beginning to prickle in memory.

This is just like in my dream.

And even though I instinctively knew I'd just excited the hunter in Anthony, I couldn't stop from turning tail and running from the room. A squeal caught in my throat as I ran down the hallway and raced into a room I'd never been in before. My heart was pounding and my whole body was shaking as I twirled back to face the door—only to froze. I'd found the library.

The doors banged open behind me and Anthony prowled inside, big and strong and far too sexy for the confined space.

My breath was already coming in short gasps. His presence added to that, and I suddenly found it immensely difficult to breathe. I turned to run but he was too fast.

He grabbed me from behind, one arm locking across my chest, the other snaking around my hips. He held me captive against his big body and whispered in my ear. "Why are you running?"

I gasped as his voice, like in every dream and fantasy I'd had before now, it made my insides turn to molten lava. I wriggled against his body, feeling his erection press into the small of my back and countered with a question of my own. "Why are you chasing me?"

He spun me around, picked me up and carried me over to the desk in the center of the room where he set me down.

I intuitively opened my legs for him to step between them, our movements as natural as breathing. As though we'd done this dance a thousand times before. My hands slid up his arms until I could cup his jaw and bring him close.

He stopped inches away from my mouth.

I pulled on him, wanting him closer; on top of me and inside of me.

My dreams are about to come true!

"I have so much I need to tell you." His voice was a whisper, his eyes exactly as I remembered from my dreams. All blue and purple swirls, intense and full of desire.

I shuddered with the erotic memories of my dreams. "Later," I whispered back, lifting my chin so that my lips were a breath away from his. "Right now, I need you to kiss me."

He complied, his kiss hard and deep and full of yearning.

My eyes slid closed, and I moaned at our connection as I opened for him. His tongue swept between my lips, tasting my mine and making me shiver in delight. I tore at his shirt buttons, wanting to feel the heat of his skin against my hands.

He pulled back, staring down at me with a blazing intensity.

I wasn't letting him stop—not now—not after months of dreaming of this moment. Of waking up with an empty body and an even lonelier heart. I didn't care what obstacles lay between us in the future. They didn't matter now. I just needed this, more than anything else in the world. "Don't wait," I said, words I'd told him so many times before in my dreams. I pushed his jacket off his shoulders and opened his shirt, reaching for his pants and running my hands over the bulge of his cock. "Please."

His growl shook his chest as he reached for my heavy skirts, pulling them up around my waist. Then his hands slid up over my thighs and his mouth claimed mine once more.

I kissed him hard, sucking on his tongue, reveling in the impossible sensation and fantasy of the moment.

Anthony's fingers dipped between my legs, teasing the hot and aching flesh there.

I gasped against his mouth, my clit throbbing desperately for his attention.

"Lay back," he commanded as he broke our kiss and pushed me to lie down on the desk.

A wave of heat flooded my cheeks, but I did as he said, lying down on the mahogany desk with my legs spread and my skirts bunched up around my underwear.

Anthony pulled at the strings on my bodice, opening the front and releasing my breasts like he'd been born to the skill. He squeezed my sensitive nipples and cupped my breasts.

I cried out with pleasure. God, he made me crazy for him.

Please, oh please!

I was ready to beg.

His hand moved between my thighs, pushing aside my underwear to slide a long finger inside me.

I screamed at the intimate touch, heedless of who else was in the castle, and arched my back, my pussy tightening around his finger as he pressed up inside me.

"God, you're so wet." Anthony groaned above me. "I can't wait to make you come all over my cock."

I covered my face with my hands, mortification and desire mixing and making me shudder with an inner fire.

Anthony kneeled on the floor and urged my thighs open wider.

I bucked beneath his hand, unable to stay still.

He finally pressed his lips to my swollen clit.

I cried out, grabbing hold of his hair to bring myself closer to his heavenly mouth.

He licked me slowly at first, building the orgasm inside of me like a master. Then he began moving his fingers, finding my g-spot and flicking his tongue on my clit at the same time until the pleasure reached maddening heights.

I was going to come. The tension in my legs was winding up and my belly was so tight I felt like it would break. With each thrust of his finger and each swipe of his tongue, he pushed me closer to Heaven. "Anthony... I'm going to..."

He stopped with the wicked ministrations of his mouth and removed his fingers, bringing me back from the brink of orgasm. But he didn't leave me empty long. He was already pulling his cock out of his pants and guiding the head to my entrance. "Not without me," he growled.

I gasped at the thickness of his cock as he thrust inside of me and lifted my legs to allow him deeper.

He reached for my thighs, pushing them back and opening me wide.

I groaned in unbridled pleasure as he filled me, reaching every aching part of my pussy and making me grip his forearms in a frantic and breathless plea. "Don't stop. Please don't stop!"

He pulled back and thrust into me again in one long move, hammering home to the hilt over and over.

I called out his name, again and again. With every thrust of his hips, he drove his thick, long cock into my wet pussy until my thoughts disintegrated and there was only rampant, raw need.

He reached between us and flicked his thumb over my clit, working it like a demon. It was too much.

My pussy clamped down on him and I was thrown into chaotic oblivion, screaming out my pleasure as he fucked me straight through my orgasm, wringing out every cry of pleasure from my lips.

Then he was fucking me harder, and harder, his own orgasm chasing him, driving him deeper and faster.

I moved against him, rocking my hips and taking him as deeply as I could. I stared up at him through lust-slitted eyes, drunk with my own pleasure.

A heartbeat later, he threw back his head and roared out his own ecstasy, the sound echoing throughout the library.

Hot spasms pulsed inside of me, throwing me into yet another round of smaller orgasms, my body desperately milking Anthony's cock for every last drop as we jerked and bucked in each other's hot embrace.

He collapsed forward, into my arms, still buried deep inside of me.

I wrapped my arms around his back, holding him close. His heart beat rapidly in his chest, the sweat coating his face and arms making him smell even more delicious than he had before. And as we came down together, the only sound in the room was that of our heavy breathing, replacing the creaking noises of the desk moments earlier.

When he finally lifted his head, his eyes were the most purple I'd ever seen them.

I cupped his face and stared at them. "God, you're beautiful."

He chuckled and gently prized himself out of my arms and back to standing, though he still stayed between my thighs. "You're the one who's beautiful, Charity." He said the words with such reverence, as if he meant every last one. The way he stroked my body as he spoke made me believe him even more.

I smiled up at him, feeling the need to be real, and honest in our post orgasmic bliss. "It was your eyes, you know..." I sighed. "I've been dreaming about you for so long. And when we met, I knew it was you."

"What do you mean?" Anthony whispered, already pulling away from me.

I sat up, confused, my brows furrowing. "I recognized you because of your eyes. The purple swirls in your eyes. They were just like that in all my dreams..."

ELEVEN

Anthony

I pulled up my trousers and fastened them quickly, fear whistling through my veins. "What do you mean, purple? I have blue eyes." I knew exactly what she was talking about, of course, and yet everything inside of me shouted out in denial. I was a dragon shifter—not a sorcerer. I didn't want my mother's curse. I didn't want purple eyes!

Charity pushed her skirts back down, a frown still marring her lovely face as covered her creamy thighs, then hopped off the desk. "Ah... what are you getting all upset about? I'm confused."

She was right. I *was* upset, and I couldn't put a lid on it. I grabbed for my shirt and my jacket, trying to distract myself by dressing so that I would have the chance to calm down. It didn't work at all. I was piquing it. "I'm fine."

"You're not fine," she snapped back, her gaze narrowed. "One minute we're having this beautiful moment and I'm telling you something important, and then you..." she waved her hand around instead of finishing.

"What?" I demanded, whirling on her and misdirecting my anger. "What did I do wrong?"

Her frown deepened. "I don't understand what's going on right now at all, Anthony. What aren't you telling me?"

"I..." My throat closed and I pushed the feeling of anxiety away. "Do not..." I shook myself, my need desperate need to fly away from here clamping down on me like a vise grip. I was losing control and fast. "I..."

"You what, Anthony?" She didn't understand why I needed to leave.

I had to, before I shifted inside the small library and hurt her. Unable to explain myself, I ran for the door. and

Charity followed me.

I ran for all I was worth, through the foyer and out onto the castle steps. There, I gave up and gave in. I didn't have the strength to fight the war waging within me between my shifter and my magic—so I let my dragon take over. He filled me up, swallowing me whole as my magic pulsed within me with too much intensity to contain.

No! I don't want this magic.

It was a curse. I was a freak.

No man has magic! How can I be the man my fated mate needs if I'm so different?

My mate stood on the top step of the castle stairs, staring at me with obvious confusion, tears in her eyes.

I didn't want to hurt her, so I opened my wings and took to the sky to vent my frustration and fly off my panic.

When will I finally be able to be me? When will she be safe from me? And how long do I have to wait until my mother will take away this curse and give us the chance to be together?

My thoughts ran wild. There was no escaping their torment. A dark cloud of guilt and feelings of being ostracized ate away at me. So, I flew and flew, until my body ached and my heart hurt; and only then, when I was already close to my limit did I turn around to glide all the way home.

When I finally arrived and shifted back to human form, I could barely lift my arms.

It was dark and the inside of the castle roared with the heat of various fireplaces, all lit and crackling with local firewood.

"Can I help you to your room, sire?" asked Thomas, one of our many servants.

I shook my head wearily. "No, but thank you." I could have used the help, but I was too ashamed to accept the strength the servant offered. And all I could think about now was that Charity was going to hate me when she found out that I'd lied to her about my magic, that I hadn't shared my issues with her—the woman who was my perfect mate. And even if I hadn't directly lied, I'd deliberately kept the truth from her, and withholding information was just as bad.

Despite my extreme exhaustion from the flight, I managed to get to my bedroom and practically fell into the shower, making the water as hot as I could stand it in an attempt to wash away the unclean mire of my thoughts. Despite the heat of the shower, I couldn't stop shaking. For a long time my body felt like the cold of the outside air had seeped inside me and filled my bones with ice.

Eventually, though, the hot water pummeling me from the shower head defrosted me all the way to my core. And I stayed under its steady stream until I could no longer physically stand. Instead, I sank to the floor and sat on the tiles beneath the heat; exhausted, devastated, overwhelmed, and somehow empty all at once.

What have I done?

"What in the gods' names are you doing?" A loud voice interrupted my reverie.

Carlak?

What was my brother doing here?

"Well?" he demanded again, stomping into the bathroom and leaning into the shower to turn off the tap with an angry flick of his wrist. "You've used a whole kingdom's worth of water. Were you seriously *that* dirty from your flight?"

I stared up at my older brother, shocked that he was back home. I'd thought he was away and quite frankly he was the last person I expected to see. Worry and misery coursed through my veins, making it almost impossible to speak, but I tried. "Carlak... I..."

With a hefty sigh he offered me a hand and heaved me to my feet. "Let's get you dry, warm, and into bed. Seriously, though, Anthony. I leave the castle for a single month and your whole life apparently falls off the edge of the world?" My brother grumbled away, shaking his head and acting like an old mother hen.

I didn't stop him. In fact, the fuss was reassuring in a strange way. Carlak was three years older than me and had always been the classic older brother. The intelligent, overly confident boy who everyone knew would one day be the king of his people. He was the responsible one. Not me. I'd never had to be, as the perennial prince. The kingdom didn't rest upon my shoulders, but his.

Finally, as he pulled back the covers and pushed me into bed, I found my voice.

"How are the twins?" I asked.

"They're fine. Don't worry about my family, little brother. It's time to worry about your own."

"Mine?" I asked in confusion. "I don't have a family. Not like that, anyway." And I feared my mate would never love me now that she knew what sort of abomination I was. Let alone the fact I was a coward, always flying away from his own problems. I was no prize prince, that's for sure.

Carlak dragged a chair from a corner of the room and set it beside my bed. There he sat, his brow furrowed and twisted as he stared at me with obvious concern. "Not yet, you don't," he said. "But you have a mate, and if you're lucky, you'll have a child soon enough. What are you doing flying around aimlessly, until you're so exhausted you can barely make it back home? What possessed you do something so stupid when your mate is here?"

I shuffled into bed to hide my discomfort, rearranging the blankets fruitlessly. I hated hearing the disappointment in his voice. In grated on my already fragile nerves and made me loathe myself even more. "How do you know all that?"

"Mother had another vision," Carlak said, as though that was a run of the mill type of thing.

It was of course—for our family—but what if Charity heard him, what would she think?

"She's worried about you, little brother. And she's even *more* worried about what's going to happen between you and Charity."

I sighed and let my head fall back against my pillow. "Thank you for coming to check on me, brother, but I'm okay. I just... needed to fly today. To get out. Get away."

Anthony groaned and muttered something incoherent.

I lifted my head and met Carlak's angry gaze.

"What are you running from?" He blasted the question at me, his words now clear as day. "Seriously, Anthony. You're always hiding and keeping yourself in check. And for what? You're not the Crown Prince. Of the two of us, you're the one who's meant to be the wild one! You're meant to be having fun and living your life free as a bird. So, what are you so worried about?"

I couldn't answer him. Truthfully, I didn't want to, but my magic had other ideas. It swelled inside of me, seeking a place amongst my family. Where it had always wanted to be. "Carlak, I..."

"Whoa. What's happening with your eyes?" He craned his neck to get a closer look.

I jerked away, staring down at my lap. Fury rushed through me at my magic's betrayal. I just wanted it to disappear, to die a quick death. And yet, it seemed to be growing stronger, more out of control than ever before and determined to make itself known. "It's nothing," I muttered, not daring to look up.

Carlak grunted. "You know, your eyes used to do that magic thing when we were kids. Just the same as Mom's... I just didn't say anything."

My head came up fast, my eyes wide. "What are you saying?"

Carlak rolled his eyes. "I'm your brother, Anthony. I shared a room with you for years. Did you seriously think you could hide your magic powers from me? Really?"

"I don't have magic!" I exclaimed, even though I knew it was stupid to deny something he was obviously already aware of. But when it came to my magic, my default setting seemed to be to lie about it. It was a touchy subject, something I'd never accepted, something that felt like a parasite in my soul and not a gift.

Carlak glared at me. "You're sitting there, lying to my damn face, when we both know the truth. I can't believe it. You've got some nerve brother." He got up, flicked his jacket to straighten it, and stalked toward the door.

"Hey! Where are you going?" I called out. "Did you seriously just fly all the way home to call me a liar, then leave again?"

Carlak turned to stare at me. He would be a great king, when the time came. He'd always been able to cow just about anyone since he was six years old with *that* look. "You *are* a liar, Anthony," he said, more gently than I expected. "You just lied to me, but saddest of all, you're lying to yourself. You've been denying who you are."

Shock coursed through me at his words. Shock... and shame. He was right, but denying my magic was so ingrained in me that I didn't know how *not* to do that. I was different and didn't want to be. Why did no one seem to understand?

He shook his head when I didn't respond. "I came home to see if I could help you, but it's obvious you're past the point of no-return. I'm sorry, brother." Then Carlak turned to leave again after delivering his cryptic pronouncement.

I groaned and ran my hand down my face. "What the hell does that mean?"

"It means grow up, Anthony," Carlak snapped at the threshold. "Face up to your demons, acknowledge who you are, and stop being afraid of it! Claim your mate, and seriously... grow the fuck up." On that note he left and slammed the door for good measure.

I sat amongst my warm blankets staring after him, my cheeks blazing. Everything he'd said was true and it hurt more than it should have. I was a lying spoilt, and immature prince—and it *was* time I grew up.

Is this how Charity sees me, too?

I needed to go see her and check if she was okay. I'd left in a huff, right after sex, and never given her an explanation. She was likely irate, and I wouldn't blame her for it. I threw back the covers and rushed to throw on some clothes. Where was Charity right now, anyway? When I'd left her...

I froze, one leg in my pants as the full impact of what I'd done to her hit me like a lightning bolt. "Oh, my God." I'd made passionate love to her, then abandoned her. And worse, I'd rejected her emotions and needs by flying away without so much as a backward glance. All because I was afraid of showing her my true self, including the magic inside of me.

But Charity wasn't of our world. To her, shifting into a dragon most likely seemed magical. Why would she be worried about whether I had a different kind of magic to other dragon shifters? If she hadn't judged me for morphing into a dragon, why would she judge me for anything else?

Shit. I've been a fool!

And Carlak? Fuck me. When had he worked out that I had the same powers as our mother? Why hadn't he ever said anything?

I'd been lying about my magic for so long, I felt trapped, and the longer it went on, the more terrified I'd become that I would be revealed to be a liar and a freak. But I *was* lying, and he'd always known it. And yet, he'd never stopped caring about me.

How have I fucked up so royally?

I owed my brother an apology, but my mate was my number one priority. I finished pulling on my pants, cold chills of dread creeping down my spine. I needed to find Charity and now.

Memories of our lovemaking began to smash through my brain, leaving my breathless. The pleasure and our connection. The way she'd moaned and shook and orgasmed around my cock.

Damn it.

The time we'd spent together in the library—however brief—had been the single most amazing experience of my life.

And I went and fucked it all up!

As soon as my sweater was over my head, I ran for the door. I pulled it open, slowed to a jog, and headed for the stairs that led back up to my mother's old tower. Would Charity still be there?

When I reached the door to her room, my heart was pounding. But I didn't stop to think. I would only start second-guessing myself, then. Instead, I knocked loudly and boldly, and pushed the door open, ready for a book to be thrown at my head, or something like it. The sight before me broke my heart in two.

Charity was lying on the bed, sobbing. The sounds, clearly wrenched from deep inside her, were bone-crushing to hear.

I swallowed hard, pushing the sudden lump down in my throat. "Sweetheart, I am *so* sorry."

As soon as my words found her, Charity scrabbled up to sit on the edge of the bed, her hands clutching at the bedcovers. "Get out of here," she said and her eyes flashed.

If I was reading her correctly, it seemed like she hated me. I couldn't blame her. *I* hated myself for what I'd done. My preciousness and inability to adapt, to become who I was always meant to be had potentially ruined everything. "Please, Charity, let me explain."

"No!" she yelled. "I don't want you to explain. I just want to get out of here. I want to go home."

Home? To the human world? Back to her thankless job and her tiny, sad apartment? "I did the wrong thing, and I know I totally fucked up." I walked toward her, holding out my hands to placate her. "Our lovemaking was absolutely beautiful, and I—" A small marble carving sailed at me, and I barely ducked out of its way before it smashed into the wall behind me.

"I don't want to hear it!" she cried out, her voice stricken and thick with emotion. "I've been dreaming about you for months... *months*, Anthony! And you don't even care about me. I thought we were meant to be, or some crap like that. You almost had me convinced. Almost..." She stopped talking and a loud sob escaped her lips.

"But we *are* meant to be!" I exclaimed, staying where I was and readying myself to duck out of the way again if I needed to. "We're fated mates. That's the truth."

"Well, I don't care anymore," she sobbed. "I just want to go home and get away from you. I want to return to my normal, boring life. No more fancy castles, dragons, magic, royalty, or anything else!"

"All right. I'll take you home," I said, though it hurt me to even say the words. "But please, *please*... just let me explain first?"

Her lower lip trembled, and her gaze found the floor.

I could see by her expression that she was seriously considering my offer.

Eventually she crossed her arms over her chest and glared at me, deferring to her hurt and pain to protect her heart. "Fine. Explain yourself. Then you can take me home."

I didn't want to remind her that taking her home would mean carrying her into the human realm, probably on my back, in my shifter form. Today had already been fraught with enough worry. She'd given me the chance to explain, so now I had to give her a reason to stay.

I took a deep breath, to steady myself. "I'm going to tell you the whole truth, and it's a long-ish story. Are you okay with that?"

She nodded, her lips pursed. "Just get on with it, Anthony."

"Okay... so, my mother is, well, she's a sorceress."

"A... what?" She blinked at me, like I'd spoken in a foreign language. And to her, I guess it was.

My heart started to race as anxiety riddled me. I'd never openly discussed this, and I wanted to get it right. The last thing I wanted was to scare her off. In the end, I decided to keep it simple. "Mom has magic."

"Like you being a dragon shifter? That sort of magic?"

"Not exactly."

"Then, um, what *is* a sorceress? Is it like... a witch or something? I think I've heard the word in a story once before."

"Sort of. She has magical powers for healing, and she can see prophecies, and the future—things like that." It was a power that she considered a blessing and curse in one.

But I had only ever seen it as a curse.

Charity's eyebrows drew together as she considered what I'd said. "She used her magic to heal me from Barry's attack, didn't she?"

I nodded, wanting her to understand.

Her expression cleared. "Well, that sounds kind of cool."

Now it was my turn to frown. "You don't... hate the very idea of it?" I asked.

"Why would I? I mean, yes, it's a shock, I'm from the human realm. But to be honest it was more of a shock to see you turn into a dragon than anything else I've experienced recently. Your mom is lovely, and she helped me in a time of need. That's pretty special, actually and I'm grateful to her for that."

"Well, yes, I suppose it could be seen that way. But my mother grew up with people using her for her abilities, and she can't shift."

Charity shrugged. "Yeah? And? And I missing something here?"

She obviously didn't understand. "Being a dragon shifter is the only thing that ties us all together, everyone in this realm. My mother was alone and felt very out of place. She was a freak among her own people."

Charity groaned, the sound full of frustration. "Anthony, can you get to the point? I'm a human! I was a waitress who worked her way up to being a manager. I didn't go to college. I'm used to hard work and pain-in-the-ass customers. Not magic and flying around the sky! So, spit it out already." She waved her hands around like she was conducting a spell herself.

Then the thought struck me. She had known what I looked like before meeting me in person... "Charity, you said you dreamed of me, right, before we met?"

She nodded, then a wash of redness flushed her cheeks.

"What sort of dreams?" I asked, suspicious of that blush. I suspected that we weren't simply *conversing* with one another in those dreams.

"None of your business," she snapped, confirming they must have been sexual in nature. "Get to your point," she added. "You have five minutes left to explain, or I'll find someone else to fly me home. You said everyone in the whole castle is a dragon shifter, right? Even the girls?"

I nodded, sick to my stomach at the idea that she would even consider flying away from me. "Yes. Someone will take you home, though I'd prefer to be the one if you still want to leave after I've finished."

She rolled her eyes and made a circular motion with her hand, gesturing for me to hurry the fuck up.

I shook myself.

Get to the point.

"Okay, so, basically, I... I... Oh fuck, this is harder to admit than I thought." I cleared my throat.

Damn it. Just say it.

"That purple swirl you see sometimes in my eyes? It's magic." The words were finally out, and I stumbled through the rest of my explanation. "I inherited my mother's magic, as well as my father's ability to shift. But I've been hiding my magic since, forever, since I was a child. I don't want it, Charity. In fact, I *hate* it. I've always hated it and kept it hidden from everyone except my parents."

There. I've gotten it all out.

It wasn't quite the relief I was hoping for, but it certainly felt like a weight lifted from my shoulders and that was something.

"But why do you hate it?" she asked, which from a human was probably a fair question.

"Because it makes me a freak in this world," I told her honestly, keeping it as simple as possible. "My mom is awesome, but she can't shift. Everyone else here can shift, but they don't have magic. You see? Yet somehow, I've ended up having both abilities, my mother's and father's. I'm different from everyone, and I don't want to be."

I took a deep breath and released it slowly. "When you saw my magic after we made love... the purple in my eyes, I lost control. I know I shouldn't have, I'm sorry. And I know you don't really understand, but I've been hiding this part of myself for my whole life, and the fact that it's now just coming to the surface whenever it wants…" I shuddered. "It scares me."

She narrowed her eyes. "So let me get this straight. You're, like, some super powerful dragon shifter, who just happens to have magic as well… making you truly incredible. And you're upset by all your awesome gifts because others don't have them? So, you worked yourself up and freaked yourself out badly enough to abandon me immediately after the most amazing sex… ever?"

Well… when she puts it like that…

I risked a smile at her, even as heat bloomed in my cheeks. "It *was* the most amazing sex ever. Every kiss, and every touch told me that you're mine, and I'm yours. It was… perfect, Charity."

"So perfect that you couldn't wait to run away from me the second we were done?" She swiped at new tears on her cheeks as if angry they'd fallen.

"I'm *so* sorry. But will you please forgive me, now that you understand why?"

"No, Anthony. I don't forgive you, and that bullshit you just gave me…? Well, let's just say if your parents were here, I'd give them a right talking to!"

"My parents?"

She began to undress, pushing her warm dress to the floor and opening a drawer to pull out the jeans and sweater that she'd worn here that very first day. The servants must have washed out the blood and grime and returned the garments to her. She pulled on her jeans, wriggling into them.

My gaze went straight to her gorgeous body as she covered it up. I wished I'd been able to have her completely naked beneath me. I would have loved every inch of her. Those delicious breasts and curvy hips. I hadn't been able to see all of her in the library since she'd still worn her dress.

She tugged on her sweater and moved to grab a warm jacket from the closet. "Yes, your parents," she said, answering the question I'd forgotten I'd just asked. Her brief nudity had distracted my thoughts.

"How could they let you get away with lying to yourself, and everyone else around you?"

I put a hand to my head, pressing against a sudden throbbing behind my temple. "What are you talking about?"

She pulled the warm jacket on and flicked the hood up over her long dark hair. "I'm talking about the fact that even children are taught better logic than that. At least, they are in the human world. You have been given these incredible gifts—the gift of magic as well as shifting—and basically, you just don't want it? You don't want to be one of a kind? You don't want to be special? Well, *bad bloody luck*! You should have been honest with everyone from the start and celebrated your magic instead of hiding who you are! Honestly, you're an idiot, and so is anyone who helped you hide an essential part of yourself."

She shook her head and pulled on fur-lined gloves she must have been given by one of the servants. "Now... take me home."

"But, I—"

"No." She held her hand out in front of her to stop me. "I listened. That was the deal. And if I'm completely honest, I think you're full of shit. I'm not going to fall in love with an idiot who's spent his whole life denying who he is and runs away the moment anyone recognizes just how special he is. Now. Are you flying me home, or am I finding another dragon to take me?"

Anger and anguish flared at the same time within my heart, fighting for supremacy, combining and growing in size.

My mate is rejecting me. She's leaving me.

My dragon and my sorcerer fought inside my human form and the fire they both created burned in my veins, desperate for release.

TWELVE

Charity

Sudden flames flared bright within Anthony's eyes and fear struck at my core like a knife to my diaphragm. I'd pushed him too far and he was fast losing control. No one could keep so much power inside themselves, deny it, hate it, and expect it to disappear without a trace! Even I knew that.

I wasn't familiar with everything in this world, but it was clear as the purple eyes in the prince's face that he was losing the battle against his magic. His dragon was beautiful, and obviously powerful; but his mother's magic thrived inside of him too... and it had been deprived of freedom and denied for far too long.

My chest rose and fell as panic set in, and my breathing came in panting breaths. My heart was hammering against my ribs like a frantic drum and adrenaline zinged along my nerves. I needed to put space between us— and fast—before Anthony did something to destroy us both.

The bedroom door was mercifully still open, so I inhaled a breath for good luck, and made a desperate run for it.

Blazing flames shot from Anthony's fingers as I ran past him, catching the plush carpet alight.

I screamed as I hurtled over the fire and bolted through the door and out in the hall. I raced down the stairs, my mind racing as I headed toward the front foyer.

I must find help!

I couldn't leave Anthony to burn down the castle. Or worse, to burn himself up. He'd denied an integral part of himself for so long that he could no longer control it, and I wouldn't have him bring an end to everything because of a stupid mistake.

There was a man standing with the butler, by the front entrance. He looked different to the servants. He was taller and wore clothes that spoke of wealth.

I grabbed his arm, gasping for air. "It's Anthony. He needs help! Please."

The man's blue eyes trained on my face.

I immediately knew who he was. "You're Carlak."

He nodded in recognition. "And you're Charity."

I nodded frantically in return. "Please. You've got to help him."

Carlak started running toward the stairs, not waiting for an answer; he asked on the move. "What happened?"

I ran behind him, breathless with worry. But still, I managed to answer him. "I think it's his magic. It's taking over! And he doesn't know how to control it." I was guessing, of course, but that explanation made the most sense to me based on what little I knew. Especially when I remembered the bright purple sparking in his eyes as I'd made a run for it.

Carlak paused at the base of the stairs, the scent of smoke filled the air. "That stupid bastard," he growled, then began taking the stairs two at a time.

I was right on his heels, my heart racing in my chest. I'd never moved so fast in my life. Outside of the attack in the alleyway after work, I'd never faced such a time-sensitive emergency. "Where is he?" I yelled out to Carlak when we both reached the top of the stairs. I covered my mouth and began to cough from the smoke as it burned my eyes and throat. It was everywhere, filling the halls and the rooms. But I still couldn't see Anthony anywhere.

"I think he's on the balcony!" Carlak called, pointing ahead of him, down the hallway.

Dredging up my courage, I took a deep breath and ran through the smoke, down the long carpet runner, in the direction Carlak had pointed. I knew I shouldn't be anywhere near this danger as a mere human, but I couldn't help but feel that this was my fault. And I couldn't bear the thought of something happening to Anthony.

He had lost control, all because I'd called him out on something that had been torturing him since he was child. Wrong or not, misguided or not, he was clearly in immense amounts of inner turmoil and pain. And I'd done nothing to help him. In fact, I'd made it worse. In my own anguish and feelings of rejection, I'd lashed out at him. Rightly so, maybe, but this was going to have devastating consequences—I could already tell.

The heat of the flames in the hallway made me flinch, but I kept running, kept pushing forward. The smoke made my eyes tear up, but I ducked and weaved around the flames until I burst through the open door and out onto the balcony.

Carlak was close behind me.

I turned a moment later to see if he was coming but an intense wall of fire and smoke rose up, cutting him off from my sight. I blew out gasping breaths, trying to steady myself and stave off panic. The night air out here in comparison to the fire inside was freezing. I shivered in shock, then turned back to find Anthony standing on the balustrade, still dressed, and there was no sign of his dragon.

"Hey," I called out, still gulping for breath, but trying to remain as calm as possible. "What are you doing out here?"

"You shouldn't have come back," Anthony said, his voice a deep growl. He didn't turn around.

I put my hand to my chest, my heart thundering beneath my hand. We were so far up. I had learned that this was the highest tower in the castle. And it was a very, very long way down. "Are you planning on flying us to safety?" I asked. "Because I'm not sure I can get back the way I came." I glanced behind me, amazed that I was managing to have such a calm conversation when the fire was burning up the castle.

Anthony didn't say anything, but his anguish permeated the air between us. He wanted me to leave, so he could stay here in his tower of solitude, stewing on his feelings. He likely wanted to be left to burn up, to escape his problems—to be free of the freak he believed himself to be.

But I wasn't having that. It was time to change tact. I'd seen *so* much beauty in this man, and I had to find a way to reach the prince who wanted my love.

He has to be inside there still...

"How strong is this fated mate bond you've been talking about?" I asked, shivering out of fear rather than because of the icy cold air. I could still feel the hot furnace behind me, threatening to engulf us whole.

"There's no stronger bond than that of a fated mate pair," Anthony said, then slowly turned, his eyes glowing with a silvery magic I'd never seen before. Previously, his eyes had flared purple.

Is this his true magic? Is he finally letting it free?

"Nothing stronger," he repeated.

"Really?" I asked, finding my strength as I crossed my arms over my chest. "Then why are you burning down the castle where your mate is?"

He pressed his lips into a thin line, remaining silent.

"What was your plan, huh?" I continued, because it was obvious he couldn't or wouldn't answer. "Burn it all and then fly away again? Or were you intending to go down in the flames too?"

He shook his head.

"Then what?" I asked, desperate to know just how dark his thoughts had turned, to see what I was dealing with. "Were you going to end it all and throw yourself off the edge?"

He didn't move or rebut my statement.

My heart gave a frightened lurch. I went on as if he'd confirmed my suspicion. "Wouldn't your dragon save you, Anthony? If you threw your-self off the edge here, would you not simply shift and fly away? Your dragon wouldn't let you die."

He shrugged. "I don't know anymore. My magic is too powerful now. I can't stop it. Maybe it would let me die? I'm not worthy of it."

I frowned at him, trying not to show how much his mood was scaring me. "You're not making any sense, Anthony. You've finally found me, and now you're just going to give up on life? On *us*?"

"You rejected me," he croaked, his voice thick with emotion. "You don't want to stay with me. You want to go home... to the human world, which you have every right to do." He sounded hollow and depressed, as if he'd lost his will and heart.

It brought tears to my eyes. I stamped my foot, desperate to get through to him, then regretted the action as pain coursed up my ankle. "Stop being such a drama queen, Anthony! We had a fight because I was mad at you—and rightly so. You made love to me, then left me! I'm allowed to be angry, but that doesn't mean you just give up on us. None of us are without flaws and couples have fights! It's normal."

His eyes burned with a fiery glow that slowly turned more red than silver. "You don't want to go home anymore?"

"Well, I kind of still do," I muttered. "But only because you're being an idiot. If you pull yourself together and deal with all this shit about your magic and stuff, then I'll stay. I mean, after all, we're meant to be together, aren't we?" I sounded like the idiot to my own ears, waxing lyrical about us being fated, but this meant something in his world, and I had to get him to listen to reason.

Anthony jumped down, landing on the stones in front of me. "But I'm an abomination."

I rolled my eyes. "You are not. You're perfect."

"Perfect?" he whispered.

"Well, for me anyway." I flipped my hair back off my face. I was sweating as the heat grew more intense. Everything was sticking to me. I couldn't tell if it was just because of the fire behind us, or the nervous tension of our possible impending doom. But right this second, I was glad of the frigid air. "Isn't that how the fated mate thing works?" I pressed. "If you're a freak, then I must be too! If fate makes no mistakes, then we're perfectly matched just the way we are."

"Anthony!" Carlak's scream penetrated our conversation.

Anthony and I jerked and turned to face the door, just as a wooden beam cracked and broke amidst the fire.

I cried out, falling back against Anthony's chest. "Your brother's still in there. You need to stop the inferno or he'll die!"

"I don't know how," he breathed, sounding desperate. But he pushed me protectively behind him and rushed toward the flames with the obvious intention of trying to help his brother regardless. He might be afraid, but it was clear he'd fight for his family—for the people he loved—and that said a lot about the man within.

"You *do* know how! You have to trust yourself!" I screamed out. "You made the fire with your magic. You can use your magic to stop it, too. I believe in you, Anthony!" I had no idea how magic realistically worked, but we had to save Carlak, and the castle, before it all collapsed into dust, taking everyone along with it. I grabbed Anthony's arm and yelled above the sound of the inferno blazing around us. "You said you're more powerful than you ever realized. You can use that power to save your brother!"

"I'm afraid," Anthony whispered, though I heard it as clear as day.

"Not as afraid as I am, or your brother is!" I cried, tears streaming down my face. I didn't know where the next words came from, perhaps a mixture of my dreams and everything I'd learned since I'd arrived. Or perhaps it was simply intuition. But I tapped into every bit of inner knowledge I had. Anthony needed me as much as I needed him. He'd saved my life and given me a second chance the night he found me. Now it was my turn to show him the way home again.

"Stop denying who you are and step up! You might not be the next king, but you're still a prince of the Black Mountains. And you're also the most powerful sorcerer this world has ever known! Use that and do some *good*!"

Anthony stared at me for a second as if digesting the hard truth with an open mind for the first time in his life, then turned to the fire and roared, thrusting his arms out in front of him and calling back the flames.

I stumbled back, staring in awe as flames blazed in Anthony's palms and he drew the fire from the tower and back into himself.

The moment all the flames were gone, he groaned, collapsing to his knees.

I grabbed for his shoulder and squeezed it tight. "You did it! Well done!"

"Go." He groaned again, hugging his middle as if in unfathomable pain. "Find Carlak."

I nodded and moved quickly, but cautiously. Smoke still filled the hallway, but I found Anthony's brother with ease. He had collapsed against a wall, and he didn't appear to be breathing. Frantically, I ran my hands over him. He didn't have any wounds that I could feel or see. His pulse was thin and weak, but it was still there.

In desperation I rolled him onto his side and belted him on the back between the shoulder blades, but it was no use. His lungs were obviously filled with smoke, and I couldn't clear them out on my own. "Anthony!" I screamed. "I need you! We've got to get him into the clear air. Help me!" I scrambled to my feet and grabbed Carlak's wrists, then began tugging him with all my might in the direction of the balcony. It was the only source of fresh air available.

He was so heavy, but I hefted him along, desperate to get him outside. "Help!" I screamed. I couldn't have my mate's brother—the future king— die on my watch.

Pounding sounded on the stairs as men ran to our aid.

"Help me get him to the balcony!" I cried.

Two of the servants lifted their future king with their combined strength and hauled him into the fresh air.

I pressed a frantic hand to his chest. "He's still not breathing. Anthony, you've got to help him. Do something!"

Anthony was as pale as a bottle of milk, clearly still recovering from the effort of containing the fire, but he crawled over to his brother and set his hands hovering over Carlak's chest area. He closed his eyes and gasped out, sounding as though he were physically drawing Carlak's pain and suffering into him just as he'd absorbed the fire. His hands glowed with silvery-white light as black tendrils of smoke lifted through Carlak's shirt and drifted up into Anthony's palms.

The servants gasped in unison, falling back. "The prince has magic!"

"Yes, he does!" I snapped at them, pinning them with my gaze. "And he's saving your future king's life, so you better hope his magic is as strong as your queen's!" I had no idea how strong Marienne's magic was, but when the servants bowed their heads, I knew I'd said the right thing.

Shocking us all, Carlak suddenly began to cough, then gasp for breath, his chest shuddering with effort.

"Sit him up!" I cried, rushing for his back and pushing him up.

The servants helped me get him to a seated position and stepped back.

He coughed some more, clearing his lungs. Finally, he opened his eyes.

Anthony fell forward, his head on his brother's thigh, his shoulders shaking with the strength of his emotions and the sheer effort and power required to save his brother.

Carlak stared down at Anthony, then up at me where I crouched next to them both.

"Are you okay?" I asked Carlak.

He nodded, then slowly put his hand on Anthony's head, resting it there in a show of reassurance to his younger sibling. "It's okay, brother. Everything's going to be okay."

With a shuddering sigh of relief, I crawled around him to Anthony,

He had rolled off Carlak, knelt in the position of prayer, and began to weep, letting out years' worth of denial and anguish.

I wrapped my arms around my mate's back and wept with him.

THIRTEEN

Anthony

I'd almost killed my brother, destroyed our family's home, and lost my mate. All because I couldn't control the magic I'd been born with. The resentment and shame that had built up over the years with my denial had almost ended us all.

Unexpectedly, a loud whooshing sound met my ears. I looked up into the sky to see my father flying toward us at a furious pace. I swiped at the tears on my face and straightened my back before standing and assisting Charity to her feet beside me.

Carlak climbed to his feet, too, and the three of us stood watching as Dad descended.

He hovered over us and turned so that we could see Mom on his back.

Her was face aghast. "Oh, my boys." She materialized beside us a moment later, her arms wrapping around both our shoulders. "My big, brave sons. I'm *so* glad you're both all right, and you too, dear Charity."

"Should we go inside?" Charity suggested gently. "Somewhere warm for us non-shifters."

I turned toward the door, to guide Charity through the ruins of the tower.

Mom reached out. "Wait. Everyone, hold hands. I'll transport us down into the dining room."

Charity grabbed hold of one of my hands, and one of Carlak's in complete trust. White light shimmered all around us, then we were downstairs beside the fireplace, a bear skin rug beneath us, and the dining table nearby.

Mom moved to inspect Carlak, running her hands over his face and head.

Charity stood up and shivered. "Well, *that* was intense," she exclaimed.

I couldn't help myself. "Which part?"

She hurried over to the fire, putting her hands out to warm her palms. "Um, well... all of it, I guess. But that transportation trick of your mom's? It is very cool."

"Very cool..." I repeated, managing to stagger sideways so that I could collapse on the large sofa near the fire. Every part of my body was slow and felt like it was dragging. Using that much magic to contain and kill the fire felt like it had drained my soul.

The doors slammed open, shattering the silence, and Dad marched in, wrapping a robe around his body as he did so. "What the hell happened up there?"

I groaned and leaned back against the sofa.

Where do I even start?

With Mom's help Dad got Carlak up and moving, walking around the room. "You okay, son?" he asked.

Carlak nodded. "Yeah, I'm fine, Dad. Thanks to Anthony and Charity."

I gripped my head, then dragged my hands down my face in mortification. "The only reason you were in danger in the first place was because of me, brother."

Carlak turned to stare at me. "I'm a dragon. I know better than to try and charge through an out-of-control fire, and risk being overwhelmed by smoke. I could have turned back and headed downstairs to get help, but I didn't. I was stupid."

My face heated with shame at his words. "You weren't the stupid one." I stood up and took a step forward with my arms open. "I'm sorry, brother."

Carlak rushed over to hug me tight.

My heart swelled with love for my older brother.

When he pulled away, he smiled softly. "I'm going to rest, then I'll go home to my wife."

"You're going to leave me with Mom and Dad?" I gaped at him, only half teasing.

Carlak laughed. "You deserve to have your ass chewed out, little brother. But it's not Mom and Dad I'd be worried about..." Carlak gave a pointed look in the direction of the fire, where Charity still stood.

I nodded.

Yeah, I'm beginning to realize just how important the fated mate bond is.

No matter how mad or disappointed my parents had been with me in the past, I'd never considered throwing myself to my death. Never. But the true devastation that came with Charity walking away from me had been overwhelming.

Mom walked over to me, reached out, and gripped both my hands. "Your magic got out of control?"

I glanced over at Charity, before I spoke.

She was watching me carefully, like she wasn't sure what to make of me anymore.

I nodded slowly. "Yes. It felt like..." I wasn't sure quite how to explain it, but I owed it to everyone to try. "Like my dragon and my magic were fighting a battle deep down inside of me, and I couldn't get either one of them to calm down."

Mom smiled gently. "It sounds like your magic won the battle, for once. You generally shift to squash your magic down and push it away, don't you?"

I gulped, my throat tightening. I didn't like the idea that my magic had defeated my dragon, but I hadn't shifted. That was true. So, what was the answer?

Mom turned to Charity, let go of one of my hands, then gestured for my mate to come closer. "May I see what happened from your perspective, Charity?"

See? Oh... crap.

Charity crept forward, her arms crossed over her chest. "Yes, you may. What do I need to do?"

"Just hold my hand," Mom said. "And I'll look into your memories, if you allow it."

Charity's gaze slid to mine.

I gave her a stiff nod. "It's safe, but if you feel uncomfortable..."

"I'm not uncomfortable with your mother's magic," Charity declared, lifting her chin and daring me to comment. "Please do whatever you need to."

Mom grabbed both of our hands, and although I tried to pull away, she didn't let me go.

I closed my eyes and tried to lift a magical shield against the visions my mother was about to share with me. I wasn't sure I was ready to see myself in that state.

But my magic was untrained and weak compared to my mother's.

Into my head flashed feelings of fear and anger, but also a deep sense of a need to help. Love, even—maybe. There was Charity rushing through the smoke and fire. Talking me down off the ledge. Seeing my magic. Wanting me to make the right choice. Then she saved Carlak, dragging him along the stones. My magic shimmered on my brother's chest and smoke filled the air.

Mom let go of my hand and staggered forward, grasping the couch for strength as she coughed and cried out, then sobbed. "My babies."

Dad wrapped her in his arms, holding her tight while whispering sweet words of reassurance and love.

I glanced at my mate who was watching my parents together with a look on her face that spoke of shock and wonder.

Their love was epic, the stuff fables were written about. I'd grown up around it and considered that sort of devotion normal. But from that look on Charity's face, she'd never seen such a love before. It was the love of a fated mate pair. The best kind of love.

When Mom could stand once more, she opened her arms to Charity.

My mate went in for a hug without hesitation.

"Thank you," Mom whispered, stroking Charity's hair as she held my mate to her shoulder. "You saved them. You saved them both."

When Charity pulled back, she had tears in her eyes. "It was my fault. I should never have—"

"No," Mom interrupted, cutting her off. "If this is anyone's fault, it is mine. I shouldn't have allowed Anthony to hide his magic from the world. I knew how strong he was, and how upset he was with the magical side of himself, and I did nothing about it. I should have…" She covered her mouth with her hand, unable to finish.

I sighed, walking toward them both. "No, Charity. No, Mom. This is my fault. All my fault. I've been a coward my whole life, and it's about time I finally accept who I am. And that means my magical side, as well as my shifter side. Instead of accepting myself, I tried to hide it from the people I love most. I lied. And it's time I took responsibility for those choices that I've made along the way and the consequences that have ensued. I lied to my brother, and my friends, even our people. It's time they all knew who I am, truly… if they don't already." I smiled tentatively at Charity.

She smiled back. "Yeah… I'm not sure how fast gossip flies around the castle? But those two guys on the roof were shocked when they saw you do your thing."

"My thing…" I laughed briefly, then shook myself. "I think I'm going to need a lot more practice before it's considered my *thing*."

Charity glanced at my mother. "Well, you have the perfect teacher, right here."

Mom nodded at me. "I would love to help teach you how to manage your magic, son. When you're ready, let me know, and I'll be right there." She cupped Charity's face and sighed. "I'm going to leave you two to talk. It's time for us to head to bed."

With that, Dad lifted Mom up in his arms and carried her from the room.

Charity stared after them for a time with a grin and a head shake. "So, that's where you get it from."

I laughed; I couldn't help it. "Yeah, well… you're too beautiful to walk. And it gives me an excuse to hold you."

Charity sobered, her expression falling. "Your mom's right, Anthony. We do need to talk."

We certainly do.

"Yes, we do. Shall we talk here? Or go to my bedroom?"

She stared at me, her eyes twin pools of shimmering uncertainty.

"How about we start here?" I suggested, taking her hand and pulling her toward the chairs in front of the fireplace.

We sat in our chairs, the fire warming our faces.

"Where should we start?" Charity asked, her voice a touch wobbly and uncertain.

I coughed a little to clear my throat. "I'll start with an apology. Though I owe you many, I'll get to the most important one first. I'm so sorry for leaving you in the library this afternoon. Making love to you was the most magnificent and important moment of my life, and I ruined it for both of us."

Charity stared down at her hands which were tightly clasped in her lap. "You kind of did, yes. It was extremely hurtful and confusing. You didn't explain... you just ran."

"Can you forgive me?" I asked around the sudden lump in my throat.

She lifted her chin. "I will, over time, I'm sure."

"And now?" I asked, my heart beating a little faster as hope blossomed in my chest. "I'll do anything for a second chance with you, Charity. Anything at all. What can I do now to make things right between us?"

She stared at me with narrowed eyes, as if considering and discarding several possible responses. And then she came out with the last thing I was expecting. "You mentioned this several minutes ago when your mom was here, but I want to confirm whether you mean it. Anthony, I want you to *accept* your magic truly and start doing lessons with your mom to control it."

I sat up straighter, a familiar fear eating at me. I knew I had to accept myself, and that meant accepting my magic as well as everything else. It was just difficult to acknowledge, when I'd spent a lifetime avoiding it. "Well... ah..."

"You've already started on that path," she continued, her tone hesitant, but encouraging. "Those two servants saw you save Carlak, and they'll tell everyone, surely?"

They might, because they knew what it meant. But they might simply keep it to themselves, thinking that's what the family would want. And I knew I couldn't rely on a couple of servants to maybe or maybe not spread the word. This was up to me. It had to be a conscious decision, which meant I had to do what she said and own up to everything—to everyone.

"What are you most afraid of?" She reached out and gripped my hand. "Surely nothing worse than what happened tonight?" Her smile was tentative, but she was right.

I thought about it, considering the situation from every angle, and couldn't quite think of why I'd held onto my secret for so long. I started talking, because often that revealed the problem. "When I was young, I didn't want to be different to my brother and all my friends. Then I grew older and... well, then I felt trapped, I think. In my own lie. It was like, the longer it went on, the harder it became to reveal the truth. And then, of course, the more I tried to hide my magic, contain it, the more it tried to get out, and my fear of losing control only grew." My heart squeezed at the realization that I'd created my own cage. "Oh, my God, I did this to myself. And everything I tried to do to control it all, only made things worse."

Charity laughed. "That's normal, Anthony. We *all* create problems in our own heads out of fear and anxiety sometimes."

"But I... I need to tell you something else." I swallowed hard. "The reason..."

Shit.

"The reason I came to find you that day was because my mother showed me a vision of you being attacked by that guy near your restaurant. I knew I had to save you."

Charity grinned at me. "Why would I be upset about that? I'm freaking *glad* your mom showed you that, or I'd likely still be in hospital somewhere, or worse."

"Worse," I whispered, shuddering at the memory of what I'd seen in that vision.

She winced a little. "Well then. Even better that you *did* come and save me," she said softly as she awaited my response.

I just sighed.

She frowned. "There's something else, isn't there?"

I nodded. "Yes. Mom showed me a vision of you... you were pregnant and wrapped in flames. She told me that if I didn't learn to control my magic then something terrible was going to happen to you. And I've been trying even harder to tamp my magic down ever since then."

A swift intake of breath was Charity's only reaction for several seconds. Eventually, she whispered, "So, does that mean that even is still coming? You know... when I'm pregnant? Or are we done now? Like, are we safe because of the decisions you're making now?"

"I don't know." I shook my head, worry for my mate filling my chest and making it hard to breathe properly.

"Can you find out?" she asked. "Can we go ask your mom, or can you do it?"

My brows rose.

Can I?

I'd looked into the future for Veronica, and I hadn't even meant to. Could I do it now for Charity? "We could try," I ventured. "And if not, we can always ask Mom in the morning." She'd help if we needed her to, I was sure of it. I stood up and held both hands out in front of me.

Charity got to her feet a little slower. She was obviously hesitant. "Does it hurt?" she ventured.

I shook my head. "It's like when Mom viewed your memory of the fire. It doesn't hurt at all. Just give me your hands and I'll see if I can do this."

She slipped her hands into mine, palm against palm.

I reached for my magic and called upon it for help, in a way I'd never done before. The power lurched up inside me in response, as if it had been waiting for just this moment all my life. It was eager and happy to provide, and the vision hit us both hard and fast.

Charity dragged her hands out of mine, stopping the slew of images. "What the hell was that?"

"That's the vision. It'll be like a movie, sort of. Flashes of the future."

She was glaring at me, not sure. "That wasn't anything like when your mom did it before."

That was probably because Mom had taken images out of Charity's head, rather than projected any into her mind. Or maybe I just wasn't good at it? "It didn't hurt, though, did it? We can wait for my mother tomorrow if you'd prefer?"

Charity shook her head and took a steadying breath. "No. It didn't hurt. It was just... unexpected. Let's try again now."

I held out my hands once more and this time it was even easier to draw upon the magic inside me. The vision flashed into both of our minds, and this time I held tight to Charity's hands, stroking my thumbs over her skin in reassurance.

There she was, standing in our bedroom, cupping her swollen belly. Pregnant and stunningly beautiful. A wave of love for her washed over me.

But what of the fire? Our future?

Charity turned to look toward the bedroom door, and I walked into the room, a huge smile on my face. In my arms were two children. A little boy of about four years old was riding high on my shoulders, and another, about two, sat in my arms wriggling like a little fish and giggling.

Our family was safe and well. The happiness in the room was a palpable, very real thing, and all of a sudden, I couldn't breathe.

I let go of Charity's hands, needing the vision to end. I fell into the chair I'd been sitting in only moments before, gasping for air.

"What's wrong?" Charity rushed to my side and kneeled. "Are you okay?"

I nodded, focusing on my chest simply breathing in and out. "Yeah. I..." I kept breathing, forcing the air in and out of my body until I could finally relax once more.

Charity stood and made a pretense of warming herself at the fire. "Please tell me you didn't just have a panic attack at the sight of us having multiple children, Anthony?" She put her hands on her hips, obviously indignant.

I started to laugh. "No sweetheart, not at all." I rose and pulled her into my arms, cupping her head with one hand and holding her to my chest. "No... I think I just became totally overwhelmed with relief. There's no destructive fire in your future, only happiness. For both of us. I was just... it shocked me, after the last terrifying vision I saw. Something has changed for us—something good."

"Did you feel that happiness in the vision? I did" she said, her voice a little shy.

"Yes. It was... beautiful," I admitted. I'd never dreamed I could be that happy. Nor that a woman as beautiful and amazing as Charity would love me and want to create a future—a family—with me.

Charity looked up at me, her face full of the longing I'd always hoped to see in my mate's eyes. "Let's go to bed. I want to see your room now."

I leaned down and pressed a loving kiss to her forehead, before stroking back her hair. The brief touch was merely a taste of what I wanted to experience with her. "I can't think of anything I'd like more, beautiful." I took her hand and guided her out of the dining room.

It's time to show my mate how much I love her.

FOURTEEN

Charity

Part of me believed I should wait before jumping straight back into bed with Anthony, especially after the tumultuous day we'd had. But I needed to reconnect with him in the most irrepressible way, and I could sense that his need was just as strong as mine.

It was as if we'd climbed a great mountain together and been given the greatest gift. We had overcome a terrible situation and discovered we were meant to be together, with almost perfect certainty. Nothing could have made me happier than to know that this man would love and cherish me forever. It was a surreal feeling, that kind of surety and safety. I'd never had anything like it in my life.

"So, I suppose we're staying here?" I joked.

Anthony dragged me down the hallway and pushed open the heavy wooden door that led to his bedroom quarters. He turned to look at me with a silver light blazing in his eyes. "If you want to return to the human world, I will come too," he said fiercely and with perfect honesty.

Hmm... Stay here and be a princess? Or go back to management in hospitality dealing with assholes like Barry? It's such a tough choice!

I chuckled to myself. The fact that Anthony would even consider though meant what we'd seen in the vision was real. We'd be together no matter where we were, and he was all in. "No, not for good," I answered. "Just to say goodbye and collect some of my personal things. Obviously, I need to sell my apartment too..."

Anthony ushered me inside, then shut the door behind us and turned to face me.

I swallowed hard, my heart singing when I saw the intense desire that permeated his features. For a fleeting moment, I lost my train of thought and was swept away by the connection between us.

What was I saying? Something about my apartment?

"Not that any of that stuff matters right now," I managed to finish.

He shook his head in agreement. "We'll work everything out, together. I promise."

I nodded deciding to give up on even trying to remember our conversation and took a step toward him. The room was warm, the fireplace crackling with delicious heat, and yet I shivered with anticipation.

Anthony stepped close, cupping my face with his large hands. "I promise I'm going to be better for you—for the amazing future we're going to have."

I nodded, too overcome with emotion to speak a moment more. I slid my hands up his chest and wrapped my arms around his neck. The time for talking was done. I was ready for the rest of our lives.

His lips crashed down onto mine and I could feel the strength of his hunger.

I lifted my chin to get even closer, thrusting my tongue between his lips, to taste him, to know him the way no one else ever would.

He moaned softly, letting go of my face and grabbing my ass with both hands. His cock was already hard and pressing into my belly, ready to claim me again.

I couldn't wait to feel him inside me once more, but there were *so* many things I wanted to do to him first. I pulled away and dropped to my knees, tugging at his pants to gain access to his hard erection.

"Charity…" he said, his tone cautious. "You don't have to do that."

I looked up at him, my heart in my throat. "Please help me remove this clothing. I want to taste you." He'd played my body like a master musician this morning and I wanted to be the one to make him moan in ecstasy this time.

Anthony stared down at me for a moment then set his hands to his waistband, untying and tugging on the material and strings until his pants dropped and his naked cock sprung up to greet me.

I stared at his beautiful length, grabbing hold of the thick shaft with one hand before I set my lips to the head and opened my mouth. He tasted like the salt of sweat, and something distinctly sweet somehow. He was delicious and everything I wanted. I moved my head and hands in unison, stroking his cock as I explored his arrow shaped head, running my tongue around the rim and along the slit, before taking him deeper, past my gag reflex and down into my throat.

"*Fuck*… that feels amazing, beautiful." He slid his fingers through my hair around my skull, cupping my head tenderly and encouraging me.

I moved harder and faster, reveling in the sensation of being able to pleasure him in return.

Anthony jerked in my grasp before pulling back and tugging me off his cock. "Oh, that's not fair. Now you're doing that *too* well. I want to come inside you, baby."

I jumped to my feet, licking my lips, the taste of him in my mouth and happiness singing in my blood. "Yeah… I suppose that's a good idea. We've got to get moving on all those babies we saw in that vision!"

He stripped off his shirt and kicked his pants away. He was now gloriously naked, and my God, he was even more sculpted and beautiful than he'd been in my dreams. He was truly perfect for me. "Are you sure about that?" he asked quietly. "I don't want to rush you into anything you're not ready for. We have as long as you need."

"Rush me?" I repeated, incredulous. Sure, we'd only met a few days ago, but… "I've been waiting my whole life for you to find me."

He crushed me against his naked body, kissing me so deeply my toes tingled, leaving me breathless.

I tugged at my clothes, desperate to remove the remaining layers between us.

He turned me around and got to work on the buttons of my gown. The dresses here were beautiful and warm, but damn, they weren't easy to get out of without assistance. When I was finally naked, Anthony stood still for a moment, studying me intently, his luminous gaze swirling with need. "You are truly beautiful, Charity."

Heat flushed my cheeks at the compliment and the sincerity of his tone.

Before I could say anything in return, he lifted me up and carried me to the bed.

Together, we scrabbled to push all the covers back until the cool sheets were beneath my back.

"Please, I need you." I pulled Anthony on top of me, and he slid between my thighs like he'd done it a hundred times before. It felt so right to have him there. It was like we belonged together.

He kissed my lips, then put his mouth next to my ear and whispered as he pressed his cock to my entrance. "You really want me to fill you with our baby?" a primal and sexy growling undertone in his voice.

I gasped as his words pierced my heart. "Yes," I whispered, unable to deny the greatest wish of my life.

He thrust deep in response and his cock filled my body.

Joy filled me at the thought of making a child with my one true soul mate. A wish I never thought would be granted. I'd dreamed, but I'd seen myself trapped in a mediocre job as the year passed me by... I never could have imagined I'd find my mate, the man who would keep my heart in the form of a dragon shifter prince from another realm!

"I love you," Anthony whispered, his breath hot against my ear as his cock surged within me once more.

I cried out, feeling his words as much as hearing them. They were like a panacea for my lonely and wounded soul.

"I love you more than anything in this world," he growled. "And I will love you when we are both old, and gray, and our children have children."

My eyes slid closed as pleasure bloomed inside my belly at the thought. I lifted my legs to wrap around his hips, allowing him to reach even deeper. I gasped aloud in ecstasy as Anthony's cock hit my g-spot. I arched my back, moaning from my very core.

Spurred on, Anthony fucked me harder and faster, until the room was filled with the sound of flesh meeting flesh, and our groans as our desire grew to a fever pitch.

I moaned and kissed Anthony's shoulder, digging my teeth into his flesh and tasting the sweetness of his skin. I wanted to taste every inch of him, to lay claim to the prince who had saved my life not just once, but twice.

He groaned loudly, thrusting deep inside me. Then his roar filled my ear as his seed pulsed inside me, pushing my orgasm over the edge and throwing me into a world of spasming an chaotic pleasure.

I screamed and gasped for air, my whole-body quaking in the aftermath of our frenzied passion as we shared a single perfect moment in time.

Anthony collapsed on top of me and then rolled to the side, so he didn't crush me with his lithe, muscular body. "Oh, my God, that was *awesome.*"

I suppressed a breathless giggle and reached for his face, cupping his cheek as I finally had the chance to gaze upon him in our post-coital bliss. "You're not going to run away this time?" I asked, my heart still racing.

Anthony shook his head, his expression serious. "Never again, Charity," he promised. "From now on, we're together—forever and always. I love you with all my heart."

My heart skipped a beat, and I leaned forward to kiss his lips, before I pulled back to say the words I'd been wanting to say in return. "I love you, too, Anthony."

EPILOGUE

Anthony
~Three Months Later~

Charity wouldn't agree to marry me until we'd known each other for over a month, and by the time she finally said 'yes', she was pregnant. We had cause for more than just one thing to celebrate! The wedding ceremony was beautiful and afterward we gathered in the Great Hall to enjoy an epic feast.

I stood by the dance floor, enjoying watching all my friends and family dancing the night away as festive cheer fille the air.

Dad had asked Charity to dance, and he was gently spinning her around in time with the music.

"Enjoying your night?" Mom asked as she walked toward me, dressed in the most royal purple, over-the-top gown I'd ever seen her wear.

"I am, Mom. Thank you, for everything."

She had been teaching me how to use my magic, and things were going well in that regard. I still had moments where I instinctively went to stifle it down, but those moments were becoming less frequent. And now that I was leaning into that side of myself, my magic seemed less prone to spill out in unexpected ways.

I was on a journey to self-learning, and while I wasn't there yet, Charity's love and positive presence, and my mom's magical guidance, were helping me along the path to self-acceptance and becoming who I was always destined to be.

She put her arms out with a broad smile.

I hugged her tightly. "I'm so happy for you, Anthony. You've found your fated mate, you're going to be a father, and our people know that there will be a sorcerer looking after them, even after I'm gone."

I pulled back and frowned down at her. "You're not dying anytime soon, Mom."

She cupped my chin and squeezed. "I know, dear. Still... you've finally stepped into being the man you were born to be. And I just want you to know that I'm so proud of you."

I looked away and laughed, afraid I might cry if she kept gazing at me like that, with all the heartfelt love of a mother who had watched we struggle for so long and was finally seeing me bloom.

"Hey, Mom. There's something I always wanted to ask you," I said to her. "Charity used to dream about me. I know she told you."

She nodded. "Yes. What's your question, sweetheart?"

"Did you put those dreams in her head to help her accept me?" I pressed. I wouldn't have been surprised if she did.

Mom raised a single eyebrow at me. "You think I'd put those types of erotic images into her mind? No, son. That was most definitely *not* me."

My cheeks heated with embarrassment.

Yikes! Awkward.

"Then who was it?"

She shrugged. "You, more than likely."

"Me?" I asked. "I didn't do that. I wouldn't even know how!"

Mom laughed. "You underestimate your magic, Anthony. Your magic, and the fated mate bond are powerful when united. I'm sure it found a way, while you were sleeping, to find your mate and get her ready for you."

The strength of that statement hit me like a brick. My dragon heart, my magic, and fate itself had worked together to bring about our ultimate happiness. "Wow, that's incredible."

"Isn't it?" She smile briefly, leaned forward and kissed my cheek. "I'll leave you to enjoy your night, my boy. I love you."

"I love you too, Mom."

She glided away and to rescue Charity from my father.

Veronica sidled up next to me, a glass of wine in her hand.

I raised an eyebrow at the girl I'd known from the moment she was born. "Hitting the alcohol now, Dragon Daughter?"

Veronica's blue eyes flared and she tossed her long blonde hair over her shoulder. "I *am* eighteen now," she said, indignation clear in her voice. "It's legal."

In European countries, anyway.

"So, what are you doing standing over here?" she asked, turning to stand by my side so we could both watch everyone enjoying themselves. "Surveying your kingdom?"

I scoffed at her. "I'm the second born son, child. This isn't my kingdom, and never will be. Haven't you learned anything by now?"

She punched me in the arm, hard.

"Hey!" I glared at her. "It's my wedding day. You're meant to be nice to me."

She didn't apologize, but she didn't punch me again, either. Instead, she went back to sipping on her drink.

"It's still your kingdom, you know," she said after a while. "Carlak might be king one day, but you're the sorcerer now, yeah?"

I shrugged. "I suppose. My mom's been teaching me how to use my magic, but I'm decades behind her when it comes to experience." The lessons had been going well, though I may have blown up a few things along the way.

"Yeah... but your mom's not going anywhere, so you have the time you need to learn."

"True," I said, already having seen a vision of the day of my parents' passing. Thankfully it was many, many years from now. I tried not to dwell on it too much.

Veronica didn't say anything more, but she didn't leave my side.

A twinge of something uncomfortable began to niggle at me. "What do you need, Dragon Daughter?" I asked, not turning to look at her.

She didn't hit me, which meant she was about to get serious. "You know when you came over for lunch that time?"

I searched my memory, unsure of which event she was talking about. But then it hit me. "Oh, you mean when I accidentally gave you a vision of your future?" I'd forgotten about that day. I'd been so consumed with my own secrets and lies that I'd pushed that very *juicy* piece of information away. Iain and Veronica were twin flames of fury. They'd burn the world down with their love...

If they could get past their long-held grudge against one another.

And now that she mentioned it... "So, what are you going to do about that?" I turned to face her and raised a querying brow.

"Nothing." She tipped back her head and finished the rest of her drink in one gulp.

"What do you mean, nothing?" I chuckled softly at her. "You know who your fated mate is and you're going to... ignore him?"

That just wasn't done. She was of legal age, and he was already five years older than her, maybe a little more. They were a perfect match, except for the fact that they were cousins. But surely fate wouldn't have gotten such a match wrong?

Veronica lifted her chin defiantly. "I've taken a job in the human world. I'm leaving next week."

My jaw dropped. "Are you kidding me?"

"Nope. I'm going to look after some kids for a family I met online. Maybe travel Europe for a while. Explore the world, you know?"

I couldn't believe it. "And your parents are just... letting you go? They're okay with this?"

Her eyes sparked with challenge. "Let them try and stop me."

I would have laughed if I didn't know her better. She was serious. And short of locking her up in a tower, her parents didn't have a hope in hell of stopping her. Perhaps this was what they'd been fighting about that day I'd 'visited.'

I shook my head at her. "You're running away from your future...

which is very interesting, Veronica. I thought you were the fearless one among us? But I won't be the one to try and talk you out of it. Hell... I've been running away from who I was my whole life—until now, anyway. I won't be the one to throw stones."

"I'm not running away from who I am," she countered.

This time I burst out laughing. "Oh, baby girl, you are. You're a dragon princess. You're the fated mate of a prince. You don't have to work a day in your life, and instead of enjoying your position and doing good in your own kingdom, and accepting your fated mate, you're going to travel and work for humans? Yeah, that makes perfect sense."

I continued to laugh until my beautiful mate walked up, pink in the cheeks from dancing too long. "What are you two talking about? Because whatever it is, count me in. I need something funny to take my mind off this nausea!"

"Did dad twirl you around too many times?" I asked with a grin.

She burped a little, then covered her mouth. "Oh, my God. Excuse me."

I put my arm around Charity's shoulders and tugged her close. "You're beautiful, even when you burp." And she was. Today had been perfect in every way.

Charity rolled her eyes. "I feel disgusting... but I'm glad you think I look pretty."

"You look amazing," Veronica said. "And congratulations on your pregnancy."

Charity grinned wide and pride shone bright in her eyes. "Thank you. We were going to keep it quiet, but the moment I hit six weeks I started being sick all the time, and well... it's been impossible to keep quiet ever since."

I kissed my mate's forehead and held her tight. "I think we should dance. I promise to take it slow." There was a soft, slow song being played, which was perfect for my bride's woozy stomach. I so desperately just wanted to hold her close and treasure her on our special day.

"Oh, that would be beautiful," Charity said before she turned toward Veronica. "It was lovely to see you again."

I threw a lop-sided smile at the Dragon Daughter, then lifted my free hand to wiggle my fingers at her. "Are you sure you don't want another vision?" Not that I'd been controlling it the first time I'd shown her who her fated mate was, but I could bring up the same images now, I was sure.

Veronica backed away so fast, shaking her head before she narrowed her eyes and playfully glared at me.

I couldn't help but laugh. "Bye then, Dragon Daughter."

"What was that about?" Charity asked.

I took her hand and led her onto the dance floor. I set my hand to my wife's still normal-sized waist and took her fingers in mine. "Long story short, I accidentally showed Veronica who her fated mate was. I couldn't control the vision at the time, it just happened. And now she's running away to the human world to avoid him."

Charity glanced around the room. "Who is it?" she whispered conspiratorially.

I glanced in the direction of Stavrok's table and Iain caught my eye with a grin before I turned back to Charity once more. "It's probably best if I don't tell you," I conceded.

My bride laughed. "Probably! I'm not sure I could keep a straight face when I saw them and it's their romance, not mine."

"He doesn't know," I told her. "Well, at least, I don't think he does. I haven't told him, anyway."

Charity tangled her fingers in the hair at the base of my neck. "I'm sure he knows."

I frowned at her, maneuvering her around the dance floor and making sure not to twirl her too fast. "What do you mean?"

Charity stared at me like I was the one not making sense. "What happens when a male dragon shifter sees his fated mate for the first time?" she queried.

"He... oh..." She was correct. There was no way that Iain didn't know Veronica was meant to be his. "You're right. Then why..." I shook my head. "No. Not tonight. They can sort out their own shit. I want to celebrate us, and our baby tonight."

Charity smiled up at me, her eyes misting with tears. "It really has been the most perfect day."

"It was." My arms tightened around her. "I'm glad you enjoyed it. And tonight, I'll hold you in our bed and count my lucky stars that you're mine forever."

Charity dropped her head then stared up at me seductively through her eyelashes. "I'm sure we can do more than just cuddle..."

My cock instantly throbbed at the mention of a *proper* wedding night. I pulled her closer and danced even slower, letting my dragon purr with happiness, his desire simmering deliciously below the surface.

That night I carried my new wife across the threshold, straight into bed, and she fell asleep in my arms. Her pregnancy made her exhausted and it had been a long day. I had every respect for her need to rest, and knew that when she awoke, there would be plenty of time to play.

Thanks to her unwavering love and the fact that she had refused to give up on me, even when I'd wanted to give up on myself, we now had the rest of our lives to enjoy one another.

8
IRE AND ICE
HIS
DRAGON
PRINCESS
USA TODAY BESTSELLING AUTHOR
AMELIA SHAW

PROLOGUE

Veronica
~18 Months Later~

My parents refused to let me leave the castle... again! I'd asked them to be reasonable. I'd begged them to understand. I'd even pleaded with them. Then, I'd started yelling.

There was no convincing them to allow me to go anywhere without them. They were leaving me with no other option than to break free of my gilded cage, whether they liked it or not. I was eighteen now, and with two older brothers to look after my parents' kingdom, what use was I?

People were speaking loudly in the dining room as I passed, and I stopped in the hallway outside the room, listening hard to try and figure out what was happening. It was breakfast time and there was an unfamiliar male voice I wasn't expecting to hear. Who could that be?

I altered my previous trajectory toward the library and, instead, pushed open the door to the dining room. My gaze fell on one of the men I'd grown up with. Not the one I always feared seeing, but a dragon prince nonetheless.

"Hi Veronica."

Despite the anger of my previous argument with my parents still boiling in my veins, seeing him made me smile. "Anthony! I didn't know you were here."

I rushed forward for a hug. The secret plans inside my head to leave the castle and the protection of my family were already making me homesick and saying goodbye to Anthony would make the farewell even worse. I clung to the man who'd been like an older brother to me when I was growing up.

The barely dressed prince pulled out of our hug and gave me an awkward smile. "It wasn't planned; I just started flying and found myself here."

That didn't sound like Anthony, but then, he had always been cagey about his emotions.

I reached for his hands and gripped his fingers, wanting him to know that he had a friend. "You know it's always good to see you."

But as soon as I said the words, blindness overtook me. The world around me dropped away to darkness, but inside my mind a vision coalesced and became strong.

I was standing by the window in our palace, upstairs in my favorite reading room. I was wearing a gown of royal purple. A dress I didn't own.

My eyes burned with hot tears as I stared at that version of myself. I was heavily pregnant and smiling in a content way. That simply couldn't be. Contentment was a feeling I'd never known. Ever.

Why would I be happy to be having a baby? This vision made no sense. How far into the future was this?

My hand rested on my huge belly, and then I turned toward the sound of footsteps echoing in the room as my heart leapt with happiness.

I didn't want to see the next part and squeezed my eyes shut. But I couldn't stop the images being projected into my mind by the prince still gripping my hands.

The father of my child stepped out of the shadows, a smile on his face that I'd never witnessed before. Iain.

Iain? No! That was impossible. He hated me. He always had.

Before I could see any more lies, I ripped my hands out of Anthony's hold and the vision stopped.

My normal eyesight immediately returned and with it I saw Anthony, looking pale and drawn and staring at me with a wary look in his eyes. Asshole!

"What the hell was that?" I yelled at him, shaking with the need to shift. My dragon was furious and confused. So many other emotions too. I couldn't even sort one hot flash of anger from other deeper feelings and it just made me—and my dragon—even more upset. I needed to shift and fly... fly far away.

Anthony ran a shaking hand through his hair. "I'm sorry. That's never happened before."

Bullshit! You know exactly what just happened! You're a sorcerer! Just like your mom.

"What happened?" Dad demanded, rushing to our side.

"Oh, it was nothing," Anthony said quickly, then looked over to me with a look of unmistakable fear.

I turned to tell my father exactly what I'd seen. "When he grabbed my hand, I saw... I saw..."

I stopped, partly out of empathy for Anthony's obvious distress over the situation, but also for my own selfish reasons. Iain was the youngest son of King Stavrok, my mother's cousin. I couldn't believe Fate would tie me into a marriage with my own cousin, surely?

But Mom and Dad would. They completely believed in fated mates. After all, their marriage was the product of Fate's choice. But I wouldn't be. No matter what they said, or demanded of me, I would not marry Iain because Anthony had 'seen' it and communicated that to me in a vision.

No.

I lifted my chin and turned to my father, changing the subject for all of our sakes. "Dad, why have I been restricted in all my flight plans this month? I tried to organize to go and see Kayla, but I was told I couldn't."

Dad turned to Mom, then glanced back at me. "Veronica, we've gone over this. You are a princess. You can't just fly off whenever you want, to God knows where. You know what happened to your mother."

I rolled my eyes and crossed my arms over my chest. "Yeah... she was kidnapped by your half-brothers, which led to the re-unification of your family, Dad. That was never a bad thing."

Mom walked over, annoyance at my attitude written all over her pale face. "Veronica. You have responsibilities here."

"I don't." I groaned, gesturing to her with my hand. "That's the problem, Mom. You do! Dad does. Even my brothers do. I have nothing to do here, absolutely nothing, except hang around and watch everyone else live life to the fullest."

Mom reached out a hand to me. "You can shadow me, learn the ropes of being a queen..."

I shook her off. "I'll never be a queen, Mom. Here or anywhere else." Even if that stupid vision was right, Iain was the youngest son and would never inherit. "I may as well learn some basic skills. Maybe cooking or sewing."

Dad groaned. "Veronica! You are a princess. Shadow your mother with her responsibilities for our people. Helping the less fortunate. Volunteering..."

I groaned and covered my face with my hands.

He didn't stop. "Or shadow me and learn about our kingdom. Politics. You have an incredibly bright mind. I don't want that going to waste."

I dropped my hands and glanced at Anthony, who looked lost in thought. Was he still stewing over the vision he'd shared? He was going to be no help here at all.

I continued to argue back and forth with my parents about being allowed out, but it was clearly useless.

At the back of my mind, a new plan was forming. Now that I'd seen what Anthony showed me, I didn't want to just leave the castle. With this new information about Iain, I needed to leave the realm.

Now I just had to work out where to go, and how I could get there.

~A month later~

Anthony's wedding was the last family event I'd agreed to attend before my trip. As I stared around at the guests, I noticed Iain standing with my brother and some other mutual friends. I decided to give them a wide berth.

But there was one person I wanted to speak to before I finally flew away.

I grabbed a glass of champagne from a nearby waiter and walked over to the groom.

Anthony raised an eyebrow at me. "Hitting the alcohol now, dragon daughter?"

I tossed my long blonde hair over her shoulder, annoyed at him after only one sentence. "I'm eighteen," I said. "It's legal in our realm, even if it isn't everywhere in the human world." Then I took a sip of champagne to prove my point.

Covering the wince that accompanied the tart taste was the hardest part.

"So, what are you doing standing over here?" I asked him, turning to stand by his side so we could both stare at the dance floor. "Surveying your kingdom?"

He scoffed. "Second born son, child. Haven't you learned how things go?"

I punched him in the arm, hard. I was third born, and a girl. Didn't he understand that I was the one who had no purpose in life?

"Hey!" Anthony glared at me. "It's my wedding day. You're meant to be nice to me."

I narrowed my eyes, but kept my mouth shut. He was right. I went back to sipping my terrible champagne and scowled at the room in general instead of specifically at him.

Anthony stared at his beautiful wife who was dancing with his father, King Erik. Love was written all over Anthony's face, making me uncomfortable.

I needed to change the focus. "It's still your kingdom, you know." I bit my lip, recalling some information my mother had passed along. Everyone knew about Anthony's magic now. "You're the sorcerer now, yeah?"

He shrugged. "I suppose. My mom's been teaching me how to use my magic, but I'm decades behind her."

I grinned. It was nice to see him finally accepting his role. It was obvious he'd been fighting his magic for a long time. "Yeah... but your mom's not going anywhere, so you have time to learn."

Marienne was barely fifty. He had many years to learn her secrets.

"True," Anthony said with a heavy sigh.

I empathized. None of us liked to think about the day our powerful parents would leave this world. I certainly didn't want to entertain the thought. My dad was the most amazing man I'd ever known. He'd rebuilt our kingdom from the ashes of war. He was more amazing than a phoenix and a sorcerer put together.

Doubt suddenly assailed me. Maybe I was doing the wrong thing? Leaving my parents and my whole world behind.

"What do you need, dragon daughter?" Anthony asked suddenly, dragging me out of my thoughts.

I glanced up at the man who'd shown me a vision I never asked for. He didn't say anything more, so I knew it was time that I asked the questions for which I'd been dying to know the answers. "You know when you came over for lunch that time, a few weeks ago?"

My heart began to pound a little harder and my stomach clenched with the stress of even bringing up this topic.

Anthony studied me. "Oh, you mean when I accidentally gave you a vision of your future?"

Yes! I wanted to scream at him, but instead I choked down another sip of champagne, and nodded mutely instead.

"So, what are you going to do about it?" Anthony asked.

"Nothing," I said, gathering my courage and tipping my head back to finish the rest of my drink. Yuck.

"What do you mean, nothing?" He chuckled softly. "You know who your fated mate is and you're going to ignore him?"

Fated mate? No! There was no way Iain was the man I was meant to marry. Anthony had to be wrong, but I wasn't about to tell the newly married sorcerer that his vision was dodgy.

Instead, I changed the subject. There was no point arguing with him. "I've taken a job in the human world," I confessed quietly. "I'm leaving next week."

Anthony's jaw dropped. "Are you kidding me?"

"Nope. I'm going to look after some kids for a family I met online. Maybe travel Europe for a while."

Anthony stared at me like I was insane. "And your parents are just... letting you go?"

They were, even if they didn't know it yet. "Let them try and stop me."

Anthony shook his head. "You're running away from your future... which is very interesting, Veronica. I thought you were the fearless one among us. But I won't be the one to try and talk you out of it. Hell, I've been running away from who I am my whole life. Until recently. I won't throw stones."

I glared at the impudent prince. "I'm not running away from who I am."

He burst out laughing. "Oh, baby girl, you are. You're a dragon princess. You're the fated mate of a prince. You don't have to work a day in your life, and instead of enjoying your position and doing good in your kingdom, you're going to escape to a whole other realm, and plan to travel and work for humans. Makes perfect sense."

My jaw dropped as I stared at Anthony. The gall! I wasn't sure what to yell at him most about. The fact that he thought I was an entitled bitch, or that he'd just called me a baby.

Before I could ask him more questions, or demand that he tell me the truth about my future, Anthony's new wife Charity walked up, red in the face from dancing too long. "What are you two talking about? Cos whatever it is, count me in. I need something funny to take my mind off this nausea."

"Dad twirl you around too many times?" Anthony asked her.

She burped a little, then covered her mouth and said, "Excuse me."

Anthony hugged his wife tightly. "You're beautiful."

Charity rolled her eyes. "I feel disgusting... but I'm glad I look pretty."

"You look amazing," I rushed to say, annoyed at myself for not extending my salutations. "And congratulations on your pregnancy. And the wedding."

Charity grinned with obvious pride. "Thanks. We were going to keep it quiet, but the moment I hit six weeks I started vomiting, and well... it's been impossible to keep quiet since."

"I think we should dance," Anthony said, and his wife beamed up at him.

"Oh, that would be lovely." She turned to me. "Lovely to see you again, Veronica."

Anthony lifted his sorcerer's hand to wriggle his fingers at me. "You sure you don't want another vision?"

Hell no! The first one had been bad enough.

I backed away so fast Anthony laughed at me and called out, "Bye, dragon daughter."

I ran away, not afraid to admit that I was nervous about spending any more time with Anthony. My future awaited and it was in the human realm, not here with Iain, or my parents, or anything to do with my dragon shifter genes.

CHAPTER
ONE

Veronica
~Current Day~

I lifted the screaming, red-faced baby up and out of her crib, bouncing on the spot as I'd been taught to do by one of the children's other nannies. "It's okay, sweetheart. Don't cry. Mommy and Daddy will be home soon."

The baby immediately calmed as I held her in my arms. I wiped her tears away with a clean face washer before resettling her for the long night ahead. This family loved having kids, but they certainly didn't hang around long enough to bond with them.

"Good girl," I cooed at the infant. "Mommy and Daddy have way too much money, don't they?"

I was one of three nannies the parents had hired to look after their five children. I wouldn't have stayed working for them as long as I had, except for the fact that they took amazing holidays to exotic destinations.

Luckily for us, the parents couldn't go anywhere without our help, so they took the nannies with them everywhere they went.

We were currently in Greece, staying on a little island I could walk around in a single day. The weather was spectacular and I had what the humans called, 'a tan.' As the daughter of the King of the Winter Palace, I'd never known my skin could be any other color than pure white. Every time I caught sight of myself in a mirror, I wanted to burst out laughing from the shock.

I had two days off every week to travel and sightsee. There weren't many jobs like this one, and my responsibilities ended and began with keeping the baby happy. Compared to running a kingdom, I counted myself blessed.

A vibrating in my back pocket caught my attention. My cell phone.

Weird. Who would be calling me at this time of night?

I placed the sleeping baby back in her crib then snuck out of the bedroom and raced down to my own tiny sleeping quarters. The text was from my older brother...

"Shit!"

There's been an accident. Dad's hurt. You need to come home.

My father was King Damon. The King of the Winter Palace. A formidable and dangerous foe.

My heart pounded sickeningly in my chest as I typed back.

What happened? Is he okay? He's healing... yeah?

As I hit send, a million thoughts raced through my mind. He couldn't be really hurt. He just... couldn't. Dragon shifters healed quickly. Supernaturally.

My brother's response took so long my fingers were white from gripping the phone by the time the shocking response came through.

No. He's not okay. He fell. Shards of glass got in his lungs. Marienne's coming. But you should come home.

A sob rose to my lips as I texted back.

I will. Is everyone else okay?

My brother wouldn't ask me to come home unless something was really wrong with Dad, so I wasn't sure why I asked about anyone else.

A final message from my brother had tears coursing down my cheeks.

Iain was working here with Dad. He's missing. No-one can find him.

I'm coming, I typed in as fast as my numb fingers and blurry eyes could manage. What did he mean that Iain was... missing? We were dragon shifters. We didn't just disappear.

True panic raced up my spine making my nerves tingle and hurt. I had to go, now. There wasn't a minute to waste.

Oh my God, oh my God. Not Dad. And not Iain.

I still hadn't reconciled Anthony's vision within my heart. I'd ignored it. Called him a liar, and a troublemaker a hundred times over. Iain couldn't be my fated mate. He just... couldn't.

But as I searched inside myself for that strange part of me that had always been too aware of Iain, I found it alight and hurting.

Damn it. That is not good.

I raced to the tiny bedroom I shared with Narelle, a blonde Dutch girl a few years older than me. "Hey, you okay?" she asked, sitting bolt upright on her bed where she was reading.

"No," I gasped out, swiping at my cheeks to dispel the wetness and proof of my grief. I had to get it together to fly home. I was no use to anyone if I couldn't find the portal. I reached for an explanation that the human would understand. "My dad's sick. I have to go home."

I grabbed my bright pink suitcase from under the bed and started throwing all my clothes inside.

Narelle jumped to her feet. "You want help?"

"Um..." I didn't know how to answer her. My whole body was shaking, and I couldn't think. I didn't have much time to decide, and I wasn't even sure I wanted to take all this stuff home with me.

"How about I do the bathroom?" she suggested.

I nodded because I didn't know how to say no.

Iain... oh God. He couldn't be dead. He couldn't be.

Beyond the panic I could hear my mother's voice inside my head, calm and strong. 'Focus, Veronica. Focus. You need to get home safe.'

I closed my eyes and took some steady breaths to slow my heart rate down. My dad was going to be fine; I just knew it. And Iain? He was probably just... maybe the wolves... I shook myself. There wasn't a good reason why he'd be missing unless he was dead. He was a prankster, after all. The youngest son who had never really cared about the kingdom... or responsibility.

But even though part of me hated him for all the pranks he'd pulled on me years ago, I couldn't believe that he'd just disappear if my father was hurt. Iain was an idiot, but he was loyal. And noble. And...

"Wooo..." I blew out my breath and opened my eyes, reaching for the box of tissues. I had to stop thinking about what was going on at home, until I could actually get back there. Crying more and allowing myself to think of the worst possible outcomes, like them both dying, was not going to get me home any faster.

I blew my nose, wiped my eyes and bit my lip. Focus on what's in front of you.

I stared down at my suitcase, letting my mom's best advice sink in. One step at a time. One job at a time. One problem at a time. And what I needed to focus on right now was tying up all my loose ends, then getting away without anyone seeing me shift or fly.

I went to grab another light sweater out of my drawers, then dropped it onto the bed beside my suitcase. Maybe I should just leave everything here? Just in case I'd be back sooner than expected?

I may fly home and simply find Iain sitting in my parents' dining room eating dinner after getting lost for a day in the woods. And my father healing and yelling out orders from his bed.

They'd allow me to return straight back here again. Surely?

But my heart knew the truth. I wouldn't be returning to the human realm any time soon. My brother wouldn't have texted me unless Dad's injuries were serious.

And if my dad was truly as hurt as my brother said, then I wasn't coming back to the human realm in the near future. Maybe not ever.

"Hey..." I called out to Narelle as she walked back into the room, zipping up my toiletry bag filled with shampoo and soaps, a worried expression on her face.

"Yeah?" She glanced down at my half empty suitcase. "Do you need help with that?"

I put my hands on my hips and stared down at the mess of summer dresses and bathing suits that I would never wear again. Damn, I was going to miss the sun.

"Well, actually, I might leave it all for you and Tania to share, if you want?"

Narelle stared at me with wide, surprised eyes. "Seriously? You're not taking any of your clothes?"

I shook my head, feeling stupid for ever thinking I should pack my clothes for the trip. "I'm from a really cold country, I'll never get to wear any of this again."

Narelle reached for one of my red sun dresses that she'd openly coveted in the past. "Thanks, Ronnie."

Now, that was a nickname I was going to miss.

"Oh!" I dove under my bed and pulled out my wallet. "Take the cash I have, too."

I pulled out the notes and coins I'd collected and tossed them down onto my bed.

"Oh, I can't do that," Narelle exclaimed. "Take it with you."

I sighed as I ran my hands over the top of my head, pulling my hair up and into a ponytail. "No. Please share it with Sarah, if you want. Have a few drinks on me."

Sarah was the other nanny, but she was older and a little crankier.

Narelle tilted her head. "Thanks, but... why?"

I shrugged. "My parents have money, so it's just not a thing." And that was the understatement of the century.

"You never told me that." She sounded hurt, but I couldn't stop to explain any more. I had to go.

I grabbed my cell phone from where it had dropped onto the floor and slid it into my pocket. "It's not important. But I have to go. Would you tell the Fredricksons that I'm sorry?"

She nodded, then reached for a sweater, pulling it on to cover her bare arms as the night air had turned cooler. "How are you getting home? Surely you need money for a plane ticket, or something?"

"My parents will sort all that out," I explained, grabbing my friend into a hug. "Thank you for everything. It's been great."

Narelle chuckled in my ear and hugged me tight. "You're a weird one, you know that?"

I smiled against her hair, then pulled back to look straight into her bright blue eyes. "Yeah, I know. You take care of yourself, okay? No going back to that asshole of an ex-boyfriend. Got it? I don't care how cute you think he is."

Narelle rolled her eyes but grinned at me as well. "Yes, Mom."

I grabbed her against me for one more hug, her warmth and comfort making tears spring to my eyes. Stop it! It was time to go.

"Bye." I hurried out the bedroom door before I could change my mind.

The house the family was renting was on the top of a large hill, and the back garden was completely private. No one would be able to see me shift and fly away from there.

I ran out the back door and into the cool night air. I hadn't shifted in the whole eighteen months I'd been here, and I could feel my dragon waking up inside of me. She was stretching her wings and shaking herself, ready to take flight for the first time in so long. And there was an awakening joy that began to infuse my blood.

I glanced around, taking mental pictures of the exotic trees and the crystal blue pool. I'd enjoyed my life in the human realm. I'd learned a lot and made some great friends. But there was no question about me going home. Not in these circumstances. If Dad was hurt, or God forbid, dying... I had to go home. Now. Mom would need me.

My heart began to pound faster as my shifter rose up and took over my body. My skin changed to scales and I grew taller, bigger, larger.

I blinked and my eyes shifted as I transformed into my dragon, with keen night vision taking over from my human side. Like any other predator.

I tried not to think of Iain as I launched up and into the air, flapping my wings to get higher. I flew toward the portal that marked the crossover point between realms, and even though I tried to keep the thoughts at bay, my dragon cried into the night.

I'm coming. Please. Don't die before I get there, Dad.

TWO

Veronica

From Greece, the trip to the portal was a lot further than I'd ever flown before, but I pushed myself higher and faster. I knew where it was; I could practically feel it in the distance, like the warmth of the sun, calling me home.

My wings were aching but I couldn't slow down. I pushed harder, and then I saw it. The portal.

I flapped my wings higher and higher, then I relaxed and let myself soar. The release of pain was almost too good, but I focused my trajectory and passed through the portal. I was back in my own realm, and my welcome wagon was the cold rain the pelted my face.

I twisted and soared toward my family home, the Winter Palace.

The air grew colder and snow began to fall. My chest was hurting from breathing the air I'd known all my life.

This is why people don't leave the realm. Because it's a long way and exhausting.

I flew further, struggling to keep flapping my wings. But then the peaks of my father's castle came into view, stretching high into the sky.

Relief sailed through me. I was almost home. I worked myself higher, using the last of my energy to get above the clouds and to rise above the freezing weather of our home.

Once up there, I could breathe a little easier and I sent a prayer of thanks to my brothers for teaching me this trick when we were younger.

I coasted along, catching my breath until I was closer to the castle, then I let myself soar down, riding the currents and wind blasts and saving my energy for the landing.

My room had a huge balcony and I aimed my landing for the stones just outside the door. I managed to land on my dragon feet, then let go of my shifter body as quickly as I could.

I stumbled, then fell... hard. "Ah..." My hands scraped along the cobblestones and I had no energy left to do anything but sob, right there on the ground.

The door opened and my brother Theo rushed over and wrapped a blanket around me. "Are you okay? I saw you flying and thought I'd bring you clothes."

I lifted my head, my eyes hot and filled with tears. "It's good to see you, brother."

Theo smiled. "Yeah, you too dragon daughter."

I groaned. "I haven't even been home five minutes..."

His chuckle was friendly as he hauled me to my feet. "Come on. Let's get you warm. You hungry?"

My teeth chattered as I shivered. "Always."

We stepped inside and the heat of the room hit me like a wave. "Whoa."

Theo shut the glass door behind us and drew me over to the fire, throwing another log into the already blazing grate.

"How's Dad?" I asked, reaching out my hands to try and warm my shivering body.

He walked to the door without answering my question, his frown when he glanced back telling me too much. "Get dressed and I'll meet you in the kitchen room, yeah?"

The kitchen room was a little dining hall that us kids had used when growing up.

I nodded, my other question stuck in my throat. Any news about Iain? But I couldn't say ask because my heart knew he hadn't been found. Theo would have led the conversation with that, I was certain.

But it was more than that. That part of me that had always been a little obsessed with Iain, my oldest brother Bernie's best friend, had begun to hurt. I'd shut down any feelings I had for Iain years ago, when he made it clear that I was nothing more than an annoying kid to him. But now that I'd opened the little Pandora-style box in which I'd tamped down my feelings, and looked inside, a rush of feeling was pouring out once more.

I raced over to my old closet, pulling out my warmest clothes. My mom liked me to wear dresses every day of the week, like a princess should. I rolled my eyes at the very thought of the rules my mom used to force upon me.

But my father had supported my desire to wear pants on occasion, and had made sure the tailors sewed me some of those as well as dresses.

I pulled out my favorite warm, black pants and several layers for my top half. A thin wool undertop, and a gray dress-like pullover with long sleeves. Lastly were thick socks and flat-heeled knee-high boots.

"That's better." I felt like myself now. And a lot warmer at least.

My pink gloves and scarf were laying on my bed, so I picked them up on my way out the door. I shivered, even in the warmth of the castle walls and my clothing. My body was going to need time to readjust to the temperature here, it seemed.

Greece had been very warm, indeed, in comparison.

I rushed along the hallway, wrapping the scarf around my neck and pulling on my gloves over my cold fingers.

The kitchen room was full of my family and the cousins I'd grown up with.

"Anselm! Vanya!" I called, running over to Stavrok's oldest kids and wrapping my arms around Vanya's shoulders. "It's so good to see you."

Vanya squeezed me so tight I squeaked with pain.

"Oh, sorry." She stepped back.

"Tell me what happened," I demanded, then stepped back to widen the circle. Jessa and Carlak stood beside me, then a hand on my shoulder had me turning around.

It was Anthony.

I couldn't help it. The look on his face. The sadness. The pity...

My fingers curled into a fist and my arm launched out at his face. I hit Anthony, hard.

The sorcerer took it on the chin and reeled back.

"You son of a bitch," I screamed at him. "How could you not protect them! How?"

Anselm grabbed me and hauled me back. "Veronica! Stop! It's not Anthony's fault."

"My dad's dying! Iain's missing!" I screamed at my cousin. "How are you all not furious!"

"We are," Vanya said, crossing her arms over her chest, glaring at me. "But you don't need to take it out on Anthony."

I covered my face with my hands, certain I was about to burst into tears. My eyes burned and my throat ached. My breath heaved inside my chest, but I didn't cry.

I dropped my hands and stared at the sorcerer, now standing far away. "I'm sorry."

Anthony rubbed his chin. "It's all good, dragon daughter." His eyes shifted into that look again, the one that said he had a vision to share, and I glanced away.

"You can use me," I told him. "To find Iain."

Silence descended on the group and when I finally looked up again, my cheeks were aflame with a hot blush.

My cousins were all looking at each other, confused.

"Why would you..."

"How would that..."

Anthony walked toward me, straight through the middle of the circle. He didn't speak and I quietly thanked him for not confirming my secret. Not yet anyway. I was still struggling with it myself.

"I don't know if it'll work." He spoke quietly, reaching for my hands anyway. "You weren't here when the accident happened."

I still didn't know what the details were, but I lifted my chin anyway. "Try. Please."

Anthony, the youngest son of Queen Marienne, nodded his head and my eyes slid shut.

There was only darkness and pain.

I gasped out and Anthony's hands squeezed my fingers tighter, as though he was going to stop me from pulling away, if that was my intention.

I squeezed back. I wasn't letting go. Not until we found him.

The visions came in flashes, like a lightning storm lighting up each picture for only a moment, before blackness fell again.

Flash. A stony path. One I hadn't seen before. Which was odd.

Flash. A river. The one that led out of town and into the forest.

Flash. A house. A cellar. Iain.

"No!" I cried out as I gazed upon him.

He looked up as though he could hear me, his bright blue eyes pinning me in place. His leg was trapped under several boulders and his hair was matted with blood.

"Iain," I whispered, then Anthony let go of my hands.

The vision and sounds of the room came rushing back to me like a giant whirlwind, knocking me around. I staggered sideways, my knees giving out beneath me.

Anselm grabbed me up and lifted me into his arms a moment, before setting me down on the couch.

"Thanks," I managed, still reeling from what I'd seen.

I glanced over at Anthony, who was standing in the same place as though frozen.

"Anthony!" I called out. "We need to go get him."

But the sorcerer wasn't moving.

"Anthony!"

The doors to our sanctuary burst open and King Erik and King Stavrok stormed in.

Erik rushed over to his son. "Anthony? What happened?"

Anselm explained what Anthony had done while I managed to get to my feet. I'd need a jacket if we were going out into the snow. I wasn't sure how long Iain would be able to hold out in these temperatures.

"How long's he been gone?" I demanded to the closest person to me. It happened to be my brother, Theo.

"Who?" he asked.

Idiot.

"Iain! How's long's he been missing? When did the accident happen?"

"Just this morning," Theo answered, going pale. "Dad and Iain went flying. They went over the forest and disappeared. Dad came back a few hours later. Bleeding. His arm and leg broken. He collapsed on arrival and hasn't woken up yet."

"So he's the only one who knows where Iain is," I whispered. Dad wouldn't have left Iain if he'd had any other choice. He'd used all his energy to fly back for help, then couldn't speak once he got here.

Marienne, the sorceress, burst into the room. "Anthony!"

She hurried over to him and I met her gaze as she reached out to touch her son. "Anthony was helping to find Iain, but I think he's in shock... or something."

Marienne laid her hands on Anthony's face. "He's used too much of his magic. I'll care for him. You all need to go."

"You know where my son is?" Stavrok demanded, staring at Marienne.

The sorceress turned her violet eyes on me, her purple magic swirling in their depths. "No. But Veronica does."

I gulped as all eyes turned on me. "He's trapped. In a cellar. Under an old house."

Stavrok reached out for my arm, squeezing painfully. "Where?"

I tugged my arm away from him and although I couldn't move far, he got the message and let go.

"I don't know. There was a stony path I've never seen before. The creek leading out of the castle. We have to go." I stumbled toward the door. "He won't last the night."

The party of family and friends followed me as we raced for the front door.

"Do we fly?" Stavrok asked me.

I wasn't sure. I didn't even know which way we were going. "I don't know. Dad and Iain flew, so perhaps it would be faster..."

Stavrok began to undress, throwing his clothes to the floor. All the men around me prepared themselves to shift.

"I'm coming with you," I said, pulling off my boots. "You won't find him without me."

None of the men around me argued, though I could tell they were hesitant to take me.

"Come on," I said, pushing the last of my own warm clothes to the ground as the servants pulled open the front door and a blast of icy cold air hit me in the face. I stifled a sigh. This weather would take some getting used to, again.

Then I thought of Iain, unprotected and in danger of dying. No time to lose.

"Let's go."

CHAPTER

THREE

Iain

I must have fallen asleep again, because I had to be dreaming if I was hearing things now. I'd heard Veronica's voice but there was no way she was here.

"It's just your own mind, idiot," I chastised myself. I hadn't meant to fall asleep. In fact, I'd promised myself I wouldn't. But between the cold, the hunger and the pain, I probably hadn't had much fight left in me. At least no one was here to see me failing.

But why hadn't anyone found me yet? Where was Damon? I'd heard him yell out after the house had caved in on us, something about going for help. But that could have been a dream, too.

My whole body was shivering again, from my lips and chattering teeth to my shaking shoulders. Even my pale white, bloodless fingers seemed to be frozen.

I didn't have clothes, or blankets, but I'd managed to pull over some rough hessian bags to cover my chest and leg a little. I wasn't sure it was doing much, but it was better than nothing.

My leg wasn't throbbing anymore, which was kind of a relief, though part of me knew that was a bad thing. The nerves were dead, or there was no blood flow any longer. Either way, I doubted I was getting out of here alive.

And even if I did, would I be looking at life without my leg?

I closed my eyes and dreamed of the only thing that ever gave me any peace. Veronica.

The dragon daughter herself. A princess.

We'd grown up together, as cousins. We'd always been told that my father Stavrok and Lucy, Veronica's mom, were first cousins.

She was seven years younger than me so when I turned eighteen and she was only eleven, the strange feelings I began to feel toward her made me feel sick. I pushed her away. Hard.

I taunted her and played tricks on her. I was mean, even as she got older. By the time she was sixteen, she hated me.

Unfortunately, it wasn't long after her sixteenth birthday that I discovered two things.

One, that the feelings I'd been fighting against for five years were the result of our fated mate bond, and two... that she wasn't really my cousin.

I'd used the blood relative excuse for years as to why finding Veronica attractive was wrong. Even though second cousins wasn't considered a close relationship, I convinced myself it was disgusting.

But then, after an offhand comment from Lucy, I realized that my father had adopted her as his cousin. My grandparents and Veronica's grandparents had been friends, so when they'd all died, Dad had taken Lucy into the castle and cared for her as he would a younger sister.

But there was no blood relationship there.

"Oh... fuck, it's cold." I shuddered against the frozen, hard ground, passing in and out as the bleak daylight slowly faded into night.

The fact that Veronica would never know the real reason I'd teased and tortured her was my only regret right now. That, and the fact that my death was going to destroy my family. I may not be the heir to the throne, or the favorite son, but my parents had loved me. Always.

"At least I had that. More than some people have."

I began to laugh, the last words of a dying man. How ridiculous. And ironic. My own voice was the last thing I'd ever hear. I had hoped it would be my wife's, or at least one of my siblings. Or perhaps a child, if I'd ever had the chance to produce my very own heir.

Being the son born five years after a set of triplets that were bonded like no other hadn't been the easiest thing. It had felt more like growing up as an only child.

But damn, what I wouldn't give to hear Anselm's voice right now, telling me what I was doing wrong. Classic older-brother-future-king type of shit.

I loved him, though. And I know he loved me.

I dashed away a tear that dropped onto my cheek. Yeah... I was going to die down here. I stared at my leg once again, considering the option to tear my body away from the limb. Would that give me more chance of survival, or less?

I closed my eyes. I was out of options. I was too weak to shift. And if I did somehow manage to get out from under this massive rock, I'd bleed out before I could crawl out of here.

"Iain! Iain!" Veronica's voice echoed in my head again.

I chuckled and lay my head back on a rock. "I'm here, sweetheart. I'm here." So, the last thing I was going to hear was my fated mate's voice inside my head. That was better than anything else.

"Iain! We're coming. Just hold on."

I opened my eyes and struggled to sit up. "Veronica?"

"Yes! It's me."

My jaw dropped and a strange surge of warmth filled my chest. "Ah... I'm dreaming again, right?"

There was a huge creak and groan as some of the huge boulders around me were lifted and firelight sparked around me.

The fire caused a silhouette highlight of dragon wings above me, moving the wood and boulders and stone. Dust clouds made me cough and I covered my mouth, trying not to breathe in any more of the crap around this abandoned house.

Footsteps sounded on the ground outside the house, and then a figure appeared.

"Veronica?"

It was truly her. How was this possible? She was naked and trembling, her body more beautiful than I could ever remember. Her time away had done her the world of good, it seemed.

I glanced away, not wanting to look at her like that, when she had no choice about her nudity after shifting.

"Iain, oh my God." She hurried down beside me, putting her hands on my face, on my arms, on my leg. "You're hurt. Your leg."

I groaned as my shifter began to rise inside of me, wanting to shift with my mate now in sight.

"Are you in pain?" she asked, shaking a little as though she was as freezing as I was.

"Yes," I said, to cover the fact that I was really struggling now. My shifter had kept to his slumber when Veronica had been underage. When he'd seen her at Anthony's wedding, I'd barely been able to keep him together.

But now... she was nineteen, she was beautiful, and she was here, rescuing me.

"Arghhh..." My spine arched as I fought off my dragon. "Fuck.... I'm going to shift."

"But... why? How?"

My eyes had already shifted and my night vision made her body even more beautiful.

"Fuck." I looked away, her pink nipples pebbled as if aching for my touch. "You know why, Veronica. Please. Help me."

She stared at me for a moment, then she stood up and screamed. "Anselm! Theo! Hurry! We need to get this boulder off his leg so he can shift and heal."

More wings disappeared and my big brother ran down the broken stairs and into the cellar. "Iain. Oh... man, it's good to see you."

My dragon settled a little, but it hovered just beneath the surface. "Help. Brother. Get this thing off me."

Anselm studied the rock as Theo appeared.

"Man, he's gonna bleed out if we lift this off him."

"He's going to die if we leave him here," Veronica snapped, all fire and brimstone. "Just do it, guys. Lift that fucking stone, I'll pull him out and he can shift before he bleeds too much."

Anselm looked at me. "Are you sure you can do it? You've lost a lot of blood."

I clenched my jaw tight and nodded. "I can. But I've only got a minute or two before I pass out. Lift the rock and run, guys. Please."

More help appeared as loud wings flapped, then my father appeared. "Son!"

Stupid tears clogged my throat. "Dad."

King Stavrok, a beast of a man, and my father, the king, dropped to his knees beside me. "Oh son, I thought we'd lost you forever."

He cupped my face in the most affectionate touch I'd received in years.

I couldn't speak, but Veronica was there, taking charge. She put a hand on Dad's shoulder and tugged him back.

"Uncle, we need to hurry. Help Anselm get this rock off him. His dragon's ready to shift, and if we don't do it now, we'll lose him."

Dad stood up. "He can't shift, not like this."

Veronica growled, her shifter as close to the surface as mine was. "He's not dying down here. You got that? Lift the rock, and get clear. I'll get him out and he'll shift."

Dad's growl was louder and more menacing and yet Veronica didn't budge.

My shifter couldn't help but be proud of the strength of my mate.

"He'll kill you when he shifts, Veronica, and that's if he can. I'm not letting you do this."

She put her hands on her hips and faced my father. "Uncle! You have to trust me. I found him. He's still alive because of me. Just listen and do as I say. One more time."

I could see my father hesitating. He believed in magic and premonitions, and although I had no idea what Veronica had done or said to get them here, obviously she believed she had the right to throw her weight around.

I added fuel to the fire. "Dad. Please. Just do what she says."

I could tell he wanted to ask why, but he didn't. He just turned toward the wreckage that had fallen on my leg.

"Okay boys. On three, we lift. Once he's clear, we run and shift, get to the sky."

Anselm and Theo nodded and grabbed sections of the boulder that lay pressed on my leg.

Dad called out. "One. Two. Three. Lift!"

Veronica grabbed under my arms and the moment the rock shifted, she pulled, hard, using her dragon strength to move me.

I half-blacked out. The pain! Oh my God, the pain! A throbbing, sharp, let-me-die-please type of pain coursed through my body.

Veronica shook my shoulders hard, and I managed to open my eyes. I was bleeding out. I could feel it. The blood gushing from my wound, draining my life force.

I was so cold, my leg throbbing with agony.

"Iain!" She screamed in my face, then she slapped me. Hard.

The pain was horrible but woke up my shifter. She was mad at me. My mate was angry.

"Get up!" she screamed. "Shift! Now!"

Then she grabbed my face and kissed me, hard. Her lips on mine were from a dream, but then she was gone and the coldness of her loss blasted me in the face.

"You will not die on me. You got that?" she whispered. "Now... fly with me."

She ran, up the stones and away from me. I saw her transform in the darkness and fly away.

My dragon shifter rose up inside me faster than ever before. My wings sprouted and my body changed, the pain in my leg dulling down to a basic thud as my dragon took over my humanity.

I could see everything now, my night vision kicking in. I roared, pain beginning to build inside my body as my shifter fought the injuries.

Fly. I heard Veronica's voice in my head. *Fly.*

I staggered up the steps, up the hole my family had made for me to get out of.

My claws gripped the cold dirt as I panted for breath. I was seeing stars, but not the ones in the night. I was going to pass out again.

A roar above my head made me look up. It was Veronica, her wings flapping hard, keeping her in place. She roared again, icy fire blasting through the nights sky.

God, she's magnificent.

She was calling to me and my dragon needed her, more than his next breath.

I jumped off the rock I stood on, launching into the sky, and followed my fated mate home.

CHAPTER

FOUR

Veronica

My heart pounded in my chest as though it was racing to its last beat. Iain was standing on the ground, unmoving. He'd managed to shift, but I wasn't sure he was going to make it.

I need to fly back down and help him.

But even as I thought the words, Iain looked up at me, his eyes blazing in the darkness of the night.

Then he was flying up, toward me. Happiness filled my heart and I started to fly home, in the direction of the Winter Palace.

Iain was slow, but he wasn't far behind me. I flew just fast enough that he could see me, but I wanted to give him something to aim for so I stayed just out of his reach.

When I landed on the doorstep of our castle, I shifted back quickly and pulled open the front door, yelling. "We need help. Bring supplies!"

Waiting servants rushed forward with a cloak for me and I wrapped it around my body. Fuck, I was freezing! Again!

Uncle Stavrok and Anselm came running toward the front entrance, barely dressed, but at least they were wearing pants.

A dragon roar met my ears and I turned on the top step to see Iain flying in fast, but he was too low.

I started waving my arms, signaling at him to land near us.

He tried to comply, but he was clearly struggling. His dragon dropped out of the sky, landing badly about a hundred feet down the path, rolling over and over in the snow and ice and coming to a halt in a flurry of white.

I grabbed a black cloak from our butler's arms and started running down the road.

Anselm, with his longer legs, ran past me and Stavrok was hard on my heels.

Iain shifted back to human form just as we reached him. "Here," I called out to them, throwing the cape over Iain's shoulders. Anselm quickly fastened the buttons, then Stavrok ducked down and lifted his son, heaving him up over his shoulder before running back to the castle entrance.

Anselm and I gaped at the speed with which he'd scooped Iain up, shared an incredulous look, then ran after them.

Stavrok bounded up the steps with ease, as if Iain weighed nothing at all. When we reached the foyer, Stavrok was already marching toward the main living room.

Inside, the fire was roaring and I rushed over to the fireplace to warm my chilled bones while Stavrok lay Iain on a nearby couch. Iain was shaking and his teeth were chattering.

I didn't think about how it would look. I ran over to the couch, jumped on top of Iain's half naked body, and lay down beside him, spreading my warm, thick cloak over the both of us to cocoon in whatever body warmth we could.

"What are you..."

"Shut up," I whispered, stealing my arm around his middle and pressing my flesh to his.

I lay my head on his shoulder and closed my eyes, embarrassed on a level I had never experienced before. But I refused to move. He needed to warm up, and fast.

Everyone was going to know about our bond now, and my cheeks flushed with heat.

"Everyone, give Iain some space," Stavrok called. "Go get the healer. Everyone else out. I'll stay."

There were some soft murmurings, but I didn't open my eyes until the noises faded away. I clung to Iain's shivering body until he began to quieten and his limbs soften beneath me.

Then I opened my eyes, slowly.

Stavrok was sitting in the large armchair next to the fireplace, staring at us, but everyone else was gone.

I lifted my chin until I could see Iain's face. He had his eyes closed and his breathing was even, as though he was sleeping. But something told me he wasn't.

I moved my arm, lower, toward his belly. His hand came up to grab my arm, stopping the movement. But it didn't stop me from feeling something warm and hard pressing up against the blankets.

"Don't move," he whispered. "Please don't move."

I relaxed again, laying my hand against his ribs. He was trembling again now, though I was pretty sure it was due to something other than cold this time.

"I'll get up. You're warm now."

"No," Iain snapped, a growl behind his words. "I'm… I can't control it. Please, just stay where you are."

My heart was pounding again, my dragon shifter recognizing the call of her mate. He wanted me. He was hurt, barely alive… but he wanted me.

Stavrok stood and walked over, slowly. "Son, I can help."

Iain growled a little deeper, his arm slipping around my shoulders and holding me to his chest now.

"Dad. Back off."

Fear shot through me, but beneath the worry was a strong pulse of desire. Of arousal. It was something I'd never felt before. Not to this level. I swallowed the moan that would have followed my next words.

"It's okay, Uncle…"

"It's not okay," Stavrok whispered, still a few feet away. "Iain… why didn't you tell anyone that Veronica was your mate?"

I glanced at the prince, whose jaw was set in the most determined angle I'd ever seen. "She was eleven when I first knew. She was a child. I was disgusted with myself."

Stavrok made a tutting noise. "Hey, it's okay. None of this is your fault. We're both so glad… so grateful you're alive."

I nodded against his neck, barely able to breathe now. My belly was quivering. His smell was just… so good.

"Iain, I know your dragon wants to claim her, but please, let her go. Give her to me. I'll take her to have a shower. To eat. You trust me, don't you?"

Stavrok's voice was soothing, but it annoyed me just the same.

"It's okay," I managed to choke out. "You can go. He can keep me."

I couldn't believe I was saying the words, but I was. I wanted him. And he wanted me. Surely that wasn't a terrible thing?

"Veronica?" Stavrok asked quietly. "Iain isn't in control, and although he doesn't want to hurt you… you're a virgin, are you not?"

I buried my face in Iain's shoulder once more. "Yes. Why?"

Iain's arms loosened on me, then he said in a growling tone, "Quickly. Go with my dad. I… need to get my dragon back under control."

I lifted my head and stared at him. "You don't want me anymore?"

All of my fears came crashing down on me once more, but the heat in his eyes called his words a liar.

"Go." He spoke louder this time. "Dad, quick. Take her before I shift."

Stavrok's arms came around me and lifted me off Iain's body.

"No!" I screamed, my arms out and grasping for my mate.

Iain turned his head away, his chest rising and falling as he took great big gasps of air.

Stavrok set me on my feet, then pulled the same move he had with Iain. He put his shoulder in my gut and lifted me up off my feet.

"Uncle Stavrok! Put. Me. Down."

He didn't comply. Instead, he marched me all the way upstairs and didn't put me down until we were in my bedroom.

I fell back on my ass on the familiar carpet, still only wearing my cloak. "Why did you do that?"

My mom came hurrying into the room, her face as white as a ghost. "Veronica? Oh my God... Veronica!"

"Mom! Is Dad..." Tears filled my eyes and squeezed my heart. I couldn't finish the question.

"He's alive." She rushed over to me, holding out her hands and hauling me to my feet.

I fell into her arms and she dragged me in for the biggest hug of my life. My mother. A dragon princess of her era. She held me as I squeezed her tight, then finally she pulled back and cupped my face in her hands.

"Are you all right?" she asked.

I nodded. "Yes. I'm fine."

Mom released me to turn and stare at Stavrok. "Iain?"

He nodded. "Thanks to Veronica, he's alive. Healing."

Mom turned toward me. "What... I'm sorry... I don't understand."

Stavrok smiled at me and bowed his head. "I'm going to go and make sure my son hasn't burned down the castle. And you can talk to your mom."

The king left me alone and somehow, strangely, I wanted to call out to him and call him a coward. Or maybe that was just how I was feeling? I didn't want to talk to Mom, or anyone else, about Iain.

"Tell me about Dad," I said to her, wandering over to the fireplace.

"How about you tell me about Iain?" she said. "After you've had a hot shower and dressed. I'll wait. Then we'll talk about Dad."

I nodded and ran into my adjoining bathroom. She was giving me room to breathe and think. Something Mom rarely did because she knew that I'd somehow try to get out of the conversation.

But there was no getting out of this one. Iain's dragon was ready to grab me the first time he next saw me, and I wasn't sure I could stop my own dragon from wanting the same thing. I was still throbbing in areas that were vastly embarrassing to admit to.

My bathroom was bigger than I remembered. There had been nothing like it in any of the places I'd visited in the human realm. The huge claw-footed bathtub called to me, but I didn't have hours to run the thing and soak. I had to get back to Mom, and everyone else.

I wanted to see my father.

I took off the cloak, put on the hot water and stepped into the huge shower. The pressure was fantastic and I stood there for too long, letting the heat soak into my bones. I washed my hair with the homemade soap and when I was finally ready to step out, I dried myself with the thick, luxurious towels my mom loved.

My wardrobe was inside my bedroom, so I wrapped towels around my hair and body and made my way back to my room. Mom was sitting on the small love seat near the fireplace, her eyes closed as if in sleep. She looked utterly exhausted.

I crept over to my wardrobe and pulled out a long winter dress and some tights. By the time I was finally dressed, she was awake and smiling at me. "Hey. Feeling better?"

I nodded. "Definitely. I'd forgotten how cold it is here."

Her smile was sad this time. "Yeah. You haven't been home in over a year."

I glanced away. "Yeah, I know. I meant to come for Christmas, but the family I was nannying for needed me, and, well…"

I should have come home when they'd asked me to over the holidays. But between Anthony's visions of Iain and my newfound freedom, I'd been partly afraid to come home, if I was being honest.

"It's okay."

"How's Dad?" I asked, sitting down beside her.

Mom sighed, deep and heavy. "He's still unconscious, but Marienne will be here soon. His body is still strong, and he's healing, but… we're all worried."

I nodded, a lump in my throat. I didn't know what to say to make my mom feel better.

But then her eyes lit up and she patted my hand. "Tell me about what's going on with you and Iain."

I opened my mouth to tell her the long story, then snapped it shut again. I'd been taught to be polite, but my own nature was rough and straight to the point.

So, I wasn't going to lie or string my mother along. I opened my mouth and told the truth. "Iain is my fated mate."

Iain

By the time Dad got back to the lounge room I'd managed to get to my feet and was limping around in my efforts to pace. My leg was killing me, but it was still attached to my body, so I was grateful.

"When were you going to tell me?" Dad roared, striding into the room, ablaze with annoyance just as I expected.

"Never!" I yelled back. "I thought she was my cousin! And she was a fucking child! My plan was to make her hate me, and marry someone else before she reached maturity."

My dad growled at me, two feet away now. "Well, that didn't fucking happen, did it?"

We were both huffing and panting when the healer and Anselm entered the room.

"My lord."

Dad turned to the healer and gestured to him to come further into the room. "Please. Come and see to my son."

The healer was a man older than my father, carrying a black bag. But he was a steady man with intelligent eyes. "Lie down on the sofa, son. Let me look at you."

I did what the healer said, mostly to avoid arguing any more with my dad.

The healer put his hands on my head, checking for a fever, then moved down my body and to my leg.

"Oh, this looks like it was very painful."

I groaned as his fingers pressed into my tender flesh. When I glanced down, I could see the thigh was red raw and the flesh was indented and crisscrossed with scarring. I had begun healing, but it was still pretty bad.

"It's not bleeding anymore," I managed to choke out in a semblance of humor. "I thought I was going to lose it, to be honest."

Anselm and Dad moved closer, sitting nearby.

"How did you shift?" Anselm asked. "I thought you'd bleed out or die before your dragon could take over. I was shit-scared, to be honest. But I wasn't going up against Veronica. She was ferocious."

Dad turned away but I could tell he was still listening.

The healer smiled and I couldn't stop my own laugh. "Yeah... even though my life was literally hanging in the balance, no one was going up against the dragon daughter."

"I did," Dad said, his voice hollow in the big room.

I laid my head back on the sofa, a wave of tiredness washing over me. "Yeah, and even you backed down."

Silence.

"You still didn't answer the question," Anselm said. "How did you manage to shift with so much blood loss, and the pain must have been... bad."

I groaned. "It was so bad I passed out."

Silence again, then my big brother poked me in the arm. "Yeah? And?"

I smiled at the memory. "Veronica slapped me and screamed in my face. So, I got up."

Dad's laugh was loud. Unmistakable in its meaning. But he didn't say anything.

It was Anselm who had the guts to ask the question. "What's with you and the dragon daughter? I thought you hated each other."

I sighed heavily then gasped as the healer rubbed some ointment into my leg and said, "Sit up and drink this tonic. It will help you to replace some of your lost blood."

I sat up and took the vial he handed me, tossing the contents back even though it smelt like a pond.

"Eek, that's vile," I said, gagging after it slid down my throat.

Dad walked away then came back a moment later with a glass of whiskey. "Here."

I grabbed it and took a large swig into my mouth, swallowing the drink down with relish.

"Thanks."

I lay back against the pillows and the healer walked over to my dad. "King Stavrok. I'm going to retire for the night, but if you need me at all, I'll be in the servants' quarters."

The man bowed and left.

I shifted on the sofa, my leg still aching like it had taken a beating. "How's Uncle Damon? No-one's said anything about him, but I assume he made it back? Told you where I was?"

Anselm and Dad shared a look, then my brother said, "Ah... no. Well, Damon made it back... just. Collapsed outside of the castle and he's still unconscious. That's why Veronica came back. Theo messaged her in the human realm and she flew straight home."

I rolled onto my side so I could face my family, the whiskey doing its job to warm my belly and relax me. "So how did you find me?"

There was a bell ringing in my head, some piece of information I wasn't piecing together.

Anselm slid forward, to the edge of his seat, and clasped his hands together. "We would never have found you, except for Veronica. Or if we had... you'd be dead. No-one knew where you and Damon had gone, and with him unconscious, we didn't even know where to start looking."

I blinked, then slowly, using my arms, pushed myself up to a seated position once more. "Is that why Veronica was yelling at Dad? She was saying something about trusting her, or something? I didn't understand and I could barely think anyway by that point."

Between the blood loss, the cold and the fact my mate had found me, I was delirious.

Two servants opened the door carrying silver platters of food and drinks. They moved things around with the tables so they could place the food within arm's reach, then bowed and left.

"Thank you!" I called out to them as they walked away, reaching for a steaming hot bowl of soup.

I was starving, but shoving thick bread and heavy meat into my gut wasn't smart. I'd start with the creamy pumpkin soup, and work up from there.

The first spoonful was pure bliss, as was the buttered roll my brother pushed my way.

I ate as much as I could, Dad and Anselm taking a thing or two, but they were obviously leaving most of it for me.

"Please. Eat," I said, gesturing to the platters. "There's enough for ten men here."

Dad smiled and grabbed a roll while Anselm poured himself some wine. The fire crackled in the grate and my belly was finally sated. I sat back with a groan and a sigh. To think, only a few hours ago, I'd truly believed my time on this planet was done. How quickly things changed. Thanks mostly to Veronica.

"I really thought we'd lost you," Anselm said, looking down on the food and not meeting my gaze.

"You weren't far away from losing me, I can tell you," I said. Then I glanced at Dad. "You still haven't explained what happened with Veronica."

"She got Anthony to hold her hands and search for you. We didn't know how or why she would help at the time. Now, of course, we do."

Anselm lifted his head, his eyes wide as realization hit him. "What... you mean... Veronica?"

I nodded and gulped down another swig of whiskey. "Yep. The dragon daughter is my mate. I've known for eight years."

"And you didn't tell me? Tell us?" Anselm demanded.

"What was I going to say?" I fired back. "That my fated mate was a fucking child? And at the time I thought she was our cousin."

"She is," Anselm said, his eyebrows furrowing. "Our second cousin."

I glanced at Dad who said simply, "Cass isn't my blood relative cousin. She was a family friend of the family, who I took in as my sister when her parents died. It never seemed like a title I needed to correct."

I shrugged. "It's fine." But it hadn't been for a long time.

"But you always seemed to hate her," Anselm went on, sounding incredulous. "You..."

"I know." I groaned, running a hand through my hair. "I was mean to her, taunted her. Pushed her away as much as I could."

"But why?"

"Because I was disgusted with myself!" I yelled at them both. "Not that I was attracted to her, like that. I wasn't. I was more, protective. Wanting to help her, shield her. But I knew what it was, the beginning of the bond. And I couldn't do it. I didn't want to feel like that."

I'd never lusted after Veronica as a child. Never. But the happiness my dragon felt when she was nearby was a sure sign she was meant to be mine. So I'd run away, figuratively. Putting as much space between her and me as I could.

"Your love for her isn't disgusting," Dad said. "You never touched her, barely spoke to her when she was young."

I made a strange choking noise, "No... I pushed her away. Hard."

"Well, she's nineteen now, almost twenty," Anselm said, sounding strangely excited. "And she obviously knows about the bond, or she wouldn't have demanded Anthony read her like a bloody crystal ball."

I couldn't help the smile that spread across my face at the image his words invoked. "She was pretty adamant, huh?"

"Adamant?" Dad repeated, snorting loudly. "She punched Anthony in the face."

I gaped at him, "No..."

Anselm smirked. "Hell yes, she did. You're gonna have fun putting some reins on her, brother."

"Reins?" came an amused voice from the doorway.

I glanced up and saw Aunt Cass watching us. She looked as lovely as ever, but much paler than usual. I smirked and held my hands up. "I didn't say it, Anselm did."

Cass chuckled. "Well, you better not let my daughter hear anyone say it... she's already frothing at the mouth over how you've treated her the past ten years."

I sobered immediately. "It wasn't... I didn't..."

Cass put up her hand to silence me, always the queen. "You don't owe me an explanation."

"Where's Veronica?" I asked, already assessing my body and trying to figure out whether I had the strength to stand up or not.

I did, but it wouldn't be pretty.

"She's with her father."

An ominous cloud descended on the whole room.

I pushed myself to my feet, my leg throbbing hard. "Take me there. Please."

If Veronica's dad died, would she ever forgive me? He'd used up every last vestige of strength to get home... to get help, for me. Would she blame me? Probably. Then where would we be?

Two fated mates unable to be together? Or something even worse?

CHAPTER
SIX

Veronica

My father's chest rose and fell like he was simply asleep, but there was a deathly pallor to his face I'd never seen before. It scared me, seeing him like this. Weak, and vulnerable. It wasn't something I was used to, with my dad. The great King Damon. The King of the North. The savior of the Winter Palace.

The door opened behind me and light footsteps on the carpet made their way to the other side of my parents' massive bed.

"I'm here, Damon. My old friend," Marienne whispered, reached out to touch my dad's hand. "Whatever has happened to you?"

I looked up at Anthony's mom, the Queen of the Black Mountains, and my eyes filled with tears. "Can you help him? Please?"

She sat on the bed and reached out to pass her hand over my father's chest, closing her eyes as her magic rippled around her like a cloak.

I waited, holding my breath. All I could hear was the thumping of my own heartbeat in my ears. The door opened again and Mom hurried in. Iain was behind her, limping his way to a chair in the corner.

My gaze was drawn to him even though I was still furious with him.

For everything.

For being so mean to me in my teenage years. For not telling me the truth. For almost dying before I could wring his neck for the other two offences.

Yet, inside my chest my dragon settled with him in the room. Almost... happy. As much as I could be, in the circumstances.

Fucking traitor.

Marienne turned toward Mom and me. "He's tired. I don't know how else to put it. His body is healing, but I can only feel how exhausted his soul is. His mind doesn't want to wake up."

Mom's sob sounded moments before she swallowed it down.

I stood up and wrapped my arms around her. "It's okay, Mom. You don't have to be strong for us. Not now."

My mother didn't cry in front of us; she never had. But it wasn't for lack of emotions, her heart beat hard and strong. The strength of her love for my father had never been in question. Even when they fought... screamed the castle down some days in their passion for a brighter, better future, we knew they loved each other.

Mom nodded, and tears slid down her pale cheeks. But she didn't make another sound.

Iain limped over to the bed, sitting near Dad's feet. He cleared his throat roughly, the cough sounding in the room. "Uncle Damon, I... I'm so sorry. It was my idea to check out the abandoned house. I had no idea it was going to collapse. It was my fault. All of this."

I stared at him, my anger and pain mixing together to become a single arrow of focused fury directed straight at Iain's heart. My mate had dragged my dad into a situation that may have killed him?

"Are you fucking kidding me?" I hissed at Iain, my hands tightening into fists.

Iain turned bloodshot eyes toward me. "I'm sorry."

I shook my head and took a step back, away from the bed. "If my dad dies, I'll never forgive you."

My father was the sun and the moon for my family, for my kingdom. And more importantly, for my mother.

Iain stood up, his voice imploring. "Veronica. Please..."

I ran from the room. I couldn't even look at him and my dragon was so fucking angry I could shift this very minute. In fact...

I turned down a hallway, running in the direction of my room, stripping off my clothes as I ran. I couldn't believe this. Theo had called me back here just in time to save my pain-in-the-ass, supposedly fated mate, only to expect me to watch my father die?

No!

I couldn't accept that outcome. I refused to watch him die. I wouldn't let it happen. I ran through my room to the balcony and for the second— or was it third?—time that day, I shifted and took to the sky. My dragon blasted fiery ice as I flapped my wings, ascending higher into the heavens.

I'd thought the year away from Iain would have calmed me, given me perspective. But it hadn't. Quite the opposite, in fact. I was as angry and confused as ever when it came to him and our connection. I flew until I was exhausted, then spiraled down, down down, until I reached the streets of the town below.

I landed near my uncle and aunt's house, and shifted back to human before hurrying up to their door.

I knocked once and Uncle Dymitri answered. "Veronica! Oh, God, come in before you freeze."

I strode inside and he handed me one of the long, thick cloaks that hung by the door. Everyone in our kingdom had such clothing to hand.

"Who is it, Dymitri?" Aunt Sarah's voice sounded moments before she saw me. "Oh! Come in, you must be freezing."

She hurried me into their cozy little lounge room where the fire blazed hot.

"It's beautiful in here," I said, rushing up to the fireplace to defrost.

Sarah laughed. "Yeah, I'm still human. That fire burns all year round."

I smiled at her, having a greater understanding now of what sort of temperatures a human was used to. "I can't believe you chose to live here. Why didn't you drag Dymitri back to your home town?"

Sarah stared at her husband with a disgusting amount of devotion. "He loves it here. Why would I have made him leave?"

I rolled my eyes at the gooey look they shared, but grinned. "Indeed."

Dymitri was my father's half-brother, and I'd grown up with his kids as my cousins. Thoughts of my dad immediately wiped the grin off my face. "Have you been up to the palace? Did you hear about Dad?"

Dymitri sat in a large armchair and Sarah poured tea from a pot already sitting on the nearby table, then handed me the cup.

"Yes, we did." Sarah spoke up for my uncle, sitting down on the sofa opposite me. "We've been up there already but came home a few hours ago. Is there any news?"

"Well, we found Iain and brought him home," I said, my throat aching with the words. Bastard. "But Dad's still... asleep."

"Iain... nice young man," Dymitri said. "He's been here for months, on and off. Helping your dad with renovations and plans."

I gulped. I hadn't known that. "Really? That's nice of him."

Dymitri chuckled. "It certainly is. His castle and lands are much milder than ours. I would have thought he'd prefer to stay home."

I nodded, not totally sure what to say to that.

"Come, sit." Sarah patted the spot next to her. "Are you warm enough now?"

I was, actually. The heat from the crackling fire in the grate had thawed me out nicely. I was also totally exhausted from the day's festivities, and then the shifting and flying. I plopped down on the couch next to my aunt, sipping the tea she'd given me.

"So, what are you really doing here, girl?" Sarah asked, picking up her knitting needles.

I avoided her question and asked, "What are you working on there?"

"A baby blanket for Tilly. Her baby's due in a few months' time."

Dymitri and Sarah had three children. Matilda was their daughter. "Oh, that's so good. God, I've missed a lot!"

Sarah and Dymitri smiled but didn't say anything. They didn't need to, though. The weight of their silence was impregnated with reproachful undertones. My guilt about being away for so long grew.

"I should have come back for Christmas," I whispered, my cup clattering as I lowered it to the saucer.

"Yes, you should have," Sarah said calmly. "But you're young. You're gonna make mistakes."

"Just try not to repeat too many of them," Dymitri said with a smile.

I sighed and tugged the cloak tighter around myself. That was good advice.

"Okay. I'll do my best."

Sarah put down one of her needles and reached for my hand. "Do you want to stay here tonight? We're empty nesters now. We have beds to fill."

I wiped away the stupid tear that had wended its way down my cheek. "No. I should get back. To Dad. I want to be there if..." I swallowed. "No, when, he wakes up."

I stood and hurried to the door. "Can I borrow the cloak? I'll bring it back tomorrow."

"Of course," Sarah said, right on my heels. "What's going on, Veronica? Why did you drop in? Not that we don't love seeing you, but I'm sure it wasn't just for the tea."

"Oh, nothing," I said, reaching for the door handle. "I just... wanted to see family, I guess."

Sarah and Dymitri had often been my safe haven when things blew up with Mom and Dad. I wasn't sure what they could do for me now, or how they'd help me with my Iain problem. I'd just come here automatically, out of habit. But it was still nice to see them.

"We'll come up in the morning," Sarah said. "Unless we hear anything before then."

Dymitri was standing by the door pulling on his coat. "I'll walk you up to the castle."

"Oh, you don't need to do that," I told him, but he ignored me.

He kissed his wife on the lips, and ushered me out with a wave of his hands. "Let's go."

I smiled my goodbyes at Sarah and headed out the door. It was really late now. Almost every house we walked past had their lights off. I hadn't realized how dark and late it had gotten.

"Thanks for the company," I said to my uncle as we walked up the steps to the castle entrance.

"What's going on, Veronica? Really?"

I sighed, knowing I hadn't fooled either Dymitri or Sarah. They could tell I needed advice.

Hmm... where to even begin? "You and Sarah are fated mates, right?"

He nodded. "Yeah. We all are. Your mom and dad. Me and Sarah. Lucian and Katerina."

"So, that's expected and normal in our family?" I asked, teasing out the discussion as long as I could.

Dymitri buttoned up his coat as we continued the walk up to the castle. It really was cold out tonight. I shivered, waiting for my uncle to answer.

The more we walked the more I realized how grateful I was for my uncle. I wouldn't have loved walking this whole way by myself.

"Have you found your fated mate, Veronica?" Dymitri asked suddenly. "Is that what this is about? Is he human?"

"What?" I asked.

"Did you find him while you were away on holidays? Because you know—"

"Oh no." I put out a hand and grabbed his arm to stop whatever he was about to say. "Nothing like that."

"Ah. Okay."

We were almost home. My time was running out to get an external opinion. "Dad said that you and Sarah didn't have the easiest road. With your relationship."

Dymitri broke into laughter. "That's an understatement. Sarah had been kidnapped and injured. We had to rescue her, then convince her that it was totally normal that dragons and other realms existed."

"What happened?" I asked. "When she found out what you were?"

"She freaked out, naturally," he said with a grin. "But when her sister dragged her out into the storm and they almost died, well... I was willing to do anything to be with her after that. Even move to the human realm if that's what she preferred."

"Anything for your fated mate, huh?" I asked. My heart sank. This is what I was partly afraid of. What would I sacrifice to be with Iain? What would he sacrifice for me? Would either or both of us be asked to sacrifice too much?

"Yeah," Dymitri said with a smile. We'd reached the top of the stairs and he stopped and turned to face me. "You happy for me to give you a little advice?"

I nodded. "Please do."

"Your dad will pull through. I know he will. Just be there for your mom and don't give your dad too much shit when he finally wakes up, okay? The poor guy's been working at putting this castle back together since he was sixteen years old. He's earned a rest, though I was hoping it wouldn't take a near-death experience to slow him down."

My throat clogged with sudden tears as I gulped and nodded. "Yeah. My dad... I always thought of him as being... you know..."

"Strong? Immortal?"

I nodded, wiping at the tears on my cheeks.

"He's not, Veronica. He's just a man. A shifter, yes. A king, most definitely. But he'll die one day, like we all will. What's important is the time you spend together before that happens."

I inhaled sharply. He was right.

"And as far as a fated mate goes, it's often the last person you expect. Look at the kings. Stavrok found Lucy in a village on the other side of the Veil. Erik's fated mate was his older brother's widow. And your father's fated mate was a young virgin under Stavrok's care."

I covered my face with my hands. "Oh my God." I mean, I knew my parents' story, of course. I just hadn't thought about it quite like that.

Dymitri laughed at my discomfort. "Your father was not ready for his mate. He was barely able to keep the lights on in the castle. But Fate has a plan and she's always right. You've just gotta have faith."

I dropped my hands down and away. "Faith, huh?"

My uncle grinned. "Yep. Always. And speaking of fated mates, I better get back to mine."

The castle's front door opened and our night butler gestured for me to come inside. I watched my uncle walk away, then finally returned to the warmth of my family home.

SEVEN

Iain

Auntie Cass had put everyone up, either in the guest quarters or sharing the family rooms. I was lying in a bed a few feet away from Anselm, who was snoring like a chimney.

Anselm's wife had given birth to their second child not long ago, and he'd said he hadn't had a full night's sleep in forever. A foreign concept to me, and every prince... everywhere.

He'd passed out and was currently snoring his head off. I'd been trying to sleep, but between Anselm's snores, the pain in my leg and Veronica's final words echoing in my mind, I was wide awake.

I climbed out of bed, hit the bathroom for a long hot shower, then quietly dressed and headed out into the dark halls. Night time in the castle was so quiet, but a skeleton staff always remained on duty.

There were a few single candles lit in the hallway sconces, making it just light enough to walk easily, and I could hear footsteps that told me there were people still moving around in other parts of the castle.

As I rounded a pillar on my way to the kitchen, I ran into Veronica. Literally.

"Oof." We bounced off each other and she grabbed for her cloak, pulling it tightly around her body. But not before I'd caught a glimpse of what lay beneath.

"What the hell, Iain?" She growled at me.

I stood frozen, not wanting to upset her or rouse my dragon. She was naked beneath that cloak and my shifter would spring to life in the most embarrassing way if I dwelled on Veronica's luscious curves.

"Sorry," I managed to mumble, and tried to move past her.

"No. Iain." She stepped into my path to block me. "We need to talk."

My chest tightened and breathing suddenly became more difficult. "Okay. Where? When?"

She bit her lip. "Um... everyone else is asleep. Do you want to chat in my room?"

Oh God. "Yeah. Okay." How the hell was I going to control my need for my mate with her bed mere steps away. And when she was wearing only that cloak?

She nodded once, stepped around me, and walked off, as if she wasn't aware of the need that thrummed inside me.

I took a breath, and a moment, then followed in the dragon daughter's wake. Her bedroom was up two flights of stairs, and deep into the wing containing the family bedrooms.

A healer was walking toward us as we neared the king's bedroom, and Veronica rushed over to him. I sped up my steps to catch the last of their words.

"There's no change, but he's not getting any worse," the healer said. "I'm going to bed for a few hours, then I'll come up and check on him again."

"Thank you," I managed to choke out.

Veronica turned right, grabbed the handle on an ornately decorated door, and opened it. I followed her, closing the door behind me, knowing I was now in her bedroom suite. My heart rate sped up a touch so to distract myself, I stared around at the room.

The space was beautiful, with a magnificent four poster bed in the center and a roaring hot fire in the huge grate off to one side. She hurried over to the fireplace, stretching out her hands to warm herself.

I wandered over to a large ruby red seat in the corner furthest away from the dragon princess and sat on the cushion. "Are you all right? Where did you fly to?"

Veronica stared at me, her blue eyes sparkling in the light of the room. "Nowhere really. I just flew until I couldn't fly anymore. Then I ended up at Sarah and Dymitri's house, and my uncle walked me home."

I shifted on my chair. "Dymitri is a great man. I've worked with him a lot over the years."

She turned away, toward the fire, so I was shown her back.

"What's wrong?" I asked, standing up to walk closer. If she wanted to talk, then I was here for her.

She chuckled softly. "What's wrong? Um... other than the fact that my father may be dying and my fated mate has hated me my whole life?"

I blinked at the unexpected accusation. "I've never hated you," I growled, my dragon thrashing inside my head at the prospect that she could believe such a thing. "Never."

She twirled back in a flash of both tears and anger, a Veronica duality that had always confused me. "Then why, Iain! Why? Why would you make me think that you hate me?"

I couldn't stand it any longer, being apart from her.

Fully aware that she might slap me in the face, I reached out for her, grabbing her body and hauling her close.

She didn't hit me. In fact, her hands came up to cling to my shirt. She stared up at me, her blue eyes wide and open, perfect for me to stare down into their gorgeous depths.

"I hated myself, not you," I whispered. "I hated believing that one day, you'd think I'd groomed you for this day. That I'd been nice only because you were my mate and that, when you were old enough, I'd take you to my bed. I needed you to be free to make a choice, Veronica. To want me. Not because Fate told you to, or because you felt like I influenced you in any way. I wanted you to have the right to choose for yourself."

She gulped, her throat working as she absorbed my words. The reasons why I'd pushed Veronica away for so long were vast and numerous.

"But…"

"But what?" I asked. "You have to see it from my angle. A grown man who worked out that a beautiful child would one day be his wife. It didn't feel right, and the only thing I could think to do was push you away."

I shook my head. That had been a bad day.

"But what about now?" she asked, tears glistening in her eyes. "Does my presence still make you feel like it's all wrong? Like you still hate yourself? Is that why you pushed me away when I wanted to stay close to you? On the couch."

"Oh, my beautiful…" I crushed her to me, holding her head to my chest and hugging her tight. "God, no. How could you even think that?"

She didn't say anything. But she nuzzled into my chest as though creating a home.

"I let my father drag you away because otherwise I would have shifted and hurt you, maybe myself or my dad, too. I could barely control my dragon around you. He wants you so bad."

I rested my chin on the top of her head, then dropped a kiss on her long blonde hair. "God, I don't hate you. I adore you."

She lifted her head and stared up at me, then she whispered, "No you don't. You're just saying that."

Oh, so that was the crux of her issue? She believed I was only saying these things because Fate decreed that I should want her. Not because I actually did. But because Fate was forcing me to feel it.

I lifted my hands and cupped her precious face. I had dreamt of it every night since she went away. "Princess Veronica, I have adored you for years. But I didn't want my feelings to force your hand. I needed you to feel as though you had a choice in our union."

Even though I didn't feel like I had a choice. Wanting Veronica was as natural to me as breathing. I'd never wanted any woman the way I wanted the dragon princess.

She bit her lip, looking fragile for the first time in her whole life. "I do… I think."

I kissed her forehead then the tip of her nose. Her eyes closed as I tilted her head to the side and pressed my lips to her left cheek, then her right. Her skin was as warm as sunshine.

I stared down at her, my heart in my throat. This was it. The moment I'd been fixated on for years. The moment when I had the opportunity to finally tell my mate the truth. And it was more heart-wrenching—more nerve-wracking—than I'd ever prepared for.

I took a deep breath and the words rushed out of me. "I love everything about you. I love how stubborn you are. I love how you fight for what you think is right. I love how much you love your family, and your loyalty knows no bounds."

Her lips parted as she took a breath.

I wanted to kiss her, but I needed to say more. "I love that you are fierce, and protective. And I love that, despite how afraid you were, you punched Anthony in the face and made him read you to find where I was. You saved my life, Veronica."

What other woman would fight for her man in such a way?

She smiled, the edge of her luscious lips curling up in an enchanting way.

Then she shrugged, like the whole lifesaving thing was no big deal.

I tilted her chin up with my fingertips and lowered my head, slowly moving in and kissing my mate on the lips for the very first time.

The first touch was a mere butterfly kiss. Testing the waters and seeing if she was going to allow more.

The next kiss was led entirely by the dragon daughter and her unexpected hunger. She grabbed my hair with two hands and hauled me down to crash upon her shores in a far stronger way than I'd started.

I wrapped my arms around her and breathed her in. Her lips opened and I swept my tongue in to taste her. I could have stopped, at our first heated kiss, if we'd simply left it there.

But then she did something that pushed past the thin veil of control and choice I was trying to hang onto.

She moaned. In the most seductive way possible.

And my need for her took over.

EIGHT

Veronica

My first kiss ever had been while I was on holidays with my nannying family. It had been awkward and horrible, in lots of ways. My second had been over Christmas when I'd met a boy and thought he was lovely. Again, I'd felt like a fish on dry land. Totally out of my depth.

My third kiss was happening now, with Iain. And it was nothing like either of the others. His lips were beautiful, somehow soft and strong at the same time. His smell was amazing. I inhaled deeply, wanting to fill my senses with his scent that rose around us.

When I opened my mouth to get closer and he swept his tongue between my lips, he didn't suffocate me. He tasted me, teased me, and made me want to reciprocate. And I did. I grabbed his head and hauled him closer, thrusting my tongue into his mouth and moaning as his delicious flavor shot through me.

This was right. This was how it was meant to feel. How it was meant to be.

I moaned again, and Iain stilled for a moment, freezing, as though he was about to pull away.

No. He wasn't doing that. He wasn't leaving me. He wasn't pulling away again.

Never again.

I pressed closer, fitting my body's soft curves against his hardness, my nipples tightening beneath the cloak where I was still naked. His hold around me tightened like a serpent, constricting until I could barely breathe, but I was damned if I'd ask him to let go.

When I broke off our kiss to gasp, his hold loosened a touch, and he ducked his head and kissed my neck, sucking on the skin lightly while moving his hands down to my ass.

He grabbed me and hauled me against his hard body. My knees gave out and I threw my head back, allowing him to hold me up as I explored his arms and back with my fingers.

My cloak was uncomfortable. The thick fabric was making me hot and creating a barrier between us that I didn't want.

I reached for the buttons at the throat, undid them and pushed the material from my shoulders, allowing it to drop.

Iain caught the cloak and held it to my partially clad body. Both of us were breathing hard. When he lifted his head, his gaze met mine, and his dragon shifter was right there at the surface. His irises were molten silver, making him look wild and sexy as hell.

"Are you sure?" Iain bit out. "Because I'm aware you're naked apart from this scrap of material, and I'm not sure I can hold myself back any longer."

"Thank God for that!" I bit out, stepping out of the circle of his arms and shoving the cloak off my body to let it drop to the floor and pool at my feet. "You've pushed me away long enough!"

He sucked in a breath, staring at my naked form, the blaze in his eyes becoming almost incandescent. I stood still, pushing any insecurity or desire to cover up down into the recesses of my mind. I was a dragon shifter, and a princess. I would not be embarrassed. I would not feel shame for the body I'd been given, even if this was the first time I'd let a man lay eyes on me in this way.

And that look in his eyes...

My desire ramped up ten-fold. Iain hurriedly began to undress, pulling his sweater over his head, then unbuttoning his shirt with fingers that I was pleased to note were shaking a little. Had I done that to him? I hoped so.

"I didn't mean to keep pushing you away," he rasped out.

I put my hands on my hips and glared at him, passion fueling my anger and vice versa, knowing that in this state I probably lost some of the heated effect of my words. But I wasn't getting dressed again. "Yes, you did. And you need to stop. Unless you want me to fly off to the human realm again?"

His growl rolled through the room and echoed off the walls as he threw his shirt to the carpet. "No. I've waited long enough. We've waited long enough."

I nodded at his pants. "Those too. I want to see you. All of you."

Iain's jaw dropped, no doubt at my imperious tone, then he grinned. "You would be the only virgin who demanded to inspect her mate first."

I uncrossed my arms and pointed at his pants. "Now."

This was the part that was embarrassing, and nerve wracking. My mother had said that sex with my mate would be natural, but I'd always thought that mating sounded like a seriously horrible and strange thing to do.

I'm about to find out if Mom was right.

Iain pushed his trousers to the floor then stood straight and tall, his cock bouncing up to attention. His very large and ready-looking cock.

I swallowed hard. Was he too... big... for my body? "Okay."

He laughed at whatever was showing in my expression, and stepped forward to take my hands in his. "We don't have to..."

I nearly slapped him. "Stop saying that! You're meant to be convincing me that you want me, not that you don't care." The old anxiety about rejection immediately reared up and I crossed my arms over my bare breasts, suddenly uncertain. "I know you don't care! You've spent eight years convincing me of it."

The lightness and humor disappeared from his face. He grabbed me and swung me up in his arms, walking the few steps to the bed and tossing me down onto the mattress.

I squealed a little as I bounced, but I wasn't alone long.

Iain knelt over me, grabbing my wrists and pinning my arms above my head.

"What are you doing?" I demanded. "If you do that, I can't touch you."

I tugged, trying to drag my arms down, and Iain gave me an inch.

I frowned at him. "Seriously, Iain. What are you doing?"

"You want me to show you how much I want you?" He growled at me.

Tiny shivers of desire moved over my body, making goosebumps rise on my flesh.

I nodded.

"I need you, Veronica. Do you understand me? I don't just want you. Being without you this past year has been fucking... horrendous."

His words made tears spring to my eyes, but memories of my childhood stepped up, demanding to be answered.

"It's hard to believe you," I whispered. "You don't need me. You don't even like me."

His nostrils flared, then he said, "Words aren't going to show you how much I need you... so I'm going to have to show you with action. Grab hold of your bedhead. And don't let go."

I narrowed my eyes at him. I didn't like being told what to do, but there was a tiny part of me that thrilled at the intent look in his gaze.

Iain rolled onto his side, bringing me with him, and still held my wrists above my head with one hand. Damn, he was strong.

"I do need you." He ran his other hand over my body, exploring my curves from shoulder down to my hip and back again.

Then his fingers stroked over one of my nipples and I shivered, before he cupped my breast and squeezed.

Pleasure sparked inside my nerves and I gasped.

"But you'll never understand how much." He continued stroking his hand slowly over my belly. "Because while you were growing up, safe and secure, fighting your parents and becoming the dragon daughter..."

He slid his fingers between my thighs, stroking flesh that I didn't know could ache in such a way. Flesh that was suddenly hot and wet and in need.

"I was lying in my bed... alone. Without my mate."

His fingers found my clit and pressed, making me cry out.

"Now," he said, and this time his authoritative tone made me suck in a breath. "Hold your head board, Veronica... my fated mate, or I'll leave."

"Okay," I said, wriggling up to wrap my fingers around the wooden head board.

He didn't laugh, or exult in his win. Instead, he rolled on top of me and pushed up so he could stare down into my face. "I love you. I know you don't love me. Not yet. But I've loved you for years. Since you grew into the young woman you are today, fiery, stubborn and beautiful."

I swallowed, speechless. But I had actions. I opened my legs, making room for his hard, muscled body.

He smiled softly, then shimmied down. "Don't let go."

I wasn't sure why he was stopping me from touching him too, but with my arms like this, my spine arched naturally, forcing my breasts up.

He moved down until he could take one of my nipples into his mouth. The moment he closed his lips around the tip, I cried out. It felt so strange... But so good!

He didn't respond except to suck harder, swiping his tongue in way that increased the sensation. Then he moved over to my other nipple and gave it the same treatment.

I moaned and gasped, unable to stop the sounds from emerging as arrows of pleasure fed into my belly, straight from my nipples to my center and down to my core.

"Oh my God... Iain... why does that feel so good?"

He chuckled against my breast, then glanced up at me and connected our gazes. "Because we're meant to be together, dragon girl. My mouth was made to pleasure you."

Before I could respond, he ducked his head and began a kissing path down my belly, heading south. I squeezed the head board tight, my fingers hurting.

I wasn't entirely naïve about what happened between a man and a woman in the bedroom. I had a phone. I had access to the internet. But feeling and experiencing it in person was entirely different to watching on a screen.

He used his elbows to force my thighs open wider, then set his lips to my clit.

I screamed at the exquisite sensation, finally letting go of the head board and grabbing onto his head. "Oh, you can't... no..."

But he wasn't listening, he was flicking his tongue over my clit and making ribbons of pleasure pulse deep inside of me.

When he lifted his hand and slid a finger down my seam and into my channel, I gripped him hard, gasping out, "Please, Iain. Stop that, please."

He instantly stopped and withdrew, pausing a moment before crawling up my body. I moaned with the pain of the loss.

"I didn't mean stop," I whispered, embarrassed. I'd wanted him to stop teasing me and show me the way to the end of this journey. "I meant, stop that, and show me the real thing. Please?"

I couldn't believe I was begging, but the feelings in my body were almost overwhelming.

Iain's eyes lit up and his lips lifted in a wicked grin. "Very glad to hear that, beautiful." He pushed up my knee, opening me up to him.

Then he reached down and grabbed his cock, rubbing the head over my body before teasing the entrance and pushing in slightly. I was slick with need and want for him.

I reached for his face, grabbing his jaw and drawing him in for a kiss.

He complied, kissing me hungrily, rolling on top of me and thrusting a little harder, pushing until all of his length was inside me. I felt so full.

"Oh, fuck." He groaned into my ear, and although I recognized his enjoyment, I wasn't sure about my body.

His eyes were closed and I stared at him, enjoying the fact that he seemed totally zoned out with pleasure, even if this part wasn't so great for me.

He wasn't moving, and his body inside of mine felt foreign, and although not painful, a bit strange.

When he finally relaxed a little and opened his eyes, I smiled at him. "That was... nice."

He chuckled, his whole chest vibrating with his laugh. "Oh, we haven't even started yet."

Really? Hmm, what if I....

I lifted my other leg, wrapping it around his waist, and he slid forward, deeper inside of me. This time a rush of pleasure ran through me. I moaned at the amazing sensation. I'd never felt anything like it.

His gaze lit up and I grabbed onto his biceps, needing an anchor in the storm I could feel moving my way.

CHAPTER
NINE

Iain

Fucking hell... my mate was hotter than I'd ever dreamed she would be. And I'd dreamed of her too often to count, in recent times.

Her innocent gasps and moans made my desire soar, and the way she grabbed me like she was ready for the ride of her life, made my soul sing.

And her body... wow. Her nipples were the color of strawberries in the spring, and her pussy was so hot and tight, I'd been lucky to grab the reins on my orgasm when I did. But now... now she was tilting her pelvis in invitation, drawing me deeper into her welcoming body, and it took everything in me to hold off just a little bit longer.

She was a virgin. I had to check on her. "Are you okay?" I clenched my teeth against my rising need, but couldn't help surging against her.

She gasped, nodding. "Yes. Can you do that again?"

Could I do that again? Hell yes.

I pulled back until only the tip of my cock was inside of her, teasing us both with the sweet torment of the moment. Then I waited until she was arching her back to try and draw me back in.

I thrust forward, slowly, enjoying every damn moment of pleasure. For both of us. God, her pussy was divine.

"Ah... God, that feels good," she whispered, thrashing her head on the pillow. "I didn't know it would feel like this."

I dropped my head and closed my eyes, trying to grab hold of my control again. It was slipping through my fingers like water in a river. Every time she moved, gasped, or clung to me, I had to fight not to release inside her.

"Keep moving. Please, Iain."

God... damn...

I opened my eyes and there she was, my little, perfect, virginal mate... begging me to fuck her. I may have been a prince, but I was also a man. There was no way I could deny her request. Not when I was already seated deep inside her. I readjusted my hands, pushing up higher above her and surging into her a little harder.

"Oh, ah..." Veronica lifted her legs even higher and tightened them around my hips, making pleasure shoot straight down my cock. "Yes... that's... Iain. What is that? It feels... oh my God..."

I groaned and dropped down on my forearms, putting my lips to her ear so I could whisper to her. "That's your orgasm, building up, ready to shatter you into a million pieces. And when you do, I'll be here to put you back together again."

Veronica moaned and grabbed my head, pulling me closer and kissing me hard. I kept sliding in and out of her, but my control was slipping away. Heat tingled down the backs of my thighs and my balls drew up in anticipation.

I fucked her hard, hard and fast. Her pussy gripped me so tight I was worried I was hurting her, but my mate was moaning and it seemed to be with pleasure. Gasping and groaning and straining against my kiss.

Thrashing her head from side to side, her cheeks flushed and her lips half parted in a way that was so fucking sexy.

The tide of heat was burning me now. I'd flown too close to the sun. I clenched my teeth and pumped into her, again and again, making her pussy squeeze with every thrust.

"Oh fuck... I can't hold on. I'm going to..." I plunged deep inside Veronica's tight pussy one last, violent time, and my orgasm shot through me with the power of a lightning storm. My seed pulsed along my cock in hot spurts, raining pleasure deep inside Veronica's body.

My mate cried out, then began to shake beneath me, her pussy rippling around my cock and milking the last of my seed from me as she came, too. I held fast, enjoying the bites of pain in my back as she dug her nails into me and grabbed on for dear life.

When she finally relaxed beneath me, I collapsed on top of her and rolled us to the side so that I didn't crush her. She still shook softly, pressing her breasts into me.

"Oh my... that was amazing." She sounded excited, while I was ready to pass out.

I withdrew from her and rearranged our positions so that I could lay on my back, let her rest her head on my chest, and drag the blankets over us. I was exhausted, but in the best possible way.

"Is it always like that?" she asked, stroking her nails over my chest.

"No." I shook my head, still recovering from the best sex of my life. "It... you... Damn girl, I can barely think straight. You're amazing."

I kissed the top of her hair, exulting in the feeling of happiness inside my heart. Only six hours ago I had been lying in the frozen wreckage of a house, truly believing I was breathing my last. And now... I was in my mate's bed. The mate I'd waited so long for. And I was sated and happy.

Veronica lifted her head and twisted to lay on top of me, staring straight into my eyes. "I feel really... great. Like, really... I can't even tell you."

I chuckled, running my hands up and down the smooth skin of her arms. "I think I have an idea how you feel, beautiful girl."

And the fact that I'd pleased her in such a way, especially for her first time, made me feel as proud as a king.

She sighed happily and I couldn't stop staring at her. She was too wonderful to believe. I lifted my hand and cupped the back of her head, running my fingers through her hair. "I've dreamt about this moment for so many years... It's hard to believe this is reality."

Her gaze dropped away, but not before I saw the light go out of her eyes.

"What's wrong?" I asked, then wanted to bite my tongue. As far as she was concerned, everything. "Sorry, let me re-phrase that. How am I going to get you to forgive me for everything I've done in the past, dragon daughter?"

She dragged her gaze back up and whispered. "Please don't ruin this."

Her words punctured my heart, making my ribs hurt. "Ruin it? How am I..."

Veronica rolled away from me, making me reach out to her in a panic. She wasn't leaving me? Surely. But she didn't leave, she simply shuffled back, putting herself into a cuddling position. "Let's try and get some sleep."

I followed her and rolled over, curling my body around hers, and listening to her breathing begin to slow. She wasn't going to easily forgive me for being mean to her for so many years, that was obvious.

But I had to look at the bright side of this. I was in Veronica's bed, wrapped around her, and she'd made love to me in a way that made my heart hurt with happiness.

Surely this wasn't the end, but only the beginning of our lives together?

I stayed awake long enough to hear her fall asleep, making cute little snuffling noises while she dreamed. And although I didn't want to miss another moment of my new life, even if it wasn't how I'd pictured it, my exhausted body finally sunk into rest.

～

THE NEXT MORNING, I woke up alone, but still in Veronica's bed. I would have loved to lie there and play over our night together in my mind, but my leg was absolutely killing me.

I managed to get up and stagger to her bathroom, then it was time for breakfast, and some more of the healer's medicine. Or my father's whiskey. I wasn't fussy, as long as it helped.

I pulled on my clothes from last night, and limped into the hallway, running straight into Queen Cassandra.

"Good morning, Iain." She spoke with one eyebrow raised.

I froze, caught. Even at my age, I was embarrassed to be found sneaking out of a girl's room and heat flooded my face. "Good morning, Aunt Cass."

Her smirk wasn't exactly regal, but she looked just like my mom when she found something humorous. "Veronica is with her father. Breakfast is still being served in the main hall... and my husband is awake."

Happiness pushed away any embarrassment I was still feeling. "Damon's awake?"

Cass actually grinned, then tipped her head in a regal nod. "Yes. But if you think that's gonna fix everything, you're dumber than you look."

Then she turned and walked away. I ran after her.

"Help me, Aunt Cass."

"Maybe stop calling me Aunt Cass, then," she said while we walked.

I coughed to clear my throat. "Ah... Cass then?"

"Or Mom," she said with a cheeky grin. "Or shall we wait for the wedding first?"

I stumbled over the hall carpet runner and Cass had to stop to wait for me to recover my footing.

I couldn't help but say, "My mom always said you had Dad's spirit, which is probably why I thought you were our blood relative."

Cass laughed, a sound I hadn't heard in a long while. "Because your father and I say exactly what's on our minds? Yes, well... being raised by a king, and becoming a queen, do have their advantages."

We kept walking along the hall toward the dining room, but slower now. "What can I do, Aunt Cass... I mean Queen..."

"Just Cass."

"Okay, Cass. What can I do?"

This time she stopped walking and reached out for my arm, holding tight. "You can eat, then go see my husband. He was very worried about you when he woke."

Oh God!

"I'll go right now." I turned, intending to rush back the way we came, but Cass held tight to my arm.

"No. You need to eat. How's your leg?"

Feels like it's on fire. "I'm okay."

She sighed. "Eat first. Then go see them. And as far as Veronica is concerned, well, all I can say is, try to be honest with her, Iain. She's most likely feeling confused and betrayed, and that's going to take time to get over."

I inhaled sharply, hating that she was right. I'd never been honest with her. Not about our connection, nor my feelings for her. Not until the past day. "Thank you. I will."

We walked together to the dining room, where my father and Erik were still eating.

"Morning, son." Dad nodded at me with a cup of coffee in his hand. "How's the leg?"

I grimaced as I pulled out a large chair and sat down. "It's still attached." And throbbing with the beat of my heart.

I reached for the waffles and cream, my appetite huge this morning. I piled up my plate and picked up my knife and fork before I noticed the other three staring at me.

"What?"

"Worked up an appetite, son?" Dad asked, his lips quirked in amusement.

I put my head down and started eating, before reaching across and grabbing some crispy rashers of bacon as well. "I didn't eat at all yesterday. I'm starving."

The older generation continued to eat and talk about the running of the fields and the kingdoms. I was lost in my own head, because very soon I was going to have to confront my mate, and her father who'd almost died trying to save my life.

CHAPTER
TEN

Veronica

I gripped my father's hand, determined to make up the ground I'd lost. "Dad, I need to apologize for running away last year, and for not coming home for Christmas. That was so wrong."

He still lay in his huge bed, his face pale and his eyes looking haunted and dark as he stared at me. He looked nothing like my father, the strong King Damon I remembered. But when he smiled, it was like the sunshine peeking around dark clouds and my heart lifted at the sight.

"Sweetheart, you don't need to apologize for leaving. You did what you needed to do, as you always have. As for Christmas, yes, that wasn't the right choice as far as we were concerned, but I have to assume there was a good reason for staying away?"

His question hung in the air, and my guilt consumed me like a ravenous animal, snapping at my flesh. "I... ah... um, no. I mean, I had to work. But really, I was just being selfish."

Dad squeezed my hand. "I don't believe you, sweetheart. You're not selfish. You may be the dragon daughter whose fierce temper everyone fears, but I have to tell you, it's always given me so much joy, and pride, to have sired the daughter that intimidates everyone else. And you, the baby, too."

Hot tears blurred my vision at his kind words, and I blinked them away. The pain of guilt constricting my chest had gotten worse since speaking to my father, not better. It felt like my heart was about to break.

"Oh Dad, I'm so sorry."

"Oh, baby, come here. Come here." He pulled me further onto the large bed and I curled up and put my head on his lap like I used to when I was little.

He stroked my hair and sighed. "When did you grow up? Huh? I feel like I blinked and I missed it."

I giggled against his leg. "Hardly, Dad. You've rebuilt your whole kingdom, and taken us along for the ride."

For a king who had more responsibilities than most, my dad had been in our lives more than any other father I knew. He'd read us stories at bedtime, taken us walking in the fields and on trips to visit with the tenants.

Anselm and his sisters had been treated like royalty since the day they were born, but often, I'd felt like a regular child growing up in the Northern Kingdom. Special, and loved, but not royal.

Not until I turned thirteen and my mother decided it was time for me to learn the responsibilities of my position as a dragon princess. That was when the world had changed for me.

"Sometimes I wish I could go back there," I whispered, not speaking specifically to my dad, but he heard me anyway.

"Back where?"

"Back to the fields, when I was ten years old. Riding the sleigh, taming the horses, running through the snow. Enjoying our lands, in the simplest and most pleasurable of ways."

My dad's sigh was heavy. "You really were made for this kingdom, weren't you, my daughter? Part of me knew it was the wrong choice to force you inside, to learn the more traditional female skills. But..." He sighed again, then chuckled. "Whatever husband you choose will have to like the outdoors. Be able to get his hands dirty... put up with your temper..."

"Dad!" I complained, whacking his leg beneath the bed covers.

"And speaking of Iain..."

I sat up and twirled around, sitting cross-legged on the massive bed and staring at my dad with shock. "What about Iain?" How had he known?

My dad's face reflected amusement, a slash of welcome color highlighting his still-too-pale cheeks. "You think I didn't know?"

I rolled my eyes. "Mom." He'd only been conscious a few hours and she'd already caught him up on all the news.

Dad shifted a little, adjusting the pillows behind him and sitting up straighter in bed. "No. It was Iain, actually."

My jaw dropped. "Sorry... what? When? He hasn't seen you yet, since you woke up." Had my father seriously found out who my fated mate was, before I had?

"He told me just before the accident."

Anger flashed through me. "Why am I the last person to know everything?"

Dad reached out and touched my hand, as if sensing my distress and wanting to reduce it. "Hey, sick man over here."

I took a deep breath to calm myself. "Yes, you're right. Okay. Sorry."

I would have something to say to that damn annoying mate of mine about this, and he wouldn't like it, I was sure. "Plus, if I might correct you... I believe you already knew he was your mate. Didn't you? Before you went away."

I looked down at my fingers, clutched around my father's weather-worn, strong, capable hand.

I nodded. I couldn't deny it. "Yes. Anthony accidentally gave me a vision about my future."

"And you didn't want to know the truth?" Dad prompted, "You didn't think to tell us, obviously."

"I didn't want it to be true!" I cried. "Iain! He... Iain—"

"Had always been mean to you, I know." Dad let out a small groan as he moved his leg.

"He wasn't just mean to me!" I said, snorting in exasperation. "He made me feel like I had the plague or something! I was already the youngest of all the cousins, and he had me thinking he hated me."

Dad leaned back against the bed's headboard. "To be honest, I feel sorry for him."

"You what?" I gasped out, blinking at my father. Did I hear that right?"

"Well, put yourself in his shoes," Dad said, then rolled his eyes. "Oh my God, strike that. For a second I forgot who I was talking to."

"Hey!" I put my hands on my hips and glared at my sick father, not an easy feat while still sitting cross-legged on his bed.

Dad chuckled, then coughed, hard.

I quickly leaned across to grab his glass of water from beside the bed, and handed it to him. "You okay?"

He took a sip, then nodded. "Yes."

I waited, then asked, "Are you going to repeat that insult?"

Dad laughed, and this time managed it without coughing. "Oh sweetheart, you've never been good at putting yourself in the shoes of anyone else. You're too hot-headed. And right now, all you're focusing on is how hard Iain was on you for all those years. But did he ever hurt you? Really? Or was it more about a bruised ego?"

I crossed my arms over my chest and pouted. A bruised ego? I wasn't sure I wanted to answer that question.

"Okay then, Veronica. Prove to me that I'm wrong. Put yourself in Iain's shoes. You're almost ten years older than your mate, and once you reach maturity, you turn around one day and gaze upon an eleven-year-old child—a boy, in your case, and realize he's your mate. How do you feel?"

I opened my mouth to snap out a response, only to realize that I really had no idea how I'd feel in that situation. I could only guess.

Shock, and maybe disbelief? Probably frustration at the stupidity of Fate making such a choice for me. But would I push the kid away by being constantly mean to him, and making him feel like I hated him? I simply wasn't sure.

I was the youngest of three siblings, and the youngest of all the cousins. I'd spent my life racing to catch up. I couldn't imagine what it would be like to have to wait for such a thing.

I realized my dad was studying me intently, and I shrugged, uncomfortable with his questions.

"I want you to think about it, baby girl, okay? Because Iain is a good man. A son to be proud of. He suits you well."

I didn't know what to say. In fact, my throat was clogged up and frozen in a most annoying way.

"Iain," my dad said, but in a greeting type of way. I frowned and turned my head, following his gaze to the door.

Iain leaned against the doorframe, watching us.

"Come in," Dad said, gesturing him over. "It is so good to see you alive and well. I apologize, Iain. I failed you."

What? My dad had failed Iain? How? I frowned at my father then turned towards my mate. My beautiful man. God, he was divine to look at. Even confused and angry and hurt, as I was right now, my heart soared upon seeing him.

"No, Uncle Damon. No. You didn't." Iain limped over to the bed, his face contorting. He was obviously still in pain.

I watched him move gingerly, and a pang of guilt assailed me. Yesterday, he'd almost died. And I'd dragged him to bed last night to find out if the bond between us was as strong as I feared. It was, and it looked like Iain was paying the price today.

"You would have died," Dad said, choking out the words. "Because of me."

"I was the one who wanted to see that house," Iain said, glancing at me as if to gauge my reaction to his words.

Dad was silent for a moment, then shook his head. "You two... no, Iain. You don't need to cover for me. We both know I was the one who wanted to check out that wreck. It was my fault we were there, and that you went down to the cellar and got hurt. And if my daughter hadn't come home and used whatever mating magic you two have to find you, you'd be dead."

Iain's surprise at my dad's admission was obvious in his widening eyes.

No doubt I sported the same shocked expression. It was Dad's fault? I managed a small smile at Iain. "You told me it was your fault. But it wasn't."

He shrugged, seeming slightly embarrassed. "It was no-one's fault. It was simply... an accident. But if King Damon had died because he tried to fly home to save me, that would have been my fault."

Tears threatened my composure again at the thought that I could have lost both of them. I slid off the bed and wandered over to the blazing fireplace to stare down into the flames. So Iain was a man of secrets and he'd been covering for my dad. Clearly, he loved my father, and from what he'd said, he loved me too.

"I don't remember getting home," Dad said, interrupting my musings about Iain. "How close did I get before passing out?"

"Close enough," Iain answered; a diplomatic answer. "Your people set off the alarm and everything after that was a chain reaction. Theo sending for Veronica. Everyone trying to track me down."

I turned to face them, my throat hurting from the effort to hold back my tears. "You're both alive, and home, which is all that matters. I'll leave you both if you don't mind. I have to go and speak to someone."

I had this intense urge to see Anthony, and I wasn't sure why.

"I'll come with you," Iain said, but I waved my hand at him.

"No, please stay with my dad and visit. I won't be long."

He nodded at me, not trying to change my mind. I'd spent my life fighting for my place in this family, and in the larger group. Now it seemed that all I'd managed to gain for myself was a reputation as a selfish child who couldn't put myself in anyone else's shoes, and wouldn't even forgive her own mate.

The truth hurts, though, doesn't it?

I managed a smile to my father and Iain, and then I ran. Not simply down the castle hallways away from my father's suite. I was also running away from my past, away from my possible future, and away from the pain that all of my choices in life had brought me so far.

ELEVEN

Veronica

While Iain stayed to chat with my father, I searched the castle to find my magical friends.

I found Marienne and Anthony chatting in the library, drinking tea and munching on chocolate chip cookies.

They looked so relaxed I was loathe to interrupt, but I really needed to speak with Anthony. I directed my gaze at him. "Can I talk to you for a minute?"

Marienne raised an eyebrow at me. "Are my services no longer good enough?"

Oh crap! "Oh no, I'm sorry Auntie Marienne. It's just that Anthony... you know."

I waved my hands around, not sure how to explain why I needed him and not her. This time, she raised both eyebrows. "You mean you're here to apologize, again, for breaking my son's nose? That wasn't very ladylike, Veronica."

I scoffed. "I've never been very ladylike, Marienne." Then I glanced at the prince I'd always considered a brother. "But I am sorry, Anthony. Truly. My temper... I'm sorry. I should never have done it. I was out of my head with worry."

Anthony stood up and smiled at me. "I'm fine, Veronica. What do you need?"

I bit my lip, chewing on the flesh while I structured my question in my mind. "I don't really know. I just had this... insane need to come see you."

He chuckled softly. "I'm already happily married, dragon daughter. Sorry."

"Oh, not like that." I whacked him, gently, on the chest.

Marienne wasn't leaving, and when I turned to her, she stayed in her seat. "I'm not leaving you alone with my son again, missy. You punched him, then sucked all the magic out of him. It's taken me all day to get him right again."

I gulped, and apologized, again. "I'm sorry about that."

"No. I'm not," Anthony said, glaring at his mother before turning back to me. "You found Iain. Saved his life. I would happily sacrifice my health for his."

Marienne huffed, but I didn't think it was because she disagreed. She was probably annoyed I hadn't asked her for help.

I looked up at Anthony, who had always been at least six inches taller than me, and said the first thing that came into my head. "Would you do the premonition for me? Again? Show me my future?"

Anthony shoved his hands in his pockets as though he was afraid to touch me.

I didn't blame him.

"Why, Veronica? I mean, I've shown you the future. What I've seen anyway. And I can't always control what I show to others. It doesn't work like that."

I inhaled sharply, a twang in my gut making me desire to see it once more. "I feel like I've made some mistakes since then. Going to the human realm. Iain being hurt. If it's at all possible, I'd like to see it again, please?"

I glanced at Marienne, my fear growing. "Or am I wrong? Couldn't my fate change? Or is what is seen, set in stone?"

Marienne shook her head and gestured to me. "Come, Veronica, sit. My son can't give you more of his magic today. He's still recovering. But I'll help you."

I rushed into the seat Anthony had been occupying. "Oh, thank you."

Marienne turned to face me, that special purple magic swirling in her eyes. "I can't guarantee I'll see the same thing as Anthony showed you. I don't have any control over my visions."

I nodded, holding out both hands. "No problem, of course. I don't mind."

Whatever she could share with me would be fine. I'd already re-lived that first vision so many times.

Marienne took my hands and there was a flash of black, then a cracking, like a tree breaking apart and falling. Despite the shock of the sound, I didn't let go. Instead, I waited for the image to come.

I was here, in my room in the castle, looking out the window. Very similar to the other vision. But I wasn't pregnant, I wasn't smiling and there wasn't a ring on my finger any more.

There were footsteps like before, and I waited with my heart in my throat, to see who would walk in the door. Last time it was Iain. Surely, he'd come this time, too?

But when the door opened and a man walked in, it was Anselm, in full mourning black, carrying a bouquet of white flowers and staring at me with pity in his expression.

"No!" I shouted, yanking my hands out of Marienne's grip and jumping to my feet. "No. That's not right. It can't be."

Marienne's face was a cloud of misery. "I'm sorry, love. But you were right that your fate isn't set in stone. Every decision we make affects it somehow."

"When was that!" I demanded to know. "Anthony's vision was in the future. Years into the future."

Marienne shook her head slowly. "My visions are more often than not... images of the near future."

My breath caught in my chest, making the pounding of my heart reverberate in my ears. "How soon? How near, Marienne?"

"Days," she whispered. "Hours, even."

I took off running down the hallway, screaming to one of the guards that stood in the halls. "Call the healer! Now! Get everyone. Go!"

Two of the men took off running in the opposite direction to me. I lifted my skirts and ran faster. I may have fought against my future, afraid of what Fate had in store for me. But they would not take Iain away from me. They would not. I wouldn't allow it.

I'd gotten my nickname through sheer grit and determination, and I'd go up against the Fates themselves if they tried to hurt my mate again.

I burst through the doors to my parents' bedroom just in time to see Iain collapse beside my father's bed.

"Veronica. Get help," Dad called out as I hurled myself across the room and crawled on my knees to my mate's side. "Iain's sick."

"He's not sick, Dad," I said, ice racing though my veins as I pressed my head to his chest and heard nothing. "He's dying."

I tilted his head back, checked his airway, then hit him over the sternum, hard.

"What are you doing?" Dad asked, throwing back the covers and sliding closer.

I put my head to his chest. Nothing. "I'm starting CPR." I put my hands into the compression position and set them to his chest. "I learnt how to do it when I went to the human realm."

One, two, three.

I pinched his nose and breathed air into his mouth. Once. Twice.

Then I was up again, doing compressions. Thirty compressions. Two breaths.

Sweat rolled down my face.

"Who taught you..."

"I did a course." I panted, getting tired already. But Iain was much bigger and stronger than me and I needed to push hard. "The family had kids. They swam. They wanted me to know how to revive them if they drowned."

"Veronica..." I could hear the awe in his voice.

"Dad. Stop. Please. I can teach everyone else too. But later."

No-one in my realm knew any type of CPR. Shifters were strong and healthy. And we didn't swim, let alone drown. Our whole realm was too cold, and especially so up in the Northern Kingdom where I lived. Every lake was frozen over, practically ten months a year.

Guards came rushing in, joined by Anthony and my brother Theo.

"What can we do?"

I glanced up, not wanting to stop, but I knew I couldn't keep up this pace. "I need some help. Come kneel beside me, Theo. I'll show you what to do."

I leaned forward, breathing into Iain's mouth. My mind was so clear I could hardly believe how calm I was, my body fuelled by panic and adrenaline.

"Put your hands like this," I said, showing Theo the posture, "then I want you to push down thirty times, and I'll breathe into him."

I counted as Theo pumped. "Twenty-nine, thirty." Then I leaned down and breathed into him again.

"What's this doing?" Anthony asked, coming to kneel down with us.

"It's keeping his body alive until we can get help." I said. "We're pumping his heart for him and pushing oxygen into his lungs."

I glanced over at Anthony, who was shoulder to shoulder with me. "You ready to take over from Theo? One, two, three, take over."

Theo jumped out of the way and Anthony hopped straight into his spot. I got my breath back, then corrected his posture. "Get up a bit more, right over him. Yeah. Like that."

"Thirty."

I pinched Iain's nose and breathed into his mouth.

More people burst into the room, including the healer and Marienne. I stared at the healer. "Please. You have to help him."

The healer rushed over. "What happened?"

Dad called out. "We were talking. Iain went pale and said his leg was killing him. Then he went down."

"Thirty," Anthony called out.

I breathed into him, once, twice.

The healer lifted Iain's pants leg and I stared down at the mangled red mess. "It didn't look like that, last night."

It had been damaged, but healing. Not red, or swollen.

"Poison," the healer whispered, opening his bag and rummaging through.

Anthony had stopped pumping when Iain's leg was revealed, and I yelled at him. "Keep going!"

I gave my mate two breaths and the sorcerer kept going again with compressions. I was starting to shake. "Please hurry."

The healer pulled out a knife and rifled through his bag until he found a vial of white fluid. "I have to cut his leg open and dump this in. But if his heart isn't pumping, he won't come back."

I staggered to my feet, all my hope leeching away. If only we had the defibrillator paddles from the human realm.

An idea began to form. "Marienne! I need you to shock Iain's heart."

The sorceress hurried over to us. Iain's lips were pale.

Stavrok came running in, barely dressed, "Where's my... no!"

I ran in front of the huge king. "I have a plan. But you need to get everyone back. Please. Help me."

The king didn't hesitate. He simply nodded and went into damage control. "Okay everyone out."

"Except Marienne and the healer," I said.

Stavrok gathered everyone up, even Anthony, and forced them all out of the room.

I continued CPR, even though my arms were shaking and I clinked teeth with Iain while trying to give him mouth to mouth.

"Healer, do the leg thing. Quickly. Don't worry about the scarring."

The healer did what I asked, slicing open Iain's leg and pouring the white liquid on his leg. There was very little blood, and what was still there, seeped out of the wound, hissing and bubbling when it mixed with the medicine.

"I'm glad he's passed out," the healer said. "That would hurt like nothing else."

"He's not passed out," I snapped at him. "He's legally dead. Now go."

The healer grabbed his bag and left. I did one more round of CPR, breathed into his mouth twice, then shuffled back on my hands like a crab.

Marienne was hovering, her long dark hair falling down her back. "What do you need me to do, Veronica?"

"I need you to shock his heart, with electricity. Like a lightning bolt."

Marienne stared at me like I was crazy. "I could kill him."

"He's already dead," I cried, pointing at Iain's prone body. "Please!"

The sorceress rubbed her hands together, the crackle and spark of her powers caressing her fingertips.

She was waiting, too long.

"Do it!" I screamed, and Marienne dropped to her knees and set her hands on Iain's chest.

CHAPTER
TWELVE

Iain

There was nothing but blackness. Cold. Calm. Which was nice in a strange way. I was at peace. No more fated mate who despised me for the things that had happened in the past. No more responsibilities. Stress. Or pain.

My body didn't hurt anymore, finally, and that was good. That was very good. It was hard to think back to the time before the pain.

But I was going to miss everyone. My mom. My dad. My... Veronica.

She would be better off without me. They were all better off without me. I was only the spare son. Anselm was the heir. And my mate had never wanted me.

White light exploded inside my mind and behind my eye lids. Oh God, it was agony. Stop! Please stop! Let me go back to the place of peace. The place without pain.

Then I was dragged back into my pain-riddled body, my leg on fucking fire.

I groaned and rolled onto my side, drawing my legs up toward my chest. "Oh... God."

"You're alive. You're back!" Veronica was practically on top of me, leaning over me, then pressing her body to my side and gripping me in a tight embrace. "Oh my God, I thought I'd lost you."

Her presence settled the strange angst inside my chest, but the pain was still there, hurting deep inside me. I moaned, unable to hold it in. "What happened?"

"You died!" she yelled, whacking me in the side.

She was angry with me, again. I didn't know why and there was an answering anger building inside me now. Even my dragon was furious.

I groaned and doors banged open around us. People came rushing in around me, touching me, prodding at my hurting body.

Leave me alone.

"Get him up on the bed," Dad said, and I was scooped up and placed on King Damon's bed.

The pain in my leg burned like my whole limb was on fire. "What did you put on my leg? It feels so much worse than it did before."

The healer pushed everyone out of the way to set his hands on me. They were cold against the heat of my skin.

"I had to treat the poison, but it's working."

Wait, what? "What poison?"

"The infection," the healer said in a soft voice. "Your wound turned septic. It was killing you from the inside out."

"It did kill you! But we brought you back." That was Veronica, shouting again. She seemed super-upset about the almost dying thing, especially given she didn't seem to like me.

"Do you need something for the pain?" the healer asked.

I nodded. "Hell yes." My head was throbbing, too. I looked down at my leg to check it wasn't actually on fire. It wasn't, but it felt like it.

The healer mixed up a drink and offered it to me. I managed to lift my head long enough to gulp down something that tasted like pond water, then lay down again.

"What the hell happened?" I gasped out.

King Damon was sitting on his bed, but everyone else was standing around the bedroom, staring at me. How embarrassing. The medicine began to work and my body started to relax, the raging fire dying down to a slow burn.

I managed to roll onto my back and half sit up against the head board.

Everyone was there. Marienne. Damon. Anthony. My father and Veronica. Even Cass.

Two kings, Two queens and their offspring.

"This is an impressive audience," I managed. "For a prince who will never be king. It's a bit much, don't you think?"

Veronica glared at me, not liking my joke, obviously.

"Hey, dragon daughter, lighten up." I smiled at her. "You should leave. I'm not worth the royal procession."

If she'd been in her shifter form, I think I may have seen smoke blow from her nostrils. "You ungrateful turd."

I gaped at her, then laughed. Oh God. This is what I came back to life for? To get more shit from my mate? Just as I had for the past decade?

"Seriously?" I growled at her. "I'm ungrateful? I crawled back from death itself, and this is the shit I have to deal with? But what's changed, right? You still hate me. Obviously, you always will."

Her mouth dropped open and her eyes shifted, the irises transforming into the shape of her dragon.

Then she turned and ran out of the room.

I felt nothing, watching her go. Actually, that wasn't quite right. I did feel something. I was glad. She should go. She didn't love me. She didn't want me.

King Damon shifted further onto the bed, his bed, and shook his head at me. "Oh, mate. You screwed that one up."

I wanted to get up. To leave. I didn't want to be there. But even the slightest movement hurt, so I just lay there and grumbled.

"I don't care," I said truthfully, rolling into the fetal position and closing my eyes. "Nothing's ever going to change with Veronica. I should have stayed dead."

Then she could have married someone else. Been happy. Without me.

"Iain!" My father's shocked disapproval was clear in his tone, but I couldn't shake the black cloud descending over me. I didn't bother to open my eyes or respond when he added, "Don't say things like that."

I should be dead.

I wish I was dead.

The voices around me changed, becoming muffled. I couldn't make them out. They were murmuring about me. About where to put me. How to deal with me. I didn't care.

The depression swallowed me up and I burrowed under the covers. They should have just left me in that abandoned house and let me die.

Veronica.

I was fuming. He'd rather be dead than be with me? I ran straight back to my bedroom, picked up the nearest thing, which happened to be a vase by the door, and hurled it across the room.

It hit the wall hard, shattering into a million pieces. Just like my heart.

"Gah!" I clenched my hands into tight fists and screamed out loud. "You fucking bastard! I knew it... I knew I couldn't trust you."

I was too angry to cry, so I stomped around the room, throwing anything I could find. Until finally, finally, there was nothing left to break, and I fell to the ground in a pile of sorrow.

I finally cried, but I was strangely numb. Cold.

When there was a knock at my door, I ignored it. I didn't even know who it was. The whole house was crawling with family and friends, so it could have been anyone.

I didn't care. I needed time out, to try and calm down.

The next knock was followed by the door opening, then a low whistle. "I thought I heard the breaking of expensive things."

I didn't look up, but I rested my face on my knees. "Mom doesn't put expensive things in here. She knows they're not safe."

King Stavrok walked into my room, then sat down on the floor beside me, resting his back against the bed.

"How are you doing, dragon daughter?"

I sniffed. "Despite the broken bits, I'm fine." I was always fine.

Stavrok nudged me with his shoulder. "You can't take the things that Iain said when he woke up just now to heart. He didn't mean any of it."

"How do you know? You didn't even know I was his fated mate. He didn't tell you. He's ashamed of me. Embarrassed I'm so... well, me."

I couldn't help the fire that burned inside of me. I'd tried to quiet my fiery nature. I'd done yoga and meditation and tried to channel my mother's calm, but it never worked.

"Hate to tell you this, kid, but you are awesome. You're so much like your mother."

I turned my head to look at the big king, still resting my cheek on my knees. "What are you talking about, Uncle Stavrok? My mother is the perfect queen. Calm. Ladylike."

My uncle laughed so hard I sat up and straightened out my legs to mimic his posture. "What are you laughing at?"

"Oh," Stavrok chuckled, "just the way time changes things. Who we all were thirty years ago is very different to how we are now."

I stared up at him, remembering a story my cousins had shared with me a few years ago. "You mean like how you killed the King of the Black Mountains to save Aunt Lucy?"

Stavrok sobered, but nodded slowly. "Yes, just like that. I may be old now, Veronica, but I wasn't always. I loved, I fought, I almost died. I made mistakes, a lot of them, but it all came out well in the end."

I waited, but I wasn't patient on my best day, and this wasn't that day. "And my mom? What was she like?"

He rested his head back against the bed. "She was a true dragon princess. Strong, opinionated, beautiful."

I smiled. "She still is."

"But she wasn't the calm lady you know now," he said. "She wouldn't settle for an ordinary life. She wanted to see the Kingdom to the North, when no-one traveled here back then. This place was in ruins... but your mom, she wasn't afraid. She fought the wolves to keep the children safe. She pulled your father back from the brink of death. She was stronger than you know, Veronica. She was just like you, but you have the advantage of growing up here. In the toughest kingdom in our realm. You're your father's daughter, but trust me, Queen Cass was a rebel in her day too. Very feisty. I could barely keep her in line."

I chuckled. "Mom, feisty? And needing to be kept in line?" That didn't sound like her.

"Exactly." He nudged me again. "Stop being so hard on yourself. You're young, and yes, you're a hothead. But that's the dragon royal blood. My children have a human mother, Erik and Marienne are a mix as well. But you... you're a dragon princess through and through."

I gulped. "But mom isn't actually your cousin."

He smiled. "Her parents were my mom's best friends and full blooded dragons, so trust me. They had the strength of our ancestors in their bones and they passed it on to Cass. And through her, to you."

I sighed and rested my head on my knees again. "So, I'll be this out of control with my emotions forever, huh?"

"Hey, are you forgetting the first part of this conversation? I'm old and tired. Your mom is calm and queenly, and your poor dad... well, he barely managed the flight home after an injury."

"That's not making me feel better!"

Stavrok chuckled again. "Dragon daughter, you are in your physical prime. You're young and healthy. Enjoy the fire that flows through your blood instead of fighting it, and please... give my son a second chance."

I pressed my lips together in a flat line.

Stavrok shook his head before hauling himself to his feet.

"Are you leaving?" I asked.

He nodded. "Yes, I need to fly home for a few days and update Lucy. She doesn't like to be left out of the loop for long."

I jumped to my feet far more quickly than he had, the difference in our physical abilities obvious in that one movement. "Why should I give Iain a second chance, Uncle Stavrok? After everything he's said and done. I don't want to be with someone who doesn't like me or want me around."

He shrugged. "Because ignoring the fated mate bond is fatal, to all that are involved, Veronica. You won't find another who will love you the way Iain does, and can. And I promise you, my son loves you dearly."

I crossed my arms over my chest, still finding it hard to believe him.

The huge king walked to the door and opened it before turning back. "Veronica, you don't have to forgive him. Hell, you can punish Iain for the rest of your lives if you choose to, but before you make a decision like that —one that will bring great sadness to both of you—I ask that you give him a second chance to prove himself. You won't be sorry."

Then King Stavrok left the room, taking all my anger with him and leaving me with nothing but my own sadness.

332

THIRTEEN

Iain

The pain in my head wouldn't stop, and the darkness of my thoughts were downright black as midnight. But I'd scared Veronica off, again, and I had no lifeline to drag me to safety. No rope.

Nothing but darkness that felt soul deep.

"Iain, please, talk to me," King Damon said again, gently shaking my shoulder.

I shrugged him off and turned away.

The healer had come to check on me again and I'd wanted to outright attack the man.

"He's alive, my lord," the healer had told Damon. "But the poison in the wound... it had already spread through his blood. His skin's burning with it. All over."

I groaned. They should have left me dead. A little niggle in the back of my mind said maybe that's why I was feeling so dark and hopeless. Maybe the poison had spread to my mind, too. It was so tiring to think at all.

"What's there to do?" Damon asked. "We have to fix this and help him. Somehow."

"I don't know what to suggest, my king. I'm sorry."

The healer left and I stayed curled up in my ball of hate and pain.

"Iain, you have to fight this."

"I wanna go home," I managed to groan. My own bed. My father's kingdom. If I was going to die, I wanted to die in the same place I'd been born.

"You can," Damon said. "When you're strong enough to travel. Could you shift? That might help detox the poison from your system."

I searched inside for my dragon but he was curled up, angry and half-dead. I shook my head. "No way." I wasn't sure my dragon would survive a shift.

"Iain, you need to get up. Have a shower. Can you stand?"

I lifted my head, a hint of humor lighting me up for just an instant. "Can you?"

Damon swung his legs off the side of the bed and got up, swaying like a tree in a strong wind.

I laughed, though there was slight bitterness in the sound. "Sit down before you fall down."

Damon picked up a pillow and tossed it at my head.

It hit me, and I batted the fluffy insult away. "Fuck off."

"What the hell is wrong with you?" Damon yelled at me. "You're young, you're a prince! You've waited ten years for your fated mate, and now that you finally have a chance with her, you're giving up?"

Finally, I uncurled and managed to push myself up enough so that my belly ached with the muscle strain. "I don't have a chance with Veronica! She hates me."

Damon laughed, the noise a stark contrast to the voice in my head. "She doesn't hate you, Iain. Quite the opposite. You're a fool if you think that."

"You're wrong," I spat back. "She won't forgive me for what I had to do to her when she was a kid, to keep her at a distance. She thinks I'm an asshole."

Damon's dragon flashed in his eyes and my breath caught in my throat at the sudden ratcheting up of tension in the room.

"My daughter is the best thing that ever happened to you, you sorry son of a bitch. She's dragged you back from the brink of death! Twice! And if, after that, you're not willing to even try to live… then damn you, Iain. Damn you to hell!"

Damon stalked out of the room as regally as his injured body would allow him.

I fell back against the pillows, my exhaustion bone deep. A soft knock at the door made me turn my head, and there she was, my mate.

Veronica stepped into the room, twisting her fingers around like she was nervous, but a tentative smile played on her lips. "And I thought I had a temper."

I snorted. "We're all a product of our parents, I suppose."

"You still hate me?" she whispered.

I shook my head, forcing myself to take slow, deep breaths. "I told you before. I've hated myself, Veronica. But never you."

She took another step forward. "I spoke to the healer. He said the poison's spread."

I ran a hand through my hair, trying hard not to scream. "I can't… my thoughts. My God, Veronica, I can't… this lethargy, this deep depressive state, where I can't seem to pull myself free… Hell, this isn't me."

I finished more quietly, "I think it's the poison. It has too strong a hold. I can't seem to shake it off."

She rushed the last few steps to the bed. "There's this place Mom and Dad took us as kids. There are hot springs and Mom always said there were healing powers in the waters."

"Hot springs?" I scoffed half-heartedly. "Here?" In the North? The Winter Palace.

She nodded, her eyes flashing with the wrath of her dragon being challenged. "You know, if you don't pull yourself together, I'll just fly back to the human realm for another couple of years. It was fun. Dancing and working and sunbathing on the beaches there. I have years before my unrequited mate instincts begin to drive me crazy."

I narrowed my eyes at the dragon daughter, opened my mouth, then shut it again before I spat something nasty at her.

She was right. I was the one fast approaching the age where I would start going crazy, needing my mate.

She wasn't. She was young. She'd run from me before. She'd do it again.

"You want to leave me?"

She widened her eyes and gave me an annoyed look. "No! Are you gonna come with me to the hot springs, or not?"

I rolled my eyes and groaned. "You don't give up, do you?"

"Nope." She grabbed the bedcovers and dragged them off me. "Now get up. Before you die, again."

She stormed back to the door and then flicked her hair over her shoulder, glaring back at me. "Or would you rather that, Iain? Die? Then I can hook up with any man I want. No mate. Just humans... maybe some dragon shifters, too."

I was on my feet before I'd made the decision to follow her.

"Over my dead body," I growled out. No one else would touch my mate. Mine.

I was her first. I'd be her only.

"That's kinda the idea," she said. "You coming?"

Then she left.

I was breathing like an old man, but my dragon had woken at the thought of another man touching Veronica, and the shifter side of me lent enough strength to my limbs to follow her. The pain was manageable and anger fueled my body as I limped to the door and out into the hallway.

Veronica was about ten steps in front of me, heading toward the stairwell. She dashed down the steps and ran over to the footman. Servants flew every which way. I staggered down the steps, one at a time, holding onto the balustrade in case my legs collapsed beneath me.

When I finally made it to the landing, my chest was heaving and my lungs were burning as I dragged in air. "Where... now?"

She offered me a fur-lined cloak. "Put this on. We're going by coach."

I dragged the cloak around me and let Veronica lead me outside and into the coach. The snow was thin on the ground, which meant the sleds weren't necessary today.

"Stay warm," Veronica said, tossing a fur blanket over me from where she sat on the opposite side.

I did as she said, though my head was still filled with hateful thoughts and my body shivered, unable to decide if I was too hot or too cold. The only thing that was saving me from keeling over at this point was my dragon, growling inside my head, mad at my mate. She'd threatened to leave us again. Be with other men. He was pushing hard to grab her and show her how much we loved her.

The poison wanted me to throw myself out of the carriage and lie down to die in the snow. The duality was maddening. I couldn't talk properly or think straight.

We rode for a while, through the town and past farming fields.

I wanted to ask about where we were going, but my jaw was practically wired shut.

I didn't trust myself to speak without saying something wrong, or hurtful.

So, we traveled in silence until, finally, the rocking of the carriage stopped.

"Where are we?" I bit out, the pain beginning to overwhelm me again. Everything hurt, throbbing hard.

"Come on. Let's go." Veronica pushed open the door and got out of the carriage.

I took a deep breath, not sure I had the strength for this next part of the journey if we had to walk far.

"Iain. Get your ass out here."

A smile quivered on my lips. There's my dragon princess.

I hauled myself up off the carriage seat and fell down the steps to the ground, moaning as pain shot through me. "Fuck... me."

"If you can get your head and your body sorted out, I might just do that again. Let's go." Veronica marched off toward the foothills, boulders and darkened cave mouths stretching ahead of us.

"Where are we?" I'd never seen this part of the Winter Kingdom before.

Veronica didn't answer; she just disappeared into the mouth of one of the caves.

It was late in the day, and the setting sun cast spectacular colors across the landscape. Burnt oranges, yellows and purple.

I inhaled the chilly air through my nose and shivered. I had no idea if this was going to do anything good, but at this point, could it get any worse?

I limped to the cave entrance, annoyed that she'd left me to make this walk by myself.

Stupid, I knew, because I wouldn't have wanted her pity, or her help. But in the moment, I wasn't thinking straight. And I knew it, so I forced the words and thoughts down and just concentrated on putting one foot in front of the other.

As soon as I stepped into the cave, a wave of relaxation washed over me and my thoughts felt less like they were tumbling around in a washer.

"You weren't joking." Steam rose from pools of crystal clear water inside the cave.

Veronica was lighting candles and lanterns. "My dad kept this as his private sanctuary for a while. The one place that was truly his, while he rebuilt his kingdom. Then he brought Mom here, and they opened it up to the people."

I glanced around. "Looks like noone really uses it now."

"No. I think the people still thought of it only as the king's place. They never really came much, but Mom and Dad did bring us here and I always felt, I don't know... healthier afterward."

I hoped she was right.

Veronica began to undress, stripping off her clothes to fold them and place them in a nearby basket.

I watched, not moving. She was spectacular to look at. Skin as smooth and beautiful as silk. I ached for her, especially with those beautiful curves this close. Then I started as I realized I hadn't thought about anything physical with her since I'd been brought back from the dead.

Maybe there really was some truth to her story about this place having healing powers. For the first time in ages, I began to feel more like myself.

Veronica's final pieces of underwear fell to the rocks at her feet and she scooped them up to put them in the box alongside the other clothes.

She stood on the side of a pool, facing me. The curve of her breast was lit up by a lantern positioned behind her. The still-angry flame in my gut began to ebb in the presence of desire unexpectedly growing once more.

"Come and swim, Iain," she said. "I'm not giving up on you. We'll get you better, no matter what. As long as you don't give up on yourself.

That's what made me so angry, earlier. I couldn't bear it if..." She shrugged and turned to the water. "Come on."

She waded into the pool, not waiting for me, the clear waters rising as she descended, caressing her hips, her back. Her breasts. Then she was submerged almost to her neck, smiling at me in anticipation, her long hair floating around her like a mermaid.

"Well? Coming?"

I began to undress. First my shirt, then my pants. And then a thought struck me and I paused. "But my poison... my blood. What if I ruin the spring, Veronica?"

She shrugged, her breasts bobbing in the water, drawing attention to her strawberry pink nipples. "A price I'll happily pay for your health, Iain. We'll drain the pools, and start again."

"A second chance?" I whispered, limping toward the spring, fully naked.

Everything still hurt, but whether it was the rocks, or the steam, or the fact my mate was forcing me into the light, I felt markedly better. Clearer in my head.

She nodded.

I stepped into the water, the heat surprising me. "Whoa... that's hot."

She smiled, reminding me of a siren calling me to throw myself into the sea. "No... it's only warm, I promise. Your body is out of whack because of the fever you've had, so the contrast will burn for a moment. It will settle. Just keep walking. Come to me."

My dragon rose up inside of me, not making me shift, but controlling my limbs; forcing me forward. I took one step, then the next, and then another, reaching for the woman who'd traveled worlds to keep me alive.

FOURTEEN

Veronica

I was playing it as calm and cool as I could, but I wanted to rip Iain's clothes off his gorgeous, damaged body. My body was on fire for him. But I had to give him time to recover. If he could recover from whatever darkness he had sunk into.

I only hoped the waters here in the hot spring were as powerful as my parents had said they were.

I'd lied to Iain, saying I could just go away and ignore my call to mate with him. Maybe I could have if I'd stayed away, but now that I'd come back, and knew how it felt to be so drawn to him, so connected on a level I'd never felt before, there was no turning back.

When he finally submerged himself in the waters, I watched his face intently. He'd had this strange, dark shadow hovering over him since he woke up. Almost not there, when I tried to stare directly at it, but it had cast a shadow over his face and left a sour taste in my mouth. But, as I stared, the shadow seemed to dissipate and his features became clear.

"How are you feeling?" I asked, worried that I was only imagining the improvement.

He leaned back, dipping his hair in the water, then dropped down to submerge himself completely.

When he finally came back up, a true Iain smile was on his lips and my heart began to pitter-patter way too fast. Was he finally coming back to being himself? "So much better," he said. "How did you know this would work?"

"I didn't. But we had to try something, didn't we?" The healer had said there was no hope and my father's advice wasn't going to do more than make Iain think twice about dying.

I had to do something drastic to help him. Say something provocative. Despite being the second son, the spare to the heir, Anselm, Iain was the king of my heart. He was a dragon, through and through. And he would protect me to his dying breath, I just knew it.

I waded over to him, unafraid now. "Kiss me."

His hands reached for my waist, dragging me closer. I slid my fingers up his arms and, when I reached his shoulders, I jumped up in the water, opened my legs, and let them float around his waist.

Iain gasped as though he was surprised at my action, but his hands moved down to grab my ass and haul me against his belly.

I got as close as I could, pressing my breasts to his chest. He still wasn't moving much. I'd asked him to kiss me and, although he hadn't fully rejected me, I could sense his resistance to getting any closer.

He couldn't hide his erect hardness, though. Not when I was crushed up against it.

I tilted my hips and began to rock, his cock pressing up between us. I rubbed myself along his length, enjoying the sensations skittling through me and hoping I was eliciting the same response from him.

From his heartfelt groan, I guessed I was doing something right.

My fingers tangled in his hair and I teased him. "You aren't going to kiss me, then, Iain?"

A growl rose in his chest and his fingers tightened on my ass. "You're driving me insane."

"Then do something about it." I nipped at his jaw with my teeth, peppering soft kisses over his face.

He had to fight for me. I'd done all I could to prove I wanted him. It was now his turn.

He groaned but stayed frozen, like a statue amongst the heat of the pool. Anger rose inside of me but I didn't give in to it. My temper had made me run from Iain before, but I wouldn't this time. I wasn't the petulant child they all thought I was. At least, not always. And I'd prove it.

"What's wrong... mate?" I whispered, leaning back and arching my back, thrusting my breasts in his face. "You don't want me anymore?"

He stood so fast I cried out. Then he climbed out of the pool and stared down at me, before reaching out a hand and pulling me out when I finally chose to clasp my hand into his.

He dragged me against his body, then turned and walked forward, backing me up against a cave wall. The stones were well worn and cool against my back.

He reached between us, grabbed his cock and ran it along my cleft, rubbing the head over my clit and making me whimper in need.

I was aching inside, becoming more frantic the more he pressed against me.

"I want you." He groaned. "But I'm... afraid."

"Of what?" I could barely formulate the sentence, but I had to know.

He grinned crookedly. "Rejection."

I sucked in a breath and let it out slowly, Ragged. Then I shook my head. "No more rejection."

He grabbed me around the waist and lifted me up, setting his lips to my nipples for deep, long sucks.

"Iain... oh my... wow." I closed my eyes and grabbed onto his head, holding tight.

Then he slid me down again, my legs still tightly gripping him around the waist, and without letting me go, he climbed back down into the water once again.

He still hadn't kissed my lips, and I found my gaze dropping from his eyes to his mouth, needing those lips on me again.

"Are you still afraid?" I whispered.

Long moments passed, the light of various lanterns flickering over the clear waters of the springs. I could see every line of his beautiful body beneath the water.

"I am," he admitted, a hoarse note in his voice.

"Really? Of what, Iain?"

He chuckled slightly, but I could tell he was dead serious when he said, "That you'll never love me the way I love you, Veronica. There's too much... muddy water between us."

I laughed and wrapped my arms around his neck, "Look down, Iain. There's nothing but clear water now."

He did look down and around us, seeing what I saw, no doubt. The cleansing water of a new beginning. If we both chose to accept that new beginning.

"See," I whispered to him, cupping his cheek and drawing him back to me. "I've saved you from death twice now. I can't do anymore to show you how much I want you in my life. Now it's your turn."

His eyes glistened with unshed tears. "What do you want?"

I blinked my own emotions away, a laugh catching in my throat. "I want everything."

His gaze hardened, filled with the Iain of old. The prince. The son of a warrior. "You'll marry me?"

My nose tingled with heat and tears, but I nodded.

His hands slid around my back and down to grab onto my ass.

"You'll have my babies? Little dragon princesses that will burn the curtains and the carpets with their temper?"

This time the laugh didn't catch, but echoed around the room. "Only princesses? You don't want any sons?"

He smiled. "I'll thank the fates every day if we're blessed with a baby, Veronica. Boy or girl. But what I truly want is a little girl. Just like you."

I couldn't wait any longer. I grabbed his head and kissed him hard, wanting to show him how much I loved him. The past would come between us and irk me forever, probably, but that wouldn't stand in the way of my future anymore.

We deserved better. He deserved better. And so did I.

Iain groaned and kissed me back. Then he fit his cock to my pussy entrance and pulled me down, impaling me on him in one hard thrust.

I broke our kiss to throw my head back and gasp out, "Yes... more. Please don't stop."

He didn't. He kissed me again, thrusting his tongue into my mouth as he fucked my body. Again and again, he possessed me, and with every moment, he forced the past further away.

"Oh God, I'm gonna..." My orgasm hit me out of nowhere, intense pleasure screaming inside my body as my legs and belly shook and I released the most insane-sounding moans and groans against the safety of Iain's chest.

Iain put his lips to my ear and kept moving inside of me. "Fuck, your pussy feels amazing. Come on, my dragon girl, come on me. Again."

I dropped my head and sank my teeth into his shoulder, riding the wave of pleasure that broke through me yet again, while he continued to move inside of me.

"You're perfect. You always were. I'm so sorry for not telling you the truth sooner."

I lifted my head and kissed him hard on the mouth, then said, "I love you, Iain. Please come back to me. Don't try and die on me again."

He groaned and surged against me, moving hard and fast beneath the water.

My belly was tightening again, moans and gasps bubbling out of me. Then he groaned, grabbing me tight as he came inside of me. The pulse of his hot seed inside my womb pushed me over the edge for a third time, and I fell down the mountain of bliss alongside him.

When we both stopped shaking and the world around us became quiet once more, Iain carried me back into the shallows.

"Can we stay here for a while?" I asked, barely able to keep my eyes open. "It's so warm. So calming."

Iain nodded and drew me over to a naturally occurring alcove where he could sit, and then he set me onto his lap and encouraged me to reat my head on his shoulder.

"You sleep, beautiful. I'll watch over you."

I smiled, my mind casting back to times when I was younger. I'd never seen it before, but Iain had always watched over me. Grabbed my parents when things got too heated with my brothers, even saved me from falling off my balcony once.

I chuckled and he whispered. "What are you laughing at?"

My eyes were closed, but I said, "You... saving me from falling that day. The balcony rescue, remember?"

He groaned. "I certainly do. You almost gave me a heart attack."

I nestled into him, hoping the water around us was healing Iain's body as it was mending the rift between us. "You yelled at me so bad, I didn't talk to you for a year after that."

The memory made me smile now.

He sighed though, sadly. "I know."

I lifted my head and forced my eyes open to look at him. "I'm sorry I didn't understand. I thought you hated me, but you were just looking out for me, weren't you?"

He nodded, his blue eyes dark with intensity. "I was trying to."

I smiled and ducked my head again, pressing against his chest. "I wish we'd been born at the same time, then we would have both known we were meant to be."

His arms squeezed tightly around me. "Sleep, my beautiful princess. Because tomorrow I'm marrying you, and you won't get much sleep after that."

I was already drifting, sleep claiming my blissed-out body. "Tomorrow, huh?"

He chuckled and kissed the top of my head. "Sleep."

CHAPTER

FIFTEEN

Iain

I wasn't kidding when I told Veronica we were getting married tomorrow. I wasn't giving her another day to start overthinking things and decide I hated her again. I could beg her to forgive me for being mean to her when she was a teenager, for the rest of our days.

Every day of our married life I'd start the morning with, "I'm sorry I ignored you for a month when you were fifteen."

She was right when she said that she'd already proven she wanted me. That she'd literally dragged me back from the brink of death, and reestablished me firmly in the land of the living. I didn't know all the details though, so when we got back to the castle I tucked a worn-out Veronica into bed, got dressed and went looking for Marienne.

The sorceress was sitting in the library with a book and a glass of wine.

I knocked on the already open door, not wanting to disturb her. She didn't even lift her head to greet me. "Come in, Iain."

I limped in, the pain in my leg so much better than it had been hours ago.

When I sat down in the armchair next to her, she finally looked up at me. "You're looking much better than you were earlier today."

I couldn't resist making a joke. "You know what they say. Love of a good woman, and all that."

Marienne assessed me, her eyes glowing violet in the light. "You're different somehow."

"Veronica took me to these hot springs, and we bathed there. I'm not sure what it did, but the pain is less. My thoughts aren't as dark. Significantly less so."

She brought her drink to her lips and took a sip. "She saved you. Again."

I nodded. "Is that twice, or three times now?"

Marienne turned in her chair toward me. "I'd count it as three, myself."

I chuckled. "All in the space of a few days. Imagine what the count will be at the end of our lives together."

Marienne's eyes widened, then a large smile spread across her lips. "Is there to be a wedding?"

I nodded. "Yes. Tomorrow. I have to speak to Damon and Cass. Would you get word to everyone else? Mom? My sisters? Everyone?"

She closed her book and stood up. "Yes. There isn't a moment to lose. When do you want everyone here? Really tomorrow, or just soon?"

I stood also, shaking out my ankle as pain tingled down to my toes. "Tomorrow."

She shook her head, but her smile was kind as she said, "As impatient as your father, you are."

Not many people compared me to my dad, King Stavrok. Those words were usually saved for Anselm. "I'll take that as a compliment."

"Oh, you should," she said. "In lots of ways, you're more like him than your siblings. You have his fire, his heart. And that's the thing that sets Stavrok above most men. His good heart."

I leaned forward and kissed Queen Marienne on the cheek. "Thank you."

We began walking toward the doors. "Let's go speak to everyone now," Marienne said. "Cass isn't going to like the fact she won't have months to plan her only daughter's wedding."

I shrugged. "I don't care so much for the party. I just want Veronica to be my wife."

Marienne's approval was obvious in the warmth of her smile. "Well said."

I reached out to stop her from floating away. "Can I ask you one more thing before we go?"

"Of course."

"What happened in Damon's bedroom? Everyone keeps saying Veronica saved my life, but all I remember is passing out, then coming to in so much pain." And the hatred in my heart had been terrible. I could still feel the shadow of it.

Marienne blew out a long breath and pressed her hand over her heart. "Oh, well that will be a story we will be telling our grandchildren. It is officially up there with Stavrok killing Magnik to save Lucy."

I gulped. "You have to tell me now."

She grinned, her white teeth flashing. "You died. The poison in your leg took over your whole body and your heart stopped."

I stared at her, barely able to believe it. "But... no-one comes back from death."

Marienne raised her eyebrows and gave me a knowing look. "Veronica has been in the human world, learnt their tricks for saving people when their hearts stop. She managed to breathe life into you, and keep your heart going while the healer flushed out your wound."

My jaw dropped. "I don't even know what to say."

She laughed. "Then she had the... audacity to ask me to create lightning with my hands, and start your heart again. I've never been so scared, in all of my life."

Now I had a hundred questions for the woman who would soon be my wife. "Sounds like Veronica learnt a lot from her time away."

Marienne nodded. "She certainly did. It is only because of her that you're here, alive and well. Your parents didn't lose a beloved son. Veronica didn't lose her fated mate. And you, lucky man, didn't lose your life."

I swallowed down the lump in my throat. I owed her far more than I'd realized. "I... I can't..."

Marienne lay her hand on my sleeve. "Let's go talk to Cass and Damon. You can thank Veronica for your life, later."

Yes. Actions spoke louder than words, always.

"You're right, Aunt Marienne. Let's go." And together we went in search of Veronica's parents.

Cass and Damon were surprised by my request, but in the end, they laughed and jumped to help. Though not before Cass let out a screech and fluttered her hands over her breasts. "Tomorrow? Tomorrow? Oh my God!" She raced off to the kitchens to get the staff started on a royal banquet and Theo offered to fly to the other kingdoms to pass on the invitations.

"Thank you, brother," I said to Theo, who punched me in the arm in return.

"You could have told me Veronica was yours."

I laughed and ran a hand through my hair, frazzled as ever. I was going to get a lot of those remarks. "Yeah, well. I was a coward, mate. What can I say?"

Theo grabbed me in a hug. "Welcome to the family."

Then he took off. It was late, and dark, but Theo wouldn't be delayed. He stripped and took to the skies, taking my invitation with him.

Tomorrow, my whole family would appear and I'd be belted by all of them for not telling them the truth about Veronica earlier.

I smiled as I walked back to my mate's bedroom and joined her in her big warm bed. Nothing mattered anymore. Not my pride. Not my fear. All that mattered was my love for the woman in my arms, and the future that we would build together.

～

THE NEXT MORNING, I told Veronica my plans and, true to character, she reacted with equal measures of violence and excitement.

"You're kidding me, right?" she said, sitting up and whacking me in the chest.

"Ow." I sat up too. "I told you yesterday I wanted to marry you tomorrow."

"Yes, but I thought you were joking!" She glared at me with all the fire she possessed.

I glared back at her. "I wasn't. I want you as my wife. Now. Today. I don't want to wait a moment longer."

"And what about what I want?" she demanded, sliding out of bed so she could stand and put her hands on her hips.

I was treated to the full Veronica glare this time, her eyes flashing with passion. She looked magnificent.

I leaned back against the headboard, still confident in my decision. "And what do you want, Veronica?"

"I want..." She huffed. "I want..."

I grinned at her. "Do you want three months so you can plan the flowers and the dresses and the..."

She groaned and threw her hands up in the air. "Hell no. I hate all that stuff."

I threw back the bedcovers, walked over to her and dropped down onto one knee. Luckily, my leg was much better since bathing in the healing spring. "Then marry me. Today. If you want a fancy party in a few months, we can do that too. But today, please... become my wife. Let me commit the rest of my life to you, and I'll do anything you want. We can go live in the human world for a few years even, if that's what you want."

She frowned down at me, then whispered. "You really love me?"

A laugh burst from my lips. "Hell yes! You've already proven you'll fight death back to save me. Now you've gotta give me the chance to prove that I love you just as much."

She moved closer, a smile playing on her lips. "What about your parents? And your sisters? Don't you want them here?"

I nodded. "Yes. Theo flew off last night to tell them."

She rolled her eyes. "Of course he did. Everyone's conspiring against me."

Slowly I rose up to my feet. "If you really don't want to marry me..."

Her hands pressed into my chest, holding me in place. "No, no, no. I'm sorry. Ask me again."

She took a step back and held her breath.

I knew I shouldn't laugh, but I was close to it. My beautiful girl had to fight her temper at every turn. I reached out and gripped her hands, which were trembling. "Veronica, Princess of the Northern Kingdom. My beloved. My fated mate. The woman I love with all of my heart. Would you do me the great honor of marrying me today?"

Her eyes glistened with sudden tears and she nodded vigorously. "Yes. I'd love that, Iain."

I swept her up into my arms, my heart soaring with joy. "Then let's get started."

She hugged me tight, but as I put her down on the bed she started pushing at me. "Don't start any of that stuff yet! You shouldn't even be seeing me today. So go, go, go!"

I gaped at her. I was still naked, and very obviously ready to make love to her. My cock ached with need.

She pointed at the door. "Quickly! It's bad luck for you to see me before the wedding and I don't even know what my dress looks like yet. Go!"

I shook my head, the blood taking its time to drain away from my groin.

Looks like we're waiting for tonight.

I scooped up my clothes and quickly dressed before heading to the door. Veronica was already in the bathroom and I heard the shower start.

"Hey! Dragon daughter! See you tonight!"

"Go!" she yelled back, and I left her room with a grin on my face. My life with Veronica would never be boring, that was for sure.

CHAPTER
SIXTEEN

Veronica

An array of dresses my mom had assembled for me to choose from were laid out on her bed. "What do you think, sweetheart?" Her voice held excitement. Clearly, I'd made her, and Dad too no doubt, very happy.

Hell, I was happy. I couldn't wait to marry my mate!

I assessed the dresses and pointed. "Great choices, Mom. But I'm thinking... this one. What do you think?"

I picked up the long flowing gown embellished with embroidered flowers and beads. It wasn't my usual style, but it called to me somehow.

Mom put her hand over her mouth like she was about to burst into tears.

"You okay?" I asked.

She nodded, and took her hand away from her mouth. "Oh, yes. I just... didn't think you'd like that one. I almost didn't put it out. But it's my favorite, for you."

I glanced over at the other plainer choices. Mom had been thoughtful in her selection, choosing dresses in a range of colors as well as white.

I smiled at her. "No. This is the best. I love it."

The seamstress rushed over and slipped it out of my hands, a big smile on her face. "This won't take long to adjust to your size, Princess. You're the same build as your mother when she wore it, and almost exactly the same age."

My mouth dropped open and I turned to Mom, stunned. It was my turn to almost burst into tears. "Is this your wedding dress, Mom? It's beautiful. Why haven't I seen it before?"

She reached out an arm to me and I grabbed her hand and squeezed it. "You were never interested in such things before," she said. "You wanted to be out in the farmlands with your father. While I..."

Her eyes were swimming with tears and I rushed into her arms to hug her tight. "I love you, Mom. Thank you for throwing this crazy wedding together for me."

She laughed and squeezed me back. "Crazy is right. A day to prepare! Though I don't blame Iain for wanting to rush. He adores you, and doesn't want to give you a chance to get away again."

When I pulled back and looked up at her, there were tears on her cheeks. "Why are you so emotional today, Mom? Because of the wedding?"

Her lower lip quivered a little as she inhaled deeply, obviously trying to get herself together. "Yes, and no. This is the start of the rest of your life, baby girl. And I'm just so... relieved."

I laughed as the seamstress began to pull my clothes off to get me into my mother's dress. "Why? Were you worried that no-one would ever have me?"

I wouldn't have been surprised if she said yes.

"Oh no." Mom helped me pull up the sleeves and began doing up the tiny buttons at my back, while the seamstress pulled out a tape measure and a little tub of pins. "It's not that. It was just... I knew that you would be uncompromising in love. That only a fated mate would do. Like your father and I."

The last of the buttons were done up and I shuffled over to the mirror, wanting to get a better look. The woman who stared back at me was someone I didn't recognize.

"Wow." I couldn't believe how beautiful the dress was. It transformed me into someone far more elegant than I usually felt. "Mom, I love it."

She kissed my hair and smiled at my reflection. "And I love you."

The seamstress fluttered her hands at my mother and she fell back to allow pins to be stuck in various places so the dress would fit me like a glove when the little alterations were done.

I took a deep breath to calm down and let the intensity of emotions caused by the beautiful dress dissipate. My mom hadn't always been super affectionate, but her love for me had always been there. Behind the words I'd taken as lectures, she'd always tried to keep me safe.

"Thank you for my life, Mom." I met her surprised gaze in the mirror. "If I'm half the mother you are, one day, my children will be blessed."

The queen's eyes suddenly became very glossy once again, and she didn't say a word. Instead her mouth wobbled, and then she nodded, squeezed my hand and quickly left the room.

I glanced down at the seamstress, who was pinning the hem. I was a little shorter than my mom, obviously. "Did I just make her cry again?"

The woman chuckled but didn't look up from her task. "At least they were happy tears."

Hmm.... true.

After the fitting, I had breakfast in my room, my mom and other servants bringing me various wedding-related things to make decision about. Flower arrangements. Colored fabrics. Food choices. She had me tasting soups, desserts, meats.

I laughed as my mother shoved yet another plate of food at me. This time, it was a platter of roast vegetables. "This is like my birthday, but ten times as lavish."

"Well, I'm trying to shove three months' worth of organization into one day, sweetheart."

I picked up the fork and readied myself to taste. "You're not mad though, are you Mom?"

She shook her head. "Oh no. We probably would have killed each other if we'd had three months to fight over table settings. Imagine it! This way, we haven't fought at all. We don't have time!"

I tasted two of the potatoes and pointed. "That one's better."

She nodded and took the plate away to replace it with pumpkins.

I looked up at her. "You really think we would have killed each other?"

She laughed. "Probably not sweetheart, but you got your forthright manner from me, and when there's a tight deadline, we both shine. So today is going to be amazing!"

She was right. I gave her my sunniest smile before digging into the roast pumpkin, then my doors burst open.

"Dragon daughter!" Vanya came marching into the room with her sister. "I can't believe you're Iain's mate! We all practically fell over when we heard."

I jumped up and ran to the girls I'd always looked up to. I launched at them, hugging them tight. "I doubt you were as shocked as me, but there is one amazing bonus to becoming Iain's wife."

"What's that?" Vanya asked.

I beamed at them. "I finally get to have you both as sisters!"

Everyone squealed and another tray was wheeled in, this time full of cocktails and wines.

Mom walked over to the trays and grabbed a drink. "Come and join the party, ladies. Time to get ready!"

The next few hours were bliss, surrounded by the powerful women in my life. My mom, Marienne and Lucy, my aunts and all their offspring. We laughed, told stories and had too many cocktails including some I'd learned to mix while nannying in Greece.

When the maids came to do my hair and makeup, my beautiful family left me alone to get ready themselves. The only one who stayed, other than the maids, was Marienne.

She sat back and watched as one of the maids curled my hair and another applied makeup to my face. "Does everything look okay?" I asked the Queen of the Black Mountains. This sort of thing was so out of my comfort zone.

"Oh yes," Marienne said, her purple eyes soft as she smiled at me. "As you know, I don't have a daughter, and on my son's wedding days, I stayed with them rather than joining in with the women. Today has been lovely."

"I'm so glad you could join us," I said, sounding far too much like my mother with the political and polite response.

I frowned, then shook myself.

Marienne laughed. "Yes, Veronica. You are a queen, in your heart and in your blood. Never doubt that."

And with those words, she stood up, kissed me on the forehead, and left the room.

I watched her go, then looked into the mirror, staring at the reflection of a woman who looked nothing like the girl I'd been yesterday. "That... I... thank you." I lifted my hand to touch my hair, amazed at how great a job they'd done.

"Now, let's get you into your dress, Princess."

The maids stood me up, pulled my dress on and did up the buttons. When I finally walked over to look at the mirror again, even I was impressed with what had been pulled together in a day.

A knock at the door and a male clearing of the throat told me my father was here. "Come in, Dad!"

When he walked in, he sported a huge grin on his face. "You always know when it's me... wow! Veronica. I... didn't expect... I remember that dress."

I turned to face him so I could meet his gaze in reality, and not just via our reflections in the mirror. "Mom said I could wear it."

He swallowed hard, his throat working a moment before he said, "You look beautiful."

"Thanks, Daddy," I whispered, my heart almost full to bursting. Then I laughed to try and reduce the emotion. "I want to hug you, but that would wreck all the work they've just done on my hair and makeup."

"Then later," he said. "After everyone else has seen you."

He held out his elbow and I walked toward him, grabbing hold of the strongest man I'd ever known, aside from Iain.

"You like Iain, right, Dad?"

King Damon smiled, "Oh sweetheart, the only thing that's important is that you like him, but yes, he is a great man. I'm definitely stealing him from Stavrok's castle and keeping him here. He's good for our people. And I'm very happy that you and he are marrying today."

I nodded. "Yes, he is a great man. It took me a while to realize that, but now..." I blinked back tears. I was becoming as emotional as Mom!

Iain liked to help people; Dad had told me that. And I knew it to be true. He had a huge heart. "He suits us, doesn't he?" I said.

Dad nodded, then frowned at me. "You're not second-guessing your choice, are you? Because if you are, we can call it off."

I squeezed his arm, hard. "Don't you dare!"

I couldn't imagine living another day without Iain. Not to mention the fact that my mind kept circling back to that first vision Anthony had shown me. I could be pregnant right now. I wouldn't know. But the thought of it filled me with joy.

Dad grinned and puffed up his chest. "That's what I want to hear. Let's do it, baby girl."

The servants opened the doors for us and we walked out of my room and down toward the ball room where the wedding and reception were being held.

"Does everything look good in there?" I asked.

"Your mother has done a wonderful job." The pride in his voice was evident now. "I think you're going to love it."

When we reached the entrance to the ballroom, the doors were decorated with ribbons and my favorite white lilies. "Oh wow, that does look great."

Dad laughed. "Oh, this is only the beginning."

He nodded at the footmen who opened the double doors. "You ready?" he asked again? "Or should we take another lap?"

I pulled his arm, forcing him forward. "I'm more than ready to be with Iain forever. Don't make me walk down this aisle by myself, Dad."

He laughed loudly and, together, we entered the ball room and walked down the aisle of red carpet my mother had managed to set up. There were rows of chairs full of people, and flowers everywhere. My favorite people in the whole world lined the aisles.

Ahead of me was Iain, standing in a suit, waiting near the elder who would perform the ceremony. As soon as I saw him, my heart soared and I had eyes for no one else. I began to walk a little faster. I wanted my father to hurry up now.

I needed to be with my mate.

When we finally reached the end of the carpet, Iain reached out a hand.

My dad took my hand and placed it in Iain's. It was a symbolic gesture that, despite my modern thinking, I loved. My father's approval of our union was important to me.

"Thank you," Iain said, gripping my fingers. Then he pulled me forward and kissed me.

A titter of laughter went up around the room and I pushed back, but not quite out of his arms. I enjoyed having him hold me in that way.

I glared at him, but playfully. "I think that part's at the end of the ceremony."

He grinned, puffing out his chest. "You've never played by the rules, beautiful. Why start now?"

"So true." I grinned back at him and glanced around, feeling the love of my family and friends swell and meet me.

When I looked back at my soon-to-be husband, I was overwhelmed with happiness. "I love you, Iain."

His eyes heated, full of promise for the future. "And I love you, beautiful Veronica."

The elder began to speak and, together, Iain and I took the first step into our new life.

EPILOGUE

In the end, we didn't get pregnant right away. Quite the opposite. We discussed it and decided we wanted time to enjoy being together, being married, being young.

So we worked side by side in my father's fields, building homes and digging trenches for new crops. Then we went traveling in the human realm and I showed him Greece, and then Spain. He loved the warmth and the beauty of the human realm as much as I did. We went swimming in ice cold oceans and drank cocktails beside swimming pools, and I had never been happier in my life.

We did things that no other dragon shifters had done, or none that I knew of, anyway.

It was amazing. And I was so blessed to have Iain by my side for the adventure of life.

When I found out I was pregnant, I had a strong hankering for my mom. I wanted to go home to my family.

So, we did. Three years almost to the day since we'd been married.

On our return, I stood in the upstairs library, my hand on my growing belly. I glanced out the window and couldn't stop the huge smile at the incredible happiness I felt. I was content with my life in a way I never thought I'd be.

Footsteps made me turn and I suddenly got an incredibly strong feeling of déjà vu, a memory of this exact moment flashing into my brain.

Oh wow, I realized. This is the moment I saw all those years ago.

Tears filled my eyes as I turned to face my husband and walked toward him.

"What's wrong?" he asked, jogging to close the distance between us as soon as he noticed my tears.

I held out my arms and he swept me into his embrace before leading me to the couches.

"Are you okay?" he asked, his hand hovering near my belly. "Is it the baby?"

I shook my head and wiped away the bothersome tears. Bloody pregnancy hormones. "No, I'm fine. So is she."

We'd both decided our baby was a little girl. We wouldn't know for sure, of course, until the day she was born, but we only had a girl's name picked out. It was going to be very awkward in that delivery room if our baby came out more like his father than expected.

"Then what is it?"

The baby shifted and rolled, so I pulled Iain's hand forward to the place on my belly where he'd be able to feel her hands and feet.

"I just realized that this is the moment I saw all those years ago. When Anthony accidentally gave me a vision before I went to the human realm. This... exactly this."

I glanced around and pointed. "I saw the stained-glass window. I saw myself, like this." I cupped my belly. "Then I heard footsteps and turned around, and it was you."

He grinned at me. "So it all came true, huh?"

"Yeah… and you know what was even more shocking to me in that vision than the fact that you were my mate?"

He huffed out a laugh. "I'm almost afraid to ask, but sure. Tell me."

I whacked him softly on the arm. "Don't be afraid to ask. It's not bad."

He gripped my chin softly, then leaned forward and kissed me on the lips. "Okay. Tell me."

"It was how happy I looked in that moment that shocked me more than anything else."

Iain pushed my hair back off my face and tucked it behind my ear in a move as gentle as it was considerate. "How come, beautiful?"

"Because back then I was so… unsettled. Angry, almost all of the time. I couldn't imagine being so happy. Pregnant. Married. It just seemed so… unbelievable. I thought it must be a lie. Or my mind playing tricks. I just… couldn't understand how I could ever reach a place of such joy."

"I'm glad." Iain put an arm around my shoulders and slid close beside me so he could stare out the window, too. "I feel exactly the same. So happy, as if life has fallen into place exactly as it was meant to, for both of us." He huffed out an amused breath. "Looks like we're meant to be after all."

I kissed my husband's cheek then lay my head on his shoulder, enjoying snuggling against him. His gorgeous scent rose around me and I drew it into my lungs. "Of course, we are. I never doubted it."

I giggled as he shook with laughter, but didn't raise my head again. My beautiful prince knew me better than anyone, but that didn't mean I couldn't still tease him a little. Life really could be as perfect as a dream, and it took our fated mate love to prove it.

9
FIRE AND ICE
THE FUTURE KING'S QUEEN
USA TODAY BESTSELLING AUTHOR
AMELIA SHAW

CHAPTER
ONE

It was strange to think that I'd been born a prince due to the changed fortunes of my bastard-born father. Strange, indeed. My gaze slid across the dining room table towards my father, a man whose enormous strength and imposing stature overshadowed most men. He was lounging casually in the chair at the head of the table, wearing naught but a peasant's shirt loose around his body and a pair of grey slacks. His hair was neither cut nor styled in any way. There was practically nothing regal about him.

He reached out for my mother's hand and lifted her delicate fingers to his lips.

She smiled at the gesture, then extended her arm a little more to touch his face tenderly.

My mother was not only a sorceress, but a true queen in every sense of the word. She wore the finest clothes, spoke with genuine authority and grace, and walked in the most regal manner.

By comparison, my father would have looked at home chopping wood or plowing fields for a living.

I shook my head. Life was odd indeed.

"What's troubling you, son?" called my father across the table.

I set my polished silver knife and fork down and wiped my hands on a cloth napkin. "Nothing much."

Dad shifted in his chair, adopting an even more casual stance, resting one elbow on the armrest and lifting his thigh so he could drape a knee over the other armrest. "You sure?" he asked again with that familiar twinkle of amusement in his eye that I'd never liked. He was teasing me.

I nodded to put an end to his line of questioning and sat up straighter, directing my gaze instead to my mother. "Mother? When can we speak of my birthday celebration plans?"

My brother, Anthony, snorted beside me. "Stop talking like a stiff."

With a sigh, I ignored the sixteen-year-old who was shoveling food into his mouth like he'd never eaten before.

"We can discuss them now, if you'd like, Carlak," my mother said.

"Nineteen in a weeks' time. I can't believe it," Dad announced haughtily, finally sitting up straight in his chair. "My son is a man, and I'm so proud."

I hadn't done anything exceptional to deserve my father's praise, but I couldn't help the flutter of happiness and pride that coursed through me to hear those words. "Thanks, Dad," I said, slipping into the more casual style of speech my father preferred.

"We didn't get the chance to celebrate your eighteenth birthday properly last year," Mom went on, "so this celebration ought to be impressive. We'll invite all the royal families, of course. And anyone else you'd like, Carlak," she added.

I'd been deathly ill over my eighteenth birthday last year and had been lucky to survive the ordeal at all, let alone manage a party. I definitely wanted to make up for lost time if I was permitted. "Yes, please, Mother. That would be most appreciated."

She glanced over at my father. "The triplets' twenty-first celebration falls on the following weekend, so perhaps we can organize for Carlak's celebration to take place in a month? That will give us an adequate amount of time to prepare and will also space out the celebrations a little."

I clenched my teeth, hearing my jaw crack under the pressure. I'd been chasing Jessa, Anselm, and Vanya my whole life. They were the children of King Stavrok and Queen Lucy, two years older than me.

Before I could comment, Anthony piped up, "Hell, yeah! We haven't had a decent party in ages. I'd forgotten about Anselm's birthday."

"And Jessa's," I corrected my brother. I couldn't believe he'd forgotten about Jessa. She wasn't exactly someone you could easily forget.

My father stared at me.

And I realized my mistake. I quickly swallowed before adding as casually as possible, "Vanya's too, of course."

Mom's gaze rested on my face and heat blossomed in my cheeks. She didn't venture to say anything, but she had no need.

I buried my embarrassment in a large glass of water. I'd always liked Jessa, probably more than I should have. We'd been raised together, not quite like siblings, but definitely like close cousins. Our parents were the best of friends, which meant I had the opportunity to see the beautiful princess and her family all the time.

"Well, I can't wait to see Iain," Anthony piped up once again, naming the youngest of Stavrok's children. "He said he'd teach me some sweet flying tricks last time he was here."

I stared at him until he grew uncomfortable.

"What?" he said.

When was I going to be able to ask him about his magic?

And why hadn't Mother reassured Anthony adequately regarding his being a sorcerer? If she had, he would be able to admit that he could both shift and have powers. I'd seen them myself on more than one occasion. After all, we'd shared a bedroom for years.

However, when I'd brought that to Mother's attention, she'd told me to remain silent on the subject. She reminded me that Anthony wasn't comfortable speaking about it, and as it was his secret to bear, I should be respectful.

The notion seemed absolutely ludicrous to me. He was who he was, and should be proud of being born a true blend of both our parents. I certainly wasn't blessed with any magical aptitude. "Nothing," I finally said to my brother, more annoyed than I previously had been.

Dad chuckled in his typical fashion and dragged himself to his feet.

I jumped up also, respecting my father's authority, and straightened my jacket. As the future king of the Black Mountains, I always made a point of trying to look and behave my best. Being the heir carried a lot of responsibilities that my younger brother didn't and likely would never understand.

"Are you spending the day with me, then?" Dad asked, arching an eyebrow.

"Yes, I'd like to," I answered, nodding at him.

Dad's smile was hesitant at first, but then he gestured toward the door. "All right, let's go."

"Aren't you going to change first?" I asked, unmoving.

Dad chuckled again. "Son, I'm king. I could walk around naked, and people would still bow to me. So, get moving. We have a meeting with the councilors."

I tried not to sigh but judging by the look of annoyance on my father's face, I wasn't too sure I'd managed to quell the sound. I said goodbye to my mother—as was polite when leaving the company of a lady—and headed out of the dining room. Together we walked the long hallway toward my father's office. "Where are we meeting?" I asked my father as he strode beside me with larger strides.

"The ballroom," Dad said,. and I almost stumbled over a rug in my surprise.

"The ballroom?" I repeated, my brow dipping. "With the councilors?"

Dad chuckled and continued walking without offering further explanation.

I was starting to feel like he was dragging me down the proverbial garden path, so to speak.

When we reached the ballroom, noise spilled through the doors.

Dad didn't stop, he just pushed through the double doors like the mountain of a man he was, and the noise amplified tenfold.

I hurried after him. This was not a meeting with the councilors at all, but a meeting with our tenants. The townspeople.

Dad greeted the people, shaking hands and smiling as he walked up through the center of the room and sat upon a throne that had been moved into the room for this occasion.

I walked up beside him and turned, staring out over the sea of faces. "This isn't the meeting I was expecting, Father."

Dad stared up at me from his place on the throne. "These are my people, Carlak. And yours. The blood of our kingdom. The workers. Its heart. Make sure you don't forget it."

"Sire," said Thomas our butler as he walked up and gestured to a couple standing beside him, "the Bourgers."

Dad sat up tall and began discussing matters with the people who'd come to speak to him.

I listened and learned as much as I could.

My father had been born a bastard of the King's mistress. He ended up an orphan on the streets living under his tyrannical half-brother for many years. Mother had told us stories in the past of the reign of terror and famine that the townspeople had endured under King Magnik.

My father had rescued these people and transformed our kingdom into one we could all be proud of. It was a place where no-one went hungry, and no-one lived destitute on the streets.

I couldn't even imagine the kingdom as my father described it previously. We were wealthy, and I found it difficult to believe there had ever existed a time when we hadn't been.

As the meeting progressed the people brought forward their crops, their garments, and all manner of offerings to their king for favors and help.

My father accepted every single gift, even pulling on items of clothing and thanking the women personally who made them for him.

It was strange and I spent much of the day feeling uncomfortable. For one thing, I was on my feet, standing in the one place, unable to move. My feet ached. And for another, my princely clothing, while usually something I was proud to wear, made me feel like a peacock amongst the crows.

My father had dressed according to his audience and although he had dressed in a similar way to attend royal events, I had to respect his ability to move amongst the townspeople as though he was one of them.

I was not. And couldn't imagine being so.

"Carlak." My father called, pulling me from my reverie.

"Yes, Father?"

"Help Nadine with her child, will you?"

I stared at the woman in front of me, heavily pregnant, with three other children in tow.

"Ah, I don't..."

The woman stumbled, losing her footing.

Dad launched himself out of his chair instantly, scooping up the sleeping child from her arms and pulling Nadine into his. "Please. Sit," he told her. "Thomas! We need some chairs here. Send for more."

The butler hurried off.

My father encouraged the exhausted woman into his throne.

Her face was pale and if she'd had the strength to do so, she would have declined. I could tell.

Dad glared at me as he deposited the sleeping child into my arms.

I gasped as the unexpectedly heavy weight slid into my arms.

"All of you gather around Carlak," Dad said, gesturing to the other children. "I'll help your mother."

The other two children, strong, healthy boys with dirty faces and long hair took a step towards me.

"You need to hold her better," the older boy said to me, touching his sleeping sister's arm. "Tight against you."

I adjusted my hold on the little girl and nodded at the child who was giving me directions.

Thomas came back with an army of men and chairs as per my dad's request.

My father barked orders to get food and drink for the townspeople, then he took the little girl from me and gave her back to her mother.

I'd never felt so out of my depth, nor so embarrassed in all my life. I felt as useless as tits on a bull! It was humiliating, so I excused myself and left the room as our servants came running in with supplies. I was to be the next King and had thought myself ready and willing to serve my people. But in a few hours my father had shown me that I was nothing more than a stuffed shirt, just like my brother said.

My pride was wounded and my ego was screaming with anger. I am my father's heir! Just because I didn't want to dress in common clothes didn't make me any less of a future king... did it?

TWO

Jessa

I stared at myself in the mirror, turning left and then right to assess the hemline of the new dress I'd been gifted for the impending celebrations. "I don't know about the length," I said, twirling around again. "What do you think, Mom?"

My mother, Queen Lucy, sat on my bed with a radiant smile on her face. "I think you and your sister are two of the most beautiful girls in the whole world. And I can't believe you're almost twenty-one! The time seems to have flown. I remember bringing you into the world like it was just yesterday. The pain, the joy, all of it."

I rolled my eyes with good-natured humor and spun around to face her. "I meant the hem, Mom. Is it too short?" Instead of opting for a traditional floor-length ballgown, I'd asked for a mid-calf ballet length dress that would show off my beautiful new shoes; but it fell flat of what I truly desired and made me feel like a little girl playing dress-ups in her mother's ill-fitting clothes.

Mom slid off the bed and came closer to get a better look at the offending garment. "Hm. You have a keen eye and may be right, darling," she said, tapping her finger against her chin in thought. "It's somehow too short and too long at the same time. It's a bit of an awkward length to be honest, neither here nor there. Perhaps we ought to get it taken up to your knee? It may be too short for the weather mind you, but our ballroom will be full of people and the fireplaces will be blazing all night long and should keep everyone well and truly warm enough."

I lifted the pink gauze up to my knee for a tentative visual and grinned at the result. "You're right. It definitely needs to be shorter. Then everyone will still be able to see my shoes and I can dance the night away without tripping myself up! It'll be perfect."

Mom chuckled and shook her head. "You and your sister are so different, polar opposites almost. Vanya is wearing black from head-to-toe, while you're celebrating in your own fluffy feminine style..." She gestured to the thin straps, flimsy gauze skirt, and the sparkles that overwhelmed the structured bodice of my dress.

I shrugged with a smile and went back to scrutinizing my reflection in the mirror. "Vanya looks beautiful in her style, but it's just not for me."

My sister loved black, and I didn't. I lived for color! She was sullen and serious, where I was not. I loved to laugh! I adored her in every sense of the word, but she was truly my opposite in everything.

"I feel exactly the same way, sister," Vanya said, sweeping into the room with her regal style; her head held high, her posture perfect. She was wearing her own new dress as well and twirled in front of my huge mirror to show off her body in the figure-hugging dress. "I love my dress, Mom. It's stunning. Thanks."

Mom came over and hugged Vanya and the two shared a moment.

I stared back at the mirror, a pout forming on my lips, and my nose scrunching. "Why'd you get all the thin genes, huh?" I complained with a defeated sigh.

Mom chuckled at my half-hearted displeasure. "Sorry sweetie, you take after me, I'm afraid. But don't worry… when the time comes, you'll find a man who loves your curves as much as your father loves mine."

"Mom! Ew! Gross." Vanya protested.

I pointed at my sister, agreeing with her sentiments entirely. "Yes. Exactly that!"

Mom shook her head and returned to sitting on the bed. "You two look amazing, and all the more so for your unique differences. You're like the dark to the light, the sun to the moon, or a rainbow in a storm." She sighed wistfully. "This party is going to be wonderful, girls."

"I agree," Vanya said. "It's been too long since we've seen everyone." And by everyone she specifically meant all our 'cousins.'

"I hope Aunt Cass comes," I added hopefully. "She missed Dad's birthday after all."

Mom laughed. "Oh, Cass wouldn't miss your party for anything or anyone," she assured us. "She was the first person to hold you three after your father, and she's loved you as long as you've all been alive. She'll be there, don't you fret."

There was a knock at the door and Vanya turned toward the sound like a dancing shadow. "That's for me. I'll be back," she said before disappearing from my room.

Mom carefully helped me out of my dress and hung it up for me.

Meanwhile I pulled on some casual, warm clothes. "Do you really think a knee length dress is okay?" I asked again. "It'll be snowing outside, and I'll be in a summer dress."

Mom shrugged. "And? You're a princess and it's your birthday. I'll make sure the fireplaces are roaring for you. Everyone else can sweat!"

I rushed for my mom and hugged her tight. "Thanks Mom."

My mother, who was human and not a shifter like all of us, hugged me with the fierceness of a dragon. "I love you so much, baby girl."

I grinned and buried my head in her neck. I had amazing parents. A big, protective dad who just happened to be a king as well. And a mother who was affectionate and present and had made me feel loved my whole life. We'd had our fights, over the years of course, who didn't disagree with their parents from time to time? But overall, I knew I was lucky. So very lucky. I sighed.

"So," Mom began, pulling away and dabbing at her eyes, "are there any boys in particular I should be steering your father away from on your birthday night?"

I choked on a laugh. "Ah... I don't know what you mean, Mom?"

She stared at me with a knowing glint in her eyes. "You have to be in someone's sights, Jessa. You're more beautiful and sparkly than all the stars in the sky; and we've invited every prince and eligible bachelor in the whole realm to this party."

I giggled, excitement and embarrassment warring within me in equal measure. "No... Mom. There's nobody special, you know that."

"Do I?" she teased, a smile teasing at her expression.

I shrugged. "I want my fated mate. I don't want just any... random guy."

Mom smiled and reached out to cup my face for a moment before settling in the armchair next to the mirror. "You know I didn't find your father until I was thirty years old."

"I know, Mom." I said, trying not to roll my eyes. I'd heard their story a hundred times.

"So, my point is that you don't have to rush, sweetheart."

"I know!" I said a little more explosively than I intended before bustling over to my drawers to pull a thick pair of socks out.

Mom sighed. "I'm not trying to upset you, Jessa. I just want you to know that it's normal to have to wait for your mate. Not only that, but it's also not super common to have a fated mate, either. Up until your father found me, it was quite rare actually."

I sat on my bed and pulled my socks over my cold feet. "Yeah... I know, but now it seems like everyone's fated. You and Dad. Auntie Cass and Uncle Damon. His brothers."

Mom smiled. "And Erik and Marienne... I know. We're all very lucky, but that doesn't mean that your generation is going to be the same. You might be more traditional."

My head came up and I stared at my mother. She wouldn't. "What do you mean, more traditional?" I asked cautiously.

She swept her long blonde hair, peppered with gray, up and into a bun on top of her head, fastening it with a large scrunchie before answering. "Well, traditionally, a dragon would just come along, claim you, and fly you back to his home."

I snorted. "Yeah right!" I dared anyone to try and take me away against my will, especially if my dad was around.

"Or… we could set up an arranged marriage if you prefer?" Mom said, her tones serious and yet there was an amused sparkle in her eyes. "Which of the princes do you like the best?"

My thoughts went immediately to Carlak, the heir to the Black Mountains. I shook my head and pulled on my slippers which had been pushed under my bed. "None of them Mom, you know that. They're all too young for me." Carlak was two years younger, which meant it may as well have been twenty. The divide between us had always felt huge.

"Well, some of the other kings have older sons. We don't see them often. But there's Rothan and Tabbath. They'll be at the party."

I stared at my mother; my mouth wide open. "You invited everyone?"

She nodded. "Yes, we did. It was your father's idea. He said that he used to have the five families around quite often; but had fallen out of touch with them all since becoming closer to Damon and Erik. And I agreed of course. Why not? More allies are always a good thing, Jessa."

My parents were a power couple, and though it could be argued, were definitely the most powerful of all the kings and queens in the realm.

I jumped to my feet and grinned at my mother. "Are you trying to get rid of me, Mom? Are you not-too-secretly hoping I'll marry some prince and have to go live somewhere far, far away?"

Mom rose to her feet in a fluid, regal movement, then made her way over to me. When she reached me, she lay her palm against my face and spoke carefully and deliberately. "Sweetheart, you are my heart. I couldn't live without you nearby. But when you fall in love, I will support you, no matter where you go."

I gulped, feeling my eyes burn with traitorous unshed tears. "Thanks Mom." I couldn't imagine leaving my home. Never.

Mom leaned forward and kissed me on the forehead. "Time for bed, darling. I'll have the dress maker come by in the morning to fix that hemline for you."

"Thanks Mom."

I watched my mother walk out of my room, before grabbing a book and jumping into my huge, lonely bed. On second thought… I jumped out again and was racing to the door when my sister appeared in her pajamas.

"Where are you going?" she asked.

I laughed. "I was just coming to find you!"

Vanya grinned. "Sleep over?"

"Absolutely."

We turned on our heels and ran for the bed, launching ourselves onto the mattress and fighting one another to get into the warm spot. When Vanya finally conceded and shuffled across to her usual side, we lay facing each other for several long moments, and neither of us spoke. There was no need. We shared a special bond.

Being a triplet wasn't something I could easily put into words. Having shared a room for most of our life, as well as everything else, including an annoying brother, meant Vanya and I were closer than anyone could ever understand—even our parents. Our strikingly opposing personalities often meant people thought we mustn't get along, but they couldn't be more wrong.

I couldn't imagine not having my sister in my life. We complimented each other perfectly; we completed one another. She was my everything, as was the rest of my family. But as we got older, and more changes came our way, it became obvious that things would never be the same again. I closed my eyes with a troubled smile and fell asleep listening to the sound of my sister breathing alongside me, safe in the knowledge that at least for now everything was still okay.

THREE

Carlak

My birthday celebration had been organized and the invitations had been sent out. Now, there were only three more weeks to wait! I was excited to finally be able to revel in my entrance to adulthood, and yet somehow, I was feeling more lost at sea than I could ever remember being before.

My father had purposely been throwing me into the deep end of scenarios I'd never had to deal with before; and I wasn't sure how best to handle them. I knew in my heart that he was doing it for my own good, to teach me what it truly meant to be a King, but every time I failed it just felt like a slap to the face; another way of implying I wasn't ready for the duty I was born to.

But my father didn't seem to understand—life wasn't a storybook—bad things happened. Stavrok had become King before he was thirty years old and I'd almost died last year, leaving my parents with Anthony as the sole heir to the Black Mountains. I loved my brother, but he had no desire to be King. He had his own demons to fight, and he didn't need the added weight of a kingdom on his shoulders as well.

I had to be ready and as soon as possible. I wouldn't rest until I knew that I could handle whatever life threw my way. So, despite feeling grossly out of my depth, I would deal with every uncomfortable situation my dad presented me.

A succinct knock at the door had me turning away from my mirror. "Come in," I called.

A hand pushed on the door and my mother entered my room. "Hello sweetheart."

"Hi, Mom," I said, before I went back to critiquing my reflection in the mirror; arranging my hair and tugging my shirt and vest into place. I was still too thin for my liking, especially when compared to my father or Anselm, but I was slowly filling out. My shirts were getting tighter by the day.

"Oh, we'll need to order you some new clothes for your birthday celebration," Mother said, sitting on my bed behind me, her long royal purple gown pooling elegantly around her feet. "You've grown taller again."

I turned to smile at her with gratitude. "That would be wonderful, thank you." I'd assumed that I would be receiving a new outfit for such an important occasion, of course, but I never wanted to seem openly entitled.

I sat on the bench seat under the window to pull on my shoes, noting the way my mom just watched me without saying anything. "Is something the matter, Mom?" I asked, glancing up to catch her eye.

She smiled. "No. I was just wondering something, that's all."

"And what is it?" I pressed, feeling the hairs on the back of my neck stand on end. I didn't have any actual, tangible magical abilities, but thanks to my mother's blood flowing through my veins, I did seem to have an uncanny knack for knowing when something was wrong.

She smiled, her lower lip trembling in a way I'd never seen before. My mother was usually warm and loving, but stoic and flawlessly regal to a fault. She rarely revealed discomfort, fear, or any other negative emotion.

"Mother, what's wrong?" I asked again, sitting down beside her. "Are you feeling ill?" She was definitely looking a little paler than normal. I reached for her hand.

She flinched away, something else she'd never done before.

I got up and took a step back, the rejection as effective as a slap to my face.

"Oh no," she cried, reaching out for me, then pulling her hand back as though I'd burn her. "Let me explain, sweetheart."

I nodded, though I was struggling to breathe through the anger and hurt that bubbled just below the surface. My mother was a strong and good Queen. Hard when she needed to be, but soft with us—her children. She was my safe space, or at least she always had been.

"I've... had a dream, Carlak. A vision of your fated mate."

My jaw dropped, my eyes grew wide, and the hurt evaporated as the situation at hand was brought to light. That had honestly been the last thing I'd ever expected her to say. "But I'm—"

"Very young," Mother said, nodding her head in agreement. "Yes. I know. Your father was much older when we met, and Stavrok was thirty-five when he met Lucy. Believe me when I say, sweetheart, I certainly didn't expect you to find her so early."

Happiness and shock warred for prime position inside my chest. Having a fated mate, especially for a king, was a true blessing. Outside of being fit to rule, nothing signified that you were more deserving of your position than if the fates saw fit to grant you a fated mate. It was viewed as a very positive and lucky omen by the people at large, even the common townsfolk.

The only problem was, I'd never even been with a woman before. My illness had stolen most of my eighteenth year from me, and I hadn't been presented with the opportunity since. Did I even want to know who she was? I was meant to have years ahead of me before I found her. Yet, here my mother was, declaring that she'd seen the woman destined to be mine.

I turned and walked away toward the window, my fist pressed to my lips in thought. I had no idea how to process my feelings right now, so chose to push them down, put them away, and squash them into something much more manageable and less intimidating.

Mom walked up behind me but didn't put her hand on my shoulder like she normally would. "Please don't feel like I'm rejecting you, Carlak. It's quite the opposite. I love you so much, but I don't want to be responsible for influencing your choice. You're my son and I only want you to be happy. I want you to choose love for yourself."

I turned to face my mother once more, her blue eyes were swirling with the lilac purple of her magic. "What will happen if you touch me?" I asked.

She bit her lip, anxiety written on her features. "It's more than likely, I will transfer the vision onto you. And I won't have any power to stop it. That is how it's always been for me, I'm afraid." She shrugged, and it was the first time I'd truly seen my mother look so powerless—but we were all powerless before the hands of fate.

I inhaled sharply, my knack tingling. I exhaled slowly as the realization dawned on me. "I'm going to meet her imminently."

She nodded; her lips pursed. "I know... but, in this case, it is going to be impossible to..." She turned and walked away unexpectedly, and began pacing the room, back and forth from my bed to the fireplace. "Stavrok was the oldest to find his mate, of all the kings, but that was because she was human. Without my interference, he might never have found her in the first place," she reasoned.

I waited, because I knew my mother well enough to know that she was just thinking aloud.

"But with you it might not make a difference," she continued. "You're already of age. As soon as you see her... your dragon's going to take flight."

I blinked at her, my head a whirlwind of confusion. "I'm sorry?" I interrupted. "What did you just say?" Do I already know her?

Mom glanced over at me but kept moving, as though she couldn't prevent herself from fidgeting. She remained silent and didn't answer.

So, I asked the question burning at the forefront of my mind. "Is my mate human... or a dragon shifter, Mom?"

My mother kept moving.

I was forced to fill in the blanks. "Well, if you think I'm going to just run into her, then that must mean she's a dragon shifter, or at least she lives in our realm."

Mother nodded and made a huffing noise I couldn't quite interpret.

"I can tell you, but... oh, your father's going to want to send you away," she said.

"Send me away?" I gaped at her. "Is my mate truly that horrible?" I couldn't imagine fate sending me a woman who could be so horrible that my father would want me separated from her. That seemed entirely counterproductive.

Mom huffed out a laugh. "No, it's not that. He just... He'll want you to have time to enjoy your adulthood! Because once you find her—"

"You'll never want another."

We both turned towards the doorway where my father was standing in his long coat. He looked like he was ready to travel outdoors.

"I came to ask if you'd like to come with me for an errand and caught the tail end of your conversation. I hope you don't mind..."

Mom looked at me.

I shook my head. "No, not at all, Father. Come in, please."

My dad moved straight over to my mother and pulled her into his strong arms. "You should have told me; I wouldn't have stopped you from telling him. Your magic is a gift, you know that."

Mother dropped her head and sobbed for a moment, clearly overwhelmed.

My father lifted her face to his and wiped away her tears.

I'd never seen them look quite so in love and tender with one another than in that moment.

"You need to tell us, my love," Dad went on. "This burden you carry is too much, I can see that plain as day."

"But it's not," Mom cried. "It's incredible and it's beautiful! I just feel so guilty for seeing everything before the time. Carlak should be the one to feel it all first, not I."

I swallowed the lump in my throat upon hearing her words. "So, it turns out well, then, Mother?" I asked.

She wiped her eyes with a handkerchief my father offered her and turned to speak with me. "Oh yes, my love. It won't be easy, but..."

"But nothing ever is," I finished for her. "However, your reassurance that I have a fated mate, and that she and I will be happy... that is enough. It's all I need."

"Are you sure?" she asked, her teary eyes sparkling.

I nodded, straightening to my full height. "I trust the fates, and I know everything will happen in its own time."

My mom smiled and wiped her watery eyes. "We are so proud of you, Carlak."

"Yes, we are," my father said, reaching out an arm for me.

I moved into my father's open embrace, careful not to touch my mom. I closed my eyes and enjoyed the rare moment of affection from my big, gruff, and strong kingly father.

He touched my head and was quiet, though I could feel his love for me.

I wanted what my parents had. True love and a wonderful marriage. My instincts tingled within me and the hairs at the base of my neck stood on end. I didn't know who fate intended for me to love, or if I was old enough to take on the responsibility of a wife, but my father had trusted the fates, as had every great king that had come before me.

This was my test, my trial by fire. We would all soon discover whether I had the balls to become the leader I'd dreamed of being. All I had to do was climb up onto the ledge of fate... and take a leap of faith off the edge. My heart raced and my guts roiled.

If baby birds can step from the nest with blind faith that the winds will catch their wings, then so can I.

I would make my great family proud and prove myself the worthy heir to the Black Mountains.

FOUR

Jessa

The doors to my bedroom flew open as Anselm stormed in. "Did you know that Mom and Dad have invited everyone from the village to our party?"

I finished applying my eye liner, not an easy task, then stared at my brother in the mirror. "Yeah? So?"

"That is hundreds of people!" Anselm complained. "Where are we meant to put them all?"

I chuckled as I perused my selection of lipsticks for the night. "What are you really worried about Anselm? That there will be too many people in the ballroom? Or that you'll have to spend the whole night talking to people you don't even know?"

Anselm crossed his arms over his chest and glared at me.

I glared right back at him in the mirror. I wasn't turning around for this ridiculous conversation when I still needed to get ready.

"You're meant to help me here, Jessa."

I laughed and selected the dark pink lipstick that would go well with my dress. "Why? Because Vanya finally told you to grow up?" Judging by the guilty look on his face, I knew I was right. Finally, I sighed and swiveled around on my chair. "Look, the first hour or two will be all pomp and ceremony. You know that and there's no avoiding it. We're the first of our generation to reach twenty-one, and our mom and dad are practically exploding with excitement to show us off. So, let."

"But..."

"Not buts," I said, standing up. "Because once the cake is cut and the speeches are done, the old folks will go home, and we'll get to enjoy the party."

Anselm dropped his arms by his side once more, heaving a sigh of his own. "Are you sure?"

"Absolutely," I assured him, stepping forward to straighten his tie. "So, no passing out drunk before the speeches."

Anselm scoffed and blushed bright red. "That was one time, Jessa!"

Our seventeenth birthday party to be precise.

"Bloody hilarious." I giggled, then stepped back. "How do I look?"

He gave me a cursory glance. "Like my sister?" He shrugged.

Ugh. "Fine! Go!" I said, shooing him away. "I'll see you at the party."

Anselm left without a backwards glance, still sour about having to deal with the pageantry of royal duty.

Not allowing him to spoil my mood, I smoothed my outfit. I'd done my own hair and makeup, but one of the maids had zipped me into my dress. A knee length, bright pink dress with a jeweled bodice and a knee-length floaty skirt made of delicate gauze. I loved it so much. The adjustments to the hem had created the outfit of my heart's desires. I felt like a real princess, even though I was a princess, it was still awesome!

I finished putting on my shoes and retouching my make up.

A butler knocked on my door.

"Come in," I sang out.

The door opened and Jarred, one of the junior staff, bowed. "Your parents are waiting for you, my lady."

I checked my reflection one more time and walked toward him, a little unsteady on my new high heels.

"Are you all right, princess?" Jarred asked as he reached out a hand to me.

I grabbed it gratefully. "Yes, I'm fine. They're just new shoes... I probably should have worn them in a little more before such a big event." Mom had suggested as much, of course. But I wasn't going to give her the satisfaction of knowing she was right after all.

Once I was steady, Jarred offered me his elbow.

Linking my arm through his, I let him lead me to my father's study. There was music playing in the ballroom as we passed and the sounds of conversation could be heard.

"Are people here already?" I asked.

Jarred stopped in front of the library door. "Yes, princess. They've been arriving for the past hour or so. The king wanted for you all to present as a family."

I thanked Jarred for the escort and pushed open the door to the study. Everyone was already there, except me. My mom, in her fabulous purple gown, Dad in a sleek black suit, and my siblings dressed in their custom party best. Anselm wore a suit similar to Dad's and my sister's floor to collar bones black dress was lovely.

"I hope they're taking photos tonight, Mom. We all look amazing."

My dad laughed and walked over to me, gently kissing the top of my head. "Happy birthday, beautiful girl."

When he stepped back, I lifted my head again and grinned up at him. "Thanks Dad." I glanced around the room and my brow furrowed. "Where's Iain?"

Vanya joined me, tugging on her long gloves as she did. "He went out early. He didn't want to miss the party."

Our younger brother was always trying to stand out in his own way, and I couldn't blame it. I didn't always admit to it, but I did have sympathy for a single son born many years after a set of triplets. It was a tough gig to follow. Anselm, Vanya, and I always stuck together. And unfortunately, Iain was ultimately left out, even though we didn't really mean for it to happen. I knew that he was and that it affected him.

I shook myself free of any negative thoughts and focused instead on my sister. "Then we better get out there before he steals all the attention," I joked.

I offered my arm to Vanya, who took it with a smile.

Anselm walked around to my other side and held his elbow out to me.

Meanwhile, Mom and Dad stared at us, their love shining upon us like a beacon of light.

I rolled my eyes, swept up in the tender family moment. "Come on guys! This is our party. Let's go."

Mom sniffled, overcome with emotion on our big day.

Dad offered her a handkerchief with a lop-sided smile.

"Our babies are all grown up," Mom simpered.

Anselm groaned. "Come on, Mom. We know you love us. And we love you too. But let's go."

Dad reached for Mom's hand. "They're right, sweetheart. Let's get to the party. It's high time we celebrate the fact that we survived twenty-one years with these little dragons!"

Mom scoffed. "The fact I survived their labor was the miracle."

"Okay, okay," Anselm said, turning a humorous shade of pink. He hated when our mother talked openly about subjects he deemed as 'girly stuff' like babies, childbirth, and breastfeeding.

I shook my head and grinned, then squeezed my brother's arm. "Come on, then. Let's go. Those issues won't concern you for a little while yet!"

"After you," Dad said, gesturing to the main door.

"Really?" I asked in surprise. There had never been a time that the King and Queen weren't the first in our family to enter an important event —it was traditional, not to mention royal protocol.

Dad took Mom's hand in his and regally strode over to open the door for us. "It's your party, children. Go out before us, please. Tonight, it would be our honor."

I glanced from my brother to my sister, pride swelling in my heart. I felt more apart of their world in that one moment than ever before. "I love you both," I whispered to them.

Neither Anselm nor Vanya said anything back, but I knew they loved me without question. These two would fight anyone for me, even our own parents. They had my back and always had... they likely always will.

So, we walked forward together, onto the small balcony that adjoined our father's study and led down into the ballroom.

The moment we stepped up to the railing, the entire ballroom went silent and everyone turned toward us.

Blood rushed to my face immediately, leaving me feeling hot and uncomfortable. But everywhere I looked, everyone's faces were lit up with happiness and love for us. All the royal families were here; Marienne and Erik, Damon and Aunt Cass, and their retinue of kids. Then my gaze fell on Carlak and Anthony, Erik's sons and my stomach tightened in the strangest way.

Then Anthony pulled Carlak away and into the crowd, as though he didn't even want to look at us.

That's weird.

"Come on, sis. Let's go," Anselm whispered to me.

As a party of three, we walked down the grand stairs.

People rushed toward us and we naturally broke apart to greet individual guests and to speak with our friends.

The next few hours were overwhelmingly busy, just as I'd first assumed they would be. I shook hands with everyone in the room and received hugs from every queen and princess in our realm, even Veronica. I squeezed the nine-year-old girl tight against my dress, her beautiful face turned up and grinning broadly.

"Happy birthday, Jessa!" she cried, her arms wrapped around my neck.

I pulled back and stared down at my little cousin. "Thanks, Veronica! How have you been?"

"Great," she said with a side-eye glance at her brothers. "Don't listen to anything they have to say about me. I've been good!"

I laughed and cuddled her again. "You do all of us girls proud, Dragon Daughter."

Veronica was tough and strong and had a temper that perfectly matched a dragon princess. She was the youngest of our crew, and with a ton of boys born before her, she fought tooth and nail for her spot in our great family.

"Hey!" she fussed, pushing back against me, her nose wrinkled.

I let her go and shrugged with a smile. "I love you, V. Don't hate on honesty."

Veronica continued to pout, but then one of her brothers pulled her piggy tails and she ran after him with an indignant scream of anger.

I could only shake my head at the fiery antics of our relatives.

Aunt Cass came to hug me and wish me a happy birthday. As usual, the queen looked positively exhausted.

"Have you been working in the fields again, Aunt Cass?" I said with a soft, playful poke at her. "You're very pale."

She stuck her nose in the air. "Not to correct the birthday girl, but I'm not pale. I'm... oh." Cass put a hand to her belly and staggered sideways.

I gasped and reached out for her, grabbing her arm at the same time as Queen Marienne came close.

"Cass," she whispered, trying not to draw attention to the scene. "You need to go lie down."

The queens exchanged a look.

I stepped nearer to my Auntie, letting her use my body for support. "Hold on to me. Let's take you to the Rose Room. It's the closest," I advised quietly.

We had a lot of guest wings in the house. But even with four kids my parents never managed to fill even half the bedrooms available in the castle. But we had a lot of family and friends that visited, so Mom always made sure the rooms were clean and well appointed.

"I don't want to be a bother," she breathed. "Oh... goodness. Ouch." She was looking paler by the moment.

"You're miscarrying," Marienne warned urgently.

My stomach plummeted. "What?" I whispered back. Aunt Cass is pregnant again?

"I know," My aunt managed in response, tears sliding down her cheeks as Marienne and I walked her discreetly as possible to the edge of the ballroom. "I suffered two before I had Veronica, and now this. I don't think my body can carry another child."

By the time we reached the exit, Uncle Damon came running, "Cass? Are you okay?" he asked, his brow creased and his eyes full of heart-rending concern.

"No, she needs to lie down," I answered. "We're taking her to the Rose Room."

Damon moved to dislodge me from his wife, but I shook him off. "Go inform my mom and dad that you guys will be staying tonight, and I'll help Aunt Cass to the bedroom. Okay?" I said with much more authority than usual.

Damon straightened and nodded. "Yes, of course," he agreed, thinking prudently. "I'll let the kids know too." He reached out to cup his wife's face and kissed her lips. "Be strong, my love. I'll see you in a moment."

Uncle Damon rushed off without delay to fulfill his mission.

Meanwhile, Marienne and I managed to help Aunt Cass down the hall and into the large Rose Room, and safely onto the bed.

"What else can I do?" I asked Marienne, wanting to be as useful as possible during such a difficult time.

She pulled back the blankets and helped Cass beneath the sheets. "Could you send a servant this way when you get the chance?" Marienne asked, putting her hand to Cass's head and feeling her forehead.

Hot tears welled up in my eyes as I looked down at my aunt. "I'm so sorry Aunt Cass." All of me wished there was something more I could do to comfort her.

She smiled and reached for my hand. "Don't be sorry, my lovely one. I have three healthy, growing children. This pregnancy wasn't planned, we just..."

I glanced down at our hands which were now linked. I couldn't imagine getting pregnant by accident. How does that even work? I wondered.

"She'll be fine, Jessa," Marienne said. "Your aunt is strong and her body will heal. Sometimes you just have to trust the will of the Universe, and it's not this child's time to be born."

I nodded but couldn't stop the tears that flowed down my cheeks. I dashed them away, feeling silly. I should be able to cope with women's business more maturely! I chastised myself.

"You are a beautiful girl," Marienne offered, reaching out to touch my arm. The moment she did, a vision flashed through my mind.

I gasped at the image before me. I saw myself in the ballroom, and I was turning to look out toward someone special, but I couldn't see who they were. The vision ended and I blinked rapidly, my sense of presence returning.

Marienne had stepped away, and now stood close to the bed head. "I'm so sorry, Jessa. Please forgive me."

"For what?" I asked. "I didn't see anything special. I just saw myself in the ballroom... Is there anything you want me to know?"

Queen Marienne was a sorceress, and the main reason my father had successfully found my mother and married her. Dad would never have found a human fated mate without the guidance of a talented magic wielder like Marienne.

Marienne shook her head, putting both hands behind her back. "No. In this case I'd rather..." She coughed to clear her throat. "Not help."

I took a step toward her. "But you know something about my future? About my..." The sentence died on my tongue and I was forced to swallow hard against the overwhelming feelings that flooded my chest. "Do I have a fated mate?" I manage to ask. The special someone I was looking for in the vision... "And do you know who they are?"

I was only twenty-one, but Aunt Cass had been nineteen when she'd married Damon. Was there ever a right age to find your 'one and only'? It seemed I might be about to find out.

FIVE

Carlak

As soon as I saw Jessa walk out onto the balcony, I knew she was my mate. I knew it the way I knew my father was my father, and my blood ran red. I needed to be near her. I needed *her*. My dragon raised his head and made my whole body shudder with the urge to shift right in the middle of the packed royal ballroom, at the triplet's twenty-first birthday party.

I clamped down on my shifter with an iron grip, something my father had taught me long ago. There were people everywhere, and the place was packed. I could hurt someone, not to mention I'd destroy the event and it would never be forgotten.

Jessa's gaze scanned the room, a beautiful smile on her lips as she surveyed her kingdom. Her dress was bright, hot pink and clung to her body in a way that made my heart pound. Between her brother and sister, she was a rose among the black of night. Then her gaze fell on me.

The surge of Fate between us clashed with the heat of an inferno. My dragon rose up inside of me hot and fierce, and I could barely breathe as I fought against him. She was exquisite. She was perfect. *And she is mine!* my dragon roared within. My hands tightened into fists, and I clenched my jaw hard, grasping for any semblance of a grip on my control.

"Come on!" Anthony grabbed my hand and tugged hard. "Brother, you need air. Quickly. *Now!*" he urged.

I allowed my younger brother to pull me away to the back of the room and outside into the cold night air.

Anthony shut the door firmly behind us and turned to face me.

I willed myself to breathe, to get as much of the icy air into my lungs, chilling my teeth and forcing my dragon back into his proverbial cave. "What..." I managed, but I couldn't speak. My teeth were partly shifted, and still sharp and too big to allow speech.

"Just breathe," Anthony instructed me calmly. "You know what Dad always says. Push the dragon back and down and focus on the damage you could do if he comes out. And I know we're outside now, but Mom won't be impressed if you rip apart your new suit."

My brother's presence helped me achieve calm faster than anything else. "How did you know?" I asked him as I rubbed my jaw, my dragon retreating faster than ever before.

"Know what?" Anthony asked, now staring at the ground like a toddler in trouble.

I took a deep breath. My brother had visions just like my mother. He hadn't told me, but I knew. I didn't think he'd told *anyone* yet. "You know about Jessa, don't you?" I asked, forcing myself to give him an out, even though I shouldn't. *It's his secret to share, not yours,* I reminded myself. "Did Mom tell you?"

Anthony's head came up and his face was flushed with relief. "Did she tell you?" he asked me.

I shivered and rubbed my hands together. With the fire of my dragon gone I was getting cold now. "No. She offered... she said she knew who my mate was."

"And you didn't find out?" Anthony gaped at me as though I were an idiot.

I wasn't the one hiding my powers from the world, but I kept a lid on it. I'd promised my mother a long time ago that I wouldn't out my brother until he was ready. And I wouldn't. The curse of the oldest child. It came with many burdens, and the responsibility I felt for my brother was immense. "No. I figured that I'd let Fate lead the way."

Anthony snorted. "Well, it led you right to her, didn't it? What are you going to do?"

I took a deep, steadying breath and pursed my lips before answering. "I honestly don't know." I was only nineteen. Did I want to sow my wild oats? The thought wasn't worth contemplating, because my stomach plummeted at the mere suggestion of bedding other women while my mate waited on the sidelines for me.

"You want to go back inside?" Anthony asked gently.

I nodded, pulling myself together. "Yeah. Let's go."

But when we got back inside, Jessa was nowhere to be seen and Iain found us instead. "You guys want to play billiards?" he asked, tilting his head toward the huge game room off the ballroom. "Most of us guys are already in there."

I took one more lingering look around the room, hoping to spot her before agreeing to go with them. I grabbed a whiskey on my way through the ballroom and drank the whole thing in one gulp. Fire burned my throat, but I grabbed another, hoping the alcohol would help dull my need to seek Jessa out and drag her off somewhere private.

Jessa and I had always gotten along well enough. She was two years older and a bit wild. Not the sort of woman I'd ever imagined as my queen. She'd never shown any real interest in me either, so I wasn't sure where this need to ravish her had sprung from. It had to be the call of Fate. It was compelling me, willing me to fulfil my destiny. *I bet her nipples taste like strawberries,* my dragon whispered. *Ugh! Stop it!* I commanded. I grabbed another whiskey and threw it down before getting to the game room and finding most of my male cousins gathered. Uncle Damon's sons, Iain, Jessa's youngest brother, and a couple of others too.

I nodded my head at them all in typical male fashion and found a place on a leather couch to make myself comfortable.

"Do you want to play the winners?" Iain called to me from the billiard table.

"Sure," I answered, nodding at them, though my head was starting to spin. I let the alcohol seep into my veins, and when the servants came around with more drinks, I grabbed at them greedily. *It's working.* I couldn't play billiards, of course, but I wasn't dying to find Jessa and strip her of her party dress, either. I desperately wanted to, but the *need* had dimmed, thanks to the liquor.

"They're doing speeches," Anthony said, coming over to kick me with his shoe.

I wasn't sure I could get up. "It's probably not a good idea for me to..." I managed to slur.

My brother grimaced. "Yeah, okay. Stay here. I'll go. And I'll be back soon with cake. Okay?"

I closed my eyes and lay my head on the armrest of the couch. Everything was spinning, and I was completely fine with that. If I saw Jessa again, I wouldn't be able to keep my dragon under control if I was sober. He'd override my willpower. But if we were both inebriated, she and everyone else would be safe. My dad would be pissed, but who cared at this point? *Not me!*

I must have passed out because the next thing I knew, Anthony was shaking me. "Wake up," he hissed.

I lifted my head, seeing double images of my baby brother now. "Whoa, there's two of you."

"Eat this," Anthony said, shoving a plate at me. "They've finished speeches and they've cut the cake, so it's party time, and people are noticing that you're missing."

"I don't care," I said with a laugh, but forked the cake and started shoving some of it into my mouth. It was rich and chocolatey, with sugared strawberries and fresh cream. "Mmmm, this is nice."

My father suddenly exploded into the room and stormed over to me. "What the hell's going on, Carlak?" he demanded.

I snorted, still pickled. "Nothing, Dad. What's going on with you?" His surprised expression and awkward half smile made me giggle a little, so I grinned to myself like a naughty child and tried to focus on eating a bit more cake.

"He's drunk," Dad said, turning towards Anthony for answers. "What happened?"

Anthony tugged on our father's sleeve, pulling him out of earshot, but I could imagine what he was saying. *Jessa... blah, blah. Mate... blah, blah, blah.*

When my dad walked back over to me and put a hand on my shoulder, his love emanated through in a way that had me gulping back tears. It felt tangible. "Congratulations, son," he said, his voice thick with emotion. "She will be a magnificent queen."

I looked up at my father, my heart in my throat.

He stared down on me with all the pride I'd always hoped to see.

"You know," I said, changing the subject with a hiccup. "You look good in formal clothes, Dad."

He chuckled and squatted down in front of me, putting us on an even eye level. "Clothes don't make a king, Carlak. It's your actions that will have people respect you, nothing else." He stood up. "I'll go get him some coffee. Are you all right to stay with him, Anthony?"

My brother scoffed. "Well, I'd much rather be dancing, but sure, Dad."

I continued to focus on my cake. The food in my belly was sobering me up, and my senses were beginning to come back in a rush. *I'm embarrassing myself and my family,* I realized with horror. I had to get up and rejoin the party. I pushed against the couch and managed to rise unsteadily to my feet, lifted my chin and tugged on my shirt, straightening myself as best I could. "Father, I apologize for my behavior. I—"

My father, King Erik, stepped toward me, put his hand on my chest, and pushed me firmly back down.

My jaw dropped and I gaped at him. "Did you just push me?"

He cracked a grin. "I'll hogtie you if I must, boy. Stay there, shut up, and when I bring you coffee, you'll drink it."

"Are you... helping me?" I slurred.

Dad laughed this time. "Carlak, you are my son, and I know you want to do everything right all the time, but I'm prouder of you in this moment than ever before."

I fell back against the couch, my lips twisted. "What do you mean?" My father had never withheld his love or approval, and yet I couldn't help but constantly strive to do better. *Be better. Be worthy.*

He glanced toward the doorway before speaking again. "Son, you are my heir, and you will be king by birthright. But tonight, you showed me that you can control your dragon around your mate, protecting all the people around you from harm and possible injury in the process."

I couldn't help but roll my eyes in a juvenile way. "Dad, that's not heroic. I had to get drunk! I couldn't handle it. This was the only I way I could think of quickly to push him back down."

My father shrugged. "No, son. You handled it well. I didn't. When I saw your mother, I shifted inside this castle, almost attacked Stavrok, then picked her up and flew her home in dragon form."

My jaw dropped at the epic imagery.

Anthony punched our father in the arm. "Whoa! That's awesome."

Our dad chuckled. "Well, tonight Carlak demonstrated that he has more inner strength than me."

I ran a hand through my hair and forced a laugh. "That's nothing, Dad. All I did was control my dragon at a party."

"Within the first moments of realizing who your mate was." Father reached out and ruffled my hair. "And if you're starting with that, Carlak, your foundation of strength makes anything possible for you. Stay here, all right? I'll get you that coffee so you'll be able to fly home." With that said, Dad turned and left.

Anthony and I sat in silence.

A servant arrived soon after with a tray of water, coffee, and buttered bread rolls. "King Erik has advised that you are to eat and drink, and theb rejoin the celebration when you feel ready."

I nodded at the servant and did my best to sober up, swallowing the bitter coffee and stuffing the fluffy bread into my mouth. "Thanks for staying with me," I managed to say to my brother around my mouthful.

"No problem," Anthony said eating more birthday cake. "Are you okay if I go say goodbye to Iain?"

"Yeah, go," I said, waving my hand at him. "I'll come out soon. I just need a minute."

Anthony grinned and left, entering the ballroom, which was now pumping out some hardcore dance music.

My heart yearned to find my mate to at least know if she was safe. I managed to stand, and although my stomach grew queasy, I had better control of my legs now. I walked to the doorway of the game room and stared out at the darkened ballroom. There were long tables of food off to one side and most of the round tables had been cleared away to make space for a large dance floor and a band.

People danced and shimmied under the flashing lights, their laughter and singing ringing out above the music.

And that's when I saw her, dancing with the only unmarried heir to the throne older than herself—*Taggath*. He was thirty and too arrogant by half. But he was tall and, according to my mother, very handsome. And he had his grubby hands on my Jessa's waist.

Rage blew through my veins, banishing the liquor, and once again, I was back to fighting my dragon for dominion over my own damn body.

Fucking hell!

Jessa

Taggath's grip on my waist grew tighter as the song wore on.

He's so hot, I can't believe he wants to dance with me!

"You should consider coming to stay at our castle over the summer months," Taggath whispered, speaking directly into my ear, and making me shiver as his hot breath coursed over my skin. "We can go skinny dipping in the hot springs."

I jerked back, my eyes wide, both mortified and pervessely flattered by his offer at the same time. "Thanks. I'll think about it," I managed to answer, though I was pretty sure my mom would stop me from staying at his castle even if I wanted to. Taggath was a known playboy in the realm, but he was also almost thirty-five years old. *Surely, he'll be getting ready to settle down soon?* Maybe I'd be the one to tame him, the way Mom had been the one for Dad.

"Can I cut in?" a voice sounded from behind Taggath, audible even over the music.

I recognized it instantly.

The dragon prince in my arms turned at the intrusion. "No. She's mine," he said haughtily.

The growl Carlak released was loud enough to be heard over the deep bass of the music.

My jaw dropped. *What the hell?*

Everyone in our immediate vicinity took a big step back, including Taggath, his expression one of shock.

There was a dark warning in that growl. A sound I'd only heard once before in my life, and it had come from my father when my mother had been threatened. *Why would Carlak be making such a sound in response to someone simply dancing with me?* I wondered. "What's going on, Carlak?" I asked, mildly annoyed that he'd driven Taggath away.

Carlak didn't respond but seemed otherwise calm. He looked like his normal self, except for his eyes. They were dark yet ablaze with a fire I'd never seen before.

The music changed from a lively, fast dance beat to something slow and sexy. I wanted to look away, to reach for Taggath again, but I was rooted in place, unable to move. I was lost, staring into Carlak's eyes, the breath knocked out of me.

Carlak moved in, sliding his hands around my waist and pressing his fingers into my bodice.

I gasped, heat searing my body even though he hadn't made contact with my skin, "Oh..."

"Put your hands around my neck," he growled quietly.

I couldn't help but do as he commanded and moved my arms up to encircle his neck, my gaze still locked with his. "You're... ah, taller, than I remember," I managed to say despite the fact my throat was thick with an emotion I couldn't identify.

Carlak remained stoically silent, but he moved to the music, and we began to dance. Without warning he stepped even closer, so that our bodies connected.

I gasped at the immediate reaction such close contact caused deep in my belly. Heat blossomed inside me, coiling restlessly like a serpent ready to strike. In confusion, I arched my back to put more space between us, and yet I couldn't prevent the wicked tightening of my nipples beneath my sparkly bodice.

He swayed like a natural and led me around the dance floor with seductive elegance. He was definitely taller than the last time I'd seen him. I was forced to look up to meet his eyes now, and his shoulders were much broader and seemed to carry an air of authority.

I coughed to clear my throat and licked my lips. "I saw your mom earlier. She looks well," I said anxiously. "We had to help Aunt Cass with a... well, she wasn't feeling well."

Carlak moved closer still, pressing his lips to my ear. "What happened to her?" he asked.

My eyes slid closed, and I gulped. I couldn't suppress the wanton shudder that overtook my body at his proximity. My nails dug into his neck and the base of his skull of their own volition, holding him close.

"Jessa?" he whispered, brushing his mouth against my skin.

I shivered again, and a moan escaped me as my knees gave out.

Carlak clutched me tightly against him, not letting me fall. "Are you all right?" he asked, a little note of alarm in his voice.

I nodded and managed to open my eyes and stare up at him again. He was so close, and his lips were just inches away from mine. "What is this?" I whispered, my heart racing as I searched his gaze for answers to this impossible feeling growing inside me.

He stared straight into my eyes, his lips parting to speak.

Then my gaze was torn away as I was physically knocked sideways.

Carlak managed to grab my hand and kept me on my feet, but we were separated now, and the spell seemed to have broken like a wave crashing on the shore.

"Sorry! Sorry," the three guys mumbled in unison, drunk and rowdy. They had barreled into us as a group.

I looked around for Carlak, but his father had come up to him with Marienne, and they were already engaged in conversation. I felt my cheeks flare with warmth as I gazed longingly after him. I wanted him to come back—to dance with me—to make me feel happy, and tingly, and *way* too aware of myself.

Someone grabbed my hand, and I turned to find my mom.

She was grinning at me, warmth sparkling in her eyes. "Are you having a good time, sweetheart?"

"Um, yeah... of course! Mom, yes! This is great," I babbled, cringing internally.

"Erik told me that their family must leave. I'll grab Anselm and Vanya. Can you meet us in the exit foyer?"

"Ah, yeah, sure." I managed to nod and smile, though it was half-hearted at best. I certainly wasn't convincing myself. *They're going? Why?* I wondered, feeling suddenly bereft. I moved through the dancing swarm of friends and family filling the ballroom, all of them smiling toward me. I put on my pretty princess face, smiling and holding their hands when they extended theirs in greeting. They expected me to be perfect, and I tried my best. But I didn't feel perfect at the moment. With every step I took toward the foyer, breathing became harder and harder.

Once I burst through the final groups of people gathered at the edge of the ballroom and made it to the foyer, I heaved in a deep breath.

"Are you okay, Jessa?" King Erik asked, walking toward me and reaching out to grab my elbow as I swayed.

The growl from behind him made us both jump.

Erik laughed softly in response as he released his gentle grip on me and backed away with a grin.

I looked from Carlak to Erik and back again. "What the hell is that?"

Erik smirked at me. "That would be my son. I'm just glad he's still in human form."

I blinked at the huge king, my fast-fraying temper snapping at the enigmatic statement. Slammed my hands on my hips, I glared up at the king. "Oh, don't you start talking in riddles too! I want to know what's going on."

Mom and Dad came rushing up behind us.

"So sorry, folks. Anselm and Vanya aren't in the ballroom, and we didn't want to make you wait," said my father.

Mom glanced at me, her eyebrows furrowing deeply. "What's happened?"

Before I could answer, Marienne rushed over to hug me, then turned to my parents apologetically. "We really must go. Carlak isn't well."

I snorted. "Isn't well... as if!"

My father came closer and bent his head to whisper. "Did something happen, sweetheart?"

A soft growl filled the air but was cut off as I looked up.

Anthony was pulling his brother to the door and throwing open the exit. "Bye, guys!" he called, waving as he stripped off his evening clothes. "Thanks for the party!"

Carlak stared at me as though he had nowhere else to look in the world. His hands were tightened into fists.

Beside me, my dad was making a strange, rumbling sound from deep in his throat.

I turned towards him, startled. "Dad! Stop it!"

King Erik interrupted and shook hands with my father. "I think we'll be seeing each other again very soon."

"Yes!" Marienne said. "For Carlak's birthday party. Did you receive the invitation?"

Mom nodded. "Yes, of course, Marienne. We'll be there."

"We better go, my love," King Erik said to his wife softly, touching her arm.

"Oh, yes." Marienne smiled and waved as she walked away, her gaze lingering on me. "I look forward to spending more time together, Jessa."

Hot tears stung my eyes, and I blinked them away in frustration as emotion overwhelmed me. What was she trying to tell me?

"Thanks for coming!" Mom called out, walking behind the royal dragon family and shutting the doors to stop the icy air from blowing inside.

I walked after her, staring out through the thick glass panels as King Erik shifted, and Queen Marienne climbed onto his back to ride him.

Carlak was the last to shift, but I watched as he stripped and stood in the snow, his back to me. As a dragon shifter myself, I knew I shouldn't be watching him, or staring at his physicality. Unless it was an emergency it was considered poor taste. But I couldn't help it. My breath caught in my throat at the sight of his tight ass and his muscular back.

He lingered a moment before he glanced over his shoulder at me and shifted into his magnificent dragon form, taking to the sky.

An unexpected and strangled squeal rose up in my throat. *He's leaving me. He's not coming back.* I had to turn away and run back to my mom before my dragon took flight and chased after him. "Mommy..." I whispered, covering my mouth with both of my hands as tears filled my eyes.

Mom grabbed my arms and stared into my eyes. "Oh, my darling girl... what happened? What's wrong?"

"He left me," I whispered, having no control over my words or my feelings.

"Who left you?" she asked.

But I couldn't speak another word.

Dad walked over to the doors, then turned back around. "Oh... *fuck*."

Mom and I both turned towards him. I still couldn't talk so my mother gathered me close. "What is it?" she asked him.

"The growl... the dance... oh my God! Why didn't I realize sooner?" Then he started laughing and shaking his head with a broad smile on his face.

I dashed away the tears on my cheeks and stared at him, willing my mouth to work. "Dad, what's going on? I don't understand!"

"You don't know?" Dad asked, staring at me.

"No," I whispered feebly, feeling stupid and small. "Why won't anyone tell me?"

Dad walked over and took my hand, squeezing tightly. "Sweetheart, can't you feel it?"

"Feel what?" I asked in frustration.

Mom reached for Dad's arm. "Are you sure?" she queried him.

"Sure of *what*?" I asked, my voice turning shrill.

Mom and Dad both turned toward me as one.

"The growl is the biggest giveaway, we're lucky you're still here. If Carlak had let his dragon shift, we might not have been able to stop him from taking you away." Dad said.

Mom snorted. "No one could have stopped you the night you grabbed me, that's for sure."

"Hang on a bloody minute," I said, stepping away from my parents to stare at them wide-eyed. "What are you saying?" Though as the question left my lips, I knew the answer would be one that would shake my world to its very core. I could feel something... something *important*. I just didn't know what it was!

My parents glanced at each other.

Dad turned to me, his expression soft but shocked. "Jessa... Carlak's your Fated mate."

CHAPTER
SEVEN

Carlak

After flying home from Jessa's birthday party, I crawled into bed and woke up several hours later with a brutal, throbbing headache. "Oh... God," I moaned as I rolled over. With a massive effort, I managed to stagger to my feet and shuffle to the bathroom before vehemently worshipping at the porcelain god's altar. When my stomach finally settled somewhat, I dragged myself into the shower and let the hot water wash away the stink of my shame.

What sort of heir to a kingdom was I? The type to get myself blind drunk at a royal event, then partially seduce my mate on the dance floor in front of everyone, apparently! I felt completely disgusted with myself—as a prince, a man, and as Jessa's mate. "Fucking hell." I groaned, pushing myself up to sit against the tiled wall of the shower before throwing my head back against the cool tiles behind me.

Jessa was my mate. *Jessa!* Of all the women, in all the worlds, it had to be the most beautiful, carefree, confident, and intelligent princess in the realm. My mind reeled, still scarcely coming to grips with the truth. I certainly didn't feel worthy of her, and that smarted more than a little.

Jessa was King Stavrok's eldest daughter, and she had the natural strength, grace, and beauty of a queen. There was no way she'd want me now, especially after my obscene behavior at her shared birthday celebration. But would our Fated mate bond force her desire me regardless? That would be horrible, and the thought made my stomach turn with revulsion. It would be even worse than if she were to reject me outright. Not to mention the fact that she was older than me by two years, which at this point in our lives seemed like a *huge* chasm to overcome.

"Carlak?" my mom's ethereal voice floated through the room, reaching my ears.

"In here," I managed to croak out, feeling morose and sorry for myself.

She let herself into the steam-filled bathroom, a chuckle on her lips. "When you and Anthony were younger," she told me, "I always swore that I wouldn't help you get rid of your hangovers when the time came. It was my opinion that you deserved to learn about the side effects of alcohol the hard way."

A cold, hard object was pressed to my shoulder, and I forced my eyes open.

"Take it and drink it all," Mom encouraged, pushing the goblet at me insistently. "It will help."

I didn't bother to ask what it was, or why she'd changed her mind suddenly now that I was grown. I was just so grateful for the assistance and motherly empathy that I just chugged the foul tasting concoction down without a second thought.

"Gah. Damn. That was nasty, but thank you," I spluttered, handing her back the cup. My eyelids still felt heavy, and my stomach churned in protest. A part of me just wanted to slither back into bed to try and elude my own suffering. But just as the bile rose in my throat once more threatening to make me sick, the medicine took full effect, and the pain leeched gloriously away, dimming to a more bearable level. I could move again without agony or feeling overwhelmingly woozy, so I took the opportunity to stagger to my feet. Facing the water spray, I washed my mouth, glad to be rid of that disgusting taste.

"I will be waiting in your room, son," my mother said from behind me. "Take your time. There is no need to rush on my account." Then she left, closing the door and giving me my privacy.

I scrubbed my body thoroughly, keen to be rid of the stench of my sickness and slick of my sweat. My stomach still felt strange and my headache lingered, but it was fuzzy and muted, rather than intense and overbearing. When I was finally clean enough to face the world again, I dried myself roughly and grabbed the black, fluffy robe hanging from the wall. With gratitude and a sigh of relief, I wrapped it around my body, comforted by the softness and warmth.

Mom was patiently waiting for me, elegantly seated in the armchair by the crackling fireplace. "You're looking much better," she offered.

I ran a hand through my still-wet hair. "In no small part thanks to you," I said.

She smiled, the light and love reaching her eyes with a sparkle. "I'm very proud of you. We all are, Carlak. It took great strength and courage to remain in your human form at the celebration last night. Being confronted by your Fated mate, especially unexpectedly is a trial by fire. We do not blame you for drinking so much. It was a clever move and the right decision, given the circumstances. You showed a maturity beyond your years, and the triplets were able to celebrate their birthday without incident, thanks to your quick thinking."

I choked on a laugh as I made my way to the bed and sat down, the mattress sinking beneath me. "It doesn't feel so clever at the moment," I answered, still acutely aware of the quiet pulsing behind my eyes.

She laughed with soft amusement. "Yes, well, the potion will certainly help alleviate the worst of the pain, darling, but even so, today is a day of rest for you. You have more than earned it."

I nodded, only too willing to agree as pain squeezed my heart like a vise.

"What's wrong sweetheart?" my mother asked, ever in-tune with her children and how we truly felt. Her senses were uncanny sometimes.

I wasn't sure how to even begin to accurately describe how I was feeling, and although Mom and I were close, I hadn't always shared my feelings with her. Now, I couldn't help but admit to needing her help. "I'm... I guess I'm just worried about Jessa."

Mom cocked her head and frowned at me, her expression one of confusion. "Worried?" she asked. "In what way?"

I clenched my jaw and inhaled sharply through my nose, the pain of having to admit my fears visceral. "I'm afraid she won't want to be my mate, especially after last night's display," I lamented.

Mom smiled, shifting on the armchair. "She will, my son. The Fated mate bond is there so that people who are meant to be together don't miss their chance."

I nodded slowly, a sickening thought occurring to me. "This is what you foresaw, wasn't it? It's what you didn't want to show me? You saw that Jessa would be forced into being my queen because of the Fated mate bond."

"Oh... no!" Mom gasped, rising to her feet gracefully. "That is not how it works at all, Carlak, my dear." She came to sit beside me on the bed but didn't touch me. "Fate does not rob you of your free will."

I was struggling to keep it together right now as it was. "Then how does it work?" I gulped out. "You've told me... and everyone else agrees... Jessa won't have a choice, will she?"

She placed a reassuring hand on my shoulder for a brief and consoling moment, then removed it just as quickly. "Sweetheart, she *will* have a choice as will you. A Fated mate bond is a gift, a chance to find and be the one who is perfectly suited to you in every way. Do you want another queen? Would it make you feel better or put your heart at ease to sever your connection with Jessa and perhaps search the town for a mate of your own choosing?"

My gaze snapped up to my mother's face just as my dragon's growl rolled low and menacing through my vocal cords.

Mom jumped, then covered her mouth with her hand as she stifled a startled laugh. "Well... I dare say that answers that question, then," she said with a rueful grin.

I forced my dragon back down and swallowed hard before answering. "I'm sorry, Mom."

"No, it's fine," she said, getting up and moving around the room. "Perhaps I should share my vision with you after all? Then you can make up your own mind about what you want and how you feel you should deal with this situation."

I wasn't sure I wanted to see anything further. "Ah... if you don't mind, I think I'd prefer to wait."

She frowned at me for the second time. "Are you certain? It might help put your mind at rest."

Did I want to know if we achieved our happily ever after? Did I want that kind of guarantee? Did I truly want to see what would become of us, for it all to be revealed before it had even happened yet? Or, rather, the question was, did I *need* to know these things? And I already knew the answer to that in my heart. There wasn't a doubt in my mind—I could wait.

I will trust in Fate.

"No thanks, Mom. Knowing that Jessa is my Fated mate is enough for now. I will make peace with it."

My mother nodded and walked toward the door. "Very well. But if you ever want to know more..." she offered, leaving the invitation open-ended.

"I'll ask," I promised with a smile of thanks.

"All right. In that case, come down and join us all for some lunch when you're dressed." she said. "I'm sure your father is looking forward to speaking with you too."

I sighed, not sure I was ready for *that* conversation just yet. But what choice did I have? The truth was... none. You couldn't pause life. This was happening, and I had to find a way to deal with it, one way or another. "Sure, Mom. Will do."

They would all want to talk to me, I was sure. My dad had grown up without a father and because of that, he always felt compelled to share his wisdom and lessons with my brother and me about everything. He wanted us to have the support he never had, and for that, I should be more grateful. I had family that genuinely cared and were here to help me navigate these crazy and unfamiliar waters.

She took her leave without further comment and shut the door.

I walked to my wardrobe to choose my clothes for the day. At least one thing was for sure—I absolutely didn't want to date anyone else. I wanted my mate. I wanted Jessa. I yearned for her so intensely that it frightened me. And if she felt at all the same way, then we wouldn't last long apart. I glanced toward the window in silent contemplation.

Perhaps I could fly out to see her today? Have a conversation with her about all this?

An image of me sweeping Jessa into my arms and devouring her with my lips came to mind and I shook my head, rejecting the idea instantly. No, my dragon would never be able to just *see* our mate then walk away. Never! I couldn't do it. He was impossibly possessive. The pull to claim her would be far too strong to resist a second time. I'd barely avoided flying off with her the first time. Shrugging my outfit on, I readied myself as best I could for the day ahead—at least what was left of it.

When I'd made myself suitably presentable, I took a step toward my bedroom door when my ears detected the unmistakable sound of flapping wings. I licked my lips and shook my head, my brow furrowing. No. It had to be the wind, surely. But then there came a loud *thud* originating from the direction of my balcony doors. I pivoted on my heel immediately and raced over to the glass doors, staring out onto my private stone balcony.

Outside, standing right there—not more than several feet from me— was the single most beautiful dragon I'd ever seen in my whole life.

She was puffing and snorting up a storm as she settled down from her flight.

A shiver raced up my spine and I knew who it was as surely as I knew dragon shifter blood flowed in my veins.

My queen is here.

CHAPTER
EIGHT

Jessa

I'd woken up with anger pulsing through me, raging like the fire that blazed within my dragon's shifter heart. I hadn't even showered or taken the pins out of my hair from the night before—our epic royal triplet birthday celebration. Not allowing myself the time to doubt my feelings, I ran for the balcony of my bedroom. Throwing open the doors, I launched myself out into the air before my dragon took over my body. Shifting mid jump, I soared through the sky and headed straight to Carlak's family's castle.

Bloody asshole. He knew! He had to. Why didn't he tell me?

I flew straight toward the Black Mountains, pumping my wings and searching my memory for the location of Carlak's bedroom. I couldn't remember in my angry, red haze, but the family bedrooms of the royals were always on the top floors for security, safety, and, of course, the best views. I circled the castle, and a warm, flickering light caught my eye from within.

Yes. There!

My wings flapped hard with exertion, and even though I was tired and hungry, I couldn't stop—not unless I wanted to plummet to my untimely death. I flew up as high as I dared, then glided down, riding the winds to land right on Carlak's personal balcony.

The prince himself walked to the glass doors and stared out at me, his eyes wide.

My dragon heart roared at the same time my throat made a strange purring noise I'd never heard nor made before. My shifter took a step forward just as Carlak pushed open the door. Fear rippled through me at his human form coming so close.

I could hurt him!

My dragon let go of her vise-like grip on my body, and my humanity re-emerged. I shrunk down into my body and as soon as I was back, the freezing cold and turbulent winds of the Black Mountains hit me like a brick wall. My nipples tightened into hard, almost painful points and my whole body shivered, the fine hairs on my arms and the back of my neck standing on end.

Carlak's gaze ran over my body like hot water in a shower making parts of me heat in embarrassing ways.

I covered myself the best I could with my shivering arms as my teeth began to chatter. "Stop looking at me like that!" I demanded.

"Oh! I'm sorry!" Carlak rushed back inside, grabbed a thick robe, and brought it to me.

I reached for the robe and turned my back to him, sliding my arms into the sleeves as fast as I was physically able. "You're not supposed to do that," I mumbled mostly to myself.

We'd been taught since a very young that being naked before or after a shift was not embarrassing. It was entirely natural and necessary. Our bodies were strong and amazing, and out of respect, most other shifters averted their gazes or simply didn't look.

Carlak, on the other hand, had been devouring my body like a man in heat, not a fellow, polite dragon shifter.

Once covered, I swung back around.

Carlak was standing inside, holding the door open for me.

I lifted my head and strode forward, stepping inside the room, and was immediately overwhelmed by the smell of Carlak. This was his bedroom, his domain, and every sense of mine was on heightened, immediate alert. The fireplace seemed like a safe place to retreat to, so I ambled over toward its welcoming flames, trying not to alert Carlak to the fact that my heart was pounding in my chest like a battle drum.

"What are you doing here, Jessa?" he asked after a time.

I twisted around and glared at him. "What were you doing out on the balcony, staring at me like you've never seen a girl before?"

His eyes shifted in that moment, revealing his inner dragon, but he stayed calm and in control. "I apologize for that lapse in protocol. I was... just surprised to see you. I'm sorry."

"Surprised?" I snorted at him. "After last night? Seriously?"

"What about last night?" he asked quietly.

I crossed my arms over my chest defensively. "Don't pretend like you don't know."

He raised an eyebrow at me. A single eyebrow. A skill that I was insanely envious that he could do, and I couldn't.

I stamped my foot in indignation. "Don't you *dare*, Carlak!" I all but spat.

He prowled closer, his eyes dark and dragon-like. "Dare what?" he whispered. "I'm doing my very best to remain calm here, Jessa. Do you have any idea how difficult that is?" With every word he stepped closer.

His scent clouded me, making me wish for things I'd never thought of before. I shook my head, hopelessly lost for words.

"No, you don't, do you?" he whispered, only a few inches from me now.

He wasn't touching me, but I could feel his breath, his warmth. And I ached for him to kiss me *so* badly.

His gaze continued to scan my face as though searching for an answer. "Why are you here, Jessa?" he repeated.

I swallowed the lump in my throat, trying to force some of the morning's anger back into my words. "I was mad at you," I admitted. "I wanted to confront you."

Carlak frowned and moved back a little, giving me air to breathe. "About what?"

"About this!" I gestured between us. "How long have you known?"

He inhaled sharply, his throat flexing as he swallowed. "That you are my Fated mate?" he asked.

It was my turn to squeak in surprise. "Ah... yes."

"I found out last night," he said, "when I saw you on the balcony."

I narrowed my eyes at him, not convinced. "Your mom didn't tell you before now?" I pressed.

"What would it matter if she had?" he said, turning and walking away.

The space between us gave me back the ability to think more clearly again, but I still ached with every bone in my body for his kiss. It was frustrating to a maddening degree.

Carlak, the young prince, and me. It makes no sense!

"You could have told me! A little warning might have been nice," I said, clenching my jaw against the wave of anger that swept over me.

"Oh, really?" he said, his tone bordering on bitter now. He paced the carpet by the foot of his bed. "And what would you have liked me to say, exactly? 'Oh, Princess Jessa, I know that you don't like me, and that I've been the bane of your existence since you were five years old, but please, will you marry me?"

My jaw dropped.

Marry him... Fuck me!

"I'm only twenty-one," I squeaked. "I've never even *kissed* a guy, Carlak."

He groaned, running a hand through his hair. "Damn... I find that such a turn on."

I stomped my foot again, a habit I really needed to kick, but now wasn't the time to hold back. "Don't say that! It's not fair."

"Not fair?" he repeated, then stalked over to me and took me in his arms, grabbing me around the waist so tightly, I could scarcely breathe.

I grabbed onto his shoulders for balance, and his heat poured over me, melting my knees and causing the place between my thighs to ache with an unfamiliar need.

"Not fair is being nineteen, Jessa. Nineteen, a virgin, and two years younger than the woman meant for me!" he growled softly. "This wasn't how it was supposed to be. I wanted to be older, wiser, and more experienced."

My nails dug into his arms as jealousy sank its claws into me. I had to tilt my head back so I could glare into his face. "Why? So, you could fuck half the palace before settling down with a woman you've been saddled with?"

"Saddled with?" he repeated. "What are you talking about?"

I wanted to push him away but my nails wouldn't comply and held him tight. "Me," I managed to whisper. "You have to marry me now, don't you? Even though you've never even liked me." I winced internally, hating the fact I sounded so weak and lost in this moment.

"Jessa..." Carlak sounded pained, now.

I ripped myself out of his grasp and turned my back on him.

Damn it.

This entire situation was worse than I first thought. I knew I didn't want to get married at twenty-one, but the idea of getting married to someone who was only with me because Fate or some celestial force that we couldn't even see or divine told him he had to... well, that was even worse! I didn't want any man *stuck* with me.

"This was a mistake," I muttered. "I don't know what I was hoping to achieve by coming here, but it's obvious that neither of us wants to be in this situation. So, maybe we should just try staying away from each other." I moved to walk back to the balcony doors.

Carlak came up behind me, his hands sliding around my waist and holding me tight.

"What are you doing?" I asked, pushing at his grip but not getting anywhere.

He set his lips close to my ear. "I *want* you Jessa, so damn much that it's crazy. I want nothing more than to kiss you, touch you... and I just wish I knew how."

I closed my eyes against the wave of longing that threatened to consume me. How were we going to do this at all if neither of us had any experience? I turned in his arms until I was facing him, and my hands went to the tie on my robe, loosening it so that the front hung open. "I think you just... touch me."

His eyes blazed with the fire of his royal dragon.

I whimpered as he slipped his hands inside the robe, his palms cool against my overheated skin and making me shiver. Unable to stop them, my hands reached for his face, and I cupped his jaw, rough with unshaven hair.

He dropped his head just as I lifted my chin. His lips pressed against mine in a kiss that stole my legs from under me.

I dropped like a dead weight, lost to his scent and touch.

Carlak grabbed my bare ass in both his hands and hauled me tightly against his clothed body.

I moaned as his tongue pressed into my mouth, and I opened my lips for him, wanting to feel everything. Wanting to know what this could be. I wound my arms around his neck and held on tightly.

Carlak's hands kneaded my ass, then he lifted me up and walked me over to his bed. When he sat back on the mattress, I was straddled over his lap, leaving me open and vulnerable to his gaze.

I didn't break the kiss, didn't want to. I was too embarrassed to see what we were doing in truth, but loved the way it felt. It felt right.

His hands moved up to my breasts, cupping them before he caressed my nipples.

I gasped and threw my head back, arching against him for more.

He dropped his head low and drew one tight, aching peak into his mouth.

"Oh my God!" I groaned, threading my fingers through his hair, and holding him there. "More."

He sucked harder, seemingly inspired by my desire.

I cried out as pleasurable sensations sizzled through me.

He stopped suddenly and lifted his head, a look of concern in his eyes. "Did I hurt you?"

I couldn't look at him, my face too hot and flushed. "No. Please... don't stop!" I pleaded.

He dropped his head again, sucking on a nipple while his hands ventured between my legs.

I was aching and hot there, as if the center of my dragon's fire blazed within.

His fingers moved over my flesh, exploring places I hadn't even dared pay much heed.

I gasped as he hit something amazing. "Oh... there. Yes!"

He rubbed the spot more at my request, the feelings of intensity growing.

I trembled on his lap. "Oh, wow," I breathed.

His other hand slipped lower, and his finger found what I knew to be my entrance.

"Can I touch you here?" he whispered against my breast, seeking permission before continuing.

I nodded, licking my lips in anticipation.

"Jessa?" he pressed.

"Yes... please," I whispered, my voice husky, and my eyes still closed as my attention focused on his hand.

He eagerly thrust a finger inside me, pushing in deep to his last knuckle.

I cried out aloud and grabbed his shoulders, convulsing with pleasure.

He pulled me down, kissing me with heated passion.

I moaned against his lips as his hands continued to work their magic between my thighs. I thrashed in his arms, feeling hot and needy, almost frenzied with desire.

"Carlak!" Anthony's voice called, sounding not too far away. Then there was a heavy knock on the door. "Mom told me to come get you."

The door opened.

I flew to my feet, wrapping the robe back around my body even as I stumbled.

Carlak was faster, grabbing my elbow to steady me as the young prince, Anthony, entered the room.

The words died on his lips as his gaze landed on us. "Ah..."

"I'll be down soon!" Carlak snapped, his tone gravelly and rough.

"Anthony?" King Erik's voice sounded behind the younger prince.

Like lightning, I ran for the balcony, throwing off the robe behind me as my dragon took hold, spurred on by the desperation of the predicament in which we'd found ourselves.

"Jessa!" my Fated mate called as he dashed out to the balcony.

I heard Carlak's voice, but I couldn't stay. Not now. Not like this. With tears of shock, desire, and shame burning in my dragon's eyes, I flew home the way I'd come.

CHAPTER
NINE

Carlak

"Fuck me..." I closed my eyes and sent up a silent prayer to anyone who could possibly hear me.

Please let my father not *be in the room when I turn around. Please!*

But I was ignored, because when I turned around, my father and brother were both standing there, gobsmacked.

My raging erection died a quick death, and I ran a frazzled hand through my hair. This entire situation was diabolical. How could this happen the first time I had the chance to touch my mate? I sighed. "You couldn't have just given me ten more minutes?" I said, beyond exasperated as the tangible loss of Jessa overwhelmed my senses.

Dad and Anthony exchanged glances, then looked back at me.

My brother remained absolutely silent.

Meanwhile, my father sniffed the air. "What did I miss?" he asked, his brow furrowed.

Anthony still didn't seem able to cobble a sentence together. "Um..." he tried, stumbling over his own tongue.

"Jessa came to me," I said, my tone sharp and irritable now. "And she... I mean, *we...*"

"Ah, say no more," Dad said and clapped his hands together. "Let's all get some lunch, then we can talk." My father turned on his heel and promptly left.

A sheepish-looking Anthony followed after him, muttering, "Sorry," on his way out.

I took a moment to wash my hands and straighten my clothes. But even after I'd used a fragrant soap, I could still smell my beautiful and incredibly sexy mate all over me. My mind was still a whirl, and I ached to hold Jessa in my arms once more. The way she'd so innocently untied and opened my black robe to reveal her perfect milky skin to me... the swell of her lovely breasts and the little nest of golden hair between her legs. It was a moment that would remain burned in my memory for all time.

Giving myself a few minutes to breathe and collect my thoughts, I sat back down on my bed, twisting my hands between my knees. My heart was still skipping wildly, and I was worried about Jessa. I could only imagine the embarrassment she must have felt, being caught in such a compromising predicament by another male. She had taken off so quickly, I'd scarcely had the time to process what'd just happened.

Seeing her toss back my robe and launch herself into the sky, her magnificent dragon form taking over, had been heartbreaking, more so than I could have ever dreamed. I didn't want her to go. I understood completely, but I yearned to hold her and protect her. To soothe her discomfort and promise her somehow, that everything would be all right. Now, I could only hope that her fiery spirit and the intimacy we had willingly shared with one another would assure her that we were truly meant to be together.

I miss you, Jessa...

When I finally pulled myself together and made my way to the dining room, lunch was already served, and the smell of a rich lamb stew reached my nose. My stomach lurched a little at the normally welcome aroma, but thanks to Mom's potion, I didn't vomit again. Instead, I managed to sit down and grabbed for a slice of the fresh bread on offer. Somehow, the warmth in my hand and the doughy scent seemed much more palatable post-hangover than the idea of consuming meat.

"Why can I smell... Jessa?" my mother suddenly asked, glancing about.

I lifted my gaze to my mother's face, and her nose wrinkled in confusion. "Oh, God," I breathed. This was going to be far more embarrassing than I'd ever thought it would be.

Goddamn it.

Dad cracked a laugh, apparently unable to contain himself.

I turned to glare at him. "No! You're not allowed to comment on this. I've never once said over breakfast how I could literally still *see* mother on your face!"

Dad lurched forward, spluttering, choking, and coughing on whatever he'd just been eating.

I got up without hesitation and slapped him a few times on the back, strangely amused to finally be able to say such a thing to my dad. I'd been holding onto that little piece of information for *years*. When I finally sat back down, Mom was still beet red, and Dad was a similar color and wore a sheepish expression.

Anthony was the only one composed enough at this point to speak, so he did. "Did she really fly *all* the way here to the Black Mountains just to... kiss you?" he asked, one brow raised.

"She kissed you?" Mom interjected with a gasp, her eyes wide with interest.

I focused on my brother and took a deep breath. "She actually flew here to yell at me for not telling her that she was my Fated mate. Then she said that I was saddled with her—whatever that means?"

Dad was back to coughing and chuckling like a teenager again, his eyes watering with mirth.

With an annoyed sigh, I served myself a scoopful of berries and picked up my silver fork.

"Is she worried about the Fated mate bond also?" our mother asked, seeming somewhat surprised in her typically elegant manner.

I mutely nodded as I bit into the blackberries, their bitter sweetness exploding on my tongue.

Dad reached for his glass of water and took a sip once he'd pulled himself together. "That's completely normal, son. Dragon shifters are stubborn by nature, so none of us like being told who we're meant to marry or not. We like to feel it's our choice."

Anthony snorted dramatically, as if this whole scenario were nonsense. "Honestly? It all sounds like a good idea to me. If it's Fated, you can't get it wrong, can you? It takes out all the guess work and any chance you might mess it up."

I turned and stared at my sixteen-year-old brother, my brows near my hairline. He was shoveling lamb stew into his mouth like it was his last meal before he stilled and looked up at us again. "What?" he asked, making a face.

"He's right," Mom said. "That's essentially what the Fated mate bond is for—to stop you walking away from the one person in the world who is right for you."

Dad snorted, resting an arm on the table as he leaned forward. "You mean like you almost did, love?"

"What do you mean?" I asked, glancing from my mother to my father for an explanation.

Mom sighed. "I knew your father was my mate for years before we officially met, but I was married. He was younger than I... and... I was afraid of what being with him would mean for either of us."

"You were afraid of true love, Marienne. Just admit it."

Mom glanced down at her hands, wringing them together for a moment, then looked up once more. "Yes, I was," she answered quietly. "My life hadn't been easy up until that point, and your love was... well, quite daunting."

I stared at my mother, shocked to hear her sounding so worried and small. My mom was a powerful sorceress, and she was a great queen. If she still remembered how daunting it had been to have my father love her, how would Jessa feel about our union? Despite what we'd shared, would she be second-guessing our bond right now? "So, what's your best advice, Mom? What do I do?" I managed to ask, though an uncomfortable silence had fallen over the table.

She picked up her cup of tea and took a long sip, something she often did when she wanted time to think before she spoke. Finally, she said, "I think you should go to her. You need to convince her that you want her because she is amazing. Because you know you need her with all your heart, and not simply because fate is forcing you choose her."

I glanced up at my father, needing a man's point of view, too. "Do you agree, Dad?"

He nodded with a smile, reaching out to squeeze my mother's hand. "Yes, I do. There is no greater gift in life than the love of a great woman, Carlak."

Mom and Dad shared a look that spoke of timeless affection and trust.

I glanced away, feeling strange for witnessing such a unique moment of tenderness between them. I filled my glass with water and picked it up. "Thank you, both. I think I'll go lay down again for a while." I stood up and pushed my chair back.

Dad jumped to his feet also. "Are you flying to Jessa's kingdom today, or do you think you'll wait a while longer?"

It was less than two weeks until my birthday, and I wasn't sure I could wait that long to feel her in my arms once more. But flying to her was a dangerous prospect. I wasn't sure how well I could control myself *or* my dragon once I got her within touching distance again. "I'll think about it," I said, then turned to leave.

"I'll walk you to your room," Dad offered, marching ahead so I couldn't object.

Anthony snorted out a laugh before returning to his lunch.

I ignored him and walked out of the room with my father, not sure what he was going to say, but almost positive that whatever it was, it was going to be cringe-worthy.

We walked side by side up the hall, a king and his heir.

Dad stayed silent the whole way.

I wasn't sure if he wanted to talk more about Mom, or what was going on between Jessa and me. Maybe I'd crossed a line when I brought up that little tidbit of information from the past... I couldn't be sure.

When we reached my bedroom, we stopped just outside my door.

I reached out to push it open. "Ah... thanks, Dad," I said.

He cleared his throat with a rough cough. "Carlak, I know we haven't had many talks about women and marriage, but if you have any questions—"

"Thanks, Dad," I said, cutting him off before he could say anything too embarrassing. "I think I'll be fine."

My father had, in fact, told us *many* stories about women and sex throughout the years, usually when he'd had far too much to drink, and often when he was sharing such drink with other men.

"Well, all right. Is there anything you want to know then, now? About... anything... before"

I'd only ever had one question in my mind that I'd wanted to ask of my father, but I'd never been capable of asking it. But now, standing here, I realized I was just a breath away from being married. I was a man now, and it was time to overcome my fear. "Father, I'd like to know if you think I will be a good king."

He turned until we were face to face, then he inhaled sharply, his shoulders thrusting back as he stood to his full height. "Yes, my son, I do. You'll be a better king than I've been."

I shook my head and tried not to let him see the tears that welled instantly in my eyes. "That's impossible, Father. You've brought this kingdom into the light, and your people love you."

"And you're a wonderful son and prince," he answered. "You'll have something I never had — parents that will stand by your side until our dying breath. You are the best of us, Carlak. You have my stubbornness and strength, and your mother's brilliance and courage. I'm very proud of you." My father opened his arms to me, a warm expression of pride on his face.

I stepped into them, letting him embrace me as though I were a young child again. Then I was stepping back and away, feeling a new path stretch out before me. "Thank you, Dad."

He nodded with a smile and lumbered away, back down the hall to join my mother.

With my heart now full to bursting with pride and hope, I went into my bedroom and lay down to plan the future ahead.

Jessa

I'd bitten my nails down to the quick and my fingers stung, smarting with pain, but that didn't stop me from tearing at the skin a little more.

Damn it!

I was agitated and it was maddening.

How long will he make me wait?

"Are you looking out that window again?" Vanya asked, walking up beside me with two steaming mugs. "I made you a hot chocolate since you missed breakfast this morning," she said, offering one to me.

I took the drink from her hand gratefully. "Thanks," I said with a forced smile, then took a small sip even though I wasn't very hungry. My appetite had almost become non-existent since the day I'd had to frantically leave Carlak's bedroom. We'd be caught in the act, exposed, embarrassed, and unsatisfied. There was no choice but to flee.

"No problem," my twin sister said.

Vanya and I stood side by side, staring out at the falling snow for several long minutes, just appreciating the icy beauty and serenity of the mystical world beyond.

I was happy with the silence. The jumbled mess of words and emotions swirling around inside my head were just far too much to process right now. Feeling lost, I didn't even know where to begin.

"Are you going to tell me what's wrong?" Vanya asked after a time, her voice soft.

"I'm fine," I managed to say, then took another forced sip of the milky beverage. My head was achy, and my mood was pretty flat and largely melancholy. With a sigh, I sank down onto the window seat and tucked my legs up under my heavy winter skirt, determined to shift the conversation on my terms if I was going to be made to talk idly. "How are you?" I ventured.

Vanya chuckled and shook her head in wry amusement. "Don't you dare lie to me, sister. You're not fine at all. You're worried sick about Carlak, aren't you?"

I frowned at her as I nursed my hot cup, absorbing its warmth through my hands. "How do you know about him?" I asked, swallowing the fast-growing lump in my throat.

"I heard Mom and Dad talking," she admitted.

My lips quirked into the smallest semblance of an amused smile, and I took another sip of the rich chocolate drink before exhaling deeply. "You've always spied on them."

Vanya shrugged. "Yeah... that was not my point, Jessa." She sat down on the window seat opposite me and pushed my leg to get me speaking again. "Why didn't you tell me that you'd found your Fated mate already?" she probed. "That's like... *insane.*"

I laughed at her choice of words and set my drink aside, pulling a blanket onto my lap to maintain my heat and expel this chill seeping into my bones. "Yes, it is. I didn't think I'd find my mate for years, to be honest."

Vanya tilted her head as though in contemplation. "Well... if our mates are all members of the royal heirs, you'd think we would have known about them already? It's not like there's many of us."

"You're right," I said, shocked I hadn't thought about it myself. "So, you and Anselm didn't... feel anything toward any of the eligible men or woman that night?"

Vanya pursed her lips and shook her head. "No, not at all. But then again, I don't know what it's supposed to feel like, so I could have missed it, perhaps?"

I laughed, because I couldn't help it. "Ah, sorry. *No.* You wouldn't, or rather, couldn't have missed it. I think it affects us less, but on male dragons... you definitely would have noticed. Trust me. They feel it intensely, and it's difficult for them to hide it."

Vanya leaned forward with a spark of interest. "Oh, that sounds intriguing. Tell me about it."

I turned my head and gazed out the window of the sitting room, longing for Carlak. "I'm not sure how to explain it, really. It's overwhelming in a lot of ways."

"Mom and Dad said Carlak showed great restraint not shifting and destroying our party." Vanya snorted, her eyes squinting with mirth.

I glanced over at her. "What's so funny?"

"Oh, it's just that Dad confided that King Erik took out *two* windows in the great dining room the first time he laid eyes on Queen Marienne. He couldn't control himself at all. He shifted right then and there into his dragon, burst through the windows, and flew Marienne off home like some kind of precious trophy."

I swallowed hard, my stomach lurching unexpectedly. "Maybe Carlak is wrong about being my Fated mate then. He's never shifted in front of me. He seems completely in control in my presence."

Annoyingly so, actually.

I was the one who'd lost control of my own body, writhing and moaning and carrying on in his lap while Carlak had remained fully clothed.

"Wouldn't that be a good thing, though?" Vanya asked, grinning at me. "If he's not actually your mate, then you're free to go after Taggath, or maybe even wait for the call to come from the human world."

The anger that snapped through my brain at her words was so intense, it almost stole the breath from my lungs. I was forced to stand up and turn away to control myself. I wanted to throw my steaming hot chocolate in her face! My chest flared with an inner fire.

"Oh, I'm sorry sister," Vanya said immediately, sensing my rage as she read my stiff and aggressive body language. "I didn't mean to offend you, I only meant—"

"I know," I interrupted her without turning around. "I *know*, sister, but he *is* my mate. And I know it's not what we planned or what I expected, but my dragon is fiercely protective over our bond so please don't even suggest..."

Vanya lay her hand on my arm in peace. "I'm sorry, Jessa. Truly."

I nodded tightly but didn't trust myself not to act out if she said something else that might trigger me. "I think I need to retire to my room for a while," I said, playing it safe. I didn't want to hurt Vanya or destroy our sisterly relationship if my dragon arced up again. "But I'll see you later, all right?"

"Yeah... of course," my sister agreed, remaining by the window and allowing me my space.

I walked away before I did something I knew I'd regret. Harming my sister was not in the cards for me today, and neither was seeing Carlak. I'd already gone to him once, I couldn't go to him again. My pride simply wouldn't allow it.

If he wants me, surely, he'll come for me?

I managed to get to my room before the tears came. Carlak had gone from being a neighbor and family friend, to a man I wanted in my bed, in my home, and in my life intimately. And it hurt more than I could describe that he was choosing to stay away. He knew where I was and that I wanted him.

I'd certainly made that abundantly clear last time.

And so the day passed into the afternoon. I had a long, leisurely bath, followed by dinner in my room. I feigned a headache to escape the inquisition that would undoubtably occur at the family dinner table. By nightfall I was fighting off the desire to cry some more and throw furniture around the room. It wasn't a good combination. If my dragon let loose her true anger, I'd cause some serious destruction.

Mom came to say goodnight, but smartly retreated soon after, realizing it was best to leave me alone.

"Argh... fuck!" I swore as I paced in front of the fireplace wearing a thin nightgown and robe, my body literally shaking with adrenaline and anxiety.

A knock at my window startled me, and I jumped, my whole body suddenly alert. "Carlak!" I breathed.

He was standing right there, in human form outside my window, gloriously naked.

I raced over to the glass door of the balcony and flung it wide open. "Quickly, inside!" I urged.

He hobbled inside, his teeth already chattering.

I closed the door behind him and quickly removed my robe, handing it to him without thinking. "Put this on and stand in front of the fire. It'll help warm you up."

He did as urged, though the robe didn't cover him the way it did me. In fact, it barely tied up at all. But he went to the fireplace and stood there defrosting, his back to me all the while.

Now that he was here, my energy had calmed, and I found myself instantly excited. My heart rate had picked up and a crazy, unparalleled amount of happiness was zinging through my veins at lightning speed. I was no longer alone.

He came for me.

"So, what are you doing here?" I asked, crossing my arms over my chest, acutely aware of the fact that my nightgown was sheer and although long, didn't do much to disguise or hide the curves of my body.

Carlak turned around and his gaze raked over me with a familiarity I wasn't used to yet.

"I came for you," he said simply. "Will we be interrupted again, or is your family in bed?"

I gasped, and my breath caught in my throat. He'd come to continue what we'd already started? That was very presumptuous of him, but at the same time, my body was already reacting to his suggestion. "Um... I think they're all in bed."

"Good." Carlak threw off my measly robe and surged forward, grabbing my face and planting a kiss on my lips that left me breathless.

I wanted to look at his body and explore. I wanted to kiss every inch of his flesh, but his kiss wiped away any chance I had of thinking rationally. His hands were all over me, grabbing my ass and opening my robe so he could push the sheer material to the floor.

Suddenly, we were both naked.

I wrapped my arms around his neck, the heat of his body pressed firmly against me. Unable to keep the sound of my pleasure inside any longer, I moaned.

Carlak picked me up and carried me to my bed.

My eyes were still closed as he bore me toward my destiny. The power of his kiss had left me reeling and feeling intoxicated.

We landed on the bed, and he rolled on top of me, settling between my legs as though he'd done so a thousand times before.

I arched my back, wanting him closer, deeper. With an enormous amount of self-restraint, I broke our kiss to groan and dig my nails into his shoulders so that I might find my voice. "Please, Carlak. I can't take this anymore. I need you."

But he wasn't going to just give me what my body was crying out for, that much was obvious as he kissed his way down my neck. His lips caressed my breasts, plumping the flesh up with his hands as he tongued my sensitive nipples.

I writhed on the bed, trying to force him up, to get him to do what I so desperately wanted him to, but I was unable.

God, he is strong.

"Carlak, please," I begged.

He looked up at me, his eyes filled with dragon fire. "But I might hurt you," he all but growled, sending a shiver through me.

"I don't care. *Please.*" And I didn't. Not one bit. My body had been on fire for a week, and it was time he put an end to these unbearable feelings of frustration and doused the fire that threatened to consume me from within. I grabbed onto his hair and tugged, determined, until he followed my lead.

Finally, he brought his mouth back to mine.

I captured his lips and kissed him hard, smashing our mouths together and sucking on his tongue, trusting raw instinct to guide my passion.

Carlak groaned and thrust against me in frustration and readiness, his hard cock sliding along my belly.

Oh, yes!

I wrapped my legs around his waist and pressed myself against him, aching to my very core and needing him in that moment more than I needed air.

Please don't make me wait any more.

Carlak

My dragon was barely staying contained beneath my skin. Everything inside me was too excited and felt far too intense. I was afraid my fiery shifter would burst free without my consent, and yet I couldn't stop. Not while Jessa was beneath me on the bed, her naked body wriggling and thrusting against me.

I broke our kiss and set my mouth into her neck, sinking my teeth into the soft flesh of her shoulder, tasting the salt of her heat. "You smell *so* perfect," I rasped.

She didn't respond with words, only with actions. Her heels dug into my ass and her moans filled my ears.

I reached between us and grabbed my cock, taking a moment to squeeze the shaft *hard*, trying to regain some control over the beast that wanted to take over.

Jessa's body was so deliciously curvy in all the right ways. She had hard, luxuriously wide hips and big, perky breasts—the perfect woman. And it was time to make her mine.

I set my cock between her thighs, following my instincts as best I could. I slid my head over her wetness, nudging at her opening.

"Oh..." Jessa gasped.

"There?" I asked, flicking my thumb over her clit to ease the tension.

She nodded her head, her teeth pressed into her lower lip.

I thrust my hips a little, edging my way into her an inch at a time, being as gentle and as patient as both versions of me would allow.

"Kiss me," Jessa coaxed, grabbing my shoulders and tugging me back to her.

The movement had me filling her up, and we both groaned loudly as my cock forged the final path inside her.

I pressed my forehead to hers, breathing hard and shivering at the surge of pure pleasure that danced along my spine. She was hot and wet and *so* tight, squeezing me like a warm glove, just right—as if she were truly made for me. I forced my eyes open and stared down at her, butterflies in my belly. "Are you okay?" I whispered.

She nodded. "Please, don't stop, Carlak."

I withdrew and surged back into her, earning a gasp from her that made my face flush with blood and heat. I captured her lips with a kiss, determined to give her as much pleasure as I could.

Her hands moved over me, caressing my shoulders and running through my hair.

Raw sensation raced up my body like lightning, and fire poured down my thighs. I kept moving, plunging into her for all I was worth, instinctively listening to Jessa's gasps and moans of pleasure and adjusting my angle and motions accordingly.

Then, just before I got to the point of no return, I pulled out and exploded in ecstasy, coming between us, our bodies creating a heated clasp that extended my orgasm for what seemed like forever. I cried out, trying not to be too loud. I buried my head in the pillows beyond her shoulder and shuddered over her as my hot seed poured between our flesh. I finally came back to myself and opened my eyes.

Jessa stroked my hair and made soft noises of comfort and satisfaction.

I rolled away from her to lay beside her, panting still. "I'm sorry," I breathed.

"Sorry?" She laughed. "What would you ever be sorry for? That was... amazing."

She hadn't finished, although my father had told me in the past that wasn't unusual. Women didn't climax as often or as reliably as men. Still, I hated the idea that my mate hadn't enjoyed herself as much as I had. I yearned for her to feel as good as I did, to experience that break of will and body that filled the world with fire and burned through to the core of your soul.

"Can we have a quick shower?" I asked, sliding from the bed and dragging myself to my feet. I so desperately didn't want to move, wanting instead to pass out with my mate's body curved around mine and fall asleep with her in my arms. But we weren't clean, and if we were discovered like this—God forbid—it would be unpleasant to say the least.

"Sure," she said, bouncing up with a lot more energy than I had. "Through here," she directed in good spirits.

I watched her luscious ass move as she walked to the bathroom, then she grabbed a blanket to cover herself.

"Oh, no," I said, striding over to tug the blanket from her body. "Don't you dare cover up. I want to see every inch of you."

"Well, there's *a lot* to see," she said self-consciously, biting her lip.

I frowned at her. "What are you talking about, Jessa? You're perfect in every conceivable way."

"But Vanya's so thin," she complained, running her hands up my chest.

I put my hands on her waist and pulled her into my body, keen to allay her fears.

"She always looks so good in her dresses, and everyone thinks she's *so* beautiful."

I chuckled and leaned forward to kiss her lips. "Sweetheart, you are a goddess, and your body is perfect for me. Literally perfect. I wouldn't wish you to be any other way than you are right at this moment. In fact, once we're both clean, I think we should do all that again."

"Again?" she asked, her eyes opening wide.

I smiled and tugged her into the shower. We didn't talk while we washed each other's bodies, but by the time we were done, I was hard again and ready to bury myself in her beautiful body once more. "Back to bed?" I asked, raising an eyebrow as I slipped my hand between her soft thighs.

"Um... actually." She grimaced. "I'm a little sore," she whispered.

I pulled my hand back, embarrassment making me stammer. "O-oh. I'm so sorry. I didn't mean to..."

She grabbed my hand and pulled it back to her breast.

I cupped the fullness of her flesh and smiled with relief.

She's not rejecting me.

"It's okay," she assured me. "I imagine it takes time to adjust, and this was only our first time. Maybe we can try again in the morning, if you're up to it." She reached out and touched my cock, hesitant and gentle, but curious.

I groaned and gathered her up against me again. "I'll *definitely* be up for it," I promised without hesitation. "Do you want me to stay?"

"Only if you want to," she answered. "I would never expect or force you."

"Oh, I want to," I said. "Believe me." I'd left a note on my bed in case my parents or my brother came looking for me and I wasn't back yet. The last thing I needed was my father on a fury-and-fear-driven rampage looking for me, his heir.

Jessa led me back to the huge bed, her fresh and beautiful body carrying with it the fragrance of the floral and fruity wash we'd used.

I climbed beneath the covers, lying on my back like a lord of leisure. "Come." I encouraged her to lay her head on my chest and I breathed in the heavenly scent of her hair. "I just can't believe how beautiful you are, Jessa."

She giggled and pulled up the blankets before settling her hand on my chest. "Carlak?"

"Hm?" I hummed, my eyes already sliding shut as fatigue spilled over me.

"Do you really think we're meant to be together?"

Her question surprised me, but I could feel her need to receive a proper answer. I kissed the top of her head and sighed. "Yes, I do. Making love to you just now was... it felt perfect. It was like finding the other half of my soul. Didn't you feel the same way?" It was a dangerous question to ask if she didn't, in fact, feel the same, but the words were out before I could recall them.

"Yes... but..." she said.

"But what?" I asked, sleep's claws digging into my brain. My body had never felt so sated, and I hadn't been sleeping well at all since Jessa had flown away from me.

"But don't you think this has all just happened too fast?" she whispered. "I mean... I just don't know."

I stroked her back once more, loving the feel of her smooth skin against mine. "Trust in the Fates, sweetheart. They know more than we do."

"Okay," she said as if still plagued by concern.

I couldn't dwell on her worry long, because darkness then consumed me, and I slept better than I had in years.

WHEN I AWOKE, I was on my back and the blankets had been flipped off. My skin was cold, except for where Jessa sat up next to me, softly touching my belly.

"Good morning," I yawned, stretching my arms above my head.

"Good morning," she repeated, grinning down at me.

Her fingers were tangled in the hair at the base of my cock and her gaze was trained on my flesh, which was hardening by the moment.

"What are you doing, mate?" I asked.

Her gaze snapped up to mine, and there I could see the cheekiness that was so exclusively Jessa. "I'm playing," she answered.

"Playing?" I repeated, then gasped.

Her hot palm wrapped around my cock, and she smiled again at my reaction.

"What are you wanting out of this?" I asked, although my voice was strained with desire.

"I want to learn about your body," she said simply, moving her hand up and down the shaft and causing an insane amount of pleasure to shoot through me.

"Oh... God," I breathed. "You already know my body," I managed.

Jessa cupped my balls with her other hand and continued to explore me. "But," she teased, "his is so much more fun." Leaning forward, she kissed the head of my cock reverently, like it was a mystical rose or something as majestic.

"Oh, no..." I groaned, trying to sit up.

My beautiful and cheeky mate quickly pushed me back down. "No?" she asked. "Am I doing it wrong?"

"No, but you're going to make me come like that, and I'm supposed to be helping you find *your* pleasure. Oh... God," I groaned.

The princess bobbed her head again and sucked the head of my cock into her mouth, running her tongue around my sensitive flesh, first one way and then the other as if it were an icy treat.

"It's your turn now," I moaned out, my fingers tangling in her hair even as her head bobbed up and down. I was going to lose my mind!

"Hm... Next time," she practically purred.

I was fast losing the battle for control, and it was abundantly clear that Jessa was determined to push me right up to the cliff's edge and then over it. I tried to get up one more time, as my own desire fulfillment warred with my desire to please her.

She shoved me down, her hand on my chest. Her lips caressed the head of my cock, increasing and decreasing the pressure as she sucked, all the while her hand milked my shaft. The combination of heat and her ready enthusiasm was an undeniable aphrodisiac.

I finally lost the battle and cried out as my orgasm slammed into me with the force of a dragon taking out the peak of a mountain top. Wave after wave of pleasure coursed over me as my seed burst forth from my cock, painting my chest and belly in milky, gleaming strands.

"Oh my God..." I shuddered.

Jessa lay down beside me, a proud and playful smile on her rosy lips.

"You are amazing," I said as I leaned over to kiss her.

She eagerly kissed me back, her tongue dancing with mine.

There was a knock at the door, then a female voice called out. "Jessa? Is everything all right?"

"Oh shit," Jessa gasped, jumping from the bed and racing for the door.

She cracked it open and whispered to whoever was on the other side before shutting the door again and turning around to me. "That was just Vanya. Apparently, everyone's waiting on me for breakfast. Do you want to join us? Or..."

I had no idea what I wanted, but sleep was on the very top of my priority list right now as the fatigue following the amazing orgasm Jessa had caused stole over me.

TWELVE

Jessa

Without further delay, I raced back to the bed and started grabbing weather-appropriate casual clothes from out of my drawers. "Vanya warned me that Mom and Dad are going to come up if I don't go downstairs. I've kind of been sulking in my room this past week, and they're growing impatient with me. I wasn't dealing well with being separated from you as it turns out."

Carlak rolled off the bed and staggered toward the bathroom, unsteady on his feet. "Ah, give me five minutes, but... I didn't bring any clothes," he said with sudden realization.

Shit!

That was definitely going to be a problem. There was no way in hell my father was catching Carlak in his birthday suit! I wracked my brain for a solution. "Oh! I could borrow some for you from Anselm, maybe?" I suggested. "You're about the same size, I think."

Or should he just go back to his castle?

"Unless you don't want to stay... because if you go out there now, Dad's going to pretty much demand that you marry me on the spot, and we're not really there yet, are we?" I quickly tugged on a pair of warm, fleece-lined black leggings and my favorite cozy purple sweater.

Carlak didn't answer me, instead just walking straight into the bathroom.

I could hear the distinct sound of water running as he began to clean himself up.

Bloody parents had the *worst* timing! And it was supremely frustrating. I'd been looking forward to spending the day in bed with Carlak, just learning about his body and committing to memory all the things that made him squirm and cry out as I literally milked the pleasure from his body with my mouth, hands, and body.

My own insides were still throbbing with a dull ache from losing my virginity to Carlak last night, but already I wanted him again. And an ache of an entirely different nature arose. Watching him come like that in my bed had been so incredibly and torturously hot.

I did that!

And I was stupidly proud of my efforts. By the time I'd put my fluffy socks and comfortable house shoes on, Carlak had returned.

He walked back into my bedroom, clean, refreshed, and slightly red from the warmth of the rushed shower. "I might just go," he said, his lips turned down in a regretful frown. "It's probably best your father doesn't toss me out of a window before I've had the chance to speak to him properly and formally about us being together. I want to be respectful about how we approach your parents with this."

I ran at him with love in my heart, throwing myself into his waiting arms and hugging him tight with all my might. It felt so good to be with him. So right.

He squeezed me in return, inhaling deeply as though to memorize my scent.

"Thank you for flying here," I whispered. "I was going insane without you. It was the best night ever." I pulled back and his genuine, charming smile made my heart sing inside my ribcage like a canary at the height of summer.

"I'll sneak away tonight if I can, though I think my father wants to have one of *those* talks with me." He sighed.

I giggled and grimaced with empathy, knowing just the ones. They were often long-winded, tiresome, and utterly cringe-worthy. "Okay. Well, I won't expect you, but I'll be missing you and hoping."

He grabbed my face with his hands and kissed me hard, then strolled away with the natural authority of a first born prince and over to the window in all his naked human glory. "You know we're never going to have any privacy if we continue to live in the castles of our parents."

I laughed.

Whoa. Talk about moving fast...

"Don't spoil the mood." I reprimanded him playfully. "Just go. We'll talk about all that stuff later on. We have a whole future ahead of us."

He waved and opened the door to the balcony, then shut it behind him again.

I stood with bated breath and watched as he transformed into a magnificent dragon.

He rose into the air with a single powerful beat of his immense wings before soaring off into the falling snow, high above the world below.

I shook myself physically, brushing the snowflakes from my outfit while trying not to squeal with the sheer excitement and happiness that threatened to spill over from inside me. The dining room wasn't far, but I hurried along the hall all the same and pushed my way into the grand room with a smile on my face. "Sorry I'm late!" I said with a happy sing-song tone to my voice as I apologized for my tardiness.

The whole family was already sitting down, patiently waiting for me to begin the first meal of the day.

I took my seat promptly and poured myself some fresh orange juice. There would be no coffee for me today, that was for sure. I didn't need it. I was far too high on life and love!

"You look... different," Anselm said, frowning at me from across the table with a hint of consternation, as if he were trying to decipher some unseen anomaly about me. "What's with your face?" he asked.

I put my hands to my cheeks, immediately flushing red with silent embarrassment. "What's wrong with my face?" I echoed innocently.

Mom put a calm hand on Anselm's shoulder. "I believe what your brother was trying to say is that you look much happier this morning, dear. Did something happen last night that you would like to share?"

I shook my head from side to side adamantly, reaching for the plate of sweet pastries and ripe fruit in front of me. "No, no. I'm fine. I'm just feeling better is all," I lied, averting my eyes as if the best night of my life hadn't just taken place.

"Yes, you certainly look fine," Dad said approvingly, obviously pleased I was finally no longer hiding away in my room like I had been most of the week, resembling more of a moody teenage princess than a grown woman who had found her fated mate.

I lifted my gaze tentatively to meet my mom's as I stabbed a juicy raspberry with my fork and popped it into my mouth.

She was smiling back at me with a very knowing look in her eyes.

What? She knows! Oh my God. How? Ugh!

That knowledge made me feel embarrassed on a whole other level, so I focused on my food, piling my plate high with delectable morsels before tucking into my meal, keeping my eyes firmly fixed on my plate.

"So, it's Carlak's birthday this weekend," Mom said, probably trying to change the subject but failing miserably. "Erik and Marienne have asked if we'd like to spend the weekend there. You girls would have to share a bedroom, due to some redecorating going on at the moment, but I think it would be nice to stay, don't you?"

"I doubt we'll end up bunking together," Vanya muttered into her hot chocolate with a smirk as she toyed with her breakfast.

I would have kicked her under the table—I *so* wanted to—but the traitor would have ratted on me. "Sounds great, Mom," I said brightly before anyone else had a chance to comment further. "That will be nice. We won't have to leave the party early then." My heart was pounding in my chest, and I couldn't help but notice the passing looks that were occurring between my parents. I waited on tenterhooks. Even though I really wanted to know what they were thinking, I wasn't bold enough to go there.

Finally, our father asked, "Jessa... are you sure there isn't anything you need to tell us about Carlak?"

I stuffed a whole mini chocolate croissant into my mouth in the most unladylike fashion and shook my head, speaking around my mouthful. "Nope."

"And you're still sure he's your mate?" Dad pressed on.

I rolled my eyes at him and swallowed down the mass of sweet, chewed-up pastry. "Dad, you're the one who told me that Carlak was acting like my mate."

"He was at the time," Dad said, then glanced at Mom and then back at me.

"What aren't you telling me?" I asked, my stomach suddenly swooping with worry.

What the hell is going on here?

Mom coughed to clear her throat. "Well, we're a little worried that perhaps we were wrong about your bond. After all," she reasoned. "Carlak didn't shift—"

"And you didn't shift either," Dad continued. "You've been a whole week apart with no signs of losing control whatsoever. It's not quite the pattern we're used to seeing around here. Not when it comes to Fated mates, at least."

They were wrong. *So* wrong. They had to be. Everything inside my entire being, my whole essence, told me they didn't understand. My hands tightened into fists, and my jaw locked down as I fought the raging urge to correct them and shout it in their faces as my dragon reared her head, making her presence known.

"Sweetheart, it's okay," Mom tried to soothe me. "There's no need to hole yourself up in your room any longer. You're still young, and Carlak has always adored you. So, if we made a mistake in our advice..."

If my mother suspected I'd slept with Carlak already, why was she doing this? Especially in front of the whole family? I stood up and went to speak my mind, but my teeth had partially shifted, and my ability to talk effectively was gone. I whirled away and stormed back to my room in frustration and denial.

Fucking idiots! How can they have no idea? Or is this some sort of joke? A game for them? Are they getting their jollies out of tormenting me?

Part of me knew that if I told them the truth about Carlak coming to me and my bed last night, they might change their mind.

Might, being the operative word.

They would still be right about the fact that he had never lost his control around me. Except for in bed... but maybe that was normal? I didn't know! It's not like I had a point of reference with which to compare.

A seed of doubt began to sow itself deep inside my belly. What if Carlak wasn't my true, Fated mate? What if he was just more like my first crush? A casual lover? Maybe this feeling was nothing more than coming of age hormones? Just because I'd lost my virginity to him didn't mean we were necessarily Fated. I'd honestly never thought of that. But my parents were Fated mates, as were Damon and Cass, and Marienne and Erik.

Surely, I have to have a Fated mate, as does Carlak?

Nothing else made any sense. It seemed to be the pattern with the royals... If we weren't each other's true mates, maybe those who were, were still out there somewhere, still waiting to be discovered? I shook my head and paced my bedroom, growling with consternation. I desperately wanted to fly, to race to my window and take flight high into the stunning winter sky to blow off some steam. But apart from the fact that my father would chase after me out of fear for my safety more than anything else, I wasn't sure I was really up to it.

And it would just invite further questioning.

I sighed. I had a flaming headache from the stress and the ridiculous emotional roller coaster I'd been on for the past few days. And I had no idea what to do. So, I ended up having a long, scorching hot shower before just crawling back into my lonely bed. Carlak would come tonight, even though he said he might not, wouldn't he? At least I hoped so.

I said I would hope.

But he didn't.

And I waited still. I left the balcony doors unlocked and woke every hour from a fretful slumber throughout the night, praying that I'd open my eyes to find him there.

But he didn't show.

I tried to console myself the next day that King Erik had probably sat Carlak down and talked at him until he'd fallen asleep in his chair, just like he suspected he might. But the seeds of doubt had now sprouted and taken a foothold within me like a creeping vine in spring, and I wasn't sure that I knew how to uncurl its sticky tendrils from around my morose and uncertain heart.

Is love supposed to be this complicated?

THIRTEEN

Carlak

My temperature was well over a hundred degrees, and my dutiful mother was forcing herbal remedies down my throat every hour on the hour, using everything she had at her disposal as a queen and sorceress to improve my failing health.

"Mom, please stop," I managed to say when she brought me one that was vomit-inducing to help clear my lungs. "I just need to rest, honestly. No more medicine."

"Your lungs are weak," she argued, shaking her head as she read through a spell book on her lap. She hadn't left my bedside for two days, once again proving that she was truly the strongest queen there was.

"My lungs aren't... weak..." I rasped before a coughing fit struck and rendered me incapable of speaking for several breathless minutes. The fucking sickness was back, and there was only two days until my party. If I didn't feel like I'd been slammed into the side of a mountain a dozen times and then left to die in the snow, I'd scream in frustration and rage.

"Oh, I didn't mean you're weak, my love," Mom went on gently. "It's just that the sickness that took you over last winter has left a mark. It took a long-term toll, and now we just need to focus on getting you well again." She flipped through the ancient tome of magic, lost in thought before speaking again. "I've spoken to your father already about cancelling your party."

"No!" I shook my head, forcing myself to sit up in bed, my eyes wide. "No, you can't. I'll be better by then, I know it."

She lifted her head to stare at me, her eyes wide with surprise. "Carlak..."

"No," I said again, this time imbuing my words with as much authority as I could muster as the heir to the throne of the Black Mountains. "I must see... Jessa."

Mom's gaze softened and she sighed. "Sweetheart, we can send for Jessa, but you don't need a huge birthday party if all you need is one person."

I shook my head stubbornly, my mind made up. "No." I'd thought of that, but I'd already done this all wrong. I needed to speak to her father, King Stavrok. I wanted to seek his permission to ask for my mate's hand in marriage.

Jessa deserves to have me do this right, for her. She deserves to be happy.

"I could send for her today," Mom urged, reaching out to hold my hand. "You might feel better if she was here. You know, being happy is a powerful magic all on its own. It has uncanny healing abilities, especially when it comes to matters of the heart. Her love could help you, darling. She could lend you her strength. Why not take the chance? It certainly couldn't hurt, Carlak."

I pursed my lips and shook my head in response.

"Why must you be so stubborn?" She sighed. "You're as ridiculously stoic as your father. It's fine not to be fine, sometimes," she stressed. "There is no shame in it!"

I wheezed, my breathing almost unbearably painful now. "I don't want her to see me like this, Mom," I gasped, wincing in the face of the pain. "*Please.*"

Her eyes welled up with tears as memories of my battle last winter swept over her.

I squeezed her hand with my fingers. "I'm *not* going to die, Mom. Just give me a few days, please. I'll recover. I'm stronger than you think. I know it. I survived this beast once and I'll do it again."

It had been the return flight from Jessa's castle that had done it. After losing our virginity together, I'd been caught in a violent and icy storm that I hadn't expected, then arrived home practically frozen solid. Even my dragon suffered. Now, I had to rebuild my strength in time for my mate and her family to arrive. It was all that mattered. I needed Jessa to know once and for all that we were truly Fated and destined to be—no ifs, buts, or maybes about it. Once she knew my heart, how I really felt, every-thing would fall into place. I was sure of it.

"Okay, baby," Mom whispered with a smile as fragile as glass. "But if Jessa's your Fated mate, she's going to want to be here by your side. She'll be mad you've hidden your illness from her. There should be no secrets between you. Honesty is paramount in a lasting union, my son. I know this from experience."

My mom was probably right. After all, she knew girls a lot better than I did. But even so, I couldn't put this on Jessa. I wanted—needed—her to choose me because *she* wanted to, not because she felt beholden to me or pressured by our parents. "It'll be all right," I assured my mom. "Please, just let me sleep and gather my strength. Time is of the essence, and I'm running out."

She kissed my forehead and whispered a quiet prayer before she headed out, casting just a quick glance over her shoulder before leaving me to my peace.

I closed my eyes and settled into my princely bed, the heaviness of fatigue weighing down upon me like a tangible blanket of lead. I was going to be King of the Black Mountains one day. I would sit the throne and have people to protect and govern. I had to recover and become stronger. The realm needed me, and I wouldn't permit this dastardly illness to rob me of my vitality, life, and purpose. The will of my inner dragon roared in agreement, unwilling to allow his wings to be clipped or accept a life half lived.

A restless, fever-fueled sleep soon claimed me, and I dreamed of my younger brother as I thrashed unconsciously in my sweat-soaked sheets. In my dream, he came to my aid, laying his hands upon my face, and somehow drawing the fever from my very body. But when I opened my eyes during a temporary lapse of unconsciousness, Anthony wasn't there. No one was. So, alone and burdened by a fire that wasn't my own, I labored through the sickness and I slept, hoping against hope that I'd be well enough to attend my own birthday celebration.

THE DAY of my party arrived, and I was still weak, but mercifully my fever had broken, and I could finally eat again without ejecting the contents of my stomach soon after.

"Son, you still look *terrible*," my father said. He always did have a way with words.

I rolled my eyes and shook my head at his lack of tact. "I'll be fine, Dad," I said, drinking the herbal soup I'd been served for lunch. "When do the royal families arrive?" I asked.

"Well, King Stavrok's family was originally meant to arrive this morning, but we sent word that we needed some more time to prepare. By way of an apology, we told them that they were welcome to stay longer after the party."

My stomach churned under the scarcely substantial weight of the soup, but I managed to keep it down by sheer force of will. I knew I couldn't recover without the sustenance of food. If I kept nothing down, I'd continue to grow weaker by the hour. "You didn't tell them I was unwell, did you Dad?" I asked, my brow furrowed.

His lips twisted. "No, I didn't, though I think we should, especially as Jessa is your mate. It seems a bad idea to hide ill health, Carlak."

I shook my head again in objection but refused to explain myself further. This was not going to plan at all, but I was determined to salvage as much of it as I could.

I can't let my Fated mate down!

I'd wanted to woo Jessa with a magical night, ask her father formally for her hand in marriage, and then propose in some dramatic, romantic way. Perhaps on a balcony beneath the stars or out in the gardens among the roses. I wanted her to feel every bit as special as she was to me, but now, all I could think about was what a raw deal she would be receiving. This sickness had almost ended me last year, and striking me down for a second time proved only that I was indeed much weaker than I'd thought, or than I'd hoped.

I wasn't sure how I was even going to begin to explain this to Jessa. Why would she want me—the weak one—when she could have her choice of any other strong prince or mighty dragon shifter in the realm and beyond? I feared now, more than anything, that if she chose to remain my mate, she'd be forever settling. Resigning her life to that of a queen forced to dutifully keep vigil in regret by the bedside of a sick king, lamenting as youth and vigor passed her by. She'd mourn me even as I lived, upset at what *could* have been, rather than being the proud wife of a warrior king—a king she and the Black Mountains could truly love—like my father.

With substantial effort, I managed to shower, finding some relaxation and relief beneath the hot water. But then I was so exhausted I needed another sleep to fortify my strength for the evening. When the call eventually came to warn us that we had just an hour left until the party, I was thankfully feeling strong enough to dress myself and prepare for the celebration ahead. The pale, drawn face that stared back at me in the mirror with shadows under his eyes was a worry, but there wasn't anything I could do about it. Except... "Mother."

I finished dressing in all my royal regalia befitting the occasion and then went in search of my parents' room. If anyone could make me look more presentable for my big night, surely Mom could? But I was already too late. By the time I arrived at their bedroom, the luxuriously appointed chamber was empty. In the nearby distance I could hear the sound of music rising from the ballroom as the musicians had begun to play, and there was a steady hum of voices that told me that people had indeed started to arrive.

I took a slow, steadying breath and lifted my chin, claiming back some semblance of control over myself as best I could. My chest ached from coughing and wheezing for days on end, and I could still sense a fever brewing once more in the sweat of my brow. But I refused to let this sickness beat me. I was taking control of my life and my fate, no matter what it cost me. No matter how great the pain, or how sick I still felt, I was walking out there like the man I was supposed to be—the heir to the throne of the Black Mountains.

I lifted my chin, straightened my suit jacket once more, and walked toward the party. They'd be waiting for me already, my family and our guests. It was time to celebrate being a man, and then I could take my next steps into the future with Jessa still hopefully willing to remain at my side. I'd find a way to heal, one way or another, for her and the realm. A strong heir is what they deserved, and it's who I wanted to be.

It's who I will be.

Despite all my hope for the future, and my dragon's yearning to see Jessa, the walk to the ballroom felt somehow more like the begrudging amble of a man climbing the stairs to greet an executioner... as the noose awaited him.

Curling my hands into fists, I felt the crescents of my nails biting into my palms.

Keep it together, man. Just hold fast. This isn't the end.

Far from it. Tonight was supposed to be a whole new beginning.

FOURTEEN

Jessa

Where was he? I'd glanced at the balcony doors a hundred times, and Carlak was still nowhere to be seen.

Marienne and Erik were greeting guests at the door like the incredibly gracious hosts they were. Rather than sit on their thrones and expect visitors to come to them, they were right there in the fray, treating everyone as equals with hearty handshakes and warm embraces.

Meanwhile, Anthony had given me the biggest grin when I'd walked in, as if to say that he knew everything that had happened between his brother and me.

I grimaced awkwardly.

He probably does.

"Stop fidgeting," my mom whispered at me as she caught me tugging at my dress for the tenth time.

"I'm not," I hissed back, even though I knew I was. I was dancing on tenterhooks, my inner dragon absolutely yearning to lay eyes on Carlak, the prince of my heart.

"You need to lower your expectations," she said, getting closer so only I could hear her. "I can see how much you want to see Carlak but—"

"Mom, I love you," I warned through gritted teeth, "But I'm going to have a fit if you don't back off."

She gasped in shock.

Her reaction gave me a moment of pause, but it was the best I could do. I wasn't in control of my body, or my dragon right now. I just needed to see the man who'd taken my virginity and never returned.

My father stepped closer, offered me an understanding nod and tactfully took my mother away.

Thanks, Dad.

I was positively vibrating with stress as it was becoming worse as the minutes wore on. I wasn't sure if I was going to kiss Carlak or kill him when I saw him. What excuse could he possibly have for not coming back to me these last four nights after showing me the pleasures that could be shared between a man and a woman?

Vanya pressed into my side and grabbed my hand, squeezing tightly in quiet support. "Just breathe, okay?" she instructed.

I nodded and forced myself to take a deep breath in through my nose. I was almost out of control, and the night hadn't even started yet!

Finally, after what seemed like an eternity, Queen Marienne and King Erik walked onto the balcony and smiled out over the gathered crowd.

We all turned toward them as they introduced Carlak, and with bated breath we all waited for him to make his grand entrance.

And he did, stepping out in a beautiful, tailored black suit, his hair slicked back, making him look sleek and handsome beyond his years. His smile was hesitant, and his cheeks were pale.

I wasn't sure what was going on, but it was obvious something was amiss with the celebrated prince.

Vanya whispered surreptitiously into my ear. "Is it just me, or does he not look well?"

She was right, of course, but I couldn't speak. Just seeing him again stirred up all kinds of emotions that I wasn't sure I could name, let alone handle.

His gaze skimmed over the large, formally dressed group, then our eyes met, and sparks flew.

My heart pounded and ached, while my dragon roared inside my head.

Carlak smiled at me but maintained his composure, nodding at my father before moving on to the rest of the group.

My breathing was labored, coming hard and fast, and made my chest rise and fall as painfully as if I'd just run a marathon. Where was he going? Why wasn't he coming straight to me? What in all the realms was he thinking? I continued to watch Carlak as he walked down the stairs with his parents and greeted all the royal families, including ours.

He nodded at my parents and smiled with his typical indifference.

I forced myself to curtsey as we all did, all the while maintaining eye contact.

Carlak reached out for my hand expectantly.

Without hesitation, despite my inner turmoil, I gave it to him.

He kissed my fingers, and although the gesture was unique and special, he kept any sort of genuine recognition from his face and voice.

When he moved on, I sighed with soul-deep disappointment.

"Well, what did you expect?" Vanya whispered at me. "A royal jig in front of everyone?"

I wasn't sure what I'd expected to be honest, but that wasn't it. Far from it.

"Jessa, how are you?" a familiar voice asked suddenly.

I turned around to greet Taggath, the dragon prince from my party. "Taggath," I said. "So nice to see you."

He leaned in too close for comfort and grinned at me salaciously. "I hope you'll consider dancing with me again, Princess. We were rudely interrupted at your party."

The mention of Carlak made my spine stiffen with unexpected defiance. My dragon was angry, and I felt it acutely. "I'd love to dance with you. That would be great."

It was obvious to everyone else it seemed that Carlak had been faking the Fated mate connection all along.

But why?

My heart burned at the thought. Perhaps he just wanted to get into my pants before anyone else could. The old "take the princess' virginity play". I didn't really know. For a stomach-churning moment, I almost didn't want to know.

"Would you like to sit with me over dinner?" Taggath asked, sliding a presumptuous hand around my waist.

A chill coursed up my back in response to his touch, and it wasn't in a thrilling way. "Ah... I'm sorry. I actually promised my parents I'd sit with them tonight, but I'll see you after?" I asked, slipping out of his hold as smoothly as I could. "For the dancing?"

He nodded and moved on without complaint, obviously feeling rather confidant tonight.

Traditionally, most of our parties consisted of mingling and dinner, cake, speeches, then dancing and more drinking, and tonight was no different. I had to endure sitting beside my sister and watch as Carlak ignored me in favor of the huge party his parents had planned for him, and it grated on my every nerve.

Dinner was delicious, but every bite was forced as I tried to engage in casual conversation and not let my need for Carlak overwhelm me. The speeches were thankfully fast and without too much pageantry, and despite waiting with bated breath for Carlak to mention me at one point or another, he never did. By the time the cake was cut and served, I was sick with disappointment and heart sore to my bones.

I was standing with my family, trying to enjoy a glass of champagne by the fireplace when Carlak finally had the gall to approach us.

"Good evening, everyone. Are you enjoying yourselves?" he asked.

I turned to stare at him. His color had improved as the night wore on. "Yes, we have, thank you," I managed to answer politely, taking another sip of my drink.

Carlak nodded and turned to my dad. "King Stavrok, may I request a moment of your time?"

"Tonight?" Dad said, sounding confused.

Carlak nodded again. "Yes, please, it's important. We can just step out of the ballroom and into the hallway if you'd rather remain close?"

Dad sounded as confused as I felt as he agreed and left with Carlak.

Hot tears filled my eyes, and I turned away from the ballroom to stare into the mesmerizing flames of the fireplace. Why was everything upside down and inside out? It didn't make any sense!

The music stopped, and there was silence for a moment before a slow, deep bass began to pound, the rhythm filling the air. We were moving onto the dance portion of the night.

Taggath's hand on my bare shoulder made me shiver, but I managed to blink the tears away and turn around. "Hi," I said, licking my lips and burying my emotions.

Taggath grinned at me.

Now that I looked closer, his teeth were extremely uneven, and I swallowed the grimace before it could reach my face. Why had I thought he was so perfect before?

"Let's do it," he said, sliding his hand around my waist and pulling me onto the dance floor.

The music was slow and sexy, but I wasn't feeling it. So as not to embarrass myself, I tried to keep with the beat, swinging my hips and tossing my hair around a little to fit in with the party vibe, but I just wanted to go home.

Taggath moved behind me and slid his hands around my waist, holding me tightly against him. "Damn, you're beautiful," he said. "And so sexy."

I swallowed hard, trying not to flinch. His touch almost felt like poison. "Thanks," I managed.

Taggath was big, strong, dominant, and a lot older than me. It felt intimidating and gross.

All the same, at an event like this, I felt it would be strange and awkward to try and tell him that I wanted him to take his hands off me. I smiled at the people around us who were watching with interest.

My sister smiled at me from the sidelines.

I desperately wanted someone to intervene but didn't know how to ask or signal her for help—not without seeming extremely rude or attracting the wrong kind of attention.

Taggath's lips pressed into the flesh of my neck.

I cringed instinctively, twisted in his arms and pushed at his chest, trying to put some distance between us. "Don't do that," I said.

"Why not?" he asked in a slithery voice. "I can smell another man on you, it's obvious you aren't a virgin anymore."

Another shudder of revulsion rippled through me at his words, and I choked down the urge to slap him in the face.

His hands moved down to my ass, and he hauled me against his hard body. "I was considering asking you to marry me... but now I think you'd be better as a casual bedmate. What do you think, hmmm?"

He dropped his head and came at me, his lips puckered in a putrid move.

I turned my head away and tossed aside any notion of remaining polite. "No! Let go!" I pushed against his shoulder, but he didn't move. In desperation, I kicked him in the shin. What else could I do? He wasn't taking no for an answer.

He staggered slightly as my hard shoe made contact with bone.

"Fuck off!" I hissed, writhing to get away from him, pushing against his chest.

Unwilling to let his quarry free so easily, he grabbed my forearm tightly. "What's wrong with you?" Taggath asked, hobbling a little as he forcefully dragged me to the edge of the dancefloor. "You can slut it up like a whore with some random cock, but you won't fuck me?"

I didn't get the chance to defend my honor because behind us everything changed. The music ground to a screeching halt, leaving the room filled with a strained silence—but not for long. Too soon, there were shouts of fear coming from all directions.

My dad yelled over the noise, his eyes wide with shock. "Jessa! Get out of the way!"

Taggath gasped and stumbled back, finally releasing my wrist.

I stumbled to the side, desperately grabbing onto my brother as he swooped in to catch me.

"We've got to get out of here," Anselm said, his tone one that defied argument as he pulled me toward the stairs.

"What's happened?" I asked in a panic, my heart pounding wildly in my chest. My gaze darted frantically around until it stopped on the dance floor, where Carlak had shifted into his enormous dragon and was slowly and menacingly stalking toward Taggath.

"No! Stop! Wait!" I demanded of Anselm, managing to tug my arm out of his protective hold.

My mate had come to save me, and for the first time... his dragon was no longer under his control.

My soul sang, despite the chaos. He'd lost control, just like the other dragon shifters. He wasn't pretending or faking our bond at all.

He IS my Fated mate!

FIFTEEN

Carlak

I was no longer in control of my body or my shifter, and I didn't fucking care. Taggath had just assaulted my mate. I'd seen his hands on her, felt her discomfort and heard her cry out as he called her a whore.

He deserves to die.

I took another step forward, watching as the snake slithered back toward the fireplace, desperately pressing himself against the bricks in fear.

People were screaming around me, but that didn't matter. Nothing mattered except avenging my mate's honor. I just had to make sure that the slimy bastard didn't get away.

All too predictably, the older prince tried to run, too cowardly to face me.

I opened my mouth and roared at him, unleashing my rage in a torrent of hot breath that all but threw him against the wall. My fire was building in my chest. I could feel the heat rising, its welcome blaze ready to burn. If Taggath tried to run again, I'd blast him without an ounce of remorse.

My parents would forgive me for damaging the castle, I was sure. Killing a fellow royal, on the other hand... well, right now, it just didn't fucking matter. That scumbag had dared to lay a hand on my woman, and I was going to make him sorry he was ever born.

"Carlak, stop!" King Stavrok shouted to the left of me.

I ignored the man that was now small beside me.

He was the largest king we had. A true giant of a man. Now, he barely made it to my shoulder, and his words no longer meant the world to me.

I'd already gotten what I'd asked for—his blessing to ask Jessa to be my queen. He'd expressed his worry that we weren't the Fated mates that he initially believed. He genuinely thought that the superior control I demonstrated over my dragon was a sign that I wasn't truly fated to Jessa. Well, he may have thought that before, but I was damn certain he wasn't thinking that anymore.

Taggath's father slid along the stone wall, slimy as his son, as though he could grab Taggath and interfere with our altercation.

I puffed smoke and growled, swiping out with one of my foreclaws.

Stavrok called out to Taggath to move back and to submit.

As if he had no spine whatsoever, Taggath sank down to his knees, trembling like the absolute coward he was. He didn't even put up a fight. The smarmy bastard just caved, crumpling like tissue paper. He wanted my woman but wasn't willing to spill blood for her—that much was clear.

I wanted to scream at him, to tell him Jessa was *mine*. He had no right to speak to her, let alone touch her, as far as my dragon was concerned. But I had no words, and no appropriate vocal cords with which to even try to communicate. There was only one sure way to show him how angry I was, and that was to hurt him. I had to make him see how royally he'd fucked up, and I'd do it here and now, in front of the whole court at my damned birthday celebration. This moment would be remembered forever.

I am not weak.

I stepped forward once more, glaring at the dragon prince with my blazing golden dragon eyes.

Fight me!

I wanted him to shift, to stand up and become the dragon he was. Then we could truly see who was the strongest—who was right for princess Jessa.

The pompous asshole was rising to his feet again.

I began to puff myself up, ready for the battle that was necessary. He'd touched my mate, and he was going to pay. He'd never lay a finger on her again when I was through with him.

The feel of a small hand splayed on my front leg had me halting. I inhaled deeply, and Jessa's familiar scent made my dragon even more determined to protect her.

She was moving slowly, around my leg, then to my chest. Her human hand was so small as she stroked my scales affectionately, moving all the way up to my head.

I lowered my gaze from my prey and looked deep into my mate's eyes.

"Hello, Carlak," she said.

I purred at the erotic, silky tone of her voice.

"You know," she began, continuing to stroke the scales of my snout. "My family thought that you weren't my Fated mate. Can you believe it? All because you controlled your dragon so well around me. Your strength fooled them all, Carlak."

I frowned, only partially understanding her words through the fog of fear at losing her and the anger directed at Taggath still clouding my head.

"Come back to me," she whispered, though I heard every word clearly. "Come back and tell them all that I'm yours. After all, you know, you've kind of been ignoring me all night... and I've been sad."

As her words soaked into my consciousness, my humanity stretched up and grabbed hold of my dragon, ready to rein him in. But he went willingly, realizing that my mate needed the kind of reassurance that only my human half could provide. My dragon form receded, and I regained my human body. A wave of brutal exhaustion flowed over me, and I staggered sideways. Shifting into my dragon had taken every last bit of my strength.

I'd been running on pure adrenaline and rage, and now my tank was empty.

Jessa rushed forward to wrap her arms around me.

My mother came over a moment later with a robe, slipping it over my shoulders. Then she put the back of her hand to my forehead and *tsked* loudly. "You're burning up, Carlak. I knew this party was a bad idea."

The crowd around us was watching with keen interest, but I tried not to let it worry me. I'd spent my whole life concerned about what my subjects would one day think of me, what my family thought of me, and now, it didn't matter. Tonight, I was as naked as the day I'd entered this realm and utterly exhausted. All I wanted was Jessa. "Jessa... I'm sorry," I whispered, struggling to speak with my dry mouth.

"The prince needs water!" she called out to the servants.

I smiled at her.

She knows me so well already.

Jessa looked at my mother for clarification. "He's been ill again, hasn't he?" she asked as her concerned gaze raked over me once more.

My mother nodded, her tone grave. "I thought we were going to lose him."

"Mom!" I managed to gasp out. "I'm *not* going anywhere. I told you I was strong enough to survive this."

Jessa's eyes filled instantly with tears. "I thought you didn't want me. I thought that was why you left and never came back. But you were sick all this time?"

I opened my mouth to respond, but movement from behind Jessa caught my eye.

Taggath was on his feet and charging toward me.

"You little runt!" the prince spewed. "I'm going to kick your ass for that."

Jessa's eyes flashed with anger as she spun around and swung at Taggath's face.

The elder prince keeled over at the unexpected blow, hitting the floor with a resounding *thud*.

My mate stood over him, her hands on her hips. "You stay away from him, and you stay away from me! And if you *ever* so much as lay a finger on me again, I'll make sure my father rips your arms off!"

"He won't be the only one vying for that honor," my dad said, coming up behind me to stand at my shoulder, his strength at my back. "I think it's high time you left, Taggath."

The prince scowled with his bleeding lip, then scampered away, leaving the party in disgrace.

He'll be lucky if he ever finds a bride now.

The servants hurried over and brought me water to gulp down.

I took the chalice from them gladly and drank the cold liquid, extinguishing the last of the fire burning in my throat.

"Well, that was certainly unexpected," my father said, grinning down at me.

King Stavrok laughed as he sidled up behind Jessa. "You know, I think Prince Carlak has a question for you, young lady."

Jessa turned to face me, her heart in her beautiful blue eyes.

I swallowed hard.

It's now or never.

I tied my robe so that I wouldn't give the rest of the gathered guests another glimpse at my naked body and walked over to Jessa.

She was staring at me with tears spilling down her flushed cheeks.

I had to tell her the truth *now*. I reached out and cupped her face. "Sweetheart, I didn't mean to make you sad. You're my everything. But I've been ill... very ill the past few days, and I couldn't visit. This sickness almost took me once, and I was determined to fight it and be as strong as I could be for you for tonight."

She sniffed and looked down. "But tonight, you ignored me."

"No, beautiful... I just wanted to ask your father for permission to propose before I did. I wanted to do everything right. You deserve the most perfect life, and I want to give it to you, if you'll let me."

Her gaze shot back up, then she let out a laugh and shook her head. "Well, you didn't do everything right! You should have just cancelled your party and invited my family over here so that I could sit with you while you were sick. We would have come without delay."

I lifted my chin, pride burning a hot hole in my chest. "I didn't want you to think I was weak, or to have your father refuse me because I'm not strong enough to be your husband."

Jessa glanced over her shoulder at her dad, then back to me, her gaze softening. "Carlak, you're my mate. It doesn't matter what anyone else thinks or does. *I* only care about *you*."

I stepped closer, cupping her beloved face again in both hands. "Well, I love you, Jessa, more than anything in this world. And I know we're young, but..."

"Yes," she whispered, not even letting me finish the question. "Yes, I'll marry you. Tonight. Tomorrow. As soon as Mom can get me a white dress, and your dad can find an Elder to marry us!"

I chuckled and brought her face closer to mine with a smile. "You're going to keep me on my toes, aren't you?"

Jessa slid her hands around my waist and brought our bodies together. "Of course I will, for the rest of our lives."

As the bliss of the scene washed over me, my brain decided that it was an opportune moment to throw everything at me, all at once—all the things I'd done wrong. "Oh, God! I should have kneeled, shouldn't I?" I blanched. My proposal was so far from perfect, it wasn't even funny.

Jessa laughed, her voice like music to my ears. "Carlak, just kiss me," she said.

"But..."

"No buts!" she countered defiantly, a huge grin splitting her face. "No more worrying about everything. You have officially had the most dramatic birthday party ever! You turned into a dragon, almost attacked another prince, and ended up naked in the middle of the ballroom. And after all that, I *still* think you're perfect."

I stared at her with so much love flowing through me, I just had to say it again. "I love you so much, Jessa."

"And I love you too, prince of my heart," she said. "Now kiss me!"

I dropped my head and pressed my lips to hers, deciding not for the first time that she was right, and the time for words was well and truly over.

Lost in the bliss of our kiss, my dragon roared with more strength and joy than I could ever remember experiencing before.

My dragon had found his mate and I'd found my queen. I was without doubt the luckiest man in the whole damn world.

CHAPTER
SIXTEEN

Jessa

Our families embraced us and there were hearty congratulations all around. The party quickly shifted into overdrive as the music was struck up once more. The servants raced around filling everyone's drinks and replacing food trays, and our immediate families retired to the library.

Carlak was hot to the touch and growing paler by the minute.

"Let's all sit," Queen Marienne suggested to my parents—who'd taken over the love seat—while my siblings stood warming themselves by the fire.

Anthony was hanging around the door, but was at least in the library with us, and Marienne and Erik were standing by the large desk.

King Erik went over to the whiskey station and began pouring drinks. "Shall we toast to the happy couple?" he asked.

"Yes, definitely," Dad said, standing up to receive the glasses for him and Mom.

"Hang on one minute," Anthony said, and ducked out the room as swift as lightning.

I glanced up at King Erik with a questioning look.

He merely shrugged. "Give him a minute. That boy has good ideas as a general rule."

And he was right. A moment later, Anthony came back with a servant in tow, carrying a bottle of champagne and some soda.

"Oh, perfect!" I said, grabbing a flute of champagne for myself and our mothers. As soon as everyone had a drink, I stood up beside Carlak, holding his hand tightly, excitement making my stomach clench.

This is it.

"Well," King Erik began, "I have to admit that Marienne and I had hoped that our families would one day be united, and it seems that our dream has come to fruition."

Marienne beamed, her smile bright. "It was meant to be."

Dad lifted his whiskey. "We are delighted that Jessa has found her mate in Carlak, the man she truly wanted," he said. "To Carlak and Jessa, may they know a great and enduring love!"

"To Carlak and Jessa!" everyone in the room echoed, clinking their glasses with one another in celebration of our union.

I made sure to touch my glass with everyone in the room, then turned to give Carlak the biggest kiss. I didn't care that it was in front of everyone. I was just so happy, I could burst.

Carlak was smiling, but his once pale skin was now turning ash gray.

I took a sip of my champagne, then placed my glass down on the coffee table, my instincts to protect my mate already rising. "I think Carlak needs to lie down. Is it okay if we head to bed?" I glanced at my Erik and Marienne my future father and mother-in-law, trying not to let the hot blush in my cheeks steal away my courage. I couldn't even look at my parents, but Carlak and I were engaged now. Surely, they wouldn't stop us?

"Ah…" Erik glanced at my dad as though asking his permission on the situation.

I finally sighed and looked at my parents. "Seriously? He's barely standing. We're not going to be doing anything. I just want to be with him."

Carlak huffed out a laugh with what little strength he had in reserve. "I'm sorry to admit it, but she is right. If I don't lie down soon, I'm afraid I'm going to keel over, and I'd rather not do that with an audience after the evening's events."

King Erik stepped forward. "I'll walk them to his bedroom. No one will dare bother the newly engaged couple if I'm escorting them."

I thanked Queen Marienne, kissed my siblings, and hugged my parents, my heart overflowing with emotion. "See you all for breakfast?" I asked, still a little embarrassed but *so* happy, I could almost fly without wings.

"Yes, we'll see you then, sweetheart," Mom said smiling at me warmly.

Vanya wasn't smiling.

In fact, I could feel her sadness as though it were a tangible, physical presence in the room. I glanced her way, my heart in my throat.

She just raised her arm and gave me a small, seemingly sullen wave. "See you tomorrow," she said.

Anselm seemed a little happier, but he wasn't smiling either.

And that's when it hit me like a blazing ball of fire to the face. The triplets were finally being split up, and much sooner than any of us thought we would be. Without reservation, I launched myself at my siblings, one arm around my sister, and the other around my brother. "I love you both. *So* much," I breathed, choking back a sob.

Vanya gripped me tightly.

Even Anselm brought his head down and pressed his forehead to mine in a rare show of affection.

We stood that way for several long moments, before the silence around us became awkward, and I pulled gently away. "I'll see you both at breakfast," I promised.

Vanya nodded, wiping the tears from her cheeks as she smiled. "See you then."

Anselm gave me a wink and a smile too.

With the fire of my heart merrily burning away inside me like a candle in the dark, I went to Carlak and gripped his hand with pride, ready to lend him my strength and guide him whenever he needed.

This is the next stage of my life...the girl is gone, and the woman has taken her place.

He smiled at me and squeezed my hand in return, his skin clammy.

Together, we walked to the door.

King Erik strode forth and opened it for us.

I turned around grinned, waving at my family one more time before stepping out of the library and into the hall beyond.

Carlak slumped against me the moment we were out.

His dad swooped in close and put an arm around his waist. "Come along, let's get you to bed, son."

I dutifully held Carlak's hand while King Erik helped him up the two floors to his bedroom.

Once inside, Carlak practically collapsed into bed, his brow dotted with sweat. "Oh, damn... I think I may have pushed it a little too far tonight," he said.

King Erik chuckled. "You think? What in God's name gives you that idea?" He ruffled Carlak's hair affectionately and said quietly, "I'm so proud of you." Then he smiled gently at me and left us alone.

I stared after him for a time, realizing that I'd always seen King Erik as the rough and tough king. I'd never seen him show such softness or kindness to anyone. It was beautiful to witness, and made me hope that Carlak also had those many layers that he would only reveal to his loved ones. I slid off the bed and stretched.

"Where are you going?" Carlak asked.

I unbuttoned my dress and allowed it to slip to the floor. "Nowhere. I'm just getting into my pajamas." And by that, of course, I meant I was getting naked. When I was in my birthday suit, I slid under the covers with him and snuggled up. It felt incredible to be so close to him again. I'd missed it far more than I dared to say.

My new fiancé groaned. "No fair. You're naked in my bed, and I can't do anything about it."

My poor love was still fully dressed, so I helped him take his jacket and shirt off, then lay down again beside him with my head resting on his naked chest. Finally, my racing heart began to slow, and I could think clearly now that it was quiet, and we were safe in each other's arms once more. "Carlak, how sick have you been?" I queried. "Your mom said she thought they might lose you."

He sighed and ran a fatigued hand through my hair. "You know that sickness I had last year?"

I nodded against his chest, recalling the memories. "My mom said you almost died."

"Yeah, well... it was very similar, but I refused to let it beat me. I had you to fight for this time. But I am sorry I didn't tell you. I shouldn't have done that. I was so worried about how weak I'd appear that I didn't think about how you would worry for me."

I nodded and tried hard not to cry. "I thought you didn't want me anymore. You said you'd try to come back if you could, and then you didn't. And then I didn't hear from you at all for days..."

He kissed my hair by way of an apology. "I'm sorry, sweetheart." His tone earnest and heartfelt.

I nodded against his chest, then lifted my face for a kiss. "You're not allowed to do that to me ever again, though, got it? No hiding stuff from me."

He pressed his lips together in a thin line, then nodded.

I settled my head back down on his chest. I knew he was proud and that he wanted to do the right thing, always. But he *had* to keep me in the loop, or I'd wallop him the same way I did Taggath! His stubborn ass wouldn't even see it coming.

"Jessa?" Carlak asked.

Sleep was just reaching its alluring hand up and began tugging me into the sweet promise of darkness and slumber. The party was still going and likely would last for hours yet. I could hear the music thrumming from here, but I didn't care. I was *exactly* where I wanted to be. "Yes, my prince?" I asked, nuzzling into his skin.

"Will Anselm and Vanya be okay without you?" A note of concern had crept into his voice.

What an incredible man!

My eyes opened at the mention of my siblings' names, and I looked up at him, marveling at his intuitive nature. He truly was his mother's son. "So, you noticed that too, huh?"

He nodded. "Yeah... you three are close, I know. I don't want to come between you."

I settled again, not wanting to focus on what I was losing but instead focus on what I was gaining. "We are and we always will be close," I assured him. "But now, I have you as well." And it wasn't like we couldn't spend time at my parents' palace. We had two castles between us now, and I didn't see any reason why we couldn't simply live between them, at least to begin with. Who knew where our wedded life would take us! It boggled the mind to even think about.

But now wasn't the time to talk about all of that. The future could wait until the future. In this moment, all I wanted was to just lie here and rejoice in the fact that Carlak was alive, healing, and had asked me to marry him.

We're going to be together forever.

My heart felt truly content. Before we lost ourselves to sleep, I got up and turned the final lamp off and rolled onto my side, getting comfortable on the impossibly soft mattress as I breathed in my mate's familiar scent.

Carlak moved in behind me, a hand gripping my hip in a possessive caress, as if he feared he might awaken to find me gone in the morning.

Every curvaceous inch of me radiated bliss. I loved feeling so protected, wanted, and treasured. It was a feeling I never wanted to lose. "Thank you for loving me," I whispered into the darkness as my eyelids grew heavy and my lashes fluttered closed like butterflies resting daintily on my cheeks.

His chuckle was soft, but incredibly sexy. "Thank you for saying you'll be my wife, Jessa. You've made me the happiest man in the realm tonight, my beautiful future queen."

I smiled wistfully and willingly allowed sleep to whisk me away into the land of dreams. Safely wrapped up in my love's arms, the sound of Carlak's rhythmic dragon heartbeat and his steady breathing lulled me into the sweetest and most joyous of dreams. Dreams of eternal love, endless skies, and forever spent by my Fated mate's side. I'd attained everything I'd ever wanted, and couldn't wait to start our lives together as husband and wife, the future king and queen of the Black Mountains.

I'm truly the luckiest woman in the world.

EPILOGUE

It had taken me months to learn all the intricacies of Jessa's beautiful form, to find out what made her arch and cry out or shudder in silent ecstasy. The female body was a mystery to solve, but I had been determined that my Fated mate would enjoy the carnal side of making love as much as I did.

Today marked our one-year wedding anniversary, so I rose early to shower and shave, then went back to bed to wake my gorgeous wife with a luxurious breakfast in bed and her special gift.

At my instruction, the servants had brought a variety of her favorite breakfast foods on gleaming silver trays and laid them on a table next to the bed before they snuck out again. I loved that my servants and I had a good rapport, and that they were only too willing to indulge me and help me surprise the woman of my dreams on such a special day.

I stripped off my robe eagerly and climbed back under the sheets to lay behind my beautiful wife. A day would never go by where I wasn't thankful just to have her nearby.

"Hm... good morning," she groaned, arching into me, and offering her supple neck for my kiss.

I obliged, kissing her lovely throat before she rolled over and I kissed her luscious lips.

"Good morning, wife," I said with a smile that reached my heart. "Happy anniversary."

Her eyes opened fully, and a smile beamed upon her face as radiant as the sun. "Yes! Oh my God! Happy anniversary, my love. Can you believe it?"

I stroked her face gently with my hand and sighed in deep content- ment. "Yes... and no," I answered honestly. "It feels like only yesterday I was dying to fly over and see you, to claim you as mine."

She stretched like a cat, lifting her arms above her head so that the blankets fell lower, exposing the creamy upper swell of her breasts. "Oh, yes," she said grimacing. "Don't remind me! I hate thinking of how desperate I was back then. The bond was so incredibly powerful, I nearly lost my mind."

I peeled the blankets down to her slender waist, then shimmied down next to her body so I could take one of her rosy nipples in my mouth. "I never want to forget how much we love each other," I purred. I lavished one tight nipple with my tongue, then suckled her, hard, just how I knew she liked it.

Jessa gasped and grabbed my head, holding me to her with fingers that curled into desperate claws. "Oh, we're starting our day like that, are we?" she delighted.

I plumped up her other breast with my hand, and transferred my lips over, eager to pleasure them both. "I can't imagine a better way."

She moaned in agreement, arching her back and threading her fingers through my hair before raking them sensually along my scalp.

My own body responded with an immense surge of heat to my groin, making my cock throb with aching need. I kissed my way down her belly until I rested between her thick, milky thighs.

Jessa opened for me willingly, biting her lower lip in anticipation.

I set my mouth to her, her radiating heat causing my cock to engorge even more in preparation for what was to come.

My wife gasped aloud, the sound of her moans like music to my ears.

She tasted like honey, and I loved licking and lapping at the sensitive flesh of her blonde nest like a spoiled cat enjoying its delicious cream. I flicked my tongue over her swollen clit, which looked ripe and wet, like a luscious cherry.

She cried out and grabbed at my hair more tightly as her pleasure built, the muscles of her sexy thighs tensing, and her toes curling against the bedsheets.

But I wasn't done yet—far from it. Almost regretfully removing my mouth from her heaven, I slid one finger inside her, then two, loving the vise-like grip of her pussy around my hand. My dragon within purred with ecstasy, already imagining the feeling of our cock being milked by that gloriously tight hole.

"Carlak!" she cried out in anguish. "Come up, *please!*"

Her hips were bucking at me now, and although I'd wanted to make her orgasm with just my mouth this morning, the desperation of her tone made me rethink my plans, not to mention the insistent throbbing of my cock yearning to be buried deep within her.

"Carlak!" she urged again, pulling at my hair now, ever my feisty queen.

I withdrew my fingers and quickly wiped my mouth on the sheets before crawling up between her legs and getting into position on top of her.

Her sigh of relief was more of a gasp as she lifted her legs and wrapped them around me, pulling my hips down and directing my cock to exactly where he wanted to be.

It was my turn to moan as a wave of lust passed over me, causing a full body shiver. "I was trying to make this last," I managed to hiss out.

Jessa reached between us and seized the girth of my cock, positioning my cum-slick head at her ready entrance. "It will," she whispered against my lips, kissing me softly. "But I need you inside me. *Now.*"

My queen's wish is my command...

I pushed up on one hand and lined myself up before sinking into her wetness with a long and steady thrust, just burying myself into her depths like a spear plundering flesh.

"Oh... God!" Jessa cried out, throwing her head back against the pillows.

She was *so* damn tight that I was struggling to maintain my control already. "Did you speak to Mom about contraception?" I asked, realizing we should have had this conversation much earlier.

Jessa nodded, opening her beautiful blue eyes to meet my gaze. "Yes, I'm safe."

Which meant I could come inside her. My heart soared to new heights, buoyed by my rocketing lust and pleasure.

Her pussy clamped down on me, and Jessa teased me, undulating her hips as she clenched and unclenched.

I dropped my head to kiss her, tasting the sweetness of her mouth. "Damn, you feel amazing."

"So do... you," she gasped out, digging her nails into my triceps as she held tightly to my arms, as if I were anchor in an endless sea.

I began to move faster, pounding her harder and pushing her higher up the mountain of bliss. With every thrust of my rock-hard cock inside her, Jessa cried out, her every gasp and moan serving only to push me even closer toward the edge myself.

"Oh, yes... *Harder*..." she groaned, lifting her pelvis higher, and tightening the wrap of her legs around me.

With a salacious grin of my own, I reached back and switched things up, pushing her thighs forward, opening her more, and tilting her pelvis just the way she liked it for a good deep fucking.

"Oh... fuck!" Jessa's eyes were squeezed shut and her skin was flushed pink as she danced upon the precipice of oblivion, readying herself for the fall.

I fucked her harder and faster, plundering her like a madman, and making the bed move now. She was *so* perfect in every way. Heat trickled down the backs of my thighs and my balls tightened. I wasn't going to last much longer.

Her pussy was gripping me hard—the perfect home for my shifter cock.

I closed my eyes and kept my thrusts short and sharp, holding onto my control by sheer force of will. If she didn't come soon, I'd have to with-draw and change position so I could last longer. But damn, I didn't want to. She was heaven in the flesh, dreams made reality.

"Carlak, I'm going to…" she rasped as her pussy tightened around me in a death grip.

I thrust deep inside her, reveling in the spasms and ripples of her pussy around my cock as her orgasm washed over her. I couldn't hold back any longer, and I didn't need to. I fucked her hard and fast, triggering my own release. Heat poured over me as my cock unleashed my seed inside her. Pleasure unlike anything I'd ever experienced, hit me hard. I cried out, growling as I shook in her arms. As the crest of my ecstasy broke over me, I fell onto Jessa's body, shuddering in the wake of my bliss.

I couldn't see anything or hear a sound, I could only feel the shivers of sensation and happiness that coursed all over my body like tiny spider-webs of lightning spreading all over me, covering me in a net of living energy. When the aftershocks finally receded, I came back into myself, cussing under my breath in awe.

Jessa was stroking my hair and holding me tightly, her legs once more locked around my waist, keeping me close.

I rolled us to the side so I was no longer squashing her, and she came with me, unwilling to be separated just yet.

"Wow," Jessa whispered. "That was amazing. It felt so good."

I was panting with exertion but gave her my biggest smile. "Yes. It was."

Finally, the inferno of heat between us smoldered down to a comfort-able warmth, and Jessa excused herself to run to the bathroom.

I cleaned myself up too and got our breakfast ready.

When she came back to bed, she had a huge and brilliant smile on her face. "Oh, this was a seriously great idea," she said in delight.

"Breakfast in bed?" I asked her, offering her a plate of fruit and croissants.

"Thank you so much," she said, bouncing into bed and taking the plate.

We sat together for a time, just eating and grinning at each other.

"Did you enjoy being able to stay inside me?" she asked between bites, bringing up a topic we'd discussed at length over the past few months.

I groaned to emphasize my words. "It was *incredible*. So much better than having to pull out at the last minute. What was it like for you?"

She actually blushed and looked even more beautiful for it. "I loved it. I didn't think I would, but I came again after you, and I could feel it pulsing inside me. It was amazing."

I chuckled, loving her open honesty and that she felt so comfortable speaking to me about our intimacies. "You're the amazing one," I said as I leaned forward and kissed her. "Thank you for making it possible."

"Well, since we agreed to wait to have babies for a while, your mom gave me a herbal medicine to take every day. She said it'll stop anything from starting, so it keeps us safe."

"That's great," I agreed, not really wanting to talk about my mother at this point in time—in bed—but grateful for her help all the same. "So, what are we doing the rest of the day? Do you want to fly home and see your parents?"

She grinned like a kid with a secret. "Actually, they're all coming here for dinner. Marienne already invited them, so they're flying over later."

"That's excellent," I said, knowing seeing her parents and siblings would just add to the joy of her day.

Jessa and I had decided to put off having kids for a while, given that we were both still very young. And with her brother and sister still single, Jessa felt somewhat strange about moving through more of life's milestones without them. Their bond was truly unique.

"So, with all that in mind, what should we do now?" I asked, glancing at the food laid out on the tables. "More breakfast or a shower?"

Jessa slid out of bed and grabbed the silver tray loaded with chocolates. "Let's have a spa bath!" she suggested, then she sauntered sexily into the bathroom, her hips swinging to and fro in a beckoning manner.

My cock stirred once more, and I chuckled as I followed her into the steamy room, only too eager to indulge in a round two. Our life was beyond amazing, and it was all thanks to the mate I was lucky enough to be blessed with before my nineteenth birthday. My soul sang as absolute peace washed over me.

I found my mate.

Some days I still couldn't believe it, and it was the best feeling in the world. And one I'd never take for granted as long as I lived.

10
FIRE AND ICE
DRAGON
OF HER
DREAMS
USA TODAY BESTSELLING AUTHOR
AMELIA SHAW

CHAPTER

ONE

Vanya

Our thirtieth birthday was just around the corner, and my siblings didn't even seem to care that such a massive milestone was approaching.

And why would they?

Anselm and Jessa were both happily married and had brought children into the world with their mates last year. My sister had been blessed with a pair of beautiful twins, and Kayla had given my brother a strapping son. My siblings were busy, content, and flourishing in their new lives.

I, on the other hand, was not. I spent far too much time trying not to compare myself—the proverbial old spinster—to my amazing brother and sister, Prince Anselm and Princess Jessa, the pride and joy of our powerful kingdom. But what made the comparisons particularly annoying and hard to deal with was the fact we weren't just any ordinary siblings. We were triplets. A natural trio born within mere minutes of each other. As a result, people had been comparing us to one another our entire lives.

And with our baby brother, Iain, now mated to Veronica, I'd definitely been left behind. I distinctly felt like I was letting everyone down. I wasn't the golden child, or the pretty child... I was the dark, waifish, and bookish outcast.

What do I have to offer my amazing family?

"Good morning, beautiful girl," Mom said, walking gracefully into the dining room for breakfast. "How'd you sleep?" Our mother had been injured last year and now walked with a steel cane to help her balance, but she was still as beautiful as ever. The kingdom adored her, as did our father.

"Pretty good," I lied, not wanting to get into it. Truthfully, I'd stayed up far too late reading a book from the library until sleep had claimed me, only to wake up in a sweat, having dreamed of a man I'd never seen before. I wasn't usually one for erotic dreams, but last night had been truly incredible, and I found myself missing the mystery man.

My mother sat down in her high-backed chair opposite me and poured herself a steaming, fragrant cup of tea—her regular morning ritual. Everyone knew that after her tea she'd have hot buttered toast with jam or a sweet pastry, then some yoghurt and fruit. She was a creature of routine and stability in our sometimes chaotic and crazy dragon shifter family, though she had her fiery side. "Have you ordered your dress for the party yet?" she asked, referring to our upcoming thirtieth.

I grabbed a piece of tasty cheese and a handful of dark purple grapes. I'd lost a little weight *again* and needed to eat enough to fill out my elegant dress. "Yes. Weeks ago, actually," I answered. "I wanted to make sure it was done in time."

When I'd spoken to the dressmaker, it had crossed my mind that my sister might want a new dress too, and I'd considered calling her to ask if she wanted to join me for a fitting or two. Then it had occurred to me that she would probably be wearing something gifted to her by Marienne, her mother-in-law.

In that moment, the chasm between us seemed even greater than ever before. My siblings were living their lives, and I was almost of a matronly age and still living with our parents... We'd gone from being a trio of best friends with the whole world ahead of us, to being grown adults with separate lives, and it hit me hard.

"Are you okay, sweetheart?" Mom asked suddenly, her serene features marred by a grimace of concern. "You look sad."

"Oh no, I'm fine," I managed to say with a forced smile, though that too was a lie. I took a fresh, still-warm bread roll from the woven basket in front of me and pulled it apart with my fingers absently. "I'm just feeling a little lonely, I guess. You know, with everyone being away at the moment."

Anselm and his wife were visiting Aunt Cass in the North, and Jessa was at Erik and Marienne's castle, like always. Jessa seemed to prefer it there, and it was hard not to take that personally. It wasn't like there were many castles to choose from. We were each other's mirror opposites. Her with blonde hair, bubbly demeanor, and penchant for pink, and me with my raven locks, reserved outlook, and love of more gothic attire.

"Well, they'll be here for the party," Mom said as she beamed to raise my spirits. "There are only a few days to wait now, and then we'll have all the company we could ever want. You'll probably find yourself craving the peace and solitude once they land. It'll be overwhelming—you know that."

I chuckled softly. "True. Very true."

Everyone was coming to the party. Not just my siblings, but all the kings and queens, their children and grandchildren. It would be an enormous event, almost as big and lavish as a wedding. It was a party to celebrate three royal birthdays, after all.

The door suddenly banged open, and Dad marched into the dining room with a harried air about him. "I'm sorry I'm late," he apologized, sitting down at the head of the table, a frown firmly in place on his usually smiling and handsome but aging visage.

"What's happened, Dad?" I asked, my own expression dropping in empathy for my father. "What's wrong?"

He straightened his jacket and sat up, shifting on his seat in annoyance, choosing not to answer immediately.

"Here, love," Mom said, pouring Dad his morning coffee and shuffling a hearty portion of crispy bacon and perfectly poached eggs onto his plate. "Take a minute, then tell us what's going on."

I smirked at my mother's demeanor as she slowly sat back down. Though she was reliable and set in her ways, she wasn't normally the calm one between my parents. But with Dad looking to fly off the handle at any moment, she was engaging her *ultra soothing* mode. She was calming his inner dragon. But what could have made my father so worried? It couldn't be...

Oh, God...

"Nothing's wrong with Jessa or any of the babies??" I demanded, my stomach lurching at the mere thought of something happening to any of my family, especially my new niece and nephews.

"Oh, no, it's nothing like that," he assured us both, reaching out to squeeze my arm in a comforting gesture, but said no more.

Mom and I waited as patiently as we could for my father to get himself together, the silence extending all around us. Was he angry? Hurt? Fearful? I couldn't tell at this point, as his expression was unreadable. But he was still processing something, that was for sure. Whatever it was, it was *big,* and that triggered a deeply unsettling feeling in my gut.

I kept eating, knowing full well there was no rushing my father. He would speak when he was good and ready and not a moment before.

Dad huffed and pushed his food around on his plate for a minute more, then finally he spoke. "I think Anselm will be bringing his family back a little earlier than expected."

My mother and I waited, expecting something more. That wasn't exactly distressing news. They were family and coming back for the party in a few days anyway.

"And?" Mom prompted, reaching out to grab Dad's hand.

"Well," Dad began again. "Cass just called me, and she's in a bit of a... well, she's having a tantrum, basically."

I lifted my glass to take a sip of my drink and chuckled directly into my orange juice, careful not to accidentally snort the bittersweet, pulpy beverage. I'd done that once before, and the sting of citrus up my sinuses was *not* something I wanted to repeat.

"Ah... more information please?" Mom said, grabbing her teacup. At this rate, we'd be waiting until lunch for the problematic part of the story.

Dad took a sip of his coffee, savoring the strong flavor as he mulled over his words. "Okay... so, to cut a long story short, a man has come forward, from the outer township, and claims to be Damon's son."

My jaw dropped at the scandal Dad had just revealed. "Seriously? How old is he?" I pressed, because surely, that was the most important thing to know.

If he's younger than twenty-eight years old, Aunt Cass is going to have a fit!

"He's older than you," Dad said, a begrudging acceptance on his face. "Thirty-two or three, I think."

Mom sighed heavily. "Well, if it is true, then at least he wasn't conceived after Damon met Cass. That would be an absolute tragedy and a disaster for their marriage."

"No, it was from years before ever he met Cass, and Damon readily admits to having slept with the boy's mother. But there's something else that is much more serious than Cass's potentially wounded ego."

"What could be worse than that?" Mom asked, sounding offended on my aunt's behalf.

"Proof that he is without question Damon's son. And why is that an issue, you ask?" Dad cut in before Mom could answer. "The line of succession is now in serious jeopardy."

"What proof?" I asked, and suddenly the dragon king tattoo flashed in my mind, the image seared into my brain like a blazing brand. It was from my dream. "No..." I gasped.

"No what?" Dad asked, his brow furrowing and my unexpected outburst.

"It's the tattoo, isn't it?" I gulped. "He bears the royal tattoo."

Dad nodded. "Yes, he does, as does Damon's oldest son with Cass, so it could be either of them that make a claim to the throne when the time comes."

"Oh, that *is* a pickle," Mom said. "Poor Cass." My parents continued to chatter about the royal bloodlines in hushed tones, but they shouldn't have bothered to try and conceal their conversation.

I couldn't hear what they were saying anyway over the sound of blood roaring in my ears, lost in my own thoughts. Fear and excitement shot through me in equal measures, making me shiver so hard I had to get up and walk over to the fire to calm myself.

Could Dad really be talking about the man I'd dreamed of last night? And every other night for the past week. He had long dark hair, bright, intense blue eyes, an incredible body, and the infamous tattoo of the dragon kings on his chest. I knew every dragon king and prince in our realm, and I hadn't recognized his face the first time I'd dreamed of him. And he still wasn't familiar. I'd assumed that meant he wasn't real, and merely a figment of my lonely and overactive imagination.

But what if he wasn't just a dream, after all, but a real man? An illegitimate prince of the North? My stomach tightened, and an unfamiliar heat blazed between my thighs, making my cheeks flush pink.

Holy crap. What do you do when dreams become reality?

TWO

Jaegar

The heat of the flames warmed my back as I stood by the fireplace, ready for the fight that was coming. I faced a group of people I never thought to meet, not by choice, at least. The reigning royal family, including a prince from Bravadok.

"So, Jaeeegarrrr..." the queen said, drawing my name out like she hadn't heard it said before.

"Jaegar," the king said quickly, his ice-blue eyes sliding to me, then back to his wife. "It's not a name you would have heard in the South."

I forced myself to stare straight ahead. I was named after a King of the

North, three generations back, and I was pretty sure the current king, Damon, knew that.

"Yes, Your Highness?" I said, raising an eyebrow at Queen Cass. "You were about to ask a question of me?"

She stared at me for another long moment before muttering a curse and walking away.

I stared after her and watched the people around me react with shock at her words.

"Aunt Cass," Prince Anselm said, his annoyance obvious.

The queen threw out her arm and pointed straight at me. "Look at him. Just look at him. He's got Damon's eyes, and that bloody thing he does with his eyebrow. I was hoping it wasn't true, but..." She crossed her arms over her chest and glared at me. "What do you want?"

I tried not to sigh too loudly, although the rush of air came out of me before I had a chance to stop it. "I never wanted to come here. My mother raised me with full knowledge of who my father was, but she is, well, *was*... proud."

The queen sank down onto the nearest couch, her face pale now. "I'm so sorry."

I nodded once in acknowledgement. "It's not the reason I'm here. I have no wish to take your son's birthright or throw your lives into a state of chaos, and I apologize for doing so." The last thing I'd ever wanted to do was come to the castle, announce my heritage, and have the king demand I strip to show them the proof of my lineage. It had been demeaning, and they were lucky I'd been able to hold my dragon shifter inside and hadn't accidentally destroyed their foyer.

"What is it you want, Jaegar?" King Damon, my sire, asked.

I stared at him, finally letting a skerrik of my dragon out. "You know, I thought you'd be taller."

The guy to my right snorted, then covered his mouth with his hand.

"Theo, this isn't funny," said Damon.

I gave my half-brother half a smile.

The guy stuck out his hand to introduce himself. "I'm Theo."

I shook his hand with another nod.

The crown prince indicated to the rest of the room. "This is my brother, Barry, and our cousin, Anselm, and his wife, Kayla."

I smiled at everyone in the room. "And Princess Veronica?"

"Our sister is travelling with her husband," Theo said.

"And this is Rocky," Kayla said, bouncing a gorgeous little boy on her hip.

"Hey, Rocky," I said, reaching out my hand.

The little boy grabbed my finger with the strength of a healthy child and gurgled with a delighted smile.

"Whoa, aren't you a strong boy?"

"Well, he's got that tattoo you all share," Kayla said, pulling aside the child's shirt to show me.

I stared at that tiny little mark, remembering all the years I'd spent covering mine up and wishing that my mother would just let me burn the stupid thing off.

"He's the next King of Bravadok?" I asked, and though I was trying to make the question sound jovial, even I could hear how stiff I sounded.

"He might be," Kayla said, holding her baby close. "I was just glad he had something that Anselm has," she said with such warmth as she glanced at her husband that I had to look away as envy twisted up in me and threatened to choke me.

"Yes, that must be nice," I managed to mutter.

"Maybe we should head home," Kayla said, putting a hand on Anselm's arm. "Give this family time before they travel for the party."

"The party?" the queen asked, throwing herself back and crossing her arms over her chest. "I'm not going anywhere—not with this hanging over the family."

I thrust a hand into my hair, frustration clawing at my gut. "I'm not here to hang anything over you... God. This was not how I wanted to do this." I'd rehearsed this conversation and many more, so many times in my head.

King Damon stepped closer. "Jaegar, tell us what you need."

I inhaled sharply and forced myself to say what I'd come here to say. "There are three reasons I'm here. Number one, I promised my mother I'd come and meet you all after she died. I'm not here to try and usurp the throne or anything. I don't want that." I shook my head violently. "It's quite the opposite. Why do you think I stayed hidden for so long?"

"Well, can I be the first to say it's nice to meet you," Barry said, smiling at me, albeit a little cooly. "But any particular reason your mother asked you to come up after she passed away, rather than before?"

I groaned at the question, as I didn't want to explain. I rocked back on my heels. "Because she was my only family. She was an orphan, without any siblings. She hated the idea of me being alone. Not that I care, of course, but she thought I needed family. And I promised. So, I'm here."

The rest of the room all looked at each other in a way that made my cheeks heat with blood.

Fuck!

I wasn't some pitiful case that needed them. This was my mother's dying wish, and if I'd loved her any less, I would have been able to ignore the request. "Look! It's not just that... I... fuck it. Forget about it." I couldn't do it. It was too difficult. My head felt like it was going to explode with the pressure of just being in the room, surrounded by them all—staring at me like I was some kind of unwanted freak. "Just forget I even exist."

I stormed for the huge double doors, my heart in my throat, ready to disappear once and for all.

But a mere breath later, King Damon flew across the room and stood in front of me, barring the way and blocking my path.

I skidded to a halt, so I didn't crash directly into him, my eyes wide. "Fuck, you're fast."

My sire lifted an eyebrow at as if to say, *"I'm the king, or did you forget?"* "You said there were three reasons you were here," he prompted.

I shook my shoulders, the hairs on the back of my neck bristling with unease as someone else approached. It was the younger of the two princes, Theo. He was about my height, which was saying something, as we weren't short men, and had kind, dark blue eyes.

"Please come back," he implored, gesturing to the couches behind us. "I know my family is a little full on, but trust me, you're lucky Veronica's not here. We're the calm bunch."

A strangled feminine giggle caught my attention, and I turned around to see a most unexpected sight, given my cold welcome.

The queen was snorting to herself on her chair as she waved me over. "Come back, Jaegar. Please forgive an old woman her jealousies. None of this is your fault."

I was drawn back to the center of the room despite my misgivings.

Anselm dragged a chair from the dining area over to the fireplace. "Here," he said, gesturing to it with a smile.

I sat, as did everyone else except the king.

He remained standing beside his wife, keeping a weathered eye on me.

I had to assume it was because he wanted the advantage if I tried to leave again. But I'd learned from my mistake. He was *fast*, shockingly so, and I'd need to be faster if I wanted to run.

The queen spoke again, her hand on her husband's. "Forgive me?" she asked again, hopefully.

I nodded stiffly, not sure how to respond to her earlier declaration. *Jealousies? What could she be jealous of?*

She was the one my father had ultimately married. She'd become queen, had three healthy children, *and* ruled over a formidable kingdom. We'd had next to nothing the entire time I was growing up. It'd been difficult and as a result, it'd made me hard, forging me into a dragon shifter not to be trifled with.

"What were the other two reasons you've come now?" Theo asked.

I sat up straighter, swallowing the lump in my throat. Now that my anger had somewhat dissipated, I was left with an unfamiliar discomfort. "Well, the second is that... well, Dymitri saw my tattoo the other day—he wasn't meant to—I'm generally very good at hiding it. But there was an accident, and my clothes were torn, and... he saw."

"Dymitri saw the tattoo?" the king asked, his lips twisting into a grimace.

I sighed. "He gave me three days to tell you, or he was, and I quote, 'dragging my sorry ass into the castle himself.'" I couldn't help but be proud that a man with such strength and integrity was my uncle. Sort of. I'd always admired Dymitri and his brother, Lucian.

The queen glanced up at her husband. "Sounds about right."

"And the third reason?" Theo asked, not letting it go.

I stared at the young prince. He was quietly tenacious, which I could see now. "Well," I coughed to clear my throat, embarrassment keeping me from announcing my news any louder. "I'm afraid that I have been dreaming of a woman. One that doesn't exist in this kingdom. Believe me, I've looked."

Anselm snorted out a laugh, unable to contain himself.

Kayla elbowed him sharply in his side. "Stop it! You princes are all the same."

The room went quiet, and I looked the human dead in the eye, my tone terse. "I'm not a prince. Never was."

"Oh, I'm sorry," Kayla said, glancing around the room, realizing her mistake. "I didn't mean…"

"It's fine sweetheart," Anselm said smoothly, gripping his wife's hand and glaring at me. "Jaegar wasn't born of the queen, but he has royal blood, which means his appetites are… healthy. You weren't wrong, my love, and there's no need to be sorry just because Jaegar is struggling with his identity. Is there, Jaegar?"

The chill that came over the room was notable, and I couldn't help but smile at the crown prince of Bravadok. That stare would have cowered many a man. But unfortunately for him, that wasn't me. I glanced across at Kayla and noticed the tears swimming in her eyes. That was what broke me. "I'm sorry, Kayla. Please forgive me for snapping at you. As the queen said, there are a lot of emotions here today."

Kayla flapped a hand at her face to banish her tears and prevent them from falling. "Oh, it's fine. Don't mind me. I'm just a bit emotional, that's all."

Anselm pulled his wife to his side and kissed her face.

She hugged her baby son to her chest, and a powerful arrow of understanding struck me straight in the heart. They were a family. A true, *loving* family. This wasn't a kingdom filled with arranged marriages and cold indifference.

There was so much love in this room, I was struggling not to crack and make a run for it again. "Forgiven?" I asked, my throat thick again.

"Oh, of course," Kayla repeated. "Now, keep telling us about the woman you were dreaming about before I rudely interrupted. I used to dream about Anselm too, before we met, and then long after, of course."

I shifted on my seat. That was what I was afraid of.

"Do you have a fated mate also?" Theo asked. "Dad's told us about them, and Iain said he dreamed of Veronica too. Isn't that right, Dad? It's a sign of a fated mate?"

Everyone turned toward King Damon, and the man nodded, not taking his eyes off me. "Yes. You're… what? Thirty-two, thirty-three, Jaegar? Without your mate you must be becoming frustrated."

"If that's what you want to call it," I answered, trying my best to keep my grouchy tone even.

"My father told us once that he was going half insane with loneliness before Marienne helped him find Mother. Perhaps she could also help you?" offered Anselm.

"Marienne?" I repeated. "The Queen of the Black Mountains?"

The queen stood up, slipping her hand into her husband's elbow crook. "Yes, Marienne, and her son, Anthony, have magic that helps them see the future. She told Stavrok that Damon and I were meant to be. Perhaps..." She glanced up at her husband. "You should come with us to the Kingdom of Bravadok in a few days. It is the triplets' thirtieth birthday, and everyone will be there. If your mate is among the nobility, she'll be present."

Everyone? As in all the kingdom's kings, queens, princes and princesses?

Oh, hell no.

I forced a smile on my face and shook my head. "Oh, I don't think—"

"Yes," the king said, cutting me off before I could finish. "That's a great idea, Cass. Marienne will be there, and she can help you, Jaegar."

"But..."

"You must come," Anselm said, standing up. "It is my birthday after all, cousin. I invite you."

I stared at the prince in front of me. Even my finest clothes would be considered rags to him. Surely, he didn't expect me to turn up at a party as the poor relation? "I can't," I said again. "I'm not family, and I wouldn't have a thing to wear to a party of that magnitude."

Kayla smiled at me sweetly. "I hate to tell you this, Jaegar, but you *are* family now. There's no point fighting it. Trust me, you won't win. These guys don't let you go once they've got you. Believe me, I've been there."

I got to my feet this time and gestured to my body. "Look, I appreciate the offer, but I cannot attend a royal party like this. I would not shame myself or bring dishonor to your family."

"Of course, you can attend," Anselm said. "Like Kayla said, you're not getting away from us now, not to mention that my sisters would kill me if I didn't bring you."

Kayla squeezed her husband's arm. "You look a similar size," she said observantly. "Perhaps Jaegar can borrow some clothes, honey?"

Anselm blinked at his wife, then at me. "Oh! Of course. If that's what you're worried about. I have—"

"No!" The king's voice boomed through the room.

We all stared at King Damon, who had frozen. "Apologies. All I meant was, my... son will have his own clothes. Isn't that right Cass, dear?"

The queen nodded. "Yes, of course. We have three days. That'll not be a problem."

"But... No... I can't..." I protested as they swept me away into their world.

Kayla walked over to me and put her hand on my shoulder. "Seriously," she advised. "Don't try and fight it. Just throw your hands up and enjoy the ride. It'll be a good one, I promise."

I stared at her, then back at the room full of now beaming royals.

Heaven help me. What have I gotten myself into?

THREE

Jaegar

Despite all my objections, Kayla had been right. The royal family were a whirlwind of power, and they wouldn't be denied. Anselm and his small family left for their home, and I was told that I had to stay in the palace.

"I have my own home, Your Majesty," I said as Queen Cass took me out of the main room and showed me to a guest room.

"I know you do," the queen said, "and call me Cass or Cassandra, if you want. You're my stepson, I suppose."

Now that we were alone, I felt I needed to apologize to her. Regardless of how well off she was, I'd upset the apple cart by showing up unwanted and unannounced. "Queen Cassandra—"

"Cass."

"Cass."

Damn, that feels weird.

"I owe you an apology. I know out of everyone, you are the most upset by the news of my existence. Believe me, if I'd been able to hide myself for the rest of my days, I would have."

The queen sighed and reached out a hand to touch my arm. "Jaegar, I never wanted to be a queen. I had plans to travel and see the world, much like Veronica, really." A soft smile graced her lips as she spoke of her daughter. "I never imagined I'd fall in love with the King of the North, whose kingdom was in complete disarray and this weather..." She shivered dramatically, acknowledging the cold.

I couldn't' help but laugh. The queen was a lot more relatable than I'd given her credit for.

"So, what I mean to say is"—she reached out and softly touched my face—"we never know where the future may take us, but I've learned to embrace the journey. Please don't think I am mad at you, or even your mother. I just... I was young and inexperienced when I met Damon, and I suppose I just ignored the fact that he was not. I always wanted another child. For some reason, I always saw us with four, but after losing several pregnancies after Veronica, we stopped trying."

I shifted a little where I stood, trying not to show the queen how uncomfortable I was. She was sharing very deeply personal information, and I wasn't quite sure how to respond, so newly welcomed into the royal fold.

She smiled. "I'm sorry, you didn't need to know any of that. All I mean to say is that you were obviously meant to be, Jaegar. So, please don't try to leave us now that you've finally found us. I'm not sure your father would allow you to get away, even if you wanted to."

"You know I'm not here to fight your son for succession," I said quickly when the thought occurred to me. "I don't want the throne. I'm just fulfilling my mother's dying wish, that's all."

Cass sighed. "I don't know the precise rules regarding succession, Jaegar, but you have the tattoo, and you are the eldest son."

"But—"

"Let's not worry about it for now," she said, pushing past me to open the doors to the largest, most opulently appointed room I'd ever seen. "I know it's not the most masculine room," she apologized, indicating the florals on the bedspread. "I'll have everything changed over tomorrow. But for now, you should be comfortable at least."

The fire in the grate was already burning, and the lights had all been lit. "You had this room prepared for me?" I asked, my heart twinging in my chest at the thought.

"Yes," she said simply. "After you arrived, I made a phone call to my cousin, then had the servants arrange this for you. Despite my foolhardy jealousies, I could see that Damon would want you to stay close. And more than anything, I want him to be happy. He's a good man and he deserves the chance to get to know you."

I nodded once. I knew that. Everyone in the kingdom knew the story of how he'd saved us from the wolves and rebuilt the kingdom from the ashes of the past. But that didn't mean I had to like him. Or forgive him for leaving my mother pregnant and alone. I wasn't sure I wanted to get to know him. All I wanted to do was respect my mother's memory and find my mate—the woman I'd be so feverishly dreaming of.

"Thank you, Cass," I said, walking over to the fire to warm myself.

"I'll have the royal tailor come by in the morning to measure you, and I'll see you at breakfast."

"You know you don't need to take me to the royal birthday party. That seems like a big step at this point in time," I tried again before she could leave.

Cass grinned at me from the doorway. "You're coming with us, Jaegar. You need to find your mate, and Marienne can help you, I'm sure of it. Plus, you never know... your mate may very well live in Bravadok."

"That would be handy. Then I wouldn't need to come home again." I regretted the barb when the queen's face fell. "Queen Cass, I—"

"No apologies," she said, holding her hand up in front of her. "I don't blame you for feeling unwelcome or unwanted. Not that it compares, but I was orphaned at a young age and remember the pain well."

"Oh, I'm sorry," I said, startled to hear such a thing.

"King Stavrok raised me as his younger sister, in a way, so I was very lucky. The royal families are all I've ever known, and for that, I am grateful."

I nodded my head, unsure of what else to say.

I'm such an ass sometimes.

"There's a private bathroom through that door," Cass said, pointing to a door I'd assumed was the closet. "So please, take a long shower, and get a good night's sleep. If I know Damon, he'll have a million questions for you over the coming days. He is very good at holding his armor in place and protecting his heart, but I have a feeling, Jaegar, that you are going to go crashing through those walls in record time."

"I..." I began to say, though I had no idea how to respond to such a thing. But I didn't get the chance to say anything more.

"Goodnight, Jaegar, sleep well." Then she left me in a room bigger than my whole house.

"Goddamn, this is crazy." I walked over to the door that she said was a bathroom and threw it open. "You've got to be kidding me." The bathroom was half the size of the bedroom and the biggest one I'd ever seen. "And this is just for guests?" I asked the emptiness, though as expected, it failed to provide me with an answer. I glanced at the bed, then back at the shower. I didn't want to use their fancy royal facilities, but I also didn't feel clean enough to sleep in their beds.

"Fuck it."

Talk about being stuck between a rock and a hard place.

I tore off my old, warm clothes, then piled them in the corner of the bathroom. The whole room was tiled with soft sandstone tiles and the floor beneath my feet was warm as I walked over the huge shower. The smell of my own body odor made me grimace.

I definitely need a shower.

I turned the knobs and adjusted the temperature until the water was just hot enough that I could step beneath the heavy spray without burning myself. The heat was heavenly, and the smell of sweet acid— ketosis—met my nostrils. I'd burned too many calories today. I'd barely eaten before arriving, then found dinner hard to swallow as the family had stared at me the whole time.

I'd sweated standing so close to the fire, but had found comfort in the move. Hearths were always safe spaces. I reached for the soap and started scrubbing away the sweat and grime of my day, even washing my long hair.

Once clean, I stood beneath the hot spray and just let the heat wash away everything, not just the suds, but also the despair and hope, fear and stress. And I remained there, just soaking, until there was nothing left but my tired body.

A vision of my woman came into my mind, and I groaned as my cock hardened in response. I'd dreamed of a dark-haired beauty for too many years to count. She had fair skin, eyes as blue as sapphires and long, dark hair that fell to her waist. She was the epitome of a gothic beauty.

I soaped up my hands and wrapped my fist around my cock. I'd searched for my mate for so long and had never found her. The loneliness was beginning to eat away at me. Anselm hadn't been wrong there. My age was advancing, as was the need for my mate. In my dreams she had lips painted red like berries, full and lush. Her body was slender but strong, and her nipples were a perfect treat for my mouth. I stroked my cock with long pulls, the pleasure tingling along my skin and making my balls tighten between my thighs.

I needed to find her—the woman who was destined to be my mate. And when I did, I would tangle my fingers in her hair and kiss her until neither of us could draw breath. Then I would lay her down and slide into her hot, wet, and welcoming body, fucking her until we both screamed out in ecstasy.

"Oh, God... fuck!" I gripped my shaft tight and pumped once more as my orgasm stole over me. Groaning softly, I watched as my seed pulsed out of me before the hot water washed everything away. I collapsed back against the tiled wall, letting the pleasure of my release eat away at every last remaining ounce of strength.

When I could finally open my eyes, I turned off the water and grabbed a towel. The material was the softest I'd ever felt, which for some reason, made me angrier than I could rationalize. Quickly drying myself, I turned off all the lights, then went into the bedroom. The bed was *massive*, far too big for one person, but there was no random woman to fill the space with tonight.

I threw back the heavy blankets and climbed underneath. The luxury of this room was overwhelming, and I rolled into my usual sleeping position so that I didn't think about the *what ifs* that had claimed my childhood. I'd always wondered how different my life might have been if my father had known of my existence. If my mother had just told him she was pregnant. Would I have grown up in the castle, surrounded by luxury and wealth? Would my parents have married and had more children, or would I still be the bastard I was today?

There were still so many questions, and as of yet, no answers in sight.

Perhaps there never would be.

And even if my sire managed to tell me the truth, would anything ever fill the gaping hole left inside my chest after all these years?

FOUR

Vanya

"But..." I stared at my sister-in-law, shocked by what she was telling me.

Kayla juggled Rocky on her lap and laughed. "But what?"

"But we can't have illegitimate kids. It's not what happens with fated mates, is it? I'm sure Dad always said..." I pressed my fingertips into my forehead where a headache pounded. My thoughts had been an absolute mess the last few days.

The door to the living room opened, and the rest of the family joined us.

I stood up, facing my parents who were walking into the room with Anselm at their side. "Hey, Dad, I thought you said that you couldn't have illegitimate kids if you were fated."

My dad's face went blank with shock at my unexpected question, then he walked over to the bar for a glass of whiskey.

I stared after him.

Did I say something wrong?

Mom came over to me, took my hand, then sat down on the couch. "Sweetheart, you need to relax. This is a lot to take in for everyone."

I ignored her placation and turned to Anselm. "Tell me about him. What's he like?" My heart was pounding like a dragon's wings reaching for the sky. Higher and faster, until I had to force myself to take a deep breath, for fear I'd suffer a heart attack before the answer was given.

"He's definitely stubborn, and a bit rough around the edges." Anselm reached out for Rocky, who went to his father with a giggle and a grin. "But he looks a lot like Damon. Same blue eyes and chin. Same height too, or maybe a bit taller even."

Mom gripped my hand tighter. "Of course, he's a bit rough around the edges, he grew up in poverty. Damon's been rebuilding his kingdom for thirty years, but there were many times when there wasn't enough food or shelter for the township."

"He's very handsome," Kayla said with a cheeky smile in my direction. "But he's got a chip on his shoulder the size of Texas, which isn't surprising, really. I can't imagine growing up like he did. Thinking he had to keep who he was a secret all those years."

"It's amazing that he managed for so long," Dad added with more empathy than I expected.

I bit my lip to keep from saying anything I'd regret.

"So, he's coming for the party then?" Mom asked.

I shot straight to my feet, my heart in my throat.

"Vanya! Are you okay?"

I hurried over to the fire, putting my hands out to warm them and settle my nerves. "Yeah, yeah, fine, Mom," I lied. "I'm just anxious about the party, let alone with a stranger coming." I turned around, letting the heat of the fire warm my back, and forced a smile to my face.

My dad frowned as he took a sip of the whiskey. "I'm not sure why

Damon wants us to invite him. It seems a more than a little bit out of line to me."

"Oh, honey, don't be like that," Mom said, walking over to our father to kiss him quickly. "This is Damon's *son*, regardless of his origins, and we should welcome him with open arms. No matter what the future brings, nothing good will come from shunning him."

Dad frowned. "But the lineage—"

"You know," Anselm interrupted, "Barry has never really wanted to be king. He and Theo often joke about abdicating and letting Veronica and Iain rule."

My jaw dropped. "You're joking?"

"No," Dad said, horror evident in his tone. "They can't do that!"

Anselm chuckled. "I'm serious. They're great guys, but they've never felt like being king was for them. Veronica's the strongest of the three, and with Iain at her side, they would make good rulers. I think part of them hopes that in time he'll step up and want to be king, so that they can get their wish."

"But Iain doesn't even want to be King of the North!" I exclaimed. This was getting out of control. How was everything suddenly so up in the air? It was like a cosmic earthquake had rocked the great dragon shifter families, and I wasn't sure I liked it. "Dad! Surely, this can't happen?"

My father rubbed his jaw as though he were thinking about it properly. "I don't know what can happen, Vanya. I was the only son, the only heir. I knew I was going to be king from the moment I knew how to speak."

"And I've always felt the same way," Anselm said, shrugging. "But what if this... how do you say his name again, Kayla?"

"*Yay-ger*," she answered, sounding his name phonetically.

"What if this Jaegar is meant to be king, Dad? He is the first-born eldest son. What then?"

The whole room fell silent, and I turned back toward the fire. I'd dreamed about my mate again last night, and it was the hottest dream I'd *ever* had. We'd enjoyed sex in a hot, steam-filled shower. And the things he'd done to me... I'd never experienced such things before. I was still mentally reeling.

"What are you thinking, sister?" Anselm called out.

I shook my head, unable and unwilling to share my inner most thoughts.

Not now, not ever!

"What's wrong, my daughter?" Dad asked, reaching out to touch my arm. "Surely, regardless of what happens, this won't affect our kingdom, so what worries you so much?"

Oh, God... he'll be here soon.

I couldn't tell him I feared that Damon's bastard son was my mate. So, I did the only thing I could do. I continued to lie. "I'm just worried about the party, Dad. This was meant to be a celebration for *us*, for everything great that has happened for our family, and now this... scandal..." My concerns made me sound more conceited than I was, but I couldn't reveal my suspicions.

"Don't you worry about it," our father said, tugging me in for one of his bear hugs. "I'll make sure that no one else finds out who Jaegar is, and I'll ask Damon to introduce him as a friend of the family. We'll keep the gossip to a minimum, I promise. All right?"

"All right, Dad," I said, closing my eyes and relishing my father's strength. I'd never known anything but unconditional love as a child. I couldn't imagine how Jaegar had grown up, knowing he was the bastard of the king and not being able to tell anyone. Kayla was right. It would have been a difficult life to endure.

I pulled back from my father's embrace and shifted the conversation slightly. "You know, there must be something in the Northern genes. With this son of Damon's, and Dymitri and Lucian being the sons of the old king, they seem to have sons everywhere they go."

Mom laughed, her eyes twinkling.

Dad smiled. "You know, you might just be right, sweetheart."

"Does anyone know when Jessa's coming home?" Kayla asked. "Is she flying over with Marienne on the day? Or earlier?"

There were only two days until the party, so unless she came today, she wasn't arriving early enough for me.

"They're all arriving the morning of the party. Marienne, Jessa and the twins are travelling by carriage," Mom said. "It will give us time to catch up before the other guests arrive and we can get ready together. The party starts at six, and although my original thoughts were to have a large sit-down dinner, I was told that a mingling party would be better. With lots of... what did you call it, Kayla?"

"Finger food!" Kayla said with a grin. "Though the way you guys do finger food puts every human restaurant I've ever seen to shame."

I managed a half-smile through the stress that was squeezing my chest. "Our men eat a lot," I said.

"Which means most of the finger food is just meat on sticks!" Kayla joked, though she was frowning as she looked at me, as if she were seeing something more.

"Well, there's only a few days to go," Mom said, clapping her hands.

The doors opened, and the servants all came in with dinner. Pots of soup, baskets of freshly baked rolls, and overflowing platters of crisp roasted vegetables and succulent meats. My father's all-time favorite spread.

"Let's eat," Dad said, taking Mom's hand and leading us all to the table.

We sat, were served, and began to eat. My stomach was gripped by anxiety, which meant I struggled to force anything down. But to avoid bringing further attention to my inner turmoil, I managed some clear, vegetable soup and a generously buttered bread roll, which for me wasn't bad.

"Are you feeling, okay?" Kayla asked from the place where she was sitting opposite me. We were at the far end of the table so Kayla could get up and attend Rocky if she needed to.

"Of course," I answered automatically. "How are you?" I glanced at Kayla's plate to find she only had some potatoes and bread. "Why aren't you eating?"

Kayla raised an eyebrow at me. "Why aren't *you*?" she countered. "I can tell you've lost weight again—and I know it's not to fit into some dress. What's wrong?"

I glanced over at Anselm, then back to Kayla. She was paler than normal, and her lack of appetite was unusual. Kayla was all curves like Mom and Jessa. She also wasn't drinking. Her wine glass was filled with water, which although it was not unusual for her to abstain from alcohol, it was creating a trail of clues I couldn't ignore. "Are you..." I didn't want to say the words "pregnant again", but from the way Kayla immediately colored bright red, I knew it was true.

"Don't tell anyone, please?" Kayla whispered across the table. "I don't want to take any of the attention away from the party."

I gaped at her. "Don't be silly!"

"What are you two talking about?" Anselm asked, turning around to question us, fork in hand.

Kayla gave me a small shake of her head.

I turned back to my brother as I grabbed another bread roll to pick at. "Nothing much. Just my lack of appetite. I'll be glad when this party has been and gone. You know how I get."

Anselm shrugged, seemingly satisfied, and went back to his discussions with Dad.

I grinned over at my sister-in-law, wanting to squeal with joy over how happy I was for her and my brother, but from the look on Kayla's face, I couldn't allow myself to show it just yet. So, I poured myself some wine and had some sips to keep the happiness locked away inside. I'd soon have another niece or nephew to dote on and spoil, which was the most wonderful news.

As the wine seeped into my soul and relaxed the ache in my chest a little, I turned to listen to my parents chatting about the kingdom and some of the meetings they'd attended during the day. The liquor worked its magic, warming my insides, and pushing away the fear and doubt of what was to come in the next few days. I'd never been one to pine away for my fated mate, but I couldn't deny that my loneliness of late had become intense. Especially with all three of my siblings being married.

My mind swam with questions. Could this Jaegar really be the man Fate had designed for me? Would I finally be happy and no longer feel so alone? What would he be like? Surely, someone who grew up in the poorest parts of Damon's Winter Kingdom would be so incredibly different from me that it would be shocking. And tough... God, he'd put my father to shame with how tough he would likely be.

We will have to be compatible if Fate means for us to be together...

I knew so little about my siblings Fated Mate journeys. Thinking back, I'd been shocked at just how quickly Jessa and Carlak had gotten together, and Kayla had just turned up pregnant and slid straight into our family.

Did they all have dreams about their mates before they met? Did they feel like they had a choice in the matter? And how did they bridge the gap between them?

Damn it, I really don't know anything about love. So much for being the daughter of a great love affair!

I glanced over at my parents and realized I really didn't know much of the things they'd overcome to be together. Perhaps it was time I asked. I needed answers more than I needed air at this point!

FIVE

Jaegar

Theo walked up next to me and bumped me with his shoulder.

I turned to glare at him.

He grinned up at me. "Are you sure you're ready for this?"

My answer came on swift wings. "Hell, no."

Theo laughed loudly and stripped off his shirt. The kid was well built but was still thin. "Veronica's going to be your biggest hassle. She won't know what to do with *another* big brother."

I looked away from his smiling face and began disrobing. Theo and Barry had already accepted me in a way that was as off-putting as it was mind-blowing. How could they just accept another brother? A bastard of all things? A man who could usurp their throne?

These men make no sense.

"You two almost ready?" Damon asked, stepping up beside us.

I nodded and swallowed hard. My father was a strong, large man who'd brought our kingdom back from the brink of complete destruction. He was respected by all, and I'd spent so many years hating him for not being there for me. It was a very strange feeling to be in his company now and to be wanted.

"Are Dymitri and Lucian coming?" I asked, coughing to clear the tightness in my throat.

"They're travelling by carriage, as their wives and children prefer it," Damon said. "So, they left days ago."

Barry came running up. "Sorry! Forgot something."

Damon nodded. "All right, you three go... Cass and I will be right behind you."

Queen Cass was nowhere to be found, and I had to assume that was due to my presence, although she'd seemed welcoming enough toward the end.

"Okay, let's do this." I stripped my too-clean body of the new pants I wore and walked through the open balcony door.

Damon's two other sons ran up behind me, standing shoulder to shoulder on the balcony.

"Let's do it," Theo said and began a count down. "Three..."

I dove straight off the side of the balcony without waiting, and closed my eyes as the wind came rushing past my face. My dragon clawed up to greet me, taking over my body. My eyes popped open as my wings materialized, stretching wide. The side of the castle's turret was straight ahead, and I banked sharply to the left, the stones missing my nose by a mere inch.

I flapped my wings and soared up and over the castle, climbing higher until I reached the clouds. Up here I was in heaven. Up here, I was free. Free from the weight of the world that had tried so hard to crush me since I was a child. As I settled and headed south, two male dragons drew up beside me, flying at my wings. I glanced over at them, their expressions impossible to read in dragon form, so I kept my head forward, flying in the direction of Bravadok.

We passed the Black Mountain Kingdom on the way, and we just kept heading south.

The dragon I believed to be Theo bumped my wing to get my attention at one point and began flying a slightly altered course.

I didn't fight him on it, having never been to any of the other kingdoms before. If he was saying King Stavrok's kingdom was that way, I'd follow. We flew on and on, until my wings ached, and I was sick to death of staring at the endless sea of trees and snow. Since flying was my freedom, it was not something I ever thought I'd find myself thinking.

The air felt warmer here, though the snow still fell. There was also much more greenery. Nature seemed to thrive in a warmer climate, where it wasn't as harsh. It had a chance to blossom, rather than merely survive, which was yet another thing I couldn't wrap my head around.

All I've ever done is survive.

Finally, up ahead, a large castle appeared. It was truly magnificent. It wasn't a crumbling, decrepit building in need of repair, but a huge, vibrant, and well-lit palace. The township below us was bustling and lively, with pops of color springing up in the form of swathes of fabric and blooming flowers.

I followed my half-brothers all the way to the top of one of the towers, letting them land first. I flapped my exhausted wings as they both shifted back to human form.

Servants appeared instantly, coming to attend to them with large, warm robes.

When they were finally safe indoors, I let my body drop, landing on the stonework, and my dragon withdrew. The air was so warm here that I barely shivered as the same servants offered me a large black robe of my own.

"Thank you." I took the robe and slipped it on, wrapping the tie before anyone could see my nude body.

"Come in," Theo called from the glass door.

"After you," I told the young male servant as he hurried indoors once more. I shut the glass door behind me, then came face-to-face with none other than King Stavrok, himself.

"You must be Jaegar," he said.

There was no one else this man could be. He was well into his older years, with graying hair and the battle of years upon his face. But he was dressed well, and he was as tall as me, looking me straight in the eye with a keen intelligence I hadn't seen often before.

"Yes, Your Majesty," I said, dipping my head, though I bowed to no one.

"You let them land first," he observed. "Why?"

I lifted my head and frowned at him. "It was the safest way."

"Weren't you tired?" he pressed.

I shrugged. I was fucking exhausted from that flight but wouldn't give him the satisfaction of knowing that.

We stared at each other for several moments before Theo broke the tension.

"Jaegar, this is our Uncle Stavrok."

The king glanced over at Damon's son, then back at me. Long, assessing moments passed before he stuck out his hand in welcome. "Call me Stavrok."

I nodded and offered him my own in return.

His hands weren't soft as I'd expected of a King of the South, but strong and roughened as though he trained daily. There was a strange look in his blue eyes. If I didn't know better, I'd say there was a growing respect kindling there, but that didn't make any sense. He didn't know me.

"Stavrok, are they here?" a woman called out, walking along the hallway. A very curvy older woman dressed in a royal purple dress stepped up next to Stavrok, a large grin on her pretty face. "Hello. You must be Jaegar. It's so nice to meet you. I'm Lucy."

This time, I offered a semi-bow. The human that had managed to claim and tame the heart of the king deserved it. "Hello," I managed to say, though I couldn't help but look around for my half-brothers, who'd disappeared.

"The boys have probably run off to look for Iain or Anselm," Stavrok said, noticing my gaze.

I clenched my jaw to stifle the groan that rose. They'd run off and left me with a foreign king and queen? Did they not know anything about me?

"Are Damon and Cass far behind you?" Lucy asked, her manner soft and friendly.

I glanced out the large window behind us, not seeing anyone yet. "Damon said they wouldn't be long."

"And how are you doing with everything?" the queen asked.

I raised my eyebrows. "In regard to?"

She laughed, "Ah... joining the royal family as the illegitimate, eldest son?"

I blinked at her.

The king took pity on me and put his arm around his wife. "Apologies. Lucy doesn't beat around the bush, as the human saying goes. Leave him be, wife."

"But I might not get any time with him later once everyone else arrives." Lucy pouted. "I understand it's a sensitive subject over here, but it's not as big a deal where I come from."

I couldn't help but smile at her. My illegitimacy was a huge deal for me, and I'd spent my life running from the implications of my birth. But I could also see the queen wasn't trying to offend. She was from a completely different realm, so I understood her curiosity. "Well, to answer the question, it has been an interesting few days, to say the least."

Lucy grinned at me warmly. "I can imagine. Your clothes arrived this morning, by the way. So, I'll show you to your room, if you'll follow me?" The queen moved to step away from her husband.

The king made a soft growling noise.

I couldn't help the reciprocal noise I made in response.

The king's eyes widened for a moment before he nodded his head at his wife. "Lucy, sweetheart, you stay here and greet Cass and Damon when they arrive. I'll take Jaegar to his room."

She raised an eyebrow at him as if unimpressed. "Do you even know where he's sleeping?"

The king rolled his eyes and got directions.

Meanwhile, I watched the entire exchange with fascination.

When they were finally done, the king clapped me on the shoulder, and we were walking down the corridor and away from the queen.

I didn't say anything at first, unsure how to approach the fact that I'd just growled at the King of Bravadok. Was that a punishable offense here?

"I'm glad you came," Stavrok said once we turned a corner and headed down a second corridor. "It took courage to seek Damon out after so many years."

I huffed a little. "Yeah, that or stupidity."

He stopped aside a dark wood door, then stared at me with an intense gaze. "Do you want the crown?" he asked.

I flinched, though I didn't mean to. "Hell, no. I never wanted anything from him."

Stavrok stared at me for another moment, then nodded. "We've got a few hours before the party, so take your time getting ready. We'll see you tonight." Then he nodded and walked away.

I watched him go because it had been a long time since I'd seen a man with the sort of strength he had. When I pushed open the door to *my room*, I stood and gaped. It wasn't quite as big as the bedroom I'd been given at Damon's palace, but considering how many people would be staying at the castle, I was shocked to see I wasn't sharing with Theo and Barry. The traitors had left me the moment they could.

Bloody bastards.

I shut the door and wandered around the space. The carpet beneath my feet was lush, and the drapes were thick and made of velvet. Everywhere you looked in this castle there was a painting or a vase, or some expensive looking trinket. It was much more opulent than the Winter Palace, that was for sure.

I checked the adjoining doors and found a small but well-appointed bathroom, for which I was grateful. I didn't want to be wandering the halls of the palace in a bath towel. After a short, hot shower, I lay down on the bed and closed my eyes. My new clothes that Queen Cass had ordered for me were hanging near the fireplace, so I had time to relax.

I didn't mean to fall asleep, but I dozed, swimming in and out of dreaming. And there she was, my fated mate. Her long, dark hair trailing over her back as she walked away from me. I reached out for her, but she threw me a soft smile and sashayed away, always just out of reach.

When my body finally felt rested, I rolled to my feet and stood by the fire, listening to the sounds around me. There were people walking above my head, and others running down the hallway outside the door. I'd lived in a tiny house my whole life, with no one except my mother for company.

It was time to do something I never thought I'd do. I was putting on royal clothes and playing dress up, going to the birthday party for the triplets of Bravadok. I reached for my tuxedo and grimaced. Would this town house the woman of my dreams? Would I finally be able to assuage

the loneliness in my soul? Or would this gamble of exposing my identity
bite me in the ass like I always thought it would?
　　Only time will tell...

CHAPTER
SIX

Vanya

I'd spent the day with Jessa and her babies, cooing over my niece and nephew until they were exhausted and fast asleep in their cribs.

"Can you believe Mom kept our cribs from when we were babies?" Jessa asked with a laugh, walking over to the mirror in the corner of my room.

"Ah... yeah I can, actually," I said with a laugh. "Mom's sentimental in that way. You know that."

Jessa was dressed in a long, flowing sapphire blue dress that accentuated her tiny waist and abundant curves.

I couldn't help what came out of my mouth next. "Your boobs look so *amazing* in that dress. Are you sure Carlak is okay with that much cleavage being on display?"

Jessa glanced down at the mounds of flesh poking out from her scooped neckline, then laughed. "He doesn't get a say in my wardrobe," she answered, poking out her tongue. "But the worst part is this isn't even half of them. Since breastfeeding the twins, I've gone up two cup sizes!"

"I'm so jealous." I stared down at my own flat chest.

Jessa scoffed. "Well, I'm jealous of you, Miss Skinny Mini. Enjoy the fact you don't need to wear a bra. It must feel amazing." She sighed with another glance down at her ample breasts.

I turned around to check out the back of my dress and smiled at my sister. "Well, I suppose there are pros and cons to both."

Jessa and I were complete opposites when it came to our physical forms. We didn't even look like sisters, let alone twins. I was the dark to her light. She was bright and curvy, and I was pale and waifish.

"Are you sure you're okay?" Jessa asked me suddenly. "You've seemed a little... off today."

"I'm fine," I managed to say, but my sister knew me better than that.

She sat on the couch and stared at me, undeterred. "You're not, that much is clear. What's going on, Van?"

I shook my head. "Stop it, Jess. My makeup's done, and if you make me cry, I'll be mad."

She stared at me a while longer before sighing and standing up, admitting to temporary defeat on my behalf. "All right... but I've spoken to Carlak about staying here for a few weeks so we can talk. I've missed you and I've missed my home."

I charged at my sister and hugged her tightly.

"Whoa." She giggled as she hugged me back.

"I've missed you," I said as I fought back the wave of tears that threatened to spill and ruin my makeup.

"Well, I'm not going anywhere," she assured me, pulling back and squeezing my hands. "You'll be begging me for some peace and quiet after a few days, mark my words."

"Doubtful," I countered. "Very doubtful." As we smiled at each other, there was a knock on the door. "Come in."

It was Anselm, dressed in his finest black suit. He looked absolutely smashing. "Are you two ready?" he asked as he stepped into the room.

I kept hold of my sister's hand and walked over to our brother. "This reminds me so much of our twenty-first."

Anselm nodded. "Yeah, me too. Boy, how things have changed, hey?"

I glanced at Jessa, then back at Anselm. "For you two, maybe."

Anselm's eyes widened, then he stumbled. "Oh, I didn't mean... I'm sorry, sis."

I reached out and squeezed his hand too. "It's fine. One day I'm sure things will change for me too." My heart certainly knew that it would, but my stubborn head was mired with negativity. It *felt* like things would never change.

Jessa slid her hand around my arm and grinned at me. "Well, shall we get this party started?" she offered.

Anselm arched an eyebrow. "Same entrance as always?"

I chuckled. "Why not?" I wasn't one for being the center of attention, but when I was one of the triplets, I never worried about facing the world. When we were together, I felt strong, like I could handle anything—even if I wasn't ready.

We walked down the hallway and toward the doors to the small balcony. My breath hitched in my throat, and I stopped, unable to take another step before asking the question on the tip of my tongue. "Have either of you seen Jaegar yet? Is he here?"

Anselm frowned at me. "I haven't, but don't worry, sister. He won't ruin the party. Despite everything, I think you're going to like him."

I sucked in a breath and nodded. I wasn't afraid of that.

I'm afraid of the opposite being true.

My heart raced.

Am I ready to meet the man who I think could be my fated mate?

Anselm stepped forward and opened the doors, pushing them wide and holding out his hand to me. The sounds of the crowd from beneath built to a roar, until suddenly there was a round of shushing, and the room fell silent.

I glanced at Jessa, and together we walked out onto the balcony that overlooked the enormous ballroom, smiling and waving as the festive space exploded with a deafening round of applause. My belly tightened and dropped as I searched the room expectantly for an unknown face.

"Let's go," Jessa said, tearing me away from my perusal, and down the steps into the ballroom below.

Why can't I see him? What does he look like? I thought I'd know him, or feel him, straight away. Maybe Jaegar isn't the fated mate I'd thought he was?

Mom and Dad were waiting at the bottom of the steps to give us hugs and kisses and to say "happy birthday" for the second time today.

Kayla stepped up next to Anselm, looking pale but beautiful. No one else might have noticed, but it seemed obvious to me that morning sickness was likely wreaking havoc with her.

"Oh, your dress is lovely, Kayla," I said, giving her a warm smile.

Carlak stepped up to draw Jessa into his side. "Happy birthday, Vanya. You look as beautiful as ever."

"Doesn't she?" Jessa said, grinning at me with her normal levels of pride and happiness.

"We all look beautiful," I responded, gesturing to all the women in the group. "And I'm just so glad we're all here together for such a special milestone."

"Speaking of," Carlak said, "Anthony and Charity were asking for us. Shall we go speak to them?"

Jessa nodded and headed off with Carlak at her side.

Then Anselm bowed out with Kayla to go and speak to other guests and perform the usual meet and greets.

And that meant I was left with my parents and a heavy feeling in the pit of my stomach. I felt so incredibly left out that it set off a pang in my heart that almost had me clutching at my chest.

I'm alone.

Mom's gaze slid behind us, and a huge smile lifted her lips. "Vanya, come and meet Jaegar. I know you've been wanting to make his acquaintance."

I froze and a whole-body shiver coursed over me, making the hairs on my arms prickle. My breathing grew shallow, and my stomach instantly filled with the sensation of a million chaotic, fluttering butterflies.

"Are you okay?" my mother asked with a look of concern.

But before I could answer her, I looked over my shoulder and slowly turned around. There, before me, standing next to Uncle Damon, was the man from my dreams. He had long, beautiful dark hair, and eyes as bright as the sapphires in my father's crown. "It's you," I breathed, my heart in my throat.

He opened his mouth to speak but was interrupted.

My father reached out to grab my arm, shocking me.

Any words Jaegar had planned to say were lost to a feral warning growl.

My father responded in kind, not letting my arm go.

Jaegar's eyes flashed from blue to silver in a mere second. He looked strong, predatory, and incredibly handsome as his inner dragon reared up within him.

My heart jumped with adrenaline, racing inside my chest like a prized stallion. If I didn't stop this, we'd end up with two fighting dragons in a room filled with people. "No!" I found the courage to say and put out a hand toward Jaegar. "Stop. He's my dad. He won't hurt me." I tugged my arm, but my father refused to let go. Then help came from an unexpected place.

"Stavrok, let her go," Mom said, her voice soothing. "Jaegar's not going to hurt her. You know that. Now, calm down." Mom tugged at Dad's arm until his fingers loosened their grip.

I stumbled toward Jaegar the moment I was freed.

He grabbed my arm and pulled me to his side so fast I was seeing stars. His arm went around my body, holding me so close, protecting me and shielding me from the world.

In such close proximity, I could smell his skin and feel his heat beneath his shirt. I didn't know this man, but as a soft moan left my lips, I tucked my nose into his neck and took a deep breath.

It's him. My mate.

My heart sang. I knew it beyond doubt. He smelled like home.

This time Jaegar's growl was more like a rolling purr, and he wrapped his second arm around me as well. "I found you," he said, sounding as though he was panting or in shock. His chest was rising and falling too fast, and although part of me was afraid that he'd shift, the dragon shifter part of me was blissfully happy at the fact.

Mom walked closer, despite my dad calling out to her. "Jaegar, sweetheart..." she was saying softly. "Can you control yourself? Or do you need to get outside?"

Jaegar was trembling and the sheer power that it took to hold his dragon inside made me smile. He was so impressive.

"I. Don't. Know," he admitted, each word punctuated with a labored and desperate pause.

Mom continued. "Vanya... darling... I think you're going to need to wake up and help Jaegar out here. I'm not a dragon, but you are. Do you know what he needs?"

I opened my eyes and stared up at him. My blood was hot, flowing in my veins like lava, and every part of me was intoxicated by the mere scent of him. I'd found him.

Finally. He's real.

"He'll need to shift," Damon interjected from beside us.

I hadn't even realized he was still there.

Jaegar wasn't growling at his father, which was interesting, but his hands tightened on me.

"Do you want to fly with me?" I whispered. "We could both go."

"My. Clothes. Queen. Cass," Jaegar gritted out as he battled for control.

Damon chuckled softly. "She won't care if you tear them to shreds, but if you have the control, Stavrok might have somewhere nearby that you can both safely disrobe before shifting."

Jaegar nodded in a jerky fashion. "Yes. Please. *Now.*"

Mom began to walk backward. "Come on. The south balcony. Quickly!" She gestured toward us, encouraging us to follow.

But Jaegar didn't move.

Somewhere deep in my foggy, intoxicated brain, I knew he needed my help. It was my turn to step up and guide my mate. "Come on, let's get out of here," I said to him, lurching after my mother. "Jaegar. *Please.*"

That got him moving. He followed me by sheer force of will, still clinging to my hands, refusing to let me go for a single moment.

Mom and Dad hurried ahead, pushing open the doors to the balcony, then pulled the curtains shut around us once more.

I burst through the curtains and inhaled sharply as the cold air blasted me in the face. It was an incredibly welcome relief to the fire I felt blazing inside.

Jaegar was already undressing, tugging at his clothes urgently as he tried to disrobe without ruining what I had to assume were very new clothes.

He was out of his jacket, vest, and shirt, the items thrown back toward the door over his shoulder. Then he set to work on getting out of his pants.

I stood back and let my gaze soak in the wonder that was my mate. He was magnificent. So huge, broad and muscular. He was literally what dreams were made of.

He momentarily turned away, so I only saw the clench of his too tight, too perfect ass, before he leapt into the air and shifted into a massive, silver-tipped dragon. Spiraling up into the air, he hovered, waiting for me.

I stared up at him, mesmerized and shivering as the cold began to seep into my body.

"Vanya?" Mom called out. "Are you going too?"

Heedless of whether my parents were watching, I simply nodded my head and unhooked the clasp at the nape of my neck, letting the dress slither to the ground. I wasn't wearing a bra, and my nipples were already tight and hard. I didn't bother with my black lace panties. I just let my dragon rise up inside my body, tearing the material apart as she broke free. I flapped my wings, and with a song in my heart, I took to the sky, chasing my fated mate into the clouds.

CHAPTER
SEVEN

Jaegar

I flew through the winter sky, my beautiful mate on my tail. In this form, all I could feel was happiness. I had no worries. There was only beauty and pleasure. It was everything I'd ever hoped for and more.

We flew up and around the castle, moving away, then flying back. Tumbling through the air and dancing through the clouds. But where should we go? I didn't want to go back to the party, and I didn't think my mate wanted to, either. But my home was too far, and as soon as I shifted back to human, I knew that I'd want my mate. Naked and in a warm bed —in that order.

Finally, we spiraled down together into the courtyard at the castle, and my mate released her dragon, shifting back into her human self. Her naked, human self. She was slender, with just the barest hint of curves, but undeniably beautiful. Her long, dark hair flowed over her body, covering her breasts. She looked like a pale, Gothic goddess.

I let go of my dragon too, knowing full well my cock wouldn't be soft.

We stood there for a time, staring at each other, caught between worlds, neither of us daring to move or breathe.

Then the door opened, and servants rushed out with robes.

My mate cast me a final, longing glance, before bustling inside and into the warmth of the castle.

I took my time, pulling the robe on and letting my body cool down, literally and figuratively. When I finally walked inside, the servants shut the doors behind me.

My mate was standing nearby, shivering hard. The poor thing didn't have an ounce of body fat to help keep her warm.

I couldn't stop myself. I walked over to her and wrapped my arms around her, tugging her into the heat of my body. "Are you all right?" I asked.

She nodded but didn't curl into me the way she'd done when we'd first met.

I smiled, unable to be sad at this moment. "You know, I don't actually know your name."

She chuckled and lifted her head, staring at me with big, soulful eyes. "I'm Vanya."

"Vanya..." I let the name roll off my tongue, enjoying the sound. Where had I heard that name before? "How are you related to everyone here?"

Her dad... she'd said someone was her dad. Who was it? I shook my head, trying to clear away the fog that surrounded our meeting.

Her jaw dropped open, and her eyes widened. "Weren't you here when I opened the party?"

I shook my head. "No, I was talking with Theo outside. Why? Did you—"

The doors to the small room burst open and two women came rushing in.

"Everyone but Jaegar and Vanya, out."

They weren't just two women. They were queens. Cass and Lucy both hustled over to us, their arms laden with clothes.

"We thought it safer for us to come than your fathers," Lucy said with a smile. "We figured we'd be less likely to set off Jaegar's shifter again."

"Thanks, Mom," Vanya said, reaching for her incredibly sexy, tight dress.

"Mom?" I repeated. "Lucy's your... mom?"

How the hell did I miss that?

Lucy laughed softly. "Did you think your fated mate would be a commoner?"

"Well... yes," I said. "Because I'm a..."

Lucy and Cass exchanged glances.

Vanya turned away to slip her dress back on, demonstrating a little modesty in front of the queens.

I forced myself not to stare as her robe dropped to the ground.

"Vanya is one of my triplets," Lucy said, grabbing my attention. "And her younger brother, Iain, is married to Veronica."

I pressed my lips together, holding in any cracks about things getting a bit incestuous. Fate obviously wanted our bloodlines joined. "Okay." I didn't know what to say or think. My mate was a princess? A princess of an incredibly wealthy kingdom?

I began to shake my head. "No... Wait. Hang on." And then as the haze of our meeting cleared, I recalled what Vanya had said when I'd growled. Stavrok was her father.

Holy shit.

Vanya was never going to agree to come back with me to live in a one-bedroom shack in the poorest part of the Winter Kingdom. Her bathroom would be larger than my whole plot of land.

"You're not a commoner, Jaegar," Vanya said, and it was the first time I'd heard her real voice. She was strong and commanding. She stared at me with a piercing gaze. "You're the eldest son of the King of the North, Jaegar. And you're my mate."

I looked from her to Lucy, to Cass, then back to Vanya once more. "Your father really is—"

"King Stavrok," she said with a nod and another lift of her proud chin.

I ran a hand through my hair, my arm shaking as I gave voice to my earlier thought. "Holy shit."

This time Lucy laughed, loudly. "You've got that right. Now... Jaegar, get dressed and come and rejoin the party. Then we can all work out where you're going to sleep tonight."

I frowned at the queen. "But I've already been assigned a bedroom."

Lucy and Cass exchanged a long, knowing look before Cass turned to me. "You have... and you're totally fine with sleeping alone tonight?"

My gut churned at the idea, and my gaze slid across to my mate, the heat of desire rising within me once more.

"Exactly," Cass said with an understanding little chuckle. "We were fated mates of dragon kings back in the day too. We know we won't be able to keep you two apart long."

Vanya growled a little. "Mother! We just met. You don't think—"

"Oh, I know, darling daughter," Queen Lucy said with a wide grin. "I remember what it was like all too well. But anyway, I think we need to give Jaegar a moment and then return to the party."

Lucy and Cass walked toward the door.

Vanya meandered behind them extremely slowly. She was playing with her hair and adjusting her dress, even though she looked absolutely perfect.

"I won't be long," I said, forcing a smile to my frozen features. How cruel could Fate be to me? My mate couldn't be the Crown Princess of Bravadok. That made no sense. And what it meant for my future was as scary as it was baffling. I'd grown up poor, while the princess had grown up entitled and rich.

I wasn't interested in living anywhere other than my mother's small, humble cottage, whereas I was almost certain that Vanya would want to live here and remain in her father's castle. Or at the very least, she'd likely expect to live in the Kingdom of Winter's refurbished castle.

We don't suit, not at all.

My head pounded, and I dressed slowly, giving myself time to think of a solution, or at least, my next few steps forward. And when no path made itself clear, I paced in front of the fireplace, unable to do what needed to be done.

"What are you doing in here?" My father's voice was so new to me, and yet so familiar somehow.

I mutely nodded, because there was no answering that question.

Damon walked up to me, and as I stared into the flickering flames of the fire, his shoulder pressed against mine. "Tell me what's going through your head."

It sounded like a command, and yet I heard the question behind the tone. "I... don't know," I said, then added, "and that's not my cowardly way of lying, because I really... don't know. It's blank inside my head and cold. I feel lost."

"You're afraid," Damon said, "And that's understandable. You spent your whole life on the outskirts of the city when you should have been in the palace. You were born a bastard when you should have been a prince."

I rolled my eyes and turned to the man I should have called my dad all these years. "I was never meant to be a prince."

Damon lifted his hand and stabbed me in the chest with his finger. "Well, that tattoo says otherwise. You can hate me all you like—fight me all you want—but as a man who has felt the pull of a fated mate in my life, I can tell you, son, you're not winning this battle. Even if you are stupid enough to run away from Vanya."

I glared at him and pushed his arm away, my temper flaring in my frustration. "I'm not stupid. And I don't run."

"Then get back out there," Damon said with a head flick towards the door. "Go and show those royal, uppity asshats that you've got more class than all of them combined."

I crossed my arms over my chest and glared at him. I didn't have the guts to tell him that not only did I not have the class, but also did not I want to go out there again. But I'd done lots of things in my life that I didn't want to, and this was going to be one of them. A man always rose to the occasion, even if it killed him. "Okay, fine. I'll go back out there and smile and pretend like everything's fine."

Damon chuckled. "Well, you don't need to pretend anything. Just don't run, okay? And maybe speak to Carlak. You might just find he may have a similar story to share."

"And Carlak is?"

Damon sighed. "Carlak is the Crown Prince of the Black Mountains—Marienne and Erik's eldest son."

And he has a similar story? That, I'd like to hear.

I nodded my head at him. "All right. Introduce me, please."

Damon nodded and turned toward the door. "Then come."

I followed him, though it irked me to do so, back into the fray, the heat, and the noise. There was nothing like the sound of dozens of people talking and music pounding in a room that still somehow seemed too small for so many personalities.

Damon made his way to the edge of the room where three young men stood, all a few years younger than me. "Carlak, this is Jaegar," Damon said, nodding between us. "I told him you'd tell him about what happened on the triplets' twenty-first birthday, while I deal with Stavrok. I'll be back." Damon turned on his heel and left me with three men, probably all princes.

I forced a smile to my lips. "Hi, I'm—"

"You're Damon's son," Carlak said, nodding his head at me, then indicated to his side. "This is my brother, Anthony."

"Nice to meet you both."

Anthony held out his hand to me.

I reached out, not willing to refuse an introduction to the Prince of the Black Mountains. But the moment my hand connected with Anthony's, I was thrown into the future. I gasped as my eyes slid shut, and a vision projected into my mind of a castle bedroom. Vanya was there, lying on the bed, crying out in pain. It was immediately evident she was in labor. Her belly was huge and swollen, and there was an alarming amount of blood on the bed.

"No!" I said out aloud and tried to pull my arm back.

"Wait!" Anthony grabbed hold of my arm with his other hand, unwilling to let me go.

My heart pounded in my chest as I waited to see if my mate was going to die. But the door opened, and I watched myself as I raced in, followed by Lucy and another woman I'd never seen before. Then people surrounded her, and I watched as Vanya pushed and strained a child into the world. A squalling, crying, happy baby that was lifted straight onto their mother's chest.

My heart swelled and tears burned in my eyes. There I was, a woman in my arms and a new baby to live for. A family.

My own family.

Anthony finally released me, and the vision faded.

"No..." I whispered as my waking vision returned and I was back in the real world, my future now nothing but a hazy image in my mind. "How..."

Anthony rubbed his hands together and smiled, a faint purple light glowing in his eyes.

"What are you?" I asked, a shiver coursing up my spine and making my shoulders shake.

"I'm a sorcerer," Anthony said as he tilted his head. "*And* a dragon shifter."

"And my husband," said a soft, female voice from the side.

I looked to my right and a beautiful woman glided up next to Anthony and slid her hand around her husband's arm. "You must be Jaegar. You're the talk of the party."

I groaned. "I didn't want that."

She smiled at me, and her eyes lit up. "You're also fated to... Vanya. Is that right?"

Carlak stared at me, his shock a palpable thing. "You're... what?"

Anthony smiled sincerely, and I had to assume that he'd shared in the vision he'd shown me. "She's waited a long time for you."

I cleared my throat loudly and looked at Carlak. "Damon said that you would share an experience with me that was similar."

Carlak nodded, suddenly as serious as the grave. "Yes. The triplets' twenty-first birthday was when I realized that Jessa was my fated mate."

There was a moment of silence, and they stared at me as though I should say something.

"Ah... okay."

Anthony's wife chuckled. "Jessa, Anselm, and Vanya are the triplets."

I began to understand. "So, Jessa is married to the Crown Prince of the Black Mountains, and Anselm married a human?"

"And Veronica is married to Iain," Carlak reminded me. "So your families are intrinsically linked."

More than I ever imagined.

"What happened on the night of their birthday?" I asked, curious more than anything else.

Carlak's lips twisted as he recalled his evening with his mate. "I got so drunk, I could barely see straight, but it helped keep my dragon in check."

"Why didn't I think of that?" I muttered, shaking my head.

Anthony laughed. "Your path is different from Carlak's."

"And how fixed are your visions?" I asked the young sorcerer. "Does what you see always come to pass?"

Anthony pressed his lips together into a thin line. "I don't know if, I'm honest. I'd have to ask my mother to know for sure. Her magic is far greater than mine."

"But if you had to guess?" I pressed, my stomach churning over the fading image of my own little family.

Long moments passed before Anthony finally answered me. "Things can always change."

And that was exactly what I was afraid of.

EIGHT

Vanya

My whole body ached for Jaegar's touch, though the more reserved royal in me didn't want to admit to it so readily.

"Here, drink this," Jessa said, thrusting a glass of champagne into my hand. "Though you may need something stronger, if memory serves."

I took a big sip then glanced over at her. "What do you mean?"

Jessa sighed wistfully. "On our twenty-first birthday I looked at Carlak and knew he was meant to be mine. I'd never felt anything like it. The feeling of when he first touched me... it was like lightning sizzling over every inch of my skin." She ran her hands up and down her arms and shivered as though remembering.

I smiled at my sister. "I never knew that. You've never talked much about it, to be honest."

Jessa shrugged. "We were young, and I was so worried about leaving you and Anselm. We'd never been apart until I found my mate. It seemed cruel in a way, to be separated."

It was my turn to heave a sigh. "It's worse being the one left behind, believe me."

Jessa stepped beside me and rested her arm against mine. "You're not being left behind anymore, Vanya. And Damon's eldest son, of all people. It's quite *scandalous*." She flicked her eyebrows up and down in a suggestive manner.

I couldn't help but laugh. "Scandalous. Me? That seems ridiculous somehow."

"Have you two arranged to meet up later this evening?"

I turned to frown at her. "Why would I?"

Jessa burst out laughing and almost snorted, her eyes twinkling with mirth. "Oh, sis! You won't be able to stay away from each other. The fated mate bond doesn't ask your permission. It just claims you, body, mind, heart, and soul."

"It certainly doesn't," I muttered. "Poor Jaegar barely contained his dragon. He would have destroyed the room if his control had been weaker."

"Well, that would have been memorable."

I opened my mouth to ask another question about Carlak, when Marienne and Erik sashayed over, arm in arm.

"Happy birthday, beautiful girl," Marienne said, leaning forward to kiss me, having already spent time with Jessa tonight.

"Thanks, Aunt Marienne."

Marienne and Erik exchanged a glance before Marienne looked over at me, her eyes twinkling with mischief. "I hear Jaegar has finally found you."

I stared at her with my jaw dropped. "You knew?"

Jessa gaped at her mother-in-law, "Why didn't you say anything?"

Marienne reached out and squeezed my hand. "I've been having dreams...

visions of Jaegar over the years. I didn't know what they meant at first, they weren't very clear. But when I heard that Damon's son had come out of the stonework, so to speak... I knew that he was the man I'd been dreaming of."

I swallowed down the feelings of unexpected hurt and betrayal that rose up within me. If I'd known my fated mate was out there, I could have gone and found him sooner.

I've been alone so long while everyone else has already started families...

"Why didn't you tell me?" I asked, unable to keep the accusatory tone from my voice.

Marienne bit her lip. "Because I wasn't sure if Jaegar would ever choose to come forward. To declare who he was. Your path with him hasn't been clear to me. Not until tonight."

"Why tonight?" I asked, biting back on my aggravation.

"He saw you," she said simply. "Now that he's touched you, he won't run. Not again."

"Again?" I repeated, dumbfounded.

"Well... Jaegar's attempted to speak to Damon many times in the past, but his pride has always gotten in the way. Now that he knows that *you* are his future, he can step into his true role."

"And what role will that be, my dear?" Erik asked with a quirked brow. "Another bastard king?"

I stared at Uncle Erik, anger blazing in my belly until I realized that I was quite literally looking at a bastard king. "Oh... you're..."

Erik smiled and inclined his head. "Yes, that's right. I was my father's bastard. I never expected to inherit his throne."

"You have been the best thing for the Black Mountains," Marienne declared, reaching up to cup her husband's face. "And for me."

"But Damon already has two legitimate sons," Jessa said, frowning at her father-in-law. "Do you really think Barry and Theo will just step aside for a man they don't even know?"

I tried not to feel angry toward my sister's tone, but I couldn't help but take exception. This was my mate she was talking about.

"We'll see," Uncle Erik said. "Normally there wouldn't even be a discussion about lineage, but with Jaegar being significantly older and baring the dragon king tattoo—"

"He could be king," Marienne said. "I've seen it. But that vision is only one possible version of the future. He could walk many paths."

"He wouldn't have to be king," I said. "He could live here with me in Bravadok."

Erik and Marienne smiled and nodded as though they agreed with me, but there was a caution in their eyes that told me there was more to the story.

But perhaps instead of getting the information second-hand, it would serve me well to speak to the man himself. "Would you all excuse me?" I said, moving to step past Marienne. But a friend of my dad's came and spoke to me, then another, then another. By the time I'd spent time with everyone who wanted to say, "Happy Birthday", and made my way over to where Carlak and Anthony were, Jaegar was nowhere to be found. "Where's he gone?" I asked.

Anthony quirked an eyebrow at me. "Hey, Vanya, how are you? We're great, thanks for asking. How's your night going?"

I glared at him, then conceded. "Sorry, that was rude."

I need to find my mate.

"If you're looking for Jaegar, he headed off with Cass a few minutes ago."

"Oh," I went up on my tiptoes, looking around frantically. My stomach gurgled as it digested little more than a glass or two of champagne.

Anthony stopped a waiter as he walked past with a plate of herbed, roast chicken sticks. "Vanya," he said, his tone commanding. "Eat something."

I didn't question the sorcerer's advice. The last thing I needed tonight was to faint in front of everyone. "All right." I grabbed some chicken and sank my teeth into the flesh, my stomach growling in response as I chewed absently.

Carlak snagged another glass of champagne from another waiter and handed it to me. "You're the birthday girl. You should be enjoying yourself as much as possible."

I nodded and kept eating, surprised at just how hungry I was. "I agree." A tingle coursed up my spine, and I swallowed the moan that rose in me as a hand slid around my waist and moved into my side. How could Jaegar be so familiar to me? It was as though I'd known him forever and shared every intimacy imaginable with him. His touch was perfect, as was the very scent of him.

And as he leaned closer, he whispered into my ear, "We need to get out of here before I ravish you in front of everyone."

I couldn't help the thrill that shot through me, but I turned my head and lifted my gaze to his. "I can't leave."

He frowned and his lips thinned as he pressed them hard together.

I could see he wanted to assert his dominance over me, but what he didn't realize was that I was the daughter of King Stavrok, and I wasn't taking orders from anyone—not even my fated mate. I straightened my spine, but still had to tilt my head to look up at him.

Damn, he's tall.

"The party will only go for a few more hours. Have something to eat and drink."

And calm down.

I knew what he was feeling. It was an incredible ache that started deep in the belly and heated the very blood. But this was my birthday, and my triplet siblings were here to celebrate with me. It was the whole reason for this event. I couldn't just run off with a man that I barely knew. He may be my fated mate, but that didn't change the fact he was a virtual stranger to me. "Have you met my sister, Jessa, yet?"

His eyebrows flickered up in the faintest expression of curiosity.

"Or Iain?" Anthony suddenly said, bursting through the bubble around us and reminding me that we weren't alone. "I think they just arrived, actually."

The doors to the hall flew open and in walked my baby brother and his fiery wife—the Dragon Daughter herself.

I couldn't help but roll my eyes and grin at Anthony. "Did they have to upstage us?"

Anthony grinned back. "Of course they did! Go, see them."

I nodded and as I stepped toward them, Jaegar's grip on my hip tightened. I glanced up at him. "It's okay. Come meet my family."

His feet were frozen in place or so it seemed.

I held out my hand to him, offering him my own strength.

He didn't move for a long moment, then finally, he took my hand in his.

I guided him over to where my parents were hugging Iain and Veronica.

"Hey, guys," I said, letting go of Jaegar's hand.

Veronica threw herself at me, almost knocking me over with the strength of her hug. "Happy birthday!" she cried before pulling back. Veronica looked tanned and vibrant.

"Vacation going well?" I asked.

"Oh yeah," she gushed. "Travelling is *amazing*."

Veronica slipped back into her place beside my brother with a smile.

Jaegar reached out for my waist once more, the protective dragon in him rising to the surface despite the fact these people were family and no threat to me.

Iain's eyebrows quirked up in question.

Before I could answer him, Veronica's lips curved into a huge smile. "And who's this?" she asked.

Dad mercifully stepped closer and made the introductions as quickly and painlessly as possible, giving a shortened version of everything leading up until this point.

Iain reached out and shook Jaegar's hand, making him let go of me for a short moment.

I thought I'd be glad for the respite, but instead, my skin ached to feel the heat of him once more. My royal personality, the one who had learned to hold her own and live with her own company, now warred with the passion of my dragon.

Veronica frowned at Jaegar. "So, how do you know my family? I've never met you before."

"Oh, ah..."

I had to laugh amicably at Jaegar's inability to answer Veronica's question. "We call Veronica the Dragon's Daughter. Ever since we were kids Veronica's been able to outrun, outfly, and outburn us all."

Iain pulled her possessively to his side. "Yep. She's amazing."

Veronica turned her face up to receive Iain's kiss, but her eyes were still glued to Jaegar. "You still didn't answer my question," she pressed.

Dad coughed loudly. "Maybe I should go and get Damon?"

"Maybe someone should answer my question," Veronica snapped. "Because if I didn't know better, I'd ask why you have my father's eyes."

Jaegar straightened beside me, tensing at Veronica's temper. "Well..."

"Jaegar is your half-brother," I explained quickly, jumping in to smooth the transition. "He was born to one of the women in your king-dom, five years before Uncle Damon met Aunt Cass."

Veronica's eyes flashed with the fire of her dragon. "Are you serious? I've got another older brother?" She rolled her eyes dramatically, then laughed, breaking the tension to smithereens. "What can I say? Welcome to the chaos!" Then she did what Veronica always did, she surprised us all. She walked across the small circle, closing the divide between her and Jaegar, and wrapped her arms around him for a hug.

He stared at me, worry-struck, clearly not used to such shows of familial affection.

I mouthed, *hug her back,* because Veronica wasn't letting go.

Jaegar's arms came around her very slowly and carefully.

When Veronica finally let go and moved back, I could almost feel him trembling at the interaction that was so foreign to him. He'd felt rejected all his life, and now he was being accepted and swept up into the biggest family unit in the realm. It would be overwhelming.

We need a breather.

I stopped a waiter as he walked past with a platter of food. "Thank you." I took one of the beautiful little quiches and indicated that everyone else should also try them.

Jaegar took one automatically, clearly grateful for how in tune we were.

Damon handed him a glass of whiskey, most likely sensing his son's discomfort.

Jaegar tossed it back like it was nothing.

Nothing like a bit of liquid courage to settle the nerves!

"Vanya!" Anselm called and came toward me.

"Yes, brother?" I let myself be pulled into the final hours of the party, never moving too far from Jaegar's side.

When it was time for people to leave, I watched them go anxiously, wishing the night over. I didn't mean to, of course. This was an important evening, and my family had spent months planning it. But my dragon was restless, as was my affection-starved body.

Every time Jaegar touched my arm or my waist, my core tingled, and a soft moan escaped my lips. Whenever his gaze met mine, a shot of heat would course over me, stirring desire within me, and a need I'd never felt before.

When the last of the guests were finally gone, my whole family turned to me and made excuses to hurry off to bed. They were all very tired, had a headache, had drank too much, or they had guests to see to.

And then I was alone with the dragon who haunted my dreams.

Jaegar

I'd held onto my dragon during the party by sheer force of will and the fear of doing damage to those around us. But now that the ballroom was empty and my beautiful mate was standing before me in her long, skintight dress, I felt overcome.

Vanya turned away from me to usher my father and his family out of the room so we could be alone.

Despite my best efforts, I couldn't wait a moment longer. I slid into position behind her and pressed my body against hers. "I need you."

She shuddered against me, whimpering softly as she turned around and reached up, placing her hands on my chest.

I gripped her waist with a sense of urgency, my heart hammering in my chest as I stared down into her magnificent blue eyes. "Is there somewhere we can go?" I asked.

Her fingers nails dug into my chest and her eyes shifted to silver as her dragon reached up to meet me, summoned by our instinctual need for one another. "Come," she said, then my mate turned and fled.

My dragon roared inside me, pleased to feel as desired as I did.

Without a moment to waste, I ran after her, hot on her heels.

She moved through the hallways at speed, and up one level until she burst through the door of a luxurious bedroom.

I growled as I stormed after her, my primal yearnings responding to the exhilaration of the chase.

"The doors!" she called back at me. "Close the doors."

I turned back just long enough to slam them shut.

Vanya ran into my arms, her own encircling my neck as she jumped up against me. She wrapped her legs around my waist and brought her lips crashing down against mine.

The taste of her was like nothing I'd ever experienced or could have possibly expected. The feeling of her burst through me, warming every cold, dark place in my soul like dragon fire.

My hands moved under her dress, feeling hot, smooth flesh, and I groaned against her mouth. Gripping her ass, I hauled her against me, my cock hard and ready to burst through my slacks.

Vanya thrust her tongue into my mouth with wild abandon and ran her nails through my hair, combing at my scalp as if she couldn't get close enough. She seemed to want me as much as I needed her.

Not needing to be encouraged any further, I walked us toward her huge bed.

She jumped down from my arms and began tugging at the buttons on my shirt. Her lips twitched as though she needed to say something, but her dragon had taken hold of her tongue.

Only too keen to assist her, I ripped off my shirt and unbuttoned my pants. My cock sprung forth as I stepped out of my clothes, ready for action. Ready to claim my fated mate.

Vanya's eyes grew wide, and she seemed to momentarily hold her breath.

"Second thoughts?" I asked her, praying to all that was heavenly that she wouldn't say yes.

Gods, I need her!

She shook her head slowly before reaching up to unclip the dress at the nape of her neck. The dark blue dress slithered to the floor, revealing my mate's magnificent body to my hungry gaze. Her breasts were small but perfect, and her hips gently curved. She wore only a small scrap of fabric that hid her innermost secrets from me.

But it won't last for long.

I surged forward and grabbed her up, throwing her on the bed so that she landed on her back with a surprised expression on her face. I crawled up between her thighs and lay down on her to feel the heat of her skin against mine. It felt like I'd waited forever for this moment and now it was finally here. A loud groan rose from my throat.

She wrapped her thighs around me, drawing me nearer.

I kissed her hard and fast, enjoying my fill of her lips before sliding down her beautiful body for more. I started with her nipples, tasting each strawberry-peaked breast, suckling until her rosy buds grew hard.

Vanya gasped and arched her back, instinctively thrusting her flesh further into my mouth.

My heart soared and my mind raced as I moved lower, pressing my lips to the supple flesh of her belly. I slid down until I could tear her tiny lacy panties off with my teeth. The scent of her arousal was so amazing to my inner beast that I buried my face between her thighs and inhaled deeply as soon as she was completely naked.

"Oh! God..." Vanya grabbed my head, to push me away or to tug me closer, I wasn't sure.

But regardless, I extended my tongue and licked her swollen flesh over and over again, swirling, suckling, and nipping.

She shuddered beneath me and moaned, clearly unafraid to express her desire.

I used my hands to pry her wider, pushing apart her thighs to grip her tight ass in my callused hands. Then I brought her pussy to my mouth and indulged in the delectable feast that she was. Her pussy lips were wet and gleaming, pink and perfect, and she tasted like paradise.

Gods, she was worth waiting for!

"Jaegar.... Please... *Please*... Come up to me!" Vanya's hands were more desperate now, tugging at my hair with need.

A deep growl rippled through me. There was no reason to make either of us wait any longer. She was clearly ready and wanting, and so was I. My cock was painfully rock-hard and pulsed against my belly with arousal. I stalked on top of her once more and lined my dick up with her wet entrance.

She raised her legs and wrapped them around my waist once more, locking me into her so neither one of us could escape. "Please," she gasped out again, arching her back as her pussy brushed against the head of my cock. "I need you, Jaegar."

I wasn't going to get a more beautiful or honest request than that. I rolled squarely onto her luscious body and surged forward, the head of my cock sliding into the heart of her. If I'd had any reservations that Vanya was made for me, the feel of her perfect cunt embracing me erased *all* doubt. A pleasure unlike any I'd ever felt washed over me as her heat consumed me.

I am home.

Vanya shivered in my arms, her hot gasps making my need for her grow.

I slid back, then thrust forward again, the tight clasp of her body welcoming me with every move. I kissed her, softly at first, then more passionately as the heat between us grew. Rocking and undulating my hips, I increased my pace.

Our tongues tangled, and her gasps began to build in volume and desperation. I fucked her sweet, delicious body harder and faster, claiming my dragon shifter princess mind, body, and soul. With each frenetic thrust, and each moan, my orgasm roared down on me, threatening to push me over the edge. But I didn't want to fall—not without her.

As if the moment couldn't be any more perfect, Vanya began to arch against me, her breathing labored as she squeezed her eyes shut tight.

My pulse quickened at the raw beauty of what I was about to witness.

"I... I..." she stammered, then her cry pierced through the haze of pleasure filling my brain. Her body bowed, then released like a spring. Her pussy rippled and spasmed around my cock, calling upon my own orgasm without remorse.

I buried myself deep in my mate's body, and with a throaty roar, I let myself ride that wave of ultimate bliss with her.

We endured ecstasy together, our bodies entwined, heart to heart, and lips to lips, before we collapsed in a pile of spent, sweaty limbs.

I rolled onto my back and pulled her on top of me.

Vanya was breathing as hard as I was, her heart thundering in her chest as she came down.

"Are you okay, my love?" I asked, struggling to slow the thumping of my own heart.

She nodded. Glancing up to meet my eyes for a moment, she lay her head back down and nuzzled into my chest. "Yeah," she assured me breathlessly. "I feel amazing."

I chuckled, relief flooding my soul as I wrapped my arms around her body and held onto her tight. "Me too, beautiful."

Vanya settled against my chest and before I knew it, her breathing settled into slow, rhythmic cadence of sleep.

But I couldn't sleep. There was no way, at least initially. I lay awake for many hours afterward, just letting her warm the long hours of the night that were often too dark. Alone in my mind, my past haunted me. My choices provided an ample feast of my thoughts.

But with Vanya's valiant heart beating against mine, and her warmth heating my skin, I eventually managed to fall asleep and made it through to sunrise without any of my usual nightmares.

www.samaiya.com

CHAPTER

TEN

Vanya

When I awoke, my heart was rapidly beating, and panic was streaking through my blood. Jaegar was beside me, naked in bed, and sound asleep. I couldn't believe that he was still here.

I eased away from him, carefully and slowly, desperate not to wake him up. Once I made it to the edge of the bed, I lifted the covers and jumped out of bed. Then I raced to the shower, eager to wash off the evidence of my lack of self-control. I'd promised myself I wouldn't jump into sex with Jaegar the minute we were alone. I'd wanted us to ease into our relationship, fated mates or not.

I'd seriously thought that Aunt Cass and Mom had been exaggerating when they'd talked about what I'd likely experience with my fated mate, but my attraction to Jaegar was even more intense than I'd expected and impossible to ignore.

I turned on the hot tap and water blasted into the huge shower cubicle. I stepped beneath the spray, needing the space and time to think. My skin was on fire, and I was trembling with the aftereffects of something I didn't understand. Was this truly how it felt when you found your fated mate?

Is it really supposed to feel so consuming?

What I felt left me breathless and overwhelmed.

How can this be normal? It's exhausting!

When I was done with washing my tender, strangely lethargic body, I crept back into my bedroom to get dressed. Jaegar was still asleep, sprawled out in bed. I quickly grabbed for some underwear and pulled a day dress out of my wardrobe to slip into.

I tried to keep my eyes on the carpet and my hands moving to dress myself, but I couldn't help but allow my gaze to be drawn back to the bed. To the huge shoulders, ripping muscles, and flat stomach of a man who'd fought to survive in the toughest kingdom in our entire realm.

My stomach lurched and my heart did an uneasy flip-flop. I still couldn't believe that this was how it was meant to feel. I felt so... uneasy. So, unlike myself.

Shaking my head, I snatched up my shoes and hurried out the door, leaving my fated mate alone in my bedroom. The hallway was mercifully empty, so I took a moment to pull on my knee-high black boots, smooth down my dress, and compose myself.

When I was finally ready, my breathing was still erratic, and I'd developed a headache. The question to answer though, was it from dehydration and too much champagne at the party? Or from the mind-blowing orgasms I'd been gifted with last night? We'd made passionate love again this morning, not long after the break of dawn. Probably why Jaegar was still fast asleep.

I'd ridden him long and hard, until he'd blown apart within me. My legs had been shaking long after, and even now I was exhausted. Sex with Jaegar was unlike anything I could have even dreamed. He was an animal in the very best possible way. As if he was ruled by his passion and instincts alone, and it set the coals of my dragon heart blazing with an unparalleled need.

"Hey, sis!" Anselm called out as he strode along the hallway. "Everything okay?" He stopped in front of me, a frown on his face.

I forced myself to nod, even though I was bursting with questions. "Yes, of course. Are we all meeting for breakfast this morning?"

He grinned at me. "Oh, you missed breakfast, but there might be a few stragglers left in the dining room."

I pressed my lips together to stop my squeal.

Oh my god!

That would have set tongues wagging with both Jaegar and I missing for the first meal of the day.

Anselm nudged me with his elbow. "Come on. Kayla asked me to go and get a plate of fruit for her to have in our room. She's feeling a little queasy."

"Hmm…" I managed to say with a smile. Did Anselm know his wife was expecting again, or was she still hiding the fact from her husband?

"The party went well last night," Anselm said, walking beside me toward the dining hall. "Jaegar's appearance has certainly set people's gossip meters into overdrive."

"I can imagine." I sighed.

A true gentleman, Anselm opened the door to the dining hall.

Inside, there were a few people still sitting at the table, while the servants quietly removed plates and glasses from guests who'd been and gone.

"Good morning, daughter," Dad said, getting up from the head of the table with a big smile. "I'm assuming you didn't sleep well?" He reached out to kiss me on the cheek.

My insides flared with heat, and I rolled my eyes. "I just slept in," I lied.

"Yeah right," Jessa said from her place next to Mom. "You *never* sleep in. What gives?" she asked, waggling her eyebrows at me.

I sat down at a spare place and reached for the roast potatoes. I didn't want to admit it to anyone, but I was starving and needed something hearty and filling. "I slept in," I repeated with a shrug. "No big deal." I wasn't ready for a family grilling on my newly blossoming love life.

Gods help me!

Mom glanced at Dad and reached for her juice glass. "And Jaegar?" she asked quietly, "is he also... sleeping in this morning?"

Heat flushed my cheeks again, and I closed my eyes to the shame with a grimace. "Mom!"

Jessa gasped aloud.

The sound made me open my eyes again and reach for the roast beef. I'd barely eaten last night, and it was catching up with me this morning.

"You slept with him?" Jessa whispered fiercely across the table, though there was no one except our family around.

"I'm going back to Kayla," Anselm said, before taking his plate of fruit with him. "Good luck, sis." His grin told me he didn't feel sorry for me.

So, I grabbed my knife and fork and started shoveling food into my mouth, hungrier than I'd ever been. Much to my mental anguish and surprise, it seemed sex really did build an appetite!

My family stared at me as though they'd never seen me eat before. Which was partially true, I supposed. They certainly weren't used to me enjoying my food with gusto.

"What?" I asked around a mouthful when no one was forthcoming.

"Oh... it's nothing," Mom said, reaching for the fruit platter.

"Come on, Van. Spill!" Jessa implored me.

I rolled my eyes. "Jessa... seriously? Here? *Now*?" I didn't want to indicate that both of our parents were sitting right here at the table, but they should know that they were the main reason I didn't want to say anything here. If Jessa and I were alone, I would have said more. In fact, I had questions.

"Oh, here he is!" Mom said with a big grin and a sidelong glance at me.

The hairs on my arms prickled up as the chair beside me was pulled out.

Jaegar sat down. "Apologies for being late," he said, shifting in his seat and getting comfortable.

His voice was like silk as it slid over me, making me want to drown in the sound.

"Did you sleep well?" Mom asked, almost managing to sound simply polite.

"I did. Thank you." Jaegar said, not moving to get any food.

I glanced at him and saw his hands folded in his lap.

Isn't he hungry?

"Would you like something different for breakfast, perhaps?" Mom asked. "We can get anything you'd like cooked."

"No. I... was just waiting in case there were some sort of... rules." Jaegar sighed heavily.

I reached over and squeezed his hand in encouragement. "Just eat. You're family here with us." I stood up and pulled the platter of meat and potatoes closer. "If you're anything like my dad, you eat a lot of meat?"

He met my gaze and nodded, heat searing me right down to my core. "Thank you."

I sat again and returned to cutting up my morning meal.

Meanwhile, Jaegar began serving himself.

Mom and Dad watched us with keen interest.

It was somewhat unnerving, and I wasn't sure what to do except change the subject. "So, where's everyone else?"

Mom answered first. "Most of the families went home last night. Marienne and Erik, Anthony and Charity."

I glanced over at Jaegar before asking. "What about Cass and Damon? Veronica and Iain?"

"They're all still here," Dad said. "But they ate early, and said they wanted to go shopping at the markets in town."

"How long are they staying for?" I pressed. Wanting to know how soon I'd be losing Jaegar, unless I could convince him to stay here, with me.

"Only another day," Mom said. "Though perhaps Jaegar might want to stay longer?"

Jaegar lifted his head and stared directly at my mom, "Oh... well, I'd planned to leave with the king and queen, but...." His gaze moved to me.

I managed to smile back at him, my heart racing at the thought of his departure. "Maybe we can talk about it later? Who knows, the way Veronica throws her weight around that family, you all might end up moving here." I meant it as a lighthearted joke, which my family seemed to understand.

They all laughed at the absurd thought.

But Jaegar reached for his glass of water and frowned. "My home is in the Northern Kingdom. I wouldn't want to live anywhere else."

The breath caught in my throat as I stared at Jessa as panic rose within me.

What does that mean for us?

"Have you travelled much?" Jessa asked him suddenly to detract from his awkward statement, fiddling with a croissant on her plate as she did so. "Have you been to any of the other kingdoms?"

"No," he answered. "Before yesterday I've never left my home."

His words settled over me and gave me hope that maybe, just maybe, I could convince him to stay here.

He doesn't know what he was missing!

"That's not unusual," My father said. "Especially for those in the North. When I had a dinner for the kingdoms, and this was many years ago, we would invite everyone. Damon was almost never able to join us. He hated coming this far south."

Jaegar nodded again. "Yes, the North is special. Have any of your been to the Northern Kingdom?"

Jessa shook her head.

I mirrored her reaction. "No."

Mom perked up and grinned. "I have, but only a few times. It's a long way for me to travel, unfortunately. But when Cass had her babies, I went to keep her company each time."

"The Northern Kingdom is wild," my father said, "and beautiful. Of all the kingdoms, it is the toughest to survive, let alone thrive in. Your ability to withstand hardship, Jaegar, is unparalleled in this room."

Jaegar shifted in his chair as though uncomfortable with the compliment. "Thank you, King Stavrok, but I know the vital role you played in saving us all from the wolves. I was only a young child, but I remember it all the same. Our people spoke of you and your bravery for many years afterward."

I glanced between the two men at the table, surprised by the kinship I could see growing already. I nudged Jaegar with my elbow. "Well, it sounds like you know more about my father than I do."

"I wouldn't say that" he said softly, "but it's safe to say that I may not be here, alive and well, if your father had not helped us on that day."

Dad coughed to clear his throat.

My heart ached for the deep feelings being shared in the room.

"The five kingdoms support one another," my dad finally managed to say, his voice thick with emotion.

"Yes. We do," Mom said, staring directly at me. "No matter where you go, you'll always have a home here."

I gave my mom a small smile, my stomach roiling.

Jessa called for some sweets and started talking about the Kingdom in the Black Mountains.

The rest of breakfast went by quickly, but it left me wanting more time alone with Jaegar. I needed to know what his plans were moving forward into the future, and if he'd consider staying here with me.

Surely, he'll stay?

ELEVEN

Jaegar

Breakfast had been a bit of a strained time, but interesting, nonetheless. Which was how all my mealtimes had been since I'd gone to the castle and told my father who I was. It seemed royal life was not short of intrigue. When the king and queen of Bravadok excused themselves, I was left alone with Vanya and her sister, Jessa.

Jessa's keen, bright gaze landed on me. "So... what are your plans now, Jaegar?" Her lips twitched as though she wanted to ask me more but didn't.

From the way Vanya stiffened beside me, I had to assume that Jessa holding back wasn't normal behavior for her. "I don't actually know," I managed to say before giving in and reaching for the coffee pot. I had a pounding headache and wasn't sure if it was the lack of sleep, or the stress of the last few days, but I needed some caffeine to help get me through, which was not something I normally would admit to.

"What do you mean?" Jessa asked, her eyebrows narrowing further. "You're Vanya's mate, so the choices are pretty clear. Either you stay here with our family, or you both go back to the Northern Kingdom. Right?"

Her tones brooked no argument, and yet, I wanted to snap back at her. There were other choices.

Always.

But I managed to take a breath and wait a heartbeat, a trick I'd learned so I didn't react on pure emotion. Instead, I said, "I think that's between Vanya and me, don't you?" When I flashed an annoyed look at her, instead of the anger I expected to see in her face in return, there was a flash of surprise, then a growing respect.

Jessa got to her feet and tossed her long blonde hair over her shoulders with a subtle smile and a nod. "You're right, of course. And I think it's high time for me to check on Rocky. I'll see you both later." Then she grinned at her sister and left the room too.

I took a long sip of hot coffee. "Damn, this is exhausting."

Vanya twisted in her chair to look at me. "Which part?"

I gestured to the huge table. "All of it, honestly. The enormous family for starters. I'm not used to being around so many people."

Vanya glanced down at the table, appearing hurt.

Damn it.

"I don't mean to imply anything against your family, Vanya. Not at all. It's just... I grew up with only my mother for company. Then I joined Damon's family a few days ago." Not intentionally, of course, but now none of them seemed to want me to go back. They wanted to keep me in their lives. "And it's just been very full on. I need more quiet and some time to think."

I didn't know how to explain it better to her. Vanya had grown up in the castle, one of four siblings. Of course, she was used to the sort of noise and bustle that came with this life.

She chuckled softly, her expression brightening. "Oh, I can totally understand what you mean. I'm the only one of my family that doesn't handle all this very well." She made a gesture with her hand to show the encompassing area around us. "I'm a little bit of a black sheep, here," she joked.

I relaxed back into my chair and took another sip of coffee, thankful that she wasn't offended and understood where I was coming from. I didn't want my mate to feel ill-at-ease so early into our relationship. "How'd you sleep?" I ventured.

She burst out laughing, then covered her mouth, saying behind her hand, "Um... very well, considering you were burning up the bed beside me. It's like sleeping with a furnace!"

I shrugged, trying not to take exception to the joke. She couldn't see that as a negative, surely? "Heat is important in the North, especially since I didn't grow up in a castle." Not that the castle had been in much better shape than the rest of the town thirty years ago. There had been huge chunks of the structure missing, and the functioning rooms were crumbling too, according to the few staff that still worked the ruins.

I wasn't half proud to admit that my sire, King Damon and his family, had rebuilt the North stone by stone. He'd worked side by side with the farmers and builders, making our kingdom strong again. My father wasn't just a royal with a crown, he was a man who wasn't afraid to get his hands dirty, and I respected that.

"What was it like?" she asked quietly. "Growing up like you did?"

"You mean with a single mother, living in poverty? Or..." I didn't want to say it but, was she wondering what it was like growing up knowing that my father was the king?

"Well... yes, I guess," she said, shrugging. "I'm sorry. I'm just trying to understand more about you."

I chuckled. "That's not really something you need to know about, sweetheart. It was hard, all of it. But my childhood, and my life, my struggles... they made me who I am today."

And I wouldn't change anything—probably.

"And who are you?" she whispered, her eyes gleaming with the hunger that I was beginning to feel stir within me also.

I didn't want to answer her question. The answer wasn't easy or pretty. So, I reached out and cupped her face, threading my fingers through her long, dark hair. "Kiss me."

She lifted her chin and leaned forward.

I met her halfway and kissed her, softly at first, then deeper.

Her fingers threaded into my hair and held me tight to her.

A loud cough made us both sit back, and I got to my feet, ready to face whoever was intruding.

It was my father, looking sheepish at witnessing our passionate display of affection.

My dragon was up and ready to protect my mate, if need be, but my father's smile soothed me in the strangest way. I knew he wouldn't hurt Vanya. Which on a logical level, made sense. But my dragon wasn't logical, he never had been. It was why I worked so hard to master my emotions and temper. "Good morning," I said, with a nod of my head.

King Damon's smile was brighter than I'd anticipated. "We were planning on staying on a few extra days and Cass asked me to come and find you, to ask if that was all right with you?"

I glanced down at Vanya,

Her beautiful face was flushed pink, her gaze still glossy with desire.

Did I want to leave her? Never.

I forced my gaze back to my father's. "Of course. I have nothing I need to rush back to."

The king grinned. "We're all getting ready to go for a walk around Bravadok. I'd appreciate your opinion on a few of the township ideas I'd like to potentially implement back home, if you can spare the time?" He lifted an eyebrow in question.

My stomach squirmed in the strangest way. "You want my advice?" I asked, scarcely believing it.

"Of course," Damon said. "You're the one who has lived in the town. You've known the stressors affecting the people, and what the weather has done to their homes. Your firsthand experience would be invaluable."

Vanya stood up next to me but didn't say anything.

Damon continued. "Dymitri and Lucian are here today but will leave early tomorrow. They'd like to see you."

Vanya smiled at me in encouragement. "I'd love to come for a walk, if you don't mind the company."

My dragon wouldn't have allowed her to stay away. I'd been sound asleep when she'd left our bed this morning, but I'd felt her absence almost immediately. "That sounds like a good plan," I said, taking Vanya's hand and pulling her close. "Shall we go now?"

Damon nodded. "Yes, we're all congregated by the entrance. Come."

I followed my sire, with my mate at my side. After so many years of being cold, and tired and lonely, I was now surrounded by family and friends and permitted access to the very best all the kingdoms had to offer. I was struggling to keep up with all the changes. The group standing in the foyer was larger than I'd expected, and my breath caught in my throat as anxiety rode me hard.

Vanya squeezed my hand.

I looked down on her for reassurance, and her subtle smile gave me the courage I needed.

Lucian was the first to come forward. "Jaegar," he said as he held out his hand.

I offered him my arm and smiled in return. "Hey, Lucian. It's good to see you."

Lucian laughed. We'd worked side by side building homes for the townsfolk many times. "You didn't think to drop the hint about you being my nephew?" he asked, one eyebrow cocked.

I shrugged as I withdrew. "Not really."

Lucian laughed and this time came forward for a hug.

I didn't pull back the way my initial instincts told me to, and instead let the man embrace me as family.

When he finally pulled back, his smile was warm and his eyes were surprisingly shiny. "Well, from one bastard son to another ,I say, welcome to the family."

It was Damon who punched his brother in the arm. "Hey!"

Lucian shook him off. "What? Someone's got to say it. Otherwise, that shit will eat you alive. Right, Jaegar?"

I suddenly felt the ease of something inside me. "Yeah, that's about right." It was the weight of carrying the secret that had always bothered me. And although I'd known that Lucian and Dymitri were my grandfather's bastards, I'd never really considered them to be the same as me. They were well liked by the town and known to the king. They were family. I wasn't. Well, I hadn't been.

Now... things are different.

"Well, let's get going," Stavrok suddenly said from the front of the group. "There's lots to see." He pushed open the front doors, and we stepped into the sunlight.

Veronica rushed to the back of the group to stand beside me and chatter away in my ear.

Even King Damon didn't go far.

The feeling was smothering but strangely soothing, and I tried to lean into the feeling rather than shy away from it. This was going to be my new life after all—full of family.

Bravadok was a beautiful, well thought out township. The king was well liked, and his people felt content to wave and speak openly with him.

The houses Damon had me confer on were interesting, though not well made for the levels of cold back home. I had a good look at everything he asked me to, and by the time we got back to the castle, I was ready to crawl straight back into bed.

TWELVE

Vanya

Watching Jaegar move through our town was a lesson in restraint. Every time he spoke with that beautiful, sexy voice I just wanted to kiss his lips right off his face.

He moved like a lion, strong and sure, ready to attack or defend at any given moment. But he was also reserved, even shy, only speaking when spoken to. He was a puzzle, that was for sure.

When we got back to the castle, he'd invited me for a nap. At first, I'd thought he meant for another hot session of lovemaking, but from the way he trudged toward his room, it became clear that he actually wanted to sleep.

Instead, I'd walked him to my room, practically tucked him under the covers, then watched as he passed out. A part of me had wanted to stay and cuddle with the furnace, but I'd been too wired and awake to sleep. So, I found myself wandering up to my favorite spot in the castle, the library on the eighth floor. But I wasn't alone for long.

"Hey, birthday girl!" Veronica called out, walking into my space, accompanied by both Charity and Kayla, former humans and now princesses of our realm.

"Hey, guys," I said, putting down my book straight away.

They sat down on the chairs and couches around me, expectant looks on their faces.

"What?" I asked, glaring especially at the Dragon Daughter. She was never hesitant in coming forward.

Veronica laughed. "We want to know about Jaegar, obviously. He's your mate, right? Does that mean he's going to live here?"

I glanced at the three girls, all looking at me with bright smiles on their faces. "Um... I don't know. We haven't really talked about all that stuff just yet."

Charity snorted. "Yeah, too busy falling into bed together, I suppose."

"Yeah, they're still in that blissful and overwhelming first stage of love," Kayla added.

I crossed my legs and stared at them with my lips pursed and my eyebrows high. "Judgey, much?"

They frowned at first, then burst out laughing.

"Oh, no!" Kayla said. "You forget that I jumped into bed with even knowing Anselm's name."

"And I was no better." Charity laughed. "Anthony had my heart the moment I saw him. The fated mate stuff is *intense*."

Together they glanced toward Veronica.

I focused on her too.

"What?" Veronica asked.

"You've never told us much about you and Iain," I countered. "We thought you two hated each other."

Veronica shrugged her slim shoulders. "Iain knew I was his mate for ages, he just didn't tell me because of my age. And when I found out, well,

I ran to the human world. I last thing I wanted was to get married off at eighteen."

I laughed. "Oh, no, you waited until you were all of nineteen. That's so different."

"Hey!" she said and reached over to whack my arm. "I *had* to come back. Dad was hurt and Iain was—" she stopped to gulp, her eyes tearing up a little at the memory.

I reached over and squeezed her hand. "I'm only teasing, Dragon Daughter. We are so glad you found Iain, and he you. You're great together."

"Yeah... but did you fall into bed together the first moment you were alone?" Kayla asked with a broad grin. "That's the real question."

Veronica rolled her eyes, then laughed. "Of course, we did. Even with Iain's injuries, we couldn't keep our hands off each other."

All the women around me sighed with longing.

Their reactions got me thinking and reminded me that I still had questions. "Does the fire, die down?" I asked, not sure what answer I was hoping for.

"Not entirely," Kayla answered. "It just simmers down, I guess, to a more manageable need."

Charity nodded in agreement.

Veronica on the other hand laughed out loud. "Speak for yourselves, ladies. I'm *still* enjoying the first year of marriage."

Kayla shifted in her seat, then returned the conversation to Jaegar and I. "Do you think he'll want to take on an active role in the Kingdom of the North? I mean... not as the king or anything, but I'm sure Damon will want him close by, yeah?"

I glanced at Veronica. "I don't really know. What do you think?"

Veronica chewed on her bottom lip for a moment. "Honestly? I don't know. I haven't had the chance to talk to my parents properly since we only arrived late yesterday. Dad seems to want to be near Jaegar, and Mom's worried, I can see that."

"And how do you feel about it all?" I asked her, only just realizing that it was Veronica's family, and her home, that Jaegar was the most threat to.

She huffed out a laugh. "Oh, I feel everything," she said. "The gamut! I'm shocked Dad has another son and angry at Jaegar's mom from keeping him from us all. But I'm also annoyed at Jaegar for not coming to the castle sooner.

Then I'm worried about the kingdom and succession, and all that. But mostly, I guess, I'm kind of just happy. It's pretty cool to have another older brother, actually. And he seems nice. Different than Barry and Theo, but nice."

I tried not to smile and simply nodded. Jaegar was holding back his true dragon king feelings, I could tell. He was exhausted just getting through the day, but things would come out soon enough.

"I'm surprised you're not with him, now," Charity said. "Anthony wouldn't let me out of his sight when we were first together."

"He wanted a nap, and I was too buzzed to sleep," I confided. "Jaegar isn't used to being around so many people, so it's draining him a little."

"And he's the center of everyone's focus, too," Charity said with a sigh. "I don't really like that part either. I can tell he's nervous, and it makes me nervous too."

"But he *is* a dragon king," Veronica interrupted, "or he could be. Surely that means that he'll get used to us, and the kingdom, and everything? He has the tattoo, right? That's how it works." She sounded hopeful for my mate, which was nice to hear.

I shrugged. "I don't know at this point. I just know that I'm grateful he came forward at all. Unlike you, Dragon Daughter, I'm thirty years old, not nineteen. I didn't think my fated mate would ever find me."

Footsteps down the hallway made us all turn as one.

"Speak of the devil," Veronica whispered, jumping to her feet to greet her brother.

He rounded the corner looking well rested and a little ruffled. "Hey," he said, nodding at the group.

"Feeling better?" I asked with a smile.

He nodded.

"How'd you find us?" Charity asked, sending me a sly look, before glancing back at Jaegar.

I had no idea why she'd ask him such a thing, but when he frowned and didn't answer immediately, I got curious.

We waited with bated breath, the silence drawing out.

"I don't know, I just started walking," he said eventually.

Veronica laughed. "You just accidentally managed to find us on the eighth floor?"

He shrugged and didn't say anything more.

"I think we'll head back downstairs. Come on, Ronnie," Charity said. "Dinner will be on soon, and I need a shower before I change clothes."

"Change clothes?" Jaegar asked, an air of panic whistling around him like a fire sparking to light.

"Yeah, everyone dresses up for dinners in the castle." Kayla answered. "But whatever you packed is fine. Stavrok and Lucy aren't ones to stand on ceremony."

Jaegar's smile was tight as they left, then he turned to me. "I didn't pack anything. The queen did everything for me."

And by "the queen," I was pretty sure he meant the Queen of the North. "Don't worry," I reassured him, "Aunt Cass is *always* prepared," I assured him. "She's been in this game a long time."

He heaved a heavy sigh and ran a hand through his long hair. "I don't like not knowing what everyone expects."

I stepped closer to him so I could touch him and placed both my hands on his chest, the heavy beat of his heart thumping beneath my palms. "That's why you have me," I said soothingly, "I grew up in this world and can help you navigate around whatever you need."

He nodded and exhaled slowly. "Okay."

So many questions were on the tip of my tongue, but I could feel how overwhelmed Jaegar was. So, instead, I offered something I'd never thought I would. "Since you've seen my kingdom now, do you want me to come home with you and see the Northern Kingdom? You know, when your family returns home?"

His eyes lit up and his hands moved to encircle my waist, pulling me closer in return. "Would you really do that?" he asked.

I laughed, glad to see him so perked up. "Of course, but I'm warning you, I don't like being cold!"

His laugh was rich and warm, just like him, and it made my heart melt. "Well, we're going to have to get you a really thick coat."

I nodded and went up on my tiptoes, lifting my chin to kiss him. When he pressed his mouth to mine, I immediately began to moan and sigh. He tasted and felt *so* good against me.

When he finally lifted his head, his eyes were glittering with silver and I could feel the hardness of his cock, pressing into my belly. "How long do we have until dinner?" he asked.

"Um... I don't know," I answered, no idea what the time was, my head swimming in desire. "A few hours maybe?"

His grin was wicked this time and my heart raced. "Time enough for me to feel your naked body against mine?"

I nodded enthusiastically and grabbed his hand, holding it tight. "Absolutely. Follow me."

We ran down the hallways, laughing like children.

I'd always thought I was happy in my life, and in my home, but the joy I felt in knowing Jaegar and being by his side, was a happiness I'd never known, and I knew without a shadow of a doubt as laughter bubbled out of us that I'd do just about anything to hold onto it.

THIRTEEN

Jaegar

I want to go home.

Damon and Cass had plans to stay longer, but even the promise of my mate's kisses and warm body against mine, couldn't make me want to stay. Vanya and I had enjoyed a deliciously sexy encounter before dinner, and after as well, but no matter how close I felt to her, or how strong our connection, something seemed to be missing. Something important and integral to my very being.

It wasn't until the next morning when I woke up feeling homesick, my heart yearning for the snow, and the familiarity of home, that I understood the feeling for what it was.

Vanya snuggled into my side, all lithe limbs and milky skin.

I kissed her hair, inhaling the scent and committing it to memory.

"Hmmm... Morning," she mumbled, rolling away and stretching her arms above her head luxuriously like a cat. The blankets slipped lower, revealing her tantalizing berry-red nipples.

I couldn't help but reach out and touch them, unable to resist the urge and desire to feel their pert peaks against my fingers. "Good morning," I returned.

She crawled back over to kiss me, then excused herself to go to the bathroom with a smile.

I waited for her to return, then did the same, taking a moment to splash some cold water on my face to try and calm the anxiety within me. I loved being with Vanya, but no matter what angle I attacked the situation from, I wasn't sure I could stay here, in her kingdom. It wasn't where I belonged, I knew it in my bones.

She'd said she wanted to visit the North with me sometime, which had temporarily lifted my spirits, earlier.

But will she come home with me today? Now?

Unfortunately, I didn't know the answer to that question, and that worried me more than anything. The uncertainty of our predicament was slowly eating away at me.

"Are you coming back?" she called out when I didn't immediately return.

I finally returned to the bedroom, feeling the weight of my fear in the pit of my stomach like a stone.

"What's wrong?" she asked when she saw my face, sitting up in bed and gathering the blankets around herself.

I took a breath, then just said what I feared to share. "I have to go home, Vanya."

She smiled. "Yeah, I know. We've already planned—"

"No. I mean, I have to go home now. Today."

Her jaw dropped, and I could see her mind ticking over as she digested my words. "But we already decided we'd all leave in a few days' time."

I nodded my head and grimaced in apology. "Yeah, I know. But I can't wait that long. I'm sorry."

She gulped, her throat working hard as she swallowed. "As in... you don't want me to come with you?"

"No!" I reassured her, rushing back to the bed to sit on the covers and face her. "I want you to come with me more than anything. I couldn't leave you, I just... I can't wait any longer. I can't explain it. Would you come with me today? This morning if possible?"

She chuckled nervously. "Um, I guess? I'd have to speak to my parents, and my sister, Jessa. She organized her life around staying here with me for two weeks because I've been missing her so much..."

I sighed, a sense of guilt overwhelming me. Vanya had a life already, family, and friends—plans she'd made. My heart ached. "I suppose I could go ahead without you, and you could catch up when everyone else flies back?" I suggested, though my stomach twisted at the thought.

She stared at me for a long moment before answering, "You really need to go home, today?"

I nodded. Though if she pressed me further as to why, I wouldn't be able to explain it rationally. I just felt a pull to the ice and snow, to the lands that had always been my home—the stomping grounds where I grew up—where I became a man.

"Okay," she said suddenly with an officious nod of decision, then slid out of the bed on the opposite side. "I need a shower and breakfast, and we'll have to send some clothes and things ahead, but I'll organize it all this morning."

I gaped at her, my heart hammering anew as a fragile hope blossomed within me.

She hurried into the shower without looking back.

I followed after her in wonder and partly because I just wanted to gaze upon the beauty of her as she bathed herself. "You'll come with me? Really? Today?"

She nodded again, already stepping beneath the hot spray of the water. "I will. Though I must warn you, I haven't flown to the North before, so I'm not sure I'm going to be able to make it in one flight. It's a long way."

I crossed my arms over my chest. I hadn't thought about that. The flight had been exhausting for me coming over, but I'd refused to be weaker than my half-brothers. "Is there a halfway point where we could rest?" I asked, having never travelled beyond my homelands.

She tilted her head as though thinking about it. "Hmm, I think the Black Mountains, technically. But that *would* mean an extra night away from your home. Though there might not be another option, the more I think about it, the less confident I feel about being able to do the flight in one day."

I wanted to rush into the shower to hug her but caught myself and my excitement. It wasn't like me to express emotion so openly, but my need to go home was swallowing me alive, one large mouthful at a time.

Vanya scrubbed her hair with soap, all business as she got on with the job.

"I don't care," I said. "As long as we're on our way home, my dragon will be satisfied."

She nodded, her face still thoughtful. "I'll talk to Marienne and Erik today. I'm sure they won't mind us stopping in for the night."

I didn't know much about the king and queen of the Black Mountains, so I kept my thoughts to myself. I just internally rejoiced that I would soon be home, and I would finally feel safe where I belonged.

As EXPECTED, everyone wanted us to stay the final few days as planned, but Vanya put her foot down and told everyone that we needed to go. The way she spoke brooked no argument, which was a wonder to see.

Our clothes and personal effects were packed and sent ahead via horse and cart. Then we said goodbye to our families and stepped out into the cold air on the top balcony, ready to fly.

I undid the sash that held my robe closed and turned to look at my beautiful mate, my heart in my throat as I tried to find the right words. "I need to say thank you," I said in a rush before I could doubt myself. "You stood up for me, you fought to give me this. So... thank you." It felt awkward as hell to say, to admit gratitude and a debt owed, which was something I definitely wasn't used to. I'd always stood on my own two feet, been my own man. To be beholden to a mate was as wonderful as it was foreign.

The brilliant smile Vanya gave me in return made up for all the tension in my heart. "Of course," she said. "I'll do everything I can to make you comfortable in this new world, please know that. I understand royal life and all its trappings are still very strange to you."

I nodded with a small smile and took one final look at the kingdom around me. "Let's go."

She smiled back and inclined her head. "You first?"

I laughed as I shook my head. "No, definitely not. Ladies first."

She shrugged and dropped her robe without hesitation, revealing her gorgeous body for mere moments before she took a step up to the balcony railing, then jumped, plunging toward the earth below.

I raced forward to watche my fated mate.

She shifted mid-fall, her gorgeous dragon extending its wings and swooping low over the village in a circle as she waited for me to join her in the air.

I turned around and raised my hand one last time, waving at my father and his family, that familiar ache stealing over my heart again.

King Damon smiled and nodded at me.

Not wanting to make Vanya wait any longer, I turned and threw my robe away at the same moment I dove off the castle walls, shifting to fly after my mate.

The flight to the Black Mountains was long and arduous, and my whole body was aching by the time we got there.

As soon as we landed, servants came running out with cloaks. "Your Highness," one of them greeted Vanya, "we got word that you were stopping here for the night."

Vanya took the cloak and quickly wrapped herself in its warmth. "Thank you, Samuel. Yes, that's right. This is Jaegar, he is King Damon's son, and my fated mate."

The servant didn't even blink, he simply nodded his head and flicked his hand, sending another servant running my way to hand me a cloak.

I took it gratefully, smiling at the young man as I wrapped myself up. "Thank you."

"Come," Samuel said. "We have made up a room and have food waiting."

It was dinnertime, and my stomach lurched with hunger at the mention of food. I definitely needed to refuel and rest. "Thank you, again."

We were shown to a large, opulent room warmed by a roaring fire.

Vanya hurried towards the fireplace, extending her hands to drink in its heat.

I walked around the room, taking in the richness of the furnishings and decor. "This place is as beautiful as your palace."

Vanya laughed, rubbing her hands together and shuffling from foot to foot, trying to warm up. "King Magnik was a tyrant, but he liked to show off his wealth. You'll see his touch throughout the palace. There's gold and jewels added to the strangest things."

"King Magnik?" I asked, having never heard of him.

"Yeah, Uncle Erik's half-brother. He was the king before—"

"Before what?" I asked, my brow creasing.

Vanya turned to me, a smile quirking her lips. "Before Uncle Erik, and before my dad killed him."

I stopped my perusing and stared at her, dumbstruck. "I'm sorry... what?"

My mate quickly recalled an event that had taken place more than thirty years ago, of a King who'd stolen Lucy from King Stavrok—out of blind greed, rage, and a thirst for power.

I growled loudly, anger rolling through my chest like an inferno at the mere thought of such a thing. "I would have killed him too," I growled. If someone ever took Vanya because she could be bartered for land and power, they'd be dead before they knew what hit them.

Vanya smiled softly at my reaction. "You're a lot like my dad, you know."

"Hmm?" I enquired, unwilling to accept such an immense compliment. King Stavrok was an excellent man, king, and father. I could never compare myself to someone such as him. I'd never even dare.

"You are," she repeated. "But I doubt I'll be able to convince you. You're as stubborn and unyielding as the mountains, though you'll see in time, I'm sure."

There was a knock at the door and a woman came in, with clothes draped over her arms. "Princess Vanya, I brought some of Queen Marienne's clothes for you. And, sir... some of the King's clothes. They are simple but—"

"They're perfect," I interrupted her. "Thank you."

She hurried away at my swift but polite dismissal.

I walked over to the bed, picking up one of the shirts laid out for me. "Simple... I don't understand."

"Uncle Erik was the bastard son of the old king. He never expected to inherit the throne," she explained. "And he doesn't like all the pomp that comes with being royalty. Much like your father I assume, he isn't comfortable in royal robes."

I didn't bother replying, afraid of what it would reveal about myself. But instead made a mental note to speak to King Erik in the future, if he would speak to me about such personal topics. "Well... these clothes are still beautiful," I said.

Vanya picked up one of the dresses and nodded her head. "Oh, yes. Marienne has beautiful taste too." She dropped her cloak and began dressing.

I feasted my eyes on her slim body before she covered it once more. I would have stripped her and taken her to bed again if my stomach wasn't empty and my body not incredibly fatigued from our trip.

"Dinner?" she suggested, as though reading my thoughts. "Then bed?" Her eyes held a mischievous twinkle, which lightened the mood considerably.

"Absolutely," I said, dropping my own cloak and not bothering to hide my half hard cock. "Seeing your beautiful body is never going to *not* affect me, sorry."

She giggled and covered her mouth with her hand as she enjoyed what was on view. "Never apologize for wanting me. I've spent my whole life around my curvy mom and sister. I know I'm lacking in places, but honestly, I just didn't have a choice in the matter. This is me." She gestured to her perfect body with a lop-sided grimace.

I reached out and grabbed her hand, guiding her to wrap her fingers around my swelling cock.

She did so and stroked me once, drawing a long groan from me.

"Sweetheart, you're perfect," I managed to say before kissing her on the lips. "He doesn't lie," I winked, glancing at my cock between us.

There was another knock on the door interrupting our moment, and we broke apart.

Vanya excused herself to speak to the staff.

Meanwhile, I quickly dressed, now impatient to get back to bed as soon as I had something in my belly to tide me over.

"Dinner?" she prompted again, pulling on some slippers and standing by the door.

I did the last of the buttons up on my borrowed shirt and grabbed the coat for extra warmth. "Yes, let's go."

We followed the servant to the dining hall where we were treated to a simple yet ample fair. Then, with our bellies full, it was time to return to bed.

FOURTEEN

Vanya

Dinner was great, and the servants were courteous and lovely, as always. My sister, Jessa, had lived with them for almost ten years on and off, so they all knew me. Jaegar earned many curious looks, but the staff were kind and tried not to stare—which I appreciated, *a lot*.

He still didn't seem to understand who he was or what he was capable of.

To me, it was obvious. He could do great things. But whether he wanted to or not was a very different question. He'd been born in poverty and thrust into the royal limelight. It was definitely a lot to digest, so my heart went out to him, though royal life was all I'd ever known.

"Are you ready for bed now?" he asked, having polished off two plates of food.

I nodded, pushing my own half full plate away. I'd served myself too much, thinking I'd be able to eat more after our long flight. "Yes, definitely. Though, I may need a shower."

Jaegar's grin was wicked as he stood up and took my hand. "A shower is a great idea."

I rose from my seat and moved away from the table.

He placed his hand on the small of my back, sending a shiver of longing through me as we made our way to our room. As soon as we stepped inside our quarters, his arms went tight around my waist.

My eyes closed on a breathy sigh, and heat washed over me.

His lips pressed to my neck, trailing luxurious kisses down the side of my throat.

I tilted my head, giving him better access, eager to be ravaged by my fated mate.

His hands came up to cup my breasts and he tweaked my nipples through the fabric of my borrowed dress.

My knees turned to water. Without a second thought, I twisted in his arms, grabbing hold of his shirt to kiss him hard. I didn't want a soft seduction tonight, I wanted to feel him inside of me, rugged and strong. I jumped up and wrapped my legs around his waist, the dress pooling between us.

"Shower?" He panted as he caught me and held me close.

I nodded, pressing my lips to his neck and tasting his sweat. The taste of his heated skin and his scent, just like everything else about him, was delicious.

He walked us into the large ensuite and put me down, and didn't step away. He simply leaned forward and kissed me, all the while stripping his clothes from his body and mine from me.

When we were finally naked, I leaped at him again, wanting to feel his rippling muscles against my fair, soft skin.

He lifted me into his arms once more and walked us into the shower, where he fiddled with the taps until water flowed over us.

I gasped out aloud at the initial blast as cold water prickled my skin, making my nipples pebble into tight peaks.

"Sorry, baby," Jaegar gasped out and pressed me against the tiles behind us.

Soon hot water began to pour over us, and I forced my heavy eyes open so I could stare up into his ice-blue eyes. They were flecked with the silver of his dragon and stole my breath away. "God, you're beautiful," I managed to say, cupping his jaw as I stared up into his face."

He didn't respond with words, instead, he kissed me hard and surged into me in a single, swift and brutal move.

I arched up into him, crying out in ecstasy, meeting his stroke with my own. His cock delved deep, filling me up and reminding me of why the fated mate link was so strong, so perfect.

He pulled out almost all the way, then thrust forward again, rolling his hips as he pinned me, fucking me against the wall.

My whole body shivered with pleasure and desire. The stark contrast of the cold tiles against my back and the heat of the water at my front made every nerve in my body stretch and yearn for greater contact.

Jaegar plowed inside of me, his strong body holding me up effort-lessly. His hands gripped my thighs, and his rugged rock-hard body pressed against my slight form as he lips captured my mouth.

Several breathless moments later, I broke our kiss to pant and cry out as my first orgasm stormed through me. My belly tightened and my pussy convulsed and contracted around him, squeezing his length over and over in undulating waves.

But he didn't stop there. He moved faster and harder, determined to drag another merciless orgasm from me as he chased his own release.

I dug my fingernails into his shoulders and held on for the ride as he pushed me further and higher into the giddy heights of pleasure once more.

The sounds of our mutual rapture filled the steam-filled room. He groaned and grunted like a beast determined to breed.

It was the hottest and most raw and carnal thing I'd ever heard. I tangled my fingers in his long, dark, wet hair and pulled him even closer, sliding my tongue between his lips to indulge in him.

His movements became erratic and even more powerful, shoving me up the wall before he finally buried himself deep inside me and came in a great deluge.

The pulsing of his cock and the surge of his seed inside of me pushed me over the edge and I came again, whimpering with the sheer power of the waves of pleasure that rolled through my belly and over my senses.

We shivered together and clung to one another for so long afterward I began to think we'd soon just sink to the floor in exhaustion and bliss to fall asleep beneath the warm water.

But Jaegar managed to summon some sort of inhuman strength and step back, carefully letting me slide to my feet. He turned the water off, grabbed some towels, and wrapped us up in fluffy white robes.

We staggered to the huge bed and fell onto the mattress.

I had just enough strength left to climb beneath the covers and lay my head on the best pillow there was—Jaegar's huge chest.

There, to the sound of his strong heart, I slept the most sated night of my life.

My new life has begun.

THE NEXT MORNING, we took it nice and slow, having a leisurely breakfast before thanking the staff, and making our way to the highest balcony.

"You know," Jaegar said to me, as he opened the balcony doors. "I've never shifted so much in my life."

"What do you mean?" I asked.

"All this flying," he said with a weary smile. "First flying to your castle, then shifting when we saw each other, then yesterday to reach this halfway point..."

I grinned at him. "Well, hopefully today is the last flight for a while, and you can rest." After all, it would be at least a week or two before we went back.

He nodded far too quickly. "Definitely! I don't think I want to make that flight again. Ever."

I forced a smile to my lips and made a non-committal sound.

Surely, he can't mean that?

I lived at Bravadok castle... and although I supported him needing to return to his homeland for a while, we'd be visiting all the time. Ultimately, I'd been holding onto the hope that he'd want to move in with me in the long run.

Perhaps it was a foolish hope?

I took a long breath and forced myself to remain calm and not spiral out of control. Jaegar was exhausted and homesick. I couldn't take what he was saying too seriously. There was a chance he'd feel differently once he'd had time to find his feet and recover. "Well, let's go then." I smiled at him one more time before jumping off the castle balcony and letting my dragon take over my body.

Once inside my shifter mind, I forgot all about him not wanting to live with me at my parents' castle. The only thing I wanted to do was to be close to him. To fly through the sky and play games. It was all I desired. In my human form, I wanted to live with him and love him, so hopefully we'd be able to work everything else out.

I hadn't been to the Northern Kingdom in years, and as it came up on the horizon, a wash of dread coursed over me. I shivered, trying to dismiss it. I'd forgotten how thick the snow fell here, and how close the dark woods were.

Lucian and Dymitri had lived in those woods for years, and I just couldn't imagine ever doing that. It would have been cold, feral, and primitive.

Jaegar began to fly lower, toward the village.

I wanted to go to the castle, where it would be warm and there would be servants around to settle us into my Uncle Damon's home.

I could seriously use the comfort...

But I wasn't there to see Aunt Cass and her family. I'd flown all this way for Jaegar and his need to go home. Perhaps this was what he'd meant? To go back to the house he'd grown up in with his mother?

I followed him down into the village, landing in a large field just outside the township where it was safe for two dragons to touch down. I shifted back to human as soon as I could and immediately regretted it as I started to shiver. "Brrr... it's freezing!"

Jaegar shifted back also, letting his magnificent dragon go. When he saw how cold and naked I was, he immediately ran to me. "Come on then, my place isn't far."

He wrapped his arms around my shoulders and hurried me over the field and up a narrow road.

The icy rocks hurt my feet, and I hobbled along like a delicate flower, a thought I hated..

He chuckled and seeing my level of discomfort, he picked me up like I weighed nothing.

I would have complained at his little show of male power if I hadn't been so cold. Instead, I stubbornly tucked my head under his chin and plastered myself to his warm chest.

"No wonder you had to learn to make more heat," I managed to say from between chattering teeth, amazed by his ability to be warm no matter what the temperature.

He laughed. "Hang in there, baby. We're almost there."

I'd never been so cold in my life, but I closed my eyes and steadied my breathing as best I could, trying not to freak out about the conditions I was enduring. I'd grown up in Bravadok. It snowed there also, but I'd never been outside for more than a few seconds in the snow before. I didn't like it and never wanted to play in it. As a result, I'd never known the sort of cold that made your fingers go numb quickly.

"Here we are," Jaegar said, setting me down on a stoop, then opening the wooden door into a little hut.

I rushed inside, and the space was only just marginally warmer than outside. "Jaegar... It's freezing..." I managed to say as I shuddered violently.

"Oh... yes," he apologized, grabbing a blanket from the small couch to wrap around my shoulders. "How about you climb into the bed, and I'll start a fire?"

I looked around and saw there was a bed pressed against the wall. I didn't have any other choice. I bolted for the bed and climbed beneath the rough, dark sheets. There were several blankets on the bed, but the sheets were icy cold to the touch and even beneath all the layers, I still shivered and shook until I rattled the teeth in my head.

Jaegar started a fire in the grate, and as the flames began to flicker and the wood began to burn, he stood up and sighed as he looked around the sad, humble abode. "It's so good to be home." He wasn't shaking, or even shivering in the slightest. He didn't look cold at all.

And yet, I was freezing and felt like the cold might be the death of me! "Can you come warm me up?" I managed to ask desperately.

He looked at me like he'd forgotten I was even there. "Oh, yes! Sorry!" Then he walked over, threw back the covers, and climbed in.

I scrambled on top of him, hugging his body and pressing my head into his chest, eager to draw every last scrap of warmth from him that I could.

He chuckled as he arranged the covers over me and brushed my hair back off my face. His hands and fingers weren't even cold.

How is that possible?

His arms went around my back and the heat of his body eventually seeped into mine.

Slowly but surely, my shaking subsided, and I could breathe more easily again.

He kissed the top of my head. "We're going to have to get you some warm clothes, aren't we?"

I nodded but didn't say much in return, because what could I say? That this was freaking horrible to me? That I hated it already? That the idea of actually trying to live in this tiny house terrified me. It was *one* room. I couldn't see a bathroom or running water, though there probably was something somewhere.

An outhouse behind, maybe?

I shuddered at the thought. All I'd seen were the dirt floors, the threadbare furniture, and the suffocatingly low ceiling. I was so cold and tired, this was absolutely the last place I wanted to be in the realm. I wanted to be back in my castle, in my huge bed, warm and safe.

Lying on top of Jaegar, I did feel safe and warm finally, but we couldn't stay in bed forever. And he couldn't be by my side every day to merely ensure my survival. If this was the kind of life he wanted, then I didn't know what I'd do. Because this was the last thing I needed.

Am I going to be a thirty year old princess living in an icy hovel like a pauper?

I closed my eyes and tried my best not to cry. The idea that he'd lived here all his life was devastating to me. Did he used to have to sleep beside his mother to keep her warm, too? Had he had enough to eat? How had he survived living here, in what was without argument the toughest kingdom in the whole realm?

I knew I was a spoiled, pampered, literal princess, but no one in our entire kingdom lived in a one-room shack. No one. My parents would never have allowed it. Everyone in Bravadok had a much higher standard of living than whatever this was.

I bit my lip and breathed through my nose, tears now dripping down my face to freeze on my cheeks like crystal. Had my beautiful man survived this world, only to now feel totally uncomfortable in the castle, and with the family he should have always been a part of?

Lying here in Jaegar's hovel, the mountain climb ahead of me now seemed impossible. I couldn't see how we'd ever be able to make our two lives work. Our differences were just too vast. There was a literal world between us. A wave of depression washed over me, drowning all the good feelings in my mind.

If this is the future my fated mate craves, I can't be a part of it.

With my tears stinging my face, I listened to the steady beat of his heart and prayed that somehow, we'd find a way.

CHAPTER

FIFTEEN

Jaegar

When I tried to get out of bed, Vanya didn't want me to get up, but I had to. "Let me just feed the fire. I'll come back straight away, and it'll heat the place up. I promise."

She nodded but didn't speak as she slid off my chest.

I tried not to worry, but something was wrong with her. I could feel it in the pit of my stomach. I rushed over to the fireplace and placed two more heavy, dry logs on the dwindling fire. The flames flickered around the wood hungrily, and I made my way back to the bed. The fire wasn't making much of an impact yet, but it would.

I climbed back under the covers and sat up against the headboard I'd made years ago.

Vanya immediately clambered back into my lap like a child, curling up into a small ball, and shivering against me.

I gathered the blankets around her once more and wrapped her up in my arms. I'd made a mistake bringing Vanya here. I saw that now. It wasn't even the middle of winter, and yet the chill of our kingdom was obviously far too much for her. I had to get her clothes that would suit her and help make her comfortable.

I needed her to get to know me properly. She was my fated mate, which meant I was meant to marry her, have children with her, and love her forever. But only if she knew who I *really* was. Not the princely façade Queen Cass draped me in.

The poor bastard side of me. The real me.

"Are you warm enough yet?" I asked her, kissing her on the head. "I might get dressed and go get you some appropriate clothes."

She looked up, her heart in her eyes. "Can we go to the castle?" she pleaded. "Veronica's clothes might fit me."

I didn't want to go to the castle, nor take other princesses' clothes to dress my mate, but Vanya looked truly miserable—so I gave in. "Of course," I said, managing to extricate myself from her clinging arms, and went straight to my dresser drawers. "But I'll have to get you a coat and some boots so we can make our way up to the castle." I had to get her a full outfit, obviously. The castle was probably an hour's walk from my home, and she wasn't going to make it without warmer attire.

"I can shift and fly up," she offered by way of an alternative option, looking relieved and hopeful for the first time since our arrival.

I clenched my teeth, stopping myself from immediately responding. "I can't shift again," I said through my teeth as calmly as I could. "I'm too tired. I'm not used to it."

"But I'm not," Vanya offered. "I could shift, and go get the clothes, then come back. Would that work?"

I bristled in annoyance. I wanted to yell from the depths of my chest.

No! It won't work.

It was just another nail in the coffin of our burgeoning bond, further proof that Vanya would never survive in my world.

Maybe fate does make mistakes.

I tried one more time. "Dymitri's house isn't far. He has daughters about your size. I could go and borrow some of their things for the journey."

Her shoulders fell, and she looked utterly crestfallen, but she nodded, resigned. "Yeah, okay. I suppose that's a good compromise."

Relieved that she wouldn't be flying off to the castle without me, I tugged on my clothes, adding an extra thin layer under my shirt in case I'd gone soft after being in the South. "I won't be long," I told her, rushing forward to kiss her pouting lips. The room was heating up, and the fire was beginning to truly blaze. "Stay here. The fire should last until I get back. Try to stay warm."

I went to the door, gave her one more smile and headed out into the cold. The temperature had dropped, even though it was barely lunchtime. Storm clouds gathered overhead, and I could smell the snow on the wind coming our way.

Great.

We weren't leaving the house today no matter what clothes I brought her. Vanya wouldn't venture out in this kind of weather.

I went straight to Dymitri's house, and his daughter, Matilda, was there darning some socks and baby clothes.

"Hey Jaegar," she called out, waving me inside. "Come on in. What can I help you with?"

"Ah... your warmest clothes," I said, with an awkward shrug. "Or something of your sister's maybe?"

Matilda raised an eyebrow and crossed her arms over her chest with a chuckle. "I don't think my dresses are going to fit you, Jaegar."

I rolled my eyes at her ridiculous sense of humor. "It's for *Vanya.*"

Matilda's eyes widened. "The princess from Bravadok?"

I nodded, immediately feeling like I was drowning. "Yeah. She came back with me and she's freezing."

Matilda tilted her head, her assessing gaze narrowing on me. "She came back with you? Why?"

I huffed and refused to answer her question. "Can you just help me? Please?"

She squinted at me, then sighed. "You know, you really need to just... share your feelings with people. Open up a bit. You're so much like my dad." Then she turned away and walked into one of the bedrooms.

I waited for a few moments, looking around at Dymitri and Sarah's beautiful home. It was small like all the homes in town, though it was probably three times the size of my own. The inside was well made, and the furnishings were brightly colored.

The contrast to my own little house was quite stark and confronting, and I was struck with the inexplicable desire to do some renovations on my mother's home. The insulation needed to be replaced, as did the front door. It was so warm in here by comparison, and I knew that Vanya would have been so much happier to have come back to a house like this.

It wasn't a palace, or even an extravagant house, but it was beautiful and comfortable. It had the feeling of a real home.

"Here you go," Matilda said, bustling back into the living area, her arms full of clothes. "If I remember correctly, Vanya is super skinny, so she'll need lots of layers. And here're my boots too." She handed everything over and stepped back to grab some socks.

I couldn't express the amount of gratitude I felt in my heart in that moment. "Thanks, Tilly. This means a lot."

She rolled her eyes at me this time. "Go on."

I rushed back to my house, noticing, not for the first time, the cracks in the front door and the missing sections of the thatched roof. For someone who'd been so desperately hoping to find his fated mate soon, I certainly hadn't done a great job of feathering my nest.

That needs to change, and soon.

I knocked once, then pushed open the door. "I'm back."

Vanya had moved over to the couch. She was still wrapped in many blankets, but she was closer to the fire and her pale skin had a hint of pink now. "Hey," she said, smiling softly.

I held out all the clothes I'd gathered. "Here you go. There's lots of layers so you'll be warm." I placed the clothes on the couch, then went back to the front door. There was a huge draft blowing through the cracks, which only added to the discomfort of the space.

What can I do to fix it on such short notice?

I went to the cupboard and grabbed an old wool blanket and a hammer. Once I found a couple of nails, I covered the door with the blanket and tacked it in place. Immediately the whistling of the wind through the door quieted. It was rudimentary at best, but it definitely helped a little. I turned back to face my mate and licked my lips, clearing my throat.

She was staring at me, unmoving.

I gestured to the door and heaved a sigh. "I'm sorry about the state of this place. It needs a little work."

She nodded but didn't say anything. She took some of the clothing into the blanket pile and began dressing within the folds of its warmth.

I missed seeing her naked beauty, but it was good to see her looking happier at least.

When she finally emerged from the blankets, she was wearing many layers, a long dress, leggings, and an overcoat. Still, she rushed for the fireplace to warm her hands like she was still suffering.

"How are you doing?" I asked, my heart aching in the strangest way.

"I'm a bit hungry," she admitted with half a smile.

Shit.

"Okay, well, let me make us something. I'm sure I have some food in the fridge." I managed to find some meat and vegetables and heated those up for us in a pot over the fire.

We ate in silence at the small table I'd grown up sitting at.

Vanya glanced around occasionally, but she was so hunched over, it was difficult to tell what she was taking in.

I cleared my throat with a rough cough. "Thank you for coming back with me."

She nodded, then shivered again.

"You know," I said, "If you want to go up to the castle after lunch. I'll walk you up. Maybe I can show you some of the village on the way?"

Vanya's head came up and her gorgeous dark eyes met with mine. "Really?" She sounded so hopeful.

I squashed any rising disappointment I felt, and instead injected a happy tone into my voice. "Of course! I wanted to show you the village and my house. So, one thing down, and then we can do the other on the way back to the castle."

She immediately brightened, eating faster and smiling.

Meanwhile, my appetite was gone, so I just drank some water and watched her.

When she'd finished her lunch, she asked me some questions about my life. "So, you grew up here, right? Your whole life?"

I nodded. "Yeah, as far as I know."

"And your mom?" she asked, gently this time. "She passed recently?"

"Yeah," I answered, the familiar pain hitting me again. "It was a few months ago, but it feels like yesterday."

"Is that why you sought out Uncle Damon?" she pressed.

I sighed and went to clean up our dishes. "Yeah... but that wasn't totally my choice. My mom made me promise that I'd go and find him after she was gone, so I'd have a family. She was worried about me."

I didn't need to tell Vanya I'd been dreaming about her too. That—more than my promise to my mother—had been the driving force. That and Dymitri threatening to out me, of course.

"Why didn't she want you to find Damon while she was alive?"

I ran a hand through my hair. "That's not an easy thing to answer."

Vanya turned toward me and waited. "Can you try? I'm not going anywhere." But she was. She'd leave me today and never come back, that was obvious.

So, what did I have to lose by telling her the truth? "Well, my mother was proud."

Vanya chuckled softly and reached across the table to touch my hand, the first sign of affection she'd shown me outside of her need to be warm. "Oh, I can't imagine that," she said with a grin.

I knew she was trying to tell me that I'd gotten it from somewhere, but I couldn't smile or laugh. Talking about my mother hurt. It likely always would. "Mom wanted to tell the king about me, but she said that the whole kingdom was struggling to survive, and as they weren't fated, she felt conflicted. And by the time I was old enough to want to know him, the king had already married Cass."

Vanya nodded and waited.

I exhaled slowly and kept going with my tale. "I wanted to meet him, of course, but I... I don't know—maybe it was pride, or ego, or something —but I didn't want to just throw myself at him as if I were desperate. And I didn't want my mother to ever think she wasn't enough for me, because she was. She was a great mother."

"Yeah... but surely she wouldn't have felt rejected if you went looking for your father too?" Vanya asked, her eyebrows drawn together. "I mean... the bigger the family, the better. Right?"

I shrugged. "I wouldn't know. My mom *was* my whole family, and she was enough." I stood up, not wanting to talk about my mother anymore. Vanya would never understand what my mom had to do to survive. How hard she worked just to feed me, to keep us alive.

I'd gone to bed hungry for most of my childhood, knowing somewhere in the castle my sire was warm and fed. It still made me angry to think about it, even though my adult brain knew that the king would have helped us if he could. If he'd only known. And that our whole kingdom was grateful for how hard he'd worked to rebuild everything.

It didn't make me feel any better though. I'd been unwanted then, and I was just as unwanted now. I forced a smile on my face. "Should we go?"

Vanya nodded and stood up, grabbing the boots Matilda had lent me and pulling them on. "Definitely! I can't wait to be back inside the castle's walls." She headed for the door enthusiastically.

I tried not to show her how disappointed I was once more. She didn't care for my heritage, my home, or my town. She was a princess, and no matter how much I wanted her to adjust to the North and accept my humble origins, it was clear that was never going to change.

She might have wanted to see my world, and I was grateful for that concession, but she just wasn't built to survive this place, and I couldn't blame her for missing what she was used to—just as I did.

CHAPTER

SIXTEEN

Vanya

Even with ten layers of clothing hidden under my dress, as well as thick socks and boots, I was *still* freezing when we stepped outside into the township. I tried not to shiver and clung to Jaegar's arm as he gave me the tour of the North Kingdom.

The streets and homes were small and unkempt when compared to my father's kingdom, but I knew it wasn't fair or reasonable to compare the two. Mom had told us stories of how badly affected the Kingdom of the North had been by King Damon's father, and how hard they'd all fought to rebuild—to keep everyone alive in the harsh and inhospitable climate.

"The homes here seem to be built differently," I said, gesturing to the stonework of the closest house. The stones were smaller and a darker blue than what our kingdom used for construction.

"Yes," Jaegar said, sounding strangely short and angry.

"Oh, I meant it more as a question," I rushed to say. "Is it for insulation? To ward against the cold?"

Jaegar softened slightly, his terse tone dropping as he explained that the external walls of each home were at least two stones thick, usually three, while the roofs were thatched and steepled, made to withstand and shed the intense amount of snow they received.

The people were dressed in plain clothes that looked thick and warm. The children were running in the streets and playing, despite the biting wind and the threatening rain overhead.

We walked up the winding streets towards the large, looming castle overheard.

I gasped when we finally stood squarely before the kingdom. "It's so... ancient," I managed to say in wonder.

Jaegar nodded. "Yeah. According to the elders, this kingdom was the first one built out of the five. But it was the first to fall, too."

I glanced over him with curiosity. "You said something about my dad saving your town from the wolves?"

He nodded. "Yes. Don't you know the story?"

I shook my head and grimaced. "Not really. Mom mentioned some things to us about that years ago, but not a lot of details. Can you tell me more?"

He lifted his arm and slung it over my shoulders, his mood seemingly slightly improved at the chance to talk about his beloved homeland. "I was only young, of course, but I remember being so afraid. The wolves from the woods came to attack the castle, and we all had to hide. My mother was terrified, but we survived."

"And my dad?" I asked again. "He was there at the time?"

Jaegar nodded. "He came and fought for us. He was the first fire dragon I'd ever seen, and he was amazing. He was injured, but once the battle was over, he still flew all the way home. I assume to go back to your mom."

I stared at him, my chest tightening with the emotions his words invoked. "They're fated mates," I whispered. "Their love is amazing."

He nodded, then turned away, offering me his arm. "Let's get you to the castle."

"Don't you want to show me anything else?" I asked, assuming he did. "You love this place. Surely you have shops... schools..." I hinted.

He shook his head and pulled me up toward the castle. "No, it's fine. Come on."

It took a while, but we wove our way, up the steps and to the huge front door of the castle.

Jaegar let go of my arm and went straight up to the ornately designed steel door, knocking hard. When the door opened, he stepped back and put his hands behind his back, clasping his hands together as though he were standing at attention.

The butler opened the main door, his eyebrows drawn together in surprise. "Sire, are you home early?" he queried.

Jaegar nodded quickly. "Yes, we arrived this morning. Could you please see to Vanya's needs until the king and queen arrive home tomorrow?"

The butler nodded. "Of course."

I stared at Jaegar. His voice was so strong, and his posture was as straight as an arrow. He had the presence and bearing of a king, even if he didn't yet realize it. I followed after the butler, walking toward the alluring warmth of the castle, only to find that Jaegar was pulling back. "Aren't you coming with me?" I asked.

He shook his head, his lips pulling tightly into a thin line. "No. I'm afraid I have some things to work on today. I can't delay."

"But you'll come sleep here with me, tonight, right?" I pressed, turning to stare at him. Surely, he didn't mean to go back to that draughty, tiny little house all on his own? Not when the castle and its royal family had welcomed him as a long lost son.

"Well, I—"

"Please, Jaegar," I said over the top of whatever excuse he was going to come up with. "I don't want to stay here without you." And I didn't, which was the truth. If I'd believed that Jaegar would abandon me the moment we'd arrived, I would never have come.

Jaegar's ice-blue gaze bored into me until finally, he nodded, a short, curt motion of his head. "All right. I'll be by later."

I took a step toward him to kiss him goodbye, but he bowed his head and rushed away to attend to whatever it was that was so important.

I stared after him, gobsmacked. What had caused such a significant turnaround?

"Come inside, Princess Vanya," the butler called out, interrupting my thoughts. "You must be cold."

Jaegar was out of sight now, so I turned and ran inside the castle. "Freezing!" I agreed, shivering for effect.

The butler hurried me into the main dining room, where a large fire heated the room.

"Oh!" I hurried over to the fireplace, putting my hands out to feel the heat on my palms. The doors behind me opened and I turned around to see who it was.

Sharon walked in, the regular housekeeper. "Princess Vanya," she greeted me, her arms full of dresses and other clothing. "I heard you had arrived and were dressed in clothes that weren't yours."

I frowned at what she held, not recognizing the garments. "Hello, Sharon. I don't think they're mine either."

She shook her head. "No, of course. Your clothing hasn't arrived yet, so I took it upon myself to go through Veronica's closet. Most of her clothes should fit you."

"Oh, thank you," I said gratefully, reaching out to touch a midnight-blue dress.

Sharon *tsked* loudly. "And whose clothes are these?"

I put my hand to the rough cloak I wore, feeling a little self-conscious. "I don't know, actually. Jaegar borrowed them from a friend, I believe." I'd been too out of my mind with the cold to ask any questions.

Sharon made a disgruntled noise. "Follow me, dear. The maids are setting up a guest room for you as we speak, and we'll get you into a nice warm bath, then into some of these clothes. You don't want to wear those any longer than you must."

I followed her but glanced down at the clothes I wore with appreciation. The boots were comfortable and well-made and had amazingly kept my feet warm and dry even though we'd walked the whole way in the snow. The cloak was made from rough and worn materials, as was the dress, but that didn't mean they were beneath me. I didn't care about being dressed in finery, especially when I'd faced freezing to death.

I would have walked up to the castle wrapped in a blanket if I'd needed to!
Sharon showed me to my bedroom and ran me a bath.

Uncle Damon's castle was the least fancy of all the castles in the realm, but it was steeped in history. The paintings, the portraits, and the architecture were simply beautiful and ancient beyond memory. The rooms were smaller, the furnishings simple. But the room was clean, and well cared for, and most of all, it was warm.

"Hop in," Sharon encouraged with a smile as she helped me undress. "You must be cold to your core."

I undressed quickly and rushed to get into the bathtub and sank beneath the hot water. Goosebumps covered my flesh, and for a moment, I simply shivered beneath the surface. But then a wave of relaxation washed over me as the heat seeped into my bones. "Oh, thank you Sharon," I said.

The housekeeper smiled and fussed with the clothes I'd borrowed, and retrieved a gown and fresh towels for me.

I sat up a little as the water began to rise, steam filling the warm room. "Sharon, can I ask you something?"

"Of course," the housekeeper answered.

"How has the family been with Jaegar? I mean, has it been difficult for them? For him?"

Sharon moved closer, her gaze sliding left then right furtively. "Why do you ask, Miss Vanya? Is it true that you are... *connected* to Jaegar?"

I chuckled softly. The servants sure loved to gossip. "Who told you?" I asked.

Sharon smiled but didn't reveal her source.

So, I told her the truth. "We are fated mates, actually. But I'm still unsure of what will happen next for us."

Sharon's eyes went wide, then a soft smile lifted her lips again. "Then it's true. He is truly the king's son."

I frowned at her. "Of course, he is. Why would you question that?"

Sharon shook her head. "We were all unsure when Jaegar came to the castle. We were afraid of what it would mean for our kingdom, for the royal bloodlines."

I nodded in understanding, though I couldn't empathize truly. My father's kingdom had always been wealthy and well run. This kingdom had many, many years of starvation and desolation. I couldn't even imagine what the servants had gone through. "So, you believe in who he is now that you know he's my fated mate?" I asked. "It is because of the royal link?"

Sharon nodded. "It makes more sense now, although, to tell you the truth..." She lowered her voice to a whisper. "I never doubted it, personally, though everyone else did. But it's in his eyes, isn't it? And in the way he holds himself. He seems to be what real kings are made of."

I sighed, running my now warm hands over the surface of the water and watching as the ripples fanned out. "I see it too. He's a royal dragon, through and through."

"I'll leave you to it, then, Miss Vanya," Sharon said. "But are you hungry? Would you like me to bring some afternoon tea to your room for when you're done?"

I nodded and smiled. "That would be wonderful. Thank you."

Sharon bobbed a curtsey and left.

I stayed in the bath until the water cooled, then got out to dry myself by the fire.

Could I live here with Uncle Damon and Aunt Cass?

Surely, it wouldn't be too difficult. I'd always been close to Veronica, and we could travel back and forth to my father's kingdom whenever I felt the need to see my family again.

Jaegar and I can find a solution, I'm certain. Fate doesn't make mistakes! And I know what I feel in my heart...

When my mate finally arrived after dinner was long past, he dragged me straight to bed. There he made love to me with a blazing passion that left me sweaty, exhausted, and breathless.

But when I awoke the next morning, he was already gone.

I'd convinced myself throughout the night that I could move up to the North to be with Jaegar, but that was only if he *chose* to be my mate, my life partner in a proactive and real way. If he was going to up and leave me alone every waking moment, I wasn't so sure that was the kind of relationship I could stand.

But what was the likelihood that I could stay away from the man that was my fated mate? Not high at all, I was certain. No one denied a fated mate bond. It was unheard of. Though if there was ever a dragon shifter tough enough to walk away and defy fate itself, it would be mine.

SEVENTEEN

Jaegar

By the time I hauled myself up to the castle for a late supper, I was starving and aching from the physical work I'd put myself through all day. I missed Vanya terribly, but my mind was too dark to consider anything more. I knocked on the main door, surprised to find the king himself opening it for me. "King Damon," I said, trying to sound neutral.

The king smiled and gestured for me to come in. "You're just in time for dinner."

"Oh?" I asked, surprised for the second time in as many moments. "I thought I'd missed it." In fact, I'd deliberately waited until I knew it would be done. The housekeeper would keep a plate for me and let me eat in the kitchen.

"No, not at all," he said. "We all just arrived, so the dining room is set up. Come."

I begrudgingly let the king drag me into the dining hall, where everyone was already seated and waited. No one had started eating, so either my timing was strangely perfect, or they'd waited for me.

"Please, sit," Damon said as he took his place at the head of the table.

Vanya was waiting, a seat next to her available for me.

"Hello, everyone," I managed to say, nodding my head to the rest of the family as I took my seat. "I didn't think you were arriving until tomorrow?"

Everyone was there, even Iain and Veronica.

Queen Cass answered my question, "We were anxious to come home."

"Please, eat," the king said.

Everyone began reaching for the platters and serving themselves.

A servant walked up and discreetly asked me if I'd like wine or whiskey.

I immediately requested whiskey, realizing I would need fortification to get through whatever conversation was coming.

"It's so great to be home," Veronica said appreciatively. "Though it's so much colder than I remembered. We've been in the human world too long again."

I smiled at her.

Veronica's gaze zoomed in on me. "Have you ever crossed the Veil, Jaegar?"

"No," I answered truthfully, reaching for the roasted potatoes slathered in melted herbed butter. "I'd never left the North... before a few days ago."

"It must have been such a shock," Vanya said quietly beside me. She was dressed in a beautiful, dark dress, her long hair piled on top of her head in an arrangement of elegant curls.

I shrugged. "Yes, it was, but I'm home now."

A strange silence followed my answer before Theo spoke. "Jaegar, can I ask you something?"

I nodded. "Of course." The creamy pasta dish I'd heaped on my plate was settling well into my cold belly, and as I took a long sip of whiskey, I sighed, finally relaxing.

"You love this kingdom, don't you?" he pressed.

I frowned at the crown prince. "Of course. It's my home."

What an odd question.

I picked up my fork and speared a chunk of potato before putting it in my mouth.

"I don't think that now is the time to talk about that," the queen said carefully.

My brow furrowed in confusion. "About what?" Were they considering kicking me out of the kingdom or something? Had they finally decided they couldn't deal with me being part of their world and wanted to be rid of me once and for all? "You're not going to ask me leave, are you?" I asked. I wasn't sure I'd survive being cast out of the only home I'd ever known.

Barry joined in on the conversation and laughed. "Oh, no. Not at all. You love this place even more than us."

I glanced sidelong at Vanya.

She gave me a soft shrug, as if to say she didn't know what they were talking about.

The king picked up his wine glass and took as sip before speaking. "My sons are trying to tell you, inelegantly I must say, that we'd all like you to take a more active role in the running of the kingdom."

I glanced at the queen, then Vanya, then back at the king. "A more active role than what I'm currently doing? Building houses for my people?" I didn't think anything was more important than that.

The queen smiled.

Veronica laughed out loud. "See! He's *just* like you, Dad."

I glanced at my half-sister and frowned. "What are you talking about?"

She rolled her eyes. "My dad, or... well, I should say *our* dad, shouldn't I? But anyway... Dad's the same as you. Mom's always said that he never wanted to live in the castle. He would have much rather lived in a field with the farmers."

I glanced at my father.

He smiled and swirled the wine in his glass. "Of course. I couldn't have rebuilt my home without getting out in the kingdom and helping."

The queen shook her head. "Sweetheart, there aren't many kings who would have literally built those first homes with their own hands and spoken to farmers while planting crops."

I looked at my father with renewed respect. I knew he'd done a lot, but I hadn't realized quite how much. I'd never known he'd dealt with the land and its people so very directly, just as I did. A man who worked with his hands and cared for his subjects had to not only be respected but appreciated. It took strength of character to be that kind of person, especially with such a heavy mantle to carry.

"You did the right thing," I said. "The North needs a king who will stand with his people from the ground up."

"Exactly our point!" Barry said loudly, grinning from ear to ear.

I took a sip of whiskey, still unsure as to where this particular strain of conversation was heading.

Then Barry added, "That's why Theo and I think you should be king instead of either of us."

The whiskey burst out from between my lips and all over the platter of pasta in front of me. "Oh, my gods, I'm so sorry," I gasped as the whiskey continued to burn in my throat, reaching out to wipe up the whiskey with my hand, though it was a pointless exercise.

The servants came forward instantly, whisking the food away and wiping everything clean.

"It's perfectly all right, sire," one of the servants assured me. "Would you like another whiskey?"

"Hell, yes." I was going to need more than a little fortification if this was what the princes wanted to talk about. I could hardly believe my fucking ears. My brain felt like it was going to explode.

Is this really happening?

Cass smiled gently. "Well, that certainly answers the question of whether you were planning to take over for Damon."

I leaned back to give the servants space to reset the table, my head spinning. "Take over... what?"

Cass gestured to the royal dining room. "The kingdom."

My stomach dropped, but this wasn't totally unexpected. I bore the tattoo, and I was the eldest son. It made sense they were worried about my intentions.

I shook my head. "No... not at all. Absolutely not. I never wanted anything from your family, and the idea of usurping my king never even occurred to me."

"This is your family too," the king said, his voice strong and sure.

I blinked at him, then looked back at his sons. "Then what is this about?"

Theo and Barry glanced at each other.

"We don't love the people the way you do," Theo finally said. "And you have the tattoo. So..."

"So... what?" I asked, my heart hammering in my chest like a war drum.

"So..." Theo tilted his head at me, frowning as though he was the one confused, rather than me. "Why don't you assume the throne after Dad?"

I stared at him, shocked beyond belief.

The crown princes want me to usurp them?

"Instead of you?" I whispered, reaching for my poor head. "Are you serious?" My quiet words were at odds with the turmoil churning inside my mind. My heart was thundering like a jackhammer in my chest, and adrenaline zinged along my veins like white-hot lightning.

Every instinct in me wanted to run. Hell, I wanted to *fight*. But who was the enemy in this situation? It didn't seem there was one. There was just the proposal of an insane notion—nothing more, nothing less.

Vanya's hand slid over my thigh.

I jerked my head over to stare at her.

She was giving me an encouraging smile but there was worry in her eyes also, as well there should be.

This was the last thing I'd expected to hear tonight. The *very* last.

"Ahhh..." I said, at an utter loss for words for the moment.

Veronica snorted out a laugh. "You're right, Mom. He definitely didn't come here to steal the crown. It doesn't even look like he wants it."

"I don't!" I immediately said without really thinking first.

My father's face fell.

I regretted my thoughtless reply instantly. "I'm sorry, that came out wrong. I mean—"

"It's all right," Cass said, reaching over to take hold her husband's hand. "We didn't expect you to feel so strongly about it, but I guess you've had a lot longer to think about all of this than us."

I nodded, gulping loudly, though they were way off the mark. I'd never thought about it. It wasn't my place. I was the bastard son, the one raised in poverty, far beyond the privilege and airs of the royal family.

Theo leaned forward in his seat, gaining my attention. He had a big frown on his face. "But... why?" he pushed, a note of desperation in his voice. "You're the oldest, by far. And you have the tattoo."

"So do you," I said, pointing out the obvious.

Doesn't the kid want the crown he was born to? This makes no sense. He's the legitimate heir.

Theo's smile was lopsided. "Yeah... I do. And I love my family and my people, but I've never looked forward to being king. I'm not a natural-born leader like you. You're a Northman in the truest sense."

I scoffed at him, slugging back my whiskey. "Not a natural? Are you kidding me? I felt like a freak at the party the other night, whereas you fit in everywhere."

"But that's not what being king is about," Damon interjected reasonably, his voice heavy.

I rounded on him, an irrational panic building in my chest. "But that's part of it, isn't it? The meetings and the royal family parties and gatherings. I grew up starving and angry at the world. I'm not meant to run a fucking kingdom!"

"Jaegar..."

I took note of the warning tone in Vanya's voice but ignored it and decided to address the whole table. "I like building houses. I like looking after my neighbors. I like getting my hands dirty. I don't want to sit on some fat pillow in a grand hall and dish out advice to people."

Damon's face flushed red.

Before he could speak, Cass sighed pointedly. "I wish Stavrok was here."

"Why?" I demanded, wanting to know her reasoning. "So, I can feel even more inferior than I do already?"

"No!" she snapped back, unperturbed by my temper or abrasiveness. "Because my cousin would tell you that you're much more like Damon than you can ever imagine!"

I stood up abruptly, Vanya's hand falling from my lap and the chair making a loud, scraping noise on the polished floor. "I'm not you!" I practically yelled at my father. "And I never will be. So, just stop... all of you, okay? And leave me alone."

The sound of soft footfalls following me out into the hallway had me turning around with clenched fists, a fire burning in my gut as I turned to confront whoever it was.

Vanya jumped back from my fury, her hands upraised in a calming gesture.

I forced myself to calm down. "Sorry," I breathed, barely containing what so desperately wanted to erupt out of me now. "I had to get out of there."

"It's all right," she soothed, reaching out to touch my arm. "But I need you to know that I think you'd be a great king, Jaegar. You're strong and fearless, and you love your people so much."

I stared at her as her words sank in. And when they finally reached my soul, I snatched my arm out of her grip in distrust and hurt. "Is that what you think?" I demanded, speaking through my teeth, which were already shifting. "That I'd do a good job sitting on a fucking throne all day? Of playing at being royal like you? That goes to show how well you know me, *mate*." And with that final barb thrown, I turned and ran from a life that was being thrust upon me. A life I never wanted.

That's not me!

I ran through the castle, back across the threshold and out into the cold. I was panting and couldn't catch my breath, and my dragon was screaming at me to fly, to take to the skies. With a racing heart and more emotions roiling within me than I'd ever felt in my whole life, I chose not to fight him.

"Jaegar! Can I help, sire?" the butler called out from the front door, a concerned expression on his face.

I turned and threw my best coat at him. "Just take care of my clothes, please." I ripped off my shirt and managed to throw it toward my coat before my dragon ripped through my body. My arms and legs shortened, and my body grew in size. My skin became gleaming scales, and my blood turned to liquid ice in my veins.

How could my own fated mate turn on me during such a pivotal moment? Was she so obsessed with marrying a royal that she'd forgotten who I really was? Where I'd come from? Because I certainly hadn't. Memories of my mother and the years we'd spent scraping to get by assaulted my mind, yanking on my heartstrings. This wasn't what she'd intended when she asked me to seek out my sire, I was sure of it.

It was time to fly, to escape, and to retreat from the suffocating glitz and glamor of the royal world to the only home I'd ever known—to the place that I belonged. My duty as a man of the North was to the people— not a throne.

EIGHTEEN

Jaegar

Pure fury saw me through the first half of the next day. I still couldn't believe that fate had sent me such a shallow, incompatible mate. Her intentions and desires were clear now. She was exactly what he'd feared she was—a pampered princess, inside and out.

She just wants a damn royal!

And for Theo to offer me the throne, in front of everyone? The way he put me on the spot like that... I hadn't been prepared at all.

The fucking gall of that kid. Doesn't he know anything?

My shoulders ached from the rocks I'd spent all day lifting, but it was a great and rewarding feeling to see the wall finally come together. A large part of the external barrier that ran around our kingdom was crumbling, and I'd been put on the team tasked with repairing it. We all still had secret worries about the wolves in the woods, even though they hadn't been seen for almost thirty years now. Behind me, I heard one of the guys speak, dragging me from my thoughts.

"Your Highness," he said. "It's good to see you."

"And you also, Tomas," Damon's already familiar voice answered.

I wiped the sweat from my brow on the sleeve of my shirt and turned around to look at the man who'd sired me. He wasn't wearing his royal rags today. Instead he'd donned a simple gray shirt, trousers, and a coat. He didn't quite look like he belonged here, but he didn't look like the king either.

"Jaegar," he greeted, nodding once, his blue eyes zeroing in on me.

I nodded back. "Hey."

The men around us seemed to disappear all at once as they made various excuses to look in on other projects, leaving me alone with my father.

I took a sip of water from my canteen, waiting for him to speak. When he didn't, I cleared my throat and spoke up. "Do you have something to say? Otherwise, I've got get back to this." There were only a few hours of daylight left before the day was over, and I was almost done, albeit I'd gotten to the hardest part of the job.

"I'll help," Damon said, pulling off his coat and laying it on the stones to his left.

"Oh, no," I said, shaking my head. "No need. I've got it."

"You need a second pair of hands to finish the top layer," the king said, walking up to me. "And don't act like you don't. I was building these walls since before you were born, son."

His words made my heart feel strange, but I shook off the sensation. An able-bodied man had offered to help me. That's all I needed to focus on. "Fine," I relented. "Hand me that rock."

He pointed to a step near the wall. "You get up first, then I'll hand it to you. We're going have to work together to get this part done before we lose the light."

I stared at him for a moment, in awe at this side of him. He was right, of course. I'd struggle to lift the remaining rocks, hefty as they were, above my head high enough to place them on the wall, especially alone. And that immediately made me wonder.

What else has he done in his lifetime? What else do I not know?

"Okay," I managed to say, then went and stood where he recommended. Then I watched as a man of at least sixty years old, albeit a dragon shifter, squatted down and wrapped his arms around the largest boulder in our vicinity. Before I could even think to tell him not to lift that one, it was done.

Damon heaved the rock up, then walked over to me, placing it into my waiting arms.

I swallowed the groan of pain caused by lifting the fucker of a thing myself. Instead, I went up and lifted the boulder above my head, placing it on the wall regardless of the strain. If my old man could do it, so could I.

Damon handed me the mortar which was a tacky sludge that would securely fill in all the gaps between the rocks.

I applied it over every crack, smoothing it down into the crevices and by the time I was done, he was back with another boulder.

We worked that way for hours, finishing more than double what I'd aimed to get done on this day.

The king—my father—was an incredibly strong man and tenacious as all hell. He didn't stop, even when I could tell he was sore and tired. He worked like a soldier, a true laborer, unrelenting in— the face of stress and physical torment.

When the sun set over the forest and darkness fell, we stood side by side, panting hard, taking a moment to silently appreciate our hard work and what we'd achieved.

"Do you want to come back to my house?" I asked him, handing him my almost empty canteen of water. "For a drink?"

He nodded, wiping sweat from his brow.

And together we staggered the short distance back to my home.

When we entered, I tried not to feel ashamed of the interior of the house. Vanya had been incredibly uncomfortable here, amongst the peasants.

But Damon walked in and sat down as though he'd been here before, groaning with the strain of the day. "Damn," he said. "I haven't worked that hard in a long time."

I poured us both a glass of water and handed him one. "But you can still do it," I said to him, lifting my glass in gratitude. "Thanks for the help."

Damon nodded in acknowledgement.

Then we drank our water in silence as the moments ticked by.

I began to wonder what else I could offer him. "We could get some dinner?" I offered. "I don't have much here, but I eat at the local most nights." We had a cheap but good little tavern not far away, and I had a lot of my meals there.

Damon smiled. "Thanks, but Cass wants me home for dinner."

I couldn't help but laugh at how absurdly casual he sounded. "You say that like you're going home to your wife, just like any other normal man."

Damon frowned at me, his lips twisting. "That's exactly what it feels like, too. Yes, we have servants, Cass isn't the one doing the cooking, and my house is bigger than most... but it's still the same, Jaegar."

I sat down on the armchair, my muscles protesting at the movement. "You know, I don't think I've worked that hard in years either." I stretched out my arms, feeling the tight and painful pull of a torn muscle.

"You should come up to the castle," Damon said. "You could use a long, hot bath."

"I'm fine here," I said stubbornly. "I have a bathroom. I'll have a shower later." I didn't have a luxurious tub to luxuriate in of course, but I had all the basic necessities I needed.

Damon nodded slowly but didn't speak. And he didn't leave either.

"Did you come to talk about something?" I asked him. "I hope you're not trying to make me become king after you, because that isn't on the cards for me. I'm sorry to disappoint."

Damon chuckled. "Really? Have you checked in with Marienne on that?"

"Oh, well..." And Anthony's vision flooded back to me of Vanya's birthing scene, inside the castle's walls. I shook my head. "It doesn't matter. That life isn't for me. Besides, Anthony said their visions change all the time. It's not like they're set in stone."

Damon sighed. "Jaegar, you don't have to be king. You don't even have to live in the castle if you don't want to. But—"

"But what?" I demanded to know. Why had he bothered to put in a hard day's labor by my side if he wasn't going to be straight with me now?

"But you'll miss out on things if you make that choice."

I lifted my chin. "Dymitri and Lucian live in town, here, with me," I pointed out.

Damon smiled, but his gaze said he knew something more. "That's true, but it wasn't to begin with. They lived with us—for years, in fact. It wasn't until we all had children, and Sarah and Katerina had personally acclimatized to our weather, that they eventually chose to live in town."

I blinked at him, momentarily taken aback. "I, ah, I didn't know that." I'd thought they'd lived it rugged and rough like I had.

Damon grinned at me. "Why would you? That was almost thirty years ago, now."

I sighed and put down my glass, resigned to the fact that this was going to be an uncomfortable conversation. "So, what's that got to do with me?"

Damon stood up and moved over to the fireplace, bending down to begin the process of building the fire for the night just like any other man. When he was done, he stood back up, groaning softly with the pain of moving. "It's got everything to do with you Jaegar. Whether you like it or not, you have royal blood flowing in your veins, a royal fated mate from another kingdom, and from what you've said, a potential future in the castle that Anthony had already seen."

I stood up and paced the room, my heart beginning to gallop. I'd been running away from this conversation for so long, unsure I was ready for it. "And?" I said, my chest tightening, "So, that means that this noose around my neck will always be there? That I have no choice in the matter?"

"You always have a choice," the king said. "But are you ready for the consequences of making those choices?"

I stared at him, then crossed my arms over my chest, an unexpected anger building in my heart. "What are you talking about?"

Long moments ticked by as Damon stared at me before he spoke again. "Do you really think you can reject your fated mate and survive?"

My throat thickened, and I swallowed hard at the solemn expression on his face. He was being deathly serious. He was giving me a warning. "But Vanya would never survive this world. She wants me to be a prince and to live in her father's castle!"

Damon shrugged. "And? What's wrong with that?" he asked.

I threw my hands up in the air in frustration. "Are you serious? You know *exactly* what's wrong with that! I'm an ice dragon! A man of the

North! I'm not living in some pampered, bullshit castle with nothing to do all day."

Damon raised an eyebrow at me. "You do realize that with all that power comes money, duty, control, and resources? Do you know what sort of changes you could make? What sort of good you could do for our people?"

I opened my mouth, then shut it again.

Damn it.

He was right, unfortunately. It was what he'd done, after all. He'd fought hard when it was required of him, then used his power to help our people. "Fine," I conceded. "But even if I wanted to help our people, I still don't want to be king."

Damon snorted. "Son, I don't intend to die for at least another good twenty years, and I'm not giving up the job until then. So, how about you don't make wide, sweeping statements that aren't relevant yet?"

I glared at him. "And yet your son seems to think I need to make that choice, now. He certainly made it an issue over dinner the other night."

"Your half-brother," Damon added, "is young and enthusiastic to have the mantle of crown prince taken off him. He wasn't lying when he intimated that he wasn't interested in ruling."

For fuck's sake...

Damon strolled over to the door and put his hand on the handle. "Look, son. I am *so* grateful that you came to us when you did. I only wish I'd known about you sooner."

"What would you have done?" I asked, my throat thick with emotion as I dared to ask the one question that had plagued me all my life.

The king's icy blue eyes looked right into the depths of my soul as he answered, "I would have brought you into my family immediately. You and your mother would have lived in the castle, and I would have looked after you the best I could. I would have made you feel welcome and made sure you knew that you were loved."

Despite my original reservations, I believed him. And it made more of a difference than I ever imagined.

But...

"I still don't want to leave the North," I said, voicing my truth. "I can't do it."

"Then you better speak to Vanya, because trust me when I say, you won't survive long without her. Especially since you've taken her to bed. That only reinforces and strengthens the intensity of the bond."

I inhaled sharply through my nose. I didn't like people telling me what I could and couldn't do. Not fate, or the king, my father.

Damon held his hand up to wave farewell. "I hope you choose the path that is right for you both," he said, then took his leave.

Out of pure stubbornness, I stayed in my humble little thatched home for the evening and climbed into my cold, empty bed to sleep away the thoughts that overwhelmed me and the pain that wracked my aching body. But sleep eluded me, and instead I lay on my lumpy, old mattress staring up at the ceiling with nothing more than the ghost of Vanya's scent and my memories to keep me company through the long, dark and icy night.

Vanya

A hot cup of tea wasn't the most appetizing breakfast, but it was all I could stomach. I excused myself from the family breakfast and went to sit in the library with my drink. There I was, curled up in a chair by the fire, when I heard someone come in.

"There you are, sweetheart," said the queen.

I smiled at the woman who was the closest thing to a second mother I had. "Hey, Aunt Cass."

She sat in the armchair opposite me and folded her hands in her lap, wasting no time in beating around the bush. "Well, this is a bit of pickle, isn't it?" she asked.

I nodded and gulped as hot tears immediately sprang to my eyes. "Yep." I couldn't say anything more without bawling my fragile heart out, so I took a long sip of tea and stared into the dancing flames of the fireplace. I'd never felt more alone in all my life, and that was saying something. When I'd gone to bed last night, I'd been certain that my mate would return to me despite the upset over dinner. I'd imagined he couldn't stay away from me.

That's how fated mates work, isn't it?

But he had, and I'd awoken to a cold bed and a pit in my stomach the size of my fist. This wasn't how it was meant to be, and my soul ached at the distance that seemed to growing like a great divide between us in the aftermath of his denial of the crown.

Cass sighed heavily, as if the weight of the world were on her own shoulders. "You know, if I'd known he was meant for you, Vanya, I would have been nicer to him in the beginning."

I chuckled out a laugh. "You weren't mean to him, surely? That's not like you."

Cass's lips quirked up at the corners. "I wasn't terrible, of course... but I did suspect he was lying to usurp my sons of their birthright. And then there was the jealousy. He's my husband's son, but not mine." She shook her head. "Oh, that's a tough beast to master." Her sad smile spoke of many things. Of stories of love and longing and fighting and life with all its many ups and downs.

Tears welled up in my eyes. "You've lived a really great life, haven't you, Aunt Cass?" I asked, though it was an observation, and more rhetorical than an actual question.

Cass, my dad's first cousin, turned to look at me. Like, *really* look at me. Her gaze ran over my face, and it felt like she was staring into my soul, looking for an answer to a question she wasn't asking aloud.

When she finally spoke, she said what I secretly hoped, "He'll come back, Vanya."

I nodded slowly and focused on sipping my tea, cupping both hands around the warmth of the porcelain in case I dropped it. I was feeling strangely woozy, and it was probably because I hadn't managed to eat properly. With Jaegar away, I just didn't have the heart in me to eat.

"He will," she reasserted, obviously seeing the flicker of uncertainty in my eyes.

"Maybe," I said with a sigh. "But I have no idea how we're going to make this work in the long run if we even make it that far. We're so different that we might as well be from entirely different worlds."

"But he's your fated mate," she said, blinking at me as though I'd just said the world was flat.

I couldn't laugh, but her wide eyes made me smile. "I know you moved here for Uncle Damon, but you had a castle, and you were always at our place. I can't move here to live in that... in that little hovel of his, Auntie Cass. I love him, but I just can't. I don't mean to sound vain, or selfish, but"

"You're not," she interrupted. "Damon saw Jaegar last night and he said that his house is one of the worst he's seen in the whole town. And considering Jaegar has literally been restoring this kingdom from the ground up, it doesn't make any sense why he's left it like that."

I pressed my lips together to stop myself from crying out, my heart lodging firmly in my throat.

Cass moved closer and put a hand out to me, "It's okay, sweetie. Talk to me. This is a no judgement zone."

"It's all about his mom," I said, "and his childhood. He's so proud. So..."

Cass chuckled. "He's a royal who is probably tougher than any king in our realm, living or dead. If he chose to lead the North, either as our king, or beside Theo, we would become the most formidable force around."

I stared at my aunt, realizing that she'd more than wrapped her head around the idea that a bastard could usurp her son. "So, you really don't care if Jaegar ends up becoming the king and Theo doesn't?"

Cass glanced away a moment, her cheeks flushing with a telling rosy pink hue. "I can't say I wasn't upset at first when Theo brought it up to me. But his points were all valid. My children have been raised, much like you and your siblings. They have been pampered in many ways. Sure, they've helped the farmers, and have gotten their boots on the ground, so to speak, but..."

"But?" I asked, hope winging in my heart with a nervous flutter.

"But the North is the toughest kingdom we have. Damon survived his father's downfall and managed to rebuild everything here, mostly due to his pure grit and determination. Like you said, I often flew down to your father's kingdom and hid there, away from the hard work and the pain of watching my husband claw back what had been so tragically lost. I wasn't as strong as I should have been, Vanya, but none of us are perfect creatures."

It was my turn to reach out and grip her hand. "Uncle Damon is lucky to have you, and it's clear he adores you. Even though you came from different walks of life, it doesn't mean you didn't make it work. After all, just look at Anselm and Kayla."

Cass laughed. "They're from literal different worlds, all right, but I'd say Sarah and Katerina have had it harder. They moved to our realm to live in the North. They've had to put up with a lot more than anyone. The adjustment period can be difficult without support. Without someone to talk to about your fears and feelings."

I nodded slowly, mulling her words over. "Maybe I need to speak to them."

Cass smiled. "You can, anytime, of course. But what they'll tell you is that they just... adapted. They got warm clothes, pushed out babies, and simply loved their men."

"And how are their houses?" I asked as nerves jangled through me.

Cass' sparkling laughter made me smile. "They're lovely, actually. Dymitri and Lucian stayed here, in the castle, for years while they bonded with Damon and built themselves new homes in town. Remember, they grew up in the woods."

I shuddered. "I can't imagine how they survived that, but at least they had each other."

She sighed. "Neither can I, honestly. They're the toughest of us all."

I set my now empty teacup down and pulled my legs up so I could rest my head on my knees. "I can't see a way through all this, Aunt Cass. I mean... you should have seen his face when I told him I thought he'd make a good king. You'd think I told him he'd hurt children or something. He was mortified and filled with rage. I've never seen him like that." I couldn't even come up with a comparison that would make him look so angry.

Cass sighed and stood up. "It's a lot to deal with at once. Within a single week, Jaegar went from being anonymous and alone in this world, to being a prince and a fated mate to foreign royalty. That would be too much for almost anyone. Maybe just try and be extra patient with him, hmm? Baby steps. Just take it a day at a time."

I lifted my head and nodded with a sigh of my own. There was an undeniable wisdom in her words. There was no point catastrophizing. "Okay, Aunt Cass."

During the night, I'd planned to fly home after lunch today, but maybe that wasn't the best choice. My mate flying away from me last night had cut me deeply. If I did the same thing to Jaegar, leaving him when he needed me the most, what sort of fated mate did that make me? What did it say of our bond if I flew back to the comforts of what I'd always known, unwilling to adapt like the other strong women that called the North their home...

AFTER LUNCH I retired to my bedroom and just cried. The smell of Jaegar's body still lingered in the sheets, and I missed him so much, it physically hurt. When a knock sounded at the door, I called out, "Just a minute!" taking the time to blow my nose and wash my face with cool water.

I probably look like hell.

My eyes were still red and my cheeks were puffy, but I opened the door anyway, assuming it was most likely one of my cousins coming to check up on me. "Jaegar," I whispered, staring up at him as if he'd disappear like mist in the morning. "Are you really here?" He'd washed his long hair, and it glistened with good health. Even with the pain in my chest upon seeing him, I wanted to reach out and tangle my fingers in his dark locks. "What are you doing here?"

His smile was sheepish and reserved. "Can I come in?" he asked.

I stepped back and waved him in, shutting the door behind him. I wasn't dressed nicely, and surely, I looked like an utter mess. But what did it matter if he was coming to tell me that we needed to break up?

Is that even a thing with fated mates? Can we break up?

He walked over to the fireplace, probably to warm up. He'd been outside all day most likely, knowing him.

I made my way over to the bed and sat down on the same mattress we'd made love on only a day ago. Part of me wished I could sit somewhere else, but my heart clung to the small and desperate hope that he'd come back to me. That he'd deny his stubborn nature and decide we were worth fighting for—that I was worth being a little uncomfortable for.

He was silent for too long.

My poor, fried nerves fizzled, and tears pricked at my eyes again. "Well? Please say something."

He walked over to where I sat, then kneeled on one knee.

My jaw dropped, and I stared up at him. "What are you doing?" I breathed.

He took my hand in his and stared back at me with those amazing blue eyes of his. "Please forgive me for the other night, Vanya. My anger was not toward you, but you copped it, and for that I'm sorry."

I nodded, gulping at the emotions lodged in my throat. "It's okay. I understand." And I had. I knew that all of this had been a lot for him to digest, but that hadn't stopped me from being quite a teary mess after. "Do you realize that I don't know you?" I asked. If I were honest, that's what had hurt the most. I could handle his anger and anxiety. I hadn't liked it, of course, but his words about not knowing my fated mate had been what had cut me to my core.

He shook his head slowly. "No, you aren't the problem here, Vanya. I am, and know that. I'm not good enough for you or this family. I'm common trash."

Horror struck my heart, and I fell onto my knees before him, taking his beloved face in my hands. "No, you're not, and you never have been." I wanted to wring his mother's neck at this point, but didn't dare voice anything disparaging against her memory. Jaegar should never have grown up believing anything other than what I was about to say next.

"Jaegar, you are my mate. You are loved. You are worthy. And you can be whoever you want to be. And if that is someone who stays relatively anonymous and lives in the village, then so be it."

His head, which had been bowed, came up to stare at me. "Do you mean that? You'd come here? Live with me?"

My lips quirked up at the edges. "I would." There was no other choice. I couldn't live without him. I knew it in my bones. I'd known for some time, despite my own discomfort and shock upon coming to the North more than a little unprepared. "But I'm sorry, we *need* a new house. Somewhere with no ghosts and no memories, and maybe even a few creature comforts."

His eyes glistened with unshed tears and his lower lip trembled ever so slightly.

And with that, I knew I'd hit the nail on the head.

He swallowed hard, his throat working overtime. "You deserve a palace."

I shrugged. "We have two of those, but it doesn't mean we have to live in them all the time. I just need you, Jaegar... and a really warm, well-insulated house."

"Two castles..." He shook his head and chuckled softly. "I can build you another house. One like Dymitri's, warm and big enough for a princess."

And a prince...

"I know you can," I said, gripping his hands. "And if you choose to step up within Damon's family, I'll stand by your side and live wherever you want us to."

He frowned at me then spoke slowly. "And if I don't want to do that?" It was clear this subject was at the heart of the conflict raging within him.

"Let's sit on the bed," I said, standing up and pulling him to his feet.

When he finally sat down on the mattress, he was stiff and wasn't touching me.

I sighed and tamped down my impatience, just as I had promised Aunt Cass I would. I had to try...

But why is he still worried about me loving him?

Instead of sitting down beside him, I stayed standing in front of him. "If you don't want to be a prince and accept those responsibilities, I'd like to spend some time at the other kingdoms throughout the year. My sister mostly lives in the Black Mountains, and my brother is home in Bravadok. Iain floats everywhere. So, I'd like to travel as much as we can to see them."

"But we could still live here, in the North, in a home of our own in town?" he asked, his voice sounding hopeful for the first time since his return.

I nodded, resolute in my decision. "Yes, of course, Jaegar."

He grabbed me around the waist and hauled me against him.

I hopped onto his lap, straddling his waist, wrapping my arms around his neck. "I love you and I'll do whatever I can to keep us together, and to make sure you're happy."

His hands pressed into my back, his breath caressing my lips. "But I want you to be happy too, Vanya."

I laughed, feeling truly happy for the first time in days. "As long as I'm with you, *and* I'm warm enough…" Something we'd have to work on. "I'll be happy."

He kissed me then, stealing the breath from me.

The passion of his touch made me moan with longing, and his kisses caused all rational thought to fly from my mind.

We're together now. That's all that matters.

I thrust my pelvis against his, wanting a deeper, more intimate connection.

He stood up then, turned around and laid me down on the mattress, his heavy body pressing into mine. When he lifted his head, I tried to pull him down to me again.

But he stopped me, holding firm in his position. "So, you really don't care if I'm a bastard?"

I shrugged, still in disbelief that he'd think that would matter. "So is Uncle Erik and he's the King of the Black Mountains."

"Or that I might never want to be a prince or do any of the royal things?"

I laughed and shook my head. "As long as you love *this* princess, nothing else matters to me. We'll figure it all out along the way, one day at a time."

He stared at me for too long, lost in my eyes.

I wriggled in his grip, wanting more. Truthfully, I wanted to get naked and feel his beautiful, hot, ripped body against mine.

"Will you marry me?" he whispered.

I stopped wriggling and ran my fingers through his hair, my happiness now impossibly complete. "Of course, I will," I answered. "When?"

He laughed. "Ah… tomorrow? Next week? How long does it take to set up a party for that sort of thing?" he asked.

"Kiss me," I whispered up at him, arching my back to feel him against me. "We can sort all that out later. For now, I just need you."

He grinned and came down on me once more, sweeping me up and away into a world of mind-blowing bliss and physical rapture that lasted so many hours, I lost count.

EPILOGUE

I threw open the doors to the servants' quarters and bolted down the hallway until I reached the medical wing. The doctor was sitting at his table, drinking a cup of tea. "You've got to come. Now!" I roared, before I turned and ran back, hearing the commotion of the staff coming behind me. The stupid doctor had left Vanya, telling her she had plenty of time before giving birth, and that she should get some sleep.

Sleep! Asshole. As if!

"Jaegar, what's happened?" Stavrok called out after me.

But I didn't dare stop. "Baby!" I yelled over my shoulder, still running.

My wife needed me, and all I could do was pray that Anthony's vision from almost a year ago would come true, and that soon we would have our beautiful child. I could hear Vanya's screams before I got to our bedroom, and they made my heart race. I burst through the doors, the king and the doctor hard on my heels. "He's coming!" I said, leaping onto the bed beside her. "I'm here, beautiful. Everything is going to be okay."

She was panting hard, her white cotton nightgown now drenched in sweat so that it clung to her body. "I think I need to push," she gasped in between breaths.

The door opened again, and the king and queen of Bravadok came in.

Lucy went around the bed to the other side of Vanya, grabbing her hand tightly. "I'm here, sweetheart," she assured her daughter.

The doctor walked in a moment later, far too cool and calm for the situation.

I almost rose up from the bed to snap his damn head off his shoulders.

"Princess Vanya, let's see what's happening here." He lifted the hem of her nightgown and reached beneath it, performing a quick physical before voicing his professional opinion. "You're fully dilated now and can push when you're ready."

"I could have told you that!" Vanya growled at him, her eyes fierce as her cheeks reddened with exertion.

I shared a look with Lucy, and we both tried not to laugh. Vanya had turned into a right mother dragon through and through the moment she'd become pregnant. She was every bit as tough and strong and as fiery as I was. And I couldn't be prouder.

She began to cry out, squeezing my hand *hard*. She strained and pushed, her big belly heaving with the effort.

The king stood behind me by the bed, nearby if we needed him.

Vanya fell back against the pillows, sobbing as her body trembled. "This is *so* hard."

"I can see the head, Vanya. A few more pushes and you'll have your baby in your arms," the doctor advised.

A servant came up beside me with a bowl of cold water and a washcloth.

I grabbed the cloth and dabbed her face and neck tenderly, hoping to ease even the smallest of discomforts. "You're doing so well, my love," I cooed, lending her whatever strength I had to give.

"Oh, no," she sobbed, her eyes wide. "It's coming again." She sat up and this time, yelled out loudly as she pushed hard, her brow creased, and her teeth bared.

"I have the head!" the doctor said.

Vanya turned her head to me. She was so exhausted, but so damn determined.

I wiped her face and kissed her brow. "Good girl," I whispered. "Good girl. You're so brave. You can do this. I believe in you, baby."

"Slowly, Vanya," the doctor said. "Small, careful pushes, and the baby will slide out."

With a final, mammoth effort, she began to bear down on her final pushes, groaning loudly until the baby slid out between her thighs and into the doctor's waiting hands.

"You have a son!" he announced, checking our child over thoroughly before cutting off the cord and wrapping the infant in a blanket the servant gave him.

I kissed Vanya, sending up prayers of thanks to the gods for the safe arrival of my son and the health of my wife.

Queen Lucy stood up and moved behind the doctor. "Watch her bleeding," she warned. "I had a lot of trouble after the triplets."

The doctor didn't say anything in response to Lucy, simply handing the baby up to my wife, and moving to check on her health.

"Oh, he's beautiful," Vanya cooed, settling into the pillows mounted up behind her. "And he looks just like you."

I chuckled out a laugh. "If he's beautiful, sweetheart, then he gets that from you." I stared down at my wife and son, the knowledge that I had a family, my own blood family, washing over me. "Thank you."

She looked away from the baby for a moment and up at me, tears shimmering in her striking dark eyes. "I love you."

Lucy came back to Vanya's side, a broad smile on her face. "Oh, sweetheart, he's just beautiful."

I slid off the bed and encouraged the king to come forward to have a look at his newest grandchild.

Vanya was literally glowing.

I'd never seen her look so happy, though our wedding day came a close second. We'd been married nine months ago in my father's kingdom, in the North, very shortly after I'd proposed.

The wedding had been emotional, and the party... absolutely epic. We'd conceived our baby that very night, the love of our fated union stronger than anything I'd ever known. Family and friends from all over the realm had come to celebrate with us, and I'd never felt so content.

Not until today.

The queen looked up at me. "Jaegar, he's beautiful."

I smiled at her. "That's all your daughter, Lucy."

"Jaegar, look!" Vanya said her breath catching in her throat as she pulled back the baby's blanket.

I didn't want to dislodge my in-laws, so I walked behind Lucy and stared down at what Vanya was trying to show me. There, on the baby's chest, was a tiny little birthmark.

"Is that..." My heart exploded and was reborn a million times over in a single breathless moment.

Vanya smiled at me, rather smugly, a gleam of pride in her eye. "Yes, my love. He is a dragon king... if he wants to be." Vanya went back to staring at our son and pulled down her shirt to offer the baby her swollen breast for his first feed.

Stavrok moved off the bed and walked around to me. "Congratulations, son."

I reached out and shook his hand, a wave of relief washing over me. "I'm just so relieved they're both okay," I said.

Stavrok looked at his wife and daughter. "Vanya, can I take your husband to my study for a drink to celebrate? We'll only be an hour."

"Oh, I don't think so..." I began to say, not wanting to leave my baby and wife quite so soon.

Vanya nodded, a tired smile on her lips. "Of course, Dad. Mom will stay with me."

"And Jessa will be here any moment now," Stavrok said, and slapped a hand on my back encouragingly.

At that moment Jessa hurried into the room, her belly swollen with her second pregnancy. "Oh my God. Vanya!" she squealed, rushing over to her side.

We left the women to coo over my beautiful son, and I let my father-in-law take me for a quick drink.

In his study, the whiskey slid down my throat like a dream. I'd been up with Vanya all night, so although she'd done all the work, my stress levels had been through the roof watching her go through so much pain and being unable to do much about it—other than being there for her. The whiskey soothed my frayed nerves, and I sighed heavily. "Thank you, that's great."

Stavok smiled. "I won't keep you from your son long, I just wanted to ask you something while I could. Damon mentioned that you are thinking of stepping up as his heir. Is that true?"

I laughed. "Of all the times to ask me."

My father-in-law grinned at me. "I'm no fool, son."

I'd been oscillating between the idea of just being my half-brother's right-hand man and stepping up as everyone so obviously wanted me to. But now, things had changed. "Well, considering I have a son who bears the Dragon King mark, who am I to go against what the fates want?"

Stavrok laughed and poured me more whiskey. "You're exactly right Jaegar. And you're precisely what your kingdom needs."

My kingdom... what a thing.

But as my father said often, a kingdom was simply a pile of rocks that housed and protected its people. The soul of the North was in our blood and in our hearts. And that was why I would stand up as their king despite my earlier reservations and desire to run from all royal duty. My people wanted me to rule, and that's why I'd do it, and not for any other reason.

I stood up, aching to get back to my family. "I want to thank you Stavrok, for everything you've done for me. For accepting me and supporting us. You're truly..." I struggled to say the words. He was like a second father to me, and as a child who'd wanted nothing more than to have one father, it was incredible gift to now have two.

Stavrok stood up and shook my hand once more. "Go to your family, Jaegar, knowing once and for all that you are a true king of fire and snow."

Lifted to dizzying heights by his words, I took my leave and went back to my son and beautiful wife, safe in the knowledge I was truly loved, and that love wasn't contingent on me being anyone other than exactly who I was.

The only thing I've ever wanted.

THE END